THE CONFIDENCE-MAN

THE
CONFIDENCE-MAN:
HIS MASQUERADE

By

HERMAN MELVILLE

Edited by Elizabeth S. Foster

HENDRICKS HOUSE, INC.

NEW YORK   1954

PREFACE

The text used in this edition is that of the first edition of *The Confidence-Man: His Masquerade*, New York, 1857; with this the almost simultaneous London edition is compared in the Textual Notes. Melville's spelling, punctuation, and grammar have been preserved, but errors that were fairly obviously typographical have been emended and accounted for in the Textual Notes. Melville did not see this novel through either the American or the British press, and probably did not read through the fair copy made for the press by his sister Augusta; therefore the text retains a number of discrepancies and peculiarities that he might have eliminated if his trip to the Mediterranean in search of health had not carried him away from such tasks as proof-reading.

The Introduction and Explanatory Notes make heavy use of my doctoral dissertation, "Herman Melville's *The Confidence-Man:* Its Origins and Meaning," Yale University, 1942. Since 1942 the researches of several other students of this novel or of parts of it have repeated some of mine and, I am happy to say, not only confirm mine by their agreement but add significant findings; these studies are Mr. Egbert S. Oliver's identification of Winsome with Emerson, Mr. John W. Shroeder's proofs of the diabolic nature of the Confidence-Man, and Mr. William Pommer's demonstration of the influence of *Paradise Lost*. A number of writers have mentioned the main source of the chapters on Indian-hating.

I wish to express my gratitude to the Committee on Higher Degrees in the History of American Civilization, Harvard University, for permission to use materials in the Melville Collection in the Harvard College Library (referred to in the notes to the Introduction and the Explanatory Notes as HCL-M); to the Massachusetts Historical Society (referred to as MHS) for

v

permission to use letters in the Shaw Collection; to the Manuscript Division of the New York Public Library for permission to use letters and diaries in the Duyckinck Collection (NYPL-D) and the Gansevoort-Lansing Collection (NYPL-GL).

My thanks for invaluable help are due to many colleagues and friends, among whom I should like to name Mr. Stanley T. Williams, Mr. Jay Leyda, Mr. Merton M. Sealts, Jr., and Mr. Howard P. Vincent.

ELIZABETH S. FOSTER

Oberlin, Ohio
May 12, 1954

CONTENTS

THE CONFIDENCE-MAN

INTRODUCTION

"Through the mouths of the dark characters of Hamlet, Timon, Lear, and Iago, he craftily says, or sometimes insinuates the things which we feel to be so terrifically true, that it were all but madness for any good man, in his own proper character, to utter, or even hint of them."

After almost a hundred years of silence, *The Confidence-Man* at length begins to make itself heard. It is the last of Melville's prose to be rescued from oblivion; that rescue is on the way is shown by the fact that recently critics have begun to mention it with respect, and sometimes with excitement.

In the 1850's Melville's contemporaries turned their backs on his vision of truth's ambiguities and the universal malice. They made fun of his "ambiguities," and then they forgot him. While he pondered the mysteries of iniquity, they for their part were too busy preparing civil war and national and international rapacity to trouble themselves with ancient, discredited bogies. Melville had won and for the most part held an enthusiastic audience with his first six books, *Typee* (1846), *Omoo* (1847), *Mardi* (1849), *Redburn* (1849), *White-Jacket* (1850), and *Moby-Dick* (1851); but he lost it with *Pierre* (1852), and he spoke to only a handful of readers in *Israel Potter* (1855) and *The Piazza Tales* (1856). In 1857, shaken in fame, in health, in courage, but not in integrity, he spoke again in *The Confidence-Man: His Masquerade*. It became his valedictory as a professional novelist.

In our relatively disillusioned times—it has become a commonplace to say—Melville's vision of the "malignity which has been from the beginning" seems less perverse than it did in the century of Emerson and Whitman. Yet it is more than pessimism that has frightened readers away from *The Confidence-Man*; an obscurity that was perhaps intentional has always hung like a smoke screen between the bright, clear, aimless story in the foreground and the somber, close-knit ulterior drama on which the form and tension of the novel depend. In the last few decades, however, scholarship and criticism have been teaching us to read Melville more deeply. Furthermore, and this is what chiefly makes this book available to the twentieth century as it was not to the nineteenth, the literature of our time has worked changes in our vision and our taste. Symbolism, fantasy, the discovery in myth and dream of "more reality, than real life itself can show"—these have undermined the realism beloved of the mid-nineteenth century; cryptic, triple-tiered, all but private styles have taught us to read polyphonic literature without much in the way of a key. Eliot and Joyce and a host of other writers have given us a taste for the intellectual excitement and imaginative extension and enlargement that lie in laminated meanings, in close-packed, multiple suggestion and ironic echo.

The Confidence-Man, which baffled and vexed Melville's contemporaries, is well worth recovering now from the dust of neglect and the murk of obscurity. Its bold and rueful question, its satire both philosophical and social, its wit, its endless irony, its style so impeccably finished and subtle and yet so fresh, its tantalizing mysteries—these repay its ransom. As a philosophical satire on optimism, it is a modern Candide, and a worthy successor of that immortal book. One must grant at once that Melville's novel lacks the clarity, the movement, and the devastating brilliance of wit of Voltaire's. These are not its weapons or its charms, as the urbane certainties and skepticisms of the eighteenth century are not its matrix. Instead, the climate of Melville's comedy is one of subtle, pervasive, elusive irony, of suggestion and understatement rather than exaggeration, of talk rather than action. Yet his baleful comedy is more inclusive as a philosophical attack than Voltaire's hilarious one, and more mordant. There are few kinds or degrees of optimistic "philosophy" that do not contribute some garment to the masquerade of Melville's Confidence Man. Moreover, to Melville the idea that this is the best of all possible worlds seemed not merely ridiculous but loaded with danger to humanity. And as for the forces that govern our destinies, Melville seems to say that, if he should ever abandon his conviction that the purposes of God are past finding out, he would be tempted to figure Him, not as the loving Father of Christian belief, not as the benevolent Creator of the Deists, not as some Arnoldian stream of tendency that makes for righteousness, but as a jokester, perhaps malevolent, perhaps indifferent.

Melville indeed was closer in mood to Shakespeare, the Shakespeare of the great tragedies and some of the later plays, which in fact lend many lines and allusions to *The Confidence-Man*, than to Voltaire. Like Shakespeare, Melville was bemused with the falseness of appearances in this life, the oppositeness of appearance and reality; his Masquerade admits us to a topsy-turvy world, where the apparent cynic is the real lover of mankind, and the real misanthrope is rigged out as Philanthropos, and every mask belies the nature of its wearer. Also, in *The Confidence-Man* the gods are ambiguous, as they are in *King Lear*. Do they kill us for their sport? And just as the forces of evil seem to have been loosed in *Lear,* freed from all check for a time, so on an April Fool's Day the legions of Satan make sport on board the world-ship which is the scene of Melville's novel. The Confidence Man himself is Melville's most ironic and bitter presentment of his half-mystical apprehension of evil at the heart of things. The evil is thrust close here; the devil goes to and fro in the earth and walks up and down in it; the "inscrutable malice" that Captain Ahab so hated, reaches out for men, plays with them, and betrays them. Two of the five interpolated stories in the novel are stories of simply unexplainable evil. The hand is the hand of Melville, but the voice is the voice of Job, and of Shakespeare.

Not tragedy, however, but comedy—though rather grim comedy indeed—is the mode of *The Confidence-Man*. "There are certain queer times and occasions in this strange mixed affair we call life when a man takes this whole universe for a vast practical joke, though the wit thereof he but dimly discerns, and more than suspects that the joke is at nobody's expense but his own." So mused Ishmael in *Moby-Dick*. "Half melancholy, half farcical—like all the rest of the world." So Melville summarized existence a few months after he finished *The Confidence-Man*; he happened to be thinking of a Mr. Dickson's Zionist dreams, but his description of the human spectacle as "half melancholy, half farcical" states the point of view from which *The Confidence-Man* was written, and is consonant with Ishmael's suspicion that the universe may be a vast practical joke. Shakespeare's tragi-comedies, *Cymbeline* and *The Winter's Tale* for example, ugly and cruel and blind as they show life to be in large part, nevertheless move on, as everybody knows, to the happiness of awakened faith, reunion, reconciliation, under gods who are "above our question." Such acceptance and affirmation were not for Melville, at any rate not yet; he could write comedy from the Slough of Despond only because, like Ishmael, he had made up his mind to grin and bear it, whatever *it* might be, and because his compassion for man the cosmic waif was balanced by his judgment, his intelligence, his humor, his sense of the absurdities of man the victim of his own follies. The "nothing too much" of the comic spirit presides in the structure of the novel, of which the first half satirizes credulity and the second half points out the evil consequences of too much distrust. Yet pessimism, never sublimated as in Shakespeare, goes hand in hand with comedy; the Confidence Man is an enemy too strong for man to vanquish, and the gods are not questioned about his appetite for human victims, only because they will not answer.

The more obvious satire of the novel, however, is like a bright surface spread over the tenebrous waters in which the darker meanings lurk. The dearth of charity among Christians, greed, gullibility—the light of satire glances constantly over these human failures and foibles. It is focused sharply and wittily from time to time on certain characteristics of Western, and particularly American and nineteenth-century civilization—the invasion of all areas of life, even religion and philanthropy, by the "Wall Street spirit," the hope of millennial enlightenment from a free press, *laissez-faire*. Not without poetic reason was the Mississippi, that very type and central artery of the United States, chosen as the scene of the story.

Another reason why *The Confidence-Man* claims our attention is that it formed and probably caused the end of Melville's career as a writer trying to support his family by his pen; that is to say, it ended the professional career of one of the great writers of the nineteenth century thirty-four years before his death. Also it is a curious document on the relation of writer and public. The indifference and hostility of the public did not turn Melville back to writing the South Sea idylls that the public demanded, but perhaps it is what pushed him into a symbolism, a kind of double-talk, that seems intended rather to darken than to illuminate meanings.

As a work of art, *The Confidence-Man* has always been undervalued because its surface story seems aimless and without tension or climax, and because the central meaning and whole emotional freight of the novel, which give it form, are hidden in the vessel's dark hold. But the structure had best be discussed later. Here it is only necessary to speak of Melville's symbolism in *The Confidence-Man*.

This symbolism is an altogether different sort from that in *Moby-Dick*. In *Moby-Dick* Melville was writing first of all the story of a mad, defiant, vindictive chase of a great white whale and the ruin wreaked upon the chasers by the whale. But in and through his story, Melville's questing mind and his defiant humanism hurled themselves against the mystery and the blank impersonality of the universe, so that, almost whether the author would or no, the moral and metaphysical dimension extended itself behind the moving scene of the whale chase. As has been said,[1] the images came and later the mean-

[1] R. W. Short, "Melville as Symbolist," *The University of Kansas City Review*, XV (1948), 38-46. Howard P. Vincent's *The Trying-out of Moby-Dick* (Boston, 1949) supports the thesis that *Moby-Dick* was rewritten and magnified, in every sense, after the first version was almost complete.

ings came into the images. In *The Confidence-Man*, however, the ideas seem to have come accompanied by their images. The very title of the book announces the allegory, and also the method, a sort of punning double reference. The first sentence begins the fantasy (if one reads at two levels), the allegorical embodiment of an idea. Throughout the novel, then, we might expect to find a "part-and-parcel allegoricalness of the whole," a system of fairly precise and constant parallels between the story and the shadow-story, between swindling men and swindling faiths; and so we do. The whole thing is schematic, as *Moby-Dick* was not; the relation between image and idea is tight, ingenious, and rational rather than loose, imaginative, evocative, as in *Moby-Dick*. It is the idiom of wit rather than of poetry; it is a method appropriate to sharp, intellectual satire.

Was it also meant to be a cipher? In some of the stories that came between *Pierre* and *The Confidence-Man*, Melville was writing one story for the public and another for himself, as recent scholarship has shown. The second half of "The Paradise of Bachelors and the Tartarus of Maids" is on the surface a description of a trip through a paper mill where the women workers were exploited, pale, and half-sick; underneath is a description of the process of child-bearing.[2] There is not here the profound union of idea, story, and symbol that there is in *Moby-Dick*, the multiple reference in which the allusions are related as the notes in a chord of music. There is only an ingenious sort of punning, a clever superimposition of one picture on another so that through a green lens you see the maids in a paper mill and through a red lens you see the gestation process. If Melville wished to share his secret of the double meaning, he had to wait eighty-five years. It seems more probable to the present writer that he did not, that the sexual references constituted for him a private joke or private jibe or private solace of some sort. Forced, if he would sell

[2] E. H. Eby, "Herman Melville's 'Tartarus of Maids,'" *Modern Language Quarterly*, I (1940), 95-100.

his wares, to write what the public's myopic eyes could read easily and in a half light, and probably contemptuous of its prudery as well as its blindness, perhaps he took an ironic revenge. Or perhaps his artistic conscience demanded three-dimensional art, and he saved it somewhat by adding this strange and private third dimension. At any rate he wrote an all but unrelated shadow-story which apparently no one understood but himself, then or for the next century minus a few years. He did the same thing again in "I and My Chimney."[3] Since the hidden meaning in this sketch is an account of his family's suspicions that he was insane and of the medical examination which they caused to be made, it is hard to believe that Melville wished to share his secret this time, even with an esoteric audience.

In *The Confidence-Man* Melville was again engaged in double-writing, and it is quite possible that he intended no one to glimpse his shadow story. Perhaps he felt that, because of the profound antagonism between his views and most of the dominant faiths of his America, it was dangerous or hopeless to try to make himself heard, but that he must nevertheless stubbornly record his convictions; if readers deplored pessimism and allegory, then parabolic meanings could be shifted beyond their focus. Perhaps he felt that what he had to say about religion was too radical for the many but that by using esoteric symbols he could convey it to the few. After all, his sophisticated friend Duyckinck had reproved him for irreverence when he said that Shakespeare was gentle, almost, as Jesus; and *Putnam's Monthly* had refused his harmless "The Two Temples" because it might offend "the religious sensibilities of the public." Or, possibly, after three or four years of seclusion among pious women, who were also of much narrower intellectual range than he, Melville lost his bearings and could not know how much or how little anyone would understand or resent.

[3] Merton M. Sealts, Jr., "Herman Melville's 'I and My Chimney,' " *American Literature*, XIII (1941), 142-154.

ii

"Bitter is it to be poor & bitter, to be reviled, & Oh bitter are these waters of Death, thought I."

To understand the mood in which *The Confidence-Man* was written, we must go back to the troubled years just before its composition in 1855-1856. Melville was living two miles from Pittsfield, Massachusetts, on his farm, Arrowhead, with his wife, his four children (born between 1849 and 1855), and his mother and sisters. He was a young man, thirty-six years old, when he wrote *The Confidence-Man*; since 1846 he had published eight novels and some short stories and essays. But the years after the publication of *Pierre*, in August 1852, had brought him bitter reverses. *Pierre* estranged his public. The outpouring of the giant energies that had gone into *Moby-Dick* and *Pierre* left him close to physical and nervous exhaustion; his health broke in the spring of 1853. The sea of metaphysical, religious, and ethical speculations into which his books had plunged him was sweeping him along into more and more fearful currents of agnosticism and pessimism. Something, probably his bad health, over-wrought nervous state, and spiritual depression, seems to have inhibited both letter-writing and visiting. To some of his family his mind seemed deranged. Some of the reviewers, with blithe condescension, called him mad. Illness, isolation, financial and apparently literary failure, an intellectual and spiritual state verging close on despair and shared or comprehended by none—one cannot think of this personal tragedy without pain.

"Dollars damn me," Melville had written to Hawthorne in 1851; "and the malicious Devil is forever grinning in upon me, holding the door ajar."[4] The Devil's grin in 1856 was wider

---

[4] The letter is printed in full in Willard Thorp, *Herman Melville: Representative Selections, with Introduction, Bibliography, and Notes* (New York, 1938), pp. 389-393. For this period in Melville's life, see Jay Leyda, *The Melville Log* (New York, 1951), 2 vols., II, 496-583; and Leon Howard, *Herman Melville* (Berkeley and Los Angeles, 1951), pp. 207-257.

and infinitely more malicious. Melville's receipts from magazine stories, it has been estimated, averaged about $240 a year from 1853 through 1856.[5] Royalties from his books had fallen off to almost nothing. On 6 March 1856, he was in debt to Harper and Brothers by $348.51; on 30 June 1857, his debt to them was $352.11, after subtraction of $16.48, his dividends on sales of *Omoo, Redburn, White-Jacket, Moby-Dick,* and *Mardi.*[6] In the summer of 1855 he tried, in vain, to sell Arrowhead to the Insane Asylum Commission as a location for a new asylum.[7] The malicious Devil grinned indeed. Small wonder that, grin and all, he is the hero of *The Confidence-Man.*

All through these years of dwindling income and nagging debts, he was dogged by illness too. This gifted author, who had trusted so confidently in his teeming pen to support his family, and who was aware now of his great powers, must, in the prime of life, be racked for many years by attacks of rheumatism, "crick in the back," sciatica, neuralgic pains, and virtual blindness. In 1853 his family and friends had tried to save his health by getting him a consular appointment; his mother wrote to her brother, Peter Gansevoort,[8]

The constant in-door confinement with little intermission to which Hermans occupation as author compels him, does not agree with him. This constant working of the brain, & excitement of the im-

[5] William Charvat, "Melville's Income," *American Literature,* XV (1943), 251-261.

[6] Melville's accounts with Harper & Brothers, HCL-M.

[7] The *Berkshire County Eagle,* 31 August 1855, reports that the Commission has examined Melville's farm for this purpose; a week later the paper says that the Insane Asylum for Western Massachusetts will be at Northampton. Jay Leyda, "White Elephant vs. White Whale," *Town & Country,* C1 (1947), 68ff., describes Melville's efforts to dispose of his farm from 1855 until its sale to his brother Allan in 1863. His *The Melville Log* also prints the significant documents, under appropriate dates.

[8] "Lansingburgh, Tuesday Eveg 20th April [1853] 10 O'clock P.M." NYPL-GL. Harrison Hayford and Merrell Davis, "Herman Melville as Office-Seeker," *Modern Language Quarterly,* X (1949), 168-183, 377-388, publish this letter in the course of a full discussion of the efforts of Melville's family and friends, and his own efforts, to obtain for him a government post between 1839 and 1866.

agination, is wearing Herman out, & you will my dear Peter be doing him a lasting benefit if by your added exersions you can procure
for him a foreign consulate. . . .

In February 1855, his wife later recorded, "he had his first
attack of severe rheumatism in his back—so that he was helpless—and in the following June an attack of sciatica. Our neigh-
bour in Pittsfield, Dr. O. W. Holmes, attended & prescribed
for him."[9] Sometime during these months *The Confidence-Man*
was probably begun. On the following 14 September, the local
newspaper reported that he was "just recovering from a severe
illness," and that "the author of Typee" had attended, not in
costume, a fancy-dress picnic at Melville Lake, on the grounds
of J. R. Morewood.[10]

The Confidence-Man was plotted and written between bouts
with the demons of pain and eye failure. By the summer of
1856, when the book was almost done, Melville's broken health
was the subject of family councils and family letters from Boston to Galena, Illinois. His father-in-law, the Hon. Lemuel
Shaw, Chief Justice of Massachusetts, wrote to his son on 1
September[11]:

I suppose you have been informed by some of the family, how
very ill, Herman has been. It is manifest to me from Elizabeth's letters, that she has felt great anxiety about him. When he is deeply
engaged in one of his literary works, he confines him[self] to hard
study many hours in the day, with little or no exercise, & this espe-

[9] Quoted in Raymond M. Weaver, *Herman Melville: Mariner and
Mystic* (New York, 1921), p. 352, from a notebook kept by Melville's
wife, Elizabeth Shaw Melville. Melville said that his eyes were "tender
as young sparrows," and that he sometimes wrote squinting at the paper
with one eye.

[10] *Berkshire County Eagle*, 14 September 1855.

[11] Hon. Lemuel S. Shaw to Samuel S. Shaw, 1 September 1856. MHS.
Herman's aunt Mary A. A. Melville, the widow of his uncle Thomas,
wrote to Shaw from Galena, Illinois, 25 October 1856: "We saw by the
papers that Herman had sailed for Europe; I most sincerely hope that
his health may be permanently benefited by the journey. . . ." MHS.
Mrs. Griggs was Herman's oldest sister, Helen Maria; Augusta, a younger
sister. Most of the documents quoted here and below may be found in
Leyda, *The Melville Log*, under the appropriate dates.

cially in winter for a great many days together. He probably thus overworks himself & brings on severe nervous affections. He has been advised strongly to break off this labor for some time, & take a voyage or a journey, & endeavor to recruit. No definite plan is arranged, but I think it may result, in this that in the autumn he will go away for four or five months, Elizabeth will come here with her younger children, Mrs. Griggs & Augusta will each take one of the boys, their house at Pittsfield will be shut up. I think he needs such a change & that it would be highly beneficial to him & probably restore him.

Melville took the advice of his family, a plan was arranged, and on 11 October he sailed from New York, to spend the winter in Mediterranean countries, on funds provided by Justice Shaw.

But let us go back to the early summer of 1855. We know that Melville proposed a novel to Dix & Edwards, perhaps for serial publication in *Putnam's Monthly*, because G. W. Curtis advised J. A. Dix, in April, May, or June: "I should decline any novel from Melville that is not extremely good."[12] This proposed novel must have been *The Confidence-Man*, unless it was a novel never written or written and destroyed. There is a bit of internal evidence which suggests that part of *The Confidence-Man* was done by the end of that summer of 1855: in Chapter 13, about one-fourth of the way through the book, Melville writes of the Crimean fortress Malakoff as though that fortress were still "secure"; it fell on 8 September 1855, and the *Berkshire County Eagle*, which had been full of the siege of "impregnable Malakoff" for several months, reported its fall on 8 October. In any case Melville was busy writing. Between

[12] In an undated letter written from Providence, where Curtis was on a reader's vacation; references within the letter indicate that it was written before July, 1855. HCL. Leyda, *The Melville Log*, p. 500, dates the letter "Mid-April?" Howard, *Herman Melville*, p. 221, thinks that Melville proposed this novel "in late March," and that Melville might have worked up "Benito Cereno" as a novel if his proposal had been accepted. Mr. Howard (on p. 226) associates the conception of *The Confidence-Man* with a costume picnic that Melville attended (in plain clothes) in September 1855; Melville's remarks about life's being "a pic-nic *en costume*" come, however, in Chapter 24.

April 1855 and May 1856, he published five stories and sketches in *Harper's New Monthly Magazine* and in *Putnam's* and, late in May 1856, *The Piazza Tales,* a collection of five stories and sketches which had previously appeared in *Putnam's* plus a sixth sketch, "The Piazza." On 16 February 1856 he sent this last piece to Dix & Edwards, the publishers of *Putnam's;* on 24 March he returned to them his signed contract and proofs of *The Piazza Tales.*[13]

By the middle of February 1856, then, though nagged by illness and financial worries, he was fairly free to devote himself to *The Confidence-Man.* He was "convinced that a residence in the country was not the thing for him," as his sister later wrote, and "could he have met with an opportunity of disposing of his place he would have done so."[14] Before the middle of July he managed to sell the western eighty acres of his hundred-and-sixty-acre farm. Also, his sister Augusta was making a fair copy of *The Confidence-Man* for the press.[15]

On 1 August, his thirty-seventh birthday, he took a vacation, and arrived at the home of his uncle Herman Gansevoort, at Gansevoort, in Saratoga County, New York, for a fortnight's visit and some short excursions to Lake George and Saratoga Springs with his brother Allan and others; on 16 August, on his way back to Arrowhead, he dined with his uncle Peter Gansevoort in Albany. Then, sometime in September, the arrangements were made for his winter abroad in pursuit of health. On 27 September, as his uncle Herman Gansevoort recorded it, "Herman Melville bro^t his little son Stanwix to remain with us to stay untill his father returns from Europe," and,

13 Merton M. Sealts, Jr., "The Publication of Melville's *Piazza Tales,*" *Modern Language Notes,* LIX (1944), 56-59.

14 Quoted in Leyda, "White Elephant vs. White Whale," p. 118.

15 Letter of Lemuel Shaw, Jr., Melville's brother-in-law, to Samuel S. Shaw, Boston, 15 July 1856: "Herman writes that he has sold the western half of his farm at Pittsfield—upon pretty good terms.—I believe is now preparing another book for the press; of which Augusta is making a fair copy for the printer & which will be published before long. I know nothing about it; but I have no great confidence in the success of his productions." MHS.

the next day, a Sunday, "Sister Maria, Fannie, Stanwix and Kate, attended Church—Self and Herman at home." On 29 September, Herman left for New York.[16]

On 1 October he was in New York, visiting friends and preparing for his trip and for the publication of his novel. His friend Evert A. Duyckinck recorded in his book of "Jottings" under this date:[17]

Herman Melville passed the evening with me—fresh from his mountain charged to the muzzle with his sailor metaphysics and jargon of things unknowable. But a good stirring evening—ploughing deep and bringing to the surface some rich fruits of thought and Experience—Melville instanced old Burton as atheistical—in the exquisite irony of his passages on some sacred matters; cited a good story from the Decameron, the *Enchantment* of the husband in the tree; a story from Judge Edmonds of a prayer meeting of female convicts at Sing Sing which the Judge was invited to witness and agreed to, provided that he was introduced where he could not be seen. It was an orgie of indecency and blasphemy. Said of Bayard Taylor that as some augur predicted the misfortunes of Charles I from the infelicity of his countenance so Taylor's prosperity "borne up by the Gods" was written in his face.

Did Melville talk about his new book with his friend? A few weeks later Duyckinck referred to the "new volume which he left behind him" as "a fine playful subject for a humourist & philosopher."[18]

[16] The information about Melville's two visits to Gansevoort comes from Herman Gansevoort's remembrancer; I am indebted to Mr. Jay Leyda for the transcription. On 24 October 1856, Priscilla Melville, an aunt of Herman who was living in Pittsfield, wrote to Justice Shaw of Herman's wife: "Lizzie is up to her eyes in business, but is hastening, as much as *possible*, the preparations for her departure—her *out-of-door* affairs, detain her *now*—" MHS. On 23 November 1856, Shaw wrote from Boston to his son Samuel S. Shaw: "Elizabeth is here with her two youngest children. . . . Elizabeth has received but one letter from her husband, written soon after his arrival at Glasgow. He expected after a few days in Scotland to proceed to Liverpool & thence to London. . . ." MHS.

[17] NYPL-D.

[18] Letter of E. A. Duyckinck to G. L. Duyckinck, 18 November 1856. NYPL-D.

Another glimpse comes from Duyckinck's "Jottings": "Oct. 9, [1856] In the evening at Mr. Shepherd, in 14th St. with Herman & Allan Melville and Tomes. Good talk Herman warming like an old sailor over the supper—He is going to Italy for the winter."[19]

And two days later Duyckinck records: "Oct. 11. Another, yet another of the series of Extraodinary fine days; sunny, mellow, quiescent. Saw Herman Melville off in the propeller Glasgow for Glasgow. . . . Melville right hearty—Pleasant fates to him on his Neapolitan way."

Before he sailed, Melville and Dix, Edwards and Co., of New York, had drafted an agreement, dated 10 October 1856, and calling for the delivery of the manuscript of The Confidence-Man to the publishers by 11 October and its publication by 15 December 1856. For some reason this arrangement was not satisfactory. Allan Melville, Herman's brother and also his attorney, signed a final and similar contract for Herman on 28 October; it promises delivery of the manuscript on 1 November 1856, and its publication by the following January.[20] The manuscript was left behind with someone, probably Allan, possibly Lizzie Melville, Herman's wife, or his sister and copyist, Augusta.[21]

From Melville's *Journal up the Straits*, his casual record of the next seven months, we learn that the *Glasgow* made the north of Ireland in fifteen days, and went up the Clyde to Glas-

[19] Daniel Shepherd, a friend of Melville's brother Allan, had just published *Saratoga: A Tale of 1787*. Robert Tomes was the author of *Panama* (New York, 1855). The "Jottings" are in NYPL-D.

[20] Both contracts are in HCL-M. Dix, Edwards and Co. were to pay expenses; Melville was to receive 12½% of the retail price of copies sold after sales had paid all costs of publication exclusive of advertising expenses; the copyright was to be Melville's sole property, subject to the contract; the stereotype plates were to be the common property of both parties but in possession of the publisher during the term of the contract, seven years.

[21] Justice Shaw wrote to his son Samuel (Boston, 17 April 1857) respecting *The Confidence-Man*: "He left the M.S. ready for publication, when he went out, last autumn. . . . I have it [the book] but have not yet read it." MHS.

gow on Sunday, 26 October.[22] By 8 November, a Saturday, he had made his way to Liverpool, where his friend Nathaniel Hawthorne had been United States Consul since 1 August 1853. On the following Monday he "Saw Mr. Hawthorne at the Consulate. Invited me to stay with him during my sojourn at Liverpool." Accordingly Melville spent Tuesday evening, Wednesday, and Thursday morning with the Hawthornes at Southport, twenty miles from Liverpool. His entry for Wednesday, though characteristically bare and brief, reminds us of the strength of the old friendship, probably the deepest and most fructifying of Melville's life: "At Southport. An agreeable day. Took a long walk by the sea. Sands & grass. Wild & desolate. A strong wind. Good talk. In the evening Stout and Fox & Geese. —Julian grown into a fine lad; Una taller than her mother. Mrs. Hawthorne not in good health. Mr. H. stayed home for me."

Hawthorne wrote a long account of this meeting in his own journal; it contains the best description that we possess, outside Melville's own writing, of his state of mind in the period of *The Confidence-Man,* and it is written by the person best fitted to comprehend the mind and feeling of Herman Melville. Melville, Hawthorne says,[23] was

looking much as he used to do (a little paler, and perhaps a little sadder), in a rough outside coat, and with his characteristic gravity and reserve of manner. . . . Melville has not been well, of late; he has been affected with neuralgic complaints in his head and limbs, and no doubt has suffered from too constant literary occupations, pursued without much success, latterly; and his writings, for a long while past, have indicated a morbid state of mind. . . . [On Wednesday] we took a pretty long walk together, and sat down in a hollow among the sand hills (sheltering ourselves from the high, cool wind) and smoked a cigar. Melville, as he always does, began to reason of Providence and futurity, and of everything that lies be-

[22] Herman Melville, *Journal up the Straits: October 11, 1856—May 5, 1857,* ed. Raymond Weaver (New York, 1935), p. 1.

[23] *The English Notebooks by Nathaniel Hawthorne,* ed. Randall Stewart (New York, 1941), pp. 432-437.

yond human ken, and informed me that he had 'pretty much made
up his mind to be annihilated'; but still he does not seem to rest in
that anticipation; and, I think, will never rest until he gets hold of a
definite belief. It is strange how he persists—and has persisted ever
since I knew him, and probably long before—in wandering to-and-
fro over these deserts, as dismal and monotonous as the sand hills
amid which we were sitting. He can neither believe, nor be comfortable in his unbelief; and he is too honest and courageous not to
try to do one or the other. If he were a religious man, he would be
one of the most truly religious and reverential; he has a very high
and noble nature, and better worth immortality than most of us.

The two friends met again in Liverpool on Friday, spent
Saturday together in Chester, and met once more on Monday.
"He said," Hawthorne writes,

that he already felt much better than in America; but observed that
he did not anticipate much pleasure in his rambles, for that the
spirit of adventure is gone out of him. He certainly is much overshadowed since I saw him last; but I hope he will brighten as he
goes onward. He sailed from Liverpool [for Constantinople] in a
steamer on Tuesday. . . .

Melville probably turned over to Hawthorne all the arrangements for the English publication of his novel.[24] If he made
any of the arrangements himself, he must have made them by
mail, for there is no evidence that he went to London until

24 "Mr. Hawthorne, when United States Consul at Liverpool, at one
time acted as Mr. Melville's agent with English publishers," according
to Arthur Stedman, writing in the World (11 October 1891) at the time
of Melville's death. Perhaps Melville confirmed Hawthorne's arrangements from Rome, where he received mail between 25 February and 21
March, in time for Hawthorne to sign the final contract for him on 20
March. According to a letter of 23 November by Justice Shaw, Melville
had "expected after a few days in Scotland to proceed to Liverpool &
thence to London"; his journal shows that after 28 October, when he
was in Glasgow, he spent some time in Edinburgh and went through
York and Lancaster on his way to Liverpool, where he arrived on 8
November. If in those ten days he also went to London, he not only
pushed himself harder than he usually did on this trip, but also, by
going from London to Liverpool by way of York, spent money more
carelessly.

after the book was published. He had brought with him "manuscript books" for publication in London, according to his wife[25]; these (presumably *The Confidence-Man* only) he almost certainly left with Hawthorne. The agreement with the London publishers of *The Confidence-Man*, Messrs. Longman, Brown, Green, Longmans and Roberts of Paternoster Row, was signed for Herman Melville by Nathaniel Hawthorne on 20 March 1857.[26]

Contrary to his usual custom, he saw neither the English nor the American edition of *The Confidence-Man* through the press; this fact probably accounts for some discrepancies in the novel.

Melville spent the winter in various Mediterranean countries, including the Holy Land, trying to recover his health and spirits. His *Journal* shows that he was able to do fairly strenuous sight-seeing in Constantinople, Egypt, and Palestine, and that his interest in the color and the absurdities, and his compassion for the pathos, of the human drama were as keen as ever. At Salonica deck passengers came on board for Constantinople, "Among others two 'beys effendi' in long furred robes of yellow, looking like Tom cats. They had their harems with them." In Constantinople, besides the crowds, the beautiful women, the beggars, the scenery, the architecture, the mementoes of history, he saw in a cemetery[27]

a woman over a new grave—no grass on it yet. Such abandonment of misery! Called to the dead, put her head down as close to it as possible; as if calling down a hatchway a cellar; besought—'Why dont you speak to me? My God!—It is I! Ah,—speak—but one word!'

---

[25] Elizabeth Melville wrote two very brief versions of her husband's biography in a little pocket diary, now belonging to her granddaughter, Mrs. Eleanor Melville Metcalf; they are partly transcribed in Raymond Weaver's *Herman Melville* and in his introduction to *Journal up the Straits*, and in Leyda, *The Melville Log*; see p. 525 in the *Log*.

[26] The contract is in HCL-M. The firm agreed to publish at their own risk and to divide profits equally with Melville.

[27] Sunday, 14 December; p. 29.

—All deaf. So much for consolation.—This woman & her cries haunt me horribly.—

At the Dead Sea he tasted the "smarting bitter of the water,—carried the bitter in my mouth all day—bitterness of life—thought of all bitter things—Bitter is it to be poor & bitter, to be reviled, & Oh bitter are these waters of Death, thought I."[28]

He tried in vain to summon up the ancient glories of history and poetry that had irradiated, in his imagination, these legend-haunted shores, "Xerxes' bridge-piers," Achilles' tomb, the isle of Patmos; arid barrenness, at Patmos, and "the penetration and acumen" of Niebuhr and Strauss robbed him "of the bloom."[29] Only the pyramids awoke his imagination to "awe & terror"; it was "in these pyramids that was conceived the idea of Jehovah. Terrible mixture of the cunning and awful."[30]

Jerusalem defeated imagination and hope. "No country will more quickly dissipate romantic expectations than Palestine—particularly Jerusalem. To some the disappointment is heart sickening."[31] The filth, the smells, the commercialism, the "indifference of Nature & Man to all that makes the spot sacred to the Christian," the defilement of places still holy to the heart, the stony, glaring aridity! Where can thirst find the springs of Christ's presence, when the Tomb is a glittering show-box, when the guides say, " 'Here is the stone Christ leaned against, & here is the English Hotel' "?[32]

In Naples on 19 February, he wrote home that his health was greatly improved.[33] But in Rome in March, pain returned to his eye and often shortened his days among the paintings and ruins and sculptures. "Eye so bad had to go to room and bed

28 P. 74.
29 Thursday, 5 February; p. 107.
30 P. 58; he saw the pyramids on 31 December.
31 P. 91f; he was in Palestine from 6 January to 25 January.
32 Pp. 79f, 88.
33 Mrs. Lemuel Shaw, Herman's mother-in-law, wrote to her son Samuel (Boston, 20 March 1857): "I am afraid that you will miss Herman as his last date was the 19 of Feby in Naples. . . . His health is improving much—if he could only be absent one whole year, I think it would restore his health." MHS.

at 5 P.M. minus dinner";[34] such notations become frequent. While he was in Italy, his book was published in New York and London.

The New York edition appeared, appropriately and ironically, on 1 April. Within a month, and before Melville returned to America, the firm of Dix, Edwards and Co., caught in the gathering panic of 1857, failed.[35]

The London edition was published on 8 April. A thousand copies were printed, and only a few more than a third of them were sold in the next fourteen months.[36] Melville arrived in London on 26 April 1857, and went the next day, a Tuesday, "To the Longman's &c." The brevity of the entries in his journal at this point suggests perhaps disappointment, perhaps only travel-weariness; on Wednesday, "to Madame Tussaud's. No where else in particular."

He saw Hawthorne again, briefly and for the last time.[37] Then, on 6 May, he sailed from Liverpool for home. He landed

[34] Thursday, 5 March; p. 135. His eyes had been pained by "the glare of the light of arid hills" in Judea. See also pp. 137, 140, 141 for mention of the return of painful ailments.

[35] In the advertisement in the New York *Daily Tribune*, 1 April 1857, Melville was ticketed as "author of 'Typee,' 'Omoo,' etc. etc.," and the book described as 12mo., cloth, price $1. Evert Duyckinck wrote to his brother George on 31 March: "Allan Melville has just this moment sent me Herman's 'Confidence Man.' It is a grand subject for a satirist like Voltaire or Swift and being a kind of original American idea might be made to evoke a picture of our life and manners. We shall see what the sea dog philosopher of Typee makes of it." NYPL-D. This copy is now in the possession of Mr. Jay Leyda.

Dix, Edwards and Co. dissolved on 27 April 1857. George William Curtis, one of the partners, continued the business with the senior partner of Miller and Holman, printers, under the new name of Miller and Co.; but this firm suspended the following August. (See *American Publishers' Circular and Literary Gazette*, III [2 May 1857], 277, and F. L. Mott, *A History of American Magazines*, Cambridge, 1938, 3 vols., II, 427.)

[36] The price was 5s retail. By June 1857, 343 copies had been sold; by June 1858, a total of 409 copies; the firm had failed to cover expenses by £24 8s. (Melville's accounts with Longman, Brown & Co. HCL-M)

[37] *Journal. . . ,* p. 175. One of the persistent errors of both Melville and Hawthorne scholarship is that they met for the last time in November 1856.

late in May on his native shores, somewhat mended in health[38] and just in time to witness the complete failure of his novel.[39]

The Confidence-Man was the last of Melville's fiction to be published during his lifetime; and, although he lived thirty-four years longer, it was the last prose that he wrote except some fragmentary sketches and, not long before his death, the short novel *Billy Budd*, first published in 1924. After the failure of *The Confidence-Man* and two subsequent years of lecturing, he did not again address the public, except at rare intervals and in verse. In 1863, in bad health, he moved from the Pittsfield farm to New York City. There he was Inspector of Customs from 1866 to 1885. He published four books of verse, *Battle-Pieces and Aspects of the War* (1866), *Clarel, A Poem and Pilgrimage in the Holy Land* (1876), *John Marr and Other Sailors*

---

[38] Letter of Melville's brother-in-law, Lemuel Shaw, Jr., to Samuel S. Shaw, Boston, 2 June 1857: ". . . Herman returned in the City of Manchester about ten or twelve days ago, he says he is better than at any time while absent, but still he is not perfectly well; he staid with us about a week & I gave a dinner party for him & had a very pleasant one, Dr. Holmes & the two Dana's &c. Herman says he is not going to write any more at present & wishes to get a place in the N.Y. Custom House. Lizzie & her children returned to Pittsfield with Herman. . . ." MHS.

[39] Melville's *Journal* implies that his ship, the *City of Manchester*, left Liverpool on 5 May. The New York *Daily Tribune* announced on 21 May 1857: "Arrived. Steamship City of Manchester (Br. screw), Petrie, Liverpool May 6. Arr. Sandy Hook 19th at 9 p.m."

If Melville ever made any comments on his intention in *The Confidence-Man* or on its reception, they have not, apparently, been preserved. Hawthorne sent him a Christmas card, on the back of which were remarks about *The Confidence-Man;* Miss Agnes Morewood, a grandniece of Melville, remembers having seen it, but it has been lost or mislaid. (*The Melville Society Newsletter*, 10 November 1947.) Melville's brother-in-law, Lemuel Shaw, Jr., perhaps expressed the general opinion of the family in a letter to his brother Samuel (Boston, 21 April 1857): "A new book by Herman called 'The Confidence Man' has recently been published. I have not yet read it; but have looked at it & dipped into it, & I fear it belongs that [sic] horribly uninteresting class of nonsensical books he is given to writing—where there are pages of crude theory & speculation to every line of narritive—& interspersed with strained & ineffectual attempts to be humorous—I wish he could or would do better, when he went away he was dispirited & ill—& this book was left completed in the publisher's hands." MHS.

(1888), and *Timoleon* (1891), the last two in editions of twenty-five copies each. He died in New York, in relative obscurity, on 28 September 1891.

iii

". . . so precious to man is the approbation of his kind, that to rest, though but under an imaginary censure applied to but a work of imagination, is no easy thing."

The Confidence-Man was reviewed in England[40] promptly and more widely than any of Melville's other works since *Moby-Dick;* in America it went almost unnoticed. The author's reputation had stood the strain of *Pierre* much better in England than at home.

Although some of the English reviewers reveal a certain respect for any work by Herman Melville, it is clear that one reason for the attention given the book in England was its sharp satire on the American scene. The novel is chiefly interesting, some of the reviewers thought, for its local color. British relish for satire on American weaknesses informs the criticisms which take this tack. The money-getting spirit is especially bad in the United States, said the *Saturday Review,* and Melville is a powerful satirist in attacking it. "Satire on many American smartnesses," said the *Spectator,* "and on the gullibility of mankind which enables those smartnesses to succeed" is what gives the book its value. "It required close knowledge of the world, and of the Yankee world, to write such a book. . . . Perhaps the moral is the gullibility of the great Republic, when taken on its own tack"; thus the *Westminster Review* praised it.

Its rather general satire on human nature, on the other hand,

---

[40] British periodicals which reviewed *The Confidence-Man* were *The Athenaeum,* XXX (11 April 1857), 462-463; *The Critic,* XVI (15 April, 1857, 174-175; *John Bull and Britannia,* 11 May 1857, p. 300; *The Leader,* VIII (11 April 1857), 356; *The Literary Gazette,* No. 2099 (11 April 1857), pp. 348-349; *The Saturday Review,* III (23 May 1857), 484; *The Spectator,* XXX (11 April 1857), 398-399; *The Westminster Review,* LXVIII (July 1857), 310-311. It was noticed in *The Examiner* (18 April 1857).

and the good talk, aphoristic and clever, of its numerous characters were its chief merits, according to a few reviewers. "Much cordial philosophy is extracted from their talk, fragrant with poetry or bitter with cynicism," the *Athenaeum* said. And the *Critic* found it "an analytical inquiry into a few social shams."

But its final meaning, to the more discerning, was a puzzle. "It may be a *bona fide* eulogy on the blessedness of reposing 'confidence'—but we are not at all confident of this. Perhaps it is a hoax on the public—an emulation of Barnum," said the *Literary Gazette.* The *Critic* spoke with prescience, saying that of all Melville's works *The Confidence-Man* was the one which "readers will find the hardest nut to crack." It added, with more sense of the book's depths than was displayed in any other review: "We are not quite sure whether we have cracked it ourselves—whether there is not another meaning hidden. . . ." The *Athenaeum* excused itself by saying that some of Mr. Melville's readers might possibly "wait for a promised sequel to the book before deciding as to the lucidity or opaqueness of the author's final meaning."

Although the *Saturday Review* felt that the tone of the book was merely fantastic, that "the eccentric transformations" of the Confidence Man were only "capers," and that Melville did not seriously intend to indict all mankind as either fools or knaves, other journals sensed misanthropy, though not the deeper pessimism, and objected to it. "There seems too great a success on the part of the rogues," said the *Spectator.* "The view of human nature is severe and sombre," the *Westminster Review* thought; the book was written "too much in the spirit of Timon."

The general failure of readers to crack the shell of this novel is best seen in the various interpretations of the Confidence Man himself. There is a series of impostors in the novel. Some reviewers thought the Confidence Man was one of these, some another. Some thought that he was one man in different disguises. The *Athenaeum* saw him as an ambassador of good, who moved among the "masqueraders . . . honeying their hearts with words of social benignity and faith." The *Saturday Review* took him to be an ordinary Mississippi "operator" or swindler, a "clever impostor" who "dupes almost everyone and makes a good deal of money." Only the *Critic* saw the darker implications: "We feel half inclined to doubt whether this apostle of geniality is not, after all, an arch-impostor of the deepest dye."

More than one critic complained that in form the book was planless, rambling, monotonous. "Nonsensical people talking nonsense," the *Literary Gazette* concluded, the composition of "a March hare with a literary turn of mind." But the reviewers were almost unanimous in their praise of the style; the style, they said, was controlled, vivid, extraordinarily powerful, graphic, fresh, and entertaining.

One notes in these reviews the praise of the style; the confusion about the central intention and the central character of the book; the almost complete failure to detect the underlying pessimism; and the absence of any suspicion that Christianity is being criticized—the *Saturday Review* rebukes Melville for his "occasionally irreverent use of Scriptural phrases" without sensing that religion itself is weighed and found wanting on every page of the book.

In America *The Confidence-Man* was greeted by a great silence. All the big magazines which had reviewed Melville's work through *Moby-Dick*, even those whose interest had survived *Pierre*, ignored *The Confidence-Man*, except, some of them, to note that it had been published. Especially in *Harper's New Monthly Magazine*, which had praised *Moby-Dick* and had printed seven of Melville's tales and sketches between 1853 and 1856, was this absence of critical comment noticeable.[41] The few periodicals that did discuss it, though they had a good word for the style, damned it more or less gently as another of Melville's "strange vagaries."

[41] Hugh H. Hetherington, "The Reputation of Herman Melville in America," unpublished doctoral dissertation, University of Michigan, 1933, p. 336, n. 2.

Putnam's Monthly Magazine, published by the publishers of *The Confidence-Man,* carried an article by Fitz-James O'Brien which surveyed Melville's books (except *Pierre* and *White-Jacket*) and found him in need of the help of a critic.[42] Melville is

a man born to see, who insists upon speculating. . . . The 'Confidence Man' is a thoroughly American story; and Mr. Melville evidently had some occult object in his mind, which he has not yet accomplished, when he began to paint the 'Masquerades' of this remarkable personage. . . . Save for its greater reasonableness and moderation, the 'Confidence Man' ought to be ranked with 'Moby Dick' and 'Mardi' as one of those books which everybody will buy, many persons read, and very few understand.

He was right in saying that the book would not be understood; perhaps his *a priori* objection to the philosophical, the fanciful, and the fantastic in Melville's books clouded his vision of Melville's "occult object." Nevertheless, he praised the realism and the strong, fine style of *The Confidence-Man.*

The rare and brief American reviews,[43] like the English reviews, said that the style was "striking, original, sinewy, compact" (as *Mrs. Stephens' New Monthly* phrased it), and that the local descriptions were "striking and picturesque" and the "oddities of thought, felicities of expression, the wit, humor, and rollicking inspirations are as abundant and original as in any of the productions of this most remarkable writer" (as

[42] "Our Authors and Authorship—Melville and Curtis," *Putnam's Monthly Magazine,* IX (April 1857), 384-393; the article is unsigned.

[43] *Mrs. Stephens' New Monthly,* II (June 1857), 288; *New York Daily Times, Supplement,* 11 April 1857, p. 1. Mr. Jay Leyda, who discovered most of these reviews, also excerpts or mentions in *The Melville Log* (pp. 566, 568, 575) reviews in the *Albany Evening Journal,* quoted in the *Salem Register* (6 April 1857), and the *Boston Daily Advertiser* (8 April, 1857), and a notice in *The Spirit of the Times* (25 April 1857). Mr. Leyda has kindly given me a copy of a manuscript review preserved among Melville's papers; it is not known who wrote it or whether it was ever published; it is favorable and rather general. He has also sent a copy of a very brief review, "probably by J. G. Holland," in the *Springfield Daily Republican,* 16 May 1857.

the *New York Daily Times* put it). Also, as in the English reviews, no one understood what the book was about or what the Confidence Man was or that the book had any pattern: "You might, without sensible inconvenience, read it backwards," Mrs. Stephens' reviewer announced, along with a frank confession of inability to understand the book or find the object of the Masquerade. The *Springfield Daily Republican* found it most ingenious but cynical.

The American comments differed from the English in being less respectful, less percipient than the best of the English, more given to lecturing Melville for becoming eccentric rather than writing more *Typees,* and of course less taken with the satire; Melville's home-town paper, the *Berkshire County Eagle,* after saying handsomely that *The Confidence-Man* "is much praised in the English papers," quoted the remarks of the *Saturday Review* on the money-getting spirit in the United States in order to refute them by saying that as a picture of American society the book is "slightly exaggerated."

Since the rediscovery of Melville in the twenties, *The Confidence-Man* has been the last of Melville's novels to draw its due of either critical study or critical acclaim. In most of the past thirty years it has been the ugly duckling, showing no promise of the swan except to one or two critics, who, however, did little more for the novel than affirm its importance. In recent years, however, one has begun to hear that there is "a strong, tough intellection at work in it"; that it is a work of high moral intelligence and that the Confidence Man himself is "one of the most extraordinary figures in American literature"; that it is "one of the most valuable of the works in Melville's canon."[44] Furthermore, though the novel had never been reprinted, except in the Standard Edition of Melville's works, in the last five years it has had three editions besides the

---

[44] William Ellery Sedgwick, *Herman Melville: The Tragedy of Mind* (Cambridge, 1944), p. 187; Richard Chase, *Herman Melville: A Critical Study* (New York, 1949), pp. 206, 185; John W. Shroeder, "Sources and Symbols for Melville's *Confidence-Man,*" *PMLA,* LXVI (1951), 363-380; p. 380.

present one—an English, an American, and a translation into French.[45]

Let us look briefly at what modern critics have made of the book. For a while *The Confidence-Man* seems to have been "regarded as a kind of bastard, to be passed over without mention or to be disposed of with an annihilating phrase."[46] As late as 1938 a student of Melville's reputation could so summarize the reception of this book in the twentieth century. Some of these annihilating phrases were: "a posthumous work," and "perverse self-indulgence of the 'spontaneous Me'"; "a laborious pseudo-narrative treatise"; "not markedly original" and "wild and whirling satire."[47] John Freeman and Van Wyck Brooks treated it less cavalierly, but not less disparagingly. Mr. Freeman called it "the vainest of satires" on "the hypocrisy and assertiveness of passengers on a steamship"; he said that it supported "Dickens' worst charges"; that the true meaning of its masquerade is "hopelessly obscure"; and that its mood was dictated by "the sense of personal failure."[48] Mr. Brooks called it "an abortion: . . . broken off in the middle, apparently, but not before the author has lost the thread of his original idea"; "the product of premature artistic senility." (Twenty years later Mr. Brooks still thought it a "laborious satire," with "its

<hr>

[45] London, John Lehmann, 1948, with an introduction by Roy Fuller; New York, Grove Press, 1949. Mr. Fuller, however, hardly recommends the novel, though he does praise the satire and, by inference, the "ambiguity remarkable in a novel published in 1851 [*sic*]." He repeats Yvor Winters' judgment on the novel, and adds what threatens to become the theme of British criticism, that its picture of commercial exploitation is verified by *Martin Chuzzlewit* and Mrs. Trollope. Besides the present edition, there have been five editions of *The Confidence-Man* in English: New York, 1857; London, 1857; London, 1923; and these two. It was translated into French, by Henri Thomas, as *Le grand escroc* (Paris, Éditions de Minuit, 1950).

[46] Hetherington, "The Reputation of Herman Melville," p. 361.

[47] In order, Weaver, *Herman Melville*, p. 348, and "Introduction," *Journal up the Straits*, p. xx; P. H. Boynton, *Literature and American Life* (Chicago, 1936), p. 472; Carl Van Doren, *The American Novel* (New York, 1921), p. 75, and in ed. of 1940, p. 99.

[48] John Freeman, *Herman Melville* (New York, 1926), pp. 140-144.

clutter of faceless characters and its dubious meaning.")[49]

Yet even in the twenties there were two dissenting voices. Carl Van Vechten, an early advocate, pointed out in 1922 that *The Confidence-Man* was the great satire on Transcendentalism.[50] Lewis Mumford treated it at some length as "a companion volume to Gulliver's Travels," as a demonstration of man's inability to lead the Christian life he professes, an "indictment of humanity . . . far more deeply corrosive than anything in Bierce or Mark Twain," as a culmination of the misanthropy and despair that began in *Moby-Dick* and increased in *Pierre*. Yet he interpreted the story in such a way as to be unable to fit some of its most important incidents into the logic of the plot, and concluded that "their existence becomes plausible only if one believes Melville's own torments and suspicions had, for a brief while, taken on a pathological character."[51]

This little trickle of recognition continued but hardly increased during the thirties. Yvor Winters maintained the importance of *The Confidence-Man* to an understanding of Melville; he treated it as a repetition of what he took to be the theme of *Pierre,* that "the world is one of moral confusion" which frustrates action; and this, he says, is "the counsel of the despairing moralist."[52] Robert Forsythe insisted that the novel should be treated as the fourth in a tetralogy with *Mardi, Moby-Dick,* and *Pierre.*[53] A French treatise on Melville's life and work by Jean Simon devoted more than a dozen pages to *The Confidence-Man,* and appraised it as faulty but far from

[49] Van Wyck Brooks, *Emerson and Others* (New York, 1927), pp. 177-179; *The Times of Melville and Whitman* ([New York], 1947), p. 169.

[50] Carl Van Vechten, *Excavations* (New York, 1926), pp. 87-88; reprinted from *The Double Dealer,* III (1922).

[51] Lewis Mumford, *Herman Melville* (New York, 1929), pp. 247-255. Lloyd Morris, in his "Melville: Promethean," *The Open Court,* XLV (1931), 514-526, said that it went "deeper than Gulliver," and praised it extravagantly in grandiloquent generalities.

[52] Yvor Winters, *Maule's Curse* (Norfolk, Conn., 1938), pp. 80, 82-85.

[53] In his review of Thorp, *Herman Melville,* in *American Literature,* XI (1939), 92-95.

negligible. Yet M. Simon offered (rather tentatively) a very curious reading of the novel which is at odds with Melville's text in many places. He took the Confidence Man to be a person who goes through life trying out various lines of conduct, and finding that roguery leads to self-scorn, that a courageous effort to cure the wickedness of men is futile and leads only to deceptions, that perhaps a smiling misanthropy that takes refuge in solitude is the best way of life.[54]

In the 1940's the little rill of sympathetic interest in *The Confidence-Man* at last began to swell a bit: a doctoral dissertation appeared, then William E. Sedgwick's brief but perceptive discussion, Egbert S. Oliver's two articles on certain chapters of the novel, an M.A. thesis, Richard Chase's bold negation of most antecedent criticism in his contention that *The Confidence-Man* is "a great book . . . a buoyant, energetic piece of writing, . . . by no means a fragment," the new editions and translation of *The Confidence-Man,* John W. Shroeder's illuminating article, and several articles on parts of the novel.[55]

Mr. Sedgwick saw in the book "a strong, tough body of

[54] Jean Simon, *Herman Melville: Marin, Métaphysicien, et Poèt* (Paris, 1939), pp. 175, 430-442.

[55] Elizabeth S. Foster, "Herman Melville's *The Confidence-Man:* Its Origins and Meaning," unpublished dissertation, Yale University, 1942; Sedgwick, *Herman Melville,* pp. 187-193; Egbert S. Oliver, "Melville's Goneril and Fanny Kemble," *New England Quarterly,* XVIII (1945), 489-500, and "Melville's Picture of Emerson and Thoreau in 'The Confidence-Man,'" *College English,* VIII (1946), 61-72; James Allen Stewart, "A Critical Study of *The Confidence-Man* by Herman Melville." M.A. thesis, University of Texas, 1946; Richard Chase, "An Approach to Melville," *Partisan Review,* XIV (1947), 284-294, p. 293; Richard Chase, "Melville's *Confidence Man,*" *Kenyon Review,* XI (1949), 122-140; Richard Chase, *Herman Melville* (New York, 1949); John W. Shroeder, "Sources and Symbols for Melville's *Confidence-Man,*" *PMLA,* LXVI (1951), 363-380; Roy Harvey Pearce, "Melville's Indian-hater: A Note on a Meaning of *The Confidence-Man,*" *PMLA,* LXVII (1952), 942-948; Dan G. Hoffman, "Melville's 'Story of China Aster,'" *American Literature,* XXII (1950), 137-149; Nathalia Wright, "The Confidence Man of Melville and Cooper: An American Indictment," *American Quarterly,* IV (1952), 266-268; Howard C. Horsford, "Evidence of Melville's Plans for a Sequel to *The Confidence-Man,*" *American Literature,* XXIV (1952), 85-89.

observed facts of human nature" and "a strong, tough intellection at work." Although he took the moral to be "that goodness, kindliness, trust, serve for nothing but springes to catch woodcocks," yet his sensitive reading discovered that here, at the dark corner of Melville's intellectual journey, Melville turned his face away from misanthropy.[56]

Mr. Chase elaborated his claims that *The Confidence-Man* is a great book and offered an extended interpretation of the story in an article and then in his book *Herman Melville*. He says he is tempted to call this novel Melville's "second-best book"; it is a book in which Melville "was able to display a ripe satirical intelligence in a style unique among his writings for its leanness, nimbleness, and jaunty vigor." Mr. Chase takes the Confidence Man to be a mythic figure standing for "the pious and irresponsible progressive," and the novel to be a series of scenes in which this mythic person "represents all that was wrong with the liberalism of Melville's day: its commercialism, its superficiality, its philistinism, its spurious optimism, its glad-handed self-congratulation, its wish-fulfilling vagueness, its fondness for uplifting rhetoric, its betrayal of all tragic or exalted human and natural values, its easy belief in automatic progress." He feels that this book ought to be "scripture" for modern liberals who wish to keep their liberalism courageous and creative. The Confidence Man is a figure of folklore, a mythic being, compounded of the Yankee peddler, Brother Jonathan, Uncle Sam, Orpheus, and Christ, a "Promethean-Orphean figure who seems to be the bringer of life and civilization to his people but who is not what he seems."[57]

Mr. Shroeder, approaching the difficulties of *The Confidence-Man* through a study of some of its sources—most illumi-

[56] Sedgwick, *Herman Melville*, pp. 187-193.
[57] Chase, Ch. 6, "The Sweet Voice," *Herman Melville*, pp. 185-209. The interpretation does not always seem to be self-consistent, at any rate to this reader. For example, I am unable to pull any meaning out of the mythology which Mr. Chase finds in the scene of the man with the gold sleeve buttons, in which, as Mr. Chase reads it, "the God of free and easy progressivism" is diddled by the Confidence Man, who, apparently, is himself a mythic figure representing free and easy progressivism.

natingly its sources in Hawthorne and Bunyan—and symbols, has let more light into this book than any other critic. Although, as he says, he has left a number of riddles unsolved and the inclusion of a number of incidents unexplained, yet his close study has enabled him to sense not only the power but also the sound architecture of *The Confidence-Man;* he calls it "a hale and well proportioned giant" among Melville's novels, and says that it "establishes a single, though complex, aim and follows that aim through with what is, for Melville, remarkable fidelity." Mr. Shroeder demonstrates beyond question the diabolic and mythic nature of the Confidence Man and the theme of his betrayal of man; to oppose this emissary of Satan, he says, Melville brings forward the dedicated hater of evil, the Indian-hater of one of the episodes.

Roy Harvey Pearce, studying the sources of Melville's Indian-hater, gives Mr. Shroeder's reading a modification. "Melville has no more praise for Indian-hating than he does for confidence," he says. "The issue of blind confidence and blind hatred is in the end identical." And "There would seem to be no way out of the darkness."

Most of the later criticism of Melville, however, has given rather meager treatment to *The Confidence-Man,* and has found little to praise. Willard Thorp considered it as a lesser novel in which Melville, surrendering to misanthropy, finds only three kinds of men in the world—knaves, fools, and misanthropes, and "exhibits his sorry examples of fraudulent humanity with a grim detachment that is more harrowing than a diatribe."[58] F. O. Matthiessen saw the novel as an example of unsuccessful realism, an attempt to portray the "cosmopolitan and confident tide" of life on the Mississippi, an attempt which produced instead only a "two dimensional travelling-salesman's world" because Melville did not know his material. "The problem was further complicated by Melville's own state of mind," a mood of Timonism. "He was too bitter, too dis-

[58] Thorp, *Herman Melville,* pp. cxvi-cxvii.

tressed personally, to keep his satire under control, and so there is no progression to his theme. . . ."[59]

In the *Literary History of the United States* Mr. Thorp calls *The Confidence-Man* a "fascinating book in what it reveals about Melville's state of mind, for the strength of its satire, and its allusive wit." Misanthropy is mainly what this brief criticism finds in the book; Melville "has now come to the point where he must abandon his humanist faith in the decency and dignity of man. . . . Where can one find in the world the mutual trust and esteem, the charity, the love, which are the cement of society?"[60] Alexander Cowie says that "although Mark Twain more savagely arraigned the creator of a cruelly iniquitous world, Melville exceeded him in sheer misanthropy," and that the book is a "potpourri of satirical commentary" and lacks "structural proportion."[61] Geoffrey Stone finds it an unfinished work in which the "opinions entertained about the Creator in the earlier books are in *The Confidence-Man* logically developed as they concern the creature, and the result is misanthropy."[62]

Newton Arvin takes it to be a still blacker book, "one of the most *infidel* books ever written by an American; one of the most completely nihilistic, morally and metaphysically." He finds this "uncomforted" allegory disappointing, because its

---

[59] F. O. Matthiessen, *American Renaissance: Art and Expression in the Age of Emerson and Whitman* (New York, 1941), pp. 409-412, 491-493. A. H. Quinn, *American Fiction* (New York, 1936), pp. 153-154, dismissed it as a dull and formless string of conversations, and as simply dull in *The Literature of the American People* (New York, 1951).

[60] Robert E. Spiller, Willard Thorp, Thomas H. Johnson, and Henry Seidel Canby, eds., *Literary History of the United States* (New York, 1948) 3 vols., I, 463-464.

[61] Alexander Cowie, *The Rise of the American Novel* (New York, 1948), pp. 393-394.

[62] Geoffrey Stone, *Melville* (New York, 1949), pp. 228-234. Gordon Beverly, in a brief letter to the London *Times Literary Supplement* (No. 2,493, 11 November 1949, p. 733) says that Melville's temper in *The Confidence-Man* is not one of "despair, or of satisfaction in denial," that the novel is a well planned, finished whole, that the conclusion is "a splendid picture of true confidence in the Universe and in Man."

satire falls short of Melville's *"ideal* purpose, the comic exposure of a long procession of frauds and shams, national frauds and contemporary shams, and particularly the quackeries of a false humanitarianism, an insensate optimism"; because it is "not a living narrative"; and because its effect is "not terror but tameness," for Melville had lost his sense of the tragic, the "vision of tragic grandeur" which informs Moby-Dick.[63]

Leon Howard found it a cynical book, the first part having been written from "a point of view which portrayed all faith as folly," and the second part being somewhat less dark in mood because Melville had become skeptical of his own cynicism. "The change of course observable in the book is more nearly explicable in terms of the author's life [his improved health during the latter part of the writing] than in terms of his art."[64]

Ronald Mason, claiming for every work of art a double validity, artistic and personal, places the importance of *The Confidence-Man* not in itself, for it is an artistic failure, but in its relation to the mind of the great man who created it. It is Melville's "baffled, disgusted recoil" from "the glaring rapacities and discordancies of the social scene in the ten years prior to the outbreak of the Civil War." It is "the embittered utterance of a bewildered mind expressing its bewilderment by bewilderment, just as the kindred imagination of Franz Kafka half a century later was to embody his own spiritual predicaments in strange unfolding symbolisms just as subtly revealing." Unable to compass Shakespeare's "serene comprehension of good and evil," Melville remains entangled in his "savage misanthropy."[65]

Lawrance Thompson's book *Melville's Quarrel with God* dis-

---

[63] Newton Arvin, *Herman Melville* ([New York], 1950), pp. 246-252. Pierre Frédérix, *Herman Melville* ([Paris], 1950), dismisses *The Confidence-Man* in half a paragraph as expressing "la misanthropie intense où a sombré son auteur."

[64] Leon Howard, *Herman Melville: A Biography* (Berkeley and Los Angeles, 1951), pp. 227-232, 237.

[65] Ronald Mason, *The Spirit Above the Dust: A Study of Herman Melville* (London, 1951), pp. 198-207.

cusses *The Confidence-Man* as another exemplification of Mr. Thompson's often repeated, central argument—that Melville came to "loathe" the Christian doctrines, that he hated God because he believed God to be a malicious tyrant, and that he wrote his books, after the first ones, in order to disclose this heavenly villainy and to vent his scorn for men who neither perceived the villainy nor understood his, Melville's, necessarily covert disclosures. *The Confidence-Man* is perhaps more important to Mr. Thompson's book than this book is to *The Confidence-Man;* for it is easier to find Mr. Thompson's argument in *The Confidence-Man* than in any of Melville's other books, partly because this novel is more obscure than any other, and partly because the swindlers who beset man in this novel are indeed cosmic, or mythic, agents or agent. Mr. Thompson assumes that they are all agents of God. He decides, for reasons not given, that one of the cynical characters, the one-legged man, is expressing Melville's views; when Melville, as narrator, says that these are the views of a "shallow unfortunate," Mr. Thompson says that the narrator of the novel must be split into two people, Melville and a stupid, "shallow Christian narrator" who must be understood to be the one who says whatever in the expository part of the novel oppugns Mr. Thompson's thesis.[66]

Looking through these twentieth-century readings of *The Confidence-Man,* one notes that most of them take Timonism or misanthropy or cynicism to be the mood or the conviction which dictated the satire and which emerges as the moral;

[66] Lawrance Thompson, *Melville's Quarrel with God* (Princeton, 1952), pp. 297-328. The argument of this book is fairly obviously circular: the author regularly assumes that any passages of an import opposed to his thesis, of which there are hundreds in Melville's works, letters, and marginalia, are ironic.

Edward Wagenknecht, *Cavalcade of the American Novel* (New York, 1952), pp. 72-73, treats *The Confidence-Man,* very briefly, as misanthropic and without coherence. Charles Feidelson, Jr., *Symbolism and American Literature* (Chicago, 1953), pp. 207-212, 341-343, discusses it rather generally as "a comedy of human thought" which is "ultimately negative," since "no verification is possible, [and] confidence and lack of confidence are equally arbitrary."

several modern critics suppose this Timonism to have been due to a pathological state of mind in Melville; one or two find a moral or metaphysical nihilism; the least sympathetic are those who assume that Melville was trying to write a realistic sketch of life on the Mississippi; hardly more sympathetic are those who understand that the book is a satiric allegory, yet criticize its art by the yardstick of realism, or measure it against the heroic and tragic grandeurs of *Moby-Dick*. Some have taken the Confidence Man himself to be one or more ordinary Mississippi swindlers; some have found him protean, a creature of fantasy, or allegoric; a few find him mythic. Many think the novel a fragment, broken off in the middle.

Obviously *The Confidence-Man* still keeps many, or most, of its secrets.[67] It keeps its secrets because its submerged meaning, it seems probable, was deliberately hidden. It needs to be decoded. Furthermore, it can be. The insights of some of the critics mentioned above will be helpful; the few scraps of manuscript that survive—bits of early drafts of parts of the novel and chapter titles, which are transcribed and discussed in the Appendix—throw light on Melville's intentions in a number of places and on the way the novel took form in his mind; to remember Melville's speculations leading up to *The Confidence-Man* and moving on from it through the poems and *Billy Budd* will clear up a few particular riddles and will also help to keep the general interpretation on the right track; finally, let us assume that Melville tried to write a coherent book—surely a reasonable assumption, and look for interpretations that satisfy every detail of the text and fit into a self-consistent whole. In the section that follows, the present editor ventures to offer the reader an interpretation that has made use of these sources of enlightenment and restriction.

It has seemed best to offer a much more detailed analysis than is usual in introductions, because for nearly a hundred

[67] Leslie A. Fiedler wrote recently that "a glance through Melville criticism would reveal on the part of his most sympathetic expounders a series of frank misreadings [of *The Confidence-Man*] and evasions of the cagiest and most transparent sort." See "Out of the Whale," *Nation*, CLXIX (1949), 494.

years this novel has hidden behind its obscurities from thousands and thousands of readers who might have been enjoying its rare qualities. Even so, the analysis attempts only to give the reader solid footing along the main paths of Melville's fantasy. As in every other work of art, the invitation to explore further and further beckons constantly from *The Confidence-Man,* and the possibilities of discovery are endless.

iv

". . . *more reality, than real life itself can show.*"

On its surface the novel is a plotless, episodic tale of the paltry swindles of a series of confidence men during a journey on an April Fool's Day down the Mississippi in a steamboat. That Melville intended this tale to have broader and satirical meanings immediately becomes clear. Like the ships in *White-Jacket* and *Moby-Dick,* his steamboat is a microcosm; its passengers, of every race, creed, and occupation, represent mankind in general, "a piebald parliament, an Anacharsis Cloots congress of all kinds of that multiform pilgrim species, man." The running satire on the difference between men's profession of Christianity and their practice is fairly obvious. The boat is named the *Fidèle;* but she looks like a white-washed fort, her windows like gun embrasures. A "lamb-like" man holds up a slate reading, "Charity thinketh no evil," and other verses from I Corinthians 13; but the passengers feel that the barber's sign, "No Trust," conveys a more appropriate sentiment. There are innumerable satirical thrusts, in the subsequent action and dialogue, at the contradiction between the love and faith on the lips of the "faithful" passengers and the skepticism and hardness in their minds and hearts. All this is clear. But the criticism of religion itself and the attack on optimistic philosophy are more deeply hidden.

The first question is: Who or what is the Confidence Man? The lamblike man disappears after his unavailing attempt to spread the gospel of love and faith, and a crippled Negro, soliciting alms with a tambourine and begging people to put confidence in him, is the first of a series of impostors who play into one another's hands and who cheat the confiding. The Negro's list of "friends" is a list of the Confidence Men to come. Melville's subtitle, *His Masquerade*, suggests that these men are one man in various disguises rather than a series of men; furthermore, they all appear mysteriously: no one ever sees them embark or disembark, although some of them speak of leaving and entering the boat, and one of them, the herb-doctor, pretends to see his predecessor step ashore.

The question whether they are one man soon loses relevance, however, as the reader begins to suspect that the Confidence Man, and also his predecessor the lamblike man, have something of the supernatural about them. No mere disguises could achieve the Confidence Man's extraordinary changes in appearance and also withstand the scrutiny of his many victims, some of whom see him in more than one phase. Besides, his motive is not money-getting (though many critics have thought it is); his most elaborate operations have as their object paltry sums, mere tokens of successfully deluded confidence. Pitch, the most thoughtful victim of the Confidence Men, recognizes them as " 'metaphysical scamps.' " Consider too Melville's parallels and oblique references. The opening sentence of the novel, describing the "sudden" appearance of the lamblike man, images the advent of a deity in its allusion to Manco Capak, the Peruvian demigod, child of the sun, and forerunner of the Inca dynasty. "In the same moment with his advent," the lamblike man steps aboard the *Fidèle;* he is, "in the extremest sense of the word, a stranger"; though he is without baggage or parcel, he looks as though he has traveled "night and day from some far country beyond the prairies."

These phrases sound so innocent that perhaps no reader, after the first few pages, would be willing to agree that Melville meant anything out of the ordinary by them; but let the reader come back to the first page after finishing the novel, or half of it, that is, after his ear has become accustomed to the whisper, and his eye to the apparitions, of Melville's "little lower layer."

One more of Melville's hints that the shadow the Confidence Man casts is a supernatural one: near the end of the novel, when the climactic avatar of the Confidence Man startles the barber into thinking him a spirit, he tells the barber not to be too sure what he is.

"You call me *man,* just as the townsfolk called the angels who, in man's form, came to Lot's house; just as the Jew rustics called the devils who, in man's form, haunted the tombs. You can conclude nothing absolute from the human form, barber."

Is he angel or devil, the Confidence Man? He goes about, in his different incarnations, preaching faith, hope, and charity, both religious and philosophic optimism; he decries all atheistic or misanthropic sentiments; he is benevolent, hopeful, meek, and gentle, the good Christian in religion and ethics, in manner and precept. But in practice he never loses an opportunity, however small, to dupe anyone who is fool enough to have faith or hope or charity. Under a pretense of Christianity, he systematically destroys the very roots of faith and brotherly love. Preaching candor, he is himself a hypocrite. Towards the end of the book he betrays his lack of faith, and therefore his hypocrisy, in a *double-entendre:* an old man, who has been reading the Bible and proclaiming his faith in man and in Providence, nevertheless supplies himself with a lock for his door, a money-belt, a counterfeit-detector, and a life-preserver; whereupon the Confidence Man says: "'In providence, as in man, you and I equally put trust.'" As with St. Paul's language on his lips he lures the greedy and the credulous, and also the generous and the thoughtful, to snatch at heaven and close their hands on hell, the old saying that the devil quotes Scripture gets a wry and Melvillean twist.

From the first chapter through the next-to-the-last, a curious emphasis is placed on the terms "original" and "original genius," always in reference to the Confidence Man; these are fingers, perhaps, pointing to the idea that the Confidence Man is a manifestation of an original or primal force in the universe.

This evil at the heart of things, this malignity that has been from the beginning, which walks the deck of the *Fidèle* behind the masks of the Confidence Man, not only puts forth the moldings of its features from behind the masks, but is sometimes tagged with an unequivocal name. Six or seven times Melville openly hints an equivalence between the Confidence Man and "that old serpent called the Devil and Satan, which deceiveth the whole world." Mr. Chase calls the Confidence Man a false Prometheus, one who falsely pretends to be the bringer of civilization and life; his interpretation of the novel in terms of the true and the false Prometheus illuminates and enlarges our vista of the social criticism, but it blacks out our view from the metaphysical or religious windows of the allegory, for Mr. Chase's Prometheus is a trope, and is limited to social reference, rather than a cosmic spirit or force. The difference between the true and the false Prometheus is not, therefore, the same as the difference between Christ and the devil, nor so terrible. At any rate, the myth by means of which Melville consciously enlarged the reach of *The Confidence-Man* is biblical; from the crippled Negro, who is made an analogue of the devil gulling Eve, to the last of the Confidence Men, who wreathes his form and sidelong crests his head like Satan in *Paradise Lost*, the myth connoted is the devil's temptation of man.

This diabolic role, however, the Confidence Man plays in such a successful disguise that numerous critics, as we have seen, have failed to guess his duplicity. Yet Melville has carefully, though very quietly, labeled each avatar, from the Negro on, as false, and most of them as swindlers.

The first advertiser of Christianity, the lamblike man, differs from those who follow him in that he commits no wrong, except perhaps unintentionally in softening victims for subsequent swindlers, and in no way, except to some people through his oddity, suggests that he is an impostor. Upon him the stigmata of the true Christian, and even of Christ himself, are patent. His message is Love. His white and "lamb-like" appearance is stressed; he seems "singularly innocent," gentle, helpless, and harmless. Though banged and nearly overthrown by some of the porters, though jeered and buffeted by his fellow-Christians, he remains meek, gentle, dreamy. In this world he is, "in the extremest sense of the word, a stranger."

This description of the lamblike man recalls what Melville had said in earlier novels about Christianity. In *Mardi* and *White-Jacket* he had in effect defined for himself the essential Christian doctrine, the message of the New Testament, as simply the ethics of universal love and passive resistance to evil, vouchsafed by a benevolent God, attested by the love of Jesus, and particularized in the Sermon on the Mount. In Serenia, the Christian Utopia of *Mardi,* the warrant for belief in Christ is, not reason or Biblical or ecclesiastical authority, but primarily the response of the human heart to His teaching; and Melville's own religious heart lifts up to an *O altitudo!* in contemplation of this heavenly ideal. His mind, however, turns its prow away from this haven and out through the breakers into the open sea of thought. Exploring that perilous unknown in *Moby-Dick* and *Pierre,* Melville finds, not a benevolent God, but enigma. God is unknowable. If He hears us, He gives no sign. The Voice of our God is Silence. That is why the lamblike man is deaf and dumb. There is another reason too: he is, in this world, "in the extremest sense of the word, a stranger." In *Pierre,* in the pamphlet on Chronometricals and Horologicals, the Christian ideal was said to be unfit for this world, or this unregenerate world for it; this thought is externalized here in the lamblike man's helpless unworldliness, his jaded air, his utter strangeness and isolation. The forever unreconcilable difference between the order of heaven and the order of earth is a theme of *White-Jacket, Pierre,* and *Billy Budd.*

At the end of the scene, as the lamblike man sleeps "like some enchanted man in his grave" at the foot of a ladder leading to a cross-wise balcony above, he calls to mind the resurrection, and also God's promise to Jacob, dreaming at Luz at the foot of the ladder to heaven, that his seed should be as the dust of the earth and that in his seed should all the families of the earth be blessed.

What, then, is Melville saying? Does he mean to include the

lamblike man among the impostors and thereby to imply that
the very founding of Christianity was an expression of the
universal malignity towards man? that God, though in an
absolute sense unknowable, is in an effective and human sense
evil? Pointing towards the inclusion of the lamblike man
among the swindlers is the fact that the placard which warns
the passengers against a "mysterious impostor," who is "quite
an original genius in his vocation," says that he comes "from
the East." This is a perhaps negligible hint, this reference to
the East. At any rate, Melville clearly differentiates between
him and the Confidence Men: he is innocent of fraud; he is
unequivocal; he is not on the Negro's list of Confidence Men.

Also, Melville clearly seems, in this scene and the next, to
be contrasting Christ and Antichrist, to be showing how the
devil makes use of Christian idealism for his own ends. The
crippled Negro with his "black fleece," coming immediately
after the lamblike man with his white, fleecy vesture, suggests
a deliberate contrast between the pure ideal of Christianity
and the black use made of it by the powers of evil, or the white
ideal and the black perversion wrought by man. Just a year
earlier, in "Benito Cereno,"[68] Melville had described another
Negro in much the same terms as this one: Don Benito's servant turns up his face "like a shepherd's dog" to his master;
our crippled Negro is "cut down to the stature of a Newfoundland dog." But Don Benito's servant conceals beneath an appearance of humble faithfulness the most profound and ele-
mental treachery, hatred, and malignity. Since these Negroes
are alike in another way, both being the ring-leaders in the
game of deception and destruction though appearing embodiments of honesty and humility, it seems that Melville carried
over from "Benito Cereno" the dog-like black man as a symbol
for the black, deceitful, universal malice masquerading as
fidelity and love. (Melville's use of both Negroes and Indians

[68] Melville sent "Benito Cereno" to *Putnam's* in April 1855 (letter of
G. W. Curtis to J. A. Dix, Providence, 17 April 1855. HCL-M); he
probably began planning *The Confidence-Man* about this time (see
above, p. xxiii).

as symbols, it ought to be made clear, has no relation to his humanitarian attitudes, expressed elsewhere, to them as people.)

Two other themes of the novel appear in this scene of the Negro's machinations. " 'Charity is one thing, and truth is another. . . ,' " the sour, gimlet-eyed, wooden-legged cynic says. " 'To where it belongs with your charity! To heaven with it! . . . Here on earth, true charity dotes, and false charity plots.' " This proposition is the one which the novel debates. It is illustrated many times in the succeeding incidents. But one notes that Melville puts it in the mouth of a "limping, gimlet-eyed, sour-faced person," whose shambling on one leg, the Methodist minister said, is emblematic of his one-sided view of humanity. And in this novel, every personal description is emblematic. Another theme, the most obvious of the novel, is the failure of Christians to be Christian. The Methodist minister, goaded into anger by the cynic, seized him and shook him "till his timber-toe clattered on the deck like a ninepin." But Melville's satire on the unchristian leaders of Christ's people is tempered by an honest tribute to the few who carry the Gospels into their acts. The Episcopal minister was steadfast in his kindness and charity—and was duped for his pains.

The next manifestation of the Confidence Man is a man in mourning. We infer his membership in the guild from his using information on a business card previously purloined by the crippled Negro and from his air of acting a part. But the mourner's essential falseness is his sentimentality. He is the man of feeling, and the feeling is a pose. In his colloquy with the sophomore, he fills out Melville's plan, for we see that the Confidence Man is armed not only with Christian but with other optimistic philosophies: the man of feeling, the graveyard sentimentalist, appropriately extols the sentimental optimism of the eighteenth century. His aesthetic definition of evil is conveyed in the Shaftesburyan parallel of wickedness and ugliness; it is to be echoed later by the final Confidence Man, the cosmopolitan. With quiet irony, Melville arrays the wisdom of the ancients in refutation of this shallow optimism.

The Confidence Man next appears as a man in a gray coat and white tie, who differs from the man in mourning by revealing "little of sorrow, though much of sanctity." He is righteousness, preying upon goodness. He betrays his falseness in a number of ways. For example, when the clergyman asks about the crippled Negro, he replies that he helped him off the boat at the last landing; but a few minutes later, he offers to find the Negro among the passengers. His arguments, like those of the rest of the Confidence Men, are pied with fallacies. But, as in the case of the man in mourning, his essential falsity lies in his contradiction of his own pretended nature: he professes charity but has none; charity is an enterprise; it is egoistic, not altruistic.

In his philosophic satire, then, Melville has moved on chronologically from Shaftesburyan to Utilitarian optimism. The benevolence of the man in the gray coat is the egoistic benevolence with which the advocates of enlightened self-interest sugared their doctrines: " 'For what creature,' " he argues, " 'but a madman would not rather do good than ill, when it is plain that, good or ill, it must return upon himself?' " This, says his auditor, is reasonable, but with mankind it won't do. " 'Then mankind are not reasonable beings,' " says the man in the gray coat, " 'if reason won't do with them.' " That is not to the point, says his sensible auditor. The optimistic Benthamite belief that man *is* a thoroughly reasonable being and the best judge of his own interests, and that seeking his own interest he is, as Adam Smith had said, "led by an invisible hand" to contribute to the public good, seems to be the butt of Melville's satire here. Just as the man of feeling was a reader of *Werther*, Shaftesbury, and Akenside, so the man in the gray coat, advocate of utilitarian optimism and free competition, even in the charity "business," appropriately has Adam Smith on his tongue, in a reference to the famous passage on making pins in *The Wealth of Nations*.

The man in the gray coat is also target for another stream of satirical bullets. More clearly visible in his make-up than the features of Jeremy Bentham and the Utilitarians are those of

William Wilberforce and the Evangelicals, a group which had in fact been brought into partial alliance with the disparate Benthamites by a common zeal for humanitarian reform. Melville mentions Wilberforce, the Evangelical philanthropist and reformer, in a passage that loosely equates him with the man in the gray coat. Like Wilberforce, who did not distress himself about the miseries of the poor in England yet devoted his life to the abolition of the slave trade and of slavery in the West Indies, our Confidence Man is promoting an exotic charity, a Widow and Orphan Asylum among the Seminoles. Like Wilberforce he is eloquent, like Wilberforce an enthusiast for foreign missions.

Melville, however, did not have to levy upon English social history for his satirical portrait of the righteous man in the role of missionary and philanthropist. He had already paid his respects, in *Omoo* chiefly, to the American and English missionaries among the Polynesians who preached no real Christianity and won no real converts. He says that he heard a missionary in a sermon in Tahiti tell the natives that Britain was so powerful and rich because she was so good, and that they would do well to bring more pigs and fruit to his house.[69] There is a double irony, too, in Melville's choice of the Seminoles. Banknotes are given to this "foreign" charity, whereas only pennies went to assuage present misfortune in the person of the crippled Negro. And the Seminole widows and orphans are pitied and comforted by a people which has forgotten that it recently widowed and orphaned them, in a war fought to take Florida from them. The so-called benevolence of the righteous man and his like in this world, those who substitute missionary zeal and cold-hearted philanthropy for the troublesome duty of really loving their fellow men, is a sort of "Protean easy-chair," which will give rest to " 'the most tormented conscience.' "

❦   ❦   ❦   ❦   ❦

One can see in Melville's story thus far not only philosophic

[69] *Omoo,* Ch. 45.

satire but also ironic reference to parts of the Sermon on the
Mount and I Corinthians 13:

Matt. 5:3. Blessed are the poor in spirit: for theirs is the kingdom
of heaven.
                4. Blessed are they that mourn: for they shall be com-
forted.
                5. Blessed are the meek: for they shall inherit the earth.
                6. Blessed are they which do hunger and thirst after
righteousness: for they shall be filled.
        I Cor. 13:1. Though I speak with the tongues of men and of
angels, and have not charity, I am become as sounding brass, or a
tinkling cymbal.
                2. And . . . though I have all faith, so that I could
remove mountains, and have no charity, I am nothing.
                3. And though I bestow all my goods to feed the poor
. . . and have not charity, it profiteth me nothing.

The Negro is one of the meek and the poor in spirit; the
man of feeling is one of them that mourn; the man in the
gray coat is righteousness and charity. And they are all spurious. In the case of the righteous man the biblical parallels are
explicit; for example, St. Paul's "the tongues of men and of
angels" becomes "a not unsilvery tongue, too, . . . with gestures that were a Pentecost of added ones, and persuasiveness before which granite hearts might crumble into gravel";
the man has, he says, " 'confidence to remove obstacles, though
mountains,' " and he has no charity.

The rest of the novel dramatizes, as a religious allegory, the
last verse of the chapter from first Corinthians with which the
novel began: "And now abideth faith, hope, and charity, these
three; but the greatest of these is charity." The man with the
big book is faith. The herb-doctor is hope. The man with the
brass plate and the cosmopolitan are charity. These virtues are
their masks; for each man is in reality his opposite.

On a slightly different plane of the allegory, each of these
swindlers to come also casts another shadow. The message
of the man with the big book is "Trust God"; that of the herb-

doctor, "Trust Nature"; and that of the man with the brass plate and the cosmopolitan, "Trust Man."

*   *   *   *   *

The man with the big book, a genial, jaunty, prosperous man who is called Mr. Truman, easily swindles a hard-hearted sophomore and the good country merchant, the merchant being disarmed by honest guilelessness as effectively as the sophomore by conceit and greed. Mr. Truman's allegorical shadow is faith in God or in the goodness of the universal order. His optimistic talk as a stock salesman enlarges into philosophic and religious significance. He talks the most flagrant optimism encountered thus far, optimism which postulates a universal goodness: of two greenhorns opposing two professional card players, he says: " 'A fresh and liberal construction would teach us to regard those four players—indeed this whole cabinful of players—as playing at games in which every player plays fair, and not a player but shall win.' "

Blind faith in this universal goodness is what Mr. Truman extols. In conversation the merchant finds that Mr. Truman will not admit that any apparent misfortunes are real misfortunes, for " 'to admit the existence of unmerited misery, more particularly if alleged to have been brought on by the unhindered arts of the wicked,' " Mr. Truman says, is " 'not prudent; since, with some, it might unfavorably bias their most important persuasions' "; and a right conviction of the divine nature and of human nature must be based " 'less on experience than intuition.' " Furthermore, one should deny present evil, he says, rather than stress the doctrine of future retribution, lest those without the true light should say that " 'Providence was not now, but was going to be.' " One should trust neither the feeling of his natural heart nor his reason in these matters, but have faith.

That is to say, in advocating blind faith Mr. Truman contrives to emphasize the blindness rather than the faith, and, like the other Confidence Men, plants the seeds of skepticism while pretending to cultivate belief.

Throughout the episode of the man with the big book, the religious allegory comes to the surface frequently and sometimes jostles the main or fictional story. The big book which is Mr. Truman's authenticator probably stands for the Bible. The merchant justifies his faith in the stock he wishes to buy by arguing: "'How, by examining the book, should I think I knew any more than I now think I do; since, if it be the true book, I think it so already; and since if it be otherwise, then I have never seen the true one, and don't know what that ought to look like.'" From this book, stock that promises fabulous rewards is sold, in language that easily translates into the familiar evangelical terms of salvation by faith. The stock in which the miser invests is one in which he must have faith, one that cannot be pried into, for it is "'a secret, a mystery.'" Mr. Truman "'in pure goodness of heart, makes people's fortunes for them—their everlasting fortunes, as the phrase goes—only charging his one small commission of confidence.'" His office is "'upstairs,'" says another Confidence Man. And finally, Melville surely intended some amusing references to hell and heaven in the "Black Rapids Coal Company," the stock of which Mr. Truman actually sells, and the "New Jerusalem" land development scheme, the stock of which Mr. Truman offers but never sells. Mr. Truman's New Jerusalem, like the one in Revelation, has its "perpetual fountain" and, if not "the tree of life," at any rate some "lignum-vitae rostrums"; and it exists—Melville puns repeatedly on this phrase—"'bona fide.'"

To complete his credentials as an avatar of the Confidence Man, Mr. Truman reveals his diabolic nature; he says to the sophomore, "'I would rather have one of your shares of coal stock than two of this other,'" that is, the New Jerusalem. He is, of course, president of the Black Rapids Coal Company. His message is "Trust God"; and the comment of the allegorist is clear: those who take stock in this belief in heaven and in universal goodness are buying shares in hell, are being diddled by the president of hell.

Next appears a herb-doctor, "his eye beaming with hope."

He sells his Omni-Balsamic Reinvigorator and his Samaritan Pain-Dissuader to the tune of "Trust Nature," just as his predecessor had sung "Trust God." Put no faith in the scientific doctors, he urges; trust the nature that God has provided: " 'Nature is health; for health is good, and nature cannot work ill. As little can she work error.' " Do not be a philosopher and demand reasons, but simply hope and trust. (Nor a logician and demand reasoning, one might add.) Hope is proportioned to faith, since the mind works on the body, and vice versa.

The herb-doctor gulls several people, who are disarmed of their natural and reasonable skepticism by faith, by hope, and by charity respectively. A consumptive recognizes a consonance between the spirit of his religion and the herb-doctor's evangelistic pleading. The miser, in spite of his avarice and the suspicion aroused by his recent dealings with Mr. Truman, believes because he longs for hope. A crippled soldier, victim of man's injustice, is softened for a moment by an act of charitable kindness, and falls dupe. But two men of close experience with nature are proof against the herb-doctor's argument that nature is benevolent. A racked invalid from one of nature's swamps cries out bitterly and angrily that the herb-doctor is a liar. A bristling, eccentric Missouri bachelor named Pitch says that the miser has been diddled with the hocus-pocus about nature, that nature gave him the cough he has, that nature makes deadly herbs as well as healing. He has confidence, he declares, neither in nature nor in man; nature made him blind and would have kept him so had not his oculist counter-plotted her; furthermore, the boys employed by him on his plantation have been so dishonest that he is on his way to buy a machine to do the work of boys.

It is hardly necessary to emphasize the herb-doctor's falseness, since Melville has so obviously made him meretricious and self-contradictory. As in the case of the other Confidence Men, his falseness is radical: he preaches confidence but instills distrust; he preaches hope, but, once sure of his victim, he cruelly plants despair. He implies that faith and hope are the crutches of cripples. Also like others of his guild, he reveals himself to the heedful reader in a *double-entendre* or two: he says, for example, that in reality he has just as much faith in nature as has Pitch, the utterly skeptical. And he says: " 'Faith, very droll, indeed, ha, ha, ha!' "

As the apostle of hope in the religious allegory, the herb-doctor's message is the Christian evangel of salvation by faith. Much of his exhortation to the consumptive contains a thinly veiled version of this doctrine: When you are weak and despairing, then is the time to get strength by faith; for your (immortal) life, rouse faith, though from ashes; hope (of salvation) is proportioned to faith. The herb-doctor concludes this colloquy by parodying a verse of Saint Paul's Epistle to the Thessalonians: "Prove all things; hold fast that which is good," and by referring to the " 'power divine' " which will effect the " 'cure.' " Double meanings may be read out of certain other phrases along here, and some readers, I think, will join me in believing that Melville intended the double reference; for example, for the herb-doctor's medicine, his "Omni-Balsamic Reinvigorator," supply "immortality" or "grace": " 'For heaven's sake, try my medicine,' " says the herb-doctor, and, " 'don't take it till night. Just before retiring is the time.' "

In the philosophical allegory, the herb-doctor is the " 'authorized agent' " of Nature, and through him Melville satirizes the nature cult of the eighteenth and nineteenth centuries, from its deistic through its romantic and transcendental phases. The herb-doctor is ushered onto the stage by an extraordinary description of natural scenery, extraordinary for its heightened poetic tone and lushness of poetic ornament unmatched anywhere else in this novel. His theme, as has been shown, is nature's benevolence, nature's harmony, nature's "final benignity,' " indeed nature's divinity. The doctrine of natural law as a universal moral order, and as the norm which human law seeks to approximate, is perhaps brought in too. Rebuking the crippled soldier for his complaints against human justice, the herb-doctor says:

"But it is never to be forgotten that human government, being subordinate to the divine, must needs, therefore, in its degree, partake of the characteristics of the divine. That is, while in general efficacious to happiness, the world's law may yet, in some cases, have, to the eye of reason, an unequal operation, just as, in the same imperfect view, some inequalities may appear in the operations of heaven's law; nevertheless, to one who has a right confidence, final benignity is, in every instance, as sure with the one law as the other."

In this speech one also recognizes an argument against evil that flourished from before Pope till after Emerson, the argument that partial evil is universal good. One more point: the protest of the nature-worshiping romantic poets against science and rationalism no doubt underlies the herb-doctor's attacks upon science and scientific doctors and upon philosophers and reasoning. But the dearest mark of Melville's satiric arrows shot at the trusters in nature is Emerson and the New England transcendentalists. Lest his satire miss this mark, Melville has the herb-doctor, with bland inconsistency after his lecture on confidence, tell the consumptive to " 'prove all the vials; trust those which are true.' " The verse from Thessalonians which this parodies had become a motto of New England transcendentalism; thus the Confidence Man again links one arm with Saint Paul and one with optimistic philosophy. The Emersonian doctrines of the issuance of good from evil and of compensation are also targets of this satire: " 'From evil comes good,' " the herb-doctor tells the consumptive; and to the Missourian Pitch, who says he has been embezzled of a plantation by the shifting of one of nature's rivers, the herb-doctor says, recalling the language of Ecclesiastes and the thought of Emerson: " 'But have you no confidence that by a reverse shifting that soil will come back after many days?' "

But Pitch, the man of experience, is proof against this optimistic nonsense about nature. The next Confidence Man, therefore, tries Pitch on another tack. The new avatar is a meanly dressed, servile, fawning, deprecating man, with a brass plate hung round his neck to proclaim him an agent of an employment agency, the Philosophical Intelligence Office. Upon his offering to engage a boy for Pitch through his office, Pitch launches a jeremiad, the theme of which is that boyhood is a natural state of rascality. But by natural laws, says the man with the brass plate, those boys who are bad outgrow their rascality, just as they outgrow their first teeth. Nonsense, says the Missourian, men are rascals too, and argument by analogy is only punning with ideas instead of words. Nevertheless, moved by the man's statement that the Philosophical Intelligence Office made a *scientific* study and moved still more strongly by his fundamental desire to believe in his fellows, the Missourian agrees to take a boy from the Office, and pays his fee for the boy's passage. Do not forget, says the man with the brass plate, that any transient vices in your boy " 'will, ere long, fall out, and be replaced by the sound, firm, even and permanent virtues.' " With these words about progress and perfectibility on his lips, he leaves the steamer near a bluff called the Devil's Joke!

Alone, the musing Missourian realizes that he has been diddled, in spite of such faithful protectors as philosophy, knowledge, and experience. His reverie even more than the preceding conversation reveals that he is the thoughtful, honest, good-hearted man whose experience with both nature and humankind has brought him to a disillusioned view of nature and a "general law of distrust systematically applied to the race." His shaggy coat, like a bearskin, his raccoon cap, his bristly chin, his gun—this rough exterior protects a kindly heart. Even his gun, which he rattles and clicks whenever optimists or hyprocrites beset him, seems a symbol less of real misanthropy than of proud, individualistic defiance of an alien world; it recalls the picture of young Redburn on the river boat, clicking the gunlock and presenting his gun at a too insolent intruder upon his poverty.

That the man with the brass plate is an incarnation of the Confidence Man is clear from the facts, among others, that he advocates the Confidence Man's philosophy, that his humility is false, that his professed charity is really cynicism. His sinister implications darken as Pitch reviews his case: If the man is a trickster, "it must be more for the love than the lucre. . . ; the insinuator's undulating flunkeyisms dovetail into those of the flunkey beast that windeth his way on his belly." This is another of the many times when the devil or the serpent of Eden is conjured up as the double of the Confidence Man. Comparison to a dog, suggested in such terms as "canine deprecation," in the man's fawning, wriggling manner, and in the brass plate hung round his neck, plus the man's shoddy garment of humility, carries the reader back to the crippled Negro like a Newfoundland dog in the second scene of the novel. One's suspicion that "dog" is meant to be symbol for "cynic" (in the popular sense) is strengthened when Pitch calls Intelligence Offices " 'swindling concerns kept by low-born cynics, under a fawning exterior wreaking their cynic malice upon mankind,' " and when Melville uses the two ideas together in speaking of Pitch himself, mumbling "his cynical mind to himself, as Apemantus's dog may have mumbled his bone." Pitch's cynicism is superficial, as external as his bear-skin coat and his hedge-hog manner. That of the man with the brass plate is radical, fundamental, and the more vicious for being disguised as eulogy of man's goodness.

The text of his discourse is clearly "Trust Man." His reasoning is "philosophical" or "scientific" rather than religious, and in the Masquerade he represents charity and brotherhood founded on such reasoning. He announces that he has made a " 'careful analytical study of man' " on " 'strictly philosophical principles' " in order to discover what is " 'the state of boyhood scientifically viewed' " and to establish " 'a new philosophy of boys.' " His conclusion is that " 'mankind . . . upon the whole . . . present as pure a moral spectacle as the purest angel could wish.' "

The man from the Philosophical Intelligence Office bases his case upon the validity of human reason, and then reasons by analogy: " 'Our theory teaches us to proceed by analogy from the physical to the moral.' " Just, he says, as the qualities of the lily are concealed in the bud, so are concealed in the boy the virtues which will sprout as surely as his beard, which is also unguessed in the child; any little vices will disappear like milk teeth. Pitch attacks the argument-by-analogy as punning with ideas, but finally falls victim to it himself because of his wish to believe in man.

Besides the optimistic postulate of the innate goodness of man, the corollary doctrines of progress and perfectibility are also broached by the man from the Philosophical Intelligence Office, and in an analogy: " 'In the natural advance of all creatures, do they not bury themselves over and over again in the endless resurrection of better and better?' " A wicked boy may become a good man; " 'he may have been a cater-pillar, but now is a butterfly.' "

" 'Pun away,' " says Pitch. " 'The butterfly is the caterpillar in a gaudy cloak; stripped of which, there lies the impostor's long spindle of a body, pretty much worm-shaped as be-fore.' "

Although in this chapter on the theory that man is in-nately good Melville had an opportunity to bring in the ro-mantic doctrine of primitivism and, in fact, by focusing his discussion on boys leads one to expect from the impostor the argument that the child, fresh from the bosom of nature, is better and wiser than the man, corrupted by arts and in-stitutions, nevertheless he avoids involving these ideas in his ridicule. What he satirizes is the theory of innate and funda-mental goodness and such corollaries as progress and per-fectibility. Perhaps he omits primitivism in the interest of con-centration; perhaps because, without subscribing to the ro-mantic tenet of innate goodness, he himself on different grounds agrees with some romantic notions about the corrupt-ing effects of civilization. The man with the gold sleeve but-tons had the very good luck to be a very good man and pre-served his symbolic whiteness by never touching the sooty world.

The man who next accosts the Missourian, slapping him on the shoulder, is the "king of travelled good-fellows, evidently"; his vesture combines many colors and the styles of many nations; the bowl of his convivial pipe is painted "with linked crests and arms of interlinked nations." He is the cosmopolitan, the climactic Confidence Man, the butterfly risen from the caterpillar, and apparently the very incarnation of charity and brotherly love. The morose Missourian Pitch speaks insultingly to him; but the cosmopolitan with good nature defends "'the spirit of fellowly gladness based on due confidence in what is above,'" for he is a man of the world, "a character which, like its opposite, the sincere Christian's, is not always swift to take offense." This reminds us, by similarity and contrast, of the "sincere Christian" with whom the novel began, the patient lamblike man. In the end Pitch spots the misanthrope under his genial mask: "'You are Diogenes,'" he says, "'Diogenes in disguise . . . masquerading as a cosmopolitan.'"

Ruefully the cosmopolitan replies: "'To you, an Ishmael . . . I came ambassador from the human race . . . but you take me not for the honest envoy, but I know not what sort of unheard-of spy.'"

More than one critic has taken this speech at face value.

As he leaves Pitch, the cosmopolitan is addressed by a stranger, whom some of the passengers suspect to be an "operator," or confidence man. This man has a bilious aspect, and wears clothes which are handsomer and finer than he appears to be. The bilious man, apropos of the misanthropy of Pitch, tells the story of Colonel John Moredock, Indian-hater, as he heard it from his father's friend, Judge James Hall.

✿   ✿   ✿   ✿   ✿

This interpolated account of Indian-hating and Colonel Moredock, which occupies Chapters XXVI and XXVII, is the turning-point of the novel at its symbolical level and the apex of the whole argument; it has been, furthermore, a stumbling-block to several critics. Therefore it will be pertinent here to examine closely Melville's treatment of the material that he borrowed from Judge Hall.

He took his "Metaphysics of Indian-hating" and his story

of Moredock largely from Hall's "Indian-hating.—Some of the sources of this animosity.—Brief account of Col. Moredock." The reader will find this essay in the Explanatory Notes. Melville says that he is using Hall's language rather closely, as he is; but the reader who compares the two treatments will find that Melville has nevertheless made important changes in style and meaning. He breathes the breath of life and drama into Hall's dry, monotonous style; he varies the tempo; he sharpens and telescopes the narrative in its less important stretches; at the dramatic moment he expands it into a memorable close-up of the hero, " 'chewing the wild news with the wild meat' "; he substitutes the specific, graphic, and connotative for the general and commonplace; he enriches with allusion and enlivens with anecdote. The skilled and experienced story-teller and stylist has transmuted Hall's sketch.

The change that Melville makes in the meaning, though not so obvious, is at least equally important. Both Melville and Hall tell the following tale: The backwoodsman's persisting hatred of the Indian, after Indian rapine has ceased, is a curious phenomenon. To understand it, one must understand the backwoodsman: from the necessities of a hard, lonely, unassisted life he has become self-reliant and independent; experience is his tutor. From infancy he has heard stories of Indian lying, theft, fraud, perfidy, blood-thirstiness, ferocity; therefore he hates and distrusts all redskins. But the pure Indian-hater is bred when to the tale of Indian atrocities wreaked upon the community is added some unendurable wrong to the backwoodsman's own family. Then he leaves his kin, commits himself to the forest, and as long as his life lasts devotes himself to his implacable vengeance—the murder of Indians. John Moredock, having lost his family in an Indian massacre, sought out the murderers one by one and killed them; after that, though he sometimes returned briefly to the settlements, he spent his life exterminating red men.

Comparison of the two versions will show that Melville keeps Hall's portrait of the Indian-hater substantially the same except for one change. Hall explains that one reason for the backwoodsman's injustice to the Indians was that the pioneers, keeping always beyond the settlements, preserved the antiquated notions of moral right which prevailed when their ancestors entered the woods in the age of conquest and discovery. Melville omits this; he rests the backwoodsman's hatred of Indians squarely upon the harm that he has suffered through Indian perfidy. But Melville's radical change is in the portrait of the Indian: Hall makes him a savage more sinned against than sinning; Melville makes him the original and irreclaimable villain. He carefully omits all of Hall's references to the initial aggressions of the whites; he deletes Hall's extenuating explanations of Indian rapine as revenge for white injustice; and he makes Indian-hating a simple and inevitable consequence of the original and unexplained wickedness of the Indians. Furthermore, through an ironic sentence about the Peace Congress, Melville links Indians with the non-human elements of nature, such as panthers, in a more meaningful way than in the casual coupling in Hall, which merely calls attention to the inimical character of both. There is in Melville's version perhaps a suggestion that the Indian is something not so much sub-human as extra-human. Finally, Melville's most conspicuous addition is the idea that the Indian hides his original, implacable malice beneath a mask of virtue and benignity in order to betray men and more easily wreak his hatred upon them: "'when a tomahawking red man advances the notion of the benignity of the red race, it is but part and parcel with that subtle strategy which he finds so useful in war, in hunting, and the general conduct of life.'" In this Indian of Melville's, readers will have recognized a type of the Confidence Man.

Melville's change in the portrait of the Indian is very significant because it is a real change, not only from its immediate source, as just shown, but also from both Hall's and Melville's customary views on the subject of Indians. Throughout Hall's work, his sympathy for the Indian victims of the determined and heartless aggression of the whites is clear. His attitude is reiterated so often that Melville's change to the antipodal interpretation must have been made with definite purpose. Furthermore, Melville did violence as much to his own views on Indians as to Hall's. So closely similar to Hall's is Melville's usual attitude towards the acculturation of savages that readers of *Typee* and *Omoo* might almost think one of Hall's passages (given in the Explanatory Notes) to be an extract from one of those books. In his review of Parkman's *Oregon Trail* in 1849,[70] Melville states concisely his own humanitarian feelings towards Indians and takes exception to Parkman's contempt for savages:

It is too often the case, that civilized beings sojourning among savages soon come to regard them with disdain and contempt. But though in many cases this feeling is most natural, it is not defensible; and it is wholly wrong. . . . Xavier and Elliott despised not the savages; and had Newton and Milton dwelt among them they would not have done so. . . . We are all of us—Anglo-Saxons, Dyaks, and Indians—sprung from one head, and made in one image. And if we regret this brotherhood now, we shall be forced to join hands hereafter.

By 1856 Melville may have repudiated the religious premise of this position, but there is no reason to believe that he repudiated the humanitarian attitude expressed here and elsewhere. He disclaims personal responsibility for the views in *The Confidence-Man* by putting them in the mouth of the Mississippi operator, who in turn specifically disclaims them and attributes them, quite unjustly, to Judge Hall. They are orphan views. Melville's portrait of the Indian, therefore, was painted, not to represent the American Indian, but to serve as a symbol appropriate to the author's ideas, a symbol, furthermore, which would clarify the argument.

Thus far, the argument of the book has run something like this: Men may choose between two ethical systems, the Christian one of mutual faith and love, announced in I Corinthians 13, and the egoistic, individualistic system epitomized in the barber's sign, "No Trust." The two emblems are the harmless,

[70] In *The Literary World*, 31 March 1849.

helpless lamblike man with his legend, "Charity thinketh no evil," and the barber with his razor. But Christian ethics appear to be ill suited to human nature; those who put their trust in the honesty and good intentions of their fellow men are all duped. Many of the dupes are themselves trustworthy people. But this is equivalent to saying that only fools are honest, and that mankind is divided into fools and knaves. And in this world, as the Missourian Pitch says, the knaves munch up the fools as horses munch up oats. St. Paul's doctrine of charity is at odds with the truth of our world as we know it, since there *is* evil in the universe and in human nature, and since some things are lies. The practice of charity merely stocks a happy hunting-ground for knaves, who take advantage of the doctrine for their selfish purpose. Consequently the doctrine itself, pragmatically viewed, is vicious, since it operates ultimately to undermine and destroy the small quantum of faith and love of which human nature is capable. Not Christianity alone is to blame for this, but all optimistic philosophies which assume that the universe is benevolent and human nature good.

In short, in the story thus far, faith, hope, and charity have been either frauds or snares; one cannot trust God, or nature, or man. Misanthropy, distrust, and a selfish, suspicious individualism have apparently been recommended. Knowledge derived from experience has been exalted and faith decried. Mankind has been divided into fools and knaves.

So simple an analysis of human nature is of course not Herman Melville's final word on "the last complications of that spirit which is affirmed by its Creator to be fearfully and wonderfully made." Some qualification of the cynicism and materialism of the main argument of the story has been made indirectly; the creed: " 'To where it belongs with your charity! To heaven with it! . . . here on earth, true charity dotes, and false charity plots,' " was put in the mouth of a soured misanthrope whose one lone leg may be " 'emblematic of his one-sided view of humanity.' " But this qualification was insufficient (as is obvious from the number of critics who speak of Melville's Timonism and his No-Trust moral in this book).

Therefore, before introducing further arguments, Melville gives us an unforgettable picture of a society without faith or charity. Look down the vista of the No-Trust philosophy and see the Indian-hater: individualist, brave, free, kind-hearted, single-minded, self-reliant, experienced, disillusioned, but lost forever to human association with family, friends, and community, and devoted forever to the Indian-hunt, creeping warily through the woods, gun in hand, preying upon his fellow creatures. This is the true philosophy of nature. This is the alternative if we jettison charity—a world of solitary, dehumanized Indian-haters.

❖ ❖ ❖ ❖ ❖

The two men who tell and listen to the story, the operator and the cosmopolitan, declare themselves to be lovers and trusters of mankind, and at the suggestion of the operator they shake hands, drink to the new friendship thus founded upon common views, and introduce themselves: the cosmopolitan, Frank Goodman; the other, Charles Arnold Noble. But the operator avoids the wine himself and slyly presses it upon his companion. The cosmopolitan pretends to honor the new and perfervid friendship by asking for a loan, and thus foils the sharper and cleverly traps him into revealing that his profession of love of mankind is a masquerade for hatred and egoism, and that his trust is a pretense for the sake of business. The operator retires in some confusion.

Charles Arnold Noble brings up a question in regard to the series of Confidence Men. The crippled Negro had listed his friends in this order: a man with a weed, a man in a gray coat and white tie, a man with a big book, a herb doctor, a man in a yellow vest, a man with a brass plate, a man in a violet robe, and a soldier. There are two discrepancies between this list and the Confidence Men who appear. The only soldier or pseudo-soldier in the novel is the Soldier of Fortune, the cripple who appears while the herb-doctor is on board and who pretends to be a veteran of the Mexican War; he qualifies perhaps as a confidence man when he collects money under slightly false pretenses, but he is a victim rather than an accomplice of the herb-doctor and hardly seems an appropriate inclusion in the Negro's list. The other missing "friend" is the man in the yellow vest. None such appears at any time; but the operator, Charles Arnold Noble, has a "violet vest, sending up sunset hues to a countenance betokening a kind of bilious habit." The significant thing about the appearance of the bilious man is the fine and glowing quality of his clothes or outside, and the mean, sour quality of the man himself; whatever Melville had in mind about the yellow vest may have been well enough represented by the "sunset hues" and the bilious face. Although indeed a confidence man, like the soldier he appears in the wrong order and is a victim rather than an accomplice of the " 'metaphysical scamps.' " It seems most likely that Melville changed or forgot his earlier intention regarding some of the subordinate arrangements of the story. It will be remembered that Melville did not see this novel through the press. Ill and sorely troubled with his eyes, perhaps he did not even read through the whole manuscript before or after Augusta copied it.

The cosmopolitan is most probably the man in the violet robe of the Negro's list; for, although his crimson garment is not the proper shade, no one else in the novel wears a violet robe, and the idea of color and extravagant oddity suggested by the term is best embodied in the strange garb of the cosmopolitan.

The cosmopolitan's courtesy, tact, perspicacity, and manner both princely and genial make him, apparently, indeed the ambassador from mankind, and in reality the subtlest and cleverest of foes. The suspicion which activates his very ingenious stratagem for unmasking the operator gives the lie, of course, to his profession of trust in men. His story of Charlemont, which is his final stroke in disarming the operator, and his comments on the story reveal the cynic behind the mask. Besides this radical contradiction, there are other clues to his falsity. Pitch spots him at once as a misanthrope masquerading as a friend of man; later, when the cosmopolitan is drawing out the operator, his picture of the philanthropist hiding his kind heart beneath a surly air and the misanthrope assuming an appearance of refinement, softness, and geniality so resembles the Missourian and himself respectively as to amount to confession. The same specious sentiment that marks the talk of the other Confidence Men appears in his conversation: he has confidence " 'in the latent benignity of that beautiful creature, the rattlesnake' "; he believes that " 'the ocean is a magnanimous element, and would scorn to assassinate a poor fellow.' " Like his predecessors, the cosmopolitan pretends to inculcate faith and optimism by refusing to believe whatever pains the sensibilities or is too horrible to be true. Like some of them, he couples his cause with religion, charity with faith. Actually he himself, however, suspects the operator, cheats the barber, and plays a very dubious protector to an old man.

But for dubbing him Confidence Man, Melville's most ingenious method, amusing for its dramatic irony, is to confront the cosmopolitan with a real Mississippi sharper, the bilious man; to draw a perfect parallel between the two, perfect except for the cosmopolitan's superior, indeed preternatural, understanding and adroitnesss,—their overfine dress, their hollow professions of philanthropic confidence and optimism, and their method of attacking a prospective victim; and then to let the reader watch a thief catch a thief, and draw his own conclusions. It is possible that by giving them Indian containers for their wine bottle and cigars, Melville meant to remind the reader that they are the Indians of the argument. Equivocations increase the irony and underline the parallel: " 'You are a man after my own heart,' " says the cosmopolitan to his obviously fraudulent friend. " 'Indeed . . . our sentiments agree so, that were they written in a book, whose was whose, few but the nicest critics might determine.' " Finally, once the relationship between the two men is clearly established, their names in conjunction have added meaning: that of the undetected cosmopolitan, Frank Goodman; that of the equally spurious philanthropist, with its visible tag of treachery, Charles Arnold Noble.

✿ ✿ ✿ ✿ ✿

Anyone in the nineteenth century waging war against optimistic philosophy must of course sooner or later single out for particular attack its great American champion, Ralph Waldo Emerson. Accordingly, Melville brings Emerson aboard the *Fidèle*, perhaps in the herb-doctor, certainly in the mystic Mark Winsome and his practical disciple Egbert, whom the cosmopolitan next encounters. Using Winsome and Egbert as his targets, Melville fires a few derisive volleys at the Emersonian metaphysics; and against the Emersonian ethics, especially Emersonian individualism, he empties the arsonal of his scorn.

In splitting Emerson's philosophy between Winsome and Egbert, whom I take to be its metaphysics and its ethics respectively, or perhaps better the abstract philosophy and its practical effect, Melville was dramatizing a dualism in Emerson that has been generally commented on from Lowell's *A Fable for Critics* (1848) to the present; and Lowell implies that he was not the first to see it. The *Fable* says that Emerson's is

> A Greek head on right Yankee shoulders, whose range
> Has Olympus for one pole, for t'other the Exchange;
> He seems, to my thinking (although I'm afraid
> The comparison must, long ere this, have been made),
> A Plotinus-Montaigne, where the Egyptian's gold mist
> And the Gascon's shrewd wit cheek-by-jowl coexist . . .;

and the recently published *Emerson Handbook,* by Frederic Ives Carpenter, stresses almost throughout its length the "two sides to Emerson's face and philosophy"; it quotes from Bliss Perry "as perhaps the first to emphasize the actual embodiment of this dualism in the physical lines of Emerson's face" (in *Emerson Today*):

His features were slightly asymmetrical. Seen from one side, it was the face of the old school, shrewd, serious, practical. . . . Seen from the other side, it was the face of a dreamer, a seer, a soul brooding on things to come, things as yet very far away.

The three main heads under which Mr. Carpenter discusses Emerson's ideas are "The Ideal and the Real," "Transcendental Idealism: Mysticism," and "Yankee Realism: Pragmatism." The "two sides" which these heads suggest are precisely those caricatured in Winsome and Egbert respectively. Parallels between the details of the Emersonian portrait in Chapters 36-41 of *The Confidence-Man* on the one hand and descriptions of Emerson by biographers and comments by Melville himself on the other will be brought out in the notes to those chapters.

Further evidence that Melville intended the mystic Winsome and his practical disciple Egbert to be different aspects of the same person, or of the same philosophy, comes from a piece of manuscript, a very early draft of "Titles for Chapters," which seems to represent a jotting down of ideas in the early stages of inventing the story. The second of these titles is "The practical mystic," and it could apply to no one except Egbert-Winsome.

This splitting was partly suggested, no doubt, by Emerson's frequent explanation that the role of the poet and philosopher should be, not participation in active and fragmentary reforms, but the generation of a moral atmosphere that would encourage each man to elevate his own nature, and also in Emerson's own reluctance to enter the practical reforms which his beliefs encouraged. Speaking of the taint of burlesque in the active representatives of virtue, Emerson had written: "Yet we are tempted to smile, and we flee from the working to the speculative reformer, to escape that same slight ridicule."[71] Melville's overt splitting of the Emersonian philosopher into the working and speculative reformer enabled him to say very earnestly that, though the metaphysics might be dismissed as moonshine, the practical ethics were operative and were charged with moral danger to mankind.

Melville is sweeping in his criticism of Emerson, and he is

[71] "The Transcendentalist," *Complete Works of Ralph Waldo Emerson*, Centenary Edition (Boston, 1903-1907), 12 vols.; I, 355.

as severe as it is possible for one to be who loves "all men who *dive*" no matter what they bring up from the depths of thought. His marginalia in his copies of Emerson's works reiterate his tribute to the nobility of Emerson's aim and of much of what Emerson had to say. But the satiric portraits of Winsome and Egbert are unrelieved by any such acknowledgment, for they embody only the faults of Emerson's mind and thought.

The satire, through Winsome, of a number of Emersonian traits is corroborated by direct comments on Emerson in Melville's letters and marginalia. Winsome is aloof, icy-cold, shrewdly opposed to philanthropy; his disciple will have " 'a head kept cool by the under ice of the heart.' " In his copy of Emerson's essay "The Poet," beside the passage beginning "Language is fossil poetry," Melville wrote:[72]

This is admirable, as many other thoughts of Mr. Emerson's are. His gross and astonishing errors & illusions spring from a self-conceit so intensely intellectual and calm that at first one hesitates to call it by its right name. Another species of Mr. Emerson's errors, or rather blindness, proceeds from a defect in the region of the heart.

Winsome's oracular, pedantic incoherencies about the Egyptians, Proclus, and Plato recall an early impression of Melville's, expressed in a letter to Evert Duyckinck, that Emerson was full of "transcendentalisms, myths & oracular gibberish," a "Plato who talks thro' his nose."[73] Winsome does not respond to the cosmopolitan's conviviality, and prefers to keep his love for wine, he says, " 'in the lasting condition of an untried abstraction.' " In the same letter to Duyckinck, Melville wrote:

You complain that Emerson tho' a denizen of the land of ginger-

[72] Melville's copies of Emerson's *Essays . . ., Essays: Second Series . . ., Poems . . .,* and *The Conduct of Life . . .,* all annotated by Melville, are in HCL-M. Most of Melville's direct comments on Emerson have been published in William Braswell, "Melville as a Critic of Emerson," *American Literature,* IX (1937), 317-334, and F. O. Matthiessen, *American Renaissance, passim.* Although these marginalia were written after *The Confidence-Man,* they are consonant with Melville's earlier impression of Emerson.

[73] Boston, 3 March 1849; NYPL-D; printed in Thorp, *Herman Melville,* pp. 371-373.

bread, is above munching a plain cake in company of jolly fellows, & swiging [*sic*] off his ale like you & me. Ah, my dear sir, that's his misfortune, not his fault. His belly, sir, is in his chest, & his brains descend down into his neck & offer an obstacle to a draught of ale or a mouthful of cake.

Melville frequently repeated such strictures. It is part of his comment on Emerson that Emerson kept many human goods, from ale to friendship, " 'in the lasting condition of an untried abstraction.' "

But it is when Winsome and Egbert discourse on self-reliance and friendship that Melville trains his artillery on Emerson. Emerson's primary ethical doctrine of self-reliance is based upon his optimistic belief that "all nature is the rapid efflux of goodness executing and organizing itself," and that the individual therefore shares in the self-existence of the Deity; in "Self-Reliance" he says:[74]

. . . we inquire the reason of self-trust. Who is the Trustee? What is the aboriginal Self, on which a universal reliance may be grounded? . . . The inquiry leads us to that source, at once the essence of genius, of virtue, and of life, which we call Spontaneity or Instinct. We denote this primary wisdom as Intuition. . . . We lie in the lap of immense intelligence, which makes us receivers of its truth and organs of its activity.

Emerson does not, of course, close his eyes to evil. But serene in his faith that "the nature of things, the eternal law" will balk wickedness and transform it in the end, Emerson urges self-reliance in spite of the evil in the Napoleons of the world. "We like to see everything do its office after its kind, whether it be a milch-cow or a rattlesnake," he says.[75] Winsome expresses admiration for the rattlesnake, implying that it would be a desirable experience to change personalities with one, " 'to sting, to kill . . . and revel for a while in the carefree, joyous life of a perfectly instinctive, unscrupulous, and irresponsible creature.' " This, Melville is saying, is your self-reliance, a

[74] "Circles," *Works*, II, 31; "Self-Reliance," *Works*, II, 63-64.
[75] "Napoleon; or, The Man of the World," *Works*, IV, 235.

reliance upon the rattlesnake spirit of nature, "'perfectly instinctive, unscrupulous, and irresponsible.'" If you think that
there is a universal benevolence that nullifies this poison, you
delude yourself criminally; in the name of an unwarranted optimism you have encouraged man to revert to the jungle. Winsome indeed says, or implies through his questions, that people
are not morally accountable, since rattlesnakes are not.

What Melville had called non-benevolence in describing
Plinlimmon in *Pierre* is the concomitant of Emerson's intense
individualism. To Emerson the relation between man and
man is important only in its bearing on the relation between
man and God. Friendships and loves are steps by which the
soul mounts, he says in several places; in "Circles" he puts it
thus:[76]

The continual effort to raise himself above himself, to work a pitch
above his last height, betrays itself in a man's relations. We thirst
for approbation, yet cannot forgive the approver. The sweet of nature is love; yet if I have a friend I am tormented by my imperfec-
tions. The love of me accuses the other party. If he were high
enough to slight me, then could I love him, and rise by my affection
to new heights. A man's growth is seen in the successive choirs of
his friends. For every friend whom he loses for truth, he gains a
better.

Melville mocks such individualism with acrid humor. Egbert
says that he agrees with his sublime master Winsome, "'Who,
in his Essay on Friendship, says so nobly, that if he want a
terrestrial convenience, not to his friend celestial (or friend
social and intellectual) would he go,'" because "'for the superior nature, which on no account can ever descend to do
good, to be annoyed with requests to do it, when the inferior
one, which by no instruction can ever rise above that capacity,
stands always inclined to it—this is unsuitable.'" One should
choose one's friends, says Egbert, as one chooses one's mutton,
"'not for its leanness, but for its fatness,'" and this is not vile
prudence but the means of preserving the delicacy of friendship. For one ever to help his friend, or to lend him money—

[76] *Works*, II, 307.

that would violate the delicacy of the relation. No true friend will ask it, as no true friend will, in platonic love, require love-rites. Emerson had written in "Friendship":[77]

We chide the citizen because he makes love a commodity. It is an exchange of gifts, of useful loans; it is good neighborhood; it watches with the sick; it holds the pall at the funeral; and quite loses sight of the delicacies and nobility of the relation.

The condition which high friendship demands is ability to do without it.

The most heartless part of this creed, according to Melville, is that it treats the individual as if he were morally responsible for what is inevitable, blandly ignores the inconsistency, and shrugs its shoulders over his suffering. A man who wants help, says Egbert, has a defect and so does not deserve help. There is "always a reason *in the man,* for his good or bad fortune," said Emerson, "and so in making money."[78] Since nature labels her harmful creatures, putting rattles on rattlesnakes, says Winsome, it is the victim's own fault if he is destroyed; and "'for a man to pity where nature is pitiless, is a little presuming.'"

In merging Emerson's ethics with the doctrines of economic individualism as he does in Egbert, Melville was not going beyond his text. A. C. Kern has demonstrated Emerson's commitment to *laissez-faire* economics.[79] The consanguinity of Emerson's philosophy with this school of thought is reasonable, since both derive from a common concept of natural law. Emerson could fit his concurrence with "the dismal science" into his serene optimism because he was sure of the goodness and beauty of the universal laws and because his scorn of materialism made it easy for him to overlook the suffering due to material causes.

But after Egbert has told the story of China Aster to prove "'the folly, on both sides, of a friend's helping a friend'" with

[77] *Works,* II, 205, 208.
[78] *Works,* VI, 100.
[79] "Emerson and Economics," *New England Quarterly,* XIII (1940), 678-696.

a useful loan, the cosmopolitan declares that he has had enough of this " 'inhuman philosophy,' " and takes his leave.

This brush between the Confidence Man and Emerson perhaps was the nucleus around which the rest of the story took shape in Melville's mind. "Titles for Chapters" (which may be seen in the Appendix) certainly looks like memoranda jotted down long before the full scheme and order of the novel came into being. Melville took a large sheet of blue paper, wrote "Titles for Chapters" at the top with a flourish, then a list of seven titles in ink; probably later, four titles in pencil and a notation near the right margin in pencil, "Dedicated to victims of Auto da Fe"; afterwards, the twelfth title in ink; finally the thirteenth in pencil. At some time he canceled them all with a pen stroke from top to bottom. All these titles except the third and fourth and the right-margin notation clearly have their counterparts in the completed novel, but in an altogether different order. The first two, "The hypothetical friends" and "The practical mystic," announce the Winsome-Egbert (or Waldo Emerson) episode. The third, "Distrust the bare basis for confidence," may have been meant to cover part of this episode or the next, or, since it states one of the morals of the story, an interpolated essay omitted in the novel. The fourth, "What confidence is in the most confiding," is, whether ironic or not, appropriate anywhere in the novel. The fifth and sixth take us backwards (in the completed book) through the skirmish between Charles Arnold Noble and the cosmopolitan, and the seventh still further back to the miser who was gulled. Then, at a later time probably, for the next group is in pencil, Melville wrote down two more titles referring to the cosmopolitan-Noble encounter, the second of these being in effect a revised version of the sixth title, above. The tenth, "A rupture," appears in the novel as the last chapter of the Winsome-Egbert episode; when he jotted down the "Titles for Chapters," Melville could have intended it for that episode or for the end of the very similar cosmopolitan-Noble affair. The last three titles represent Chapter 19, Chapter 1, and Chapter 24 in the book.

I think we may assume that the order of these titles shows

us the chronological order in which Melville invented the incidents they refer to, or at least the order of their importance or interest to him, and not a merely fortuitous and meaningless order. The list gives several indications that the story was in the early stages of invention, that Melville was feeling around for the materials he needed: two titles and perhaps the parts of the story that they covered were later discarded; "The soldier of fortune," the eleventh title, stands for a part of the story in which Melville later must have shifted his plan, as has been explained; finally, after jotting down a title for the opening scene of the book, "A mute goes on board a boat on the Mississippi," and the central paradox, "The Philanthropist & Misanthrope. The Rifle and Pipe," he was ready to discard the whole list. It makes sense, at any rate, to suppose that after he hit upon these last two ideas, he saw his story moving forward in a different sequence, perhaps the one in the completed novel, and with richer possibilities of satire.

What emerges pretty clearly from all this is that, when Melville thought out his story, the scene that came first in his mind, either in order of time or in order of importance, was a scene in which someone exposed the ethical and social bearings of Emerson's philosophy by means of a hypothetical case, a case of friend calling upon friend for help. He must have had in mind from the beginning to play on the meaning of "confidence man," since the word "confidence" (rather than "optimism," "faith," or "trust") appears four times, and "confiding" once, in his first group of seven titles. Emerson, though indeed a man of "confidence" in God, nature, and man, could not have been this initial confidence man, because he could not have been the protagonist in the next episodes in this group (ending with the gulling of the miser). Therefore we have, I think, good reason for supposing that from the beginning Melville saw what was to be either the first or a very important scene of his novel as a scene in which a confidence man tackles the famous American proponent of a philosophy of confidence and discovers that " 'moonshiny as it in theory may be, yet a very practical philosophy it turns out in effect.' " Practical, heartless, and inhuman, in fact; a swindle, in effect, for the cosmopolitan's experience with Winsome-Egbert is a close replica of his experience with the swindler Charles Arnold Noble.

Another thing that "Titles for Chapters" shows us is the close relation in Melville's mind between these two episodes. The book also stresses the parallel between them, in every subtle way: the same appeal for help in each; even the use of the same names, Frank and Charlie, in both dialogues; the story of bankruptcy interpolated in each; the same result when the friend, who had seemed rich, asks for a loan: Noble cries out that he was " 'never so deceived in a man in my life,' " and Egbert's words are " ' "I have been deceived, fraudulently deceived, in this man." ' " The parallel is Melville's complex, ironic, bitter comment on Emersonian optimism and individualism.

It came naturally to Melville's mind to think of Christ when he wanted an opposite pole from some of Emerson's ideas. Emerson wrote: "The good, compared to the evil [which a man sees], is as his own good to his own evil"; Melville commented: "A Perfectly Good being therefore would see no evil.— But what did Christ see? He saw what made him weep—To annihilate all this nonsense read the Sermon on the Mount, and consider what it implies." Melville read in a book by William Alger that

even the kindly Emerson illustrated the temptation of the great to scorn the commonalty, when he speaks of "enormous populations, like moving cheese,—the more, the worse"; "the guano-races of mankind"; "the worst of charity is, that the lives you are asked to preserve are not worth preserving"; "masses! the calamity is the masses; I do not wish any shovel-handed, narrow-brained, gin-drinking mass at all."

Melville's notation was: "These expressions attributed to the 'kindly Emerson' are somewhat different from the words of Christ to the multitude on the Mount.—Abhor pride, abhor malignity, but not grief and poverty, and the natural vices these

generate."[80] This antinomy—Christian brotherly love, that suffereth long and is kind, that seeketh not her own, the helping
hand and the feeling heart, this on the one hand, and on the
other, Emersonian individualism, which is, after all, only a
rarefied form of enlightened self-interest—this antinomy is
central to *The Confidence-Man* and perhaps, as we have seen,
primary. It is a more sardonic, a more mordant, version of the
contrast between chronometrical and horological ethics in
Pierre. In the morning a lamblike man appealing to men to love
their neighbors; in the evening—in the nineteenth century—a
practical mystic teaching men, in effect, to love themselves.

So inhuman have Winsome and Egbert shown themselves
that the cosmopolitan begins to look like the true champion of
magnanimity and benevolence after all. Melville's quiet reminder, at the end of the scene with Egbert, that the cosmopolitan is playing a role is hardly clear or strong enough to de-
throne him now in the reader's sympathy. A number of readers
have been blinded, even to his dubious performance in the
ensuing scenes, by the dazzle of his humane sentiments in this
one. Melville wrote the cosmopolitan's lines about the helping
hand and the feeling heart and about the troughs and crests of
vicissitude with an eloquence that came from his own heart.
But it is clear that he does not intend, by making the Emersonian individualist seem worse than the Confidence Man, to
whitewash the latter, but rather to underline the inhumanity of
the former. That the philosophy of Mark Winsome, the practice
of the Mississippi swindler, and the machinations of our "metaphysical scamps" the Confidence Men, all tend to the same end,
an atomistic world of trustless, loveless misanthropes, should
not be obscured by the cosmopolitan's bland, benevolent mask.

*   *   *   *   *

However hypnotic the cosmopolitan's professions may have
become for the reader, the prudent, case-hardened barber,
whom he next visits, is proof against his honeyed sentiments
and refuses to take down his own "No Trust" sign. Then the

[80] These passages and marginalia are quoted in Matthiessen, *American Renaissance*, pp. 184, 401 f.

cosmopolitan exerts a sort of magical fascination, "not wholly unlike the manner of certain creatures in nature," and the barber signs an agreement to keep the "No Trust" placard hidden for the rest of the trip. But when the cosmopolitan defrauds him of the price of a shave, the barber, loosed from the charm, restores the placard to its conspicuous peg.

The opening tableau of the book, the lamblike man holding up his legend, "Charity thinketh no evil," beside the barber's "No Trust" sign, is brought to mind as the final Confidence Man plays his professed Christian philosophy against the same misanthropic proclamation. In this reminiscent scene, Melville draws more darkly than previously some of the Confidence Man's features. The man himself hints that he is supernatural, either angel or devil. His resorting to a kind of hypnotism or fascination to achieve his purpose when all other means have failed has a sinister implication that is more ominous as one examines it. "Hard to say exactly what the [cosmopolitan's] manner was, any more than to hint it was a sort of magical."

Melville names the chapter "Very Charming." How important he considered the incident of the fascination is revealed by an early draft of the chapter title: "In which the Cosmopolitan . . . earns the title of the man-charmer in the same sense that certain East Indians are called snake-charmers [two or three indecipherable words] pretty much in the same rank with the snak[e]." Probably his difficulty with this title was that, in the case of the East Indian's charming, the roles of man and reptile are the reverse of what he needed if he was to keep the Confidence Man pretty much in the same rank with the snake; he added "but not" in front of "in the same sense. . . ," but finally drew a line through most of what he had written.

He had already suggested the affinity of snake and Confidence Man when the cosmopolitan said that he was

"so eccentric as to have confidence in the latent benignity of that beautiful creature, the rattle-snake, whose lithe neck and burnished maze of tawny gold, as he sleekly curls aloft in the sun, who on the prairie can behold without wonder?"

As he breathed these words, he seemed so to enter into their

spirit—as some earnest descriptive speakers will—as unconsciously
to wreathe his form and sidelong crest his head, till he all but
seemed the creature he described.

Moreover, since Melville knew his Milton, and since rattle-
snakes are not gold, it is no accident that the cosmopolitan is
so much like the serpent in whose form Satan appeared to Eve
and cost her Paradise:[81]

> Fold above fold a surging *maze,* his *head*
> *Crested* aloft, and carbuncle his eyes;
> With *burnished* neck of verdant *gold,* erect
> Amidst his circling spires.

The title of the last chapter of the novel, "The Cosmopolitan
Increases in Seriousness," and some of Melville's earlier drafts
of this caption, "Very Long & serious," and "is as serious as anything before; if anything a little more so," emphasize, in their
unemphatic way, his intentions in the final scene. In this scene
Melville builds up some of the most obvious and most significant symbolism of the book. It is in the gentlemen's cabin,
which is illuminated by the one light left burning, a "solar
lamp"; this lamp represents the light of the Old and New Testaments, the horned altar among its decorations standing for the
Old, and the robed man with a halo for the New. Other lamps,
"barren planets," perhaps dead religions, are dark. The extinction of this light of the world, the steward tells a man who
wishes it, would make the cabin a dangerous place, and it is
desired, he hints, only by those who would reap a profit from
a world left in darkness. This is as clear a prefiguration of Melville's pessimistic apocalypse at the end as anyone could ask.

As the cosmopolitan talks with an old man who has "a countenance like that which imagination ascribes to good Simeon,
when, having at last beheld the Master of Faith, he blessed him
and departed in peace," and who has been reading the ship's
Bible under the solar lamp, strange interruptions come from
one of the surrounding berths, where men are trying to sleep.
When the cosmopolitan observes that the Bible carries the best

[81] *Paradise Lost,* IX, 499-502; italics mine.

of news, a voice from a berth objects: " 'Too good to be true.' "
When the cosmopolitan reads from Ecclesiasticus:

With much communication he will tempt thee; he will smile upon
thee, and speak thee fair, and say What wantest thou? If thou be
for his profit he will use thee; he will make thee bear, and will not
be sorry for it. Observe and take good heed. When thou hearest
these things, awake in thy sleep,

the voice speaks again: " 'Who's that describing the confidence
man?' " And the cosmopolitan observes: " 'Awake in his sleep,
sure enough, ain't he?' " When the book of Ecclesiasticus is
disposed of as apocryphal, " 'What's that about the Apocalypse?' " comes from the berth. Since the first two interruptions
are improbable in a realistic scene but highly significant as
brief recapitulations of themes of the novel, one suspects that
the third conveys something important. "Apocalypse" may be
meant to suggest to the sharp-eyed reader that the novel has an
esoteric double meaning; or to call to mind those prototypes of
the Confidence Man, the false Christs and the Antichrist who
are foretold in apocalyptic passages in the New Testament.
Probably, considering the context about seeing visions, Melville meant to remind the reader of writings which prophesy, in
a parabolic way, the end or future state of the world, and to
prepare for his own gloomy adumbration at the close of the
novel, when the Confidence Man extinguishes the light of
Christian faith in this world.

For one last time Melville brings together the Confidence
Man, a dupe, and a cynic. The old man is soon to be fleeced,
one fears; he has refused the cosmopolitan's offer to help him
put his money in his money belt, but in the end the cosmopolitan is to lead him away in the dark. A ragged boy selling safety
devices is the last cynic; his wits have been sharpened and his
trust destroyed by hard experience beyond his years. "All
pointed and fluttering, the rags of the little fellow's red-flannel
shirt, mixed with those of his yellow coat, flamed about him
like the painted flames in the robes of a victim in *auto-da-fe.*"
He is sharp, disillusioned, scornful of the old man's ignorant

simplicity, undeceived by the cosmopolitan's pretense of virtue and benevolence—in short, like the gimlet-eyed man, like Pitch, like the Indian-hater, one rendered more or less cynical by experience but thus protected against fraud. There is perhaps also a suggestion of the Shakespearean fool in motley about him when he breaks into impudent, witty repartee; like Lear's "bitter fool," he sees the old man's folly, knows how misplaced his confidence is, and in effect warns him—he gives him a Counterfeit Detector. His auto-da-fé reminds us, at the end of our day on the *Fidèle,* of the crimes that have been committed in the name of Christian faith in the past. The ragged, houseless poverty of a child is a no less ironic testimonial of Christian brotherhood in the present.

When Melville jotted down "Dedicated to victims of Auto da Fe," in his "Titles for Chapters," perhaps he meant to make this boy the subject of a whole chapter, or perhaps he intended to dedicate his novel to victims of "acts of faith" (as well he might have done except that it would have brought his religious allegory dangerously close to the surface). In any case he seems to have originally expected to make greater use of the idea than he finally did.

The end of the novel is the end of religion, the extinction of faith and of hope. Will this also be the extinction of charity? Christianity is dead, or never born, in the old man, who—good, simple, Bible-reading communicant that he is and fair enough representative of the best of us—has neither real trust in his fellow men nor real faith in God: with a profession of confidence still warm on his lips, he looks about for a life-preserver. Christianity is dying throughout the world, and the Confidence Man extinguishes it. The solar lamp, the last light left burning, dims. " 'We are being left in the dark here,' " says the cosmopolitan. " 'Pah! what a smell, too.' " And he puts out the light.

The next moment, the waning light expired, and with it the waning flames of the horned altar, and the waning halo round the robed man's brow; while in the darkness which ensued, the cosmopolitan kindly led the old man away. Something further may follow of this Masquerade.

The argument and design of the Masquerade are complete now. The startling final sentence could hardly be the half-promise of a sequel that some have thought it might be.[82] Coming as it does in the same paragraph with the cosmopolitan "kindly" leading the old man away in the darkness, it attaches its ominous meaning to that old man's fate, and to ours. The *Fidèle,* mankind, all are left darkling. The good Simeon departs in peace, but also in darkness, and into the power of darkness.

v

". . . the sad consequences which might, upon occasion, ensue from the cabin being left in darkness. . . ."

A few months after finishing *The Confidence-Man,* Melville made the following notation about the Beautiful, or Golden, Gate in Jerusalem, which the Turks had walled up:[83]

One of the most interesting things in Jerusalem—seems expressive of the finality of Christianity, as if this was the last religion of the world,—no other, possible.

His apprehension of the doom of Christianity, of all religion, was not uncommon among the contemporaries of Arnold and Huxley. But, in spite of his criticism of the pitfalls of faith, it is not apparent that he thought the disappearance of religion would be a good thing.

In the glooms and wasteland through which Melville is groping in *The Confidence-Man,* some of the murkier shapes that rise up are questions rather than affirmations. Is all life only a vast practical joke, a joke played perhaps by the President of the Immortals himself, an Aristophanes of the universe, who for his April Fool's Day sport looses the deceiver amongst us? If so, the devil, always an ironist, would employ in the Christian dispensation, not the plagues of Job, but the Christian doc-

[82] Howard C. Horsford, "Evidence of Melville's Plans for a Sequel to *The Confidence-Man,*" brings together all such evidence, and it is considerable.

[83] *Journal up the Straits,* p. 82.

trine of love in order to destroy love in men's hearts; the most heartless irony of all is the corruption of the good man through his idealism.

The probability that the Christian promise of immortality is fraudulent is not, I take it, what mainly distressed Melville. True, the novel begins with the faith of I Corinthians and ends with the old man retiring into the darkness on the arm of our transcendent cheat the Confidence Man; and throughout the novel are intimations of the hopelessness of Christian hope. But much stronger and more continual is the emphasis upon charity. Furthermore, Melville faced the prospect of annihilation, his talk with Hawthorne in Liverpool suggests, reluctantly but without the anguish with which that prospect has stricken many, from Tennyson to Unamuno. " 'What is man that he should live out the lifetime of his God?' "[84] What moved Melville was the prospect of a world without charity.

Western man has perhaps never seemed more safe and secure in the universe than towards the middle of the nineteenth century; Christian belief made him the child of an ever-loving Father and the inheritor of heaven, the scientists made him the confident master of nature and the inheritor of the earth. But as Melville saw it, man lives, like the Indian-hater, amidst a smiling, sly, circumambient, inscrutable malice. Ahab and the Indian-hater take the path of hatred and vengeance and forswear their humanity. The embattled Pitch keeps both his wits and a piece of his heart, but at the cost of ceaseless wariness and a hedge-hog near-misanthropy. Where is the path to a decent human society, sustained by the helping hand and warmed by the feeling heart?

The nineteenth century saw a divinely assured progress, or a deterministic progress, or blind self-confidence and "enlightened" self interest to be the wide gate and the broad way that leadeth to perfection; Melville saw more clearly where these ways led, and who was the Confidence Man who enticed pilgrims along them. What he saw was the need for skepticism, for unremitting truth-seeking, for whatever will protect us against the tempting and deceiving bedazzlements of Bright

[84] The end of Father Mapple's sermon, *Moby-Dick,* Ch. 9.

Future; " 'Ah,' " cried the good country merchant, " 'wine is good, and confidence is good; but can wine or confidence percolate down through all the stony strata of hard considerations, and drop warmly and ruddily into the cold cave of truth? Truth will *not* be comforted.' " He saw the injury done by all cheating optimisms to man's humanity; Pitch, finding himself trapped and defrauded, draws his misanthropic bearskin closer about him and clicks his misanthropic rifle more fiercely; the Indian-hater sloughs off his humane self altogether. And though Melville exalted skepticism, he saw the inhuman coldness of Winsome-Egbert's world, where the head is " 'kept cool by the under ice of the heart.' " The climax of pessimism comes when these men walk the deck where the lamblike man long since went to sleep.

Yet, however disillusioned, Melville stops short of Timonism. One cannot trust God; one cannot trust nature; but one must cling to some faith in man, for the alternative is too frightful. One has the feeling throughout this novel that man is victim rather than villain, that Melville's attitude is pity rather than scorn. There are "all kinds of that multiform pilgrim species, man" aboard the *Fidèle:* pickpockets, a miser, two dishonest beggars, an ordinary confidence man, the hard of heart, the greedy, the foolish; but also the good and honest country merchant, the Episcopal minister trying to help the crippled Negro at the risk of ridicule, the charitable lady reading her Bible and sharing her purse, the "very good man" with the gold sleeve buttons, who was generous without being credulous, the irascible but honest and good-hearted Pitch. The villain is the Ambassador, not from mankind (though he gives himself that title) but from whatever those heartless immensities are that surround man's unfriended life. This, I take it, is not misanthropy but a sort of last-ditch humanism. Melville's grief is Homer's grief, but the voice that utters it is pitched very low, and the battle to which we return again tomorrow is as terrible to the least of men as to the greatest.

Every reader of Melville must have been struck by the change in stature of his protagonist in the works that followed *Pierre.* From being heroic, larger than life, more gifted or more

favored than others, as Taji, Ahab, Pierre, he becomes suddenly the most insignificant of beings, most humble, most un-
distinguished, most forgotten, as Bartleby, the projected Aga-
tha, the Chola widow, Israel Potter, Merrymusk. From being
the man of passionate action, who flings himself against the
injurious gods, he becomes the helpless victim, the one to
whom things happen. Like Pip, bobbing about alone in the
vast Pacific, he is dwarfed to an atom of suffering amidst the
immense, passionless unknown. All the short stories are irradiated by Melville's pity for man. The mood of *Redburn*, with its
sympathy for the oppressed and exploited, reappears, but there
is a deeper and wider pity now, the matrix of *Israel Potter*. It
comes from a sense that man's role in the universe is a helpless
and perhaps meaningless endurance.

The *Confidence-Man* was written, probably, along with some
of these stories. It continues their strain, and reverses the
action of *Moby-Dick* and *Pierre*, for in *The Confidence-Man* the
injurious gods come on stage, in the title role, to get man. None
of its people is victimized so painfully as Benito Cereno or the
Chola widow—its ostensible genre is comedy, not tragedy; but
victimized they are. Their posture is not the posture of endurance of outrageous fortune, but the posture of bafflement, puz-
zlement, uncomfortable misgiving before the ambiguous smile
of the Confidence Man. The reader knows more about their
outrageous fortune than they do. If Melville now found the
tragic hero to be, not the great man flexing mighty muscles,
but the mere human being, and the universal tragedy to be
what happens to the least of these, his choice of little men for
characters is the outward sign, neither of mental decline from
concern with the grand to concern with the petty, nor of misanthropy, but of an immense compassion.

vi

"How unreal all this is! Who did ever dress or act like your cosmo-
politan? And who, it might be returned, did ever dress or act like
harlequin?"

As a work of art *The Confidence-Man* has suffered in critical

opinion because the surface story is an aimless string of episodes, without tension, suspense, variation in pace, or climax,
and the dialectic of the novel, which gives it its structure, is
submerged with the allegory. Once the allegory surfaces, a
final irony emerges too: *The Confidence-Man,* in appearance
without form or pattern or progression, is in reality as formal as
a fugue, richly patterned, a progression from the ideal to the
presently real, from Christian charity and brotherhood to Emersonian individualism and the extinction of Christianity, from
arguments for the necessity for skepticism to the one argument for the necessity for charity—the intolerable heartlessness
and inhumanity of Winsome-Egbert's world of complacent
egoists.

In the large framework of the novel, the tale of the Indian-
hater stands as the rooftree, being the culminating argument
for skepticism and the forecast of a world without charity.
Forming this large structure is a close-joined sequence of
double swindles (both philosophic and religious) which moves
through a survey of modern optimisms and at almost the same
time through the Faith, Hope, Charity, the Trust God, Trust
Nature, Trust Man patterns. Observe also the symmetry in
the beginning and ending of the novel. The first scene brings
the lamblike man aboard and juxtaposes him and his message
of faith and charity with the barber's "No Trust" sign and its
open razor; the last pair of scenes brings the cosmopolitan, the
man of the world (the opposite, Melville says, of the sincere
Christian), into the barber's shop, sets up his insincere message
of charity and faith against the "No Trust" philosophy of the
barber, and dims and extinguishes the light of the world. The
second protagonist at the beginning is the crippled Negro,
who is cut down to the stature of a Newfoundland dog and
who makes a passenger think of the devil gulling Eve; the next-
to-last avatar of the Confidence Man has a brass plate round
his neck like a dog, fawns and wriggles like a dog, and makes
the reader remember the snake in Genesis, and the last avatar
reminds the reader of the serpent in *Paradise Lost.* Melville's
device of making the final scenes suggest incidents and ideas
of the beginning but in reverse order mostly, as though the

novel were being unrolled towards the beginning at the same time as towards the end, is less elaborate than Homer's identical device in the first and last books of the *Iliad*, but is equally unforced and natural-seeming with Homer's, and, like his, richly suggestive.

But even the inchoate form of the external story has a certain traditional appropriateness. For the external novel is a picaresque tale, and merely conforms to type when it strings roguish episodes loosely on the thread of a single character. It is also like the picaresque romances in its social satire and in making use of some of the stock characters who are traditional objects of satire and ridicule in rogue fiction—the barber, the miser, the quack doctor. Melville's long-continued interest in this genre shows in his reading and also in his appropriation of the idiom from time to time, most fundamentally in *Omoo*, *Israel Potter*, and *The Confidence-Man*. In the last two, roguery has become a symbol of larger evil.[85] Reminiscences of the form and content of the romances of roguery increase the understatement of Melville's allegory of the cosmic *pícaro*.

The Confidence-Man has also been disparaged by numerous critics who say that Melville did not know life on the Mississippi, and so missed an opportunity to join the local color school. It would be irrelevant to reply that Melville had seen the Mississippi in 1840,[86] that he could read a dozen descriptions and anecdotes of the Mississippi any day in the 1850's that he chose to open magazines or books, and that he obviously had read a good many of these. It hardly matters that he was much less remote from the Mississippi than Shakespeare from the seacoast of Bohemia. For though it is not Mark Twain's river of snags and stars that he describes, nor Mike Fink's, nor Banvard's, it is the river he needed for his story. It is the type

[85] Richard J. Foster, "Melville and Roguery: A Study of the Relation of Melville's Writings to Picaresque Fiction" (M.A. thesis, Oberlin College, 1950) makes these points.

[86] When he visited his uncle Thomas Melville in Galena, Illinois. (See Harrison Hayford and Merrell Davis, "Herman Melville as Office-Seeker," p. 168.) In 1855 one of his Galena cousins was connected with the river-steamboat business. See also John W. Nichol, "Melville and The Midwest," *PMLA*, LXVI (1951), 613-625.

of "the dashing and all-fusing spirit of the West"; it unites "the streams of the most distant and opposite zones," and "pours them along, helter-skelter, in one cosmopolitan and confident tide." It is the River, and it flows with unmistakable reality past bluffs and shot towers and vine-covered banks in one kind of geography, and, in another kind, past the Delectable Mountains.[87]

Again, the art of *The Confidence-Man* has been slighted whenever critics have tried, more or less consciously, to fit it into the pigeonholes of the realistic or the dramatic novel. Its characters are not treated as Fielding, or Dostoevsky, or Henry James might have treated them; but neither are Everyman, Duessa, Apollyon, Anna Livia Plurabelle: Melville was at pains to tell his readers that *The Confidence-Man* is not a psychological or a realistic novel. The characters are conceived to represent that multiform pilgrim species, man, and for the parts they have to play in the pageant of the *Fidèle*. For this, they are brilliantly realized, out of very human stuff, and with an economy that is the soul of wit, even though some of them have very difficult parts requiring them to be on two or three levels of the stage at once. They are as vivid to the eye as Hogarth could have made them; they are individual in gesture, voice, word, and deed. But, since this is an allegory, their deepest inner reality, unlike the inner reality of characters in a dramatic novel, is moral and representative rather than moral-psychological and individual.

The style of *The Confidence-Man* has unwavering distinction. There is not a listless, nerveless sentence in the novel. The spontaneity of Melville's first books is gone, the gusto and exuberance of *Moby-Dick* are played out, the emotions are bridled by weariness and disillusion. But gone too are the lapses into rhetoric that sometimes blemish even *Moby-Dick*. Yet Melville has lost none of his old picturesqueness and boldness, as the descriptions show; and he has found, or rather, achieved, a new elegance. The drafts of Chapter 14 which survive show

[87] John W. Shroeder points out connections between Bunyan and *The Confidence-Man* in his "Sources and Symbols for Melville's *Confidence-Man*."

what care, what labor, went to perfect this art of the pruned, deft, subtle style where the voice is never raised.

But the charm—and also bane—of this novel is its irony as delicate and intricate as a spider web, with radiating and concentric threads; if one breaks a thread, it is as softly entangling. Yet once the reader feels certain of Melville's intention, he may take a rare delight in the equivocations, the paradoxes, the quiet inversions of meaning, in ironic echo, parallel, and contrast. Much of the subtle air of falseness that Melville has contrived to throw over his hero, which is one of the marvels of craftsmanship in this book, derives from ironic implication and equivocation. Irony is the very stuff of a world where deceit masquerades as faith, misanthropy as universal brotherhood, and cynicism as philanthropy, and the misanthropic Pitch is the true lover of his fellow men. What are in their appearance only petty swindles, paltry cheats, are in their reality the nullification of every large hope of humanity. It is understatement to call this mode of writing understatement. But the finest and quietest irony of the book is a sort of constant whisper; it is disarming; it lies in the very manner of the book, which in a style suggesting kindliness and impartial good nature and gentle, sometimes jaunty, ease, leads quietly up to the most bitter conclusions.

Streams more diverse than those the Mississippi musters, flow into *The Confidence-Man*. The Bible, *Pilgrim's Progress*, Shakespeare, and *Paradise Lost* mingle with all varieties of picaresque fiction, from coney-catching anecdotes to *Don Quixote*;[88] Hawthorne's fine-wrought allegorical stories inter-

[88] Melville, who had probably read *Don Quixote* earlier, if one may judge from references in his writings, bought a copy which he inscribed "H. Melville Sep 18. '55." "Pencillings throughout the two volumes seem to indicate that Melville . . . gave the novel a careful rereading" shortly after purchasing this copy. His significant annotation is to Don Quixote's remark that "a knight-errant without a mistress is like a tree without leaves, a building without cement, a shadow without a body that causes it"; Melville wrote: "or as Confucius said 'a dog without a master,' or, to drop both Cervantes & Confucius parables—a god-like mind without a God." (See Harry Levin, " 'Don Quixote' and 'Moby Dick,' " *Cervantes Across the Centuries*, ed. Angel Flores and M. J. Benardete [New York, 1947], p. 220.)

mix with the raw histories of frontier settlement, Indian massacre, river bandits, steamboat con men; the wisdom of the
ancients, Lucian's irony and Tacitus' pessimism, flow beside the
brash confidence of the new Western world, the Wall Street
spirit, sentimental optimism, Emerson's blind faith. The opposites in *The Confidence-Man* are as paradoxical as the blub-
ber and poetry of *Moby-Dick*, and the art which unites them
all is no less skilful than in *Moby-Dick*, though less great.
Moby-Dick is greater because epic and tragedy are higher
regions than allegory and satire. But within its domain, the art
of *The Confidence-Man* is unique, and finished. The perfect
keeping of theme, mood, and story—each reinforcing the others
—derives, one may be sure, not only from mature and accomplished craftsmanship but from something felt very deeply
in mind, heart, and imagination.

But let us board the *Fidèle* and watch the Masquerade for
ourselves.

THE CONFIDENCE-MAN: HIS MASQUERADE

CHAPTER I

A MUTE GOES ABOARD A BOAT ON THE MISSISSIPPI

AT sunrise on a first of April, there appeared, suddenly as Manco Capac at the lake Titicaca, a man in cream-colors, at the water-side in the city of St. Louis.

His cheek was fair, his chin downy, his hair flaxen, his hat a white fur one, with a long fleecy nap. He had neither trunk, valise, carpet-bag, nor parcel. No porter followed him. He was unaccompanied by friends. From the shrugged shoulders, titters, whispers, wonderings of the crowd, it was plain that he was, in the extremest sense of the word, a stranger.

In the same moment with his advent, he stepped aboard the favorite steamer Fidèle, on the point of starting for New Orleans. Stared at, but unsaluted, with the air of one neither courting nor shunning regard, but evenly pursuing the path of duty, lead it through solitudes or cities, he held on his way along the lower deck until he chanced to come to a placard nigh the captain's office, offering a reward for the capture of a mysterious imposter, supposed to have recently arrived from the East; quite an original genius in his vocation, as would appear, though wherein his originality consisted was not clearly given; but what purported to be a careful description of his person followed.

As if it had been a theatre-bill, crowds were gathered about the announcement, and among them certain chevaliers, whose eyes, it was plain, were on the capitals, or, at least, earnestly

1

seeking sight of them from behind intervening coats; but as for their fingers, they were enveloped in some myth; though, during a chance interval, one of these chevaliers somewhat showed his hand in purchasing from another chevalier, ex-officio a peddler of money-belts, one of his popular safe-guards, while another peddler, who was still another versatile chevalier, hawked, in the thick of the throng, the lives of Measan, the bandit of Ohio, Murrel, the pirate of the Mississippi, and the brothers Harpe, the Thugs of the Green River country, in Kentucky—creatures, with others of the sort, one and all exterminated at the time, and for the most part, like the hunted generations of wolves in the same regions, leaving comparatively few successors; which would seem cause for unalloyed gratulation, and is such to all except those who think that in new countries, where the wolves are killed off, the foxes increase.

Pausing at this spot, the stranger so far succeeded in threading his way, as at last to plant himself just beside the placard, when, producing a small slate and tracing some words upon it, he held it up before him on a level with the placard, so that they who read the one might read the other. The words were these:—

"Charity thinketh no evil."

As, in gaining his place, some little perseverance, not to say persistence, of a mildly inoffensive sort, had been unavoidable, it was not with the best relish that the crowd regarded his apparent intrusion; and upon a more attentive survey, perceiving no badge of authority about him, but rather something quite the contrary—he being of an aspect so singularly innocent; an aspect, too, which they took to be somehow inappropriate to the time and place, and inclining to the notion that his writing was of much the same sort: in short, taking him for some strange kind of simpleton, harmless enough, would he keep to himself, but not wholly unobnoxious as an intruder—they made no scruple to jostle him aside; while one, less kind than the rest, or more of a wag, by an unobserved stroke, dexterously flattened down his fleecy hat upon his head. Without readjusting it, the stranger quietly turned, and writing anew upon the slate, again held it up:—

"Charity suffereth long, and is kind."

Illy pleased with his pertinacity, as they thought it, the crowd a second time thrust him aside, and not without epithets and some buffets, all of which were unresented. But, as if at last despairing of so difficult an adventure, wherein one, apparently a non-resistant, sought to impose his presence upon fighting characters, the stranger now moved slowly away, yet not before altering his writing to this:—

"Charity endureth all things."

Shield-like bearing his slate before him, amid stares and jeers he moved slowly up and down, at his turning points again changing his inscription to—

"Charity believeth all things."
and then—
"Charity never faileth."

The word charity, as originally traced, remained throughout uneffaced, not unlike the left-hand numeral of a printed date, otherwise left for convenience in blank.

To some observers, the singularity, if not lunacy, of the stranger was heightened by his muteness, and, perhaps also, by the contrast to his proceedings afforded in the actions— quite in the wonted and sensible order of things—of the barber of the boat, whose quarters, under a smoking-saloon, and over against a bar-room, was next door but two to the captain's office. As if the long, wide, covered deck, hereabouts built up on both sides with shop-like windowed spaces, were some Constantinople arcade or bazaar, where more than one trade is plied, this river barber, aproned and slippered, but rather crusty-looking for the moment, it may be from being newly out of bed, was throwing open his premises for the day, and suitably arranging the exterior. With business-like dispatch, having rattled down his shutters, and at a palm-tree angle set out in the iron fixture his little ornamental pole, and this without over-much tenderness for the elbows and toes of the crowd, he con-cluded his operations by bidding people stand still more aside, when, jumping on a stool, he hung over his door, on the cus-tomary nail, a gaudy sort of illuminated pasteboard sign, skill-fully executed by himself, gilt with the likeness of a razor elbowed in readiness to shave, and also, for the public benefit, with two words not unfrequently seen ashore gracing other shops besides barbers':—

"NO TRUST."

An inscription which, though in a sense not less intrusive than the contrasted ones of the stranger, did not, as it seemed, provoke any corresponding derision or surprise, much less in-dignation; and still less, to all appearances, did it gain for the inscriber the repute of being a simpleton.

Meanwhile, he with the slate continued moving slowly up and down, not without causing some stares to change into jeers, and some jeers into pushes, and some pushes into punches; when suddenly, in one of his turns, he was hailed from behind by two porters carrying a large trunk; but as the summons, though loud, was without effect, they accidentally or otherwise swung their burden against him, nearly overthrowing him; when, by a quick start, a peculiar inarticulate moan, and a pathetic telegraphing of his fingers, he involuntarily betrayed that he was not alone dumb, but also deaf.

Presently, as if not wholly unaffected by his reception thus far, he went forward, seating himself in a retired spot on the forecastle, nigh the foot of a ladder there leading to a deck above, up and down which ladder some of the boatmen, in discharge of their duties, were occasionally going.

From his betaking himself to this humble quarter, it was evi-dent that, as a deck-passenger, the stranger, simple though he seemed, was not entirely ignorant of his place, though his tak-ing a deck-passage might have been partly for convenience; as, from his having no luggage, it was probable that his destina-tion was one of the small wayside landings within a few hours' sail. But, though he might not have a long way to go, yet he seemed already to have come from a very long distance.

Though neither soiled nor slovenly, his cream-colored suit had a tossed look, almost linty, as if, traveling night and day from some far country beyond the prairies, he had long been without the solace of a bed. His aspect was at once gentle and jaded, and, from the moment of seating himself, increasing in tired abstraction and dreaminess. Gradually overtaken by slumber, his flaxen head drooped, his whole lamb-like figure relaxed, and, half reclining against the ladder's foot, lay motionless, as some sugar-snow in March, which, softly stealing down over night, with its white placidity startles the brown farmer peering out from his threshold at daybreak.

CHAPTER II

"Odd fish!"

"Poor fellow!"

"Who can he be?"

"Casper Hauser."

"Bless my soul!"

"Uncommon countenance."

"Green prophet from Utah."

"Humbug!"

"Singular innocence."

"Means something."

"Spirit-rapper."

"Moon-calf."

"Piteous."

"Trying to enlist interest."

"Beware of him."

"Fast asleep here, and, doubtless, pick-pockets on board."

"Kind of daylight Endymion."

"Escaped convict, worn out with dodging."

"Jacob dreaming at Luz."

Such the epitaphic comments, conflictingly spoken or thought, of a miscellaneous company, who, assembled on the overlooking, cross-wise balcony at the forward end of the upper deck near by, had not witnessed preceding occurrences.

Meantime, like some enchanted man in his grave, happily oblivious of all gossip, whether chiseled or chatted, the deaf and dumb stranger still tranquilly slept, while now the boat started on her voyage.

The great ship-canal of Ving-King-Ching, in the Flowery

Kingdom, seems the Mississippi in parts, where, amply flowing between low, vine-tangled banks, flat as tow-paths, it bears the huge toppling steamers, bedizened and lacquered within like imperial junks.

Pierced along its great white bulk with two tiers of small embrasure-like windows, well above the waterline, the Fidèle, though, might at distance have been taken by strangers for some whitewashed fort on a floating isle.

Merchants on 'change seem the passengers that buzz on her decks, while, from quarters unseen, comes a murmur as of bees in the comb. Fine promenades, domed saloons, long galleries, sunny balconies, confidential passages, bridal chambers, state-rooms plenty as pigeon-holes, and out-of-the-way retreats like secret drawers in an escritoire, present like facilities for publicity or privacy. Auctioneer or coiner, with equal ease, might somewhere here drive his trade.

Though her voyage of twelve hundred miles extends from apple to orange, from clime to clime, yet, like any small ferry-boat, to right and left, at every landing, the huge Fidèle still receives additional passengers in exchange for those that disembark; so that, though always full of strangers, she continually, in some degree, adds to, or replaces them with strangers still more strange; like Rio Janeiro fountain, fed from the Co-covarde mountains, which is ever overflowing with strange waters, but never with the same strange particles in every part.

Though hitherto, as has been seen, the man in cream-colors had by no means passed unobserved, yet by stealing into retirement, and there going asleep and continuing so, he seemed to have courted oblivion, a boon not often withheld from so humble an applicant as he. Those staring crowds on the shore were now left far behind, seen dimly clustering like swallows on eaves; while the passengers' attention was soon drawn away to the rapidly shooting high bluffs and shot-towers on the Missouri shore, or the bluff-looking Missourians and towering Kentuckians among the throngs on the decks.

By-and-by—two or three random stoppages having been made, and the last transient memory of the slumberer vanished, and he himself, not unlikely, waked up and landed ere now—the crowd, as is usual, began in all parts to break up from a concourse into various clusters or squads, which in some cases disintegrated again into quartettes, trios, and couples, or even solitaires; involuntarily submitting to that natural law which ordains dissolution equally to the mass, as in time to the member.

As among Chaucer's Canterbury pilgrims, or those oriental ones crossing the Red Sea towards Mecca in the festival month, there was no lack of variety. Natives of all sorts, and foreigners; men of business and men of pleasure; parlor men and back-woodsmen; farm-hunters and fame-hunters; heiress-hunters, gold-hunters, buffalo-hunters, bee-hunters, happiness-hunters, truth-hunters, and still keener hunters after all these hunters. Fine ladies in slippers, and moccasined squaws; Northern spec-ulators and Eastern philosophers; English, Irish, German, Scotch, Danes; Santa Fé traders in striped blankets, and Broad-way bucks in cravats of cloth of gold; fine-looking Kentucky boatmen, and Japanese-looking Mississippi cotton-planters; Quakers in full drab, and United States soldiers in full regi-mentals; slaves, black, mulatto, quadroon; modish young Span-ish Creoles, and old-fashioned French Jews; Mormons and Papists; Dives and Lazarus; jesters and mourners, teetotalers and convivialists, deacons and blacklegs; hard-shell Baptists and clay-eaters; grinning negroes, and Sioux chiefs solemn as high-priests. In short, a piebald parliament, an Anacharsis Cloots congress of all kinds of that multiform pilgrim species, man.

As pine, beech, birch, ash, hackmatack, hemlock, spruce, bass-wood, maple, interweave their foliage in the natural wood, so these varieties of mortals blended their varieties of visage and garb. A Tartar-like picturesqueness; a sort of pagan aban-donment and assurance. Here reigned the dashing and all-fus-ing spirit of the West, whose type is the Mississippi itself, which, uniting the streams of the most distant and opposite zones, pours them along, helter-skelter, in one cosmopolitan and confident tide.

CHAPTER III

In the forward part of the boat, not the least attractive object, for a time, was a grotesque negro cripple, in tow-cloth attire and an old coal-sifter of a tambourine in his hand, who, owing to something wrong about his legs, was, in effect, cut down to the stature of a Newfoundland dog; his knotted black fleece and goodnatured, honest black face rubbing against the upper part of people's thighs as he made shift to shuffle about, making music, such as it was, and raising a smile even from the gravest. It was curious to see him, out of his very deformity, indigence, and houselessness, so cheerily endured, raising mirth in some of that crowd, whose own purses, hearths, hearts, all their possessions, sound limbs included, could not make gay.

"What is your name, old boy?" said a purple-faced drover, putting his large purple hand on the cripple's bushy wool, as if it were the curled forehead of a black steer.

"Der Black Guinea dey calls me, sar."

"And who is your master, Guinea?"

"Oh sar, I am der dog widout massa."

"A free dog, eh? Well, on your account, I'm sorry for that, Guinea. Dogs without masters fare hard."

"So dey do, sar; so dey do. But you see, sar, dese here legs? What ge'mman want to own dese here legs?"

"But where do you live?"

"All 'long shore, sar; dough now I'se going to see brodder at der landing; but chiefly I libs in der city."

"St. Louis, ah? Where do you sleep there of nights?"

"On der floor of der good baker's oven, sar."

"In an oven? whose, pray? What baker, I should like to know,

9

bakes such black bread in his oven, alongside of his nice white rolls, too. Who is that too charitable baker, pray?"

"Dar he be," with a broad grin lifting his tambourine high over his head.

"The sun is the baker, eh?"

"Yes sar, in der city dat good baker warms der stones for dis ole darkie when he sleeps out on der pabements o' nights."

"But that must be in the summer only, old boy. How about winter, when the cold Cossacks come clattering and jingling? How about winter, old boy?"

"Den dis poor old darkie shakes werry bad, I tell you, sar. Oh sar, oh! don't speak ob der winter," he added, with a reminiscent shiver, shuffling off into the thickest of the crowd, like a half-frozen black sheep nudging itself a cozy berth in the heart of the white flock.

Thus far not very many pennies had been given him, and, used at last to his strange looks, the less polite passengers of those in that part of the boat began to get their fill of him as a curious object; when suddenly the negro more than revived their first interest by an expedient which, whether by chance or design, was a singular temptation at once to *diversion* and charity, though, even more than his crippled limbs, it put him on a canine footing. In short, as in appearance he seemed a dog, so now, in a merry way, like a dog he began to be treated. Still shuffling among the crowd, now and then he would pause, throwing back his head and opening his mouth like an elephant for tossed apples at a menagerie; when, making a space before him, people would have a bout at a strange sort of pitch-penny game, the cripple's mouth being at once target and purse, and he hailing each expertly-caught copper with a cracked bravura from his tambourine. To be the subject of alms-giving is trying, and to feel in duty bound to appear cheerfully grateful under the trial, must be still more so; but whatever his secret emotions, he swallowed them, while still retaining each copper this side the œsophagus. And nearly always he grinned, and only once or twice did he wince, which was when certain coins, tossed by more playful almoners, came inconveniently nigh to his teeth, an accident whose unwelcomeness was not unedged by the circumstance that the pennies thus thrown proved buttons.

While this game of charity was yet at its height, a limping, gimlet-eyed, sour-faced person—it may be some discharged custom-house officer, who, suddenly stripped of convenient means of support, had concluded to be avenged on government and humanity by making himself miserable for life, either by hating or suspecting everything and everybody—this shallow unfortunate, after sundry sorry observations of the negro, began to croak out something about his deformity being a sham, got up for financial purposes, which immediately threw a damp upon the frolic benignities of the pitch-penny players.

But that these suspicions came from one who himself on a wooden leg went halt, this did not appear to strike anybody present. That cripples, above all men should be companionable, or, at least, refrain from picking a fellow-limper to pieces, in short, should have a little sympathy in common misfortune, seemed not to occur to the company.

Meantime, the negro's countenance, before marked with even more than patient good-nature, drooped into a heavy-hearted expression, full of the most painful distress. So far abased beneath its proper physical level, that Newfoundland-dog face turned in passively hopeless appeal, as if instinct told it that the right or the wrong might not have overmuch to do with whatever wayward mood superior intelligences might yield to.

But instinct, though knowing, is yet a teacher set below reason, which itself says, in the grave words of Lysander in the comedy, after Puck has made a sage of him with his spell:—

"The will of man is by his reason swayed."

So that, suddenly change as people may, in their dispositions, it is not always waywardness, but improved judgment, which, as in Lysander's case, or the present, operates with them.

Yes, they began to scrutinize the negro curiously enough; when, emboldened by this evidence of the efficacy of his words, the wooden-legged man hobbled up to the negro, and, with the air of a beadle, would, to prove his alleged imposture on the spot, have stripped him and then driven him away, but was prevented by the crowd's clamor, now taking part with the poor fellow, against one who had just before turned nearly all minds the other way. So he with the wooden leg was forced to retire; when the rest, finding themselves left sole judges in the case, could not resist the opportunity of acting the part: not because it is a human weakness to take pleasure in sitting in judgment upon one in a box, as surely this unfortunate negro now was, but that it strangely sharpens human perceptions, when, instead of standing by and having their fellow-feelings touched by the sight of an alleged culprit severely handled by some one justiciary, a crowd suddenly come to be all justiciaries in the same case themselves; as in Arkansas once, a man proved guilty, by law, of murder, but whose condemnation was deemed unjust by the people, so that they rescued him to try him themselves; whereupon, they, as it turned out, found him even guiltier than the court had done, and forthwith proceeded to execution; so that the gallows presented the truly warning spectacle of a man hanged by his friends.

But not to such extremities, or anything like them, did the present crowd come; they, for the time, being content with putting the negro fairly and discreetly to the question; among other things, asking him, had he any documentary proof, any plain paper about him, attesting that his case was not a spurious one.

"No, no, dis poor ole darkie haint none o' dem waloable papers," he wailed.

"But is there not some one who can speak a good word for you?" here said a person newly arrived from another part of the boat, a young Episcopal clergyman, in a long, straight-bodied black coat; small in stature, but manly; with a clear face and blue eye; innocence, tenderness, and good sense triumvirate in his air.

"Oh yes, oh yes, ge'mmen," he eagerly answered, as if his memory, before suddenly frozen up by cold charity, as suddenly thawed back into fluidity at the first kindly word. "Oh yes, oh yes, dar is aboard here a werry nice, good ge'mman wid a weed, and a ge'mman in a gray coat and white tie, what knows all about me; and a ge'mman wid a big book, too; and a yarb-doctor; and a ge'mman in a yaller west; and a ge'mman wid a brass plate; and a ge'mman in a wiolet robe; and a ge'mman as is a sodjer; and ever so many good, kind, honest ge'mmen more abord what knows me and will speak for me, God bress 'em; yes, and what knows me as well as dis poor old darkie knows hisself, God bress him! Oh, find 'em, find 'em," he earn-estly added, "and let 'em come quick, and show you all, ge'm-men, dat dis poor ole darkie is werry well wordy of all you kind ge'mmen's kind confidence."

"But how are we to find all these people in this great crowd?" was the question of a bystander, umbrella in hand; a middle-aged person, a country merchant apparently, whose natural good-feeling had been made at least cautious by the unnatural ill-feeling of the discharged custom-house officer.

"Where are we to find them?" half-rebukefully echoed the young Episcopal clergyman. "I will go find one to begin with," he quickly added, and, with kind haste suiting the action to the word, away he went.

"Wild goose chase!" croaked he with the wooden leg, now again drawing nigh. "Don't believe there's a soul of them aboard. Did ever beggar have such heaps of fine friends? He can walk fast enough when he tries, a good deal faster than I; but he can lie yet faster. He's some white operator, betwisted and painted up for a decoy. He and his friends are all hum-bugs."

"Have you no charity, friend?" here in self-subdued tones, singularly contrasted with his unsubdued person, said a Method-ist minister, advancing; a tall, muscular, martial-looking man, a Tennessean by birth, who in the Mexican war had been volunteer chaplain to a volunteer rifle-regiment.

"Charity is one thing, and truth is another," rejoined he with the wooden leg: "he's a rascal, I say."

"But why not, friend, put as charitable a construction as one can upon the poor fellow?" said the soldier-like Methodist, with increased difficulty maintaining a pacific demeanor towards one whose own asperity seemed so little to entitle him to it: "he looks honest, don't he?"

"Looks are one thing, and facts are another," snapped out the other perversely; "and as to your constructions, what construction can you put upon a rascal, but that a rascal he is?"

"Be not such a Canada thistle," urged the Methodist, with something less of patience than before. "Charity, man, charity."

"To where it belongs with your charity! to heaven with it!" again snapped out the other, diabolically; "here on earth, true charity dotes, and false charity plots. Who betrays a fool with a kiss, the charitable fool has the charity to believe is in love with him, and the charitable knave on the stand gives charitable testimony for his comrade in the box."

"Surely, friend," returned the noble Methodist, with much ado restraining his still waxing indignation—"surely, to say the least, you forget yourself. Apply it home," he continued, with exterior calmness tremulous with inkept emotion. "Suppose, now, I should exercise no charity in judging your own character by the words which have fallen from you; what sort of vile, pitiless man do you think I would take you for?"

"No doubt"—with a grin—"some such pitiless man as has lost his piety in much the same way that the jockey loses his honesty."

"And how is that, friend?" still conscientiously holding back the old Adam in him, as if it were a mastiff he had by the neck.

"Never you mind how it is"—with a sneer; "but all horses aint virtuous, no more than all men kind; and come close to, and much dealt with, some things are catching. When you find me a virtuous jockey, I will find you a benevolent wise man."

"Some insinuation there."

"More fool you that are puzzled by it."

"Reprobate!" cried the other, his indignation now at last almost boiling over; "godless reprobate! if charity did not restrain me, I could call you by names you deserve."

"Could you, indeed?" with an insolent sneer.

"Yea, and teach you charity on the spot," cried the goaded

Methodist, suddenly catching this exasperating opponent by
his shabby coat-collar, and shaking him till his timber-toe clattered on the deck like a nine-pin. "You took me for a non-com-
batant did you?—thought, seedy coward that you are, that you
could abuse a Christian with impunity. You find your mistake"—with another hearty shake.

"Well said and better done, church militant!" cried a voice.

"The white cravat against the world!" cried another.

"Bravo, bravo!" chorused many voices, with like enthusiasm
taking sides with the resolute champion.

"You fools!" cried he with the wooden leg, writhing himself
loose and inflamedly turning upon the throng; "you flock of
fools, under this captain of fools, in this ship of fools!"

With which exclamations, followed by idle threats against his
admonisher, this condign victim to justice hobbled away, as
disdaining to hold further argument with such a rabble. But
his scorn was more than repaid by the hisses that chased him, in
which the brave Methodist, satisfied with the rebuke already
administered, was, to omit still better reasons, too magnanimous
to join. All he said was, pointing towards the departing recu-
sant, "There he shambles off on his one lone leg, emblematic
of his one-sided view of humanity."

"But trust your painted decoy," retorted the other from a
distance, pointing back to the black cripple, "and I have my
revenge."

"But we ain't agoing to trust him!" shouted back a voice.

"So much the better," he jeered back. "Look you," he added,
coming to a dead halt where he was; "look you, I have been
called a Canada thistle. Very good. And a seedy one: still better. And the seedy Canada thistle has been pretty well shaken
among ye: best of all. Dare say some seed has been shaken out;
and won't it spring though? And when it does spring, do you
cut down the young thistles, and won't they spring the more?
It's encouraging and coaxing 'em. Now, when with my thistles
your farms shall be well stocked, why then—you may abandon
'em!"

"What does all that mean, now?" asked the country merchant, staring.

"Nothing; the foiled wolf's parting howl," said the Methodist. "Spleen, much spleen, which is the rickety child of his evil heart of unbelief: it has made him mad. I suspect him for one naturally reprobate. Oh, friends," raising his arms as in the pulpit, "oh beloved, how are we admonished by the melancholy spectacle of this raver. Let us profit by the lesson; and is it not this: that if, next to mistrusting Providence, there be aught that man should pray against, it is against mistrusting his fellow-man. I have been in mad-houses full of tragic mopers, and seen there the end of suspicion: the cynic, in the moody madness muttering in the corner; for years a barren fixture there; head lopped over, gnawing his own lip, vulture of himself; while, by fits and starts, from the corner opposite came the grimace of the idiot at him."

"What an example," whispered one.

"Might deter Timon," was the response.

"Oh, oh, good ge'mmen, have you no confidence in dis poor ole darkie?" now wailed the returning negro, who, during the late scene, had stumped apart in alarm.

"Confidence in you?" echoed he who had whispered, with abruptly changed air turning short round; "that remains to be seen."

"I tell you what it is, Ebony," in similarly changed tones said he who had responded to the whisperer, "yonder churl," pointing toward the wooden leg in the distance, "is, no doubt, a churlish fellow enough, and I would not wish to be like him; but that is no reason why you may not be some sort of black Jeremy Diddler."

"No confidence in dis poor ole darkie, den?"

"Before giving you our confidence," said a third, "we will wait the report of the kind gentleman who went in search of one of your friends who was to speak for you."

"Very likely, in that case," said a fourth, "we shall wait here till Christmas. Shouldn't wonder, did we not see that kind gentleman again. After seeking awhile in vain, he will conclude he has been made a fool of, and so not return to us for pure shame. Fact is, I begin to feel a little qualmish about the darkie myself. Something queer about this darkie, depend upon it."

Once more the negro wailed, and turning in despair from the last speaker, imploringly caught the Methodist by the skirt of his coat. But a change had come over that before impassioned intercessor. With an irresolute and troubled air, he mutely eyed the suppliant; against whom, somehow, by what seemed instinctive influences, the distrusts first set on foot were now generally reviving, and, if anything, with added severity.

"No confidence in dis poor ole darkie," yet again wailed the negro, letting go the coat-skirts and turning appealingly all round him.

"Yes, my poor fellow, *I* have confidence in you," now exclaimed the country merchant before named, whom the negro's appeal, coming so piteously on the heel of pitilessness, seemed at last humanely to have decided in his favor. "And here, here is some proof of my trust," with which, tucking his umbrella under his arm, and diving down his hand into his pocket, he fished forth a purse, and, accidentally, along with it, his business card, which, unobserved, dropped to the deck. "Here, here, my poor fellow," he continued, extending a half dollar.

Not more grateful for the coin than the kindness, the cripple's face glowed like a polished copper saucepan, and shuffling a pace nigher, with one upstretched hand he received the alms, while, as unconsciously, his one advanced leather stump covered the card.

Done in despite of the general sentiment, the good deed of the merchant was not, perhaps, without its unwelcome return from the crowd, since that good deed seemed somehow to convey to them a sort of reproach. Still again, and more pertinaciously than ever, the cry arose against the negro, and still again he wailed forth his lament and appeal; among other things, repeating that the friends, of whom already he had partially run off the list, would freely speak for him, would anybody go find them.

"Why don't you go find 'em yourself?" demanded a gruff boatman.

"How can I go find 'em myself? Dis poor ole game-legged darkie's friends must come to him. Oh, whar, whar is dat good friend of dis darkie's, dat good man wid de weed?"

At this point, a steward ringing a bell came along, summoning all persons who had not got their tickets to step to the captain's office; an announcement which speedily thinned the throng about the black cripple, who himself soon forlornly stumped out of sight, probably on much the same errand as the rest.

CHAPTER IV

RENEWAL OF OLD ACQUAINTANCE

"How do you do, Mr. Roberts?"

"Eh?"

"Don't you know me?"

"No, certainly."

The crowd about the captain's office, having in good time melted away, the above encounter took place in one of the side balconies astern, between a man in mourning clean and respectable, but none of the glossiest, a long weed on his hat, and the country-merchant before-mentioned, whom, with the familiarity of an old acquaintance, the former had accosted.

"Is it possible, my dear sir," resumed he with the weed, "that you do not recall my countenance? why yours I recall distinctly as if but half an hour, instead of half an age, had passed since I saw you. Don't you recall me, now? Look harder."

"In my conscience—truly—I protest," honestly bewildered, "bless my soul, sir, I don't know you—really, really. But stay, stay," he hurriedly added, not without gratification, glancing up at the crape on the stranger's hat, "stay—yes—seems to me, though I have not the pleasure of personally knowing you, yet I am pretty sure I have at least *heard* of you, and recently too, quite recently. A poor negro aboard here referred to you, among others, for a character, I think."

"Oh, the cripple. Poor fellow, I know him well. They found me. I have said all I could for him. I think I abated their distrust. Would I could have been of more substantial service. And apropos, sir," he added, "now that it strikes me, allow me to ask, whether the circumstance of one man, however humble, referring for a character to another man, however afflicted, does not argue more or less of moral worth in the latter?"

19

The good merchant looked puzzled.

"Still you don't recall my countenance?"

"Still does truth compel me to say that I cannot, despite my best efforts," was the reluctantly-candid reply.

"Can I be so changed? Look at me. Or is it I who am mistaken?—Are you not, sir, Henry Roberts, forwarding merchant, of Wheeling, Pennsylvania? Pray, now, if you use the advertisement of business cards, and happen to have one with you, just look at it, and see whether you are not the man I take you for."

"Why," a bit chafed, perhaps, "I hope I know myself."

"And yet self-knowledge is thought by some not so easy. Who knows, my dear sir, but for a time you may have taken yourself for somebody else? Stranger things have happened."

The good merchant stared.

"To come to particulars, my dear sir, I met you, now some six years back, at Brade Brothers & Co.'s office, I think. I was traveling for a Philadelphia house. The senior Brade introduced us, you remember; some business-chat followed, then you forced me home with you to a family tea, and a family time we had. Have you forgotten about the urn, and what I said about Werter's Charlotte, and the bread and butter, and that capital story you told of the large loaf. A hundred times since, I have laughed over it. At least you must recall my name—Ringman, John Ringman."

"Large loaf? Invited you to tea? Ringman? Ringman? Ring? Ring?"

"Ah sir," sadly smiling, "don't ring the changes that way. I see you have a faithless memory, Mr. Roberts. But trust in the faithfulness of mine."

"Well, to tell the truth, in some things my memory ain't of the very best," was the honest rejoinder. "But still," he perplexedly added, "still I—"

"Oh sir, suffice it that it is as I say. Doubt not that we are all well acquainted."

"But—but I don't like this going dead against my own memory; I—"

"But didn't you admit, my dear sir, that in some things this memory of yours is a little faithless? Now, those who have faithless memories, should they not have some little confidence in the less faithless memories of others?"

"But, of this friendly chat and tea, I have not the slightest—"

"I see, I see; quite erased from the tablet. Pray, sir," with a sudden illumination, "about six years back, did it happen to you to receive any injury on the head? Surprising effects have arisen from such a cause. Not alone unconsciousness as to events for a greater or less time immediately subsequent to the injury, but likewise—strange to add—oblivion, entire and incurable, as to events embracing a longer or shorter period immediately preceding it; that is, when the mind at the time was perfectly sensible of them, and fully competent also to register them in the memory, and did in fact so do; but all in vain, for all was afterwards bruised out by the injury."

After the first start, the merchant listened with what appeared more than ordinary interest. The other proceeded:

"In my boyhood I was kicked by a horse, and lay insensible for a long time. Upon recovering, what a blank! No faintest trace in regard to how I had come near the horse, or what horse it was, or where it was, or that it was a horse at all that had brought me to that pass. For the knowledge of those particulars I am indebted solely to my friends, in whose statements, I need not say, I place implicit reliance, since particulars of some sort there must have been, and why should they deceive me? You see, sir, the mind is ductile, very much so: but images, ductilely received into it, need a certain time to harden and bake in their impressions, otherwise such a casualty as I speak of will in an instant obliterate them, as though they had never been. We are but clay, sir, potter's clay, as the good book says, clay, feeble, and too-yielding clay. But I will not philosophize. Tell me, was it your misfortune to receive any concussion upon the brain about the period I speak of? If so, I will with pleasure supply the void in your memory by more minutely rehearsing the circumstances of our acquaintance."

The growing interest betrayed by the merchant had not relaxed as the other proceeded. After some hesitation, indeed, something more than hesitation, he confessed that, though he had never received any injury of the sort named, yet, about the time in question, he had in fact been taken with a brain fever, losing his mind completely for a considerable interval. He was continuing, when the stranger with much animation exclaimed:

"There now, you see, I was not wholly mistaken. That brain fever accounts for it all."

"Nay; but—"

"Pardon me, Mr. Roberts," respectfully interrupting him, "but time is short, and I have something private and particular to say to you. Allow me."

Mr. Roberts, good man, could but acquiesce, and the two having silently walked to a less public spot, the manner of the man with the weed suddenly assumed a seriousness almost painful. What might be called a writhing expression stole over him. He seemed struggling with some disastrous necessity in-kept. He made one or two attempts to speak, but words seemed to choke him. His companion stood in humane surprise, wondering what was to come. At length, with an effort mastering his feelings, in a tolerably composed tone he spoke.

"If I remember, you are a mason, Mr. Roberts?"

"Yes, yes."

Averting himself a moment, as to recover from a return of agitation, the stranger grasped the other's hand; "and would you not loan a brother a shilling if he needed it?"

The merchant started, apparently, almost as if to retreat.

"Ah, Mr. Roberts, I trust you are not one of those business men, who make a business of never having to do with un-fortunates. For God's sake don't leave me. I have something on my heart—on my heart. Under deplorable circumstances thrown among strangers, utter strangers. I want a friend in whom I may confide. Yours, Mr. Roberts, is almost the first known face I've seen for many weeks."

It was so sudden an outburst; the interview offered such a contrast to the scene around, that the merchant, though not used to be very indiscreet, yet, being not entirely inhumane, remained not entirely unmoved.

The other, still tremulous, resumed:

"I need not say, sir, how it cuts me to the soul, to follow up a social salutation with such words as have just been mine. I know that I jeopardize your good opinion. But I can't help it: necessity knows no law, and heeds no risk. Sir, we are masons, one more step aside; I will tell you my story."

In a low, half-suppressed tone, he began it. Judging from his auditor's expression, it seemed to be a tale of singular interest, involving calamities against which no integrity, no forethought, no energy, no genius, no piety, could guard.

At every disclosure, the hearer's commiseration increased. No sentimental pity. As the story went on, he drew from his wallet a bank note, but after a while, at some still more unhappy revelation, changed it for another, probably of a somewhat larger amount; which, when the story was concluded, with an air studiously disclamatory of alms-giving, he put into the stranger's hands; who, on his side, with an air studiously disclamatory of alms-taking, put it into his pocket.

Assistance being received, the stranger's manner assumed a kind and degree of decorum which, under the circumstances, seemed almost coldness. After some words, not over ardent, and yet not exactly inappropriate, he took leave, making a bow which had one knows not what of a certain chastened independence about it; as if misery, however burdensome, could not break down self-respect, nor gratitude, however deep, humiliate a gentleman.

He was hardly yet out of sight, when he paused as if thinking; then with hastened steps returning to the merchant, "I am just reminded that the president, who is also transfer-agent, of the Black Rapids Coal Company, happens to be on board here, and, having been subpœnaed as witness in a stock case on the docket in Kentucky, has his transfer-book with him. A month since, in a panic contrived by artful alarmists, some credulous stock-holders sold out; but, to frustrate the aim of the alarmists, the Company, previously advised of their scheme, so managed it as to get into its own hands those sacrificed shares, resolved that, since a spurious panic must be, the panic-makers should be no gainers by it. The Company, I hear, is now ready, but not anxious, to redispose of those shares; and having obtained them at their depressed value, will now sell them at par, though, prior to the panic, they were held at a handsome figure above. That the readiness of the Company to do this is not generally known, is shown by the fact that the stock still stands on the transfer-book in the Company's name, offering to one in funds a rare chance for investment. For, the panic subsiding more and more every day, it will daily be seen how it originated; confidence will be more than restored; there will be a reaction; from the stock's descent its rise will be higher than from no fall, the holders trusting themselves to fear no second fate."

Having listened at first with curiosity, at last with interest, the merchant replied to the effect, that some time since, through friends concerned with it, he had heard of the company, and heard well of it, but was ignorant that there had latterly been fluctuations. He added that he was no speculator; that hitherto he had avoided having to do with stocks of any sort, but in the present case he really felt something like being tempted. "Pray," in conclusion, "do you think that upon a pinch anything could be transacted on board here with the transfer-agent? Are you acquainted with him?"

"Not personally. I but happened to hear that he was a passenger. For the rest, though it might be somewhat informal, the gentleman might not object to doing a little business on board. Along the Mississippi, you know, business is not so ceremonious as at the East."

"True," returned the merchant, and looked down a moment in thought, then, raising his head quickly, said, in a tone not so benign as his wonted one, "This would seem a rare chance, indeed; why, upon first hearing it, did you not snatch at it? I mean for yourself!"

"I?—would it had been possible!"

Not without some emotion was this said, and not without some embarrassment was the reply. "Ah, yes, I had forgotten."

Upon this, the stranger regarded him with mild gravity, not a little disconcerting; the more so, as there was in it what seemed the aspect not alone of the superior, but, as it were, the rebuker; which sort of bearing, in a beneficiary towards his benefactor, looked strangely enough; none the less, that, somehow, it sat not altogether unbecomingly upon the beneficiary, being free from anything like the appearance of assumption, and mixed with a kind of painful conscientiousness, as though nothing but a proper sense of what he owed to himself swayed him. At length he spoke:

"To reproach a penniless man with remissness in not availing himself of an opportunity for pecuniary investment—but, no, no; it was forgetfulness; and this, charity will impute to some lingering effect of that unfortunate brain-fever, which, as to occurrences dating yet further back, disturbed Mr. Roberts's memory still more seriously."

"As to that," said the merchant, rallying, "I am not—"

"Pardon me, but you must admit, that just now, an unpleasant distrust, however vague, was yours. Ah, shallow as it is, yet, how subtle a thing is suspicion, which at times can invade the humanest of hearts and wisest of heads. But, enough. My object, sir, in calling your attention to this stock, is by way of acknowledgment of your goodness. I but seek to be grateful; if my information leads to nothing, you must remember the motive."

He bowed, and finally retired, leaving Mr. Roberts not wholly without self-reproach, for having momentarily indulged injurious thoughts against one who, it was evident, was possessed of a self-respect which forbade his indulging them himself.

CHAPTER V

"WELL, there is sorrow in the world, but goodness too; and goodness that is not greenness, either, no more than sorrow is. Dear good man. Poor beating heart!"

It was the man with the weed, not very long after quitting the merchant, murmuring to himself with his hand to his side like one with the heart-disease.

Meditation over kindness received seemed to have softened him something, too, it may be, beyond what might, perhaps, have been looked for from one whose unwonted self-respect in the hour of need, and in the act of being aided, might have appeared to some not wholly unlike pride out of place; and pride, in any place, is seldom very feeling. But the truth, perhaps, is, that those who are least touched with that vice, besides being not unsusceptible to goodness, are sometimes the ones whom a ruling sense of propriety makes appear cold, if not thankless, under a favor. For, at such a time, to be full of warm, earnest words, and heart-felt protestations, is to create a scene; and well-bred people dislike few things more than that; which would seem to look as if the world did not relish earnestness; but, not so; because the world, being earnest itself, likes an earnest scene, and an earnest man, very well, but only in their place—the stage. See what sad work they make of it, who, ignorant of this, flame out in Irish enthusiasm and with Irish sincerity, to a benefactor, who, if a man of sense and respectability, as well as kindliness, can but be more or less annoyed by it; and, if of a nervously fastidious nature, as some are, may be led to think almost as much less favorably of the beneficiary

26

paining him by his gratitude, as if he had been guilty of its contrary, instead only of an indiscretion. But, beneficiaries who know better, though they may feel as much, if not more, neither inflict such pain, nor are inclined to run any risk of so doing. And these, being wise, are the majority. By which one sees how inconsiderate those persons are, who, from the absence of its officious manifestations in the world, complain that there is not much gratitude extant; when the truth is, that there is as much of it as there is of modesty; but, both being for the most part votarists of the shade, for the most part keep out of sight.

What started this was, to account, if necessary, for the changed air of the man with the weed, who, throwing off in private the cold garb of decorum, and so giving warmly loose to his genuine heart, seemed almost transformed into another being. This subdued air of softness, too, was toned with melancholy, melancholy unreserved; a thing which, however at variance with propriety, still the more attested his earnestness; for one knows not how it is, but it sometimes happens that, where earnestness is, there, also, is melancholy.

At the time, he was leaning over the rail at the boat's side, in his pensiveness, unmindful of another pensive figure near—a young gentleman with a swan-neck, wearing a lady-like open shirt collar, thrown back, and tied with a black ribbon. From a square, tableted broach, curiously engraved with Greek characters, he seemed a collegian—not improbably, a sophomore—on his travels; possibly, his first. A small book bound in Roman vellum was in his hand.

Overhearing his murmuring neighbor, the youth regarded him with some surprise, not to say interest. But, singularly for a collegian, being apparently of a retiring nature, he did not speak; when the other still more increased his diffidence by changing from soliloquy to colloquy, in a manner strangely mixed of familiarity and pathos.

"Ah, who is this? You did not hear me, my young friend, did you? Why, you, too, look sad. My melancholy is not catching!"

"Sir, sir," stammered the other.

"Pray, now," with a sort of sociable sorrowfulness, slowly sliding along the rail, "Pray, now, my young friend, what volume have you there? Give me leave," gently drawing it from him. "Tacitus!" Then opening it at random, read: "In general a black and shameful period lies before me." "Dear young sir," touching his arm alarmedly, "don't read this book. It is poison, moral poison. Even were there truth in Tacitus, such truth would have the operation of falsity, and so still be poison, moral poison. Too well I know this Tacitus. In my college-days he came near souring me into cynicism. Yes, I began to turn down my collar, and go about with a disdainfully joyless expression."

"Sir, sir, I—I—"

"Trust me. Now, young friend, perhaps you think that Tacitus, like me, is only melancholy; but he's more—he's ugly. A vast difference, young sir, between the melancholy view and the ugly. The one may show the world still beautiful, not so the other. The one may be compatible with benevolence, the other not. The one may deepen insight, the other shallows it. Drop Tacitus. Phrenologically, my young friend, you would seem to have a well-developed head, and large; but cribbed within the ugly view, the Tacitus view, your large brain, like your large ox in the contracted field, will but starve the more. And don't dream, as some of you students may, that, by taking this same ugly view, the deeper meanings of the deeper books will so alone become revealed to you. Drop Tacitus. His subtlety is falsity. To him, in his double-refined anatomy of human nature, is well applied the Scripture saying—'There is a subtle man, and the same is deceived.' Drop Tacitus. Come, now, let me throw the book overboard."

"Sir, I—I—"

"Not a word; I know just what is in your mind, and that is just what I am speaking to. Yes, learn from me that, though the sorrows of the world are great, its wickedness—that is, its ugliness—is small. Much cause to pity man, little to distrust him. I myself have known adversity, and know it still. But for that, do I turn cynic? No, no: it is small beer that sours. To my fellow-creatures I owe alleviations. So, whatever I may have undergone, it but deepens my confidence in my kind. Now, then" (winningly), "this book—will you let me drown it for you?"

"Really, sir—I—"

"I see, I see. But of course you read Tacitus in order to aid you in understanding human nature—as if truth was ever got at by libel. My young friend, if to know human nature is your object, drop Tacitus and go north to the cemeteries of Auburn and Greenwood."

"Upon my word, I—I—"

"Nay, I foresee all that. But you carry Tacitus, that shallow Tacitus. What do I carry? See"—producing a pocket-volume— "Akenside—his 'Pleasures of Imagination.' One of these days you will know it. Whatever our lot, we should read serene and cheery books, fitted to inspire love and trust. But Tacitus! I have long been of opinion that these classics are the bane of colleges; for—not to hint of the immorality of Ovid, Horace, Anacreon, and the rest, and the dangerous theology of Eschylus and others—where will one find views so injurious to human nature as in Thucydides, Juvenal, Lucian, but more particularly Tacitus? When I consider that, ever since the revival of learning, these classics have been the favorites of successive generations of students and studious men, I tremble to think of that mass of unsuspected heresy on every vital topic which for centuries must have simmered unsurmised in the heart of Christendom. But Tacitus—he is the most extraordinary example of a heretic; not one iota of confidence in his kind. What a mockery that such an one should be reputed wise, and Thucydides be esteemed the statesman's manual! But Tacitus—I hate Tacitus; not, though, I trust, with the hate that sins, but a righteous hate. Without confidence himself, Tacitus destroys it in all his readers. Destroys confidence, paternal confidence, of which God knows that there is in this world none to spare. For, comparatively inexperienced as you are, my dear young friend, did you never observe how little, very little, confidence, there is? I mean between man and man—more particularly between stranger and stranger. In a sad world it is the saddest fact. Confidence! I have sometimes almost thought that confidence is fled; that confidence is the New Astrea—emigrated—vanished—gone." Then softly sliding nearer, with the softest air, quivering down and looking up, "could you now, my dear young sir, under such circumstances, by way of experiment, simply have confidence in *me?*"

From the outset, the sophomore, as has been seen, had struggled with an ever-increasing embarrassment, arising, perhaps, from such strange remarks coming from a stranger—such persistent and prolonged remarks, too. In vain had he more than once sought to break the spell by venturing a deprecatory or leave-taking word. In vain. Somehow, the stranger fascinated him. Little wonder, then, that, when the appeal came, he could hardly speak, but, as before intimated, being apparently of a retiring nature, abruptly retired from the spot, leaving the chagrined stranger to wander away in the opposite direction.

CHAPTER VI

—"You—pish! Why will the captain suffer these begging fellows on board?"

These pettish words were breathed by a well-to-do gentleman in a ruby-colored velvet vest, and with a ruby-colored cheek, a ruby-headed cane in his hand, to a man in a gray coat and white tie, who, shortly after the interview last described, had accosted him for contributions to a Widow and Orphan Asylum recently founded among the Seminoles. Upon a cursory view, this last person might have seemed, like the man with the weed, one of the less unrefined children of misfortune; but, on a closer observation, his countenance revealed little of sorrow, though much of sanctity.

With added words of touchy disgust, the well-to-do gentleman hurried away. But, though repulsed, and rudely, the man in gray did not reproach, for a time patiently remaining in the chilly loneliness to which he had been left, his countenance, however, not without token of latent though chastened reliance.

At length an old gentleman, somewhat bulky, drew nigh, and from him also a contribution was sought.

"Look, you," coming to a dead halt, and scowling upon him. "Look, you," swelling his bulk out before him like a swaying balloon, "look, you, you on others' behalf ask for money; you, a fellow with a face as long as my arm. Hark ye, now: there is such a thing as gravity, and in condemned felons it may be genuine; but of long faces there are three sorts; that of grief's drudge, that of the lantern-jawed man, and that of the imposter. You know best which yours is."

31

"Heaven give you more charity, sir."

"And you less hypocrisy, sir."

With which words, the hard-hearted old gentleman marched off.

While the other still stood forlorn, the young clergyman, before introduced, passing that way, catching a chance sight of him, seemed suddenly struck by some recollection; and, after a moment's pause, hurried up with: "Your pardon, but shortly since I was all over looking for you."

"For me?" as marveling that one of so little account should be sought for.

"Yes, for you; do you know anything about the negro, apparently a cripple, aboard here? Is he, or is he not, what he seems to be?"

"Ah, poor Guinea! have you, too, been distrusted? you, upon whom nature has placarded the evidence of your claims?"

"Then you do really know him, and he is quite worthy? It relieves me to hear it—much relieves me. Come, let us go find him, and see what can be done."

"Another instance that confidence may come too late. I am sorry to say that at the last landing I myself—just happening to catch sight of him on the gangway-plank—assisted the cripple ashore. No time to talk, only to help. He may not have told you, but he has a brother in that vicinity."

"Really, I regret his going without my seeing him again; regret it, more, perhaps, than you can readily think. You see, shortly after leaving St. Louis, he was on the forecastle, and there, with many others, I saw him, and put trust in him; so much so, that, to convince those who did not, I, at his entreaty, went in search of you, you being one of several individuals he mentioned, and whose personal appearance he more or less described, individuals who he said would willingly speak for him. But, after diligent search, not finding you, and catching no glimpse of any of the others he had enumerated, doubts were at last suggested; but doubts indirectly originating, as I can but think, from prior distrust unfeelingly proclaimed by another. Still, certain it is, I began to suspect."

"Ha, ha, ha!"

A sort of laugh more like a groan than a laugh; and yet, some-how, it seemed intended for a laugh.

Both turned, and the young clergyman started at seeing the wooden-legged man close behind him, morosely grave as a criminal judge with a mustard-plaster on his back. In the pres-ent case the mustard-plaster might have been the memory of certain recent biting rebuffs and mortifications.

"Wouldn't think it was I who laughed, would you?"

"But who was it you laughed at? or rather, tried to laugh at?" demanded the young clergyman, flushing, "me?"

"Neither you nor any one within a thousand miles of you. But perhaps you don't believe it."

"If he were of a suspicious temper, he might not," interposed the man in gray calmly, "it is one of the imbecilities of the sus-picious person to fancy that every stranger, however absent-minded, he sees so much as smiling or gesturing to himself in any odd sort of way, is secretly making him his butt. In some moods, the movements of an entire street, as the suspicious man walks down it, will seem an express pantomimic jeer at him. In short, the suspicious man kicks himself with his own foot."

"Whoever can do that, ten to one he saves other folks' sole-leather," said the wooden-legged man with a crusty attempt at humor. But with augmented grin and squirm, turning directly upon the young clergyman, "you still think it was *you* I was laughing at, just now. To prove your mistake, I will tell you what I *was* laughing at; a story I happened to call to mind just then."

Whereupon, in his porcupine way, and with sarcastic details, unpleasant to repeat, he related a story, which might, perhaps, in a good-natured version, be rendered as follows:

A certain Frenchman of New Orleans, an old man, less slender in purse than limb, happening to attend the theatre one evening, was so charmed with the character of a faithful wife, as there represented to the life, that nothing would do but he must marry upon it. So, marry he did, a beautiful girl from Ten-nessee, who had first attracted his attention by her liberal mould, and was subsequently recommended to him through her kin, for her equally liberal education and disposition. Though large, the praise proved not too much. For, ere long, rumor more than corroborated it, by whispering that the lady was liberal to a fault. But though various circumstances, which by most Benedicts would have been deemed all but conclusive, were duly recited to the old Frenchman by his friends, yet such was his confidence that not a syllable would he credit, till, chancing one night to return unexpectedly from a journey, upon entering his apartment, a stranger burst from the alcove: "Begar!" cried he, "now I *begin* to suspec."

His story told, the wooden-legged man threw back his head, and gave vent to a long, gasping, rasping sort of taunting cry, intolerable as that of a high-pressure engine jeering off steam; and that done, with apparent satisfaction hobbled away.

"Who is that scoffer," said the man in gray, not without warmth. "Who is he, who even were truth on his tongue, his way of speaking it would make truth almost offensive as false-hood. Who is he?"

"He who I mentioned to you as having boasted his suspicion of the negro," replied the young clergyman, recovering from disturbance, "in short, the person to whom I ascribe the origin of my own distrust; he maintained that Guinea was some white scoundrel, betwisted and painted up for a decoy. Yes, these were his very words, I think."

"Impossible! he could not be so wrong-headed. Pray, will you call him back, and let me ask him if he were really in earnest?"

The other complied; and, at length, after no few surly objections, prevailed upon the one-legged individual to return for a moment. Upon which, the man in gray thus addressed him: "This reverend gentleman tells me, sir, that a certain cripple, a poor negro, is by you considered an ingenious impostor. Now, I am not unaware that there are some persons in this world, who, unable to give better proof of being wise, take a strange delight in showing what they think they have sagaciously read in mankind by uncharitable suspicions of them. I hope you

are not one of these. In short, would you tell me now, whether
you were not merely joking in the notion you threw out about
the negro. Would you be so kind?"

"No, I won't be so kind, I'll be so cruel."

"As you please about that."

"Well, he's just what I said he was."

"A white masquerading as a black?"

"Exactly."

The man in gray glanced at the young clergyman a moment,
then quietly whispered to him, "I thought you represented your
friend here as a very distrustful sort of person, but he appears
endued with a singular credulity.—Tell me, sir, do you really
think that a white could look the negro so? For one, I should
call it pretty good acting."

"Not much better than any other man acts."

"How? Does all the world act? Am *I*, for instance, an actor?
Is my reverend friend here, too, a performer?"

"Yes, don't you both perform acts? To do, is to act; so all
doers are actors."

"You trifle.—I ask again, if a white, how could he look the
negro so?"

"Never saw the negro-minstrels, I suppose?"

"Yes, but they are apt to overdo the ebony; exemplifying
the old saying, not more just than charitable, that 'the devil is
never so black as he is painted.' But his limbs, if not a cripple,
how could he twist his limbs so?"

"How do other hypocritical beggars twist theirs? Easy
enough to see how they are hoisted up."

"The sham is evident, then?"

"To the discerning eye," with a horrible screw of his gimlet
one.

"Well, where is Guinea?" said the man in gray; "where is
he? Let us at once find him, and refute beyond cavil this injurious hypothesis."

"Do so," cried the one-eyed man, "I'm just in the humor now
for having him found, and leaving the streaks of these fingers

on his paint, as the lion leaves the streaks of his nails on a Caffre. They wouldn't let me touch him before. Yes, find him, I'll make wool fly, and him after."

"You forget," here said the young clergyman to the man in gray, "that yourself helped poor Guinea ashore."

"So I did, so I did; how unfortunate. But look now," to the other, "I think that without personal proof I can convince you of your mistake. For I put it to you, is it reasonable to suppose that a man with brains, sufficient to act such a part as you say, would take all that trouble, and run all that hazard, for the mere sake of those few paltry coppers, which, I hear, was all he got for his pains, if pains they were?"

"That puts the case irrefutably," said the young clergyman, with a challenging glance towards the one-legged man.

"You two green-horns! Money, you think, is the sole motive to pains and hazard, deception and deviltry, in this world. How much money did the devil make by gulling Eve?"

Whereupon he hobbled off again with a repetition of his intolerable jeer.

The man in gray stood silently eyeing his retreat a while, and then, turning to his companion, said: "A bad man, a dangerous man; a man to be put down in any Christian community. —And this was he who was the means of begetting your distrust? Ah, we should shut our ears to distrust, and keep them open only for its opposite."

"You advance a principle, which, if I had acted upon it this morning, I should have spared myself what I now feel.—That but one man, and he with one leg, should have such ill power given him; his one sour word leavening into congenial sourness (as, to my knowledge, it did) the dispositions, before sweet enough, of a numerous company. But, as I hinted, with me at the time his ill words went for nothing; the same as now; only afterwards they had effect; and I confess, this puzzles me."

"It should not. With humane minds, the spirit of distrust works something as certain potions do; it is a spirit which may enter such minds, and yet, for a time, longer or shorter, lie in them quiescent; but only the more deplorable its ultimate activity."

"An uncomfortable solution; for, since that baneful man did but just now anew drop on me his bane, how shall I be sure that my present exemption from its effects will be lasting?"

"You cannot be sure, but you can strive against it."

"How?"

"By strangling the least symptom of distrust, of any sort, which hereafter, upon whatever provocation, may arise in you."

"I will do so." Then added as in soliloquy, "Indeed, indeed, I was to blame in standing passive under such influences as that one-legged man's. My conscience upbraids me.—The poor negro: You see him occasionally, perhaps?"

"No, not often; though in a few days, as it happens, my engagements will call me to the neighborhood of his present retreat; and, no doubt, honest Guinea, who is a grateful soul, will come to see me there."

"Then you have been his benefactor?"

"His benefactor? I did not say that. I have known him."

"Take this mite. Hand it to Guinea when you see him; say it comes from one who has full belief in his honesty, and is sincerely sorry for having indulged, however transiently, in a contrary thought."

"I accept the trust. And, by-the-way, since you are of this truly charitable nature, you will not turn away an appeal in behalf of the Seminole Widow and Orphan Asylum?"

"I have not heard of that charity."

"But recently founded."

After a pause, the clergyman was irresolutely putting his hand in his pocket, when, caught by something in his companion's expression, he eyed him inquisitively, almost uneasily.

"Ah, well," smiled the other wanly, "if that subtle bane, we were speaking of but just now, is so soon beginning to work, in vain my appeal to you. Good-bye."

"Nay," not untouched, "you do me injustice; instead of indulging present suspicions, I had rather make amends for previous ones. Here is something for your asylum. Not much; but every drop helps. Of course you have papers?"

"Of course," producing a memorandum book and pencil. "Let me take down name and amount. We publish these names. And now let me give you a little history of our asylum, and the providential way in which it was started."

CHAPTER VII

A GENTLEMAN WITH GOLD SLEEVE-BUTTONS

At an interesting point of the narration, and at the moment when, with much curiosity, indeed, urgency, the narrator was being particularly questioned upon that point, he was, as it happened, altogether diverted both from it and his story, by just then catching sight of a gentleman who had been standing in sight from the beginning, but, until now, as it seemed, without being observed by him.

"Pardon me," said he, rising, "but yonder is one who I know will contribute, and largely. Don't take it amiss if I quit you."

"Go: duty before all things," was the conscientious reply.

The stranger was a man of more than winsome aspect. There he stood apart and in repose, and yet, by his mere look, lured the man in gray from his story, much as, by its graciousness of bearing, some full-leaved elm, alone in a meadow, lures the noon sickleman to throw down his sheaves, and come and apply for the alms of its shade.

But, considering that goodness is no such rare thing among men—the world familiarly know the noun; a common one in every language—it was curious that what so signalized the stranger, and made him look like a kind of foreigner, among the crowd (as to some it may make him appear more or less unreal in this portraiture), was but the expression of so prevalent a quality. Such goodness seemed his, allied with such fortune, that, so far as his own personal experience could have gone, scarcely could he have known ill, physical or moral; and as for knowing or suspecting the latter in any serious degree (supposing such degree of it to be), by observation or philosophy; for that, probably, his nature, by its opposition, was imperfectly qualified, or from it wholly exempted. For the rest, he might have been five and fifty, perhaps sixty, but tall, rosy, between plump and portly, with a primy, palmy air, and for the time and place, not to hint of his years, dressed with a strangely festive finish and elegance. The inner-side of his coat-skirts was of white satin, which might have looked especially inappropriate, had it not seemed less a bit of mere tailoring than something of an emblem, as it were; an involuntary emblem, let us say, that what seemed so good about him was not all outside; no, the fine covering had a still finer lining. Upon one hand he wore a white kid glove, but the other hand, which was ungloved, looked hardly less white. Now, as the Fidèle, like most steamboats, was upon deck a little soot-streaked here and there, especially about the railings, it was a marvel how, under such circumstances, these hands retained their spotlessness. But, if you watched them a while, you noticed that they avoided touching anything; you noticed, in short, that a certain negro body-servant, whose hands nature had dyed black, perhaps with the same purpose that millers wear white, this negro servant's hands did most of his master's handling for him; having to do with dirt on his account, but not to his prejudice. But if, with the same unde-filedness of consequences to himself, a gentleman could also sin by deputy, how shocking would that be! But it is not per-mitted to be; and even if it were, no judicious moralist would make proclamation of it.

This gentleman, therefore, there is reason to affirm, was one who, like the Hebrew governor, knew how to keeps his hands clean, and who never in his life happened to be run suddenly against by hurrying house-painter, or sweep; in a word, one whose very good luck it was to be a very good man.

Not that he looked as if he were a kind of Wilberforce at all; that superior merit, probably, was not his; nothing in his man-ner bespoke him righteous, but only good, and though to be good is much below being righteous, and though there is a difference between the two, yet not, it is to be hoped, so incom-patible as that a righteous man can not be a good man; though, conversely, in the pulpit it has been with much cogency urged, that a merely good man, that is, one good merely by his nature, is so far from thereby being righteous, that nothing short of a total change and conversion can make him so; which is something which no honest mind, well read in the history of righteousness, will care to deny; nevertheless, since St. Paul himself, agreeing in a sense with the pulpit distinction, though not altogether in the pulpit deduction, and also pretty plainly intimating which of the two qualities in question enjoys his apostolic preference; I say, since St. Paul has so meaningly said, that, "scarcely for a righteous man will one die, yet peradventure for a good man some would even dare to die;" therefore, when we repeat of this gentleman, that he was only a good man, whatever else by severe censors may be objected to him, it is still to be hoped that his goodness will not at least be considered criminal in him. At all events, no man, not even a righteous man, would think it quite right to commit this gentleman to prison for the crime, extraordinary as he might deem it; more especially, as, until everything could be known, there would be some chance that the gentleman might after all be quite as innocent of it as he himself.

It was pleasant to mark the good man's reception of the salute of the righteous man, that is, the man in gray; his inferior, apparently, not more in the social scale than in stature. Like the benign elm again, the good man seemed to wave the canopy of his goodness over that suitor, not in conceited condescension, but with that even amenity of true majesty, which can be kind to any one without stooping to it.

To the plea in behalf of the Seminole widows and orphans, the gentleman, after a question or two duly answered, responded by producing an ample pocketbook in the good old capacious style, of fine green French morocco and workmanship, bound with silk of the same color, not to omit bills crisp with newness, fresh from the bank, no muckworms' grime upon them. Lucre those bills might be, but as yet having been kept unspotted from the world, not of the filthy sort. Placing now three of those virgin bills in the applicant's hands, he hoped that the smallness of the contribution would be pardoned; to tell the

truth, and this at last accounted for his toilet, he was bound
but a short run down the river, to attend, in a festive grove,
the afternoon wedding of his niece: so did not carry much
money with him.

The other was about expressing his thanks when the gentleman in his pleasant way checked him: the gratitude was on the
other side. To him, he said, charity was in one sense not an
effort, but a luxury; against too great indulgence in which his
steward, a humorist, had sometimes admonished him.

In some general talk which followed, relative to organized
modes of doing good, the gentleman expressed his regrets that
so many benevolent societies as there were, here and there
isolated in the land, should not act in concert by coming together, in the way that already in each society the individuals
composing it had done, which would result, he thought, in like
advantages upon a larger scale. Indeed, such a confederation
might, perhaps, be attended with as happy results as politically
attended that of the states.

Upon his hitherto moderate enough companion, this suggestion had an effect illustrative in a sort of that notion of Socrates,
that the soul is a harmony; for as the sound of a flute, in any
particular key, will, it is said, audibly affect the corresponding
chord of any harp in good tune, within hearing, just so now did
some string in him respond, and with animation.

Which animation, by the way, might seem more or less out
of character in the man in gray, considering his unsprightly
manner when first introduced, had he not already, in certain
after colloquies, given proof, in some degree, of the fact, that,
with certain natures, a soberly continent air at times, so far
from arguing emptiness of stuff, is good proof it is there, and
plenty of it, because unwasted, and may be used the more effectively, too, when opportunity offers. What now follows on
the part of the man in gray will still further exemplify, perhaps
somewhat strikingly, the truth, or what appears to be such, of
this remark.

"Sir," said he eagerly, "I am before you. A project, not dissimilar to yours, was by me thrown out at the World's Fair in London."

"World's Fair? You there? Pray how was that?"

"First, let me—"

"Nay, but first tell me what took you to the Fair?"

"I went to exhibit an invalid's easy-chair I had invented."

"Then you have not always been in the charity business?"

"Is it not charity to ease human suffering? I am, and always have been, as I always will be, I trust, in the charity business, as you call it; but charity is not like a pin, one to make the head, and the other the point; charity is a work to which a good workman may be competent in all its branches. I invented my Protean easy-chair in odd intervals stolen from meals and sleep."

"You call it the Protean easy-chair; pray describe it."

"My Protean easy-chair is a chair so all over bejointed, behinged, and bepadded, everyway so elastic, springy, and docile to the airiest touch, that in some one of its endlessly-changeable accommodations of back, seat, footboard, and arms, the most restless body, the body most racked, nay, I had almost added the most tormented conscience must, somehow and somewhere, find rest. Believing that I owed it to suffering humanity to make known such a chair to the utmost, I scraped together my little means and off to the World's Fair with it."

"You did right. But your scheme; how did you come to hit upon that?"

"I was going to tell you. After seeing my invention duly catalogued and placed, I gave myself up to pondering the scene about me. As I dwelt upon that shining pageant of arts, and moving concourse of nations, and reflected that here was the pride of the world glorying in a glass house, a sense of the fragility of worldly grandeur profoundly impressed me. And I said to myself, I will see if this occasion of vanity cannot supply a hint toward a better profit than was designed. Let some world-wide good to the world-wide cause be now done. In short, inspired by the scene, on the fourth day I issued at the World's Fair my prospectus of the World's Charity."

"Quite a thought. But, pray explain it."

"The World's Charity is to be a society whose members shall comprise deputies from every charity and mission extant; the one object of the society to be the methodization of the world's benevolence; to which end, the present system of voluntary and promiscuous contribution to be done away, and the Society to be empowered by the various governments to levy, annually, one grand benevolence tax upon all mankind; as in Augustus Cæsar's time, the whole world to come up to be taxed; a tax which, for the scheme of it, should be something like the income-tax in England, a tax, also, as before hinted, to be a consolidation-tax of all possible benevolence taxes; as in America here, the state-tax, and the county-tax, and the town-tax, and the poll-tax, are by the assessors rolled into one. This tax, according to my tables, calculated with care, would result in the yearly raising of a fund little short of eight hundred millions; this fund to be annually applied to such objects, and in such modes, as the various charities and missions, in general congress represented, might decree; whereby, in fourteen years, as I estimate, there would have been devoted to good works the sum of eleven thousand two hundred millions; which would warrant the dissolution of the society, as that fund judiciously expended, not a pauper or heathen could remain the round world over."

"Eleven thousand two hundred millions! And all by passing round a *hat*, as it were."

"Yes, I am no Fourier, the projector of an impossible scheme, but a philanthropist and a financier setting forth a philanthropy and a finance which are practicable."

"Practicable?"

"Yes. Eleven thousand two hundred millions; it will frighten none but a retail philanthropist. What is it but eight hundred millions for each of fourteen years? Now eight hundred millions—what is that, to average it, but one little dollar a head for the population of the planet? And who will refuse, what Turk or Dyak even, his own little dollar for sweet charity's sake? Eight hundred millions! More than that sum is yearly expended by mankind, not only in vanities, but miseries. Consider that bloody spendthrift, War. And are mankind so stupid, so wicked, that, upon the demonstration of these things they will not, amending their ways, devote their superfluities to blessing the world instead of cursing it? Eight hundred millions! They have not to make it, it is theirs already; they have but to direct it from ill to good. And to this, scarce a self-denial is demanded. Actually, they would not in the mass be one farthing the poorer for it; as certainly would they be all the better and happier. Don't you see? But admit, as you must, that mankind is not mad, and my project is practicable. For, what creature but a madman would not rather do good than ill, when it is plain that, good or ill, it must return upon himself?"

"Your sort of reasoning," said the good gentleman, adjusting his gold sleeve-buttons, "seems all reasonable enough, but with mankind it won't do."

"Then mankind are not reasoning beings, if reason won't do with them."

"That is not to the purpose. By-the-way, from the manner in which you alluded to the world's census, it would appear that, according to your world-wide scheme, the pauper not less than the nabob is to contribute to the relief of pauperism, and the heathen not less than the Christian to the conversion of heathenism. How is that?"

"Why, that—pardon me—is quibbling. Now, no philanthropist likes to be opposed with quibbling."

"Well, I won't quibble any more. But, after all, if I understand your project, there is little specially new in it, further than the magnifying of means now in operation."

"Magnifying and energizing. For one thing, missions I would thoroughly reform. Missions I would quicken with the Wall street spirit."

"The Wall street spirit?"

"Yes; for if, confessedly, certain spiritual ends are to be gained but through the auxiliary agency of worldly means, then, to the surer gaining of such spiritual ends, the example of worldly policy in worldly projects should not by spiritual projectors be slighted. In brief, the conversion of the heathen, so far, at least, as depending on human effort, would, by the world's charity, be let out on contract. So much by bid for converting India, so much for Borneo, so much for Africa. Competition allowed, stimulus would be given. There would be no lethargy of monopoly. We should have no mission-house or tract-house of which slanderers could, with any plausibility, say that it had degenerated in its clerkships into a sort of custom-house. But the main point is the Archimedean money-power that would be brought to bear."

"You mean the eight hundred million power?"

"Yes. You see, this doing good to the world by driblets amounts to just nothing. I am for doing good to the world with a will. I am for doing good to the world once for all and having done with it. Do but think, my dear sir, of the eddies and maël-stroms of pagans in China. People here have no conception of it. Of a frosty morning in Hong Kong, pauper pagans are found dead in the streets like so many nipped peas in a bin of peas. To be an immortal being in China is no more distinction than to be a snow-flake in a snow-squall. What are a score or two of missionaries to such a people? A pinch of snuff to the kraken. I am for sending ten thousand missionaries in a body and converting the Chinese *en masse* within six months of the debarkation. The thing is then done, and turn to something else."

"I fear you are too enthusiastic."

"A philanthropist is necessarily an enthusiast; for without enthusiasm what was ever achieved but commonplace? But again: consider the poor in London. To that mob of misery, what is a joint here and a loaf there? I am for voting to them twenty thousand bullocks and one hundred thousand barrels of flour to begin with. They are then comforted, and no more hunger for one while among the poor of London. And so all round."

"Sharing the character of your general project, these things, I take it, are rather examples of wonders that were to be wished, than wonders that will happen."

"And is the age of wonders passed? Is the world too old? Is it barren? Think of Sarah."

"Then I am Abraham reviling the angel (with a smile). But still, as to your design at large, there seems a certain audacity."

"But if to the audacity of the design there be brought a commensurate circumspectness of execution, how then?"

"Why, do you really believe that your world's charity will ever go into operation?"

"I have confidence that it will."

"But may you not be over-confident?"

"For a Christian to talk so!"

"But think of the obstacles!"

"Obstacles? I have confidence to remove obstacles, though mountains. Yes, confidence in the world's charity to that degree, that, as no better person offers to supply the place, I have nominated myself provisional treasurer, and will be happy to receive subscriptions, for the present to be devoted to striking off a million more of my prospectuses."

The talk went on; the man in gray revealed a spirit of benevolence which, mindful of the millennial promise, had gone abroad over all the countries of the globe, much as the diligent spirit of the husbandman, stirred by forethought of the coming seed-time, leads him, in March reveries at his fireside, over every field of his farm. The master chord of the man in gray had been touched, and it seemed as if it would never cease vibrating. A not unsilvery tongue, too, was his, with gestures that were a Pentecost of added ones, and persuasiveness before which granite hearts might crumble into gravel.

Strange, therefore, how his auditor, so singularly good-hearted as he seemed, remained proof to such eloquence; though not, as it turned out, to such pleadings. For, after listening a while longer with pleasant incredulity, presently, as the boat touched his place of destination, the gentleman, with a look half humor, half pity, put another bank-note into his hands; charitable to the last, if only to the dreams of enthusiasm.

CHAPTER VIII

A CHARITABLE LADY

I<small>F</small> a drunkard in a sober fit is the dullest of mortals, an enthusiast in a reason-fit is not the most lively. And this, without prejudice to his greatly improved understanding; for, if his elation was the height of his madness, his despondency is but the extreme of his sanity. Something thus now, to all appearance, with the man in gray. Society his stimulus, loneliness was his lethargy. Loneliness, like the sea-breeze, blowing off from a thousand leagues of blankness, he did not find, as veteran solitaires do, if anything, too bracing. In short, left to himself, with none to charm forth his latent lymphatic, he insensibly resumes his original air, a quiescent one, blended of sad humility and demureness.

Ere long he goes laggingly into the ladies' saloon, as in spiritless quest of somebody; but, after some disappointed glances about him, seats himself upon a sofa with an air of melancholy exhaustion and depression.

At the sofa's further end sits a plump and pleasant person, whose aspect seems to hint that, if she have any weak point, it must be anything rather than her excellent heart. From her twilight dress, neither dawn nor dark, apparently she is a widow just breaking the chrysalis of her mourning. A small gilt testament is in her hand, which she has just been reading. Half-relinquished, she holds the book in reverie, her finger inserted at the xiii. of 1st Corinthians, to which chapter possibly her attention might have recently been turned, by witnessing the scene of the monitory mute and his slate.

The sacred page no longer meets her eye; but, as at evening, when for a time the western hills shine on though the sun be set, her thoughtful face retains its tenderness though the teacher is forgotten.

Meantime, the expression of the stranger is such as ere long to attract her glance. But no responsive one. Presently, in her somewhat inquisitive survey, her volume drops. It is restored. No encroaching politeness in the act, but kindness, unadorned. The eyes of the lady sparkle. Evidently, she is not now unprepossessed. Soon, bending over, in a low, sad tone, full of deference, the stranger breathes, "Madam, pardon my freedom, but there is something in that face which strangely draws me. May I ask, are you a sister of the Church?"

"Why—really—you—"

In concern for her embarrassment, he hastens to relieve it, but, without seeming so to do. "It is very solitary for a brother here," eyeing the showy ladies brocaded in the background, "I find none to mingle souls with. It may be wrong—I *know* it is— but I cannot force myself to be easy with the people of the world. I prefer the company, however silent, of a brother or sister in good standing. By the way, madam, may I ask if you have confidence?"

"Really, sir—why, sir—really—I—"

"Could you put confidence in *me* for instance?"

"Really, sir—as much—I mean, as one may wisely put in a—a —stranger, an entire stranger, I had almost said," rejoined the lady, hardly yet at ease in her affability, drawing aside a little in body, while at the same time her heart might have been drawn as far the other way. A natural struggle between charity and prudence.

"Entire stranger!" with a sigh. "Ah, who would be a stranger? In vain, I wander; no one will have confidence in me."

"You interest me," said the good lady, in mild surprise. "Can I any way befriend you?"

"No one can befriend me, who has not confidence."

"But I—I have—at least to that degree—I mean that—"

"Nay, nay, you have none—none at all. Pardon, I see it. No confidence. Fool, fond fool that I am to seek it!"

"You are unjust, sir," rejoins the good lady with heightened interest; "but it may be that something untoward in your experiences has unduly biased you. Not that I would cast reflections. Believe me, I—yes, yes—I may say—that—that—"

"That you have confidence? Prove it. Let me have twenty dollars."

"Twenty dollars!"

"There, I told you, madam, you had no confidence."

The lady was, in an extraordinary way, touched. She sat in a sort of restless torment, knowing not which way to turn. She began twenty different sentences, and left off at the first syllable of each. At last, in desperation, she hurried out, "Tell me, sir, for what you want the twenty dollars?"

"And did I not—" then glancing at her half-mourning, "for the widow and the fatherless. I am traveling agent of the Widow and Orphan Asylum, recently founded among the Seminoles."

"And why did you not tell me your object before?" As not a little relieved. "Poor souls—Indians, too—those cruelly-used Indians. Here, here; how could I hesitate. I am so sorry it is no more."

"Grieve not for that, madam," rising and folding up the banknotes. "This is an inconsiderable sum, I admit, but," taking out his pencil and book, "though I here but register the amount, there is another register, where is set down the motive. Good-bye; you have confidence. Yea, you can say to me as the apostle said to the Corinthians, 'I rejoice that I have confidence in you in all things.'"

CHAPTER IX

TWO BUSINESS MEN TRANSACT A LITTLE BUSINESS

—"PRAY, sir, have you seen a gentleman with a weed hereabouts, rather a saddish gentleman? Strange where he can have gone to. I was talking with him not twenty minutes since."

By a brisk, ruddy-cheeked man in a tasseled traveling-cap, carrying under his arm a ledger-like volume, the above words were addressed to the collegian before introduced, suddenly accosted by the rail to which not long after his retreat, as in a previous chapter recounted, he had returned, and there remained.

"Have you seen him, sir?"

Rallied from his apparent diffidence by the genial jauntiness of the stranger, the youth answered with unwonted promptitude: "Yes, a person with a weed was here not very long ago."

"Saddish?"

"Yes, and a little cracked, too, I should say."

"It was he. Misfortune, I fear, has disturbed his brain. Now quick, which way did he go?"

"Why just in the direction from which you came, the gangway yonder."

"Did he? Then the man in the gray coat, whom I just met, said right: he must have gone ashore. How unlucky!"

He stood vexedly twitching at his cap-tassel, which fell over by his whisker, and continued: "Well, I am very sorry. In fact, I had something for him here."—Then drawing nearer, "you see, he applied to me for relief, no, I do him injustice, not that, but he began to intimate, you understand. Well, being very busy just then, I declined; quite rudely, too, in a cold, morose, unfeeling way, I fear. At all events, not three minutes afterwards

I felt self-reproach, with a kind of prompting, very peremptory, to deliver over into that unfortunate man's hands a ten-dollar bill. You smile. Yes, it may be superstition, but I can't help it; I have my weak side, thank God. Then again," he rapidly went on, "we have been so very prosperous lately in our affairs—by we, I mean the Black Rapids Coal Company—that, really, out of my abundance, associative and individual, it is but fair that a charitable investment or two should be made, don't you think so?"

"Sir," said the collegian without the least embarrassment, "do I understand that you are officially connected with the Black Rapids Coal Company?"

"Yes, I happen to be president and transfer-agent."

"You are?"

"Yes, but what is it to you? You don't want to invest?"

"Why, do you sell the stock?"

"Some might be bought, perhaps; but why do you ask? you don't want to invest?"

"But supposing I did," with cool self-collectedness, "could you do up the thing for me, and here?"

"Bless my soul," gazing at him in amaze, "really, you are quite a business man. Positively, I feel afraid of you."

"Oh, no need of that.—You could sell me some of that stock, then?"

"I don't know, I don't know. To be sure, there are a few shares under peculiar circumstances bought in by the Company; but it would hardly be the thing to convert this boat into the Company's office. I think you had better defer investing. So," with an indifferent air, "you have seen the unfortunate man I spoke of?"

"Let the unfortunate man go his ways.—What is that large book you have with you?"

"My transfer-book. I am subpœnaed with it to court."

"Black Rapids Coal Company," obliquely reading the gilt inscription on the back; "I have heard much of it. Pray do you happen to have with you any statement of the condition of your company."

"A statement has lately been printed."

"Pardon me, but I am naturally inquisitive. Have you a copy with you?"

"I tell you again, I do not think that it would be suitable to convert this boat into the Company's office.—That unfortunate man, did you relieve him at all?"

"Let the unfortunate man relieve himself.—Hand me the statement."

"Well, you are such a business-man, I can hardly deny you. Here," handing a small, printed pamphlet.

The youth turned it over sagely.

"I hate a suspicious man," said the other, observing him; "but I must say I like to see a cautious one."

"I can gratify you there," languidly returning the pamphlet; "for, as I said before, I am naturally inquisitive; I am also circumspect. No appearances can deceive me. Your statement," he added "tells a very fine story; but pray, was not your stock a little heavy a while ago? downward tendency? Sort of low spirits among holders on the subject of that stock?"

"Yes, there was a depression. But how came it? who devised it? The 'bears,' sir. The depression of our stock was solely owing to the growling, the hypocritical growling, of the bears."

"How, hypocritical?"

"Why, the most monstrous of all hypocrites are these bears: hypocrites by inversion; hypocrites in the simulation of things dark instead of bright; souls that thrive, less upon depression, than the fiction of depression; professors of the wicked art of manufacturing depressions; spurious Jeremiahs; sham Heraclituses, who, the lugubrious day done, return, like sham Lazaruses among the beggars, to make merry over the gains got by their pretended sore heads—scoundrelly bears!"

"You are warm against these bears?"

"If I am, it is less from the remembrance of their stratagems as to our stock, than from the persuasion that these same destroyers of confidence, and gloomy philosophers of the stock-market, though false in themselves, are yet true types of most destroyers of confidence and gloomy philosophers, the world over. Fellows who, whether in stocks, politics, bread-stuffs, morals, metaphysics, religion—be it what it may—trump up their black panics in the naturally-quiet brightness, solely with a view to some sort of covert advantage. That corpse of calamity which the gloomy philosopher parades, is but his Good-Enough-Morgan."

"I rather like that," knowingly drawled the youth. "I fancy these gloomy souls as little as the next one. Sitting on my sofa after a champagne dinner, smoking my plantation cigar, if a gloomy fellow come to me—what a bore!"

"You tell him it's all stuff, don't you?"

"I tell him it ain't natural. I say to him, you are happy enough, and you know it; and everybody else is as happy as you, and you know that, too; and we shall all be happy after we are no more, and you know that, too; but no, still you must have your sulk."

"And do you know whence this sort of fellow gets his sulk? not from life; for he's often too much of a recluse, or else too young to have seen anything of it. No, he gets it from some of those old plays he sees on the stage, or some of those old books he finds up in garrets. Ten to one, he has lugged home from auction a musty old Seneca, and sets about stuffing himself with that stale old hay; and, thereupon, thinks it looks wise and antique to be a croaker, thinks it's taking a stand way above his kind."

"Just so," assented the youth. "I've lived some, and seen a good many such ravens at second hand. By the way, strange how that man with the weed, you were inquiring for, seemed to take me for some soft sentimentalist, only because I kept quiet, and thought, because I had a copy of Tacitus with me, that I was reading him for his gloom, instead of his gossip. But I let him talk. And, indeed, by my manner humored him."

"You shouldn't have done that, now. Unfortunate man, you must have made quite a fool of him."

"His own fault if I did. But I like prosperous fellows, comfortable fellows; fellows that talk comfortably and prosperously, like you. Such fellows are generally honest. And, I say now, I happen to have a superfluity in my pocket, and I'll just—"

"—Act the part of a brother to that unfortunate man?"

"Let the unfortunate man be his own brother. What are you dragging him in for all the time? One would think you didn't care to register any transfers, or dispose of any stock—mind running on something else. I say I will invest."

"Stay, stay, here come some uproarious fellows—this way, this way."

And with off-handed politeness the man with the book escorted his companion into a private little haven removed from the brawling swells without.

Business transacted, the two came forth, and walked the deck.

"Now tell me, sir," said he with the book, "how comes it that a young gentleman like you, a sedate student at the first appearance, should dabble in stocks and that sort of thing?"

"There are certain sophomorean errors in the world," drawled the sophomore, deliberately adjusting his shirt-collar, "not the least of which is the popular notion touching the nature of the modern scholar, and the nature of the modern scholastic sedateness."

"So it seems, so it seems. Really, this is quite a new leaf in my experience."

"Experience, sir," originally observed the sophomore, "is the only teacher."

"Hence am I your pupil; for it's only when experience speaks, that I can endure to listen to speculation."

"My speculations, sir," dryly drawing himself up, "have been chiefly governed by the maxim of Lord Bacon; I speculate in those philosophies which come home to my business and bosom —pray, do you know of any other good stocks?"

"You wouldn't like to be concerned in the New Jerusalem, would you?"

"New Jerusalem?"

"Yes, the new and thriving city, so called, in northern Minnesota. It was originally founded by certain fugitive Mormons. Hence the name. It stands on the Mississippi. Here, here is the map," producing a roll. "There—there, you see are the public buildings—here the landing—there the park—yonder the botanic gardens—and this, this little dot here, is a perpetual fountain, you understand. You observe there are twenty asterisks. Those are for the lyceums. They have lignum-vitæ rostrums."

"And are all these buildings now standing?"

"All standing—*bona fide.*"

"These marginal squares here, are they the water-lots?"

"Water-lots in the city of New Jerusalem? All terra firma—you don't seem to care about investing, though?"

"Hardly think I should read my title clear, as the law students say," yawned the collegian.

"Prudent—you are prudent. Don't know that you are wholly out, either. At any rate, I would rather have one of your shares of coal stock than two of this other. Still, considering that the first settlement was by two fugitives, who had swum over naked from the opposite shore—it's a surprising place. It is, *bona fide.* —But dear me, I must go. Oh, if by possibility you should come across that unfortunate man—"

"—In that case," with drawling impatience, "I will send for the steward, and have him and his misfortunes consigned overboard."

"Ha ha!—now were some gloomy philosopher here, some theological bear, forever taking occasion to growl down the stock of human nature (with ulterior views, d'ye see, to a fat benefice in the gift of the worshipers of Ariamius), he would pronounce that the sign of a hardening heart and a softening brain. Yes, that would be his sinister construction. But it's nothing more than the oddity of a genial humor—genial but dry. Confess it. Good-bye."

CHAPTER X

STOOLS, settees, sofas, divans, ottomans; occupying them are clusters of men, old and young, wise and simple; in their hands are cards spotted with diamonds, spades, clubs, hearts; the favorite games are whist, cribbage, and brag. Lounging in arm-chairs or sauntering among the marble-topped tables, amused with the scene, are the comparatively few, who, instead of having hands in the games, for the most part keep their hands in their pockets. These may be the philosophes. But here and there, with a curious expression, one is reading a small sort of handbill of anonymous poetry, rather wordily entitled:—

"O D E
ON THE INTIMATIONS
OF
DISTRUST IN MAN,
UNWILLINGLY INFERRED FROM REPEATED REPULSES,
IN DISINTERESTED ENDEAVORS
TO PROCURE HIS
CONFIDENCE."

On the floor are many copies, looking as if fluttered down from a balloon. The way they came there was this: A somewhat elderly person, in the quaker dress, had quietly passed through the cabin, and, much in the manner of those railway book-peddlers who precede their proffers of sale by a distribution of puffs, direct or indirect, of the volumes to follow, had, without speaking, handed about the odes, which, for the most part, after a cursory glance, had been disrespectfully tossed aside, as no doubt, the moonstruck production of some wandering rhapsodist.

In due time, book under arm, in trips the ruddy man with the traveling-cap, who, lightly moving to and fro, looks animatedly about him, with a yearning sort of gratulatory affinity and longing, expressive of the very soul of sociality; as much as to say, "Oh, boys, would that I were personally acquainted with each mother's son of you, since what a sweet world, to make sweet acquaintance in, is ours, my brothers; yea, and what dear, happy dogs are we all!"

And just as if he had really warbled it forth, he makes fraternally up to one lounging stranger or another, exchanging with him some pleasant remark.

"Pray, what have you there?" he asked of one newly accosted, a little, dried-up man, who looked as if he never dined.

"A little ode, rather queer, too," was the reply, "of the same sort you see strewn on the floor here."

"I did not observe them. Let me see;" picking one up and looking it over. "Well now, this is pretty; plaintive, especially the opening:—

> 'Alas for man, he hath small sense
> Of genial trust and confidence.'

—If it be so, alas for him, indeed. Runs off very smoothly, sir. Beautiful pathos. But do you think the sentiment just?"

"As to that," said the little dried-up man, "I think it a kind of queer thing altogether, and yet I am almost ashamed to add, it really has set me to thinking; yes and to feeling. Just now, somehow, I feel as it were trustful and genial. I don't know that ever I felt so much so before. I am naturally numb in my sensibilities; but this ode, in its way, works on my numbness not unlike a sermon, which, by lamenting over my lying dead in trespasses and sins, thereby stirs me up to be all alive in well-doing."

"Glad to hear it, and hope you will do well, as the doctors say. But who snowed the odes about here?"

"I cannot say; I have not been here long."

"Wasn't an angel, was it? Come, you say you feel genial, let us do as the rest, and have cards."

"Thank you, I never play cards."

"A bottle of wine?"

"Thank you, I never drink wine."

"Cigars?"

"Thank you, I never smoke cigars."

"Tell stories?"

"To speak truly, I hardly think I know one worth telling."

"Seems to me, then, this geniality you say you feel waked in you, is as water-power in a land without mills. Come, you had better take a genial hand at the cards. To begin, we will play for as small a sum as you please; just enough to make it interesting."

"Indeed, you must excuse me. Somehow I distrust cards."

"What, distrust cards? Genial cards? Then for once I join with our sad Philomel here:—

> 'Alas for man, he hath small sense
> Of genial trust and confidence.'

Good-bye!"

Sauntering and chatting here and there, again, he with the book at length seems fatigued, looks round for a seat, and spying a partly-vacant settee drawn up against the side, drops down there; soon, like his chance neighbor, who happens to be the good merchant, becoming not a little interested in the scene more immediately before him; a party at whist; two cream-faced, giddy, unpolished youths, the one in a red cravat, the other in a green, opposed to two bland, grave, handsome, self-possessed men of middle age, decorously dressed in a sort of professional black, and apparently doctors of some eminence in the civil law.

By-and-by, after a preliminary scanning of the new comer next him the good merchant, sideways leaning over, whispers behind a crumpled copy of the Ode which he holds: "Sir, I don't like the looks of those two, do you?"

"Hardly," was the whispered reply; "those colored cravats are not in the best taste, at least not to mine; but my taste is no rule for all."

"You mistake; I mean the other two, and I don't refer to dress, but countenance. I confess I am not familiar with such gentry any further than reading about them in the papers—but those two are—are sharpers, ain't they?"

"Far be from us the captious and fault-finding spirit, my dear sir."

"Indeed, sir, I would not find fault; I am little given that way; but certainly, to say the least, these two youths can hardly be adepts, while the opposed couple may be even more."

"You would not hint that the colored cravats would be so bungling as to lose, and the dark cravats so dextrous as to cheat?—Sour imaginations, my dear sir. Dismiss them. To little purpose have you read the Ode you have there. Years and experience, I trust, have not sophisticated you. A fresh and liberal construction would teach us to regard those four players—indeed, this whole cabin-full of players—as playing at games in which every player plays fair, and not a player but shall win."

"Now, you hardly mean that; because games in which all may win, such games remain as yet in this world uninvented, I think."

"Come, come," luxuriously laying himself back, and casting a free glance upon the players, "fares all paid; digestion sound; care, toil, penury, grief, unknown; lounging on this sofa, with waistband relaxed, why not be cheerfully resigned to one's fate, nor peevishly pick holes in the blessed fate of the world?"

Upon this, the good merchant, after staring long and hard, and then rubbing his forehead, fell into meditation, at first uneasy, but at last composed, and in the end, once more addressed his companion: "Well, I see it's good to out with one's private thoughts now and then. Somehow, I don't know why, a certain misty suspiciousness seems inseparable from most of one's private notions about some men and some things; but once out with these misty notions, and their mere contact with other men's soon dissipates, or, at least, modifies them."

"You think I have done you good, then? may be, I have. But don't thank me, don't thank me. If by words, casually delivered in the social hour, I do any good to right or left, it is but involuntary influence—locust-tree sweetening the herbage under it; no merit at all; mere wholesome accident, of a wholesome nature.—Don't you see?"

Another stare from the good merchant, and both were silent again.

Finding his book, hitherto resting on his lap, rather irksome there, the owner now places it edgewise on the settee, between himself and neighbor; in so doing, chancing to expose the lettering on the back—"*Black Rapids Coal Company*"—which the good merchant, scrupulously honorable, had much ado to avoid reading, so directly would it have fallen under his eye, had he not conscientiously averted it. On a sudden, as if just reminded of something, the stranger starts up, and moves away, in his haste leaving his book; which the merchant observing, without delay takes it up, and, hurrying after, civilly returns it; in which act he could not avoid catching sight by an involuntary glance of part of the lettering.

"Thank you, thank you, my good sir," said the other, receiving the volume, and was resuming his retreat, when the merchant spoke: "Excuse me, but are you not in some way connected with the—the Coal Company I have heard of?"

"There is more than one Coal Company that may be heard of, my good sir," smiled the other, pausing with an expression of painful impatience, disinterestedly mastered.

"But you are connected with one in particular.—The 'Black Rapids,' are you not?"

"How did you find that out?"

"Well, sir, I have heard rather tempting information of your Company."

"Who is your informant, pray," somewhat coldly.

"A—a person by the name of Ringman."

"Don't know him. But, doubtless, there are plenty who know our Company, whom our Company does not know; in the same way that one may know an individual, yet be unknown to him. —Known this Ringman long? Old friend, I suppose.—But pardon, I must leave you."

"Stay, sir, that—that stock."

"Stock?"

"Yes, it's a little irregular, perhaps, but—"

"Dear me, you don't think of doing any business with me, do you? In my official capacity I have not been authenticated to you. This transfer-book, now," holding it up so as to bring the lettering in sight, "how do you know that it may not be a bogus one? And I, being personally a stranger to you, how can you have confidence in me?"

"Because," knowingly smiled the good merchant, "if you were other than I have confidence that you are, hardly would you challenge distrust that way."

"But you have not examined my book."

"What need to, if already I believe that it is what it is lettered to be?"

"But you had better. It might suggest doubts."

"Doubts, may be, it might suggest, but not knowledge; for how, by examining the book, should I think I knew any more than I now think I do; since, if it be the true book, I think it so already; and since if it be otherwise, then I have never seen the true one, and don't know what that ought to look like."

"Your logic I will not criticize, but your confidence I admire, and earnestly, too, jocose as was the method I took to draw it out. Enough, we will go to yonder table, and if there be any business which, either in my private or official capacity, I can help you do, pray command me."

CHAPTER XI

THE transaction concluded, the two still remained seated, falling into familiar conversation, by degrees verging into that confidential sort of sympathetic silence, the last refinement and luxury of unaffected good feeling. A kind of social superstition, to suppose that to be truly friendly one must be saying friendly words all the time, any more than be doing friendly deeds continually. True friendliness, like true religion, being in a sort independent of works.

At length, the good merchant, whose eyes were pensively resting upon the gay tables in the distance, broke the spell by saying that, from the spectacle before them, one would little divine what other quarters of the boat might reveal. He cited the case, accidentally encountered but an hour or two previous, of a shrunken old miser, clad in shrunken old moleskin, stretched out, an invalid, on a bare plank in the emigrants' quarters, eagerly clinging to life and lucre, though the one was gasping for outlet, and about the other he was in torment lest death, or some other unprincipled cut-purse, should be the means of his losing it; by like feeble tenure holding lungs and pouch, and yet knowing and desiring nothing beyond them; for his mind, never raised above mould, was now all but mouldered away. To such a degree, indeed, that he had no trust in anything, not even in his parchment bonds, which, the better to preserve from the tooth of time, he had packed down and sealed up, like brandy peaches, in a tin case of spirits.

The worthy man proceeded at some length with these dispiriting particulars. Nor would his cheery companion wholly deny that there might be a point of view from which such a case of extreme want of confidence might, to the humane mind, present features not altogether welcome as wine and olives after dinner. Still, he was not without compensatory considerations, and, upon the whole, took his companion to task for evincing what, in a good-natured, round-about way, he hinted to be a somewhat jaundiced sentimentality. Nature, he added, in Shakespeare's words, had meal and bran; and, rightly regarded, the bran in its way was not to be condemned.

The other was not disposed to question the justice of Shakespeare's thought, but would hardly admit the propriety of the application in this instance, much less of the comment. So, after some further temperate discussion of the pitiable miser, finding that they could not entirely harmonize, the merchant cited another case, that of the negro cripple. But his companion suggested whether the alleged hardships of that alleged unfortunate might not exist more in the pity of the observer than the experience of the observed. He knew nothing about the cripple, nor had seen him, but ventured to surmise that, could one but get at the real state of his heart, he would be found about as happy as most men, if not, in fact, full as happy as the speaker himself. He added that negroes were by nature a singularly cheerful race; no one ever heard of a native-born African Zimmermann or Torquemada; that even from religion they dismissed all gloom; in their hilarious rituals they danced, so to speak, and, as it were, cut pigeon-wings. It was improbable, therefore, that a negro, however reduced to his stumps by fortune, could be ever thrown off the legs of a laughing philosophy.

Foiled again, the good merchant would not desist, but ventured still a third case, that of the man with the weed, whose story, as narrated by himself, and confirmed and filled out by the testimony of a certain man in a gray coat, whom the merchant had afterwards met, he now proceeded to give; and that, without holding back those particulars disclosed by the second informant, but which delicacy had prevented the unfortunate man himself from touching upon.

But as the good merchant could, perhaps, do better justice to the man than the story, we shall venture to tell it in other words than his, though not to any other effect.

CHAPTER XII

STORY OF THE UNFORTUNATE MAN, FROM WHICH MAY BE
GATHERED WHETHER OR NO HE HAS BEEN JUSTLY SO ENTITLED

It appeared that the unfortunate man had had for a wife
one of those natures, anomalously vicious, which would almost
tempt a metaphysical lover of our species to doubt whether the
human form be, in all cases, conclusive evidence of humanity,
whether, sometimes, it may not be a kind of unpledged and indifferent tabernacle, and whether, once for all to crush the saying of Thrasea, (an unaccountable one, considering that he
himself was so good a man) that "he who hates vice, hates
humanity," it should not, in self-defense, be held for a reasonable maxim, that none but the good are human.

Goneril was young, in person lithe and straight, too straight,
indeed, for a woman, a complexion naturally rosy, and which
would have been charmingly so, but for a certain hardness and
bakedness, like that of the glazed colors on stone-ware. Her
hair was of a deep, rich chestnut, but worn in close, short curls
all round her head. Her Indian figure was not without its impairing effect on her bust, while her mouth would have been
pretty but for a trace of moustache. Upon the whole, aided by
the resources of the toilet, her appearance at distance was such,
that some might have thought her, if anything, rather beautiful,
though of a style of beauty rather peculiar and cactus-like.

It was happy for Goneril that her more striking peculiarities
were less of the person than of temper and taste. One hardly
knows how to reveal, that, while having a natural antipathy to
such things as the breast of chicken, or custard, or peach, or
grape, Goneril could yet in private make a satisfactory lunch
on hard crackers and brawn of ham. She liked lemons, and the

only kind of candy she loved were little dried sticks of blue clay, secretly carried in her pocket. Withal she had hard, steady health like a squaw's, with as firm a spirit and resolution. Some other points about her were likewise such as pertain to the women of savage life. Lithe though she was, she loved supineness, but upon occasion could endure like a stoic. She was taciturn, too. From early morning till about three o'clock in the afternoon she would seldom speak—it taking that time to thaw her, by all accounts, into but talking terms with humanity. During the interval she did little but look, and keep looking out of her large, metallic eyes, which her enemies called cold as a cuttle-fish's, but which by her were esteemed gazelle-like; for Goneril was not without vanity. Those who thought they best knew her, often wondered what happiness such a being could take in life, not considering the happiness which is to be had by some natures in the very easy way of simply causing pain to those around them. Those who suffered from Goneril's strange nature, might, with one of those hyberboles to which the resentful incline, have pronounced her some kind of toad; but her worst slanderers could never, with any show of justice, have accused her of being a toady. In a large sense she possessed the virtue of independence of mind. Goneril held it flattery to hint praise even of the absent, and even if merited; but honesty, to fling people's imputed faults into their faces. This was thought malice, but it certainly was not passion. Passion is human. Like an icicle-dagger, Goneril at once stabbed and froze; so at least they said; and when she saw frankness and innocence tyrannized into sad nervousness under her spell, according to the same authority, inly she chewed her blue clay, and you could mark that she chuckled. These peculiarities were strange and unpleasing; but another was alleged, one really incomprehensible. In company she had a strange way of touching, as by accident, the arm or hand of comely young men, and seemed to reap a secret delight from it, but whether from the humane satisfaction of having given the evil-touch, as it is called, or whether it was something else in her, not equally wonderful, but quite as deplorable, remained an enigma.

Needless to say what distress was the unfortunate man's, when, engaged in conversation with company, he would suddenly perceive his Goneril bestowing her mysterious touches, especially in such cases where the strangeness of the thing seemed to strike upon the touched person, notwithstanding good-breeding forbade his proposing the mystery, on the spot, as a subject of discussion for the company. In these cases, too, the unfortunate man could never endure so much as to look upon the touched young gentleman afterwards, fearful of the mortification of meeting in his countenance some kind of more or less quizzingly-knowing expression. He would shudderingly shun the young gentleman. So that here, to the husband, Goneril's touch had the dread operation of the heathen taboo. Now Goneril brooked no chiding. So, at favorable times, he, in a wary manner, and not indelicately, would venture in private interviews gently to make distant allusions to this questionable propensity. She divined him. But, in her cold loveless way, said it was witless to be telling one's dreams, especially foolish ones; but if the unfortunate man liked connubially to rejoice his soul with such chimeras, much connubial joy might they give him. All this was sad—a touching case—but all might, perhaps, have been borne by the unfortunate man—conscientiously mindful of his vow—for better or for worse—to love and cherish his dear Goneril so long as kind heaven might spare her to him —but when, after all that had happened, the devil of jealousy entered her, a calm, clayey, cakey devil, for none other could possess her, and the object of that deranged jealousy, her own child, a little girl of seven, her father's consolation and pet; when he saw Goneril artfully torment the little innocent, and then play the maternal hypocrite with it, the unfortunate man's patient long-suffering gave way. Knowing that she would neither confess nor amend, and might, possibly, become even worse than she was, he thought it but duty as a father, to withdraw the child from her; but, loving it as he did, he could not do so without accompanying it into domestic exile himself. Which, hard though it was, he did. Whereupon the whole female neighborhood, who till now had little enough admired dame Goneril, broke out in indignation against a husband, who, without assigning a cause, could deliberately abandon the wife of his bosom, and sharpen the sting to her, too, by depriving her of the solace of retaining her offspring. To all this, self-respect, with Christian charity towards Goneril, long kept the unfortunate man dumb. And well had it been had he continued so; for when, driven to desperation, he hinted something of the truth of the case, not a soul would credit it; while for Goneril, she pronounced all he said to be a malicious invention. Ere long, at the suggestion of some woman's-rights women, the injured wife began a suit, and, thanks to able counsel and accommodating testimony, succeeded in such a way, as not only to recover custody of the child, but to get such a settlement awarded upon a separation, as to make penniless the unfortunate man (so he averred), besides, through the legal sympathy she enlisted, effecting a judicial blasting of his private reputation. What made it yet more lamentable was, that the unfortunate man, thinking that, before the court, his wisest plan, as well as the most Christian besides, being, as he deemed, not at variance with the truth of the matter, would be to put forth the plea of the mental derangement of Goneril, which done, he could, with less of mortification to himself, and odium to her, reveal in self-defense those eccentricities which had led to his retirement from the joys of wedlock, had much ado in the end to prevent this charge of derangement from fatally recoiling upon himself—especially, when, among other things, he alleged her mysterious touchings. In vain did his counsel, striving to make out the derangement to be where, in fact, if anywhere, it was, urge that, to hold otherwise, to hold that such a being as Goneril was sane, this was constructively a libel upon womankind. Libel be it. And all ended by the unfortunate man's subsequently getting wind of Goneril's intention to procure him to be permanently committed for a lunatic. Upon which he fled, and was now an innocent outcast, wandering forlorn in the great valley of the Mississippi, with a weed on his hat for the loss of his Goneril; for he had lately seen by the papers that she was dead, and thought it but proper to comply with the prescribed form of mourning in such cases. For some days past he had been trying to get money enough to return to his child, and was but now started with inadequate funds.

Now all of this, from the beginning, the good merchant could not but consider rather hard for the unfortunate man.

CHAPTER XIII

THE MAN WITH THE TRAVELING-CAP EVINCES MUCH HUMANITY,
AND IN A WAY WHICH WOULD SEEM TO SHOW HIM TO BE ONE
OF THE MOST LOGICAL OF OPTIMISTS

Years ago, a grave American savan, being in London, observed at an evening party there, a certain coxcombical fellow, as he thought, an absurd ribbon in his lapel, and full of smart persiflage, whisking about to the admiration of as many as were disposed to admire. Great was the savan's disdain; but, chancing ere long to find himself in a corner with the jackanapes, got into conversation with him, when he was somewhat ill-prepared for the good sense of the jackanapes, but was altogether thrown aback, upon subsequently being whispered by a friend that the jackanapes was almost as great a savan as himself, being no less a personage than Sir Humphrey Davy.

The above anecdote is given just here by way of an anticipative reminder to such readers as, from the kind of jaunty levity, or what may have passed for such, hitherto for the most part appearing in the man with the traveling-cap, may have been tempted into a more or less hasty estimate of him; that such readers, when they find the same person, as they presently will, capable of philosophic and humanitarian discourse—no mere casual sentence or two as heretofore at times, but solidly sustained throughout an almost entire sitting; that they may not, like the American savan, be thereupon betrayed into any surprise incompatible with their own good opinion of their previous penetration.

The merchant's narration being ended, the other would not deny but that it did in some degree affect him. He hoped he was not without proper feeling for the unfortunate man. But he begged to know in what spirit he bore his alleged calamities. Did he despond or have confidence?

The merchant did not, perhaps, take the exact import of the last member of the question; but answered, that, if whether the unfortunate man was becomingly resigned under his affliction or no, was the point, he could say for him that resigned he was, and to an exemplary degree: for not only, so far as known, did he refrain from any one-sided reflections upon human goodness and human justice, but there was observable in him an air of chastened reliance, and at times tempered cheerfulness.

Upon which the other observed, that since the unfortunate man's alleged experience could not be deemed very conciliatory towards a view of human nature better than human nature was, it largely redounded to his fair-mindedness, as well as piety, that under the alleged dissuasives, apparently so, from philanthropy, he had not, in a moment of excitement, been warped over to the ranks of the misanthropes. He doubted not, also, that with such a man his experience would, in the end, act by a complete and beneficent inversion, and so far from shaking his confidence in his kind, confirm it, and rivet it. Which would the more surely be the case, did he (the unfortunate man) at last become satisfied (as sooner or later he probably would be) that in the distraction of his mind his Goneril had not in all respects had fair play. At all events, the description of the lady, charity could not but regard as more or less exaggerated, and so far unjust. The truth probably was that she was a wife with some blemishes mixed with some beauties. But when the blemishes were displayed, her husband, no adept in the female nature, had tried to use reason with her, instead of something far more persuasive. Hence his failure to convince and convert. The act of withdrawing from her, seemed, under the circumstances, abrupt. In brief, there were probably small faults on both sides, more than balanced by large virtues; and one should not be hasty in judging.

When the merchant, strange to say, opposed views so calm and impartial, and again, with some warmth, deplored the case of the unfortunate man, his companion, not without seriousness, checked him, saying, that this would never do; that, though but in the most exceptional case, to admit the existence of unmerited misery, more particularly if alleged to have been brought about by unhindered arts of the wicked, such an admission was, to say the least, not prudent; since, with some, it might unfavorably bias their most important persuasions. Not that those persuasions were legitimately servile to such influences. Because, since the common occurrences of life could never, in the nature of things, steadily look one way and tell one story, as flags in the trade-wind; hence, if the conviction of a Providence, for instance, were in any way made dependent upon such variabilities as everyday events, the degree of that conviction would, in thinking minds, be subject to fluctuations akin to those of the stock-exchange during a long and uncertain war. Here he glanced aside at his transfer-book, and after a moment's pause continued. It was of the essence of a right conviction of the divine nature, as with a right conviction of the human, that, based less on experience than intuition, it rose above the zones of weather.

When now the merchant, with all his heart, coincided with this (as being a sensible, as well as religious person, he could not but do), his companion expressed satisfaction, that, in an age of some distrust on such subjects, he could yet meet with one who shared with him, almost to the full, so sound and sublime a confidence.

Still, he was far from the illiberality of denying that philosophy duly bounded was not permissible. Only he deemed it at least desirable that, when such a case as that alleged of the unfortunate man was made the subject of philosophic discussion, it should be so philosophized upon, as not to afford handles to those unblessed with the true light. For, but to grant that there was so much as a mystery about such a case, might by those persons be held for a tacit surrender of the question. And as for the apparent license temporarily permitted sometimes, to the bad over the good (as was by implication alleged with regard to Goneril and the unfortunate man), it might be injudicious there to lay too much polemic stress upon the doctrine of future retribution as the vindication of present impunity. For though, indeed, to the right-minded that doctrine was true, and of sufficient solace, yet with the perverse the polemic mention of it might but provoke the shallow, though mischievous conceit, that such a doctrine was but tantamount to the one which should affirm that Providence was not now, but was going to be. In short, with all sorts of cavilers, it was best, both for them and everybody, that whoever had the true light should stick behind the secure Malakoff of confidence, nor be tempted forth to hazardous skirmishes on the open ground of reason. Therefore, he deemed it unadvisable in the good man, even in the privacy of his own mind, or in communion with a congenial one, to indulge in too much latitude of philosophizing, or, indeed, of compassionating, since this might beget an indiscreet habit of thinking and feeling which might unexpectedly betray him upon unsuitable occasions. Indeed, whether in private or public, there was nothing which a good man was more bound to guard himself against than, on some topics, the emotional unreserve of his natural heart; for, that the natural heart, in certain points, was not what it might be, men had been authoritatively admonished.

But he thought he might be getting dry.

The merchant, in his good-nature, thought otherwise, and said that he would be glad to refresh himself with such fruit all day. It was sitting under a ripe pulpit, and better such a seat than under a ripe peach-tree.

The other was pleased to find that he had not, as he feared, been prosing; but would rather not be considered in the formal light of a preacher; he preferred being still received in that of the equal and genial companion. To which end, throwing still more of sociability into his manner, he again reverted to the unfortunate man. Take the very worst view of that case; admit that his Goneril was, indeed, a Goneril; how fortunate to be at last rid of this Goneril, both by nature and by law? If he were acquainted with the unfortunate man, instead of condoling with him, he would congratulate him. Great good fortune had this unfortunate man. Lucky dog, he dared say, after all.

To which the merchant replied, that he earnestly hoped it might be so, and at any rate he tried his best to comfort himself with the persuasion that, if the unfortunate man was not happy in this world, he would, at least, be so in another.

His companion made no question of the unfortunate man's happiness in both worlds; and, presently calling for some champagne, invited the merchant to partake, upon the playful plea that, whatever notions other than felicitous ones he might associate with the unfortunate man, a little champagne would readily bubble away.

At intervals they slowly quaffed several glasses in silence and thoughtfulness. At last the merchant's expressive face flushed, his eye moistly beamed, his lips trembled with an imaginative and feminine sensibility. Without sending a single fume to his head, the wine seemed to shoot to his heart, and begin soothsaying there. "Ah," he cried, pushing his glass from him, "Ah, wine is good, and confidence is good; but can wine or confidence percolate down through all the stony strata of hard considerations, and drop warmly and ruddily into the cold cave of truth? Truth will *not* be comforted. Led by dear charity, lured by sweet hope, fond fancy essays this feat; but in vain; mere dreams and ideals, they explode in your hand, leaving naught but the scorching behind!"

"Why, why, why!" in amaze, at the burst; "bless me, if *In vino veritas* be a true saying, then, for all the fine confidence you professed with me, just now, distrust, deep distrust, underlies it; and ten thousand strong, like the Irish Rebellion, breaks out in you now. That wine, good wine, should do it! Upon my soul," half seriously, half humorously, securing the bottle, "you shall drink no more of it. Wine was meant to gladden the heart, not grieve it; to heighten confidence, not depress it."

Sobered, shamed, all but confounded, by this raillery, the most telling rebuke under such circumstances, the merchant stared about him, and then, with altered mien, stammeringly confessed, that he was almost as much surprised as his companion, at what had escaped him. He did not understand it; was quite at a loss to account for such a rhapsody popping out of him unbidden. It could hardly be the champagne; he felt his brain unaffected; in fact, if anything, the wine had acted upon it something like white of egg in coffee, clarifying and brightening.

"Brightening? brightening it may be, but less like the white of egg in coffee, than like stove-lustre on a stove—black, brightening seriously, I repent calling for the champagne. To a temperament like yours, champagne is not to be recommended. Pray, my dear sir, do you feel quite yourself again? Confidence restored?"

"I hope so; I think I may say it is so. But we have had a long talk, and I think I must retire now."

So saying, the merchant rose, and making his adieus, left the table with the air of one, mortified at having been tempted by his own honest goodness, accidentally stimulated into making mad disclosures—to himself as to another—of the queer, unaccountable caprices of his natural heart.

CHAPTER XIV

As the last chapter was begun with a reminder looking forwards, so the present must consist of one glancing backwards.

To some, it may raise a degree of surprise that one so full of confidence, as the merchant has throughout shown himself, up to the moment of his late sudden impulsiveness, should, in that instance, have betrayed such a depth of discontent. He may be thought inconsistent, and even so he is. But for this, is the author to be blamed? True, it may be urged that there is nothing a writer of fiction should more carefully see to, as there is nothing a sensible reader will more carefully look for, than that, in the depiction of any character, its consistency should be preserved. But this, though at first blush, seeming reasonable enough, may, upon a closer view, prove not so much so. For how does it couple with another requirement—equally insisted upon, perhaps—that, while to all fiction is allowed some play of invention, yet, fiction based on fact should never be contradictory to it; and is it not a fact, that, in real life, a consistent character is a *rara avis*? Which being so, the distaste of readers to the contrary sort in books, can hardly arise from any sense of their untrueness. It may rather be from perplexity as to understanding them. But if the acutest sage be often at his wits' ends to understand living character, shall those who are not sages expect to run and read character in those mere phantoms which flit along a page, like shadows along a wall? That fiction, where every character can, by reason of its consistency, be comprehended at a glance, either exhibits but sec-

76

tions of character, making them appear for wholes, or else is very untrue to reality; while, on the other hand, that author who draws a character, even though to common view incongruous in its parts, as the flying-squirrel, and, at different periods, as much at variance with itself as the butterfly is with the caterpillar into which it changes, may yet, in so doing, be not false but faithful to facts.

If reason be judge, no writer has produced such inconsistent characters as nature herself has. It must call for no small sagacity in a reader unerringly to discriminate in a novel between the inconsistencies of conception and those of life as elsewhere. Experience is the only guide here; but as no one man can be coextensive with *what is*, it may be unwise in every case to rest upon it. When the duck-billed beaver of Australia was first brought stuffed to England, the naturalists, appealing to their classifications, maintained that there was, in reality, no such creature; the bill in the specimen must needs be, in some way, artificially stuck on.

But let nature, to the perplexity of the naturalists, produce her duck-billed beavers as she may, lesser authors, some may hold, have no business to be perplexing readers with duck-billed characters. Always, they should represent human nature not in obscurity, but transparency, which, indeed, is the practice with most novelists, and is, perhaps, in certain cases, someway felt to be a kind of honor rendered by them to their kind. But whether it involve honor or otherwise might be mooted, considering that, if these waters of human nature can be so readily seen through, it may be either that they are very pure or very shallow. Upon the whole, it might rather be thought, that he, who, in view of its inconsistencies, says of human nature the same that, in view of its contrasts, is said of the divine nature, that it is past finding out, thereby evinces a better appreciation of it than he who, by always representing it in a clear light, leaves it to be inferred that he clearly knows all about it.

But though there is a prejudice against inconsistent characters in books, yet the prejudice bears the other way, when what seemed at first their inconsistency, afterwards, by the skill of the writer, turns out to be their good keeping. The great masters excel in nothing so much as in this very particular. They challenge astonishment at the tangled web of some character, and then raise admiration still greater at their satisfactory unraveling of it; in this way throwing open, sometimes to the understanding even of school misses, the last complications of that spirit which is affirmed by its Creator to be fearfully and wonderfully made.

At least, something like this is claimed for certain psychological novelists; nor will the claim be here disputed. Yet, as touching this point, it may prove suggestive, that all those sallies of ingenuity, having for their end the revelation of human nature on fixed principles, have, by the best judges, been excluded with contempt from the ranks of the sciences—palmistry, physiognomy, phrenology, psychology. Likewise, the fact, that in all ages such conflicting views have, by the most eminent minds, been taken of mankind, would, as with other topics, seem some presumption of a pretty general and pretty thorough ignorance of it. Which may appear the less improbable if it be considered that, after poring over the best novels professing to portray human nature, the studious youth will still run risk of being too often at fault upon actually entering the world; whereas, had he been furnished with a true delineation, it ought to fare with him something as with a stranger entering, map in hand, Boston town; the streets may be very crooked, he may often pause; but, thanks to his true map, he does not hopelessly lose his way. Nor, to this comparison, can it be an adequate objection, that the twistings of the town are always the same, and those of human nature subject to variation. The grand points of human nature are the same to-day they were a thousand years ago. The only variability in them is in expression, not in feature.

But as, in spite of seeming discouragement, some mathematicians are yet in hopes of hitting upon an exact method of determining the longitude, the more earnest psychologists may, in the face of previous failures, still cherish expectations with regard to some mode of infallibly discovering the heart of man.

But enough has been said by way of apology for whatever may have seemed amiss or obscure in the character of the merchant; so nothing remains but to turn to our comedy, or, rather, to pass from the comedy of thought to that of action.

CHAPTER XV

THE merchant having withdrawn, the other remained seated
alone for a time, with the air of one who, after having conversed
with some excellent man, carefully ponders what fell from him,
however intellectually inferior it may be, that none of the profit
may be lost; happy if from any honest word he has heard he
can derive some hint, which, besides confirming him in the
theory of virtue, may, likewise, serve for a finger-post to virtuous action.

Ere long his eye brightened, as if some such hint was now
caught. He rises, book in hand, quits the cabin, and enters upon
a sort of corridor, narrow and dim, a by-way to a retreat less
ornate and cheery than the former; in short, the emigrants'
quarters; but which, owing to the present trip being a down-
river one, will doubtless be found comparatively tenantless.
Owing to obstructions against the side windows, the whole
place is dim and dusky; very much so, for the most part; yet,
by starts, haggardly lit here and there by narrow, capricious
sky-lights in the cornices. But there would seem no special
need for light, the place being designed more to pass the night
in, than the day; in brief, a pine barrens dormitory, of knotty
pine bunks, without bedding. As with the nests in the geometri-
cal towns of the associate penguin and pelican, these bunks
were disposed with Philadelphian regularity, but, like the
cradle of the oriole, they were pendulous, and, moreover, were,
so to speak, three-story cradles; the description of one of which
will suffice for all.

Four ropes, secured to the ceiling, passed downwards

80

through auger-holes bored in the corners of three rough planks, which at equal distances rested on knots vertically tied in the ropes, the lowermost plank but an inch or two from the floor, the whole affair resembling, on a large scale, rope book-shelves; only, instead of hanging firmly against a wall, they swayed to and fro at the least suggestion of motion, but were more especially lively upon the provocation of a green emigrant sprawling into one, and trying to lay himself out there, when the cradling would be such as almost to toss him back whence he came. In consequence, one less inexperienced, essaying repose on the uppermost shelf, was liable to serious disturbance, should a raw beginner select a shelf beneath. Sometimes a throng of poor emigrants, coming at night in a sudden rain to occupy these oriole nests, would—through ignorance of their peculiarity—bring about such a rocking uproar of carpentry, joining to it such an uproar of exclamations, that it seemed as if some luckless ship, with all its crew, was being dashed to pieces among the rocks. They were beds devised by some sardonic foe of poor travelers, to deprive them of that tranquillity which should precede, as well as accompany, slumber.—Procrustean beds, on whose hard grain humble worth and honesty writhed, still invoking repose, while but torment responded. Ah, did any one make such a bunk for himself, instead of having it made for him, it might be just, but how cruel, to say, You must lie on it!

But, purgatory as the place would appear, the stranger advances into it; and, like Orpheus in his gay descent to Tartarus, lightly hums to himself an opera snatch.

Suddenly there is a rustling, then a creaking, one of the cradles swings out from a murky nook, a sort of wasted penguin-flipper is supplicatingly put forth, while a wail like that of Dives is heard:—"Water, water!"

It was the miser of whom the merchant had spoken.

Swift as a sister-of-charity, the stranger hovers over him:—

"My poor, poor sir, what can I do for you?"

"Ugh, ugh—water!"

Darting out, he procures a glass, returns, and, holding it to the sufferer's lips, supports his head while he drinks: "And did they let you lie here, my poor sir, racked with this parching thirst?"

The miser, a lean old man, whose flesh seemed salted cod-fish, dry as combustibles; head, like one whittled by an idiot out of a knot; flat, bony mouth, nipped between buzzard nose and chin; expression, flitting between hunks and imbecile—now one, now the other—he made no response. His eyes were closed, his cheek lay upon an old white moleskin coat, rolled under his head like a wizened apple upon a grimy snow-bank.

Revived at last, he inclined towards his ministrant, and, in a voice disastrous with a cough, said:—"I am old and miserable, a poor beggar, not worth a shoe-string—how can I repay you?"

"By giving me your confidence."

"Confidence!" he squeaked, with changed manner, while the pallet swung, "little left at my age, but take the stale re-mains, and welcome."

"Such as it is, though, you give it. Very good. Now give me a hundred dollars."

Upon this the miser was all panic. His hands groped towards his waist, then suddenly flew upward beneath his moleskin pillow, and there lay clutching something out of sight. Mean-time, to himself he incoherently mumbled:—"Confidence? Cant, gammon! Confidence? hum, bubble!—Confidence? fetch, gouge! —Hundred dollars?—hundred devils!"

Half spent, he lay mute awhile, then feebly raising himself, in a voice for the moment made strong by the sarcasm, said, "A hundred dollars? rather high price to put upon confidence. But don't you see I am a poor, old rat here, dying in the wain-scot? You have served me; but, wretch that I am, I can but cough you my thanks,—ugh, ugh, ugh!"

This time his cough was so violent that its convulsions were imparted to the plank, which swung him about like a stone in a sling preparatory to its being hurled.

"Ugh, ugh, ugh!"

"What a shocking cough. I wish, my friend, the herb-doctor

was here now; a box of his Omni-Balsamic Reinvigorator would
do you good."

"Ugh, ugh, ugh!"

"I've a good mind to go find him. He's aboard somewhere. I
saw his long, snuff-colored surtout. Trust me, his medicines are
the best in the world."

"Ugh, ugh, ugh!"

"Oh, how sorry I am."

"No doubt of it," squeaked the other again, "but go, get your
charity out on deck. There parade the pursy peacocks; they
don't cough down here in desertion and darkness, like poor old
me. Look how scaly a pauper I am, clove with this churchyard
cough. Ugh, ugh, ugh!"

"Again, how sorry I feel, not only for your cough, but your
poverty. Such a rare chance made unavailable. Did you have
but the sum named, how I could invest it for you. Treble profits.
But confidence—I fear that, even had you the precious cash,
you would not have the more precious confidence I speak of."

"Ugh, ugh, ugh!" flightily raising himself. "What's that? How,
how? Then you don't want the money for yourself?

"My dear, *dear* sir, how could you impute to me such preposterous self-seeking? To solicit out of hand, for my private be-
hoof, an hundred dollars from a perfect stranger? I am not mad,
my dear sir."

"How, how?" still more bewildered, "do you, then, go about
the world, gratis, seeking to invest people's money for them?"

"My humble profession, sir. I live not for myself; but the
world will not have confidence in me, and yet confidence in me
were great gain."

"But, but," in a kind of vertigo, "what do—do you do—do with
people's money? Ugh, ugh! How is the gain made?"

"To tell that would ruin me. That known, every one would
be going into the business, and it would be overdone. A secret,
a mystery—all I have to do with you is to receive your confidence, and all you have to do with me is, in due time, to receive it back, thrice paid in trebling profits."

"What, what?" imbecility in the ascendant once more; "but the vouchers, the vouchers," suddenly hunkish again.

"Honesty's best voucher is honesty's face."

"Can't see yours, though," peering through the obscurity.

From this last alternating flicker of rationality, the miser fell back, sputtering, into his previous gibberish, but it took now an arithmetical turn. Eyes closed, he lay muttering to himself—

"One hundred, one hundred—two hundred, two hundred—three hundred, three hundred."

He opened his eyes, feebly stared, and still more feebly said—

"It's a little dim here, ain't it? Ugh, ugh! But, as well as my poor old eyes can see, you look honest."

"I am glad to hear that."

"If—if, now, I should put"—trying to raise himself, but vainly, excitement having all but exhausted him—"if, if now, I should put, put—"

"No ifs. Downright confidence, or none. So help me heaven, I will have no half-confidences."

He said it with an indifferent and superior air, and seemed moving to go.

"Don't, don't leave me, friend; bear with me; age can't help some distrust; it can't, friend, it can't. Ugh, ugh, ugh! Oh, I am so old and miserable. I ought to have a guardeean. Tell me, if—"

"If? No more!"

"Stay! how soon—ugh, ugh!—would my money be trebled? How soon, friend?"

"You won't confide. Good-bye!"

"Stay, stay," falling back now like an infant, "I confide, I confide; help, friend, my distrust!"

From an old buckskin pouch, tremulously dragged forth, ten hoarded eagles, tarnished into the appearance of ten old horn-buttons, were taken, and half-eagerly, half-reluctantly, offered.

"I know not whether I should accept this slack confidence," said the other coldly, receiving the gold, "but an eleventh-hour confidence, a sick-bed confidence, a distempered, death-bed confidence, after all. Give me the healthy confidence of healthy men, with their healthy wits about them. But let that pass. All right. Good-bye!"

"Nay, back, back—receipt, my receipt! Ugh, ugh, ugh! Who are you? What have I done? Where go you? My gold, my gold! Ugh, ugh, ugh!"

But, unluckily for this final flicker of reason, the stranger was now beyond ear-shot, nor was any one else within hearing of so feeble a call.

CHAPTER XVI

THE sky slides into blue, the bluffs into bloom; the rapid Mississippi expands; runs sparkling and gurgling, all over in eddies; one magnified wake of a seventy-four. The sun comes out, a golden huzzar, from his tent, flashing his helm on the world. All things, warmed in the landscape, leap. Speeds the dædal boat as a dream.

But, withdrawn in a corner, wrapped about in a shawl, sits an unparticipating man, visited, but not warmed, by the sun— a plant whose hour seems over, while buds are blowing and seeds are astir. On a stool at his left sits a stranger in a snuff-colored surtout, the collar thrown back; his hand waving in persuasive gesture, his eye beaming with hope. But not easily may hope be awakened in one long tranced into hopelessness by a chronic complaint.

To some remark the sick man, by word or look, seemed to have just made an impatiently querulous answer, when, with a deprecatory air, the other resumed:

"Nay, think not I seek to cry up my treatment by crying down that of others. And yet, when one is confident he has truth on his side, and that it is not on the other, it is no very easy thing to be charitable; not that temper is the bar, but conscience; for charity would beget toleration, you know, which is a kind of implied permitting, and in effect a kind of countenancing; and that which is countenanced is so far furthered. But should untruth be furthered? Still, while for the world's good I refuse to further the cause of these mineral doctors, I would fain regard them, not as willful wrong-doers, but good

86

Samaritans erring. And is this—I put it to you, sir—is this the view of an arrogant rival and pretender?"

His physical power all dribbled and gone, the sick man replied not by voice or by gesture; but, with feeble dumb-show of his face, seemed to be saying "Pray leave me; who was ever cured by talk?"

But the other, as if not unused to make allowances for such despondency, proceeded; and kindly, yet firmly:

"You tell me, that by advice of an eminent physiologist in Louisville, you took tincture of iron. For what? To restore your lost energy. And how? Why, in healthy subjects iron is naturally found in the blood, and iron in the bar is strong; ergo, iron is the source of animal invigoration. But you being deficient in vigor, it follows that the cause is deficiency of iron. Iron, then, must be put into you; and so your tincture. Now as to the theory here, I am mute. But in modesty assuming its truth, and then, as a plain man viewing that theory in practice, I would respectfully question your eminent physiologist: 'Sir,' I would say, 'though by natural processes, lifeless natures taken as nutriment become vitalized, yet is a lifeless nature, under any circumstances, capable of a living transmission, with all its qualities as a lifeless nature unchanged? If, sir, nothing can be incorporated with the living body but by assimilation, and if that implies the conversion of one thing to a different thing (as, in a lamp, oil is assimilated into flame), is it, in this view, likely, that by banqueting on fat, Calvin Edson will fatten? That is, will what is fat on the board prove fat on the bones? If it will, then, sir, what is iron in the vial will prove iron in the vein.' Seems that conclusion too confident?"

But the sick man again turned his dumb-show look, as much as to say, "Pray leave me. Why, with painful words, hint the vanity of that which the pains of this body have too painfully proved?"

But the other, as if unobservant of that querulous look, went on:

"But this notion, that science can play farmer to the flesh, making there what living soil it pleases, seems not so strange as that other conceit—that science is now-a-days so expert that, in consumptive cases, as yours, it can, by prescription of the inhalation of certain vapors, achieve the sublimest act of omnipotence, breathing into all but lifeless dust the breath of life. For did you not tell me, my poor sir, that by order of the great chemist in Baltimore, for three weeks you were never driven out without a respirator, and for a given time of every day sat bolstered up in a sort of gasometer, inspiring vapors generated by the burning of drugs? as if this concocted atmosphere of man were an antidote to the poison of God's natural air. Oh, who can wonder at that old reproach against science, that it is atheistical? And here is my prime reason for opposing these chemical practitioners, who have sought out so many inventions. For what do their inventions indicate, unless it be that kind and degree of pride in human skill, which seems scarce compatible with reverential dependence upon the power above? Try to rid my mind of it as I may, yet still these chemical practitioners with their tinctures, and fumes, and braziers, and occult incantations, seem to me like Pharaoh's vain sorcerers, trying to beat down the will of heaven. Day and night, in all charity, I intercede for them, that heaven may not, in its own language, be provoked to anger with their inventions; may not take vengeance of their inventions. A thousand pities that you should ever have been in the hands of these Egyptians."

But again came nothing but the dumb-show look, as much as to say, "Pray leave me; quacks, and indignation against quacks, both are vain."

But, once more, the other want on: "How different we herb-doctors! who claim nothing, invent nothing; but staff in hand, in glades, and upon hillsides, go about in nature, humbly seeking her cures. True Indian doctors, though not learned in names, we are not unfamiliar with essences—successors of Solomon the Wise, who knew all vegetables from the cedar of Lebanon, to the hyssop on the wall. Yes, Solomon was the first of herb-doctors. Nor were the virtues of herbs unhonored by yet older ages. Is it not writ, that on a moonlight night,

"Medea gathered the enchanted herbs
That did renew old Æson?"

Ah, would you but have confidence, you should be the new
Æson, and I your Medea. A few vials of my Omni-Balsamic
Reinvigorator would, I am certain, give you some strength."

Upon this, indignation and abhorrence seemed to work by
their excess the effect promised of the balsam. Roused from that
long apathy of impotence, the cadaverous man started, and, in
a voice that was as the sound of obstructed air gurgling through
a maze of broken honey-combs, cried: "Begone! You are all
alike. The name of doctor, the dream of helper, condemns you.
For years I have been but a gallipot for you experimentizers
to rinse your experiments into, and now, in this livid skin, partake of the nature of my contents. Begone! I hate ye."

"I were inhuman, could I take affront at a want of confidence,
born of too bitter an experience of betrayers. Yet, permit one
who is not without feeling—"

"Begone! Just in that voice talked to me, not six months ago,
the German doctor at the water cure, from which I now return, six months and sixty pangs nigher my grave."

"The water-cure? Oh, fatal delusion of the well-meaning
Preisnitz!—Sir, trust me—"

"Begone!"

"Nay, an invalid should not always have his own way. Ah,
sir, reflect how untimely this distrust in one like you. How weak
you are; and weakness, is it not the time for confidence? Yes,
when through weakness everything bids despair, then is the
time to get strength by confidence."

Relenting in his air, the sick man cast upon him a long
glance of beseeching, as if saying, "With confidence must come
hope; and how can hope be?"

The herb-doctor took a sealed paper box from his surtout
pocket, and holding it towards him, said solemnly, "Turn not
away. This may be the last time of health's asking. Work upon
yourself; invoke confidence, though from ashes; rouse it; for
your life, rouse it, and invoke it, I say."

The other trembled, was silent; and then, a little commanding himself, asked the ingredients of the medicine.

"Herbs."

"What herbs? And the nature of them? And the reason for giving them?"

"It cannot be made known."

"Then I will none of you."

Sedately observant of the juiceless, joyless form before him, the herb-doctor was mute a moment, then said:—"I give up."

"How?"

"You are sick, and a philosopher."

"No, no;—not the last."

"But, to demand the ingredient, with the reason for giving, is the mark of a philosopher; just as the consequence is the penalty of a fool. A sick philosopher is incurable."

"Why?"

"Because he has no confidence."

"How does that make him incurable?"

"Because either he spurns his powder, or, if he take it, it proves a blank cartridge, though the same given to a rustic in like extremity, would act like a charm. I am no materialist; but the mind so acts upon the body, that if the one have no confidence, neither has the other."

Again, the sick man appeared not unmoved. He seemed to be thinking what in candid truth could be said to all this. At length, "You talk of confidence. How comes it that when brought low himself, the herb-doctor, who was most confident to prescribe in other cases, proves least confident to prescribe in his own; having small confidence in himself for himself?"

"But he has confidence in the brother he calls in. And that he does so, is no reproach to him, since he knows that when the body is prostrated, the mind is not erect. Yes, in this hour the herb-doctor does distrust himself, but not his art."

The sick man's knowledge did not warrant him to gainsay this. But he seemed not grieved at it; glad to be confuted in a way tending towards his wish.

"Then you give me hope?" his sunken eye turned up.

"Hope is proportioned to confidence. How much confidence you give me, so much hope do I give you. For this," lifting the box, "if all depended upon this, I should rest. It is nature's own."

"Nature!"

"Why do you start?"

"I know not," with a sort of a shudder, "but I have heard of a book entitled 'Nature in Disease.'"

"A title I cannot approve; it is suspiciously scientific. 'Nature in Disease?' As if nature, divine nature, were aught but health; as if through nature disease is decreed! But did I not before hint of the tendency of science, that forbidden tree? Sir, if despondency is yours from recalling that title, dismiss it. Trust me, nature is health; for health is good, and nature cannot work ill. As little can she work error. Get nature, and you get well. Now, I repeat, this medicine is nature's own."

Again the sick man could not, according to his light, conscientiously disprove what was said. Neither, as before, did he seem over-anxious to do so; the less, as in his sensitiveness it seemed to him, that hardly could he offer so to do without something like the appearance of a kind of implied irreligion; nor in his heart was he ungrateful, that since a spirit opposite to that pervaded all the herb-doctor's hopeful words, therefore, for hopefulness, he (the sick man) had not alone medical warrant, but also doctrinal.

"Then you do really think," hectically, "that if I take this medicine," mechanically reaching out for it, "I shall regain my health?"

"I will not encourage false hopes," relinquishing to him the box, "I will be frank with you. Though frankness is not always the weakness of the mineral practitioner, yet the herb doctor must be frank, or nothing. Now then, sir, in your case, a radical cure—such a cure, understand, as should make you robust—such a cure, sir, I do not and cannot promise."

"Oh, you need not! only restore me the power of being something else to others than a burdensome care, and to myself a droning grief. Only cure me of this misery of weakness; only make me so that I can walk about in the sun and not draw the flies to me, as lured by the coming of decay. Only do that—but that."

"You ask not much; you are wise; not in vain have you suffered. That little you ask, I think, can be granted. But remember, not in a day, nor a week, nor perhaps a month, but sooner or later; I say not exactly when, for I am neither prophet nor charlatan. Still, if, according to the directions in your box there, you take my medicine steadily, without assigning an especial day, near or remote, to discontinue it, then may you calmly look for some eventual result of good. But again I say, you must have confidence."

Feverishly he replied that he now trusted he had, and hourly should pray for its increase. When suddenly relapsing into one of those strange caprices peculiar to some invalids, he added: "But to one like me, it is so hard, so hard. The most confident hopes so often have failed me, and as often have I vowed never, no, never, to trust them again. Oh," feebly wringing his hands, "you do not know, you do not know."

"I know this, that never did a right confidence come to naught. But time is short; you hold your cure, to retain or reject."

"I retain," with a clinch, "and now how much?"

"As much as you can evoke from your heart and heaven."

"How?—the price of this medicine?"

"I thought it was confidence you meant; how much confidence you should have. The medicine,—that is half a dollar a vial. Your box holds six."

The money was paid.

"Now, sir," said the herb-doctor, "my business calls me away, and it may so be that I shall never see you again; if then—"

He paused, for the sick man's countenance fell blank.

"Forgive me," cried the other, "forgive that imprudent phrase 'never see you again.' Though I solely intended it with reference to myself, yet I had forgotten what your sensitiveness might be. I repeat, then, that it may be that we shall not soon have a second interview, so that hereafter, should another of my boxes be needed, you may not be able to replace it except by purchase at the shops; and, in so doing, you may run more or less risk of taking some not salutary mixture. For such is the popularity of the Omni-Balsamic Reinvigorator—thriving not by the credulity of the simple, but the trust of the wise—that certain contrivers have not been idle, though I would not, indeed, hastily affirm of them that they are aware of the sad consequences to the public. Homicides and murderers, some call those contrivers; but I do not; for murder (if such a crime be possible) comes from the heart, and these men's motives come from the purse. Were they not in poverty, I think they would hardly do what they do. Still, the public interests forbid that I should let their needy device for a living succeed. In short, I have adopted precautions. Take the wrapper from any of my vials and hold it to the light, you will see water-marked in capitals the word 'confidence,' which is the countersign of the medicine, as I wish it was of the world. The wrapper bears that mark or else the medicine is counterfeit. But if still any lurking doubt should remain, pray enclose the wrapper to this address," handing a card, "and by return mail I will answer."

At first the sick man listened, with the air of vivid interest, but gradually, while the other was still talking, another strange caprice came over him, and he presented the aspect of the most calamitous dejection.

"How now?" said the herb-doctor.

"You told me to have confidence, said that confidence was indispensable, and here you preach to me distrust. Ah, truth will out!"

"I told you, you must have confidence, unquestioning confidence, I meant confidence in the genuine medicine, and the genuine me."

"But in your absence, buying vials purporting to be yours, it seems I cannot have unquestioning confidence."

"Prove all the vials; trust those which are true."

"But to doubt, to suspect, to prove—to have all this wearing work to be doing continually—how opposed to confidence. It is evil!"

"From evil comes good. Distrust is a stage to confidence. How has it proved in our interview? But your voice is husky; I have let you talk too much. You hold your cure; I leave you. But stay—when I hear that health is yours, I will not, like some I know, vainly make boasts; but, giving glory where all glory is due, say, with the devout herb-doctor, Japus in Virgil, when, in the unseen but efficacious presence of Venus, he with simples healed the wound of Æneas:—

'This is no mortal work, no cure of mine,
Nor art's effect, but done by power divine.' "

CHAPTER XVII

TOWARDS THE END OF WHICH THE HERB-DOCTOR PROVES
HIMSELF A FORGIVER OF INJURIES

In a kind of ante-cabin, a number of respectable looking people, male and female, way-passengers, recently come on board, are listlessly sitting in a mutually shy sort of silence.

Holding up a small, square bottle, ovally labeled with the engraving of a countenance full of soft pity as that of the Romish-painted Madonna, the herb-doctor passes slowly among them, benignly urbane, turning this way and that, saying:—

"Ladies and gentlemen, I hold in my hand here the Samaritan Pain Dissuader, thrice-blessed discovery of that disinterested friend of humanity whose portrait you see. Pure vegetable extract. Warranted to remove the acutest pain within less than ten minutes. Five hundred dollars to be forfeited on failure. Especially efficacious in heart disease and tic-douloureux. Observe the expression of this pledged friend of humanity.—Price only fifty cents."

In vain. After the first idle stare, his auditors—in pretty good health, it seemed—instead of encouraging his politeness, appeared, if anything, impatient of it; and, perhaps, only diffidence, or some small regard for his feelings, prevented them from telling him so. But, insensible to their coldness, or charitably overlooking it, he more wooingly than ever resumed: "May I venture upon a small supposition? Have I your kind leave, ladies and gentlemen?"

To which modest appeal, no one had the kindness to answer a syllable.

"Well," said he resignedly, "silence is at least not denial, and may be consent. My supposition is this: possibly some lady, here present, has a dear friend at home, a bed-ridden sufferer from spinal complaint. If so, what gift more appropriate to that sufferer than this tasteful little bottle of Pain Dissuader?"

Again he glanced about him, but met much the same reception as before. Those faces, alien alike to sympathy or surprise, seemed patiently to say, "We are travelers; and, as such, must expect to meet, and quietly put up with, many antic fools, and more antic quacks."

"Ladies and gentlemen," (deferentially fixing his eyes upon their now self-complacent faces), "ladies and gentlemen, might I, by your kind leave, venture upon one other small supposition? It is this: that there is scarce a sufferer, this noonday, writhing on his bed, but in his hour he sat satisfactorily healthy and happy; that the Samaritan Pain Dissuader is the one only balm for that to which each living creature—who knows?—may be a draughted victim, present or prospective. In short:—Oh, Happiness on my right hand, and oh, Security on my left, can ye wisely adore a Providence, and not think it wisdom to provide? —Provide!" (Uplifting the bottle.)

What immediate effect, if any, this appeal might have had, is uncertain. For just then the boat touched at a houseless landing, scooped, as by a land-slide, out of sombre forests; back through which led a road, the sole one, which, from its narrowness, and its being walled up with story on story of dusk, matted foliage, presented the vista of some cavernous old gorge in a city, like haunted Cock Lane in London. Issuing from that road, and crossing that landing, there stooped his shaggy form in the door-way, and entered the ante-cabin, with a step so burdensome that shot seemed in his pockets, a kind of invalid Titan in homespun; his beard blackly pendant, like the Carolina-moss, and dank with cypress dew; his countenance tawny and shadowy as an iron-ore country in a clouded day. In one hand he carried a heavy walking-stick of swamp-oak; with the other, led a puny girl, walking in moccasins, not improbably his child, but evidently of alien maternity, perhaps Creole, or even Camanche. Her eye would have been large for a woman, and was inky as the pools of falls among mountain-pines. An Indian blanket, orange-hued, and fringed with lead tassel-work, appeared that morning to have shielded the child from heavy showers. Her limbs were tremulous; she seemed a little Cassandra, in nervousness.

No sooner was the pair spied by the herb-doctor, than with a cheerful air, both arms extended like a host's, he advanced, and taking the child's reluctant hand, said, trippingly: "On your travels, ah, my little May Queen? Glad to see you. What pretty moccasins. Nice to dance in." Then with a half caper sang—

> " 'Hey diddle, diddle, the cat and the fiddle;
> The cow jumped over the moon.'

Come, chirrup, chirrup, my little robin!"

Which playful welcome drew no responsive playfulness from the child, nor appeared to gladden or conciliate the father; but rather, if anything, to dash the dead weight of his heavy-hearted expression with a smile hypochondriacally scornful.

Sobering down now, the herb-doctor addressed the stranger in a manly, business-like way—a transition which, though it might seem a little abrupt, did not appear constrained, and, indeed, served to show that his recent levity was less the habit of a frivolous nature, than the frolic condescension of a kindly heart.

"Excuse me," said he, "but, if I err not, I was speaking to you the other day;—on a Kentucky boat, wasn't it?"

"Never to me," was the reply; the voice deep and lonesome enough to have come from the bottom of an abandoned coal-shaft.

"Ah!—But am I again mistaken, (his eye falling on the swamp-oak stick,) or don't you go a little lame, sir?"

"Never was lame in my life."

"Indeed? I fancied I had perceived not a limp, but a hitch, a slight hitch;—some experience in these things—divined some hidden cause of the hitch—buried bullet, may be—some dragoons in the Mexican war discharged with such, you know.

—Hard fate!" he sighed, "little pity for it, for who sees it?—have you dropped anything?"

Why, there is no telling, but the stranger was bowed over, and might have seemed bowing for the purpose of picking up something, were it not that, as arrested in the imperfect posture, he for the moment so remained; slanting his tall stature like a mainmast yielding to the gale, or Adam to the thunder.

The little child pulled him. With a kind of a surge he righted himself, for an instant looked toward the herb-doctor; but, either from emotion or aversion, or both together, withdrew his eyes, saying nothing. Presently, still stooping, he seated himself, drawing his child between his knees, his massy hands tremulous, and still averting his face, while up into the compassionate one of the herb-doctor the child turned a fixed, melancholy glance of repugnance.

The herb-doctor stood observant a moment, then said:

"Surely you have pain, strong pain, somewhere; in strong frames pain is strongest. Try, now, my specific," (holding it up). "Do but look at the expression of this friend of humanity. Trust me, certain cure for any pain in the world. Won't you look?"

"No," choked the other.

"Very good. Merry time to you, little May Queen."

And so, as if he would intrude his cure upon no one, moved pleasantly off, again crying his wares, nor now at last without result. A new-comer, not from the shore, but another part of the boat, a sickly young man, after some questions, purchased a bottle. Upon this, others of the company began a little to wake up as it were; the scales of indifference or prejudice fell from their eyes; now, at last, they seemed to have an inkling that here was something not undesirable which might be had for the buying.

But while, ten times more briskly bland than ever, the herb-doctor was driving his benevolent trade, accompanying each sale with added praises of the thing traded, all at once the dusk giant, seated at some distance, unexpectedly raised his voice with—

"What was that you last said?"

The question was put distinctly, yet resonantly, as when a great clock-bell—stunning admonisher—strikes one; and the stroke, though single, comes bedded in the belfry clamor.

All proceedings were suspended. Hands held forth for the specific were withdrawn, while every eye turned towards the direction whence the question came. But, no way abashed, the herb-doctor, elevating his voice with even more than wonted self-possession, replied—

"I was saying what, since you wish it, I cheerfully repeat, that the Samaritan Pain Dissuader, which I here hold in my hand, will either cure or ease any pain you please, within ten minutes after its application."

"Does it produce insensibility?"

"By no means. Not the least of its merits is, that it is not an opiate. It kills pain without killing feeling."

"You lie! Some pains cannot be eased but by producing insensibility, and cannot be cured but by producing death."

Beyond this the dusk giant said nothing; neither, for impairing the other's market, did there appear much need to. After eyeing the rude speaker a moment with an expression of mingled admiration and consternation, the company silently exchanged glances of mutual sympathy under unwelcome conviction. Those who had purchased looked sheepish or ashamed; and a cynical-looking little man, with a thin flaggy beard, and a countenance ever wearing the rudiments of a grin, seated alone in a corner commanding a good view of the scene, held a rusty hat before his face.

But, again, the herb-doctor, without noticing the retort, overbearing though it was, began his panegyrics anew, and in a tone more assured than before, going so far now as to say that his specific was sometimes almost as effective in cases of mental suffering as in cases of physical; or rather, to be more precise, in cases when, through sympathy, the two sorts of pain coöperated into a climax of both—in such cases, he said, the specific had done very well. He cited an example: Only three bottles, faithfully taken, cured a Louisiana widow (for three weeks sleepless in a darkened chamber) of neuralgic sorrow for the loss of husband and child, swept off in one night by the last epidemic. For the truth of this, a printed voucher was produced, duly signed.

While he was reading it aloud, a sudden side-blow all but felled him.

It was the giant, who, with a countenance lividly epileptic with hypochondriac mania, exclaimed—

"Profane fiddler on heart-strings! Snake!"

More he would have added, but, convulsed, could not; so, without another word, taking up the child, who had followed him, went with a rocking pace out of the cabin.

"Regardless of decency, and lost to humanity!" exclaimed the herb-doctor, with much ado recovering himself. Then, after a pause, during which he examined his bruise, not omitting to apply externally a little of his specific, and with some success, as it would seem, plained to himself:

"No, no, I won't seek redress; innocence is my redress. But," turning upon them all, "if that man's wrathful blow provokes me to no wrath, should his evil distrust arouse you to distrust? I do devoutly hope," proudly raising voice and arm, "for the honor of humanity—hope that, despite this coward assault, the Samaritan Pain Dissuader stands unshaken in the confidence of all who hear me!"

But, injured as he was, and patient under it, too, somehow his case excited as little compassion as his oratory now did enthusiasm. Still, pathetic to the last, he continued his appeals, notwithstanding the frigid regard of the company, till, suddenly interrupting himself, as if in reply to a quick summons from without, he said hurriedly, "I come, I come," and so, with every token of precipitate dispatch, out of the cabin the herb-doctor went.

CHAPTER XVIII

INQUEST INTO THE TRUE CHARACTER OF THE HERB-DOCTOR

"SHA'N'T see that fellow again in a hurry," remarked an auburn-haired gentleman, to his neighbor with a hook-nose. "Never knew an operator so completely unmasked."

"But do you think it the fair thing to unmask an operator that way?"

"Fair? It is right."

"Supposing that at high 'change on the Paris Bourse, Asmodeus should lounge in, distributing hand-bills, revealing the true thoughts and designs of all the operators present—would that be the fair thing in Asmodeus? Or, as Hamlet says, were it 'to consider the thing too curiously?'"

"We won't go into that. But since you admit the fellow to be a knave—"

"I don't admit it. Or, if I did, I take it back. Shouldn't wonder if, after all, he is no knave at all, or, but little of one. What can you prove against him?"

"I can prove that he makes dupes."

"Many held in honor do the same; and many, not wholly knaves, do it too."

"How about that last?"

"He is not wholly at heart a knave, I fancy, among whose dupes is himself. Did you not see our quack friend apply to himself his own quackery? A fanatic quack; essentially a fool, though effectively a knave."

Bending over, and looking down between his knees on the floor, the auburn-haired gentleman meditatively scribbled there awhile with his cane, then, glancing up, said:

101

"I can't conceive how you, in any way, can hold him a fool. How he talked—so glib, so pat, so well."

"A smart fool always talks well: takes a smart fool to be tonguey."

In much the same strain the discussion continued—the hook-nosed gentleman talking at large and excellently, with a view of demonstrating that a smart fool always talks just so. Ere long he talked to such purpose as almost to convince.

Presently, back came the person of whom the auburn-haired gentleman had predicted that he would not return. Conspicuous in the door-way he stood, saying, in a clear voice, "Is the agent of the Seminole Widow and Orphan Asylum within here?"

No one replied.

"Is there within here any agent or any member of any charitable institution whatever?"

No one seemed competent to answer, or, no one thought it worth while to.

"If there be within here any such person, I have in my hand two dollars for him."

Some interest was manifested.

"I was called away so hurriedly, I forgot this part of my duty. With the proprietor of the Samaritan Pain Dissuader it is a rule, to devote, on the spot, to some benevolent purpose, the half of the proceeds of sales. Eight bottles were disposed of among this company. Hence, four half-dollars remain to charity. Who, as steward, takes the money?"

One or two pair of feet moved upon the floor, as with a sort of itching; but nobody rose.

"Does diffidence prevail over duty? If, I say, there be any gentleman, or any lady, either, here present, who is in any connection with any charitable institution whatever, let him or her come forward. He or she happening to have at hand no certificate of such connection, makes no difference. Not of a suspicious temper, thank God, I shall have confidence in whoever offers to take the money."

A demure-looking woman, in a dress rather tawdry and

rumpled, here drew her veil well down and rose; but, marking every eye upon her, thought it advisable, upon the whole, to sit down again.

"Is it to be believed that, in this Christian company, there is no one charitable person? I mean, no one connected with any charity? Well, then, is there no object of charity here?"

Upon this, an unhappy-looking woman, in a sort of mourning, neat, but sadly worn, hid her face behind a meagre bundle, and was heard to sob. Meantime, as not seeing or hearing her, the herb-doctor again spoke, and this time not unpathetically:

"Are there none here who feel in need of help, and who, in accepting such help, would feel that they, in their time, have given or done more than may ever be given or done to them? Man or woman, is there none such here?"

The sobs of the woman were more audible, though she strove to repress them. While nearly every one's attention was bent upon her, a man of the appearance of a day-laborer, with a white bandage across his face, concealing the side of the nose, and who, for coolness' sake, had been sitting in his red-flannel shirt-sleeves, his coat thrown across one shoulder, the darned cuffs drooping behind—this man shufflingly rose, and, with a pace that seemed the lingering memento of the lock-step of convicts, went up for a duly-qualified claimant.

"Poor wounded huzzar!" sighed the herb-doctor, and dropping the money into the man's clam-shell of a hand turned and departed.

The recipient of the alms was about moving after, when the auburn-haired gentleman staid him: "Don't be frightened, you; but I want to see those coins. Yes, yes; good silver, good silver. There, take them again, and while you are about it, go bandage the rest of yourself behind something. D'ye hear? Consider yourself, wholly, the scar of a nose, and be off with yourself."

Being of a forgiving nature, or else from emotion not daring to trust his voice, the man silently, but not without some precipitancy, withdrew.

"Strange," said the auburn-haired gentleman, returning to his friend, "the money was good money."

"Aye, and where your fine knavery now? Knavery to devote the half of one's receipts to charity? He's a fool I say again."

"Others might call him an original genius."

"Yes, being original in his folly. Genius? His genius is a cracked pate, and, as this age goes, not much originality about that."

"May he not be knave, fool, and genius altogether?"

"I beg pardon," here said a third person with a gossiping expression who had been listening, "but you are somewhat puzzled by this man, and well you may be."

"Do you know anything about him?" asked the hook-nosed gentleman.

"No, but I suspect him for something."

"Suspicion. We want knowledge."

"Well, suspect first and know next. True knowledge comes but by suspicion or revelation. That's my maxim."

"And yet," said the auburn-haired gentleman, "since a wise man will keep even some certainties to himself, much more some suspicions, at least he will at all events so do till they ripen into knowledge."

"Do you hear that about the wise man?" said the hook-nosed gentleman, turning upon the new comer. "Now what is it you suspect of this fellow?"

"I shrewdly suspect him," was the eager response, "for one of those Jesuit emissaries prowling all over our country. The better to accomplish their secret designs, they assume, at times, I am told, the most singular masques; sometimes, in appearance, the absurdest."

This, though indeed for some reason causing a droll smile upon the face of the hook-nosed gentleman, added a third angle to the discussion, which now became a sort of triangular duel, and ended, at last, with but a triangular result.

CHAPTER XIX

A SOLDIER OF FORTUNE

"Mexico? Molino del Rey? Resaca de la Palma?"

"Resaca de la *Tombs!*"

Leaving his reputation to take care of itself, since, as is not seldom the case, he knew nothing of its being in debate, the herb-doctor, wandering towards the forward part of the boat, had there espied a singular character in a grimy old regimental coat, a countenance at once grim and wizened, interwoven paralyzed legs, stiff as icicles, suspended between rude crutches, while the whole rigid body, like a ship's long barometer on gimbals, swung to and fro, mechanically faithful to the motion of the boat. Looking downward while he swung, the cripple seemed in a brown study.

As moved by the sight, and conjecturing that here was some battered hero from the Mexican battle-fields, the herb-doctor had sympathetically accosted him as above, and received the above rather dubious reply. As, with a half moody, half surly sort of air that reply was given, the cripple, by a voluntary jerk, nervously increased his swing (his custom when seized by emotion), so that one would have thought some squall had suddenly rolled the boat and with it the barometer.

"Tombs? my friend," exclaimed the herb-doctor in mild surprise. "You have not descended to the dead, have you? I had imagined you a scarred campaigner, one of the noble children of war, for your dear country a glorious sufferer. But you are Lazarus, it seems."

"Yes, he who had sores."

"Ah, the *other* Lazarus. But I never knew that either of them was in the army," glancing at the dilapidated regimentals.

105

"That will do now. Jokes enough."

"Friend," said the other reproachfully, "you think amiss. On principle, I greet unfortunates with some pleasant remark, the better to call off their thoughts from their troubles. The physician who is at once wise and humane seldom unreservedly sympathizes with his patient. But come, I am a herb-doctor, and also a natural bone-setter. I may be sanguine, but I think I can do something for you. You look up now. Give me your story. Ere I undertake a cure, I require a full account of the case."

"You can't help me," returned the cripple gruffly. "Go away."

"You seem sadly destitute of—"

"No I ain't destitute; to-day, at least, I can pay my way."

"The Natural Bone-setter is happy, indeed, to hear that. But you were premature. I was deploring your destitution, not of cash, but of confidence. You think the Natural Bone-setter can't help you. Well, suppose he can't, have you any objection to telling him your story? You, my friend, have, in a signal way, experienced adversity. Tell me, then, for my private good, how, without aid from the noble cripple, Epictetus, you have arrived at this heroic sang-froid in misfortune."

At these words the cripple fixed upon the speaker the hard ironic eye of one toughened and defiant in misery, and, in the end, grinned upon him with his unshaven face like an ogre.

"Come, come, be sociable—be human, my friend. Don't make that face; it distresses me."

"I suppose," with a sneer, "you are the man I've long heard of—The Happy Man."

"Happy? my friend. Yes, at least I ought to be. My conscience is peaceful. I have confidence in everybody. I have confidence that, in my humble profession, I do some little good to the world. Yes, I think that, without presumption, I may venture to assent to the proposition that I am the Happy Man— the Happy Bone-setter."

"Then you shall hear my story. Many a month I have longed to get hold of the Happy Man, drill him, drop the powder, and leave him to explode at his leisure."

"What a demoniac unfortunate," exclaimed the herb-doctor retreating. "Regular infernal machine!"

"Look ye," cried the other, stumping after him, and with his horny hand catching him by a horn button, "my name is Thomas Fry. Until my—"

—"Any relation of Mrs. Fry?" interrupted the other. "I still correspond with that excellent lady on the subject of prisons. Tell me, are you anyway connected with *my* Mrs. Fry?"

"Blister Mrs. Fry! What do them sentimental souls know of prisons or any other black fact? I'll tell ye a story of prisons. Ha, ha!"

The herb-doctor shrank, and with reason, the laugh being strangely startling.

"Positively, my friend," said he, "you must stop that; I can't stand that; no more of that. I hope I have the milk of kindness, but your thunder will soon turn it."

"Hold, I haven't come to the milk-turning part yet. My name is Thomas Fry. Until my twenty-third year I went by the nick-name of Happy Tom—happy—ha, ha! They called me Happy Tom, d'ye see? because I was so good-natured and laughing all the time, just as I am now—ha, ha!"

Upon this the herb-doctor would, perhaps, have run, but once more the hyæna clawed him. Presently, sobering down, he continued:

"Well, I was born in New York, and there I lived a steady, hard-working man, a cooper by trade. One evening I went to a political meeting in the Park—for you must know, I was in those days a great patriot. As bad luck would have it, there was trouble near, between a gentleman who had been drinking wine, and a pavior who was sober. The pavior chewed tobacco, and the gentleman said it was beastly in him, and pushed him, wanting to have his place. The pavior chewed on and pushed back. Well, the gentleman carried a sword-cane, and presently the pavior was down—skewered."

"How was that?"

"Why you see the pavior undertook something above his strength."

"The other must have been a Samson then. 'Strong as a pavior,' is a proverb."

"So it is, and the gentleman was in body a rather weakly man, but, for all that, I say again, the pavior undertook something above his strength."

"What are you talking about? He tried to maintain his rights, didn't he?"

"Yes; but, for all that, I say again, he undertook something above his strength."

"I don't understand you. But go on."

"Along with the gentleman, I, with other witnesses, was taken to the Tombs. There was an examination, and, to appear at the trial, the gentleman and witnesses all gave bail—I mean all but me."

"And why didn't you?"

"Couldn't get it."

"Steady, hard-working cooper like you; what was the reason you couldn't get bail?"

"Steady, hard-working cooper hadn't no friends. Well, souse I went into a wet cell, like a canal-boat splashing into the lock; locked up in pickle, d'ye see? against the time of the trial."

"But what had you done?"

"Why, I hadn't got any friends, I tell ye. A worse crime than murder, as ye'll see afore long."

"Murder? Did the wounded man die?"

"Died the third night."

"Then the gentleman's bail didn't help him. Imprisoned now, wasn't he?"

"Had too many friends. No, it was *I* that was imprisoned.— But I was going on: They let me walk about the corridor by day; but at night I must into lock. There the wet and the damp struck into my bones. They doctored me, but no use. When the trial came, I was boosted up and said my say."

"And what was that?"

"My say was that I saw the steel go in, and saw it sticking in."

"And that hung the gentleman."

"Hung him with a gold chain! His friends called a meeting in the Park, and presented him with a gold watch and chain upon his acquittal."

"Acquittal?"

"Didn't I say he had friends?"

There was a pause, broken at last by the herb-doctor's saying: "Well, there is a bright side to everything. If this speak prosaically for justice, it speaks romantically for friendship! But go on, my fine fellow."

"My say being said, they told me I might go. I said I could not without help. So the constables helped me, asking *where* would I go? I told them back to the 'Tombs.' I knew no other place. 'But where are your friends?' said they. 'I have none.' So they put me into a hand-barrow with an awning to it, and wheeled me down to the dock and on board a boat, and away to Blackwell's Island to the Corporation Hospital. There I got worse—got pretty much as you see me now. Couldn't cure me. After three years, I grew sick of lying in a grated iron bed alongside of groaning thieves and mouldering burglars. They gave me five silver dollars, and these crutches, and I hobbled off. I had an only brother who went to Indiana, years ago. I begged about, to make up a sum to go to him; got to Indiana at last, and they directed me to his grave. It was on a great plain, in a log-church yard with a stump fence, the old gray roots sticking all ways like moose-antlers. The bier, set over the grave, it being the last dug, was of green hickory; bark on, and green twigs sprouting from it. Some one had planted a bunch of violets on the mound, but it was a poor soil (always choose the poorest soils for grave-yards), and they were all dried to tinder. I was going to sit and rest myself on the bier and think about my brother in heaven, but the bier broke down, the legs being only tacked. So, after driving some hogs out of the yard that were rooting there, I came away, and, not to make too long a story of it, here I am, drifting down stream like any other bit of wreck."

The herb-doctor was silent for a time, buried in thought. At last, raising his head, he said: "I have considered your whole story, my friend, and strove to consider it in the light of a commentary on what I believe to be the system of things; but it so jars with all, is so incompatible with all, that you must pardon me, if I honestly tell you, I cannot believe it."

"That don't surprise me."

"How?"

"Hardly anybody believes my story, and so to most I tell a different one."

"How, again?"

"Wait here a bit and I'll show ye."

With that, taking off his rag of a cap, and arranging his tattered regimentals the best he could, off he went stumping among the passengers in an adjoining part of the deck, saying with a jovial kind of air: "Sir, a shilling for Happy Tom, who fought at Buena Vista. Lady, something for General Scott's soldier, crippled in both pins at glorious Contreras."

Now, it so chanced that, unbeknown to the cripple, a primlooking stranger had overheard part of his story. Beholding him, then, on his present begging adventure, this person, turning to the herb-doctor, indignantly said: "Is it not too bad, sir, that yonder rascal should lie so?"

"Charity never faileth, my good sir," was the reply. "The vice of this unfortunate is pardonable. Consider, he lies not out of wantonness."

"Not out of wantonnness. I never heard more wanton lies. In one breath to tell you what would appear to be his true story, and, in the next, away and falsify it."

"For all that, I repeat he lies not out of wantonness. A ripe philosopher, turned out of the great Sorbonne of hard times, he thinks that woes, when told to strangers for money, are best sugared. Though the inglorious lock-jaw of his knee-pans in a wet dungeon is a far more pitiable ill than to have been crippled at glorious Contreras, yet he is of opinion that this lighter and false ill shall attract, while the heavier and real one might repel."

"Nonsense; he belongs to the Devil's regiment; and I have a great mind to expose him."

"Shame upon you. Dare to expose that poor unfortunate, and by heaven—don't you do it, sir."

Noting something in his manner, the other thought it more prudent to retire than retort. By-and-by, the cripple came back, and with glee, having reaped a pretty good harvest.

"There," he laughed, "you know now what sort of soldier I am."

"Aye, one that fights not the stupid Mexican, but a foe worthy your tactics—Fortune!"

"Hi, hi!" clamored the cripple, like a fellow in the pit of a sixpenny theatre, then said, "don't know much what you meant, but it went off well."

This over, his countenance capriciously put on a morose ogreness. To kindly questions he gave no kindly answers. Unhandsome notions were thrown out about "free Ameriky," as he sarcastically called his country. These seemed to disturb and pain the herb-doctor, who, after an interval of thoughtfulness, gravely addressed him in these words:

"You, my worthy friend, to my concern, have reflected upon the government under which you live and suffer. Where is your patriotism? Where your gratitude? True, the charitable may find something in your case, as you put it, partly to account for such reflections as coming from you. Still, be the facts how they may, your reflections are none the less unwarrantable. Grant, for the moment, that your experiences are as you give them; in which case I would admit that government might be thought to have more or less to do with what seems undesirable in them. But it is never to be forgotten that human government, being subordinate to the divine, must needs, therefore, in its degree, partake of the characteristics of the divine. That is, while in general efficacious to happiness, the world's law may yet, in some cases, have, to the eye of reason, an unequal operation, just as, in the same imperfect view, some inequalities may appear in the operations of heaven's law; nevertheless, to one who has a right confidence, final benignity is, in every instance, as sure with the one law as the other. I expound the point at some length, because these are the considerations, my poor fellow, which, weighed as they merit, will enable you to sustain with unimpaired trust the apparent calamities which are yours."

"What do you talk your hog-latin to me for?" cried the cripple, who, throughout the address, betrayed the most illiterate obduracy; and, with an incensed look, anew he swung himself.

Glancing another way till the spasm passed, the other continued:

"Charity marvels not that you should be somewhat hard of conviction, my friend, since you, doubtless, believe yourself hardly dealt by; but forget not that those who are loved are chastened."

"Mustn't chasten them too much, though, and too long, because their skin and heart get hard, and feel neither pain nor tickle."

"To mere reason, your case looks something piteous, I grant. But never despond; many things—the choicest—yet remain. You breathe this bounteous air, are warmed by this gracious sun, and, though poor and friendless, indeed, nor so agile as in your youth, yet, how sweet to roam, day by day, through the groves, plucking the bright mosses and flowers, till forlornness itself becomes a hilarity, and, in your innocent independence, you skip for joy."

"Fine skipping with these 'ere horse-posts—ha ha!"

"Pardon; I forgot the crutches. My mind, figuring you after receiving the benefit of my art, overlooked you as you stand before me."

"Your art? You call yourself a bone-setter—a natural bone-setter, do ye? Go, bone-set the crooked world, and then come bone-set crooked me."

"Truly, my honest friend, I thank you for again recalling me to my original object. Let me examine you," bending down; "ah, I see, I see; much such a case as the negro's. Did you see him? Oh no, you came aboard since. Well, his case was a little something like yours. I prescribed for him, and I shouldn't wonder at all if, in a very short time, he were able to walk almost as well as myself. Now, have you no confidence in my art?"

"Ha, ha!"

The herb-doctor averted himself; but, the wild laugh dying away, resumed:

"I will not force confidence on you. Still, I would fain do the friendly thing by you. Here, take this box; just rub that liniment on the joints night and morning. Take it. Nothing to pay. God bless you. Good-bye."

"Stay," pausing in his swing, not untouched by so unexpected an act; "stay—thank'ee—but will this really do me good? Honor bright, now; will it? Don't deceive a poor fellow," with changed mien and glistening eye.

"Try it. Good-bye."

"Stay, stay! *Sure* it will do me good?"

"Possibly, possibly; no harm in trying. Good-bye."

"Stay, stay; give me three more boxes, and here's the money."

"My friend," returning towards him with a sadly pleased sort of air, "I rejoice in the birth of your confidence and hopeful-ness. Believe me that, like your crutches, confidence and hope-fulness will long support a man when his own legs will not. Stick to confidence and hopefulness, then, since how mad for the cripple to throw his crutches away. You ask for three more boxes of my liniment. Luckily, I have just that number remain-ing. Here they are. I sell them at half-a-dollar apiece. But I shall take nothing from you. There; God bless you again; good-bye."

"Stay," in a convulsed voice, and rocking himself, "stay, stay! You have made a better man of me. You have borne with me like a good Christian, and talked to me like one, and all that is enough without making me a present of these boxes. Here is the money. I won't take nay. There, there; and may Almighty goodness go with you."

As the herb-doctor withdrew, the cripple gradually subsided from his hard rocking into a gentle oscillation. It expressed, per-haps, the soothed mood of his reverie.

CHAPTER XX

THE herb-doctor had not moved far away, when, in advance of him, this spectacle met his eye. A dried-up old man, with the stature of a boy of twelve, was tottering about like one out of his mind, in rumpled clothes of old moleskin, showing recent contact with bedding, his ferret eyes, blinking in the sunlight of the snowy boat, as imbecilely eager, and, at intervals, coughing, he peered hither and thither as if in alarmed search for his nurse. He presented the aspect of one who, bed-rid, has, through overruling excitement, like that of a fire, been stimulated to his feet.

"You seek some one," said the herb-doctor, accosting him. "Can I assist you?"

"Do, do; I am so old and miserable," coughed the old man. "Where is he? This long time I've been trying to get up and find him. But I haven't any friends, and couldn't get up till now. Where is he?"

"Who do you mean?" drawing closer, to stay the further wanderings of one so weakly.

"Why, why, why," now marking the other's dress, "why you, yes you—you, you—ugh, ugh, ugh!"

"I?"

"Ugh, ugh, ugh!—you are the man he spoke of. Who is he?"

"Faith, that is just what I want to know."

"Mercy, mercy!" coughed the old man, bewildered, "ever since seeing him, my head spins round so. I ought to have a guard*ee*an. Is this a snuff-colored surtout of yours, or ain't it? Somehow, can't trust my senses any more, since trusting him—ugh, ugh, ugh!"

"Oh, you have trusted somebody? Glad to hear it. Glad to

hear of any instance of that sort. Reflects well upon all men. But you inquire whether this is a snuff-colored surtout. I answer it is; and will add that a herb-doctor wears it."

Upon this the old man, in his broken way, replied that then he (the herb-doctor) was the person he sought—the person spoken of by the other person as yet unknown. He then, with flighty eagerness, wanted to know who this last person was, and where he was, and whether he could be trusted with money to treble it.

"Aye, now, I begin to understand; ten to one you mean my worthy friend, who, in pure goodness of heart, makes people's fortunes for them—their everlasting fortunes, as the phrase goes—only charging his one small commission of confidence. Aye, aye; before intrusting funds with my friend, you want to know about him. Very proper—and, I am glad to assure you, you need have no hesitation; none, none, just none in the world; *bona fide*, none. Turned me in a trice a hundred dollars the other day into as many eagles."

"Did he? did he? But where is he? Take me to him."

"Pray, take my arm! The boat is large! We may have something of a hunt! Come on! Ah, is that he?"

"Where? where?"

"O, no; I took yonder coat-skirts for his. But no, my honest friend would never turn tail that way. Ah!—"

"Where? where?"

"Another mistake. Surprising resemblance. I took yonder clergyman for him. Come on!"

Having searched that part of the boat without success, they went to another part, and, while exploring that, the boat sided up to a landing, when, as the two were passing by the open guard, the herb-doctor suddenly rushed towards the disembarking throng, crying out: "Mr. Truman, Mr. Truman! There he goes—that's he. Mr. Truman, Mr. Truman!—Confound that steam-pipe. Mr. Truman! for God's sake, Mr. Truman!—No, no. —There, the plank's in—too late—we're off."

With that, the huge boat, with a mighty, walrus wallow, rolled away from the shore, resuming her course.

"How vexatious!" exclaimed the herb-doctor, returning. "Had we been but one single moment sooner.—There he goes, now, towards yon hotel, his portmanteau following. You see him, don't you?"

"Where? where?"

"Can't see him any more. Wheel-house shot between. I am very sorry. I should have so liked you to have let him have a hundred or so of your money. You would have been pleased with the investment, believe me."

"Oh, I *have* let him have some of my money," groaned the old man.

"You have? My dear sir," seizing both the miser's hands in both his own and heartily shaking them. "My dear sir, how I congratulate you. You don't know."

"Ugh, ugh! I fear I don't," with another groan. His name is Truman, is it?"

"John Truman."

"Where does he live?"

"In St. Louis."

"Where's his office?"

"Let me see. Jones street, number one hundred and—no, no —anyway, it's somewhere or other up-stairs in Jones street."

"Can't you remember the number? Try, now."

"One hundred—two hundred—three hundred—"

"Oh, my hundred dollars! I wonder whether it will be one hundred, two hundred, three hundred, with them! Ugh, ugh! Can't remember the number?"

"Positively, though I once knew, I have forgotten, quite forgotten it. Strange. But never mind. You will easily learn in St. Louis. He is well known there."

"But I have no receipt—ugh, ugh! Nothing to show—don't know where I stand—ought to have a guard*ee*an—ugh, ugh! Don't know anything. Ugh, ugh!"

"Why, you know that you gave him your confidence, don't you?"

"Oh, yes."

"Well, then?"

"But what, what—how, how—ugh, ugh!"

"Why, didn't he tell you?"

"No."

"What! Didn't he tell you that it was a secret, a mystery?"

"Oh—yes."

"Well, then?"

"But I have no bond."

"Don't need any with Mr. Truman. Mr. Truman's word is his bond."

"But how am I to get my profits—ugh, ugh!—and my money back? Don't know anything. Ugh, ugh!"

"Oh, you must have confidence."

"Don't say that word again. Makes my head spin so. Oh, I'm so old and miserable, nobody caring for me, everybody fleecing me, and my head spins so—ugh, ugh!—and this cough racks me so. I say again, I ought to have a guardeean."

"So you ought; and Mr. Truman is your guardian to the extent you invested with him. Sorry we missed him just now. But you'll hear from him. All right. It's imprudent, though, to expose yourself this way. Let me take you to your berth."

Forlornly enough the old miser moved slowly away with him. But, while descending a stairway, he was seized with such coughing that he was fain to pause.

"That is a very bad cough."

"Church-yard—ugh, ugh!—church-yard cough.—Ugh!"

"Have you tried anything for it?"

"Tired of trying. Nothing does me any good—ugh! ugh! Not even the Mammoth Cave. Ugh! ugh! Denned there six months, but coughed so bad the rest of the coughers—ugh! ugh!—blackballed me out. Ugh, ugh! Nothing does me good."

"But have you tried the Omni-Balsamic Reinvigorator, sir?"

"That's what that Truman—ugh, ugh!—said I ought to take. Yarb-medicine; you are that yarb-doctor, too?"

"The same. Suppose you try one of my boxes now. Trust me, from what I know of Mr. Truman, he is not the gentleman to recommend, even in behalf of a friend, anything of whose excellence he is not conscientiously satisfied."

"Ugh!—how much?"

"Only two dollars a box."

"Two dollars? Why don't you say two millions? ugh, ugh! Two dollars, that's two hundred cents; that's eight hundred farthings; that's two thousand mills; and all for one little box of yarb-medicine. My head, my head!—oh, I ought to have a guardeean for my head. Ugh, ugh, ugh, ugh!"

"Well, if two dollars a box seems too much, take a dozen boxes at twenty dollars; and that will be getting four boxes for nothing, and you need use none but those four, the rest you can retail out at a premium, and so cure your cough, and make money by it. Come, you had better do it. Cash down. Can fill an order in a day or two. Here now," producing a box; "pure herbs."

At that moment, seized with another spasm, the miser snatched each interval to fix his half distrustful, half hopeful eye upon the medicine, held alluringly up. "Sure—ugh! Sure it's all nat'ral? Nothing but yarbs? If I only thought it was a purely nat'ral medicine now—all yarbs—ugh, ugh!—oh this cough, this cough—ugh, ugh!—shatters my whole body. Ugh, ugh, ugh!"

"For heaven's sake try my medicine, if but a single box. That it is pure nature you may be confident. Refer you to Mr. Truman."

"Don't know his number—ugh, ugh, ugh, ugh! Oh this cough. He did speak well of this medicine though; said solemnly it would cure me—ugh, ugh, ugh, ugh!—take off a dollar and I'll have a box."

"Can't sir, can't."

"Say a dollar-and-half. Ugh!"

"Can't. Am pledged to the one-price system, only honorable one."

"Take off a shilling—ugh, ugh!"

"Can't."

"Ugh, ugh, ugh—I'll take it.—There."

Grudgingly he handed eight silver coins, but while still in his hand, his cough took him, and they were shaken upon the deck.

One by one, the herb-doctor picked them up, and, examining them, said: "These are not quarters, these are pistareens; and clipped, and sweated, at that."

"Oh don't be so miserly—ugh, ugh!—better a beast than a miser—ugh, ugh!"

"Well, let it go. Anything rather than the idea of your not being cured of such a cough. And I hope, for the credit of humanity, you have not made it appear worse than it is, merely with a view to working upon the weak point of my pity, and so getting my medicine the cheaper. Now, mind, don't take it till night. Just before retiring is the time. There, you can get along now, can't you? I would attend you further, but I land presently, and must go hunt up my luggage."

CHAPTER XXI

A HARD CASE

"Yarbs, yarbs; natur, natur; you foolish old file you! He diddled you with that hocus-pocus, did he? Yarbs and natur will cure your incurable cough, you think."

It was a rather eccentric-looking person who spoke; somewhat ursine in aspect; sporting a shaggy spencer of the cloth called bear's-skin; a high-peaked cap of raccoon-skin, the long bushy tail switching over behind; raw-hide leggings; grim stubble chin; and to end, a double-barreled gun in hand—a Missouri bachelor, a Hoosier gentleman, of Spartan leisure and fortune, and equally Spartan manners and sentiments; and, as the sequel may show, not less acquainted, in a Spartan way of his own, with philosophy and books, than with woodcraft and rifles.

He must have overheard some of the talk between the miser and the herb-doctor; for, just after the withdrawal of the one, he made up to the other—now at the foot of the stairs leaning against the baluster there—with the greeting above.

"Think it will cure me?" coughed the miser in echo; "why shouldn't it? The medicine is nat'ral yarbs, pure yarbs; yarbs must cure me."

"Because a thing is nat'ral, as you call it, you think it must be good. But who gave you that cough? Was it, or was it not, nature?"

"Sure, you don't think that natur, Dame Natur, will hurt a body, do you?"

"Natur is good Queen Bess; but who's responsible for the cholera?"

"But yarbs, yarbs; yarbs are good?"

"What's deadly-nightshade? Yarb, ain't it?"

"Oh, that a Christian man should speak agin natur and yarbs—ugh, ugh, ugh!—ain't sick men sent out into the country; sent out to natur and grass?"

"Aye, and poets send out the sick spirit to green pastures, like lame horses turned out unshod to the turf to renew their hoofs. A sort of yarb-doctors in their way, poets have it that for sore hearts, as for sore lungs, nature is the grand cure. But who froze to death my teamster on the prairie? And who made an idiot of Peter the Wild Boy?"

"Then you don't believe in these 'ere yarb-doctors?"

"Yarb-doctors? I remember the lank yarb-doctor I saw once on a hospital-cot in Mobile. One of the faculty passing round and seeing who lay there, said with professional triumph, "Ah, Dr. Green, your yarbs don't help ye now, Dr. Green. Have to come to us and the mercury now, Dr. Green.—Natur! Y-a-r-b-s!""

"Did I hear something about herbs and herb-doctors?" here said a flute-like voice, advancing.

It was the herb-doctor in person. Carpet-bag in hand, he happened to be strolling back that way.

"Pardon me," addressing the Missourian, "but if I caught your words aright, you would seem to have little confidence in nature; which, really, in my way of thinking, looks like carrying the spirit of distrust pretty far."

"And who of my sublime species may you be?" turning short round upon him, clicking his rifle-lock, with an air which would have seemed half cynic, half wild-cat, were it not for the grotesque excess of the expression, which made its sincerity appear more or less dubious.

"One who has confidence in nature, and confidence in man, with some little modest confidence in himself."

"That's your Confession of Faith, is it? Confidence in man, eh? Pray, which do you think are most, knaves or fools?"

"Having met with few or none of either, I hardly think I am competent to answer."

"I will answer for you. Fools are most."

"Why do you think so?"

"For the same reason that I think oats are numerically more than horses. Don't knaves munch up fools just as horses do oats?"

"A droll, sir; you are a droll. I can appreciate drollery—ha, ha, ha!"

"But I'm in earnest."

"That's the drollery, to deliver droll extravagance with an earnest air—knaves munching up fools as horses oats.—Faith, very droll, indeed, ha, ha, ha! Yes, I think I understand you now, sir. How silly I was to have taken you seriously, in your droll conceits, too, about having no confidence in nature. In reality you have just as much as I have."

"*I* have confidence in nature? *I?* I say again there is nothing I am more suspicious of. I once lost ten thousand dollars by nature. Nature embezzled that amount from me; absconded with ten thousand dollars' worth of my property; a plantation on this stream, swept clean away by one of those sudden shiftings of the banks in a freshet; ten thousand dollars' worth of alluvion thrown broad off upon the waters."

"But have you no confidence that by a reverse shifting that soil will come back after many days?—ah, here is my venerable friend," observing the old miser, "not in your berth yet? Pray, if you *will* keep afoot, don't lean against that baluster; take my arm."

It was taken; and the two stood together; the old miser leaning against the herb-doctor with something of that air of trustful fraternity with which, when standing, the less strong of the Siamese twins habitually leans against the other.

The Missourian eyed them in silence, which was broken by the herb-doctor.

"You look surprised, sir. Is it because I publicly take under my protection a figure like this? But I am never ashamed of honesty, whatever his coat."

"Look you," said the Missourian, after a scrutinizing pause, "you are a queer sort of chap. Don't know exactly what to make of you. Upon the whole though, you somewhat remind me of the last boy I had on my place."

"Good, trustworthy boy, I hope?"

"Oh, very! I am now started to get me made some kind of machine to do the sort of work which boys are supposed to be fitted for."

"Then you have passed a veto upon boys?"

"And men, too."

"But, my dear sir, does not that again imply more or less lack of confidence?—(Stand up a little, just a very little, my venerable friend; you lean rather hard.)—No confidence in boys, no confidence in men, no confidence in nature. Pray, sir, who or what may you have confidence in?"

"I have confidence in distrust; more particularly as applied to you and your herbs."

"Well," with a forbearing smile, "that is frank. But pray, don't forget that when you suspect my herbs you suspect nature."

"Didn't I say that before?"

"Very good. For the argument's sake I will suppose you are in earnest. Now, can you, who suspect nature, deny, that this same nature not only kindly brought you into being, but has faithfully nursed you to your present vigorous and independent condition? Is it not to nature that you are indebted for that robustness of mind which you so unhandsomely use to her scandal? Pray, is it not to nature that you owe the very eyes by which you criticise her?"

"No! for the privilege of vision I am indebted to an oculist, who in my tenth year operated upon me in Philadelphia. Nature made me blind and would have kept me so. My oculist counterplotted her."

"And yet, sir, by your complexion, I judge you live an out-of-door life; without knowing it, you are partial to nature; you fly to nature, the universal mother."

"Very motherly! Sir, in the passion-fits of nature, I've known birds fly from nature to me, rough as I look; yes, sir, in a tempest, refuge here," smiting the folds of his bearskin. "Fact, sir, fact. Come, come, Mr. Palaverer, for all your palavering, did you yourself never shut out nature of a cold, wet night? Bar her out? Bolt her out? Lint her out?"

"As to that," said the herb-doctor calmly, "much may be said."

"Say it, then," ruffling all his hairs. "You can't, sir, can't." Then, as in apostrophe: "Look you, nature! I don't deny but your clover is sweet, and your dandelions don't roar; but whose hailstones smashed my windows?"

"Sir," with unimpaired affability, producing one of his boxes, "I am pained to meet with one who holds nature a dangerous character. Though your manner is refined your voice is rough; in short, you seem to have a sore throat. In the calumniated name of nature, I present you with this box; my venerable friend here has a similar one; but to you, a free gift, sir. Through her regularly-authorized agents, of whom I happen to be one, Nature delights in benefiting those who most abuse her. Pray, take it."

"Away with it! Don't hold it so near. Ten to one there is a torpedo in it. Such things have been. Editors been killed that way. Take it further off, I say."

"Good heavens! my dear sir—"

"I tell you I want none of your boxes," snapping his rifle.

"Oh, take it—ugh, ugh! do take it," chimed in the old miser; "I wish he would give me one for nothing."

"You find it lonely, eh," turning short round; "gulled yourself, you would have a companion."

"How can he find it lonely," returned the herb-doctor, "or how desire a companion, when here I stand by him; I, even I, in whom he has trust. For the gulling, tell me, is it humane to talk so to this poor old man? Granting that his dependence on my medicine is vain, is it kind to deprive him of what, in mere imagination, if nothing more, may help eke out, with hope, his disease? For you, if you have no confidence, and, thanks to your native health, can get along without it, so far, at least, as trusting in my medicine goes; yet, how cruel an argument to use, with this afflicted one here. Is it not for all the world as if some brawny pugilist, aglow in December, should rush in and put out a hospital-fire, because, forsooth, he feeling no need of artificial heat, the shivering patients shall have none? Put it to your conscience, sir, and you will admit, that, whatever be the nature of this afflicted one's trust, you, in opposing it, evince either an erring head or a heart amiss. Come, own, are you not pitiless?"

"Yes, poor soul," said the Missourian, gravely eyeing the old man—"yes, it *is* pitiless in one like me to speak too honestly to one like you. You are a late sitter-up in this life; past man's usual bed-time; and truth, though with some it makes a wholesome breakfast, proves to all a supper too hearty. Hearty food, taken late, gives bad dreams."

"What, in wonder's name—ugh, ugh!—is he talking about?" asked the old miser, looking up to the herb-doctor.

"Heaven be praised for that!" cried the Missourian.

"Out of his mind, ain't he?" again appealed the old miser.

"Pray, sir," said the herb-doctor to the Missourian, "for what were you giving thanks just now?"

"For this: that, with some minds, truth is, in effect, not so cruel a thing after all, seeing that, like a loaded pistol found by poor devils of savages, it raises more wonder than terror—its peculiar virtue being unguessed, unless, indeed, by indiscreet handling, it should happen to go off of itself."

"I pretend not to divine your meaning there," said the herb-doctor, after a pause, during which he eyed the Missourian with a kind of pinched expression, mixed of pain and curiosity, as if he grieved at his state of mind, and, at the same time, wondered what had brought him to it, "but this much I know," he added, "that the general cast of your thoughts is, to say the least, unfortunate. There is strength in them, but a strength, whose source, being physical, must wither. You will yet recant."

"Recant?"

"Yes, when, as with this old man, your evil days of decay come on, when a hoary captive in your chamber, then will you, something like the dungeoned Italian we read of, gladly seek the breast of that confidence begot in the tender time of your youth, blessed beyond telling if it return to you in age."

"Go back to nurse again, eh? Second childhood, indeed. You are soft."

"Mercy, mercy!" cried the old miser, "what is all this!—ugh, ugh! Do talk sense, my good friends. Ain't you," to the Missourian, "going to buy some of that medicine?"

"Pray, my venerable friend," said the herb-doctor, now trying to straighten himself, "don't lean *quite* so hard; my arm grows numb; abate a little, just a very little."

"Go," said the Missourian, "go lay down in your grave, old man, if you can't stand of yourself. It's a hard world for a leaner."

"As to his grave," said the herb-doctor, "that is far enough off, so he but faithfully take my medicine."

"Ugh, ugh, ugh!—He says true. No, I ain't—ugh! a going to die yet—ugh, ugh, ugh! Many years to live yet, ugh, ugh, ugh!"

"I approve your confidence," said the herb-doctor; "but your coughing distresses me, besides being injurious to you. Pray, let me conduct you to your berth. You are best there. Our friend here will wait till my return, I know."

With which he led the old miser away, and then, coming back, the talk with the Missourian was resumed.

"Sir," said the herb-doctor, with some dignity and more feeling, "now that our infirm friend is withdrawn, allow me, to the full, to express my concern at the words you allowed to escape you in his hearing. Some of those words, if I err not, besides being calculated to beget deplorable distrust in the patient, seemed fitted to convey unpleasant imputations against me, his physician."

"Suppose they did?" with a menacing air.

"Why, then—then, indeed," respectfully retreating, "I fall back upon my previous theory of your general facetiousness. I have the fortune to be in company with a humorist—a wag."

"Fall back you had better, and wag it is," cried the Missourian, following him up, and wagging his raccoon tail almost into the herb-doctor's face, "look you!"

"At what?"

"At this coon. Can you, the fox, catch him?"

"If you mean," returned the other, not unselfpossessed, "whether I flatter myself that I can in any way dupe you, or impose upon you, or pass myself off upon you for what I am not, I, as an honest man, answer that I have neither the inclination nor the power to do aught of the kind."

"Honest man? Seems to me you talk more like a craven."

"You in vain seek to pick a quarrel with me, or put any affront upon me. The innocence in me heals me."

"A healing like your own nostrums. But you are a queer man —a very queer and dubious man; upon the whole, about the most so I ever met."

The scrutiny accompanying this seemed unwelcome to the diffidence of the herb-doctor. As if at once to attest the absence of resentment, as well as to change the subject, he threw a kind of familiar cordiality into his air, and said: "So you are going to get some machine made to do your work? Philanthropic scruples, doubtless, forbid your going as far as New Orleans for slaves?"

"Slaves?" morose again in a twinkling, "won't have 'em! Bad enough to see whites ducking and grinning round for a favor, without having those poor devils of niggers congeeing round for their corn. Though, to me, the niggers are the freer of the two. You are an abolitionist, ain't you?" he added, squaring himself with both hands on his rifle, used for a staff, and gazing in the herb-doctor's face with no more reverence than if it were a target. "You are an abolitionist, ain't you?"

"As to that, I cannot so readily answer. If by abolitionist you mean a zealot, I am none; but if you mean a man, who, being a man, feels for all men, slaves included, and by any lawful act, opposed to nobody's interest, and therefore, rousing nobody's enmity, would willingly abolish suffering (supposing it, in its degree, to exist) from among mankind, irrespective of color, then am I what you say."

"Picked and prudent sentiments. You are the moderate man, the invaluable understrapper of the wicked man. You, the moderate man, may be used for wrong, but are useless for right."

"From all this," said the herb-doctor, still forgivingly, "I infer, that you, a Missourian, though living in a slave-state, are without slave sentiments."

"Aye, but are you? Is not that air of yours, so spiritlessly enduring and yielding, the very air of a slave? Who is your master, pray; or are you owned by a company?"

"*My* master?"

"Aye, for come from Maine or Georgia, you come from a slave-state, and a slave-pen, where the best breeds are to be bought up at any price from a livelihood to the Presidency. Abolitionism, ye gods, but expresses the fellow-feeling of slave for slave."

"The back-woods would seem to have given you rather eccentric notions," now with polite superiority smiled the herb-doctor, still with manly intrepidity forbearing each unmanly thrust, "but to return; since, for your purpose, you will have neither man nor boy, bond nor free, truly, then some sort of machine for you is all there is left. My desires for your success attend you, sir.—Ah!" glancing shoreward, "here is Cape Giradeau; I must leave you."

CHAPTER XXII

IN THE POLITE SPIRIT OF THE TUSCULAN DISPUTATIONS

—" 'PHILOSOPHICAL INTELLIGENCE OFFICE'—novel idea! But how did you come to dream that I wanted anything in your absurd line, eh?"

About twenty minutes after leaving Cape Giradeau, the above was growled out over his shoulder by the Missourian to a chance stranger who had just accosted him; a round-backed, baker-kneed man, in a mean five-dollar suit, wearing, collar-wise by a chain, a small brass plate, inscribed P. I. O., and who, with a sort of canine deprecation, slunk obliquely behind.

"How did you come to dream that I wanted anything in your line, eh?"

"Oh, respected sir," whined the other, crouching a pace nearer, and, in his obsequiousness, seeming to wag his very coat-tails behind him, shabby though they were, "oh, sir, from long experience, one glance tells me the gentleman who is in need of our humble services."

"But suppose I did want a boy—what they jocosely call a good boy—how could your absurd office help me?—Philosophical Intelligence Office?"

"Yes, respected sir, an office founded on strictly philosophical and physio—"

"Look you—come up here—how, by philosophy or physiology either, make good boys to order? Come up here. Don't give me a crick in the neck. Come up here, come, sir, come," calling as if to his pointer. "Tell me, how put the requisite assortment of good qualities into a boy, as the assorted mince into the pie?"

"Respected sir, our office—"

"You talk much of that office. Where is it? On board this boat?"

"Oh no, sir, I just came aboard. Our office—"

"Came aboard at that last landing, eh? Pray, do you know a herb-doctor there? Smooth scamp in a snuff-colored surtout?"

"Oh, sir, I was but a sojourner at Cape Giradeau. Though, now that you mention a snuff-colored surtout, I think I met such a man as you speak of stepping ashore as I stepped aboard, and 'pears to me I have seen him somewhere before. Looks like a very mild Christian sort of person, I should say. Do you know him, respected sir?"

"Not much, but better than you seem to. Proceed with your business."

With a low, shabby bow, as grateful for the permission, the other began: "Our office—"

"Look you," broke in the bachelor with ire, "have you the spinal complaint? What are you ducking and groveling about? Keep still. Where's your office?"

"The branch one which I represent, is at Alton, sir, in the free state we now pass," (pointing somewhat proudly ashore).

"Free, eh? You a freeman, you flatter yourself? With those coat-tails and that spinal complaint of servility? Free? Just cast up in your private mind who is your master, will you?"

"Oh, oh, oh! I don't understand—indeed—indeed. But, respected sir, as before said, our office, founded on principles wholly new—"

"To the devil with your principles! Bad sign when a man begins to talk of his principles. Hold, come back, sir; back here, back, sir, back! I tell you no more boys for me. Nay, I'm a Mede and Persian. In my old home in the woods I'm pestered enough with squirrels, weasels, chipmunks, skunks. I want no more wild vermin to spoil my temper and waste my substance. Don't talk of boys; enough of your boys; a plague of your boys; chilblains on your boys! As for Intelligence Offices, I've lived in the East, and know 'em. Swindling concerns kept by low-born cynics, under a fawning exterior wreaking their cynic malice upon mankind. You are a fair specimen of 'em."

"Oh dear, dear, dear!"

"Dear? Yes, a thrice dear purchase one of your boys would be to me. A rot on your boys!"

"But, respected sir, if you will not have boys, might we not, in our small way, accommodate you with a man?"

"Accommodate? Pray, no doubt you could accommodate me with a bosom-friend too, couldn't you? Accommodate! Obliging word accommodate: there's accommodation notes now, where one accommodates another with a loan, and if he don't pay it pretty quickly, accommodates him with a chain to his foot. Accommodate! God forbid that I should ever be accommodated. No, no. Look you, as I told that cousin-german of yours, the herb-doctor, I'm now on the road to get me made some sort of machine to do my work. Machines for me. My cider-mill—does that ever steal my cider? My mowing-machine—does that ever lay a-bed mornings? My corn-husker—does that ever give me insolence? No: cider-mill, mowing-machine, corn-husker—all faithfully attend to their business. Disinterested, too; no board, no wages; yet doing good all their lives long; shining examples that virtue is its own reward—the only practical Christians I know."

"Oh dear, dear, dear, dear!"

"Yes, sir:—boys? Start my soul-bolts, what a difference, in a moral point of view, between a corn-husker and a boy! Sir, a corn-husker, for its patient continuance in well-doing, might not unfitly go to heaven. Do you suppose a boy will?"

"A corn-husker in heaven! (turning up the whites of his eyes). Respected sir, this way of talking as if heaven were a kind of Washington patent-office museum—oh, oh, oh!—as if mere machine-work and puppet-work went to heaven—oh, oh, oh! Things incapable of free agency, to receive the eternal reward of well-doing—oh, oh, oh!"

"You Praise-God-Barebones you, what are you groaning about? Did I say anything of that sort? Seems to me, though you talk so good, you are mighty quick at a hint the other way, or else you want to pick a polemic quarrel with me."

"It may be so or not, respected sir," was now the demure reply; "but if it be, it is only because as a soldier out of honor is quick in taking affront, so a Christian out of religion is quick, sometimes perhaps a little too much so, in spying heresy."

"Well," after an astonished pause, "for an unaccountable pair, you and the herb-doctor ought to yoke together."

So saying, the bachelor was eyeing him rather sharply, when he with the brass plate recalled him to the discussion by a hint, not unflattering, that he (the man with the brass plate) was all anxiety to hear him further on the subject of servants.

"About that matter," exclaimed the impulsive bachelor, going off at the hint like a rocket, "all thinking minds are, now-a-days, coming to the conclusion—one derived from an immense hereditary experience—see what Horace and others of the ancients say of servants—coming to the conclusion, I say, that boy or man, the human animal is, for most work-purposes, a losing animal. Can't be trusted; less trustworthy than oxen; for conscientiousness a turn-spit dog excels him. Hence these thousand new inventions—carding machines, horse-shoe machines, tunnel-boring machines, reaping machines, apple-paring machines, boot-blacking machines, sewing machines, shaving machines, run-of-errand machines, dumb-waiter machines, and the Lord-only-knows-what machines; all of which announce the era when that refractory animal, the working or serving man, shall be a buried by-gone, a superseded fossil. Shortly prior to which glorious time, I doubt not that a price will be put upon their peltries as upon the knavish 'possums,' especially the boys. Yes, sir (ringing his rifle down on the deck), I rejoice to think that the day is at hand, when, prompted to it by law, I shall shoulder this gun and go out a boy-shooting."

"Oh, now! Lord, Lord, Lord!—But *our* office, respected sir, conducted as I ventured to observe—"

"No, sir," bristlingly settling his stubble chin in his coon-skins. "Don't try to oil me; the herb-doctor tried that. My experience, carried now through a course—worse than salivation—a course of five and thirty boys, proves to me that boyhood is a natural state of rascality."

"Save us, save us!"

"Yes, sir, yes. My name is Pitch; I stick to what I say. I speak from fifteen years' experience; five and thirty boys; American, Irish, English, German, African, Mulatto; not to speak of that China boy sent me by one who well knew my perplexities, from California; and that Lascar boy from Bombay. Thug! I found him sucking the embryo life from my spring eggs. All rascals, sir, every soul of them; Caucasian or Mongol. Amazing the endless variety of rascality in human nature of the juvenile sort. I remember that, having discharged, one after another, twenty-nine boys—each, too, for some wholly unforeseen species of viciousness peculiar to that one peculiar boy—I remember saying to myself: Now, then, surely, I have got to the end of the list, wholly exhausted it; I have only now to get me a boy, any boy different from those twenty-nine preceding boys, and he infallibly shall be that virtuous boy I have so long been seeking. But, bless me! this thirtieth boy—by the way, having at the time long forsworn your intelligence offices, I had him sent to me from the Commissioners of Emigration, all the way from New York, culled out carefully, in fine, at my particular request, from a standing army of eight hundred boys, the flowers of all nations, so they wrote me, temporarily in barracks on an East River island—I say, this thirtieth boy was in person not ungraceful; his deceased mother a lady's maid, or something of that sort; and in manner, why, in a plebeian way, a perfect Chesterfield; very intelligent, too—quick as a flash. But, such suavity; 'Please sir! please sir!' always bowing and saying, 'Please sir.' In the strangest way, too, combining a filial affection with a menial respect. Took such warm, singular interest in my affairs. Wanted to be considered one of the family—sort of adopted son of mine, I suppose. Of a morning, when I would go out to my stable, with what childlike good nature he would trot out my nag, 'Please sir, I think he's getting fatter and fatter.' 'But, he don't look very clean, does he?' unwilling to be downright harsh with so affectionate a lad; 'and he seems a little hollow inside the haunch there, don't he? or no, perhaps I don't see plain this morning.' 'Oh, please sir, it's just there I think he's gaining so, please.' Polite scamp! I soon found he never gave that wretched nag his oats of nights; didn't bed him either. Was above that sort of chambermaid work. No end to his willful neglects. But the more he abused my service, the more polite he grew."

"Oh, sir, some way you mistook him."

"Not a bit of it. Besides, sir, he was a boy who under a Chesterfieldian exterior hid strong destructive propensities. He cut up my horse-blanket for the bits of leather, for hinges to his chest. Denied it point-blank. After he was gone, found the shreds under his mattress. Would slyly break his hoe-handle, too, on purpose to get rid of hoeing. Then be so gracefully penitent for his fatal excess of industrious strength. Offer to mend all by taking a nice stroll to the nighest settlement—cherry-trees in full bearing all the way—to get the broken thing cobbled. Very politely stole my pears, odd pennies, shillings, dollars, and nuts; regular squirrel at it. But I could prove nothing. Expressed to him my suspicions. Said I, moderately enough, 'A little less politeness, and a little more honesty would suit me better.' He fired up; threatened to sue for libel. I won't say anything about his afterwards, in Ohio, being found in the act of gracefully putting a bar across a rail-road track, for the reason that a stoker called him the rogue that he was. But enough: polite boys or saucy boys, white boys or black boys, smart boys or lazy boys, Caucasian boys or Mongol boys—all are rascals."

"Shocking, shocking!" nervously tucking his frayed cravat-end out of sight. "Surely, respected sir, you labor under a deplorable hallucination. Why, pardon again, you seem to have not the slightest confidence in boys. I admit, indeed, that boys, some of them at least, are but too prone to one little foolish foible or other. But, what then, respected sir, when, by natural laws, they finally outgrow such things, and wholly?"

Having until now vented himself mostly in plaintive dissent of canine whines and groans, the man with the brass-plate seemed beginning to summon courage to a less timid encounter. But, upon his maiden essay, was not very encouragingly handled, since the dialogue immediately continued as follows:

"Boys outgrow what is amiss in them? From bad boys spring good men? Sir, 'the child is father of the man;' hence, as all boys are rascals, so are all men. But, God bless me, you must know these things better than I; keeping an intelligence office as you do; a business which must furnish peculiar facilities for studying mankind. Come, come up here, sir; confess you know these things pretty well, after all. Do you not know that all men are rascals, and all boys, too?"

"Sir," replied the other, spite of his shocked feelings seeming to pluck up some spirit, but not to an indiscreet degree, "Sir, heaven be praised, I am far, very far from knowing what you say. True," he thoughtfully continued, "with my associates, I keep an intelligence office, and for ten years, come October, have, one way or other, been concerned in that line; for no small period in the great city of Cincinnati, too; and though, as you hint, within that long interval, I must have had more or less favorable opportunity for studying mankind—in a business way, scanning not only the faces, but ransacking the lives of several thousands of human beings, male and female, of various nations, both employers and employed, genteel and ungenteel, educated and uneducated; yet—of course, I candidly admit, with some random exceptions, I have, so far as my small observation goes, found that mankind thus domestically viewed, confidentially viewed, I may say; they, upon the whole—making some reasonable allowances for human imperfection—present as pure a moral spectacle as the purest angel could wish. I say it, respected sir, with confidence."

"Gammon! You don't mean what you say. Else you are like a landsman at sea: don't know the ropes, the very things everlastingly pulled before your eyes. Serpent-like, they glide about, traveling blocks too subtle for you. In short, the entire ship is a riddle. Why, you green ones wouldn't know if she were unseaworthy; but still, with thumbs stuck back into your arm-holes, pace the rotten planks, singing, like a fool, words put into your green mouth by the cunning owner, the man who, heavily insuring it, sends his ship to be wrecked—

'A wet sheet and a flowing sea!'—

and, sir, now that it occurs to me, your talk, the whole of it, is but a wet sheet and a flowing sea, and an idle wind that follows fast, offering a striking contrast to my own discourse."

"Sir," exclaimed the man with the brass-plate, his patience now more or less tasked, "permit me with deference to hint that some of your remarks are injudiciously worded. And thus we say to our patrons, when they enter our office full of abuse of us because of some worthy boy we may have sent them— some boy wholly misjudged for the time. Yes, sir, permit me to remark that you do not sufficiently consider that, though a small man, I may have my small share of feelings."

"Well, well, I didn't mean to wound your feelings at all. And that they are small, very small, I take your word for it. Sorry, sorry. But truth is like a thrashing-machine; tender sensibilities must keep out of the way. Hope you understand me. Don't want to hurt you. All I say is, what I said in the first place, only now I swear it, that all boys are rascals."

"Sir," lowly replied the other, still forbearing like an old lawyer badgered in court, or else like a good-hearted simpleton, the butt of mischievous wags, "Sir, since you come back to the point, will you allow me, in my small, quiet way, to submit to you certain small, quiet views of the subject in hand?"

"Oh, yes!" with insulting indifference, rubbing his chin and looking the other way. "Oh, yes; go on."

"Well, then, respected sir," continued the other, now assuming as genteel an attitude as the irritating set of his pinched five-dollar suit would permit; "well, then, sir, the peculiar principles, the strictly philosophical principles, I may say," guardedly rising in dignity, as he guardedly rose on his toes, "upon which our office is founded, has led me and my associates, in our small, quiet way, to a careful and analytical study of man, conducted, too, on a quiet theory, and with an unobtrusive aim wholly our own. That theory I will not now at large set forth. But some of the discoveries resulting from it, I will, by your permission, very briefly mention; such of them, I mean, as refer to the state of boyhood scientifically viewed."

"Then you have studied the thing? expressly studied boys, eh? Why didn't you out with that before?"

"Sir, in my small business way, I have not conversed with so many masters, gentlemen masters, for nothing. I have been taught that in this world there is a precedence of opinions as well as of persons. You have kindly given me your views, I am now, with modesty, about to give you mine."

"Stop flunkying—go on."

"In the first place, sir, our theory teaches us to proceed by analogy from the physical to the moral. Are we right there, sir? Now, sir, take a young boy, a young male infant rather, a man-child in short—what sir, I respectfully ask, do you in the first place remark?"

"A rascal, sir! present and prospective, a rascal!"

"Sir, if passion is to invade, surely science must evacuate. May I proceed? Well, then, what, in the first place, in a general view, do you remark, respected sir, in that male baby or man-child?"

The bachelor privily growled, but this time, upon the whole, better governed himself than before, though not, indeed, to the degree of thinking it prudent to risk an articulate response.

"What do you remark? I respectfully repeat." But, as no answer came, only the low, half-suppressed growl, as of Bruin in a hollow trunk, the questioner continued: "Well, sir, if you will permit me, in my small way, to speak for you, you remark, respected sir, an incipient creation; loose sort of sketchy thing; a little preliminary rag-paper study, or careless cartoon, so to speak, of a man. The idea, you see, respected sir, is there; but, as yet, wants filling out. In a word, respected sir, the man-child is at present but little, every way; I don't pretend to deny it; but, then, he *promises* well, does he not? Yes, promises very well indeed, I may say. (So, too, we say to our patrons in reference to some noble little youngster objected to for being a *dwarf*.) But, to advance one step further," extending his thread-bare leg, as he drew a pace nearer, "we must now drop the figure of the rag-paper cartoon, and borrow one—to use presently, when wanted—from the horticultural kingdom. Some bud, lily-bud, if you please. Now, such points as the new-born man-child has—as yet not all that could be desired, I am free to confess—still, such as they are, there they are, and palpable as those of an adult. But we stop not here," taking another step. "The man-child not only possesses these present points, small though they are, but, likewise—now our horticultural image comes into play—like the bud of the lily, he contains concealed rudiments of others; that is, points at present invisible, with beauties at present dormant."

"Come, come, this talk is getting too horticultural and beautiful altogether. Cut it short, cut it short!"

"Respected sir," with a rustily martial sort of gesture, like a decayed corporal's, "when deploying into the field of discourse the vanguard of an important argument, much more in evolving the grand central forces of a new philosophy of boys, as I may say, surely you will kindly allow scope adequate to the movement in hand, small and humble in its way as that movement may be. Is it worth my while to go on, respected sir?"

"Yes, stop flunkying and go on."

Thus encouraged, again the philosopher with the brass-plate proceeded:

"Supposing, sir, that worthy gentleman (in such terms, to an applicant for service, we allude to some patron we chance to have in our eye), supposing, respected sir, that worthy gentleman, Adam, to have been dropped overnight in Eden, as a calf in the pasture; supposing that, sir—then how could even the learned serpent himself have foreknown that such a downy-chinned little innocent would eventually rival the goat in a beard? Sir, wise as the serpent was, that eventuality would have been entirely hidden from his wisdom."

"I don't know about that. The devil is very sagacious. To judge by the event, he appears to have understood man better even than the Being who made him."

"For God's sake, don't say that, sir! To the point. Can it now

with fairness be denied that, in his beard, the man-child prospectively possesses an appendix, not less imposing than patriar-
chal; and for this goodly beard, should we not by generous anticipation give the man-child, even in his cradle, credit? Should
we not now, sir? respectfully I put it."

"Yes, if like pig-weed he mows it down soon as it shoots,"
porcinely rubbing his stubble-chin against his coon-skins.

"I have hinted at the analogy," continued the other, calmly
disregardful of the digression; "now to apply it. Suppose a boy
evince no noble quality. Then generously give him credit for
his prospective one. Don't you see? So we say to our patrons
when they would fain return a boy upon us as unworthy:
'Madam, or sir, (as the case may be) has this boy a beard?'
'No.' 'Has he, we respectfully ask, as yet, evinced any noble
quality?' 'No, indeed.' 'Then, madam, or sir, take him back, we
humbly beseech; and keep him till that same noble quality
sprouts; for, have confidence, it, like the beard, is in him.'"

"Very fine theory," scornfully exclaimed the bachelor, yet in
secret, perhaps, not entirely undisturbed by these strange new
views of the matter; "but what trust is to be placed in it?"

"The trust of perfect confidence, sir. To proceed. Once more,
if you please, regard the man-child."

"Hold!" paw-like thrusting out his bearskin arm, "don't intrude that man-child upon me too often. He who loves not
bread, dotes not on dough. As little of your man-child as your
logical arrangements will admit."

"Anew regard the man-child," with inspired intrepidity repeated he with the brass-plate, "in the perspective of his developments, I mean. At first the man-child has no teeth, but
about the sixth month—am I right, sir?"

"Don't know anything about it."

"To proceed then: though at first deficient in teeth, about
the sixth month the man-child begins to put forth in that particular. And sweet those tender little puttings-forth are."

"Very, but blown out of his mouth directly, worthless
enough."

"Admitted. And, therefore, we say to our patrons returning

with a boy alleged not only to be deficient in goodness, but redundant in ill: 'The lad, madam or sir, evinces very corrupt qualities, does he?' 'No end to them.' 'But, have confidence, there will be; for pray, madam, in this lad's early childhood, were not those frail first teeth, then his, followed by his present sound, even, beautiful and permanent set. And the more objectionable those first teeth became, was not that, madam, we respectfully submit, so much the more reason to look for their speedy substitution by the present sound, even, beautiful and permanent ones.' 'True, true, can't deny that.' 'Then, madam, take him back, we respectfully beg, and wait till, in the now swift course of nature, dropping those transient moral blemishes you complain of, he replacingly buds forth in the sound, even, beautiful and permanent virtues.' "

"Very philosophical again," was the contemptuous reply—the outward contempt, perhaps, proportioned to the inward misgiving. "Vastly philosophical, indeed, but tell me—to continue your analogy—since the second teeth followed—in fact, came from—the first, is there no chance the blemish may be transmitted?"

"Not at all." Abating in humility as he gained in the argument. "The second teeth follow, but do not come from, the first; successors, not sons. The first teeth are not like the germ blossom of the apple, at once the father of, and incorporated into, the growth it foreruns; but they are thrust from their place by the independent undergrowth of the succeeding set—an illustration, by the way, which shows more for me than I meant, though not more than I wish."

"What does it show?" Surly-looking as a thunder-cloud with the inkept unrest of unacknowledged conviction.

"It shows this, respected sir, that in the case of any boy, especially an ill one, to apply unconditionally the saying, that the 'child is father of the man', is, besides implying an uncharitable aspersion of the race, affirming a thing very wide of—"

"—Your analogy," like a snapping turtle.

"Yes, respected sir."

"But is analogy argument? You are a punster."

"Punster, respected sir?" with a look of being aggrieved.

"Yes, you pun with ideas as another man may with words."

"Oh well, sir, whoever talks in that strain, whoever has no confidence in human reason, whoever despises human reason, in vain to reason with him. Still, respected sir," altering his air, "permit me to hint that, had not the force of analogy moved you somewhat, you would hardly have offered to contemn it."

"Talk away," disdainfully; "but pray tell me what has that last analogy of yours to do with your intelligence office business?"

"Everything to do with it, respected sir. From that analogy we derive the reply made to such a patron as, shortly after being supplied by us with an adult servant, proposes to return him upon our hands; not that, while with the patron, said adult has given any cause of dissatisfaction, but the patron has just chanced to hear something unfavorable concerning him from some gentleman who employed said adult long before, while a boy. To which too fastidious patron, we, taking said adult by the hand, and graciously reintroducing him to the patron, say: 'Far be it from you, madam, or sir, to proceed in your censure against this adult, in anything of the spirit of an ex-postfacto law. Madam, or sir, would you visit upon the butterfly the sins of the caterpillar? In the natural advance of all creatures, do they not bury themselves over and over again in the endless resurrection of better and better? Madam, or sir, take back this adult; he may have been a caterpillar, but is now a butterfly."

"Pun away; but even accepting your analogical pun, what does it amount to? Was the caterpillar one creature, and is the butterfly another? The butterfly is the caterpillar in a gaudy cloak; stripped of which, there lies the impostor's long spindle of a body, pretty much worm-shaped as before."

"You reject the analogy. To the facts then. You deny that a youth of one character can be tranformed into a man of an opposite character. Now then—yes, I have it. There's the founder of La Trappe, and Ignatius Loyola; in boyhood, and someway into manhood, both devil-may-care bloods, and yet, in the end, the wonders of the world for anchoritish self-command. These two examples, by-the-way, we cite to such patrons as would hastily return rakish young waiters upon us. 'Madam, or sir—patience; patience,' we say; 'good madam, or sir, would you discharge forth your cask of good wine, because, while working, it riles more or less? Then discharge not forth this young waiter; the good in him is working.' 'But he is a sad rake.' 'Therein is his promise; the rake being crude material for the saint.'"

"Ah, you are a talking man—what I call a wordy man. You talk, talk."

"And with submission, sir, what is the greatest judge, bishop or prophet, but a talking man? He talks, talks. It is the peculiar vocation of a teacher to talk. What's wisdom itself but table-talk? The best wisdom in this world, and the last spoken by its teacher, did it not literally and truly come in the form of table-talk?"

"You, you you!" rattling down his rifle.

"To shift the subject, since we cannot agree. Pray, what is your opinion, respected sir, of St. Augustine?"

"St. Augustine? What should I, or you either, know of him? Seems to me, for one in such a business, to say nothing of such a coat, that though you don't know a great deal, indeed, yet you know a good deal more than you ought to know, or than you have a right to know, or than it is safe or expedient for you to know, or than, in the fair course of life, you could have honestly come to know. I am of opinion you should be served like a Jew in the middle ages with his gold; this knowledge of yours, which you haven't enough knowledge to know how to make a right use of, it should be taken from you. And so I have been thinking all along."

"You are merry, sir. But you have a little looked into St. Augustine I suppose."

"St. Augustine on Original Sin is my text book. But you, I ask again, where do you find time or inclination for these out-of-the-way speculations? In fact, your whole talk, the more I think of it, is altogether unexampled and extraordinary."

"Respected sir, have I not already informed you that the

quite new method, the strictly philosophical one, on which our
office is founded, has led me and my associates to an enlarged
study of mankind. It was my fault, if I did not, likewise, hint,
that these studies directed always to the scientific procuring of
good servants of all sorts, boys included, for the kind gentlemen, our patrons—that these studies, I say, have been conducted equally among all books of all libraries, as among all
men of all nations. Then, you rather like St. Augustine, sir?"

"Excellent genius!"

"In some points he was; yet, how comes it that under his own
hand, St. Augustine confesses that, until his thirtieth year, he
was a very sad dog?"

"A saint a sad dog?"

"Not the saint, but the saint's irresponsible little forerunner—
the boy."

"All boys are rascals, and so are all men," again flying off at
his tangent; "my name is Pitch; I stick to what I say."

"Ah, sir, permit me—when I behold you on this mild summer's eve, thus eccentrically clothed in the skins of wild beasts,
I cannot but conclude that the equally grim and unsuitable
habit of your mind is likewise but an eccentric assumption,
having no basis in your genuine soul, no more than in nature
herself."

"Well, really, now—really," fidgeted the bachelor, not unaffected in his conscience by these benign personalities, "really,
really, now, I don't know but that I may have been a little bit
too hard upon those five and thirty boys of mine."

"Glad to find you a little softening, sir. Who knows now, but
that flexile gracefulness, however questionable at the time of
that thirtieth boy of yours, might have been the silky husk
of the most solid qualities of maturity. It might have been with
him as with the ear of the Indian corn."

"Yes, yes, yes," excitedly cried the bachelor, as the light of
this new illustration broke in, "yes, yes; and now that I think
of it, how often I've sadly watched my Indian corn in May,
wondering whether such sickly, half-eaten sprouts, could ever
thrive up into the stiff, stately spear of August."

"A most admirable reflection, sir, and you have only, according to the analogical theory first started by our office, to apply it to that thirtieth boy in question, and see the result. Had you but kept that thirtieth boy—been patient with his sickly virtues, cultivated them, hoed round them, why what a glorious guerdon would have been yours, when at last you should have had a St. Augustine for an ostler."

"Really, really—well, I am glad I didn't send him to jail, as at first I intended."

"Oh that would have been too bad. Grant he was vicious. The petty vices of boys are like the innocent kicks of colts, as yet imperfectly broken. Some boys know not virtue only for the same reason they know not French; it was never taught them. Established upon the basis of parental charity, juvenile asylums exist by law for the benefit of lads convicted of acts which, in adults, would have received other requital. Why? Because, do what they will, society, like our office, at bottom has a Christian confidence in boys. And all this we say to our patrons."

"Your patrons, sir, seem your marines to whom you may say anything," said the other, relapsing. "Why do knowing employers shun youths from asylums, though offered them at the smallest wages? I'll none of your reformado boys."

"Such a boy, respected sir, I would not get for you, but a boy that never needed reform. Do not smile, for as whooping-cough and measles are juvenile diseases, and yet some juveniles never have them, so are there boys equally free from juvenile vices. True, for the best of boys, measles may be contagious, and evil communications corrupt good manners; but a boy with a sound mind in a sound body—such is the boy I would get you. If hitherto, sir, you have struck upon a peculiarly bad vein of boys, so much the more hope now of your hitting a good one."

"That sounds a kind of reasonable, as it were—a little so, really. In fact, though you have said a great many foolish things, very foolish and absurd things, yet, upon the whole, your conversation has been such as might almost lead one less distrustful than I to repose a certain conditional confidence in you, I had almost added in your office, also. Now, for the humor of it, supposing that even I, I myself, really had this sort of conditional confidence, though but a grain, what sort of a boy, in sober fact, could you send me? And what would be your fee?"

"Conducted," replied the other somewhat loftily, rising now in eloquence as his proselyte, for all his pretenses, sunk in conviction, "conducted upon principles involving care, learning, and labor, exceeding what is usual in kindred institutions, the Philosophical Intelligence Office is forced to charges somewhat higher than customary. Briefly, our fee is three dollars in advance. As for the boy, by a lucky chance, I have a very promising little fellow now in my eye—a very likely little fellow, indeed."

"Honest?"

"As the day is long. Might trust him with untold millions. Such, at least, were the marginal observations on the phrenological chart of his head, submitted to me by the mother."

"How old?"

"Just fifteen."

"Tall? Stout?"

"Uncommonly so, for his age, his mother remarked."

"Industrious?"

"The busy bee."

The bachelor fell into a troubled reverie. At last, with much hesitancy, he spoke:

"Do you think now, candidly, that—I say candidly—candidly —could I have some small, limited—some faint, conditional degree of confidence in that boy? Candidly, now?"

"Candidly, you could."

"A sound boy? A good boy?"

"Never knew one more so."

The bachelor fell into another irresolute reverie; then said: "Well, now, you have suggested some rather new views of boys, and men, too. Upon those views in the concrete I at present decline to determine. Nevertheless, for the sake purely of a scientific experiment, I will try that boy. I don't think him an angel, mind. No, no. But I'll try him. There are my three dollars, and here is my address. Send him along this day two weeks. Hold, you will be wanting the money for his passage. There," handing it somewhat reluctantly.

"Ah, thank you. I had forgotten his passage;" then, altering in manner, and gravely holding the bills, continued: "Respected sir, never willingly do I handle money not with perfect willingness, nay, with a certain alacrity, paid. Either tell me that you have a perfect and unquestioning confidence in me (never mind the boy now) or permit me respectfully to return these bills."

"Put 'em up, put 'em up!"

"Thank you. Confidence is the indispensable basis of all sorts of business transactions. Without it, commerce between man and man, is between country and country, would, like a watch, run down and stop. And now, supposing that against present expectation the lad should, after all, evince some little undesirable trait, do not, respected sir, rashly dismiss him. Have but patience, have but confidence. Those transient vices will, ere long, fall out, and be replaced by the sound, firm, even and permanent virtues. Ah," glancing shoreward, towards a grotesquely-shaped bluff, "there's the Devil's Joke, as they call it; the bell for landing will shortly ring. I must go look up the cook I brought for the inn-keeper at Cairo."

CHAPTER XXIII

IN WHICH THE POWERFUL EFFECT OF NATURAL SCENERY IS EVINCED
IN THE CASE OF THE MISSOURIAN, WHO, IN VIEW OF THE REGION
ROUNDABOUT CAIRO, HAS A RETURN OF HIS CHILLY FIT

AT Cairo, the old established firm of Fever & Ague is still
settling up its unfinished business; that Creole grave-digger,
Yellow Jack—his hand at the mattock and spade has not lost
its cunning; while Don Saturninus Typhus taking his constitutional with Death, Calvin Edson and three undertakers, in the
morass, snuffs up the mephitic breeze with zest.

In the dank twilight, fanned with mosquitoes, and sparkling
with fire-flies, the boat now lies before Cairo. She has landed
certain passengers, and tarries for the coming of expected ones.
Leaning over the rail on the inshore side, the Missourian eyes
through the dubious medium that swampy and squalid domain;
and over it audibly mumbles his cynical mind to himself, as
Apemantus' dog may have mumbled his bone. He bethinks
him that the man with the brass-plate was to land on this vil-
lainous bank, and for that cause, if no other, begins to suspect
him. Like one beginning to rouse himself from a dose of chloro-
form treacherously given, he half divines, too, that he, the
philosopher, had unwittingly been betrayed into being an unphilosophical dupe. To what vicissitudes of light and shade is
man subject! He ponders the mystery of human subjectivity
in general. He thinks he perceives with Crossbones, his favorite author, that, as one may wake up well in the morning, very
well, indeed, and brisk as a buck, I thank you, but ere bed-time
get under the weather, there is no telling how—so one may
wake up wise, and slow of assent, very wise and very slow, I assure you, and for all that, before night, by like trick in the at-

147

mosphere, be left in the lurch a ninny. Health and wisdom equally precious, and equally little as unfluctuating possessions to be relied on.

But where was slipped in the entering wedge? Philosophy, knowledge, experience—were those trusty knights of the castle recreant? No, but unbeknown to them, the enemy stole on the castle's south side, its genial one, where Suspicion, the warder, parleyed. In fine, his too indulgent, too artless and companionable nature betrayed him. Admonished by which, he thinks he must be a little splenetic in his intercourse henceforth.

He revolves the crafty process of sociable chat, by which, as he fancies, the man with the brass-plate wormed into him, and made such a fool of him as insensibly to persuade him to waive, in his exceptional case, that general law of distrust systematically applied to the race. He revolves, but cannot comprehend, the operation, still less the operator. Was the man a trickster, it must be more for the love than the lucre. Two or three dirty dollars the motive to so many nice wiles? And yet how full of mean needs his seeming. Before his mental vision the person of that threadbare Talleyrand, that impoverished Machiavelli, that seedy Rosicrucian—for something of all these he vaguely deems him—passes now in puzzled review. Fain, in his disfavor, would he make out a logical case. The doctrine of analogies recurs. Fallacious enough doctrine when wielded against one's prejudices, but in corroboration of cherished suspicions not without likelihood. Analogically, he couples the slanting cut of the equivocator's coat-tails with the sinister cast in his eye; he weighs slyboot's sleek speech in the light imparted by the oblique import of the smooth slope of his worn boot-heels; the insinuator's undulating flunkyisms dovetail into those of the flunky beast that windeth his way on his belly.

From these uncordial reveries he is roused by a cordial slap on the shoulder, accompanied by a spicy volume of tobacco-smoke, out of which came a voice, sweet as a seraph's:

"A penny for your thoughts, my fine fellow."

CHAPTER XXIV

"Hands off!" cried the bachelor, involuntarily covering dejection with moroseness.

"Hands off? that sort of label won't do in our Fair. Whoever in our Fair has fine feelings loves to feel the nap of fine cloth, especially when a fine fellow wears it."

"And who of my fine-fellow species may you be? From the Brazils, ain't you? Toucan fowl. Fine feathers on foul meat."

This ungentle mention of the toucan was not improbably suggested by the parti-hued, and rather plumagy aspect of the stranger, no bigot it would seem, but a liberalist, in dress, and whose wardrobe, almost anywhere than on the liberal Mississippi, used to all sorts of fantastic informalities, might, even to observers less critical than the bachelor, have looked, if anything, a little out of the common; but not more so perhaps, than, considering the bear and raccoon costume, the bachelor's own appearance. In short, the stranger sported a vesture barred with various hues, that of the cochineal predominating, in style participating of a Highland plaid, Emir's robe, and French blouse; from its plaited sort of front peeped glimpses of a flowered regatta-shirt, while, for the rest, white trowsers of ample duck flowed over maroon-colored slippers, and a jaunty smoking-cap of regal purple crowned him off at top; king of traveled good-fellows, evidently. Grotesque as all was, nothing looked stiff or unused; all showed signs of easy service, the least wonted thing setting like a wonted glove. That genial hand, which had just been laid on the ungenial shoulder, was now carelessly thrust down before him, sailor-fashion, into a sort of Indian belt, confining the redundant vesture; the other held, by its long bright cherry-stem, a Nuremburgh pipe in blast, its great porcelain bowl painted in miniature with linked crests and arms of interlinked nations—a florid show. As by subtle saturations of its mellowing essence the tobacco had ripened the bowl, so it looked as if something similar of the interior spirit came rosily out on the cheek. But rosy pipe-bowl, or rosy countenance, all was lost on that unrosy man, the bachelor, who, waiting a moment till the commotion, caused by the boat's renewed progress, had a little abated, thus continued:

"Hark ye," jeeringly eyeing the cap and belt, "did you ever see Signor Marzetti in the African pantomime?"

"No;—good performer?"

"Excellent; plays the intelligent ape till he seems it. With such naturalness can a being endowed with an immortal spirit enter into that of a monkey. But where's your tail? In the pantomime, Marzetti, no hypocrite in his monkery, prides himself on that."

The stranger, now at rest, sideways and genially, on one hip, his right leg cavalierly crossed before the other, the toe of his vertical slipper pointed easily down on the deck, whiffed out a long, leisurely sort of indifferent and charitable puff, betokening him more or less the mature man of the world, a character which, like its opposite, the sincere Christian's, is not always swift to take offense; and then, drawing near, still smoking, again laid his hand, this time with mild impressiveness, on the ursine shoulder, and not unamiably said: "That in your address there is a sufficiency of the *fortiter in re* few unbiased observers will question; but that this is duly attempered with the *suaviter in modo* may admit, I think, of an honest doubt. My dear fellow," beaming his eyes full upon him, "what injury have I done you, that you should receive my greeting with a curtailed civility?"

"Off hands;" once more shaking the friendly member from him. "Who in the name of the great chimpanzee, in whose likeness, you, Marzetti, and the other chatterers are made, who in thunder are you?"

"A cosmopolitan, a catholic man; who, being such, ties himself to no narrow tailor or teacher, but federates, in heart as in costume, something of the various gallantries of men under various suns. Oh, one roams not over the gallant globe in vain. Bred by it, is a fraternal and fusing feeling. No man is a stranger. You accost anybody. Warm and confiding, you wait not for measured advances. And though, indeed, mine, in this instance, have met with no very hilarious encouragement, yet the principle of a true citizen of the world is still to return good for ill.—My dear fellow, tell me how I can serve you."

"By dispatching yourself, Mr. Popinjay-of-the-world, into the heart of the Lunar Mountains. You are another of them. Out of my sight!"

"Is the sight of humanity so very disagreeable to you then? Ah, I may be foolish, but for my part, in all its aspects, I love it. Served up à la Pole, or à la Moor, à la Ladrone, or à la Yankee, that good dish, man, still delights me; or rather is man a wine I never weary of comparing and sipping; wherefore am I a pledged cosmopolitan, a sort of London-Dock-Vault connoisseur, going about from Teheran to Natchitoches, a taster of races; in all his vintages, smacking my lips over this racy creature, man, continually. But as there are teetotal palates which have a distaste even for Amontillado, so I suppose there may be teetotal souls which relish not even the very best brands of humanity. Excuse me, but it just occurs to me that you, my dear fellow, possibly lead a solitary life."

"Solitary?" starting as at a touch of divination.

"Yes: in a solitary life one insensibly contracts oddities,— talking to one's self now."

"Been eaves-dropping, eh?"

"Why, a soliloquist in a crowd can hardly but be overheard, and without much reproach to the hearer."

"You are an eaves-dropper."

"Well. Be it so."

"Confess yourself an eaves-dropper?"

"I confess that when you were muttering here I, passing by, caught a word or two, and, by like chance, something previous of your chat with the Intelligence-office man;—a rather sensible fellow, by the way; much of my style of thinking; would, for his own sake, he were of my style of dress. Grief to good minds, to see a man of superior sense forced to hide his light under the bushel of an inferior coat.—Well, from what little I heard, I said to myself, Here now is one with the unprofitable philosophy of disesteem for man. Which disease, in the main, I have observed—excuse me—to spring from a certain lowness, if not sourness, of spirits inseparable from sequestration. Trust me, one had better mix in, and do like others. Sad business, this holding out against having a good time. Life is a pic-nic *en costume;* one must take a part, assume a character, stand ready in a sensible way to play the fool. To come in plain clothes, with a long face, as a wiseacre, only makes one a discomfort to himself, and a blot upon the scene. Like your jug of cold water among the wine-flasks, it leaves you unelated among the elated ones. No, no. This austerity won't do. Let me tell you too—*en confidance*—that while revelry may not always merge into ebriety, soberness, in too deep potations, may become a sort of sottishness. Which sober sottishness, in my way of thinking, is only to be cured by beginning at the other end of the horn, to tipple a little."

"Pray, what society of vintners and old topers are you hired to lecture for?"

"I fear I did not give my meaning clearly. A little story may help. The story of the worthy old woman of Goshen, a very moral old woman, who wouldn't let her shoats eat fattening apples in fall, for fear the fruit might ferment upon their brains, and so make them swinish. Now, during a green Christmas, inauspicious to the old, this worthy old woman fell into a moping decline, took to her bed, no appetite, and refused to see her best friends. In much concern her good man sent for the doctor, who, after seeing the patient and putting a question or two, beckoned the husband out, and said: 'Deacon, do you want her cured?' 'Indeed I do.' 'Go directly, then, and buy a jug of Santa Cruz.' 'Santa Cruz? my wife drink Santa Cruz?' 'Either that or die.' 'But how much?' 'As much as she can get down.' 'But

she'll get drunk!' 'That's the cure.' Wise men, like doctors, must
be obeyed. Much against the grain, the sober deacon got the
unsober medicine, and, equally against her conscience, the
poor old woman took it; but, by so doing, ere long recovered
health and spirits, famous appetite, and glad again to see her
friends; and having by this experience broken the ice of arid
abstinence, never afterwards kept herself a cup too low."

This story had the effect of surprising the bachelor into interest, though hardly into approval.

"If I take your parable right," said he, sinking no little of his
former churlishness, "the meaning is, that one cannot enjoy life
with gusto unless he renounce the too-sober view of life. But
since the too-sober view is, doubtless, nearer true than the too-
drunken; I, who rate truth, though cold water, above untruth,
though Tokay, will stick to my earthen jug."

"I see," slowly spirting upward a spiral staircase of lazy
smoke, "I see; you go in for the lofty."

"How?"

"Oh, nothing! but if I wasn't afraid of prosing, I might tell
another story about an old boot in a pieman's loft, contracting
there between sun and oven an unseemly, dry-seasoned curl
and warp. You've seen such leathery old garretteers, haven't
you? Very high, sober, solitary, philosophic, grand, old boots,
indeed; but I, for my part, would rather be the pieman's trod-
den slipper on the ground. Talking of piemen, humble-pie before proud-cake for me. This notion of being lone and lofty is
a sad mistake. Men I hold in this respect to be like roosters; the
one that betakes himself to a lone and lofty perch is the hen-
pecked one, or the one that has the pip."

"You are abusive!" cried the bachelor, evidently touched.

"Who is abused? You, or the race? You won't stand by and
see the human race abused? Oh, then, you have some respect
for the human race."

"I have some respect for *myself*," with a lip not so firm as
before.

"And what race may *you* belong to? now don't you see, my
dear fellow, in what inconsistencies one involves himself by af-

fecting disesteem for men. To a charm, my little stratagem succeeded. Come, come, think better of it, and, as a first step to a new mind, give up solitude. I fear, by the way, you have at some time been reading Zimmermann, that old Mr. Megrims of a Zimmermann, whose book on Solitude is as vain as Hume's on Suicide, as Bacon's on Knowledge; and, like these, will betray him who seeks to steer soul and body by it, like a false religion. All they, be they what boasted ones you please, who, to the yearning of our kind after a founded rule of content, offer aught not in the spirit of fellowly gladness based on due confidence in what is above, away with them for poor dupes, or still poorer impostors."

His manner here was so earnest that scarcely any auditor, perhaps, but would have been more or less impressed by it, while, possibly, nervous opponents might have a little quailed under it. Thinking within himself a moment, the bachelor replied: "Had you experience, you would know that your tippling theory, take it in what sense you will, is poor as any other. And Rabelais's pro-wine Koran no more trustworthy than Mahomet's anti-wine one."

"Enough," for a finality knocking the ashes from his pipe, "we talk and keep talking, and still stand where we did. What do you say for a walk? My arm, and let's a turn. They are to have dancing on the hurricane-deck to-night. I shall fling them off a Scotch jig, while, to save the pieces, you hold my loose change; and following that, I propose that you, my dear fellow, stack your gun, and throw your bearskins in a sailor's hornpipe—I holding your watch. What do you say?"

At this proposition the other was himself again, all raccoon.

"Look you," thumping down his rifle, "are you Jeremy Diddler No. 3?"

"Jeremy Diddler? I have heard of Jeremy the prophet, and Jeremy Taylor the divine, but your other Jeremy is a gentleman I am unacquainted with."

"You are his confidential clerk, ain't you?"

"*Whose*, pray? Not that I think myself unworthy of being confided in, but I don't understand."

"You are another of them. Somehow I meet with the most extraordinary metaphysical scamps to-day. Sort of visitation of them. And yet that herb-doctor Diddler somehow takes off the raw edge of the Diddlers that come after him."

"Herb-doctor? who is he?"

"Like you—another of them."

"Who?" Then drawing near, as if for a good long explanatory chat, his left hand spread, and his pipe-stem coming crosswise down upon it like a ferule, "You think amiss of me. Now to undeceive you, I will just enter into a little argument and—"

"No you don't. No more little arguments for me. Had too many little arguments to-day."

"But put a case. Can you deny—I dare you to deny—that the man leading a solitary life is peculiarly exposed to the sorriest misconceptions touching strangers?"

"Yes, I *do* deny it," again, in his impulsiveness, snapping at the controversial bait, "and I will confute you there in a trice. Look, you—"

"Now, now, now, my dear fellow," thrusting out both vertical palms for double shields, "you crowd me too hard. You don't give one a chance. Say what you will, to shun a social proposition like mine, to shun society in any way, evinces a churlish nature—cold, loveless; as, to embrace it, shows one warm and friendly, in fact, sunshiny."

Here the other, all agog again, in his perverse way, launched forth into the unkindest references to deaf old worldlings keeping in the deafening world; and gouty gluttons limping to their gouty gormandizings; and corseted coquettes clasping their corseted cavaliers in the waltz, all for disinterested society's sake; and thousands, bankrupt through lavishness, ruining themselves out of pure love of the sweet company of man—no envies, rivalries, or other unhandsome motive to it.

"Ah, now," deprecating with his pipe, "irony is so unjust; never could abide irony; something Satanic about irony. God defend me from Irony, and Satire, his bosom friend."

"A right knave's prayer, and a right fool's, too," snapping his rifle-lock.

"Now be frank. Own that was a little gratuitous. But, no, no, you didn't mean it; any way, I can make allowances. Ah, did you but know it, how much pleasanter to puff at this philanthropic pipe, than still to keep fumbling at that misanthropic rifle. As for your worldling, glutton, and coquette, though, doubtless, being such, they may have their little foibles—as who has not?—yet not one of the three can be reproached with that awful sin of shunning society; awful I call it, for not seldom it presupposes a still darker thing than itself—remorse."

"Remorse drives man away from man? How came your fellow-creature, Cain, after the first murder, to go and build the first city? And why is it that the modern Cain dreads nothing so much as solitary confinement?"

"My dear fellow, you get excited. Say what you will, I for one must have my fellow-creatures round me. Thick, too—I must have them thick."

"The pick-pocket, too, loves to have his fellow-creatures round him. Tut, man! no one goes into the crowd but for his end; and the end of too many is the same as the pick-pocket's —a purse."

"Now, my dear fellow, how can you have the conscience to say that, when it is as much according to natural law that men are social as sheep gregarious. But grant that, in being social, each man has his end, do you, upon the strength of that, do you yourself, I say, mix with man, now, immediately, and be your end a more genial philosophy. Come, let's take a turn."

Again he offered his fraternal arm; but the bachelor once more flung it off, and, raising his rifle in energetic invocation, cried: "Now the high-constable catch and confound all knaves in towns and rats in grain-bins, and if in this boat, which is a human grain-bin for the time, any sly, smooth, philandering rat be dodging now, pin him, thou high rat-catcher, against this rail."

"A noble burst! shows you at heart a trump. And when a card's that, little matters it whether it be spade or diamond. You are good wine that, to be still better, only needs a shaking up. Come, let's agree that we'll to New Orleans, and there embark for London—I staying with my friends nigh Primrose-hill, and you putting up at the Piazza, Covent Garden—Piazza, Covent Garden; for tell me—since you will not be a disciple to the full—tell me, was not that humor, of Diogenes, which led him to live, a merry-andrew, in the flower-market, better than that of the less wise Athenian, which made him a skulking scare-crow in pine-barrens? An injudicious gentleman, Lord Timon."

"Your hand!" seizing it.

"Bless me, how cordial a squeeze. It is agreed we shall be brothers, then?"

"As much so as a brace of misanthropes can be," with another and terrific squeeze. "I had thought that the moderns had degenerated beneath the capacity of misanthropy. Rejoiced, though but in one instance, and that disguised, to be undeceived."

The other stared in blank amaze.

"Won't do. You are Diogenes, Diogenes in disguise. I say—Diogenes masquerading as a cosmopolitan."

With ruefully altered mien, the stranger still stood mute awhile. At length, in a pained tone, spoke: "How hard the lot of that pleader who, in his zeal conceding too much, is taken to belong to a side which he but labors, however ineffectually, to convert!" Then with another change of air: "To you, an Ishmael, disguising in sportiveness my intent, I came ambassador from the human race, charged with the assurance that for your mislike they bore no answering grudge, but sought to conciliate accord between you and them. Yet you take me not for the honest envoy, but I know not what sort of unheard-of spy. Sir," he less lowly added, "this mistaking of your man should teach you how you may mistake all men. For God's sake," laying both hands upon him, "get you confidence. See how distrust has duped you. I, Diogenes? I he who, going a step beyond misanthropy, was less a man-hater than a man-hooter? Better were I stark and stiff!"

With which the philanthropist moved away less lightsome than he had come, leaving the discomfited misanthrope to the solitude he held so sapient.

CHAPTER XXV

THE COSMOPOLITAN MAKES AN ACQUAINTANCE

In the act of retiring, the cosmopolitan was met by a passenger, who, with the bluff *abord* of the West, thus addressed him, though a stranger.

"Queer 'coon, your friend. Had a little skrimmage with him myself. Rather entertaining old 'coon, if he wasn't so deuced analytical. Reminded me somehow of what I've heard about Colonel John Moredock, of Illinois, only your friend ain't quite so good a fellow at bottom, I should think."

It was in the semicircular porch of a cabin, opening a recess from the deck, lit by a zoned lamp swung overhead, and sending its light vertically down, like the sun at noon. Beneath the lamp stood the speaker, affording to any one disposed to it no unfavorable chance for scrutiny; but the glance now resting on him betrayed no such rudeness.

A man neither tall nor stout, neither short nor gaunt; but with a body fitted, as by measure, to the service of his mind. For the rest, one less favored perhaps in his features than his clothes; and of these the beauty may have been less in the fit than the cut; to say nothing of the fineness of the nap, seeming out of the keeping with something the reverse of fine in the skin; and the unsuitableness of a violet vest, sending up sunset hues to a countenance betokening a kind of bilious habit.

But, upon the whole, it could not be fairly said that his appearance was unprepossessing; indeed, to the congenial, it would have been doubtless not uncongenial; while to others, it could not fail to be at least curiously interesting, from the warm air of florid cordiality, contrasting itself with one knows not what kind of aguish sallowness of saving discretion lurking behind it. Ungracious critics might have thought that the manner flushed the man, something in the same fictitious way that the vest flushed the cheek. And though his teeth were singularly good, those same ungracious ones might have hinted that they were too good to be true; or rather, were not so good as they might be; since the best false teeth are those made with at least two or three blemishes, the more to look like life. But fortunately for better constructions, no such critics had the stranger now in eye; only the cosmopolitan, who, after, in the first place, acknowledging his advances with a mute salute—in which acknowledgment, if there seemed less of spirit than in his way of accosting the Missourian, it was probably because of the saddening sequel of that late interview—thus now replied: "Colonel John Moredock," repeating the words abstractedly; "that surname recalls reminiscences. Pray," with enlivened air, "was he anyway connected with the Moredocks of Moredock Hall, Northamptonshire, England?"

"I know no more of the Moredocks of Moredock Hall than of the Burdocks of Burdock Hut," returned the other, with the air somehow of one whose fortunes had been of his own making; "all I know is, that the late Colonel John Moredock was a famous one in his time; eye like Lochiel's; finger like a trigger; nerve like a catamount's; and with but two little oddities—seldom stirred without his rifle, and hated Indians like snakes."

"Your Moredock, then, would seem a Moredock of Misanthrope Hall—the Woods. No very sleek creature, the colonel, I fancy."

"Sleek or not, he was no uncombed one, but silky bearded and curly headed, and to all but Indians juicy as a peach. But Indians—how the late Colonel John Moredock, Indian-hater of Illinios, did hate Indians, to be sure!"

"Never heard of such a thing. Hate Indians? Why should he or anybody else hate Indians? *I* admire Indians. Indians I have always heard to be one of the finest of the primitive races, possessed of many heroic virtues. Some noble women, too. When I think of Pocahontas, I am ready to love Indians. Then there's Massasoit, and Philip of Mount Hope, and Tecumseh, and Red-

Jacket, and Logan— all heroes; and there's the Five Nations, and Araucanians—federations and communities of heroes. God bless me; hate Indians? Surely the late Colonel John Moredock must have wandered in his mind."

"Wandered in the woods considerably, but never wandered elsewhere, that I ever heard."

"Are you in earnest? Was there ever one who so made it his particular mission to hate Indians that, to designate him, a special word has been coined—Indian-hater?"

"Even so."

"Dear me, you take it very calmly.—But really, I would like to know something about this Indian-hating. I can hardly believe such a thing to be. Could you favor me with a little history of the extraordinary man you mentioned?"

"With all my heart," and immediately stepping from the porch, gestured the cosmopolitan to a settee near by, on deck. "There, sir, sit you there, and I will sit here beside you—you desire to hear of Colonel John Moredock. Well, a day in my boyhood is marked with a white stone—the day I saw the colonel's rifle, powder-horn attached, hanging in a cabin on the West bank of the Wabash river. I was going westward a long journey through the wilderness with my father. It was nigh noon, and we had stopped at the cabin to unsaddle and bait. The man at the cabin pointed out the rifle, and told whose it was, adding that the colonel was that moment sleeping on wolf-skins in the corn-loft above, so we must not talk very loud, for the colonel had been out all night hunting (Indians, mind), and it would be cruel to disturb his sleep. Curious to see one so famous, we waited two hours over, in hopes he would come forth; but he did not. So, it being necessary to get to the next cabin before nightfall, we had at last to ride off without the wished-for satisfaction. Though, to tell the truth, I, for one, did not go away entirely ungratified, for, while my father was watering the horses, I slipped back into the cabin, and stepping a round or two up the ladder, pushed my head through the trap, and peered about. Not much light in the loft; but off, in the further corner, I saw what I took to be the wolf-skins, and on them a bundle of something, like a drift of leaves; and at one end, what seemed a moss-ball; and over it, deer-antlers branched; and close by, a small squirrel sprang out from a maple-bowl of nuts, brushed the moss-ball with his tail, through a hole, and vanished, squeaking. That bit of woodland scene was all I saw. No Colonel Moredock there, unless that moss-ball was his curly head, seen in the back view. I would have gone clear up, but the man below had warned me, that though, from his camping habits, the colonel could sleep through thunder, he was for the same cause amazing quick to waken at the sound of footsteps, however soft, and especially if human."

"Excuse me," said the other, softly laying his hand on the narrator's wrist, "but I fear the colonel was of a distrustful na-ture—little or no confidence. He *was* a little suspicious-minded, wasn't he?"

"Not a bit. Knew too much. Suspected nobody, but was not ignorant of Indians. Well: though, as you may gather, I never fully saw the man, yet, have I, one way and another, heard about as much of him as any other; in particular, have I heard his history again and again from my father's friend, James Hall, the judge, you know. In every company being called upon to give this history, which none could better do, the judge at last fell into a style so methodic, you would have thought he spoke less to mere auditors than to an invisible amanuensis; seemed talking for the press; very impressive way with him indeed. And I, having an equally impressible memory, think that, upon a pinch, I can render you the judge upon the colonel almost word for word."

"Do so, by all means," said the cosmopolitan, well pleased.

"Shall I give you the judge's philosophy, and all?"

"As to that," rejoined the other gravely, pausing over the pipe-bowl he was filling, "the desirableness, to a man of a cer-tain mind, of having another man's philosophy given, depends considerably upon what school of philosophy that other man belongs to. Of what school or system was the judge, pray?"

"Why, though he knew how to read and write, the judge

never had much schooling. But, I should say he belonged, if anything, to the free-school system. Yes, a true patriot, the judge went in strong for free-schools."

"In philosophy? The man of a certain mind, then, while respecting the judge's patriotism, and not blind to the judge's capacity for narrative, such as he may prove to have, might, perhaps, with prudence, waive an opinion of the judge's probable philosophy. But I am no rigorist; proceed, I beg; his philosophy or not, as you please."

"Well, I would mostly skip that part, only, to begin, some reconnoitering of the ground in a philosophical way the judge always deemed indispensable with strangers. For you must know that Indian-hating was no monopoly of Colonel Moredock's; but a passion, in one form or other, and to a degree, greater or less, largely shared among the class to which he belonged. And Indian-hating still exists; and, no doubt, will continue to exist, so long as Indians do. Indian-hating, then, shall be my first theme, and Colonel Moredock, the Indian-hater, my next and last."

With which the stranger, settling himself in his seat, commenced—the hearer paying marked regard, slowly smoking, his glance, meanwhile, steadfastly abstracted towards the deck, but his right ear so disposed towards the speaker that each word came through as little atmospheric intervention as possible. To intensify the sense of hearing, he seemed to sink the sense of sight. No complaisance of mere speech could have been so flattering, or expressed such striking politeness as this mute eloquence of thoroughly digesting attention.

CHAPTER XXVI

CONTAINING THE METAPHYSICS OF INDIAN-HATING, ACCORDING TO
THE VIEWS OF ONE EVIDENTLY NOT SO PREPOSSESSED AS ROUSSEAU
IN FAVOR OF SAVAGES

"THE judge always began in these words: 'The backwoodsman's hatred of the Indian has been a topic for some remark. In the earlier times of the frontier the passion was thought to be readily accounted for. But Indian rapine having mostly ceased through regions where it once prevailed, the philanthropist is surprised that Indian-hating has not in like degree ceased with it. He wonders why the backwoodsman still regards the red man in much the same spirit that a jury does a murderer, or a trapper a wild cat—a creature, in whose behalf mercy were not wisdom; truce is vain; he must be executed.

" 'A curious point,' the judge would continue, 'which perhaps not everybody, even upon explanation, may fully understand; while, in order for any one to approach to an understanding, it is necessary for him to learn, or if he already know, to bear in mind, what manner of man the backwoodsman is; as for what manner of man the Indian is, many know, either from history or experience.

" 'The backwoodsman is a lonely man. He is a thoughtful man. He is a man strong and unsophisticated. Impulsive, he is what some might call unprincipled. At any rate, he is self-willed; being one who less hearkens to what others may say about things, than looks for himself, to see what are things themselves. If in straits, there are few to help; he must depend upon himself; he must continually look to himself. Hence self-reliance, to the degree of standing by his own judgment, though it stand alone. Not that he deems himself infallible; too many mistakes in following trails prove the contrary; but he thinks that nature destines such sagacity as she has given him, as she destines it to the 'possum. To these fellow-beings of the wilds their untutored sagacity is their best dependence. If with either it prove faulty, if the 'possum's betray it to the trap, or the backwoodsman's mislead him into ambuscade, there are consequences to be undergone, but no self-blame. As with the 'possum, instincts prevail with the backwoodsman over precepts. Like the 'possum, the backwoodsman presents the spectacle of a creature dwelling exclusively among the works of God, yet these, truth must confess, breed little in him of a godly mind. Small bowing and scraping is his, further than when with bent knee he points his rifle, or picks its flint. With few companions, solitude by necessity his lengthened lot, he stands the trial—no slight one, since, next to dying, solitude, rightly borne, is perhaps of fortitude the most rigorous test. But not merely is the backwoodsman content to be alone, but in no few cases is anxious to be so. The sight of smoke ten miles off is provocation to one more remove from man, one step deeper into nature. Is it that he feels that whatever man may be, man is not the universe? that glory, beauty, kindness, are not all engrossed by him? that as the presence of man frights birds away, so, many bird-like thoughts? Be that how it will, the backwoodsman is not without some fineness to his nature. Hairy Orson as he looks, it may be with him as with the Shetland seal—beneath the bristles lurks the fur.

"'Though held in a sort a barbarian, the backwoodsman would seem to America what Alexander was to Asia—captain in the vanguard of conquering civilization. Whatever the nation's growing opulence or power, does it not lackey his heels? Pathfinder, provider of security to those who come after him, for himself he asks nothing but hardship. Worthy to be compared with Moses in the Exodus, or the Emperor Julian in Gaul, who on foot, and bare-browed, at the head of covered or mounted legions, marched so through the elements, day after day. The tide of emigration, let it roll as it will, never overwhelms the backwoodsman into itself; he rides upon advance, as the Polynesian upon the comb of the surf.

" 'Thus, though he keep moving on through life, he maintains with respect to nature much the same unaltered relation throughout; with her creatures, too, including panthers and Indians. Hence, it is not unlikely that, accurate as the theory of the Peace Congress may be with respect to those two varieties of beings, among others, yet the backwoodsman might be qualified to throw out some practical suggestions.

" 'As the child born to a backwoodsman must in turn lead his father's life—a life which, as related to humanity, is related mainly to Indians—it is thought best not to mince matters, out of delicacy; but to tell the boy pretty plainly what an Indian is, and what he must expect from him. For however charitable it may be to view Indians as members of the Society of Friends, yet to affirm them such to one ignorant of Indians, whose lonely path lies a long way through their lands, this, in the event, might prove not only injudicious but cruel. At least something of this kind would seem the maxim upon which backswoods' education is based. Accordingly, if in youth the backwoodsman incline to knowledge, as is generally the case, he hears little from his schoolmasters, the old chroniclers of the forest, but histories of Indian lying, Indian theft, Indian double-dealing, Indian fraud and perfidy, Indian want of conscience, Indian blood-thirstiness, Indian diabolism—histories which, though of wild woods, are almost as full of things unangelic as the Newgate Calendar or the Annals of Europe. In these Indian narratives and traditions the lad is thoroughly grounded. "As the twig is bent the tree's inclined." The instinct of antipathy against an Indian grows in the backwoodsman with the sense of good and bad, right and wrong. In one breath he learns that a brother is to be loved, and an Indian to be hated.

" 'Such are the facts,' the judge would say, 'upon which, if one seek to moralize, he must do so with an eye to them. It is terrible that one creature should so regard another, should make it conscience to abhor an entire race. It is terrible; but is it surprising? Surprising, that one should hate a race which he believes to be red from a cause akin to that which makes some tribes of garden insects green? A race whose name is upon the frontier a *memento mori;* painted to him in every evil light; now a horse-thief like those in Moyamensing; now an assassin like a New York rowdy; now a treaty-breaker like an Austrian; now a Palmer with poisoned arrows; now a judicial murderer and Jeffries, after a fierce farce of trial condemning his victim to bloody death; or a Jew with hospitable speeches cozening some fainting stranger into ambuscade, there to burk him, and account it a deed grateful to Manitou, his god.

" 'Still, all this is less advanced as truths of the Indians than as examples of the backwoodsman's impression of them—in which the charitable may think he does them some injustice. Certain it is, the Indians themselves think so; quite unanimously, too. The Indians, indeed, protest against the backwoodsman's view of them; and some think that one cause of their returning his antipathy so sincerely as they do, is their moral indignation at being so libeled by him, as they really believe and say. But whether, on this or any point, the Indians should be permitted to testify for themselves, to the exclusion of other testimony, is a question that may be left to the Supreme Court. At any rate, it has been observed that when an Indian becomes a genuine proselyte to Christianity (such cases, however, not being very many; though, indeed, entire tribes are sometimes nominally brought to the true light,) he will not in that case conceal his enlightened conviction, that his race's portion by nature is total depravity; and, in that way, as much as admits that the backwoodsman's worst idea of it is not very far from true; while, on the other hand, those red men who are the greatest sticklers for the theory of Indian virtue, and Indian loving-kindness, are someimes the arrantest horse-thieves and tomahawkers among them. So, at least, avers the backwoodsman. And though, knowing the Indian nature, as he thinks he does, he fancies he is not ignorant that an Indian may in some points deceive himself almost as effectually as in bush-tactics he can another, yet his theory and his practice as above contrasted seem to involve an inconsistency so extreme, that the backwoodsman only accounts for it on the supposition that when a tomahawking red man advances the notion of the benignity of the red race, it is but part and parcel with that subtle strategy which he finds so useful in war, in hunting, and the general conduct of life.'

"In further explanation of that deep abhorrence with which the backwoodsman regards the savage, the judge used to think it might perhaps a little help, to consider what kind of stimulus to it is furnished in those forest histories and traditions before spoken of. In which behalf, he would tell the story of the little colony of Wrights and Weavers, originally seven cousins from Virginia, who, after successive removals with their families, at last established themselves near the southern frontier of the Bloody Ground, Kentucky: 'They were strong, brave men; but, unlike many of the pioneers in those days, theirs was no love of conflict for conflict's sake. Step by step they had been lured to their lonely resting-place by the ever-beckoning seductions of a fertile and virgin land, with a singular exemption, during the march, from Indian molestation. But clearings made and houses built, the bright shield was soon to turn its other side. After repeated persecutions and eventual hostilities, forced on them by a dwindled tribe in their neighborhood—persecutions resulting in loss of crops and cattle; hostilities in which they lost two of their number, illy to be spared, besides others getting painful wounds—the five remaining cousins made, with some serious concessions, a kind of treaty with Mocmohoc, the chief—being to this induced by the harryings of the enemy, leaving them no peace. But they were further prompted, indeed, first incited, by the suddenly changed ways of Mocmohoc, who, though hitherto deemed a savage almost perfidious as Cæsar Borgia, yet now put on a seeming the reverse of this, engaging to bury the hatchet, smoke the pipe, and be friends forever; not friends in the mere sense of renouncing enmity, but in the sense of kindliness, active and familiar.

" 'But what the chief now seemed, did not wholly blind them to what the chief had been; so that, though in no small degree influenced by his change of bearing, they still distrusted him enough to covenant with him, among other articles on their side, that though friendly visits should be exchanged between the wigwams and the cabins, yet the five cousins should never, on any account, be expected to enter the chief's lodge together. The intention was, though they reserved it, that if ever, under the guise of amity, the chief should mean them mischief, and effect it, it should be but partially; so that some of the five might survive, not only for their families' sake, but also for retribution's. Nevertheless, Mocmohoc did, upon a time, with such fine art and pleasing carriage win their confidence, that he brought them all together to a feast of bear's meat, and there, by stratagem, ended them. Years after, over their calcined bones and those of all their families, the chief, reproached for his treachery by a proud hunter whom he had made captive, jeered out, "Treachery? pale face! 'Twas they who broke their covenant first, in coming all together; they that broke it first, in trusting Mocmohoc."'

"At this point the judge would pause, and lifting his hand, and rolling his eyes, exclaim in a solemn enough voice, 'Circling wiles and bloody lusts. The acuteness and genius of the chief but made him the more atrocious.'

"After another pause, he would begin an imaginary kind of dialogue between a backwoodsman and a questioner:

"'But are all Indians like Mocmohoc?—Not all have proved such; but in the least harmful may lie his germ. There is an Indian nature. "Indian blood is in me," is the half-breed's threat.—But are not some Indians kind?—Yes, but kind Indians are mostly lazy, and reputed simple—at all events, are seldom chiefs; chiefs among the red men being taken from the active, and those accounted wise. Hence, with small promotion, kind Indians have but proportionate influence. And kind Indians may be forced to do unkind biddings. So "beware the Indian, kind or unkind," said Daniel Boone, who lost his sons by them.—But, have all you backwoodsmen been some way victimized by Indians?—No.—Well, and in certain cases may not at least some few of you be favored by them?—Yes, but scarce one among us so self-important, or so selfish-minded, as to hold his personal exemption from Indian outrage such a set-off against the contrary experience of so many others, as that he must needs, in a general way, think well of Indians; or, if he do, an arrow in his flank might suggest a pertinent doubt.

" 'In short,' according to the judge, 'if we at all credit the backwoodsman, his feeling against Indians, to be taken aright, must be considered as being not so much on his own account as on others', or jointly on both accounts. True it is, scarce a family he knows but some member of it, or connection, has been by Indians maimed or scalped. What avails, then, that some one Indian, or some two or three, treat a backwoodsman friendly-like? He fears me, he thinks. Take my rifle from me, give him motive, and what will come? Or if not so, how know I what involuntary preparations may be going on in him for things as unbeknown in present time to him as me—a sort of chemical preparation in the soul for malice, as chemical preparation in the body for malady.'

"Not that the backwoodsman ever used those words, you see, but the judge found him expression for his meaning. And this point he would conclude with saying, that, 'what is called a "friendly Indian" is a very rare sort of creature; and well it was so, for no ruthlessness exceeds that of a "friendly Indian" turned enemy. A coward friend, he makes a valiant foe.

" 'But, thus far the passion in question has been viewed in a general way as that of a community. When in his due share of this the backwoodsman adds his private passion, we have then the stock out of which is formed, if formed at all, the Indian-hater *par excellence.*'

"The Indian-hater *par excellence* the judge defined to be one 'who, having with his mother's milk drank in small love for red men, in youth or early manhood, ere the sensibilities become osseous, receives at their hand some signal outrage, or, which in effect is much the same, some of his kin have, or some friend. Now, nature all around him by her solitudes wooing or bidding him muse upon this matter, he accordingly does so, till the thought develops such attraction, that much as straggling vapors troop from all sides to a storm-cloud, so straggling thoughts of other outrages troop to the nucleus thought, assimilate with it, and swell it. At last, taking counsel with the elements, he comes to his resolution. An intenser Hannibal, he makes a vow, the hate of which is a vortex from whose suction scarce the remotest chip of the guilty race may reasonably feel secure. Next, he declares himself and settles his temporal affairs. With the solemnity of a Spaniard turned monk, he takes leave of his kin; or rather, these leave-takings have something of the still more impressive finality of death-bed adieus. Last, he commits himself to the forest primeval; there, so long as life shall be his, to act upon a calm, cloistered scheme of strategical, implacable, and lonesome vengeance. Ever on the noiseless trail; cool, collected, patient; less seen than felt; snuffing, smelling—a Leather-stocking Nemesis. In the settlements he will not be seen again; in eyes of old companions tears may start at some chance thing that speaks of him; but they never look for him, nor call; they know he will not come. Suns and seasons fleet; the tiger-lily blows and falls; babes are born and leap in their mothers' arms; but, the Indian-hater is good as gone to his long home, and "Terror" is his epitaph.'

"Here the judge, not unaffected, would pause again, but presently resume: 'How evident that in strict speech there can be no biography of an Indian-hater *par excellence,* any more than one of a sword-fish, or other deep-sea denizen; or, which is still less imaginable, one of a dead man. The career of the Indian-hater *par excellence* has the impenetrability of the fate of a lost steamer. Doubtless, events, terrible ones, have happened, must have happened; but the powers that be in nature have taken order that they shall never become news.

" 'But, luckily for the curious, there is a species of diluted Indian-hater, one whose heart proves not so steely as his brain. Soft enticements of domestic life too often draw him from the ascetic trail; a monk who apostatizes to the world at times. Like a mariner, too, though much abroad, he may have a wife and family in some green harbor which he does not forget. It is with him as with the Papist converts in Senegal; fasting and mortification prove hard to bear.'

"The judge, with his usual judgment, always thought that the intense solitude to which the Indian-hater consigns himself, has, by its overawing influence, no little to do with relaxing his vow. He would relate instances where, after some months' lonely scoutings, the Indian-hater is suddenly seized with a sort of calenture; hurries openly towards the first smoke, though he knows it is an Indian's, announces himself as a lost hunter, gives the savage his rifle, throws himself upon his charity, embraces him with much affection, imploring the privilege of living a while in his sweet companionship. What is too often the sequel of so distempered a procedure may be best known by those who best know the Indian. Upon the whole, the judge, by two and thirty good and sufficient reasons, would maintain that there was no known vocation whose consistent following calls for such self-containings as that of the Indian-hater *par excellence*. In the highest view, he considered such a soul one peeping out but once an age.

"For the diluted Indian-hater, although the vacations he permits himself impair the keeping of the character, yet, it should not be overlooked that this is the man who, by his very infirmity, enables us to form surmises, however inadequate, of what Indian-hating in its perfection is."

"One moment," gently interrupted the cosmopolitan here, "and let me refill my calumet."

Which being done, the other proceeded:—

CHAPTER XXVII

SOME ACCOUNT OF A MAN OF QUESTIONABLE MORALITY, BUT WHO,
NEVERTHELESS, WOULD SEEM ENTITLED TO THE ESTEEM OF THAT
EMINENT ENGLISH MORALIST WHO SAID HE LIKED A GOOD HATER

"COMING to mention the man to whose story all thus far said was but the introduction, the judge, who, like you, was a great smoker, would insist upon all the company taking cigars, and then lighting a fresh one himself, rise in his place, and, with the solemnest voice, say—'Gentlemen, let us smoke to the memory of Colonel John Moredock;' when, after several whiffs taken standing in deep silence and deeper reverie, he would resume his seat and his discourse, something in these words:

"'Though Colonel John Moredock was not an Indian-hater *par excellence*, he yet cherished a kind of sentiment towards the red man, and in that degree, and so acted out his sentiment as sufficiently to merit the tribute just rendered to his memory.

"'John Moredock was the son of a woman married thrice, and thrice widowed by a tomahawk. The three successive husbands of this woman had been pioneers, and with them she had wandered from wilderness to wilderness, always on the frontier. With nine children, she at last found herself at a little clearing, afterwards Vincennes. There she joined a company about to remove to the new country of Illinois. On the eastern side of Illinois there were then no settlements; but on the west side, the shore of the Mississippi, there were, near the mouth of the Kaskaskia, some old hamlets of French. To the vicinity of those hamlets, very innocent and pleasant places, a new Arcadia, Mrs. Moredock's party was destined; for thereabouts, among the vines, they meant to settle. They embarked upon the Wabash in boats, proposing descending that stream into the

Ohio, and the Ohio into the Mississippi, and so, northwards, towards the point to be reached. All went well till they made the rock of the Grand Tower on the Mississippi, where they had to land and drag their boats round a point swept by a strong current. Here a party of Indians, lying in wait, rushed out and murdered nearly all of them. The widow was among the victims with her children, John excepted, who, some fifty miles distant, was following with a second party.

"'He was just entering upon manhood, when thus left in nature sole survivor of his race. Other youngsters might have turned mourners; he turned avenger. His nerves were electric wires—sensitive, but steel. He was one who, from self-possession, could be made neither to flush nor pale. It is said that when the tidings were brought him, he was ashore sitting beneath a hemlock eating his dinner of venison—and as the tidings were told him, after the first start he kept on eating, but slowly and deliberately, chewing the wild news with the wild meat, as if both together, turned to chyle, together should sinew him to his intent. From that meal he rose an Indian-hater. He rose; got his arms, prevailed upon some comrades to join him, and without delay started to discover who were the actual transgressors. They proved to belong to a band of twenty renegades from various tribes, outlaws even among Indians, and who had formed themselves into a maurauding crew. No opportunity for action being at the time presented, he dismissed his friends; told them to go on, thanking them, and saying he would ask their aid at some future day. For upwards of a year, alone in the wilds, he watched the crew. Once, what he thought a favorable chance having occurred—it being midwinter, and the savages encamped, apparently to remain so—he anew mustered his friends, and marched against them; but, getting wind of his coming, the enemy fled, and in such panic that everything was left behind but their weapons. During the winter, much the same thing happened upon two subsequent occasions. The next year he sought them at the head of a party pledged to serve him for forty days. At last the hour came. It was on the shore of the Mississippi. From their covert, Moredock and his men dimly descried the gang of Cains in the red dusk of evening, paddling over to a jungled island in mid-stream, there the more securely to lodge; for Moredock's retributive spirit in the wilderness spoke ever to their trepidations now, like the voice calling through the garden. Waiting until dead of night, the whites swam the river, towing after them a raft laden with their arms. On landing, Moredock cut the fastenings of the enemy's canoes, and turned them, with his own raft, adrift; resolved that there should be neither escape for the Indians, nor safety, except in victory, for the whites. Victorious the whites were; but three of the Indians saved themselves by taking to the stream. Moredock's band lost not a man.

"'Three of the murderers survived. He knew their names and persons. In the course of three years each successively fell by his own hand. All were now dead. But this did not suffice. He made no avowal, but to kill Indians had become his passion. As an athlete, he had few equals; as a shot, none; in single combat, not to be beaten. Master of that woodland-cunning enabling the adept to subsist where the tyro would perish, and expert in all those arts by which an enemy is pursued for weeks, perhaps months, without once suspecting it, he kept to the forest. The solitary Indian that met him, died. When a murder was descried, he would either secretly pursue their track for some chance to strike at least one blow; or if, while thus engaged, he himself was discovered, he would elude them by superior skill.

"'Many years he spent thus; and though after a time he was, in a degree, restored to the ordinary life of the region and period, yet it is believed that John Moredock never let pass an opportunity of quenching an Indian. Sins of commission in that kind may have been his, but none of omission.

"'It were to err to suppose,' the judge would say, 'that this gentleman was naturally ferocious, or peculiarly possessed of those qualities, which, unhelped by provocation of events, tend to withdraw man from social life. On the contrary, Moredock was an example of something apparently self-contradicting, certainly curious, but, at the same time, undeniable: namely,

that nearly all Indian-haters have at bottom loving hearts; at
any rate, hearts, if anything, more generous than the average.
Certain it is, that, to the degree in which he mingled in the
life of the settlements, Moredock showed himself not without
humane feelings. No cold husband or colder father, he; and,
though often and long away from his household, bore its needs
in mind, and provided for them. He could be very convivial;
told a good story (though never of his more private exploits),
and sung a capital song. Hospitable, not backward to help a
neighbor; by report, benevolent, as retributive, in secret; while,
in a general manner, though sometimes grave—as is not unusual
with men of his complexion, a sultry and tragical brown—yet
with nobody, Indians excepted, otherwise than courteous in
a manly fashion; a moccasined gentleman, admired and loved.
In fact, no one more popular, as an incident to follow may
prove.

"'His bravery, whether in Indian fight or any other, was
unquestionable. An officer in the ranging service during the
war of 1812, he acquitted himself with more than credit. Of
his soldierly character, this anecdote is told: Not long after
Hull's dubious surrender at Detroit, Moredock with some of his
rangers rode up at night to a log-house, there to rest till morning. The horses being attended to, supper over, and sleeping-
places assigned the troop, the host showed the colonel his best
bed, not on the ground like the rest, but a bed that stood on
legs. But out of delicacy, the guest declined to monopolize it,
or, indeed, to occupy it at all; when, to increase the inducement,
as the host thought, he was told that a general officer had once
slept in that bed. "Who, pray?" asked the colonel. "General
Hull." "Then you must not take offense," said the colonel, buttoning up his coat, "but, really, no coward's bed, for me, however comfortable." Accordingly he took up with valor's bed—
a cold one on the ground.

"'At one time the colonel was a member of the territorial
council of Illinois, and at the formation of the state government,
was pressed to become candidate for governor, but begged
to be excused. And, though he declined to give his reasons for

declining, yet by those who best knew him the cause was not wholly unsurmised. In his official capacity he might be called upon to enter into friendly treaties with Indian tribes, a thing not to be thought of. And even did no such contingency arise, yet he felt there would be an impropriety in the Governor of Illinois stealing out now and then, during a recess of the legislative bodies, for a few days' shooting at human beings, within the limits of his paternal chief-magistracy. If the governorship offered large honors, from Moredock it demanded larger sacrifices. These were incompatibles. In short, he was not unaware that to be a consistent Indian-hater involves the renunciation of ambition, with its objects—the pomps and glories of the world; and since religion, pronouncing such things vanities, accounts it merit to renounce them, therefore, so far as this goes, Indian-hating, whatever may be thought of it in other respects, may be regarded as not wholly without the efficacy of a devout sentiment.' "

Here the narrator paused. Then, after his long and irksome sitting, started to his feet, and regulating his disordered shirt-frill, and at the same time adjustingly shaking his legs down in his rumpled pantaloons, concluded: "There, I have done; having given you, not my story, mind, or my thoughts, but another's. And now, for your friend Coonskins, I doubt not, that, if the judge were here, he would pronounce him a sort of comprehensive Colonel Moredock, who, too much spreading his passion, shallows it."

CHAPTER XXVIII

MOOT POINTS TOUCHING THE LATE COLONEL JOHN MOREDOCK

"Charity, charity!" exclaimed the cosmopolitan, "never a sound judgment without charity. When man judges man, charity is less a bounty from our mercy than just allowance for the insensible lee-way of human fallibility. God forbid that my eccentric friend should be what you hint. You do not know him, or but imperfectly. His outside deceived you; at first it came near deceiving even me. But I seized a chance, when, owing to indignation against some wrong, he laid himself a little open; I seized that lucky chance, I say, to inspect his heart, and found it an inviting oyster in a forbidding shell. His outside is but put on. Ashamed of his own goodness, he treats mankind as those strange old uncles in romances do their nephews—snapping at them all the time and yet loving them as the apple of their eye."

"Well, my words with him were few. Perhaps he is not what I took him for. Yes, for aught I know, you may be right."

"Glad to hear it. Charity, like poetry, should be cultivated, if only for its being graceful. And now, since you have renounced your notion, I should be happy would you, so to speak, renounce your story, too. That story strikes me with even more incredulity than wonder. To me some parts don't hang together. If the man of hate, how could John Moredock be also the man of love? Either his lone campaigns are fabulous as Hercules'; or else, those being true, what was thrown in about his geniality is but garnish. In short, if ever there was such a man as Moredock, he, in my way of thinking, was either misanthrope or nothing; and his misanthropy the more intense from being focused on one race of men. Though, like suicide,

man-hatred would seem peculiarly a Roman and a Grecian
passion—that is, Pagan; yet, the annals of neither Rome nor
Greece can produce the equal in man-hatred of Colonel Moredock, as the judge and you have painted him. As for this Indian-hating in general, I can only say of it what Dr. Johnson
said of the alleged Lisbon earthquake: 'Sir, I don't believe it.' "

"Didn't believe it? Why not? Clashed with any little prejudice of his?"

"Doctor Johnson had no prejudice; but, like a certain other
person," with an ingenuous smile, "he had sensibilities, and
those were pained."

"Dr. Johnson was a good Christian, wasn't he?"

"He was."

"Suppose he had been something else."

"Then small incredulity as to the alleged earthquake."

"Suppose he had been also a misanthrope?"

"Then small incredulity as to the robberies and murders alleged to have been perpetrated under the pall of smoke and
ashes. The infidels of the time were quick to credit those reports and worse. So true is it that, while religion, contrary to
the common notion, implies, in certain cases, a spirit of slow
reserve as to assent, infidelity, which claims to despise credulity,
is sometimes swift to it."

"You rather jumble together misanthropy and infidelity."

"I do not jumble them; they are coördinates. For misanthropy, springing from the same root with disbelief of religion,
is twin with that. It springs from the same root, I say; for, set
aside materialism, and what is an atheist, but one who does not,
or will not, see in the universe a ruling principle of love; and
what a misanthrope, but one who does not, or will not, see in
man a ruling principle of kindness? Don't you see? In either
case the vice consists in a want of confidence."

"What sort of a sensation is misanthropy?"

"Might as well ask me what sort of sensation is hydrophobia.
Don't know; never had it. But I have often wondered what it
can be like. Can a misanthrope feel warm, I ask myself; take
ease? be companionable with himself? Can a misanthrope

smoke a cigar and muse? How fares he in solitude? Has the
misanthrope such a thing as an appetite? Shall a peach refresh
him? The effervescence of champagne, with what eye does he
behold it? Is summer good to him? Of long winters how much
can he sleep? What are his dreams? How feels he, and what
does he, when suddenly awakened, alone, at dead of night, by
fusilades of thunder?"

"Like you," said the stranger, "I can't understand the misanthrope. So far as my experience goes, either mankind is worthy
one's best love, or else I have been lucky. Never has it been my
lot to have been wronged, though but in the smallest degree.
Cheating, backbiting, superciliousness, disdain, hard-hearted-
ness, and all that brood, I know but by report. Cold regards
tossed over the sinister shoulder of a former friend, ingratitude
in a beneficiary, treachery in a confidant—such things may be;
but I must take somebody's word for it. Now the bridge that has
carried me so well over, shall I not praise it?"

"Ingratitude to the worthy bridge not to do so. Man is a
noble fellow, and in an age of satirists, I am not displeased to
find one who has confidence in him, and bravely stands up for
him."

"Yes, I always speak a good word for man; and what is more,
am always ready to do a good deed for him."

"You are a man after my own heart," responded the cosmopolitan, with a candor which lost nothing by its calmness.
"Indeed," he added, "our sentiments agree so, that were they
written in a book, whose was whose, few but the nicest critics
might determine."

"Since we are thus joined in mind," said the stranger, "why
not be joined in hand?"

"My hand is always at the service of virtue," frankly extending it to him as to virtue personified.

"And now," said the stranger, cordially retaining his hand,
"you know our fashion here at the West. It may be a little
low, but it is kind. Briefly, we being newly-made friends must
drink together. What say you?"

"Thank you; but indeed, you must excuse me."

"Why?"

"Because, to tell the truth, I have to-day met so many old friends, all free-hearted, convivial gentlemen, that really, really, though for the present I succeed in mastering it, I am at bottom almost in the condition of a sailor who, stepping ashore after a long voyage, ere night reels with loving welcomes, his head of less capacity than his heart."

At the allusion to old friends, the stranger's countenance a little fell, as a jealous lover's might at hearing from his sweetheart of former ones. But rallying, he said: "No doubt they treated you to something strong; but wine—surely, that gentle creature, wine; come, let us have a little gentle wine at one of these little tables here. Come, come." Then assaying to roll about like a full pipe in the sea, sang in a voice which had had more of good-fellowship, had there been less of a latent squeak to it:

"Let us drink of the wine of the vine benign,
That sparkles warm in Zansovine."

The cosmopolitan, with longing eye upon him, stood as sorely tempted and wavering a moment; then, abruptly stepping towards him, with a look of dissolved surrender, said: "When mermaid songs move figure-heads, then may glory, gold, and women try their blandishments on me. But a good fellow, singing a good song, he woos forth my every spike, so that my whole hull, like a ship's, sailing by a magnetic rock, caves in with acquiescence. Enough: when one has a heart of a certain sort, it is in vain trying to be resolute."

CHAPTER XXIX

THE wine, port, being called for, and the two seated at the little table, a natural pause of convivial expectancy ensued; the stranger's eye turned towards the bar near by, watching the red-cheeked, white-aproned man there, blithely dusting the bottle, and invitingly arranging the salver and glasses; when, with a sudden impulse turning round his head towards his companion, he said, "Ours is friendship at first sight, ain't it?"

"It is," was the placidly pleased reply: "and the same may be said of friendship at first sight as of love at first sight: it is the only true one, the only noble one. It bespeaks confidence. Who would go sounding his way into love or friendship, like a strange ship by night, into an enemy's harbor?"

"Right. Boldly in before the wind. Agreeable, how we always agree. By-the-way, though but a formality, friends should know each other's names. What is yours, pray?"

"Francis Goodman. But those who love me, call me Frank. And yours?"

"Charles Arnold Noble. But do you call me Charlie."

"I will, Charlie; nothing like preserving in manhood the fraternal familiarities of youth. It proves the heart a rosy boy to the last."

"My sentiments again. Ah!"

It was a smiling waiter, with the smiling bottle, the cork drawn; a common quart bottle, but for the occasion fitted at bottom into a little bark basket, braided with porcupine quills, gayly tinted in the Indian fashion. This being set before the entertainer, he regarded it with affectionate interest, but seemed not to understand, or else to pretend not to, a handsome red label pasted on the bottle, bearing the capital letters, P.W.

"P. W.," said he at last, perplexedly eying the pleasing poser, "now what does P. W. mean?"

"Shouldn't wonder," said the cosmopolitan gravely, "if it stood for port wine. You called for port wine, didn't you?"

"Why so it is, so it is!"

"I find some little mysteries not very hard to clear up," said the other, quietly crossing his legs.

This commonplace seemed to escape the stranger's hearing, for, full of his bottle, he now rubbed his somewhat sallow hands over it, and with a strange kind of cackle, meant to be a chirrup, cried: "Good wine, good wine; is it not the peculiar bond of good feeling?" Then brimming both glasses, pushed one over, saying, with what seemed intended for an air of fine disdain: "Ill betide those gloomy skeptics who maintain that now-a-days pure wine is unpurchasable; that almost every variety on sale is less the vintage of vineyards than laboratories; that most bar-keepers are but a set of male Brinvilliarses, with complaisant arts practicing against the lives of their best friends, their customers."

A shade passed over the cosmopolitan. After a few minutes' down-cast musing, he lifted his eyes and said: "I have long thought, my dear Charlie, that the spirit in which wine is regarded by too many in these days is one of the most painful examples of want of confidence. Look at these glasses. He who could mistrust poison in this wine would mistrust consumption in Hebe's cheek. While, as for suspicions against the dealers in wine and sellers of it, those who cherish such suspicions can have but limited trust in the human heart. Each human heart they must think to be much like each bottle of port, not such port as this, but such port as they hold to. Strange traducers, who see good faith in nothing, however sacred. Not medicines, not the wine in sacraments, has escaped them. The doctor with his phial, and the priest with his chalice, they deem equally the unconscious dispensers of bogus cordials to the dying."

"Dreadful!"

"Dreadful indeed," said the cosmopolitan solemnly. "These distrusters stab at the very soul of confidence. If this wine," impressively holding up his full glass, "if this wine with its bright promise be not true, how shall man be, whose promise can be no brighter? But if wine be false, while men are true, whither shall fly convivial geniality? To think of sincerely-genial souls drinking each other's health at unawares in perfidious and murderous drugs!"

"Horrible!"

"Much too much so to be true, Charlie. Let us forget it. Come, you are my entertainer on this occasion, and yet you don't pledge me. I have been waiting for it."

"Pardon, pardon," half confusedly and half ostentatiously lifting his glass. "I pledge you, Frank, with my whole heart, believe me," taking a draught too decorous to be large, but which, small though it was, was followed by a slight involuntary wryness to the mouth.

"And I return you the pledge, Charlie, heart-warm as it came to me, and honest as this wine I drink it in," reciprocated the cosmopolitan with princely kindliness in his gesture, taking a generous swallow, concluding in a smack, which, though audible, was not so much so as to be unpleasing.

"Talking of alleged spuriousness of wines," said he, tranquilly setting down his glass, and then sloping back his head and with friendly fixedness eyeing the wine, "perhaps the strangest part of those allegings is, that there is, as claimed, a kind of man who, while convinced that on this continent most wines are shams, yet still drinks away at them; accounting wine so fine a thing, that even the sham article is better than none at all. And if the temperance people urge that, by this course, he will sooner or later be undermined in health, he answers, 'And do you think I don't know that? But health without cheer I hold a bore; and cheer, even of the spurious sort, has its price, which I am willing to pay.'"

"Such a man, Frank, must have a disposition ungovernably bacchanalian."

"Yes, if such a man there be, which I don't credit. It is a fable, but a fable from which I once heard a person of less genius than grotesqueness draw a moral even more extravagant than the fable itself. He said that it illustrated, as in a parable, how that a man of a disposition ungovernably good-natured might still familiarly associate with men, though, at the same time, he believed the greater part of men false-hearted—accounting society so sweet a thing that even the spurious sort was better than none at all. And if the Rochefoucaultites urge that, by this course, he will sooner or later be undermined in security, he answers, 'And do you think I don't know that? But security without society I hold a bore; and society, even of the spurious sort, has its price, which I am willing to pay.'"

"A most singular theory," said the stranger with a slight fidget, eyeing his companion with some inquisitiveness, "indeed, Frank, a most slanderous thought," he exclaimed in sudden heat and with an involuntary look almost of being personally aggrieved.

"In one sense it merits all you say, and more," rejoined the other with wonted mildness, "but, for a kind of drollery in it, charity might, perhaps, overlook something of the wickedness. Humor is, in fact, so blessed a thing, that even in the least virtuous product of the human mind, if there can be found but nine good jokes, some philosophers are clement enough to affirm that those nine good jokes should redeem all the wicked thoughts, though plenty as the populace of Sodom. At any rate, this same humor has something, there is no telling what, of beneficence in it, it is such a catholicon and charm—nearly all men agreeing in relishing it, though they may agree in little else—and in its way it undeniably does such a deal of familiar good in the world, that no wonder it is almost a proverb, that a man of humor, a man capable of a good loud laugh—seem how he may in other things—can hardly be a heartless scamp."

"Ha, ha, ha!" laughed the other, pointing to the figure of a pale pauper-boy on the deck below, whose pitiableness was touched, as it were, with ludicrousness by a pair of monstrous boots, apparently some mason's discarded ones, cracked with drouth, half eaten by lime, and curled up about the toe like a bassoon. "Look—ha, ha, ha!"

"I see," said the other, with what seemed quiet appreciation, but of a kind expressing an eye to the grotesque, without blindness to what in this case accompanied it, "I see; and the way in which it moves you, Charlie, comes in very apropos to point the proverb I was speaking of. Indeed, had you intended this effect, it could not have been more so. For who that heard that laugh, but would as naturally argue from it a sound heart as sound lungs? True, it is said that a man may smile, and smile, and smile, and be a villain; but it is not said that a man may laugh, and laugh, and laugh, and be one, is it, Charlie?"

"Ha, ha, ha!—no no, no no."

"Why Charlie, your explosions illustrate my remarks almost as aptly as the chemist's imitation volcano did his lectures. But even if experience did not sanction the proverb, that a good laugher cannot be a bad man, I should yet feel bound in confidence to believe it, since it is a saying current among the people, and I doubt not originated among them, and hence *must* be true; for the voice of the people is the voice of truth. Don't you think so?"

"Of course I do. If Truth don't speak through the people, it never speaks at all; so I heard one say."

"A true saying. But we stray. The popular notion of humor, considered as index to the heart, would seem curiously confirmed by Aristotle—I think, in his "Politics," (a work, by-the-by, which, however it may be viewed upon the whole, yet, from the tenor of certain sections, should not, without precaution, be placed in the hands of youth)—who remarks that the least lovable men in history seem to have had for humor not only a disrelish, but a hatred; and this, in some cases, along with an extraordinary dry taste for practical punning. I remember it is related of Phalaris, the capricious tyrant of Sicily, that he once caused a poor fellow to be beheaded on a horse-block, for no other cause than having a horse-laugh."

"Funny Phalaris!"

"Cruel Phalaris!"

As after fire-crackers, there was a pause, both looking downward on the table as if mutually struck by the contrast of exclamations and pondering upon its significance, if any. So, at least, it seemed; but on one side it might have been otherwise: for presently glancing up, the cosmopolitan said: "In the instance of the moral, drolly cynic, drawn from the queer bacchanalian fellow we were speaking of, who had his reasons for still drinking spurious wine, though knowing it to be such—there, I say, we have an example of what is certainly a wicked thought, but conceived in humor. I will now give you one of a wicked thought conceived in wickedness. You shall compare the two, and answer, whether in the one case the sting is not neutralized by the humor, and whether in the other the absence of humor does not leave the sting free play. I once heard a wit, a mere wit, mind, an irreligious Parisian wit, say, with regard to the temperance movement, that none, to their personal benefit, joined it sooner than niggards and knaves; because, as he affirmed, the one by it saved money and the other made money, as in ship-owners cutting off the spirit ration without giving its equivalent, and gamblers and all sorts of subtle tricksters sticking to cold water, the better to keep a cool head for business."

"A wicked thought, indeed!" cried the stranger, feelingly.

"Yes," leaning over the table on his elbow and genially gesturing at him with his forefinger: "yes, and, as I said, you don't remark the sting of it?"

"I do, indeed. Most calumnious thought, Frank!"

"No humor in it?"

"Not a bit!"

"Well now, Charlie," eying him with moist regard, "let us drink. It appears to me you don't drink freely."

"Oh, oh—indeed, indeed—I am not backward there. I protest, a freer drinker than friend Charlie you will find nowhere," with feverish zeal snatching his glass, but only in the sequel to dally with it. "By-the-way, Frank," said he, perhaps, or perhaps not, to draw attention from himself, "by-the-way, I saw a good thing the other day; capital thing; a panegyric on the press. It pleased me so, I got it by heart at two readings. It is a kind of poetry, but in a form which stands in something the same relation to blank verse which that does to rhyme. A sort of free-and-easy chant with refrains to it. Shall I recite it?"

"Anything in praise of the press I shall be happy to hear," rejoined the cosmopolitan, "the more so," he gravely proceeded, "as of late I have observed in some quarters a disposition to disparage the press."

"Disparage the press?"

"Even so; some gloomy souls affirming that it is proving with that great invention as with brandy or eau-de-vie, which, upon its first discovery, was believed by the doctors to be, as its French name implies, a panacea—a notion which experience, it may be thought, has not fully verified."

"You surprise me, Frank. Are there really those who so decry the press? Tell me more. Their reasons."

"Reasons they have none, but affirmations they have many; among other things affirming that, while under dynastic despotisms, the press is to the people little but an improvisatore, under popular ones it is too apt to be their Jack Cade. In fine, these sour sages regard the press in the light of a Colt's revolver, pledged to no cause but his in whose chance hands it may be; deeming the one invention an improvement upon the pen, much akin to what the other is upon the pistol; involving, along with the multiplication of the barrel, no consecration of the aim. The term 'freedom of the press' they consider on a par with *freedom of Colt's revolver*. Hence, for truth and the right, they hold, to indulge hopes from the one is little more sensible than for Kossuth and Mazzini to indulge hopes from the other. Heart-breaking views enough, you think; but their refutation is in every true reformer's contempt. Is it not so?"

"Without doubt. But go on, go on. I like to hear you," flatteringly brimming up his glass for him.

"For one," continued the cosmopolitan, grandly swelling his chest, "I hold the press to be neither the people's improvisatore, nor Jack Cade; neither their paid fool, nor conceited drudge. I think interest never prevails with it over duty. The press still speaks for truth though impaled, in the teeth of lies though intrenched. Disdaining for it the poor name of cheap diffuser of news, I claim for it the independent apostleship of

Advancer of Knowledge:—the iron Paul! Paul, I say; for not only does the press advance knowledge, but righteousness. In the press, as in the sun, resides, my dear Charlie, a dedicated principle of beneficent force and light. For the Satanic press, by its coappearance with the apostolic, it is no more an aspersion to that, than to the true sun is the coappearance of the mock one. For all the baleful-looking parhelion, god Apollo dispenses the day. In a word, Charlie, what the sovereign of England is titularly, I hold the press to be actually—Defender of the Faith!—defender of the faith in the final triumph of truth over error, metaphysics over superstition, theory over falsehood, machinery over nature, and the good man over the bad. Such are my views, which, if stated at some length, you, Charlie, must pardon, for it is a theme upon which I cannot speak with cold brevity. And now I am impatient for your panegyric, which, I doubt not, will put mine to the blush."

"It is rather in the blush-giving vein," smiled the other; "but such as it is, Frank, you shall have it."

"Tell me when you are about to begin," said the cosmopolitan, "for, when at public dinners the press is toasted, I always drink the toast standing, and shall stand while you pronounce the panegyric."

"Very good, Frank; you may stand up now."

He accordingly did so, when the stranger likewise rose, and uplifting the ruby wine-flask, began.

CHAPTER XXX

OPENING WITH A POETICAL EULOGY OF THE PRESS AND CONTINUING
WITH TALK INSPIRED BY THE SAME

" 'PRAISE be unto the press, not Faust's, but Noah's; let us extol and magnify the press, the true press of Noah, from which breaketh the true morning. Praise be unto the press, not the black press but the red; let us extol and magnify the press, the red press of Noah, from which cometh inspiration. Ye pressmen of the Rhineland and the Rhine, join in with all ye who tread out the glad tidings on isle Madeira or Mitylene.—Who giveth redness of eyes by making men long to tarry at the fine print?—Praise be unto the press, the rosy press of Noah, which giveth rosiness of hearts, by making men long to tarry at the rosy wine.—Who hath babblings and contentions? Who, without cause, inflicteth wounds? Praise be unto the press, the kindly press of Noah, which knitteth friends, which fuseth foes.—Who may be bribed?—Who may be bound?—Praise be unto the press, the free press of Noah, which will not lie for tyrants, but make tyrants speak the truth.—Then praise be unto the press, the frank old press of Noah; then let us extol and magnify the press, the brave old press of Noah; then let us with roses garland and enwreath the press, the grand old press of Noah, from which flow streams of knowledge which give man a bliss no more unreal than his pain.' "

"You deceived me," smiled the cosmopolitan, as both now resumed their seats; "you roguishly took advantage of my simplicity; you archly played upon my enthusiasm. But never mind; the offense, if any, was so charming, I almost wish you would offend again. As for certain poetic left-handers in your panegyric, those I cheerfully concede to the indefinite privi-

189

leges of the poet. Upon the whole, it was quite in the lyric style—a style I always admire on account of that spirit of Sibyllic confidence and assurance which is, perhaps, its prime ingredient. But come," glancing at his companion's glass, "for a lyrist, you let the bottle stay with you too long."

"The lyre and the vine forever!" cried the other in his rapture, or what seemed such, heedless of the hint, "the vine, the vine! is it not the most graceful and bounteous of all growths? And, by its being such, is not something meant—divinely meant? As I live, a vine, a Catawba vine, shall be planted on my grave!"

"A genial thought; but your glass there."

"Oh, oh," taking a moderate sip, "but you, why don't you drink?"

"You have forgotten, my dear Charlie, what I told you of my previous convivialities to-day."

"Oh," cried the other, now in manner quite abandoned to the lyric mood, not without contrast to the easy sociability of his companion. "Oh, one can't drink too much of good old wine— the genuine, mellow old port. Pooh, pooh! drink away."

"Then keep me company."

"Of course," with a flourish, taking another sip—"suppose we have cigars. Never mind your pipe there; a pipe is best when alone. I say, waiter, bring some cigars—your best."

They were brought in a pretty little bit of western pottery, representing some kind of Indian utensil, mummy-colored, set down in a mass of tobacco leaves, whose long, green fans, fancifully grouped, formed with peeps of red the sides of the receptacle.

Accompanying it were two accessories, also bits of pottery, but smaller, both globes; one in guise of an apple flushed with red and gold to the life, and, through a cleft at top, you saw it was hollow. This was for the ashes. The other, gray, with wrinkled surface, in the likeness of a wasp's nest, was the match-box.

"There," said the stranger, pushing over the cigar-stand, "help yourself, and I will touch you off," taking a match.

"Nothing like tobacco," he added, when the fumes of the cigar began to wreathe, glancing from the smoker to the pottery, "I will have a Virginia tobacco-plant set over my grave beside the Catawba vine."

"Improvement upon your first idea, which by itself was good—but you don't smoke."

"Presently, presently—let me fill your glass again. You don't drink."

"Thank you; but no more just now. Fill *your* glass."

"Presently, presently; do you drink on. Never mind me. Now that it strikes me, let me say, that he who, out of superfine gentility or fanatic morality, denies himself tobacco, suffers a more serious abatement in the cheap pleasures of life than the dandy in his iron boot, or the celibate on his iron cot. While for him who would fain revel in tobacco, but cannot, it is a thing at which philanthropists must weep, to see such an one, again and again, madly returning to the cigar, which, for his incompetent stomach, he cannot enjoy, while still, after each shameful repulse, the sweet dream of the impossible good goads him on to his fierce misery once more—poor eunuch!"

"I agree with you," said the cosmopolitan, still gravely social, "but you don't smoke."

"Presently, presently, do you smoke on. As I was saying about—"

"But *why* don't you smoke—come. You don't think that tobacco, when in league with wine, too much enhances the latter's vinous quality—in short, with certain constitutions tends to impair self-possession, do you?"

"To think that, were treason to good fellowship," was the warm disclaimer. "No, no. But the fact is, there is an unpropitious flavor in my mouth just now. Ate of a diabolical ragout at dinner, so I shan't smoke till I have washed away the lingering memento of it with wine. But smoke away, you, and pray, don't forget to drink. By-the-way, while we sit here so companionably, giving loose to any companionable nothing, your uncompanionable friend, Coonskins, is, by pure contrast, brought to recollection. If he were but here now, he would see how much of real heart-joy he denies himself by not hob-a-nobbing with his kind."

"Why," with loitering emphasis, slowly withdrawing his cigar, "I thought I had undeceived you there. I thought you had come to a better understanding of my eccentric friend."

"Well, I thought so, too; but first impressions will return, you know. In truth, now that I think of it, I am led to conjecture from chance things which dropped from Coonskins, during the little interview I had with him, that he is not a Missourian by birth, but years ago came West here, a young misanthrope from the other side of the Alleghanies, less to make his fortune, than to flee man. Now, since they say trifles sometimes effect great results, I shouldn't wonder, if his history were probed, it would be found that what first indirectly gave his sad bias to Coonskins was his disgust at reading in boyhood the advice of Polonius to Laertes—advice which, in the selfishness it inculcates, is almost on a par with a sort of ballad upon the economies of money-making, to be occasionally seen pasted against the desk of small retail traders in New England."

"I do hope now, my dear fellow," said the cosmopolitan with an air of bland protest, "that, in my presence at least, you will throw out nothing to the prejudice of the sons of the Puritans."

"Hey-day and high times indeed," exclaimed the other, nettled, "sons of the Puritans forsooth! And who be Puritans, that I, an Alabamaian, must do them reverence? A set of sourly conceited old Malvolios, whom Shakespeare laughs his fill at in his comedies."

"Pray, what were you about to suggest with regard to Polonius," observed the cosmopolitan with quiet forbearance, expressive of the patience of a superior mind at the petulance of an inferior one; "how do you characterize his advice to Laertes?"

"As false, fatal, and calumnious," exclaimed the other, with a degree of ardor befitting one resenting a stigma upon the family escutcheon, "and for a father to give his son—monstrous. The case you see is this: The son is going abroad, and for the first. What does the father? Invoke God's blessing upon him? Put the blessed Bible in his trunk? No. Crams him with maxims smacking of my Lord Chesterfield, with maxims of France, with maxims of Italy."

"No, no, be charitable, not that. Why, does he not among other things say:—

> 'The friends thou hast, and their adoption tried,
> Grapple them to thy soul with hooks of steel'?

Is that compatible with maxims of Italy?"

"Yes it is, Frank. Don't you see? Laertes is to take the best care of his friends—his proved friends, on the same principle that a wine-corker takes the best of care of his proved bottles. When a bottle gets a sharp knock and don't break, he says, 'Ah, I'll keep that bottle.' Why? Because he loves it? No, he has particular use for it."

"Dear, dear!" appealingly turning in distress, "that—that kind of criticism is—is—in fact—it won't do."

"Won't truth do, Frank? You are so charitable with everybody, do but consider the tone of the speech. Now I put it to you, Frank; is there anything in it hortatory to high, heroic, disinterested effort? Anything like 'sell all thou hast and give to the poor?' And, in other points, what desire seems most in the father's mind, that his son should cherish nobleness for himself, or be on his guard against the contrary thing in others? An irreligious warner, Frank—no devout counselor, is Polonius. I hate him. Nor can I bear to hear your veterans of the world affirm, that he who steers through life by the advice of old Polonius will not steer among the breakers."

"No, no—I hope nobody affirms that," rejoined the cosmopolitan, with tranquil abandonment; sideways reposing his arm at full length upon the table. "I hope nobody affirms that; because, if Polonius' advice be taken in your sense, then the recommendation of it by men of experience would appear to involve more or less of an unhandsome sort of reflection upon human nature. And yet," with a perplexed air, "your suggestions have put things in such a strange light to me as in fact a little to disturb my previous notions of Polonius and what he says. To be frank, by your ingenuity you have unsettled me there, to that degree that were it not for our coincidence of opinion in general, I should almost think I was now at length beginning to feel the ill effect of an immature mind, too much consorting with a mature one, except on the ground of first principles in common."

"Really and truly," cried the other with a kind of tickled modesty and pleased concern, "mine is an understanding too weak to throw out grapnels and hug another to it. I have indeed heard of some great scholars in these days, whose boast is less that they have made disciples than victims. But for me, had I the power to do such things, I have not the heart to desire."

"I believe you, my dear Charlie. And yet, I repeat, by your commentaries on Polonius you have, I know not how, unsettled me; so that now I don't exactly see how Shakespeare meant the words he puts in Polonius' mouth."

"Some say that he meant them to open people's eyes; but I don't think so."

"Open their eyes?" echoed the cosmopolitan, slowly expanding his; "what is there in this world for one to open his eyes to? I mean in the sort of invidious sense you cite?"

"Well, others say he meant to corrupt people's morals; and still others, that he had no express intention at all, but in effect opens their eyes and corrupts their morals in one operation. All of which I reject."

"Of course you reject so crude an hypothesis; and yet, to confess, in reading Shakespeare in my closet, struck by some passage, I have laid down the volume, and said: 'This Shakespeare is a queer man.' At times seeming irresponsible, he does not always seem reliable. There appears to be a certain—what shall I call it?—hidden sun, say, about him, at once enlightening and mystifying. Now, I should be afraid to say what I have sometimes thought that hidden sun might be."

"Do you think it was the true light?" with clandestine geniality again filling the other's glass.

"I would prefer to decline answering a categorical question

there. Shakespeare has got to be a kind of deity. Prudent minds, having certain latent thoughts concerning him, will reserve them in a condition of lasting probation. Still, as touching avowable speculations, we are permitted a tether. Shakespeare himself is to be adored, not arraigned; but, so we do it with humility, we may a little canvass his characters. There's his Autolycus now, a fellow that always puzzled me. How is one to take Autolycus? A rogue so happy, so lucky, so triumphant, of so almost captivatingly vicious a career that a virtuous man reduced to the poor-house (were such a contingency conceivable), might almost long to change sides with him. And yet, see the words put into his mouth: 'Oh,' cries Autolycus, as he comes galloping, gay as a buck, upon the stage, 'oh,' he laughs, 'oh what a fool is Honesty, and Trust, his sworn brother, a very simple gentleman.' Think of that. Trust, that is, confidence—that is, the thing in this universe the sacredest—is rattlingly pronounced just the simplest. And the scenes in which the rogue figures seem purposely devised for verification of his principles. Mind, Charlie, I do not say it *is* so, far from it; but I *do* say it seems so. Yes, Autolycus would seem a needy varlet acting upon the persuasion that less is to be got by invoking pockets than picking them, more to be made by an expert knave than a bungling beggar; and for this reason, as he thinks, that the soft heads outnumber the soft hearts. The devil's drilled recruit, Autolycus is joyous as if he wore the livery of heaven. When disturbed by the character and career of one thus wicked and thus happy, my sole consolation is in the fact that no such creature ever existed, except in the powerful imagination which evoked him. And yet, a creature, a living creature, he is, though only a poet was his maker. It may be, that in that paper-and-ink investiture of his, Autolycus acts more effectively upon mankind than he would in a flesh-and-blood one. Can his influence be salutary? True, in Autolycus there is humor; but though, according to my principle, humor is in general to be held a saving quality, yet the case of Autolycus is an exception; because it is his humor which, so to speak, oils his mischievousness. The bravadoing mischievousness of Autolycus is slid into the world on humor, as a pirate schooner, with colors flying, is launched into the sea on greased ways."

"I approve of Autolycus as little as you," said the stranger, who, during his companion's commonplaces, had seemed less attentive to them than to maturing within his own mind the original conceptions destined to eclipse them. "But I cannot believe that Autolycus, mischievous as he must prove upon the stage, can be near so much so as such a character as Polonius."

"I don't know about that," bluntly, and yet not impolitely, returned the cosmopolitan; "to be sure, accepting your view of the old courtier, then if between him and Autolycus you raise the question of unprepossessingness, I grant you the latter comes off best. For a moist rogue may tickle the midriff, while a dry worldling may but wrinkle the spleen."

"But Polonius is not dry," said the other excitedly; "he drules. One sees the fly-blown old fop drule and look wise. His vile wisdom is made the viler by his vile rheuminess. The bowing and cringing, time-serving old sinner—is such an one to give manly precepts to youth? The discreet, decorous, old dotard-of-state; senile prudence; fatuous soullessness! The ribanded old dog is paralytic all down one side, and that the side of nobleness. His soul is gone out. Only nature's automatonism keeps him on his legs. As with some old trees, the bark survives the pith, and will still stand stiffly up, though but to rim round punk, so the body of old Polonius has outlived his soul."

"Come, come," said the cosmopolitan with serious air, almost displeased; "though I yield to none in admiration of earnestness, yet, I think, even earnestness may have limits. To human minds, strong language is always more or less distressing. Besides, Polonius is an old man—as I remember him upon the stage—with snowy locks. Now charity requires that such a figure—think of it how you will—should at least be treated with civility. Moreover, old age is ripeness, and I once heard say, 'Better ripe than raw.'"

"But not better rotten than raw!" bringing down his hand with energy on the table.

"Why, bless me," in mild surprise contemplating his heated comrade, "how you fly out against this unfortunate Polonius—a being that never was, nor will be. And yet, viewed in a Christian light," he added pensively, "I don't know that anger against this man of straw is a whit less wise than anger against a man of flesh. Madness, to be mad with anything."

"That may be, or may not be," returned the other, a little testily, perhaps; "but I stick to what I said, that it is better to be raw than rotten. And what is to be feared on that head, may be known from this: that it is with the best of hearts as with the best of pears—a dangerous experiment to linger too long upon the scene. This did Polonius. Thank fortune, Frank, I am young, every tooth sound in my head, and if good wine can keep me where I am, long shall I remain so."

"True," with a smile. "But wine, to do good, must be drunk. You have talked much and well, Charlie; but drunk little and indifferently—fill up."

"Presently, presently," with a hasty and preoccupied air. "If I remember right, Polonius hints as much as that one should, under no circumstances, commit the indiscretion of aiding in a pecuniary way an unfortunate friend. He drules out some stale stuff about 'loan losing both itself and friend,' don't he? But our bottle; is it glued fast? Keep it moving, my dear Frank. Good wine, and upon my soul I begin to feel it, and through me old Polonius—yes, this wine, I fear, is what excites me so against that detestable old dog without a tooth."

Upon this, the cosmopolitan, cigar in mouth, slowly raised the bottle, and brought it slowly to the light, looking at it steadfastly, as one might at a thermometer in August, to see not how low it was, but how high. Then whiffing out a puff, set it down, and said: "Well, Charlie, if what wine you have drunk came out of this bottle, in that case I should say that if—supposing a case—that if one fellow had an object in getting another fellow fuddled, and this fellow to be fuddled was of your capacity, the operation would be comparatively inexpensive. What do you think, Charlie?"

"Why, I think I don't much admire the supposition," said

Charlie, with a look of resentment; "it ain't safe, depend upon it, Frank, to venture upon too jocose suppositions with one's friends."

"Why, bless you, Frank, my supposition wasn't personal, but general. You mustn't be so touchy."

"If I am touchy it is the wine. Sometimes, when I freely drink, it has a touchy effect on me, I have observed."

"Freely drink? you haven't drunk the perfect measure of one glass, yet. While for me, this must be my fourth or fifth, thanks to your importunity; not to speak of all I drank this morning, for old acquaintance' sake. Drink, drink; you must drink."

"Oh, I drink while you are talking," laughed the other; "you have not noticed it, but I have drunk my share. Have a queer way I learned from a sedate old uncle, who used to tip off his glass unperceived. Do you fill up, and my glass, too. There! Now away with that stump, and have a new cigar. Good fellowship forever!" again in the lyric mood. "Say, Frank, are we not men? I say are we not human? Tell me, were they not human who engendered us, as before heaven I believe they shall be whom we shall engender? Fill up, up, up, my friend. Let the ruby tide aspire, and all ruby aspirations with it! Up, fill up! Be we convivial. And conviviality, what is it? The word, I mean; what expresses it? A living together. But bats live together, and did you ever hear of convivial bats?"

"If I ever did," observed the cosmopolitan, "it has quite slipped my recollection."

"But why did you never hear of convivial bats, nor anybody else? Because bats, though they live together, live not together genially. Bats are not genial souls. But men are; and how delightful to think that the word which among men signifies the highest pitch of geniality, implies, as indispensable auxiliary, the cheery benediction of the bottle. Yes, Frank, to live together in the finest sense, we must drink together. And so, what wonder that he who loves not wine, that sober wretch has a lean heart—a heart like a wrung-out old bluing-bag, and loves not his kind? Out upon him, to the rag-house with him, hang him—the ungenial soul!"

"Oh, now, now, can't you be convivial without being censorious? I like easy, unexcited conviviality. For the sober man, really, though for my part I naturally love a cheerful glass, I will not prescribe my nature as the law to other natures. So don't abuse the sober man. Conviviality is one good thing, and sobriety is another good thing. So don't be one-sided."

"Well, if I am one-sided, it is the wine. Indeed, indeed, I have indulged too genially. My excitement upon slight provocation shows it. But yours is a stronger head; drink you. By the way, talking of geniality, it is much on the increase in these days, ain't it?"

"It is, and I hail the fact. Nothing better attests the advance of the humanitarian spirit. In former and less humanitarian ages—the ages of amphitheatres and gladiators—geniality was mostly confined to the fireside and table. But in our age—the age of joint-stock companies and free-and-easies—it is with this precious quality as with precious gold in old Peru, which Pizarro found making up the scullion's sauce-pot as the Inca's crown. Yes, we golden boys, the moderns, have geniality everywhere—a bounty broadcast like noonlight."

"True, true; my sentiments again. Geniality has invaded each department and profession. We have genial senators, genial authors, genial lecturers, genial doctors, genial clergyman, genial surgeons, and the next thing we shall have genial hangmen."

"As to the last-named sort of person," said the cosmopolitan, "I trust that the advancing spirit of geniality will at last enable us to dispense with him. No murderers—no hangmen. And surely, when the whole world shall have been genialized, it will be as out of place to talk of murderers, as in a Christianized world to talk of sinners."

"To pursue the thought," said the other, "every blessing is attended with some evil, and—"

"Stay," said the cosmopolitan, "that may be better let pass for a loose saying, than for hopeful doctrine."

"Well, assuming the saying's truth, it would apply to the future supremacy of the genial spirit, since then it will fare with the hangman as it did with the weaver when the spinning-jenny whizzed into the ascendant. Thrown out of employment, what could Jack Ketch turn his hand to? Butchering?"

"That he could turn his hand to it seems probable; but that, under the circumstances, it would be appropriate, might in some minds admit of a question. For one, I am inclined to think—and I trust it will not be held fastidiousness—that it would hardly be suitable to the dignity of our nature, that an individual, once employed in attending the last hours of human unfortunates, should, that office being extinct, transfer himself to the business of attending the last hours of unfortunate cattle. I would suggest that the individual turn valet —a vocation to which he would, perhaps, appear not wholly inadapted by his familiar dexterity about the person. In particular, for giving a finishing tie to a gentleman's cravat, I know few who would, in all likelihood, be, from previous occupation, better fitted than the professional person in question."

"Are you in earnest?" regarding the serene speaker with unaffected curiosity; "are you really in earnest?"

"I trust I am never otherwise," was the mildly earnest reply; "but talking of the advance of geniality, I am not without hopes that it will eventually exert its influence even upon so difficult a subject as the misanthrope."

"A genial misanthrope! I thought I had stretched the rope pretty hard in talking of genial hangmen. A genial misanthrope is no more conceivable than a surly philanthropist."

"True," lightly depositing in an unbroken little cylinder the ashes of his cigar, "true, the two you name are well opposed."

"Why, you talk as if there was such a being as a surly philanthropist."

"I do. My eccentric friend, who you call Coonskins, is an example. Does he not, as I explained to you, hide under a surly air a philanthropic heart? Now, the genial misanthrope, when, in the process of eras, he shall turn up, will be the converse of this; under an affable air, he will hide a misanthropical heart. In short, the genial misanthrope will be a new kind of monster, but still no small improvement upon the original one, since, instead of making faces and throwing stones at people, like that poor old crazy man, Timon, he will take steps, fiddle in hand, and set the tickled world a' dancing. In a word, as the progress of Christianization mellows those in manner whom it cannot mend in mind, much the same will it prove with the progress of genialization. And so, thanks to geniality, the misanthrope, reclaimed from his boorish address, will take on refinement and softness—to so genial a degree, indeed, that it may possibly fall out that the misanthrope of the coming century will be almost as popular as, I am sincerely sorry to say, some philanthropists of the present time would seem not to be, as witness my eccentric friend named before."

"Well," cried the other, a little weary, perhaps, of a speculation so abstract, "well, however it may be with the century to come, certainly in the century which is, whatever else one may be, he must be genial or he is nothing. So fill up, fill up, and be genial!"

"I am trying my best," said the cosmopolitan, still calmly companionable. "A moment since, we talked of Pizarro, gold, and Peru; no doubt, now, you remember that when the Spaniard first entered Atahalpa's treasure-chamber, and saw such profusion of plate stacked up, right and left, with the wantonness of old barrels in a brewer's yard, the needy fellow felt a twinge of misgiving, of want of confidence, as to the genuineness of an opulence so profuse. He went about rapping the shining vases with his knuckles. But it was all gold, pure gold, good gold, sterling gold, which how cheerfully would have been stamped such at Goldsmiths' Hall. And just so those needy minds, which, through their own insincerity, having no confidence in mankind, doubt lest the liberal geniality of this age be spurious. They are small Pizarros in their way—by the very princeliness of men's geniality stunned into distrust of it."

"Far be such distrust from you and me, my genial friend," cried the other fervently; "fill up, fill up!"

"Well, this all along seems a division of labor," smiled the cosmopolitan. "I do about all the drinking, and you do about all—the genial. But yours is a nature competent to do that to a large population. And now, my friend," with a peculiarly grave air, evidently foreshadowing something not unimportant, and very likely of close personal interest; "wine, you know, opens the heart, and—"

"Opens it!" with exultation, "it thaws it right out. Every heart is ice-bound till wine melt it, and reveal the tender grass and sweet herbage budding below, with every dear secret, hidden before like a dropped jewel in a snow-bank, lying there unsuspected through winter till spring."

"And just in that way, my dear Charlie, is one of my little secrets now to be shown forth."

"Ah!" eagerly moving round his chair, "what is it?"

"Be not so impetuous, my dear Charlie. Let me explain. You see, naturally, I am a man not overgifted with assurance; in general, I am, if anything, diffidently reserved; so, if I shall presently seem otherwise, the reason is, that you, by the geniality you have evinced in all your talk, and especially the noble way in which, while affirming your good opinion of men, you intimated that you never could prove false to any man, but most by your indignation at a particularly illiberal passage in Polonius' advice—in short, in short," with extreme embarrassment, "how shall I express what I mean, unless I add that by your whole character you impel me to throw myself upon your nobleness; in one word, put confidence in you, a generous confidence?"

"I see, I see," with heightened interest, "something of moment you wish to confide. Now, what is it, Frank? Love affair?"

"No, not that."

"What, then, my *dear* Frank? Speak—depend upon me to the last. Out with it."

"Out it shall come, then," said the cosmopolitan, "I am in want, urgent want, of money."

CHAPTER XXXI

A METAMORPHOSIS MORE SURPRISING THAN ANY IN OVID

"IN want of money!" pushing back his chair as from a suddenly-disclosed man-trap or crater.

"Yes," naïvely assented the cosmopolitan, "and you are going to loan me fifty dollars. I could almost wish I was in need of more, only for your sake. Yes, my dear Charlie, for your sake; that you might the better prove your noble kindliness, my dear Charlie."

"None of your dear Charlies," cried the other, springing to his feet, and buttoning up his coat, as if hastily to depart upon a long journey.

"Why, why, why?" painfully looking up.

"None of your why, why, whys!" tossing out a foot, "go to the devil, sir! Beggar, impostor!—never so deceived in a man in my life."

CHAPTER XXXII

WHILE speaking or rather hissing those words, the boon companion underwent much such a change as one reads of in fairybooks. Out of old materials sprang a new creature. Cadmus glided into the snake.

The cosmopolitan rose, the traces of previous feeling vanished; looked steadfastly at his transformed friend a moment, then, taking ten half-eagles from his pocket, stooped down, and laid them, one by one, in a circle round him; and, retiring a pace, waved his long tasseled pipe with the air of a necromancer, an air heightened by his costume, accompanying each wave with a solemn murmur of cabalistical words.

Meantime, he within the magic-ring stood suddenly rapt, exhibiting every symptom of a successful charm—a turned cheek, a fixed attitude, a frozen eye; spellbound, not more by the waving wand than by the ten invincible talismans on the floor.

"Reappear, reappear, reappear, oh, my former friend! Replace this hideous apparition with thy blest shape, and be the token of thy return the words, 'My dear Frank.'"

"My dear Frank," now cried the restored friend, cordially stepping out of the ring, with regained self-possession regaining lost identity, "My dear Frank, what a funny man you are; full of fun as an egg of meat. How could you tell me that absurd story of your being in need? But I relish a good joke too well to spoil it by letting on. Of course, I humored the thing; and, on my side, put on all the cruel airs you would have me. Come, this little episode of fictitious estrangement

204

will but enhance the delightful reality. Let us sit down again, and finish our bottle."

"With all my heart," said the cosmopolitan, dropping the necromancer with the same facility with which he had assumed it. "Yes," he added, soberly picking up the gold pieces and returning them with a chink to his pocket, "yes, I am something of a funny man now and then; while for you, Charlie," eying him in tenderness, "what you say about your humoring the thing is true enough; never did man second a joke better than you did just now. You played your part better than I did mine; you played it, Charlie, to the life."

"You see, I once belonged to an amateur play company; that accounts for it. But come, fill up, and let's talk of something else."

"Well," acquiesced the cosmopolitan, seating himself, and quietly brimming his glass, "what shall we talk about?"

"Oh, anything you please," a sort of nervously accommodating.

"Well, suppose we talk about Charlemont?"

"Charlemont? What's Charlemont? Who's Charlemont?"

"You shall hear, my dear Charlie," answered the cosmopolitan. "I will tell you the story of Charlemont, the gentleman-madman."

CHAPTER XXXIII

WHICH MAY PASS FOR WHATEVER IT MAY PROVE TO BE WORTH

But ere be given the rather grave story of Charlemont, a reply must in civility be made to a certain voice which methinks I hear, that, in view of past chapters, and more particularly the last, where certain antics appear, exclaims: How unreal all this is! Who did ever dress or act like your cosmopolitan? And who, it might be returned, did ever dress or act like harlequin?

Strange, that in a work of amusement, this severe fidelity to real life should be exacted by any one, who, by taking up such a work, sufficiently shows that he is not unwilling to drop real life, and turn, for a time, to something different. Yes, it is, indeed, strange that any one should clamor for the thing he is weary of; that any one, who, for any cause, finds real life dull, should yet demand of him who is to divert his attention from it, that he should be true to that dullness.

There is another class, and with this class we side, who sit down to a work of amusement tolerantly as they sit at a play, and with much the same expectations and feelings. They look that fancy shall evoke scenes different from those of the same old crowd round the custom-house counter, and same old dishes on the boarding-house table, with characters unlike those of the same old acquaintances they meet in the same old way every day in the same old street. And as, in real life, the proprieties will not allow people to act out themselves with that unreserve permitted to the stage; so, in books of fiction, they look not only for more entertainment, but, at bottom, even for more reality, than real life itself can show. Thus, though they want novelty, they want nature, too; but nature unfettered, exhilarated, in effect transformed. In this way of thinking, the people in a fiction, like the people in a play, must dress as nobody exactly dresses, talk as nobody exactly talks, act as nobody exactly acts. It is with fiction as with religion: it should present another world, and yet one to which we feel the tie.

If, then, something is to be pardoned to well-meant endeavor, surely a little is to be allowed to that writer who, in all his scenes, does but seek to minister to what, as he understands it, is the implied wish of the more indulgent lovers of entertainment, before whom harlequin can never appear in a coat too parti-colored, or cut capers too fantastic.

One word more. Though every one knows how bootless it is to be in all cases vindicating one's self, never mind how convinced one may be that he is never in the wrong; yet, so precious to man is the approbation of his kind, that to rest, though but under an imaginary censure applied to but a work of imagination, is no easy thing. The mention of this weakness will explain why all such readers as may think they perceive something inharmonious between the boisterous hilarity of the cosmopolitan with the bristling cynic, and his restrained good-nature with the boon-companion, are now referred to that chapter where some similar apparent inconsistency in another character is, on general principles, modestly endeavored to be apologized for.

CHAPTER XXXIV

"CHARLEMONT was a young merchant of French descent, living in St. Louis—a man not deficient in mind, and possessed of that sterling and captivating kindliness, seldom in perfection seen but in youthful bachelors, united at times to a remarkable sort of gracefully devil-may-care and witty good-humor. Of course, he was admired by everybody, and loved, as only mankind can love, by not a few. But in his twenty-ninth year a change came over him. Like one whose hair turns gray in a night, so in a day Charlemont turned from affable to morose. His acquaintances were passed without greeting; while, as for his confidential friends, them he pointedly, unscrupulously, and with a kind of fierceness, cut dead.

"One, provoked by such conduct, would fain have resented it with words as disdainful; while another, shocked by the change, and, in concern for a friend, magnanimously overlooking affronts, implored to know what sudden, secret grief had distempered him. But from resentment and from tenderness Charlemont alike turned away.

"Ere long, to the general surprise, the merchant Charlemont was gazetted, and the same day it was reported that he had withdrawn from town, but not before placing his entire property in the hands of responsible assignees for the benefit of creditors.

"Whither he had vanished, none could guess. At length, nothing being heard, it was surmised that he must have made away with himself—a surmise, doubtless, originating in the remembrance of the change some months previous to his bankruptcy—a change of a sort only to be ascribed to a mind suddenly thrown from its balance.

"Years passed. It was spring-time, and lo, one bright morning, Charlemont lounged into the St. Louis coffee-houses—gay, polite, humane, companionable, and dressed in the height of costly elegance. Not only was he alive, but he was himself again. Upon meeting with old acquaintances, he made the first advances, and in such a manner that it was impossible not to meet him half-way. Upon other old friends, whom he did not chance casually to meet, he either personally called, or left his card and compliments for them; and to several, sent presents of game or hampers of wine.

"They say the world is sometimes harshly unforgiving, but it was not so to Charlemont. The world feels a return of love for one who returns to it as he did. Expressive of its renewed interest was a whisper, an inquiring whisper, how now, exactly, so long after his bankruptcy, it fared with Charlemont's purse. Rumor, seldom at a loss for answers, replied that he had spent nine years in Marseilles in France, and there acquiring a second fortune, had returned with it, a man devoted henceforth to genial friendships.

"Added years went by, and the restored wanderer still the same; or rather, by his noble qualities, grew up like golden maize in the encouraging sun of good opinions. But still the latent wonder was, what had caused that change in him at a period when, pretty much as now, he was, to all appearance, in the possession of the same fortune, the same friends, the same popularity. But nobody thought it would be the thing to question him here.

"At last, at a dinner at his house, when all the guests but one had successively departed; this remaining guest, an old acquaintance, being just enough under the influence of wine to set aside the fear of touching upon a delicate point, ventured, in a way which perhaps spoke more favorably for his heart than his tact, to beg of his host to explain the one enigma of his life. Deep melancholy overspread the before cheery face of Charlemont; he sat for some moments tremulously silent; then pushing a full decanter towards the guest, in a choked voice, said: 'No, no! when by art, and care, and time, flowers are made to bloom over a grave, who would seek to dig all up again only to know the mystery?—The wine.' When both glasses were filled, Charlemont took his, and lifting it, added lowly: 'If ever, in days to come, you shall see ruin at hand, and, thinking you understand mankind, shall tremble for your friendships, and tremble for your pride; and, partly through love for the one and fear for the other, shall resolve to be beforehand with the world, and save it from a sin by prospectively taking that sin to yourself, then will you do as one I now dream of once did, and like him will you suffer; but how fortunate and how grateful should you be, if like him, after all that had happened, you could be a little happy again.'

"When the guest went away, it was with the persuasion, that though outwardly restored in mind as in fortune, yet, some taint of Charlemont's old malady survived, and that it was not well for friends to touch one dangerous string."

CHAPTER XXXV

"WELL, what do you think of the story of Charlemont?"
mildly asked he who had told it.

"A very strange one," answered the auditor, who had been
such not with perfect ease, "but is it true?"

"Of course not; it is a story which I told with the purpose of
every story-teller—to amuse. Hence, if it seem strange to you,
that strangeness is the romance; it is what contrasts it with
real life; it is the invention, in brief, the fiction as opposed to
the fact. For do but ask yourself, my dear Charlie," lovingly
leaning over towards him, "I rest it with your own heart now,
whether such a forereaching motive as Charlemont hinted he
had acted on in his change—whether such a motive, I say, were
a sort of one at all justified by the nature of human society?
Would you, for one, turn the cold shoulder to a friend—a convivial one, say, whose pennilessness should be suddenly revealed to you?"

"How can you ask me, my dear Frank? You know I would
scorn such meanness." But rising somewhat disconcerted—
"really, early as it is, I think I must retire; my head," putting
up his hand to it, "feels unpleasantly; this confounded elixir
of logwood, little as I drank of it, has played the deuce with
me."

"Little as you drank of this elixir of logwood? Why, Charlie,
you are losing your mind. To talk so of the genuine, mellow old
port. Yes, I think that by all means you had better away, and
sleep it off. There—don't apologize—don't explain—go, go—I
understand you exactly. I will see you to-morrow."

211

CHAPTER XXXVI

As, not without some haste, the boon companion withdrew,
a stranger advanced, and touching the cosmopolitan, said: "I
think I heard you say you would see that man again. Be
warned; don't you do so."

He turned, surveying the speaker; a blue-eyed man, sandy-
haired, and Saxon-looking; perhaps five and forty; tall, and,
but for a certain angularity, well made; little touch of the
drawing-room about him, but a look of plain propriety of a
Puritan sort, with a kind of farmer dignity. His age seemed
betokened more by his brow, placidly thoughtful, than by his
general aspect, which had that look of youthfulness in maturity, peculiar sometimes to habitual health of body, the original gift of nature, or in part the effect or reward of steady temperance of the passions, kept so, perhaps, by constitution as
much as morality. A neat, comely, almost ruddy cheek, coolly
fresh, like a red clover-blossom at coolish dawn—the color of
warmth preserved by the virtue of chill. Toning the whole
man, was one-knows-not-what of shrewdness and mythiness,
strangely jumbled; in that way, he seemed a kind of cross between a Yankee peddler and a Tartar priest, though it seemed
as if, at a pinch, the first would not in all probability play second fiddle to the last.

"Sir," said the cosmopolitan, rising and bowing with slow
dignity, "if I cannot with unmixed satisfaction hail a hint
pointed at one who has just been clinking the social glass with
me, on the other hand, I am not disposed to underrate the
motive which, in the present case, could alone have prompted
such an intimation. My friend, whose seat is still warm, has

212

retired for the night, leaving more or less in his bottle here. Pray, sit down in his seat, and partake with me; and then, if you choose to hint aught further unfavorable to the man, the genial warmth of whose person in part passes into yours, and whose genial hospitality meanders through you—be it ·so."

"Quite beautiful conceits," said the stranger, now scholastically and artistically eying the picturesque speaker, as if he were a statue in the Pitti Palace; "very beautiful:" then with the gravest interest, "yours, sir, if I mistake not, must be a beautiful soul—one full of all love and truth; for where beauty is, there must those be."

"A pleasing belief," rejoined the cosmopolitan, beginning with an even air, "and to confess, long ago it pleased me. Yes, with you and Schiller, I am pleased to believe that beauty is at bottom incompatible with ill, and therefore am so eccentric as to have confidence in the latent benignity of that beautiful creature, the rattle-snake, whose lithe neck and burnished maze of tawny gold, as he sleekly curls aloft in the sun, who on the prairie can behold without wonder?"

As he breathed these words, he seemed so to enter into their spirit—as some earnest descriptive speakers will—as unconsciously to wreathe his form and sidelong crest his head, till he all but seemed the creature described. Meantime, the stranger regarded him with little surprise, apparently, though with much contemplativeness of a mystical sort, and presently said: "When charmed by the beauty of that viper, did it never occur to you to change personalities with him? to feel what it was to be a snake? to glide unsuspected in grass? to sting, to kill at a touch; your whole beautiful body one iridescent scabbard of death? In short, did the wish never occur to you to feel yourself exempt from knowledge, and conscience, and revel for a while in the care-free, joyous life of a perfectly instinctive, unscrupulous, and irresponsible creature?"

"Such a wish," replied the other, not perceptibly disturbed, "I must confess, never consciously was mine. Such a wish, indeed, could hardly occur to ordinary imaginations, and mine I cannot think much above the average."

"But now that the idea is suggested," said the stranger, with infantile intellectuality, "does it not raise the desire?"

"Hardly. For though I do not think I have any uncharitable prejudice against the rattle-snake, still, I should not like to be one. If I were a rattle-snake now, there would be no such thing as being genial with men—men would be afraid of me, and then I should be a very lonesome and miserable rattle-snake."

"True, men would be afraid of you. And why? Because of your rattle, your hollow rattle—a sound, as I have been told, like the shaking together of small, dry skulls in a tune of the Waltz of Death. And here we have another beautiful truth. When any creature is by its make inimical to other creatures, nature in effect labels that creature, much as an apothecary does a poison. So that whoever is destroyed by a rattle-snake, or other harmful agent, it is his own fault. He should have respected the label. Hence that significant passage in Scripture, 'Who will pity the charmer that is bitten with a serpent?' "

"*I* would pity him," said the cosmopolitan, a little bluntly, perhaps.

"But don't you think," rejoined the other, still maintaining his passionless air, "don't you think, that for a man to pity where nature is pitiless, is a little presuming?"

"Let casuists decide casuistry, but the compassion the heart decides for itself. But, sir," deepening in seriousness, "as I now for the first realize, you but a moment since introduced the word irresponsible in a way I am not used to. Now, sir, though, out of a tolerant spirit, as I hope, I try my best never to be frightened at any speculation, so long as it is pursued in honesty, yet, for once, I must acknowledge that you do really, in the point cited, cause me uneasiness; because a proper view of the universe, that view which is suited to breed a proper confidence, teaches, if I err not, that since all things are justly presided over, not very many living agents but must be some way accountable."

"Is a rattle-snake accountable?" asked the stranger with such a preternaturally cold, gemmy glance out of his pellucid blue eye, that he seemed more a metaphysical merman than a feeling man; "is a rattle-snake accountable?"

"If I will not affirm that it is," returned the other, with the caution of no inexperienced thinker, "neither will I deny it. But if we suppose it so, I need not say that such accountability is neither to you, nor me, nor the Court of Common Pleas, but to something superior."

He was proceeding, when the stranger would have interrupted him; but as reading his argument in his eye, the cosmopolitan, without waiting for it to be put into words, at once spoke to it: "You object to my supposition, for but such it is, that the rattle-snake's accountability is not by nature manifest; but might not much the same thing be urged against man's? A *reductio ad absurdum*, proving the objection vain. But if now," he continued, "you consider what capacity for mischief there is in a rattle-snake (observe, I do not charge it with being mischievous, I but say it has the capacity), could you well avoid admitting that that would be no symmetrical view of the universe which should maintain that, while to man it is forbidden to kill, without judicial cause, his fellow, yet the rattle-snake has an implied permit of unaccountability to murder any creature it takes capricious umbrage at—man included?—But," with a wearied air, "this is no genial talk; at least it is not so to me. Zeal at unawares embarked me in it. I regret it. Pray, sit down, and take some of this wine."

"Your suggestions are new to me," said the other, with a kind of condescending appreciativeness, as of one who, out of devotion to knowledge, disdains not to appropriate the least crumb of it, even from a pauper's board; "and, as I am a very Athenian in hailing a new thought, I cannot consent to let it drop so abruptly. Now, the rattle-snake—"

"Nothing more about rattle-snakes, I beseech," in distress; "I must positively decline to reënter upon that subject. Sit down, sir, I beg, and take some of this wine."

"To invite me to sit down with you is hospitable," collectedly acquiescing now in the change of topics; "and hospitality being fabled to be of oriental origin, and forming, as it does, the subject of a pleasing Arabian romance, as well as being a very romantic thing in itself—hence I always hear the expressions of hospitality with pleasure. But, as for the wine, my regard for that beverage is so extreme, and I am so fearful of letting it sate me, that I keep my love for it in the lasting condition of an untried abstraction. Briefly, I quaff immense draughts of wine from the page of Hafiz, but wine from a cup I seldom as much as sip."

The cosmopolitan turned a mild glance upon the speaker, who, now occupying the chair opposite him, sat there purely and coldly radiant as a prism. It seemed as if one could almost hear him vitreously chime and ring. That moment a waiter passed, whom, arresting with a sign, the cosmopolitan bid go bring a goblet of ice-water. "Ice it well, waiter," said he; "and now," turning to the stranger, "will you, if you please, give me your reason for the warning words you first addressed to me?"

"I hope they were not such warnings as most warnings are," said the stranger; "warnings which do not forewarn, but in mockery come after the fact. And yet something in you bids me think now, that whatever latent design your impostor friend might have had upon you, it as yet remains unaccomplished. You read his label."

"And what did it say? 'This is a genial soul.' So you see you must either give up your doctrine of labels, or else your prejudice against my friend. But tell me," with renewed earnestness, "what do you take him for? What is he?"

"What are you? What am I? Nobody knows who anybody is. The data which life furnishes, towards forming a true estimate of any being, are as insufficient to that end as in geometry one side given would be to determine the triangle."

"But is not this doctrine of triangles someway inconsistent with your doctrine of labels?"

"Yes; but what of that? I seldom care to be consistent. In a philosophical view, consistency is a certain level at all times, maintained in all the thoughts of one's mind. But, since nature is nearly all hill and dale, how can one keep naturally advancing in knowledge without submitting to the natural inequalities in the progress? Advance into knowledge is just like advance upon the grand Erie canal, where, from the character of the country, change of level is inevitable; you are locked up and locked down with perpetual inconsistencies, and yet all the time you get on; while the dullest part of the whole route is what the boatmen call the 'long level'—a consistently-flat surface of sixty miles through stagnant swamps."

"In one particular," rejoined the cosmopolitan, "your simile is, perhaps, unfortunate. For, after all these weary lockings-up and lockings-down, upon how much of a higher plain do you finally stand? Enough to make it an object? Having from youth been taught reverence for knowledge, you must pardon me if, on but this one account, I reject your analogy. But really you someway betwitch me with your tempting discourse, so that I keep straying from my point unawares. You tell me you cannot certainly know who or what my friend is; pray, what do you conjecture him to be?"

"I conjecture him to be what, among the ancient Egyptians, was called a ——" using some unknown word.

"A ——! And what is that?"

"A —— is what Proclus, in a little note to his third book on the theology of Plato, defines as —— ——" coming out with a sentence of Greek.

Holding up his glass, and steadily looking through its transparency, the cosmopolitan rejoined: "That, in so defining the thing, Proclus set it to modern understandings in the most crystal light it was susceptible of, I will not rashly deny; still, if you could put the definition in words suited to perceptions like mine, I should take it for a favor."

"A favor!" slightly lifting his cool eyebrows; "a bridal favor I understand, a knot of white ribands, a very beautiful type of the purity of true marriage; but of other favors I am yet to learn; and still, in a vague way, the word, as you employ it, strikes me as unpleasingly significant in general of some poor, unheroic submission to being done good to."

Here the goblet of iced-water was brought, and, in compliance with a sign from the cosmopolitan, was placed before the stranger, who, not before expressing acknowledgments, took a draught, apparently refreshing—its very coldness, as with some is the case, proving not entirely uncongenial.

At last, setting down the goblet, and gently wiping from his lips the beads of water freshly clinging there as to the valve of a coral-shell upon a reef, he turned upon the cosmopolitan, and, in a manner the most cool, self-possessed, and matter-of-fact possible, said: "I hold to the metempsychosis; and whoever I may be now, I feel that I was once the stoic Arrian, and have inklings of having been equally puzzled by a word in the current language of that former time, very probably answering to your word *favor*."

"Would you favor me by explaining?" said the cosmopolitan, blandly.

"Sir," responded the stranger, with a very slight degree of severity, "I like lucidity, of all things, and am afraid I shall hardly be able to converse satisfactorily with you, unless you bear it in mind."

The cosmopolitan ruminatingly eyed him awhile, then said: "The best way, as I have heard, to get out of a labyrinth, is to retrace one's steps. I will accordingly retrace mine, and beg you will accompany me. In short, once again to return to the point: for what reason did you warn me against my friend?"

"Briefly, then, and clearly, because, as before said, I conjecture him to be what, among the ancient Egyptians—"

"Pray, now," earnestly deprecated the cosmopolitan, "pray, now, why disturb the repose of those ancient Egyptians? What to us are their words or their thoughts? Are we pauper Arabs, without a house of our own, that, with the mummies, we must turn squatters among the dust of the Catacombs?"

"Pharaoh's poorest brick-maker lies proudlier in his rags than the Emperor of all the Russias in his hollands," oracularly said the stranger; "for death, though in a worm, is majestic; while life, though in a king, is contemptible. So talk not against mummies. It is a part of my mission to teach mankind a due reverence for mummies."

Fortunately, to arrest these incoherencies, or rather, to vary them, a haggard, inspired-looking man now approached—a crazy beggar, asking alms under the form of peddling a rhapsodical tract, composed by himself, and setting forth his claims to some rhapsodical apostleship. Though ragged and dirty, there was about him no touch of vulgarity; for, by nature, his manner was not unrefined, his frame slender, and appeared the more so from the broad, untanned frontlet of his brow, tangled over with a disheveled mass of raven curls, throwing a still deeper tinge upon a complexion like that of a shriveled berry. Nothing could exceed his look of picturesque Italian ruin and dethronement, heightened by what seemed just one glimmering peep of reason, insufficient to do him any lasting good, but enough, perhaps, to suggest a torment of latent doubts at times, whether his addled dream of glory were true.

Accepting the tract offered him, the cosmopolitan glanced over it, and, seeming to see just what it was, closed it, put it in his pocket, eyed the man a moment, then, leaning over and presenting him with a shilling, said to him, in tones kind and considerate: "I am sorry, my friend, that I happen to be engaged just now; but, having purchased your work, I promise myself much satisfaction in its perusal at my earliest leisure."

In his tattered, single-breasted frock-coat, buttoned meagerly up to his chin, the shatter-brain made him a bow, which, for courtesy, would not have misbecome a viscount, then turned with silent appeal to the stranger. But the stranger sat more like a cold prism than ever, while an expression of keen Yankee cuteness, now replacing his former mystical one, lent added icicles to his aspect. His whole air said: "Nothing from me." The repulsed petitioner threw a look full of resentful pride and cracked disdain upon him, and went his way.

"Come, now," said the cosmopolitan, a little reproachfully, "you ought to have sympathized with that man; tell me, did you feel no fellow-feeling? Look at his tract here, quite in the transcendental vein."

"Excuse me," said the stranger, declining the tract, "I never patronize scoundrels."

"Scoundrels?"

"I detected in him, sir, a damning peep of sense—damning, I say; for sense in a seeming madman is scoundrelism. I take him for a cunning vagabond, who picks up a vagabond living by adoitly playing the madman. Did you not remark how he flinched under my eye?"

"Really," drawing a long, astonished breath, "I could hardly have divined in you a temper so subtlely distrustful. Flinched? to be sure he did, poor fellow; you received him with so lame a welcome. As for his adroitly playing the madman, invidious critics might object the same to some one or two strolling magi of these days. But that is a matter I know nothing about. But, once more, and for the last time, to return to the point: why sir, did you warn me against my friend? I shall rejoice, if, as I think it will prove, your want of confidence in my friend rests upon a basis equally slender with your distrust of the lunatic. Come, why did you warn me? Put it, I beseech, in few words, and those English."

"I warned you against him because he is suspected for what on these boats is known—so they tell me—as a Mississippi operator."

"An operator, ah? he operates, does he? My friend, then, is something like what the Indians call a Great Medicine, is he? He operates, he purges, he drains off the repletions."

"I perceive, sir," said the stranger, constitutionally obtuse to the pleasant drollery, "that your notion, of what is called a Great Medicine, needs correction. The Great Medicine among the Indians is less a bolus than a man in grave esteem for his politic sagacity."

"And is not my friend politic? Is not my friend sagacious? By your own definition, is not my friend a Great Medicine?"

"No, he is an operator, a Mississippi operator; an equivocal character. That he is such, I little doubt, having had him pointed out to me as such by one desirous of initiating me into any little novelty of this western region, where I never before traveled. And, sir, if I am not mistaken, you also are a stranger here (but, indeed, where in this strange universe is not one a stranger?) and that is a reason why I felt moved to warn you against a companion who could not be otherwise than perilous to one of a free and trustful disposition. But I repeat the hope, that, thus far at least, he has not succeeded with you, and trust that, for the future, he will not."

"Thank you for your concern; but hardly can I equally thank you for so steadily maintaining the hypothesis of my friend's objectionableness. True, I but made his acquaintance for the first to-day, and know little of his antecedents; but that would seem no just reason why a nature like his should not of itself inspire confidence. And since your own knowledge of the gentleman is not, by your account, so exact as it might be, you will pardon me if I decline to welcome any further suggestions unflattering to him. Indeed, sir," with friendly decision, "let us change the subject."

CHAPTER XXXVII

"BOTH, the subject and the interlocutor," replied the stranger rising, and waiting the return towards him of a promenader, that moment turning at the further end of his walk.

"Egbert!" said he, calling.

Egbert, a well-dressed, commercial-looking gentleman of about thirty, responded in a way strikingly deferential, and in a moment stood near, in the attitude less of an equal companion apparently than a confidential follower.

"This," said the stranger, taking Egbert by the hand and leading him to the cosmopolitan, "this is Egbert, a disciple. I wish you to know Egbert. Egbert was the first among mankind to reduce to practice the principles of Mark Winsome—principles previously accounted as less adapted to life than the closet. Egbert," turning to the disciple, who, with seeming modesty, a little shrank under these compliments, "Egbert, this," with a salute towards the cosmopolitan, "is, like all of us, a stranger. I wish you, Egbert, to know this brother stranger; be communicative with him. Particularly if, by anything hitherto dropped, his curiosity has been roused as to the precise nature of my philosophy, I trust you will not leave such curiosity ungratified. You, Egbert, by simply setting forth your practice, can do more to enlighten one as to my theory, than I myself can by mere speech. Indeed, it is by you that I myself best understand myself. For to every philosophy are certain rear parts, very important parts, and these, like the rear of one's head, are best seen by reflection. Now, as in a glass, you, Egbert, in your life, reflect to me the more important part of my system. He, who approves you, approves the philosophy of Mark Winsome."

222

Though portions of this harangue may, perhaps, in the phraseology seem self-complacent, yet no trace of self-complacency was perceptible in the speaker's manner, which throughout was plain, unassuming, dignified, and manly; the teacher and prophet seemed to lurk more in the idea, so to speak, than in the mere bearing of him who was the vehicle of it.

"Sir," said the cosmopolitan, who seemed not a little interested in this new aspect of matters, "you speak of a certain philosophy, and a more or less occult one it may be, and hint of its bearing upon practical life; pray, tell me, if the study of this philosophy tends to the same formation of character with the experiences of the world?"

"It does; and that is the test of its truth; for any philosophy that, being in operation contradictory to the ways of the world, tends to produce a character at odds with it, such a philosophy must necessarily be but a cheat and a dream."

"You a little surprise me," answered the cosmopolitan; "for, from an occasional profundity in you, and also from your allusions to a profound work on the theology of Plato, it would seem but natural to surmise that, if you are the originator of any philosophy, it must needs so partake of the abstruse, as to exalt it above the comparatively vile uses of life."

"No uncommon mistake with regard to me," rejoined the other. Then meekly standing like a Raphael: "If still in golden accents old Memnon murmurs his riddle, none the less does the balance-sheet of every man's ledger unriddle the profit or loss of life. Sir," with calm energy, "man came into this world, not to sit down and muse, not to befog himself with vain subtleties, but to gird up his loins and to work. Mystery is in the morning, and mystery in the night, and the beauty of mystery is everywhere; but still the plain truth remains, that mouth and purse must be filled. If, hitherto, you have supposed me a visionary, be undeceived. I am no one-ideaed one, either; no more than the seers before me. Was not Seneca a usurer? Bacon a courtier? and Swedenborg, though with one eye on the invisible, did he not keep the other on the main chance?

Along with whatever else it may be given me to be, I am a man of serviceable knowledge, and a man of the world. Know me for such. And as for my disciple here," turning towards him, "if you look to find any soft Utopianisms and last year's sunsets in him, I smile to think how he will set you right. The doctrines I have taught him will, I trust, lead him neither to the madhouse nor the poor-house, as so many other doctrines have served credulous sticklers. Furthermore," glancing upon him paternally, "Egbert is both my disciple and my poet. For poetry is not a thing of ink and rhyme, but of thought and act, and, in the latter way, is by any one to be found anywhere, when in useful action sought. In a word, my disciple here is a thriving young merchant, a practical poet in the West India trade. There," presenting Egbert's hand to the cosmopolitan, "I join you, and leave you." With which words, and without bowing, the master withdrew.

CHAPTER XXXVIII

THE DISCIPLE UNBENDS, AND CONSENTS TO ACT A SOCIAL PART

In the master's presence the disciple had stood as one not ignorant of his place; modesty was in his expression, with a sort of reverential depression. But the presence of the superior withdrawn, he seemed lithely to shoot up erect from beneath it, like one of those wire men from a toy snuff-box.

He was, as before said, a young man of about thirty. His countenance of that neuter sort, which, in repose, is neither prepossessing nor disagreeable; so that it seemed quite uncertain how he would turn out. His dress was neat, with just enough of the mode to save it from the reproach of originality; in which general respect, though with a readjustment of details, his costume seemed modeled upon his master's. But, upon the whole, he was, to all appearances, the last person in the world that one would take for the disciple of any transcendental philosophy; though, indeed, something about his sharp nose and shaved chin seemed to hint that if mysticism, as a lesson, ever came in his way, he might, with the characteristic knack of a true New-Englander, turn even so profitless a thing to some profitable account.

"Well," said he, now familiarly seating himself in the vacated chair, "what do you think of Mark? Sublime fellow, ain't he?"

"That each member of the human guild is worthy respect my friend," rejoined the cosmopolitan, "is a fact which no admirer of that guild will question; but that, in view of higher natures, the word sublime, so frequently applied to them, can, without confusion, be also applied to man, is a point which man will decide for himself; though, indeed, if he decide it in the affirmative, it is not for me to object. But I am curious to know more of that philosophy of which, at present, I have but inklings. You, its first disciple among men, it seems, are peculiarly qualified to expound it. Have you any objections to begin now?"

"None at all," squaring himself to the table. "Where shall I begin? At first principles?"

"You remember that it was in a practical way that you were represented as being fitted for the clear exposition. Now, what you call first principles, I have, in some things, found to be more or less vague. Permit me, then, in a plain way, to suppose some common case in real life, and that done, I would like you to tell me how you, the practical disciple of the philosophy I wish to know about, would, in that case, conduct."

"A business-like view. Propose the case."

"Not only the case, but the persons. The case is this: There are two friends, friends from childhood, bosom-friends; one of whom, for the first time, being in need, for the first time seeks a loan from the other, who, as far as fortune goes, is more than competent to grant it. And the persons are to be you and I: you, the friend from whom the loan is sought—I, the friend who seeks it; you, the disciple of the philosophy in question—I, a common man, with no more philosophy than to know that when I am comfortably warm I don't feel cold, and when I have the ague I shake. Mind, now, you must work up your imagination, and, as much as possible, talk and behave just as if the case supposed were a fact. For brevity, you shall call me Frank, and I will call you Charlie. Are you agreed?"

"Perfectly. You begin."

The cosmopolitan paused a moment, then, assuming a serious and care-worn air, suitable to the part to be enacted, addressed his hypothesized friend.

CHAPTER XXXIX

THE HYPOTHETICAL FRIENDS

"Charlie, I am going to put confidence in you."

"You always have, and with reason. What is it Frank?"

"Charlie, I am in want—urgent want of money."

"That's not well."

"But it *will* be well, Charlie, if you loan me a hundred dollars. I would not ask this of you, only my need is sore, and you and I have so long shared hearts and minds together, however unequally on my side, that nothing remains to prove our friendship than, with the same inequality on my side, to share purses. You will do me the favor, won't you?"

"Favor? What do you mean by asking me to do you a favor?"

"Why Charlie, you never used to talk so."

"Because, Frank, you on your side, never used to talk so."

"But won't you loan me the money?"

"No, Frank."

"Why?"

"Because my rule forbids. I give away money, but never loan it; and of course the man who calls himself my friend is above receiving alms. The negotiation of a loan is a business transaction. And I will transact no business with a friend. What a friend is, he is socially and intellectually; and I rate social and intellectual friendship too high to degrade it on either side into a pecuniary make-shift. To be sure there are, and I have, what is called business friends; that is, commercial acquaintances, very convenient persons. But I draw a red-ink line between them and my friends in the true sense—my friends social and intellectual. In brief, a true friend has nothing to do with loans; he should have a soul above loans. Loans are such unfriendly accommodations as are to be had from the soulless corporation of a bank, by giving the regular security and paying the regular discount."

"An *unfriendly* accommodation? Do those words go together handsomely?"

"Like the poor farmer's team, of an old man and a cow—not handsomely, but to the purpose. Look, Frank, a loan of money on interest is a sale of money on credit. To sell a thing on credit may be an accommodation, but where is the friendliness? Few men in their senses, except operators, borrow money on interest, except upon a necessity akin to starvation. Well, now, where is the friendliness of my letting a starving man have, say, the money's worth of a barrel of flour upon the condition that, on a given day, he shall let me have the money's worth of a barrel and a half of flour; especially if I add this further proviso, that if he fail so to do, I shall then, to secure to myself the money's worth of my barrel and his half barrel, put his heart up at public auction, and, as it is cruel to part families, throw in his wife's and children's?"

"I understand," with a pathetic shudder; "but even did it come to that, such a step on the creditor's part, let us, for the honor of human nature, hope, were less the intention than the contingency."

"But, Frank, a contingency not unprovided for in the taking beforehand of due securities."

"Still, Charlie, was not the loan in the first place a friend's act?"

"And the auction in the last place an enemy's act. Don't you see? The enmity lies couched in the friendship, just as the ruin in the relief."

"I must be very stupid to-day, Charlie, but really, I can't understand this. Excuse me, my dear friend, but it strikes me that in going into the philosophy of the subject, you go somewhat out of your depth."

"So said the incautious wader-out to the ocean; but the ocean replied: 'It is just the other way, my wet friend,' and drowned him."

"That, Charlie, is a fable about as unjust to the ocean, as some of Æsop's are to the animals. The ocean is a magnanimous element, and would scorn to assassinate a poor fellow, let alone taunting him in the act. But I don't understand what you say about enmity couched in friendship, and ruin in relief."

"I will illustrate, Frank. The needy man is a train slipped off the rail. He who loans him money on interest is the one who, by way of accommodation, helps get the train back where it belongs; but then, by way of making all square, and a little more, telegraphs to an agent, thirty miles ahead by a precipice, to throw just there, on his account, a beam across the track. Your needy man's principle-and-interest friend is, I say again, a friend with an enmity in reserve. No, no, my dear friend, no interest for me. I scorn interest."

"Well, Charlie, none need you charge. Loan me without interest."

"That would be alms again."

"Alms, if the sum borrowed is returned?"

"Yes: an alms, not of the principle, but the interest."

"Well, I am in sore need, so I will not decline the alms. Seeing that it is you, Charlie, gratefully will I accept the alms of the interest. No humiliation between friends."

"Now, how in the refined view of friendship can you suffer yourself to talk so, my dear Frank. It pains me. For though I am not of the sour mind of Solomon, that, in the hour of need, a stranger is better than a brother; yet, I entirely agree with my sublime master, who, in his Essay on Friendship, says so nobly, that if he want a terrestrial convenience, not to his friend celestial (or friend social and intellectual) would he go; no: for his terrestial convenience, to his friend terrestrial (or humbler business-friend) he goes. Very lucidly he adds the reason: Because, for the superior nature, which on no account can ever descend to do good, to be annoyed with requests to do it, when the inferior one, which by no instruction can ever rise above that capacity, stands always inclined to it —this is unsuitable."

"Then I will not consider you as my friend celestial, but as the other."

"It racks me to come to that; but, to oblige you, I'll do it. We are business friends; business is business. You want to negotiate a loan. Very good. On what paper? Will you pay three per cent. a month? Where is your security?"

"Surely, you will not exact those formalities from your old schoolmate—him with whom you have so often sauntered down the groves of Academe, discoursing of the beauty of virtue, and the grace that is in kindliness—and all for so paltry a sum. Security? Our being fellow-academics, and friends from childhood up, is security."

"Pardon me, my dear Frank, our being fellow-academics is the worst of securities; while, our having been friends from childhood up is just no security at all. You forget we are now business friends."

"And you, on your side, forget, Charlie, that as your business friend I can give you no security; my need being so sore that I cannot get an indorser."

"No indorser, then, no business loan."

"Since then, Charlie, neither as the one nor the other sort of friend you have defined, can I prevail with you; how if, combining the two, I sue as both?"

"Are you a centaur?"

"When all is said then, what good have I of your friendship, regarded in what light you will?"

"The good which is in the philosophy of Mark Winsome, as reduced to practice by a practical disciple."

"And why don't you add, much good may the philosophy of Mark Winsome do me? Ah," turning invokingly, "what is friendship, if it be not the helping hand and the feeling heart, the good Samaritan pouring out at need the purse as the vial!"

"Now, my dear Frank, don't be childish. Through tears never did man see his way in the dark. I should hold you unworthy that sincere friendship I bear you, could I think that friendship in the ideal is too lofty for you to conceive. And let me tell you, my dear Frank, that you would seriously shake the foundations of our love, if ever again you should repeat the present scene. The philosophy, which is mine in the strongest way, teaches plain-dealing. Let me, then, now, as at the most suitable time, candidly disclose certain circumstances you seem in ignorance of. Though our friendship began in boyhood, think not that, on my side at least, it began injudiciously. Boys are little men, it is said. You, I juvenilely picked out for my friend, for your favorable points at the time; not the least of which were your good manners, handsome dress, and your parents' rank and repute of wealth. In short, like any grown man, boy though I was, I went into the market and chose me my mutton, not for its leanness, but its fatness. In other words, there seemed in you, the schoolboy who always had silver in his pocket, a reasonable probability that you would never stand in lean need of fat succor; and if my early impression has not been verified by the event, it is only because of the caprice of fortune producing a fallibility of human expectations, however discreet."

"Oh, that I should listen to this cold-blooded disclosure!"

"A little cold blood in your ardent veins, my dear Frank, wouldn't do you any harm, let me tell you. Cold-blooded? You say that, because my disclosure seems to involve a vile prudence on my side. But not so. My reason for choosing you in part for the points I have mentioned, was solely with a view of preserving inviolate the delicacy of the connection. For—do but think of it—what more distressing to delicate friendship, formed early, than your friend's eventually, in manhood, dropping in of a rainy night for his little loan of five dollars or so? Can delicate friendship stand that? And, on the other side, would delicate friendship, so long as it retained its delicacy, do that? Would you not instinctively say of your dripping friend in the entry, 'I have been deceived, fraudulently deceived, in this man; he is no true friend that, in platonic love to demand love-rites?' "

"And rites, doubly rights, they are, cruel Charlie!"

"Take it how you will, heed well how, by too importunately claiming those rights, as you call them, you shake those foundations I hinted of. For though, as it turns out, I, in my early friendship, built me a fair house on a poor site; yet such pains and cost have I lavished on that house, that, after all, it is dear to me. No, I would not lose the sweet boon of your friendship, Frank. But beware."

"And of what? Of being in need? Oh, Charlie! you talk not to a god, a being who in himself holds his own estate, but to a man who, being a man, is the sport of fate's wind and wave, and who mounts towards heaven or sinks towards hell, as the billows roll him in trough or on crest."

"Tut! Frank. Man is no such poor devil as that comes to—no poor drifting sea-weed of the universe. Man has a soul; which, if he will, puts him beyond fortune's finger and the future's spite. Don't whine like fortune's whipped dog, Frank, or by the heart of a true friend, I will cut ye."

"Cut me you have already, cruel Charlie, and to the quick. Call to mind the days we went nutting, the times we walked in the woods, arms wreathed about each other, showing trunks invined like the trees:—oh, Charlie!"

"Pish! we were boys."

"Then lucky the fate of the first-born of Egypt, cold in the grave ere maturity struck them with a sharper frost.—Charlie?"

"Fie! you're a girl."

"Help, help, Charlie, I want help!"

"Help? to say nothing of the friend, there is something wrong about the man who wants help. There is somewhere a defect, a want, in brief, a need, a crying need, somewhere about that man."

"So there is, Charlie.—Help, Help!"

"How foolish a cry, when to implore help, is itself the proof of undesert of it.

"Oh, this, all along, is not you, Charlie, but some ventriloquist who usurps your larynx. It is Mark Winsome that speaks, not Charlie."

"If so, thank heaven, the voice of Mark Winsome is not alien but congenial to my larynx. If the philosophy of that illustrious teacher find little response among mankind at large, it is less that they do not possess teachable tempers, than because they are so unfortunate as not to have natures predisposed to accord with him."

"Welcome, that compliment to humanity," exclaimed Frank with energy, "the truer because unintended. And long in this respect may humanity remain what you affirm it. And long it will; since humanity, inwardly feeling how subject it is to straits, and hence how precious is help, will, for selfishness' sake, if no other, long postpone ratifying a philosophy that banishes help from the world. But Charlie, Charlie! speak as you used to; tell me you will help me. Were the case reversed, not less freely would I loan you the money than you would ask me to loan it."

"*I* ask? *I* ask a loan? Frank, by this hand, under no circumstances would I accept a loan, though without asking pressed on me. The experience of China Aster might warn me."

"And what was that?"

"Not very unlike the experience of the man that built himself a palace of moon-beams, and when the moon set was surprised that his palace vanished with it. I will tell you about China Aster. I wish I could do so in my own words, but unhappily the original story-teller here has so tyrannized over me, that it is quite impossible for me to repeat his incidents without sliding into his style. I forewarn you of this, that you may not think me so maudlin as, in some parts, the story would seem to make its narrator. It is too bad that any intellect, especially in so small a matter, should have such power to impose itself upon another, against its best exerted will, too. However, it is satisfaction to know that the main moral, to which all tends, I fully approve. But, to begin."

CHAPTER XL

"CHINA ASTER was a young candle-maker of Marietta, at the
mouth of the Muskingum—one whose trade would seem a kind
of subordinate branch of that parent craft and mystery of the
hosts of heaven, to be the means, effectively or otherwise, of
shedding some light through the darkness of a planet benighted. But he made little money by the business. Much ado
had poor China Aster and his family to live; he could, if he
chose, light up from his stores a whole street, but not so easily
could he light up with prosperity the hearts of his household.

"Now, China Aster, it so happened, had a friend, Orchis, a
shoemaker; one whose calling it is to defend the understandings of men from naked contact with the substance of things:
a very useful vocation, and which, spite of all the wiseacres
may prophecy, will hardly go out of fashion so long as rocks
are hard and flints will gall. All at once, by a capital prize in
a lottery, this useful shoemaker was raised from a bench to a
sofa. A small nabob was the shoemaker now, and the understandings of men, let them shift for themselves. Not that Orchis
was, by prosperity, elated into heartlessness. Not at all. Because, in his fine apparel, strolling one morning into the candlery, and gayly switching about at the candle-boxes with his
gold-headed cane—while poor China Aster, with his greasy
paper cap and leather apron, was selling one candle for one
penny to a poor orange-woman, who, with the patronizing
coolness of a liberal customer, required it to be carefully rolled
up and tied in a half sheet of paper—lively Orchis, the woman

234

being gone, discontinued his gay switchings and said: 'This
is poor business for you, friend China Aster; your capital is
too small. You must drop this vile tallow and hold up pure
spermaceti to the world. I tell you what it is, you shall have
one thousand dollars to extend with. In fact, you must make
money, China Aster. I don't like to see your little boy paddling
about without shoes, as he does.'

"'Heaven bless your goodness, friend Orchis,' replied the
candle-maker, 'but don't take it illy if I call to mind the word
of my uncle, the blacksmith, who, when a loan was offered him,
declined it, saying: "To ply my own hammer, light though it
be, I think best, rather than piece it out heavier by welding to
it a bit off a neighbor's hammer, though that may have some
weight to spare; otherwise, were the borrowed bit suddenly
wanted again, it might not split off at the welding, but too
much to one side or the other."'

"'Nonsense, friend China Aster, don't be so honest; your boy
is barefoot. Besides, a rich man lose by a poor man? Or a friend
be the worse by a friend? China Aster, I am afraid that, in
leaning over into your vats here, this morning, you have spilled
out your wisdom. Hush! I won't hear any more. Where's your
desk? Oh, here.' With that, Orchis dashed off a check on his
bank, and off-handedly presenting it, said: 'There, friend
China Aster, is your one thousand dollars; when you make it
ten thousand, as you soon enough will (for experience the only
true knowledge, teaches me that, for every one, good luck is
in store), then, China Aster, why, then you can return me the
money or not, just as you please. But, in any event, give yourself no concern, for I shall never demand payment.'

"Now, as kind heaven will so have it that to a hungry man
bread is a great temptation, and, therefore, he is not too harshly
to be blamed, if, when freely offered, he take it, even though it
be uncertain whether he shall ever be able to reciprocate; so,
to a poor man, proffered money is equally enticing, and the
worst that can be said of him, if he accept it, is just what can
be said in the other case of the hungry man. In short, the poor
candle-maker's scrupulous morality succumbed to his un-

scrupulous necessity, as is now and then apt to be the case. He took the check, and was about carefully putting it away for the present, when Orchis, switching about again with his gold-headed cane, said: 'By-the-way, China Aster, it don't mean anything, but suppose you make a little memorandum of this; won't do any harm, you know.' So China Aster gave Orchis his note for one thousand dollars on demand. Orchis took it, and looked at it a moment, 'Pooh, I told you, friend China Aster, I wasn't going ever to make any *demand*.' Then tearing up the note, and switching away again at the candle-boxes, said, carelessly; 'Put it at four years.' So China Aster gave Orchis his note for one thousand dollars at four years. 'You see I'll never trouble you about this,' said Orchis, slipping it in his pocket-book, 'give yourself no further thought, friend China Aster, than how best to invest your money. And don't forget my hint about spermaceti. Go into that, and I'll buy all my light of you,' with which encouraging words, he, with wonted, rattling kindness, took leave.

"China Aster remained standing just where Orchis had left him; when, suddenly, two elderly friends, having nothing better to do, dropped in for a chat. The chat over, China Aster, in greasy cap and apron, ran after Orchis, and said: 'Friend Orchis, heaven will reward you for your good intentions, but here is your check, and now give me my note.'

" 'Your honesty is a bore, China Aster,' said Orchis, not without displeasure. 'I won't take the check from you.'

" 'Then you must take it from the pavement, Orchis,' said China Aster; and, picking up a stone, he placed the check under it on the walk.

" 'China Aster,' said Orchis, inquisitively eyeing him, 'after my leaving the candlery just now, what asses dropped in there to advise with you, that now you hurry after me, and act so like a fool? Shouldn't wonder if it was those two old asses that the boys nickname Old Plain Talk and Old Prudence.'

" 'Yes, it was those two, Orchis, but don't call them names.'

" 'A brace of spavined old croakers. Old Plain Talk had a shrew for a wife, and that's made him shrewish; and Old Pru-

dence, when a boy, broke down in an applestall, and that dis-
couraged him for life. No better sport for a knowing spark
like me than to hear Old Plain Talk wheeze out his sour old
saws, while Old Prudence stands by, leaning on his staff, wagging his frosty old pow, and chiming in at every clause.'

" 'How can you speak so, friend Orchis, of those who were
my father's friends?'

" 'Save me from my friends, if those old croakers were Old
Honesty's friends. I call your father so, for every one used to.
Why did they let him go in his old age on the town? Why,
China Aster, I've often heard from my mother, the chronicler,
that those two old fellows, with Old Conscience—as the boys
called the crabbed old quaker, that's dead now—they three
used to go to the poor-house when your father was there, and
get round his bed, and talk to him for all the world as Eliphaz,
Bildad, and Zophar did to poor old pauper Job. Yes, Job's com-
forters were Old Plain Talk, and Old Prudence, and Old Conscience, to your poor old father. Friends? I should like to know
who you call foes? With their everlasting croaking and re-
proaching they tormented poor Old Honesty, your father, to
death.'

"At these words, recalling the sad end of his worthy parent,
China Aster could not restrain some tears. Upon which Orchis
said: 'Why, China Aster, you are the dolefulest creature. Why
don't you, China Aster, take a bright view of life? You will
never get on in your business or anything else, if you don't
take the bright view of life. It's the ruination of a man to take
the dismal one.' Then, gayly poking at him with his gold-
headed can, 'Why don't you, then? Why don't you be bright
and hopeful, like me? Why don't you have confidence, China
Aster?'

" 'I'm sure I don't know, friend Orchis,' soberly replied
China Aster, 'but may be my not having drawn a lottery-prize,
like you, may make some difference.

" 'Nonsense! before I knew anything about the prize I was
gay as a lark, just as gay as I am now. In fact, it has always
been a principle with me to hold to the bright view.'

"Upon this, China Aster looked a little hard at Orchis, because the truth was, that until the lucky prize came to him, Orchis had gone under the nickname of Doleful Dumps, he having been beforetimes of a hypochondriac turn, so much so as to save up and put by a few dollars of his scanty earnings against that rainy day he used to groan so much about.

" 'I tell you what it is, now, friend China Aster,' said Orchis, pointing down to the check under the stone, and then slapping his pocket, 'the check shall lie there if you say so, but your note shan't keep it company. In fact, China Aster, I am too sincerely your friend to take advantage of a passing fit of the blues in you. You *shall* reap the benefit of my friendship.' With which, buttoning up his coat in a jiffy, away he ran, leaving the check behind.

"At first, China Aster was going to tear it up, but thinking that this ought not to be done except in the presence of the drawer of the check, he mused a while, and picking it up, trudged back to the candlery, fully resolved to call upon Orchis soon as his day's work was over, and destroy the check before his eyes. But it so happened that when China Aster called, Orchis was out, and, having waited for him a weary time in vain, China Aster went home, still with the check, but still resolved not to keep it another day. Bright and early next morning he would a second time go after Orchis, and would, no doubt, make a sure thing of it, by finding him in his bed; for since the lottery-prize came to him, Orchis, besides becoming more cheery, had also grown a little lazy. But as destiny would have it, that same night China Aster had a dream, in which a being in the guise of a smiling angel, and holding a kind of cornucopia in her hand, hovered over him, pouring down showers of small gold dollars, thick as kernels of corn. 'I am Bright Future, friend China Aster,' said the angel, 'and if you do what friend Orchis would have you do, just see what will come of it.' With which Bright Future, with another swing of her cornucopia, poured such another shower of small gold dollars upon him, that it seemed to bank him up all round, and he waded about in it like a maltster in malt.

"Now, dreams are wonderful things, as everybody knows—
so wonderful, indeed, that some people stop not short of ascrib-
ing them directly to heaven; and China Aster, who was of a
proper turn of mind in everything, thought that in consideration of the dream, it would be but well to wait a little, ere seeking Orchis again. During the day, China Aster's mind dwelling
continually upon the dream, he was so full of it, that when
Old Plain Talk dropped in to see him, just before dinner-time,
as he often did, out of the interest he took in Old Honesty's
son, China Aster told all about his vision, adding that he could
not think that so radiant an angel could deceive; and, indeed,
talked at such a rate that one would have thought he believed
the angel some beautiful human philanthropist. Something in
this sort Old Plain Talk understood him, and accordingly, in
his plain way, said: 'China Aster, you tell me that an angel
appeared to you in a dream. Now, what does that amount to
but this, that you dreamed an angel appeared to you? Go
right away, China Aster, and return the check, as I advised
you before. If friend Prudence were here, he would say just
the same thing.' With which words Old Plain Talk went off to
find friend Prudence, but not succeeding, was returning to
the candlery himself, when, at distance mistaking him for a
dun who had long annoyed him, China Aster in a panic barred
all his doors, and ran to the back part of the candlery, where
no knock could be heard.

"By this sad mistake, being left with no friend to argue the
other side of the question, China Aster was so worked upon
at last, by musing over his dream, that nothing would do but
he must get the check cashed, and lay out the money the very
same day in buying a good lot of spermaceti to make into
candles, by which operation he counted upon turning a better
penny than he ever had before in his life; in fact, this he
believed would prove the foundation of that famous fortune
which the angel had promised him.

"Now, in using the money, China Aster was resolved punctu-
ally to pay the interest every six months till the principal
should be returned, howbeit not a word about such a thing had

been breathed by Orchis; though, indeed, according to custom, as well as law, in such matters, interest would legitimately accrue on the loan, nothing to the contrary having been put in the bond. Whether Orchis at the time had this in mind or not, there is no sure telling; but, to all appearance, he never so much as cared to think about the matter, one way or other.

"Though the spermaceti venture rather disappointed China Aster's sanguine expectations, yet he made out to pay the first six months' interest, and though his next venture turned out still less prosperously, yet by pinching his family in the matter of fresh meat, and, what pained him still more, his boys' schooling, he contrived to pay the second six months' interest, sincerely grieved that integrity, as well as its opposite, though not in an equal degree, costs something, sometimes.

"Meanwhile, Orchis had gone on a trip to Europe by advice of a physician; it so happening that, since the lottery-prize came to him, it had been discovered to Orchis that his health was not very firm, though he had never complained of anything before but a slight ailing of the spleen, scarce worth talking about at the time. So Orchis, being abroad, could not help China Aster's paying his interest as he did, however much he might have been opposed to it; for China Aster paid it to Orchis's agent, who was of too business-like a turn to decline interest regularly paid in on a loan.

"But overmuch to trouble the agent on that score was not again to be the fate of China Aster; for, not being of that skeptical spirit which refuses to trust customers, his third venture resulted, through bad debts, in almost a total loss—a bad blow for the candle-maker. Neither did Old Plain Talk, and Old Prudence neglect the opportunity to read him an uncheerful enough lesson upon the consequences of his disregarding their advice in the matter of having nothing to do with borrowed money. 'It's all just as I predicted,' said Old Plain Talk, blowing his old nose with his old bandana. 'Yea, indeed is it,' chimed in Old Prudence, rapping his staff on the floor, and then leaning upon it, looking with solemn forebodings upon China Aster. Low-spirited enough felt the poor candle-maker; till all at once who should come with a bright face to him but his bright friend, the angel, in another dream. Again the cornucopia poured out its treasure, and promised still more. Revived by the vision, he resolved not to be downhearted, but up and at it once more—contrary to the advice of Old Plain Talk, backed as usual by his crony, which was to the effect, that, under present circumstances, the best thing China Aster could do, would be to wind up his business, settle, if he could, all his liabilities, and then go to work as a journeyman, by which he could earn good wages, and give up, from that time henceforth, all thoughts of rising above being a paid subordinate to men more able than himself, for China Aster's career thus far plainly proved him the legitimate son of Old Honesty, who, as every one knew, had never shown much business-talent, so little, in fact, that many said of him that he had no business to be in business. And just this plain saying Plain Talk now plainly applied to China Aster, and Old Prudence never disagreed with him. But the angel in the dream did, and, maugre Plain Talk, put quite other notions into the candle-maker.

"He considered what he should do towards reëstablishing himself. Doubtless, had Orchis been in the country, he would have aided him in this strait. As it was, he applied to others; and as in the world, much as some may hint to the contrary, an honest man in misfortune still can find friends to stay by him and help him, even so it proved with China Aster, who at last succeeded in borrowing from a rich old farmer the sum of six hundred dollars, at the usual interest of money-lenders, upon the security of a secret bond signed by China Aster's wife and himself, to the effect that all such right and title to any property that should be left her by a well-to-do childless uncle, an invalid tanner, such property should, in the event of China Aster's failing to return the borrowed sum on the given day, be the lawful possession of the money-lender. True, it was just as much as China Aster could possibly do to induce his wife, a careful woman, to sign this bond; because she had always regarded her promised share in her uncle's estate as an

anchor well to windward of the hard times in which China
Aster had always been more or less involved, and from which,
in her bosom, she never had seen much chance of his freeing
himself. Some notion may be had of China Aster's standing in
the heart and head of his wife, by a short sentence commonly
used in reply to such persons as happened to sound her on
the point. 'China Aster,' she would say, 'is a good husband,
but a bad business man!' Indeed, she was a connection on the
maternal side of Old Plain Talk's. But had not China Aster
taken good care not to let Old Plain Talk and Old Prudence
hear of his dealings with the old farmer, ten to one they would,
in some way, have interfered with his success in that quarter.

"It has been hinted that the honesty of China Aster was
what mainly induced the money-lender to befriend him in his
misfortune, and this must be apparent; for, had China Aster
been a different man, the money-lender might have dreaded
lest, in the event of his failing to meet his note, he might some
way prove slippery—more especially as, in the hour of distress,
worked upon by remorse for so jeopardizing his wife's money,
his heart might prove a traitor to his bond, not to hint that it
was more than doubtful how such a secret security and claim,
as in the last resort would be the old farmer's, would stand in
a court of law. But though one inference from all this may be,
that had China Aster been something else than what he was,
he would not have been trusted, and, therefore, he would have
been effectually shut out from running his own and wife's
head into the usurer's noose; yet those who, when everything
at last came out, maintained that, in this view and to this
extent, the honesty of the candle-maker was no advantage to
him, in so saying, such persons said what every good heart
must deplore, and no prudent tongue will admit.

"It may be mentioned, that the old farmer made China Aster
take part of his loan in three old dried-up cows and one lame
horse, not improved by the glanders. These were thrown in at
a pretty high figure, the old money-lender having a singular
prejudice in regard to the high value of any sort of stock raised
on his farm. With a great deal of difficulty, and at more loss,

China Aster disposed of his cattle at public auction, no private purchaser being found who could be prevailed upon to invest. And now, raking and scraping in every way, and working early and late, China Aster at last started afresh, nor without again largely and confidently extending himself. However, he did not try his hand at the spermaceti again, but, admonished by experience, returned to tallow. But, having bought a good lot of it, by the time he got it into candles, tallow fell so low, and candles with it, that his candles per pound barely sold for what he had paid for the tallow. Meantime, a year's unpaid interest had accrued on Orchis' loan, but China Aster gave himself not so much concern about that as about the interest now due to the old farmer. But he was glad that the principal there had yet some time to run. However, the skinny old fellow gave him some trouble by coming after him every day or two on a scraggy old white horse, furnished with a musty old saddle, and goaded into his shambling old paces with a withered old raw hide. All the neighbors said that surely Death himself on the pale horse was after poor China Aster now. And something so it proved; for, ere long, China Aster found himself involved in troubles mortal enough.

"At this juncture Orchis was heard of. Orchis, it seemed, had returned from his travels, and clandestinely married, and, in a kind of queer way, was living in Pennsylvania among his wife's relations, who, among other things, had induced him to join a church, or rather semi-religious school, of Come-Outers; and what was still more, Orchis, without coming to the spot himself, had sent word to his agent to dispose of some of his property in Marietta, and remit him the proceeds. Within a year after, China Aster received a letter from Orchis, commending him for his punctuality in paying the first year's interest, and regretting the necessity that he (Orchis) was now under of using all his dividends; so he relied upon China Aster's paying the next six months' interest, and of course with the back interest. Not more surprised than alarmed, China Aster thought of taking steamboat to go and see Orchis, but he was saved that expense by the unexpected arrival in Marietta of Orchis in person, suddenly called there by that strange kind of capriciousness lately characterizing him. No sooner did China Aster hear of his old friend's arrival than he hurried to call upon him. He found him curiously rusty in dress, sallow in cheek, and decidedly less gay and cordial in manner, which the more surprised China Aster, because, in former days, he had more than once heard Orchis, in his light rattling way, declare that all he (Orchis) wanted to make him a perfectly happy, hilarious, and benignant man, was a voyage to Europe and a wife, with a free development of his inmost nature.

"Upon China Aster's stating his case, his rusted friend was silent for a time; then, in an odd way, said that he would not crowd China Aster, but still his (Orchis') necessities were urgent. Could not China Aster mortgage the candlery? He was honest, and must have moneyed friends; and could he not press his sales of candles? Could not the market be forced a little in that particular? The profits on candles must be very great. Seeing, now, that Orchis had the notion that the candle-making business was a very profitable one, and knowing sorely enough what an error was here, China Aster tried to undeceive him. But he could not drive the truth into Orchis—Orchis being very obtuse here, and, at the same time, strange to say, very melancholy. Finally, Orchis glanced off from so unpleasing a subject into the most unexpected reflections, taken from a religious point of view, upon the unstableness and deceitfulness of the human heart. But having, as he thought, experienced something of that sort of thing, China Aster did not take exception to his friend's observations, but still refrained from so doing, almost as much for the sake of sympathetic sociality as anything else. Presently, Orchis, without much ceremony, rose, and saying he must write a letter to his wife, bade his friend good-bye, but without warmly shaking him by the hand as of old.

"In much concern at the change, China Aster made earnest inquiries in suitable quarters, as to what things, as yet unheard of, had befallen Orchis, to bring about such a revolution; and learned at last that, besides traveling, and getting married, and joining the sect of Come-Outers, Orchis had somehow got a bad dyspepsia, and lost considerable property through a breach of trust on the part of a factor in New York. Telling these things to Old Plain Talk, that man of some knowledge of the world shook his old head, and told China Aster that, though he hoped it might prove otherwise, yet it seemed to him that all he had communicated about Orchis worked together for bad omens as to his future forbearance—especially, he added with a grim sort of smile, in view of his joining the sect of Come-Outers; for, if some men knew what was their inmost natures, instead of coming out with it, they would try their best to keep it in, which, indeed, was the way with the prudent sort. In all which sour notions Old Prudence, as usual, chimed in.

"When interest-day came again, China Aster, by the utmost exertions, could only pay Orchis' agent a small part of what was due, and a part of that was made up by his children's gift money (bright tenpenny pieces and new quarters, kept in their little money-boxes), and pawning his best clothes, with those of his wife and children, so that all were subjected to the hardship of staying away from church. And the old usurer, too, now beginning to be obstreperous, China Aster paid him his interest and some other pressing debts with money got by, at last, mortgaging the candlery.

"When next interest-day came round for Orchis, not a penny could be raised. With much grief of heart, China Aster so informed Orchis' agent. Meantime, the note to the old usurer fell due, and nothing from China Aster was ready to meet it; yet, as heaven sends its rain on the just and unjust alike, by a coincidence not unfavorable to the old farmer, the well-to-do uncle, the tanner, having died, the usurer entered upon possession of such part of his property left by will to the wife of China Aster. When still the next interest-day for Orchis came round, it found China Aster worse off than ever; for, besides his other troubles, he was now weak with sickness. Feebly dragging himself to Orchis' agent, he met him in the street, told him just how it was; upon which the agent, with a grave enough face, said that he had instructions from his employer not to crowd him about the interest at present, but to say to him that about the time the note would mature, Orchis would have heavy liabilities to meet, and therefore the note must at that time be certainly paid, and, of course, the back interest with it; and not only so, but, as Orchis had had to allow the interest for good part of the time, he hoped that, for the back interest, China Aster would, in reciprocation, have no objections to allowing interest on the interest annually. To be sure, this was not the law; but, between friends who accommodate each other, it was the custom.

"Just then, Old Plain Talk with Old Prudence turned the corner, coming plump upon China Aster as the agent left him; and whether it was a sun-stroke, or whether they accidentally ran against him, or whether it was his being so weak, or whether it was everything together, or how it was exactly, there is no telling, but poor China Aster fell to the earth, and, striking his head sharply, was picked up senseless. It was a day in July; such a light and heat as only the midsummer banks of the inland Ohio know. China Aster was taken home on a door; lingered a few days with a wandering mind, and kept wandering on, till at last, at dead of night, when nobody was aware, his spirit wandered away into the other world.

"Old Plain Talk and Old Prudence, neither of whom ever omitted attending any funeral, which, indeed, was their chief exercise—these two were among the sincerest mourners who followed the remains of the son of their ancient friend to the grave.

"It is needless to tell of the executions that followed; how that the candlery was sold by the mortgagee; how Orchis never got a penny for his loan; and how, in the case of the poor widow, chastisement was tempered with mercy; for, though she was left penniless, she was not left childless. Yet, unmindful of the alleviation, a spirit of complaint, at what she impatiently called the bitterness of her lot and the hardness of the world, so preyed upon her, as ere long to hurry her from the obscurity of indigence to the deeper shades of the tomb.

"But though the straits in which China Aster had left his family had, besides apparently dimming the world's regard, likewise seemed to dim its sense of the probity of its deceased head, and though this, as some thought, did not speak well for the world, yet it happened in this case, as in others, that, though the world may for a time seem insensible to that merit which lies under a cloud, yet, sooner or later, it always renders honor where honor is due; for, upon the death of the widow, the freemen of Marietta, as a tribute of respect for China Aster, and an expression of their conviction of his high moral worth, passed a resolution, that, until they attained maturity, his children should be considered the town's guests. No mere verbal compliment, like those of some public bodies; for, on the same day, the orphans were officially installed in that hospitable edifice where their worthy grandfather, the town's guest before them, had breathed his last breath.

"But sometimes honor may be paid to the memory of an honest man, and still his mound remain without a monument. Not so, however, with the candle-maker. At an early day, Plain Talk had procured a plain stone, and was digesting in his mind what pithy word or two to place upon it, when there was discovered, in China Aster's otherwise empty wallet, an epitaph, written, probably, in one of those disconsolate hours, attended with more or less mental aberration, perhaps, so frequent with him for some months prior to his end. A memorandum on the back expressed the wish that it might be placed over his grave. Though with the sentiment of the epitaph Plain Talk did not disagree, he himself being at times of a hypochondriac turn—at least, so many said—yet the language struck him as too much drawn out; so, after consultation with Old Prudence, he decided upon making use of the epitaph, yet not without verbal retrenchments. And though, when these were made, the thing still appeared wordy to him, nevertheless, thinking that, since a dead man was to be spoken about, it was but just to let him speak for himself, especially when he spoke sincerely, and when, by so doing, the more salutary lesson would be given, he had the retrenched inscription chiseled as follows upon the stone.

'HERE LIE

THE REMAINS OF

CHINA ASTER THE CANDLE-MAKER,

WHOSE CAREER

WAS AN EXAMPLE OF THE TRUTH OF SCRIPTURE, AS FOUND

IN THE

SOBER PHILOSOPHY

OF

SOLOMON THE WISE;

FOR HE WAS RUINED BY ALLOWING HIMSELF TO BE PERSUADED,

AGAINST HIS BETTER SENSE,

INTO THE FREE INDULGENCE OF CONFIDENCE,

AND

AN ARDENTLY BRIGHT VIEW OF LIFE,

TO THE EXCLUSION

OF

THAT COUNSEL WHICH COMES BY HEEDING

THE

OPPOSITE VIEW.'

"This inscription raised some talk in the town, and was rather severely criticised by the capitalist—one of a very cheerful turn—who had secured his loan to China Aster by the mortgage; and though it also proved obnoxious to the man who, in town-meeting, had first moved for the compliment to China Aster's memory, and, indeed, was deemed by him a sort of slur upon the candle-maker, to that degree that he refused to believe that the candle-maker himself had composed it, charging Old Plain Talk with the authorship, alleging that the internal evidence showed that none but that veteran old croaker could have penned such a jeremiad—yet, for all this, the stone stood. In everything, of course, Old Plain Talk was seconded by Old Prudence; who, one day going to the grave-yard, in great-coat and overshoes—for, though it was a sun-shiny morning, he thought that, owing to heavy dews, damp-ness might lurk in the ground—long stood before the stone, sharply leaning over on his staff, spectacles on nose, spelling out the epitaph word by word; and, afterwards meeting Old Plain Talk in the street, gave a great rap with his stick, and said: 'Friend, Plain Talk, that epitaph will do very well. Never-theless, one short sentence is wanting.' Upon which, Plain Talk said it was too late, the chiseled words being so arranged, after the usual manner of such inscriptions, that nothing could be interlined. 'Then,' said Old Prudence, 'I will put it in the shape of a postscript.' Accordingly, with the approbation of Old Plain Talk, he had the following words chiseled at the left-hand corner of the stone, and pretty low down:

'The root of all was a friendly loan.' "

CHAPTER XLI

"With what heart," cried Frank, still in character, "have you told me this story? A story I can no way approve; for its moral, if accepted, would drain me of all reliance upon my last stay, and, therefore, of my last courage in life. For, what was that bright view of China Aster but a cheerful trust that, if he but kept up a brave heart, worked hard, and ever hoped for the best, all at last would go well? If your purpose, Charlie, in telling me this story, was to pain me, and keenly, you have succeeded; but, if it was to destroy my last confidence, I praise God you have not."

"Confidence?" cried Charlie, who, on his side, seemed with his whole heart to enter into the spirit of the thing, "what has confidence to do with the matter? That moral of the story, which I am for commending to you, is this: the folly, on both sides, of a friend's helping a friend. For was not that loan of Orchis to China Aster the first step towards their estrangement? And did it not bring about what in effect was the enmity of Orchis? I tell you, Frank, true friendship, like other precious things, is not rashly to be meddled with. And what more meddlesome between friends than a loan? A regular marplot. For how can you help that the helper must turn out a creditor? And creditor and friend, can they ever be one? no, not in the most lenient case; since, out of lenity to forego one's claim, is less to be a friendly creditor than to cease to be a creditor at all. But it will not do to rely upon this lenity, no, not in the best man; for the best man, as the worst, is subject to all mortal contingencies. He may travel, he may marry, he may join the Come-Outers, or some equally untoward school or sect, not to

250

speak of other things that more or less tend to new-cast the character. And were there nothing else, who shall answer for his digestion, upon which so much depends?"

"But Charlie, dear Charlie—"

"Nay, wait.—You have hearkened to my story in vain, if you do not see that, however indulgent and right-minded I may seem to you now, that is no guarantee for the future. And into the power of that uncertain personality which, through the mutability of my humanity, I may hereafter become, should not common sense dissuade you, my dear Frank, from putting yourself? Consider. Would you, in your present need, be willing to accept a loan from a friend, securing him by a mortgage on your homestead, and do so, knowing that you had no reason to feel satisfied that the mortgage might not eventually be transferred into the hands of a foe? Yet the difference between this man and that man is not so great as the difference between what the same man be to-day and what he may be in days to come. For there is no bent of heart or turn of thought which any man holds by virtue of an unalterable nature or will. Even those feelings and opinions deemed most identical with eternal right and truth, it is not impossible but that, as personal persuasions, they may in reality be but the result of some chance tip of Fate's elbow in throwing her dice. For, not to go into the first seeds of things, and passing by the accident of parentage predisposing to this or that habit of mind, descend below these, and tell me, if you change this man's experiences or that man's books, will wisdom go surety for his unchanged convictions? As particular food begets particular dreams, so particular experiences or books particular feelings or beliefs. I will hear nothing of that fine babble about development and its laws; there is no development in opinion and feeling but the developments of time and tide. You may deem all this talk idle, Frank; but conscience bids me show you how fundamental the reasons for treating you as I do."

"But Charlie, dear Charlie, what new notions are these? I thought that man was no poor drifting weed of the universe, as you phrased it; that, if so minded, he could have a will, a way, a thought, and a heart of his own? But now you have turned everything upside down again, with an inconsistency that amazes and shocks me."

"Inconsistency? Bah!"

"There speaks the ventriloquist again," sighed Frank, in bitterness.

Illy pleased, it may be, by this repetition of an allusion little flattering to his originality, however much so to his docility, the disciple sought to carry it off by exclaiming: "Yes, I turn over day and night, with indefatigable pains, the sublime pages of my master, and unfortunately for you, my dear friend, I find nothing *there* that leads me to think otherwise than I do. But enough: in this matter the experience of China Aster teaches a moral more to the point than anything Mark Winsome can offer, or I either."

"I cannot think so, Charlie; for neither am I China Aster, nor do I stand in his position. The loan to China Aster was to extend his business with; the loan I seek is to relieve my necessities."

"Your dress, my dear Frank, is respectable; your cheek is not gaunt. Why talk of necessities when nakedness and starvation beget the only real necessities?"

"But I need relief, Charlie; and so sorely, that I now conjure you to forget that I was ever your friend, while I apply to you only as a fellow-being, whom, surely, you will not turn away."

"That I will not. Take off your hat, bow over to the ground, and supplicate an alms of me in the way of London streets, and you shall not be a sturdy beggar in vain. But no man drops pennies into the hat of a friend, let me tell you. If you turn beggar, then, for the honor of noble friendship, I turn stranger."

"Enough," cried the other, rising, and with a toss of his shoulders seeming disdainfully to throw off the character he had assumed. "Enough. I have had my fill of the philosophy of Mark Winsome as put into action. And moonshiny as it in theory may be, yet a very practical philosophy it turns out in effect, as he himself engaged I should find. But, miserable for my race should I be, if I thought he spoke truth when he claimed, for proof of the soundness of his system, that the study of it tended to much the same formation of character with the experiences of the world.—Apt disciple! Why wrinkle the brow, and waste the oil both of life and the lamp, only to turn out a head kept cool by the under ice of the heart? What your illustrious magian has taught you, any poor, old, broken-down, heart-shrunken dandy might have lisped. Pray, leave me, and with you take the last dregs of your inhuman philosophy. And here, take this shilling, and at the first wood-landing buy yourself a few chips to warm the frozen natures of you and your philosopher by."

With these words and a grand scorn the cosmopolitan turned on his heel, leaving his companion at a loss to determine where exactly the fictitious character had been dropped, and the real one, if any, resumed. If any, because, with pointed meaning, there occurred to him, as he gazed after the cosmopolitan, these familiar lines:

> "All the world's a stage,
> And all the men and women merely players,
> Who have their exits and their entrances,
> And one man in his time plays many parts."

CHAPTER XLII

UPON THE HEEL OF THE LAST SCENE THE COSMOPOLITAN ENTERS
THE BARBER'S SHOP, A BENEDICTION ON HIS LIPS

"BLESS you, barber!"

Now, owing to the lateness of the hour, the barber had been all alone until within the ten minutes last passed; when, finding himself rather dullish company to himself, he thought he would have a good time with Souter John and Tam O'Shanter, otherwise called Somnus and Morpheus, two very good fellows, though one was not very bright, and the other an arrant rattle-brain, who, though much listened to by some, no wise man would believe under oath.

In short, with back presented to the glare of his lamps, and so to the door, the honest barber was taking what are called cat-naps, and dreaming in his chair; so that, upon suddenly hearing the benediction above, pronounced in tones not un-angelic, starting up, half awake, he stared before him, but saw nothing, for the stranger stood behind. What with cat-naps, dreams, and bewilderments, therefore, the voice seemed a sort of spiritual manifestation to him; so that, for the moment, he stood all agape, eyes fixed, and one arm in the air.

"Why, barber, are you reaching up to catch birds there with salt?"

"Ah!" turning round disenchanted, "it is only a man, then."

"*Only* a man? As if to be but man were nothing. But don't be too sure what I am. You call me *man*, just as the townsfolk called the angels who, in man's form, came to Lot's house; just as the Jew rustics called the devils who, in man's form, haunted the tombs. You can conclude nothing absolute from the human form, barber."

"But I can conclude something from that sort of talk, with that sort of dress," shrewdly thought the barber, eying him with regained self-possession, and not without some latent touch of apprehension at being alone with him. What was passing in his mind seemed divined by the other, who now, more rationally and gravely, and as if he expected it should be attended to, said: "Whatever else you may conclude upon, it is my desire that you conclude to give me a good shave," at the same time loosening his neck-cloth. "Are you competent to a good shave, barber?"

"No broker more so, sir," answered the barber, whom the business-like proposition instinctively made confine to business-ends his views of the visitor.

"Broker? What has a broker to do with lather? A broker I have always understood to be a worthy dealer in certain papers and metals."

"He, he!" taking him now for some dry sort of joker, whose jokes, he being a customer, it might be as well to appreciate, "he, he! You understand well enough sir. Take this seat, sir," laying his hand on a great stuffed chair, high-backed and high-armed, crimson-covered, and raised on a sort of dais, and which seemed but to lack a canopy and quarterings, to make it in aspect quite a throne, "take this seat, sir."

"Thank you," sitting down; "and now, pray, explain that about the broker. But look, look—what's this?" suddenly rising, and pointing, with his long pipe, towards a gilt notification swinging among colored flypapers from the ceiling, like a tavern sign, *No Trust?* No trust means distrust; distrust means no confidence, Barber," turning upon him excitedly, "what fell suspiciousness prompts this scandalous confession? My life!" stamping his foot, "if but to tell a dog that you have no confidence in him be matter for affront to the dog, what an insult to take that way the whole haughty race of man by the beard! By my heart, sir! but at least you are valiant; backing the spleen of Thersites with the pluck of Agamemnon."

"Your sort of talk, sir, is not exactly in my line," said the barber, rather ruefully, being now again hopeless of his customer, and not without return of uneasiness; "not in my line, sir," he emphatically repeated.

"But the taking of mankind by the nose is; a habit, barber, which I sadly fear has insensibly bred in you a disrespect for man. For how, indeed, may respectful conceptions of him coexist with the perpetual habit of taking him by the nose? But, tell me, though I, too, clearly see the import of your notification, I do not, as yet, perceive the object. What is it?"

"Now you speak a little in my line, sir," said the barber, not unrelieved at this return to plain talk; "that notification I find very useful, sparing me much work which would not pay. Yes, I lost a good deal, off and on, before putting that up," gratefully glancing towards it.

"But what is its object? Surely, you don't mean to say, in so many words, that you have no confidence? For instance, now," flinging aside his neck-cloth, throwing back his blouse, and reseating himself on the tonsorial throne, at sight of which proceeding the barber mechanically filled a cup with hot water from a copper vessel over a spirit-lamp, "for instance, now, suppose I say to you, 'Barber, my dear barber, unhappily I have no small change by me to-night, but shave me, and depend upon your money to-morrow'—suppose I should say that now, you would put trust in me, wouldn't you? You would have confidence?"

"Seeing that it is you, sir," with complaisance replied the barber, now mixing the lather, "seeing that it is *you*, sir, I won't answer that question. No need to."

"Of course, of course—in that view. But, as a supposition— you would have confidence in me, wouldn't you?"

"Why—yes, yes."

"Then why that sign?"

"Ah, sir, all people ain't like you," was the smooth reply, at the same time, as if smoothly to close the debate, beginning smoothly to apply the lather, which operation, however, was, by a motion, protested against by the subject, but only out of a desire to rejoin, which was done in these words:

"All people ain't like me. Then I must be either better or worse than most people. Worse, you could not mean; no, barber, you could not mean that; hardly that. It remains, then, that you think me better than most people. But that I ain't vain enough to believe; though, from vanity, I confess, I could never yet, by my best wrestlings, entirely free myself; nor, indeed, to be frank, am I at bottom over anxious to—this same vanity, barber, being so harmless, so useful, so comfortable, so pleasingly preposterous a passion."

"Very true, sir; and upon my honor, sir, you talk very well. But the lather is getting a little cold, sir."

"Better cold lather, barber, than a cold heart. Why that cold sign? Ah, I don't wonder you try to shirk the confession. You feel in your soul how ungenerous a hint is there. And yet, barber, now that I look into your eyes—which somehow speak to me of the mother that must have so often looked into them before me—I dare say, though you may not think it, that the spirit of that notification is not one with your nature. For look now, setting business views aside, regarding the thing in an abstract light; in short, supposing a case, barber; supposing, I say, you see a stranger, his face accidentally averted, but his visible part very respectable-looking; what now, barber—I put it to your conscience, to your charity—what would be your impression of that man, in a moral point of view? Being in a signal sense a stranger, would you, for that, signally set him down for a knave?"

"Certainly not, sir; by no means," cried the barber, humanely resentful.

"You would upon the face of him—"

"Hold, sir," said the barber, "nothing about the face; you remember, sir, that is out of sight."

"I forgot that. Well then, you would, upon the *back* of him, conclude him to be, not improbably, some worthy sort of person; in short, an honest man; wouldn't you?"

"Not unlikely I should, sir."

"Well now—don't be so impatient with your brush, barber—

suppose that honest man meet you by night in some dark corner of the boat where his face would still remain unseen, asking you to trust him for a shave—how then?"

"Wouldn't trust him, sir."

"But is not an honest man to be trusted?"

"Why—why—yes, sir."

"There! don't you see, now?"

"See what?" asked the disconcerted barber, rather vexedly.

"Why, you stand self-contradicted, barber; don't you?"

"No," doggedly.

"Barber," gravely, and after a pause of concern, "the enemies of our race have a saying that insincerity is the most universal and inveterate vice of man—the lasting bar to real amelioration, whether of individuals or of the world. Don't you now, barber, by your stubbornness on this occasion, give color to such a calumny?"

"Hity-tity!" cried the barber, losing patience, and with it respect; "stubbornness?" Then clattering round the brush in the cup, "Will you be shaved, or won't you?"

"Barber, I will be shaved, and with pleasure; but, pray, don't raise your voice that way. Why, now, if you go through life gritting your teeth in that fashion, what a comfortless time you will have."

"I take as much comfort in this world as you or any other man," cried the barber, whom the other's sweetness of temper seemed rather to exasperate than soothe.

"To resent the imputation of anything like unhappiness I have often observed to be peculiar to certain orders of men," said the other pensively, and half to himself, "just as to be indifferent to that imputation, from holding happiness but for a secondary good and inferior grace, I have observed to be equally peculiar to other kinds of men. Pray, barber," innocently looking up, "which think you is the superior creature?"

"All this sort of talk," cried the barber, still unmolified, "is, as I told you once before, not in my line. In a few minutes I shall shut up this shop. Will you be shaved?"

"Shave away, barber. What hinders?" turning up his face like a flower.

The shaving began, and proceeded in silence, till at length it became necessary to prepare to relather a little—affording an opportunity for resuming the subject, which, on one side, was not let slip.

"Barber," with a kind of cautious kindliness, feeling his way, "barber, now have a little patience with me; do; trust me, I wish not to offend. I have been thinking over that supposed case of the man with the averted face, and I cannot rid my mind of the impression that, by your opposite replies to my questions at the time, you showed yourself much of a piece with a good many other men—that is, you have confidence, and then again, you have none. Now, what I would ask is, do you think it sensible standing for a sensible man, one foot on confidence and the other on suspicion? Don't you think, barber, that you ought to elect? Don't you think consistency requires that you should either say 'I have confidence in all men,' and take down your notification; or else say, 'I suspect all men,' and keep it up."

This dispassionate, if not deferential, way of putting the case, did not fail to impress the barber, and proportionately conciliate him. Likewise, from its pointedness, it served to make him thoughtful; for, instead of going to the copper vessel for more water, as he had proposed, he halted half-way towards it, and, after a pause, cup in hand, said: "Sir, I hope you would not do me injustice. I don't say, and can't say, and wouldn't say, that I suspect all men; but I *do* say that strangers are not to be trusted, and so," pointing up to the sign, "no trust."

"But look, now, I beg, barber," rejoined the other deprecatingly, not presuming too much upon the barber's changed temper; "look, now; to say that strangers are not to be trusted, does not that imply something like saying that mankind is not to be trusted; for the mass of mankind, are they not necessarily strangers to each individual man? Come, come, my friend," winningly, "you are no Timon to hold the mass of mankind untrustworthy. Take down your notification; it is misanthropical; much the same sign that Timon traced with charcoal on the forehead of a skull stuck over his cave. Take it down, barber; take it down to-night. Trust men. Just try the experiment of trusting men for this one little trip. Come now, I'm a philanthropist, and will insure you against losing a cent."

The barber shook his head dryly, and answered, "Sir, you must excuse me. I have a family."

CHAPTER XLIII

VERY CHARMING

"So you are a philanthropist, sir," added the barber with an illuminated look; "that accounts, then, for all. Very odd sort of man the philanthropist. You are the second one, sir, I have seen. Very odd sort of man, indeed, the philanthropist. Ah, sir," again meditatively stirring in the shaving-cup, "I sadly fear, lest you philanthropists know better what goodness is, than what men are." Then, eying him as if he were some strange creature behind cage-bars, "So you are a philanthropist, sir."

"I am Philanthropos, and love mankind. And, what is more than you do, barber, I trust them."

Here the barber, casually recalled to his business, would have replenished his shaving-cup, but finding now that on his last visit to the water-vessel he had not replaced it over the lamp, he did so now; and, while waiting for it to heat again, became almost as sociable as if the heating water were meant for whisky-punch; and almost as pleasantly garrulous as the pleasant barbers in romances.

"Sir," said he, taking a throne beside his customer (for in a row there were three thrones on the dais, as for the three kings of Cologne, those patron saints of the barber), "sir, you say you trust men. Well, I suppose I might share some of your trust, were it not for this trade, that I follow, too much letting me in behind the scenes."

"I think I understand," with a saddened look; "and much the same thing I have heard from persons in pursuits different from yours—from the lawyer, from the congressman, from the editor, not to mention others, each, with a strange kind of

261

melancholy vanity, claiming for his vocation the distinction of affording the surest inlets to the conviction that man is no better than he should be. All of which testimony, if reliable, would, by mutual corroboration, justify some disturbance in a good man's mind. But no, no; it is a mistake—all a mistake."

"True, sir, very true," assented the barber.

"Glad to hear that," brightening up.

"Not so fast, sir," said the barber; "I agree with you in thinking that the lawyer, and the congressman, and the editor, are in error, but only in so far as each claims peculiar facilities for the sort of knowledge in question; because, you see, sir, the truth is, that every trade or pursuit which brings one into contact with the facts, sir, such trade or pursuit is equally an avenue to those facts."

"*How* exactly is that?"

"Why, sir, in my opinion—and for the last twenty years I have, at odd times, turned the matter over some in my mind—he who comes to know man, will not remain in ignorance of man. I think I am not rash in saying that; am I, sir?"

"Barber, you talk like an oracle—obscurely, barber, obscurely."

"Well, sir," with some self-complacency, "the barber has always been held an oracle, but as for the obscurity, that I don't admit."

"But pray, now, by your account, what precisely may be this mysterious knowledge gained in your trade? I grant you, indeed, as before hinted, that your trade, imposing on you the necessity of functionally tweaking the noses of mankind, is, in that respect, unfortunate, very much so; nevertheless, a well-regulated imagination should be proof even to such a provocation to improper conceits. But what I want to learn from you, barber, is, how does the mere handling of the outside of men's heads lead you to distrust the inside of their hearts?"

"What, sir, to say nothing more, can one be forever dealing in macassar oil, hair dyes, cosmetics, false moustaches, wigs, and toupees, and still believe that men are wholly what they

look to be? What think you, sir, are a thoughtful barber's reflections, when, behind a careful curtain, he shaves the thin,
dead stubble off a head, and then dismisses it to the world,
radiant in curling auburn? To contrast the shamefaced air behind the curtain, the fearful looking forward to being possibly
discovered there by a prying acquaintance, with the cheerful
assurance and challenging pride with which the same man
steps forth again, a gay deception, into the street, while some
honest, shock-headed fellow humbly gives him the wall. Ah,
sir, they may talk of the courage of truth, but my trade teaches
me that truth sometimes is sheepish. Lies, lies, sir, brave lies
are the lions!"

"You twist the moral, barber; you sadly twist it. Look, now;
take it this way: A modest man thrust out naked into the street,
would he not be abashed? Take him in and clothe him; would
not his confidence be restored? And in either case, is any
reproach involved? Now, what is true of the whole, holds pro-
portionably true of the part. The bald head is a nakedness
which the wig is a coat to. To feel uneasy at the possibility of
the exposure of one's nakedness at top, and to feel comforted
by the consciousness of having it clothed—these feelings, instead of being dishonorable to a bold man, do, in fact, but
attest a proper respect for himself and his fellows. And as for
the deception, you may as well call the fine roof of a fine
chateau a deception, since, like a fine wig, it also is an artificial
cover to the head, and equally, in the common eye, decorates
the wearer.—I have confuted you, my dear barber; I have confounded you."

"Pardon," said the barber, "but I do not see that you have.
His coat and his roof no man pretends to palm off as a part of
himself, but the bald man palms off hair, not his, for his own."

"Not *his*, barber? If he have fairly purchased his hair, the
law will protect him in its ownership, even against the claims of
the head on which it grew. But it cannot be that you believe
what you say, barber; you talk merely for the humor. I could
not think so of you as to suppose that you would contentedly
deal in the impostures you condemn."

"Ah, sir, I must live."

"And can't you do that without sinning against your conscience, as you believe? Take up some other calling."

"Wouldn't mend the matter much, sir."

"Do you think, then, barber, that, in a certain point, all the trades and callings of men are much on a par? Fatal, indeed," raising his hand, "inexpressibly dreadful, the trade of the barber, if to such conclusions it necessarily leads. Barber," eying him not without emotion, "you appear to me not so much a misbeliever, as a man misled. Now, let me set you on the right track; let me restore you to trust in human nature, and by no other means than the very trade that has brought you to suspect it."

"You mean, sir, you would have me try the experiment of taking down that notification," again pointing to it with his brush; "but, dear me, while I sit chatting here, the water boils over."

With which words, and such a well-pleased, sly, snug, expression, as they say some men have when they think their little stratagem has succeeded, he hurried to the copper vessel, and soon had his cup foaming up with white bubbles, as if it were a mug of new ale.

Meantime, the other would have fain gone on with the discourse; but the cunning barber lathered him with so generous a brush, so piled up the foam on him, that his face looked like the yeasty crest of a billow, and vain to think of talking under it, as for a drowning priest in the sea to exhort his fellow-sinners on a raft. Nothing would do, but he must keep his mouth shut. Doubtless, the interval was not, in a meditative way, unimproved; for, upon the traces of the operation being at last removed, the cosmopolitan rose, and, for added refreshment, washed his face and hands; and having generally readjusted himself, began, at last, addressing the barber in a manner different, singularly so, from his previous one. Hard to say exactly what the manner was, any more than to hint it was a sort of magical; in a benign way, not wholly unlike the manner, fabled or otherwise, of certain creatures in nature, which have

the power of persuasive fascination—the power of holding another creature by the button of the eye, as it were, despite the
serious disinclination, and, indeed, earnest protest, of the victim. With this manner the conclusion of the matter was not
out of keeping; for, in the end, all argument and expostulation
proved vain, the barber being irresistibly persuaded to agree
to try, for the remainder of the present trip, the experiment of
trusting men, as both phrased it. True, to save his credit as a
free agent, he was loud in averring that it was only for the
novelty of the thing that he so agreed, and he required the
other, as before volunteered, to go security to him against any
loss that might ensue; but still the fact remained, that he engaged to trust men, a thing he had before said he would not
do, at least not unreservedly. Still the more to save his credit,
he now insisted upon it, as a last point, that the agreement
should be put in black and white, especially the security part.
The other made no demur; pen, ink, and paper were provided,
and grave as any notary the cosmopolitan sat down, but, ere
taking the pen, glanced up at the notification, and said: "First
down with that sign, barber—Timon's sign, there; down with
it."

This, being in the agreement, was done—though a little reluctantly—with an eye to the future, the sign being carefully
put away in a drawer.

"Now, then, for the writing," said the cosmopolitan, squaring
himself. "Ah," with a sigh, "I shall make a poor lawyer, I fear.
Ain't used, you see, barber, to a business which, ignoring the
principle of honor, holds no nail fast till clinched. Strange,
barber," taking up the blank paper, "that such flimsy stuff as
this should make such strong hawsers; vile hawsers, too. Barber," starting up, "I won't put it in black and white. It were
a reflection upon our joint honor. I will take your word, and
you shall take mine."

"But your memory may be none of the best, sir. Well for
you, on your side, to have it in black and white, just for a
memorandum like, you know."

"That, indeed! Yes, and it would help *your* memory, too,

wouldn't it, barber? Yours, on your side, being a little weak, too, I dare say. Ah, barber! how ingenious we human beings are; and how kindly we reciprocate each other's little delicacies, don't we? What better proof, now, that we are kind, considerate fellows, with responsive fellow-feelings—eh, barber? But to business. Let me see. What's your name, barber?"

"William Cream, sir."

Pondering a moment, he began to write; and, after some corrections, leaned back, and read aloud the following:

"AGREEMENT
"Between
"FRANK GOODMAN, Philanthropist, and Citizen of the World,
"and
"WILLIAM CREAM, Barber of the Mississippi steamer, Fidèle.

"The first hereby agrees to make good to the last any loss that may come from his trusting mankind, in the way of his vocation, for the residue of the present trip; PROVIDED that William Cream keep out of sight, for the given term, his notification of 'No TRUST,' and by no other mode convey any, the least hint or intimation, tending to discourage men from soliciting trust from him, in the way of his vocation, for the time above specified; but, on the contrary, he do, by all proper and reasonable words, gestures, manners, and looks, evince a perfect confidence in all men, especially strangers; otherwise, this agreement to be void.

"Done, in good faith, this 1st day of April, 18—, at a quarter to twelve o'clock, P.M., in the shop of said William Cream, on board the said boat, Fidèle."

"There, barber; will that do?"

"That will do," said the barber, "only now put down your name."

Both signatures being affixed, the question was started by the barber, who should have custody of the instrument; which point, however, he settled for himself, by proposing that both should go together to the captain, and give the document into his hands—the barber hinting that this would be a safe proceeding, because the captain was necessarily a party disinterested, and, what was more, could not, from the nature of the present case, make anything by a breach of trust. All of which was listened to with some surprise and concern.

"Why, barber," said the cosmopolitan, "this don't show the right spirit; for me, I have confidence in the captain purely because he is a man; but he shall have nothing to do with our affair; for if you have no confidence in me, barber, I have in you. There, keep the paper yourself," handing it magnanimously.

"Very good," said the barber, "and now nothing remains but for me to receive the cash."

Though the mention of that word, or any of its singularly numerous equivalents, in serious neighborhood to a requisition upon one's purse, is attended with a more or less noteworthy effect upon the human countenance, producing in many an abrupt fall of it—in others, a writhing and screwing up of the features to a point not undistressing to behold, in some, attended with a blank pallor and fatal consternation—yet no trace of any of these symptoms was visible upon the countenance of the cosmopolitan, notwithstanding nothing could be more sudden and unexpected than the barber's demand.

"You speak of cash, barber; pray in what connection?"

"In a nearer one, sir," answered the barber, less blandly, "than I thought the man with the sweet voice stood, who wanted me to trust him once for a shave, on the score of being a sort of thirteenth cousin."

"Indeed, and what did you say to him?"

"I said, 'Thank you, sir, but I don't see the connection.'"

"How could you so unsweetly answer one with a sweet voice?"

"Because, I recalled what the son of Sirach says in the True Book: 'An enemy speaketh sweetly with his lips;' and so I did what the son of Sirach advises in such cases: 'I believed not his many words.'"

"What, barber, do you say that such cynical sort of things

are in the True Book, by which, of course, you mean the Bible?"

"Yes, and plenty more to the same effect. Read the Book of Proverbs."

"That's strange, now, barber; for I never happen to have met with those passages you cite. Before I go to bed this night, I'll inspect the Bible I saw on the cabin-table, to-day. But mind, you mustn't quote the True Book that way to people coming in here; it would be impliedly a violation of the contract. But you don't know how glad I feel that you have for one while signed off all that sort of thing."

"No, sir; not unless you down with the cash."

"Cash again! What do you mean?"

"Why, in this paper here, you engage, sir, to insure me against a certain loss, and—"

"Certain? Is it so *certain* you are going to lose?"

"Why, that way of taking the word may not be amiss, but I didn't mean it so. I meant a *certain* loss; you understand, a CERTAIN loss; that is to say, a certain loss. Now then, sir, what use your mere writing and saying you will insure me, unless beforehand you place in my hands a money-pledge, sufficient to that end?"

"I see; the material pledge."

"Yes, and I will put it low; say fifty dollars."

"Now what sort of a beginning is this? You, barber, for a given time engage to trust man, to put confidence in men, and, for your first step, make a demand implying no confidence in the very man you engage with. But fifty dollars is nothing, and I would let you have it cheerfully, only I unfortunately happen to have but little change with me just now."

"But you have money in your trunk, though?"

"To be sure. But you see—in fact, barber, you must be consistent. No, I won't let you have the money now; I won't let you violate the inmost spirit of our contract, that way. So goodnight, and I will see you again."

"Stay, sir"—humming and hawing—"you have forgotten something."

"Handkerchief?—gloves? No, forgotten nothing. Good-night."

"Stay, sir—the—the shaving."

"Ah, I *did* forget that. But now that it strikes me, I shan't pay you at present. Look at your agreement; you must trust. Tut! against loss you hold the guarantee. Good-night, my dear barber."

With which words he sauntered off, leaving the barber in a maze, staring after.

But it holding true in fascination as in natural philosophy, that nothing can act where it is not, so the barber was not long now in being restored to his self-possession and senses; the first evidence of which perhaps was, that, drawing forth his notification from the drawer, he put it back where it belonged; while, as for the agreement, that he tore up; which he felt the more free to do from the impression that in all human probability he would never again see the person who had drawn it. Whether that impression proved well-founded or not, does not appear. But in after days, telling the night's adventure to his friends, the worthy barber always spoke of his queer customer as the man-charmer—as certain East Indians are called snake-charmers—and all his friends united in thinking him QUITE AN ORIGINAL.

CHAPTER XLIV

IN WHICH THE LAST THREE WORDS OF THE LAST CHAPTER ARE MADE THE TEXT OF DISCOURSE, WHICH WILL BE SURE OF RECEIVING MORE OR LESS ATTENTION FROM THOSE READERS WHO DO NOT SKIP IT

"QUITE AN ORIGINAL:" A phrase, we fancy, rather oftener used by the young, or the unlearned, or the untraveled, than by the old, or the well-read, or the man who has made the grand tour. Certainly, the sense of originality exists at its highest in an infant, and probably at its lowest in him who has completed the circle of the sciences.

As for original characters in fiction, a grateful reader will, on meeting with one, keep the anniversary of that day, True, we sometimes hear of an author who, at one creation, produces some two or three score such characters; it may be possible. But they can hardly be original in the sense that Hamlet is, or Don Quixote, or Milton's Satan. That is to say, they are not, in a thorough sense, original at all. They are novel, or singular, or striking, or captivating, or all four at once.

More likely, they are what are called odd characters; but for that, are no more original, than what is called an odd genius, in his way, is. But, if original, whence came they? Or where did the novelist pick them up?

Where does any novelist pick up any character? For the most part, in town, to be sure. Every great town is a kind of man-show, where the novelist goes for his stock, just as the agriculturist goes to the cattle-show for his. But in the one fair, new species of quadrupeds are hardly more rare, than in the other are new species of characters—that is, original ones. Their rarity may still the more appear from this, that, while characters, merely singular, imply but singular forms so to speak, original ones, truly so, imply original instincts.

In short, a due conception of what is to be held for this sort of personage in fiction would make him almost as much of a prodigy there, as in real history is a new law-giver, a revolutionizing philosopher, or the founder of a new religion.

In nearly all the original characters, loosely accounted such in works of invention, there is discernible something prevailingly local, or of the age; which circumstance, of itself, would seem to invalidate the claim, judged by the principles here suggested.

Furthermore, if we consider, what is popularly held to entitle characters in fiction to being deemed original, is but something personal—confined to itself. The character sheds not its characteristic on its surroundings, whereas, the original character, essentially such, is like a revolving Drummond light, raying away from itself all round it—everything is lit by it, everything starts up to it (mark how it is with Hamlet), so that, in certain minds, there follows upon the adequate conception of such a character, an effect, in its way, akin to that which in Genesis attends upon the beginning of things.

For much the same reason that there is but one planet to one orbit, so can there be but one such original character to one work of invention. Two would conflict to chaos. In this view, to say that there are more than one to a book, is good presumption there is none at all. But for new, singular, striking, odd, eccentric, and all sorts of entertaining and instructive characters, a good fiction may be full of them. To produce such characters, an author, beside other things, must have seen much, and seen through much: to produce but one original character, he must have had much luck.

There would seem but one point in common between this sort of phenomenon in fiction and all other sorts: it cannot be born in the author's imagination—it being as true in literature as in zoology, that all life is from the egg.

In the endeavor to show, if possible, the impropriety of the phrase, *Quite an Original,* as applied by the barber's friends, we have, at unawares, been led into a dissertation bordering upon the prosy, perhaps upon the smoky. If so, the best use the smoke can be turned to, will be, by retiring under cover of it, in good trim as may be, to the story.

CHAPTER XLV

IN the middle of the gentlemen's cabin burned a solar lamp, swung from the ceiling, and whose shade of ground glass was all round fancifully variegated, in transparency, with the image of a horned altar, from which flames rose, alternate with the figure of a robed man, his head encircled by a halo. The light of this lamp, after dazzlingly striking on a marble, snow-white and round—the slab of a centre-table beneath—on all sides went rippling off with ever-diminishing distinctness, till, like circles from a stone dropped in water, the rays died dimly away in the furthest nook of the place.

Here and there, true to their place, but not to their function, swung other lamps, barren planets, which had either gone out from exhaustion, or been extinguished by such occupants of berths as the light annoyed, or who wanted to sleep, not see.

By a perverse man, in a berth not remote, the remaining lamp would have been extinguished as well, had not a steward forbade, saying that the commands of the captain required it to be kept burning till the natural light of day should come to relieve it. This steward, who, like many in his vocation, was apt to be a little free-spoken at times, had been provoked by the man's pertinacity to remind him, not only of the sad consequences which might, upon occasion, ensue from the cabin being left in darkness, but, also, of the circumstance that, in a place full of strangers, to show one's self anxious to produce darkness there, such an anxiety was, to say the least, not becoming. So the lamp—last survivor of many—burned on, inwardly blessed by those in some berths, and inwardly execrated by those in others.

272

Keeping his lone vigils beneath his lone lamp, which lighted his book on the table, sat a clean, comely, old man, his head snowy as the marble, and a countenance like that which imagination ascribes to good Simeon, when, having at last beheld the Master of Faith, he blesssed him and departed in peace. From his hale look of greenness in winter, and his hands ingrained with the tan, less, apparently, of the present summer, than of accumulated ones past, the old man seemed a well-to-do farmer, happily dismissed, after a thrifty life of activity, from the fields to the fireside—one of those who, at three-score-and-ten, are fresh-hearted as at fifteen; to whom seclusion gives a boon more blessed than knowledge, and at last sends them to heaven untainted by the world, because ignorant of it; just as a countryman putting up at a London inn, and never stirring out of it as a sight-seer, will leave London at last without once being lost in its fog, or soiled by its mud.

Redolent from the barber's shop, as any bridegroom tripping to the bridal chamber might come, and by his look of cheeriness seeming to dispense a sort of morning through the night, in came the cosmopolitan; but marking the old man, and how he was occupied, he toned himself down, and trod softly, and took a seat on the other side of the table, and said nothing. Still, there was a kind of waiting expression about him.

"Sir," said the old man, after looking up puzzled at him a moment, "sir," said he, "one would think this was a coffee-house, and it was war-time, and I had a newspaper here with great news, and the only copy to be had, you sit there looking at me so eager."

"And so you *have* good news there, sir—the very best of good news."

"Too good to be true," here came from one of the curtained berths.

"Hark!" said the cosmopolitan. "Some one talks in his sleep."

"Yes," said the old man, "and you—*you* seem to be talking in a dream. Why speak you, sir, of news, and all that, when you must see this is a book I have here—the Bible, not a newspaper?"

"I know that; and when you are through with it—but not a moment sooner—I will thank you for it. It belongs to the boat, I believe—a present from a society."

"Oh, take it, take it!"

"Nay, sir, I did not mean to touch you at all. I simply stated the fact in explanation of my waiting here—nothing more. Read on, sir, or you will distress me."

This courtesy was not without effect. Removing his spectacles, and saying he had about finished his chapter, the old man kindly presented the volume, which was received with thanks equally kind. After reading for some minutes, until his expression merged from attentiveness into seriousness, and from that into a kind of pain, the cosmopolitan slowly laid down the book, and turning to the old man, who thus far had been watching him with benign curiosity, said: "Can you, my aged friend, resolve me a doubt—a disturbing doubt?"

"There are doubts, sir," replied the old man, with a changed countenance, "there are doubts, sir, which, if man have them, it is not man that can solve them."

"True; but look, now, what my doubt is. I am one who thinks well of man. I love man. I have confidence in man. But what was told me not a half-hour since? I was told that I would find it written—'Believe not his many words—an enemy speaketh sweetly with his lips'—and also I was told that I would find a good deal more to the same effect, and all in this book. I could not think it; and, coming here to look for myself, what do I read? Not only just what was quoted, but also, as was engaged, more to the same purpose, such as this: 'With much communication he will tempt thee; he will smile upon thee, and speak thee fair, and say What wantest thou? If thou be for his profit he will use thee; he will make thee bear, and will not be sorry for it. Observe and take good heed. When thou hearest these things, awake in thy sleep.'"

"Who's that describing the confidence-man?" here came from the berth again.

"Awake in his sleep, sure enough, ain't he?" said the cosmopolitan, again looking off in surprise. "Same voice as before, ain't it? Strange sort of dreamy man, that. Which is his berth, pray?"

"Never mind *him*, sir," said the old man anxiously, "but tell me truly, did you, indeed, read from the book just now?"

"I did," with changed air, "and gall and wormwood it is to me, a truster in man; to me, a philanthropist."

"Why," moved, "you don't mean to say, that what you repeated is really down there? Man and boy, I have read the good book this seventy years, and don't remember seeing anything like that. Let me see it," rising earnestly, and going round to him.

"There it is; and there—and there"—turning over the leaves, and pointing to the sentences one by one; "there—all down in the 'Wisdom of Jesus, the Son of Sirach.'"

"Ah!" cried the old man, brightening up, "now I know. Look," turning the leaves forward and back, till all the Old Testament lay flat on one side, and all the New Testament flat on the other, while in his fingers he supported vertically the portion between, "look, sir, all this to the right is certain truth, and all this to the left is certain truth, but all I hold in my hand here is apocrypha."

"Apocrypha?"

"Yes; and there's the word in black and white," pointing to it. "And what says the word? It says as much as 'not warranted;' for what do college men say of anything of that sort? They say it is apocryphal. The word itself, I've heard from the pulpit, implies something of uncertain credit. So if your disturbance be raised from aught in this apocrypha," again taking up the pages, "in that case, think no more of it, for it's apocrypha."

"What's that about the Apocalypse?" here, a third time, came from the berth.

"He's seeing visions now, ain't he?" said the cosmopolitan, once more looking in the direction of the interruption. "But, sir," resuming, "I cannot tell you how thankful I am for your reminding me about the apocrypha here. For the moment, its being such escaped me. Fact is, when all is bound up together, it's sometimes confusing. The uncanonical part should be bound distinct. And, now that I think of it, how well did those learned doctors who rejected for us this whole book of Sirach. I never read anything so calculated to destroy man's confidence in man. This son of Sirach even says—I saw it but just now; 'Take heed of thy friends;' not, observe, thy seeming friends, thy hypocritical friends, thy false friends, but thy *friends,* thy real friends—that is to say, not the truest friend in the world is to be implicitly trusted. Can Rochefoucault equal that? I should not wonder if his view of human nature, like Machiavelli's, was taken from this Son of Sirach. And to call it wisdom —the Wisdom of the Son of Sirach! Wisdom, indeed! What an ugly thing wisdom must be! Give me the folly that dimples the cheek, say I, rather than the wisdom that curdles the blood. But no, no; it ain't wisdom; it's apocrypha, as you say, sir. For how can that be trustworthy that teaches distrust?"

"I tell you what it is," here cried the same voice as before, only more in less of mockery, "if you two don't know enough to sleep, don't be keeping wiser men awake. And if you want to know what wisdom is, go find it under your blankets."

"Wisdom?" cried another voice with a brogue; "arrah, and is't wisdom the two geese are gabbling about all this while? To bed with ye, ye divils, and don't be after burning your fingers with the likes of wisdom."

"We must talk lower," said the old man; "I fear we have annoyed these good people."

"I should be sorry if wisdom annoyed any one," said the other; "but we will lower our voices, as you say. To resume: taking the thing as I did, can you be surprised at my uneasiness in reading passages so charged with the spirit of distrust?"

"No, sir, I am not surprised," said the old man; then added: "from what you say, I see you are something of my way of thinking—you think that to distrust the creature, is a kind of distrusting of the Creator. Well, my young friend, what is it? This is rather late for you to be about. What do you want of me?"

These questions were put to a boy in the fragment of an old

linen coat, bedraggled and yellow, who, coming in from the deck barefooted on the soft carpet, had been unheard. All pointed and fluttering, the rags of the little fellow's red-flannel shirt, mixed with those of his yellow coat, flamed about him like the painted flames in the robes of a victim in *auto-da-fe*. His face, too, wore such a polish of seasoned grime, that his sloe-eyes sparkled from out it like lustrous sparks in fresh coal. He was a juvenile peddler, or *marchand*, as the polite French might have called him, of travelers' conveniences; and, having no allotted sleeping-place, had, in his wanderings about the boat, spied, through glass doors, the two in the cabin; and, late though it was, thought it might never be too much so for turning a penny.

Among other things, he carried a curious affair—a miniature mahogany door, hinged to its frame, and suitably furnished in all respects but one, which will shortly appear. This little door he now meaningly held before the old man, who, after staring at it a while, said: "Go thy ways with thy toys, child."

"Now, may I never get so old and wise as that comes to," laughed the boy through his grime; and, by so doing, disclosing leopard-like teeth, like those of Murillo's wild beggar-boy's.

"The divils are laughing now, are they?" here came the brogue from the berth. "What do the divils find to laugh about in wisdom, begorrah? To bed with ye, ye divils, and no more of ye."

"You see, child, you have disturbed that person," said the old man; "you mustn't laugh any more."

"Ah, now," said the cosmopolitan, "don't, pray, say that; don't let him think that poor Laughter is persecuted for a fool in this world."

"Well," said the old man to the boy, "you must, at any rate, speak very low."

"Yes, that wouldn't be amiss, perhaps," said the cosmopolitan; "but, my fine fellow, you were about saying something to my aged friend here; what was it?"

"Oh," with a lowered voice, cooly opening and shutting his little door, "only this: when I kept a toystand at the fair in

Cincinnati last month, I sold more than one old man a child's rattle."

"No doubt of it," said the old man. "I myself often buy such things for my little grandchildren."

"But these old men I talk of were old bachelors."

The old man stared at him a moment; then, whispering to the cosmopolitan: "Strange boy, this; sort of simple, ain't he? Don't know much, hey?"

"Not much," said the boy, "or I wouldn't be so ragged."

"Why, child, what sharp ears you have!" exclaimed the old man.

"If they were duller, I would hear less ill of myself," said the boy.

"You seem pretty wise, my lad," said the cosmopolitan; "why don't you sell your wisdom, and buy a coat?"

"Faith," said the boy, "that's what I did to-day, and this is the coat that the price of my wisdom bought. But won't you trade? See, now, it is not the door I want to sell; I only carry the door round for a specimen, like. Look now, sir," standing the thing up on the table, "supposing this little door is your state-room door; well," opening it, "you go in for the night; you close your door behind you—thus. Now, is all safe?"

"I suppose so, child," said the old man.

"Of course it is, my fine fellow," said the cosmopolitan.

"All safe. Well. Now, about two o'clock in the morning, say, a soft-handed gentleman comes softly and tries the knob here —thus; in creeps my soft-handed gentleman; and hey, presto! how comes on the soft cash?"

"I see, I see, child," said the old man; "your fine gentleman is a fine thief, and there's no lock to your little door to keep him out;" with which words he peered at it more closely than before.

"Well, now," again showing his white teeth, "well, now, some of you old folks are knowing 'uns, sure enough; but now comes the great invention," producing a small steel contrivance, very simple but ingenious, and which, being clapped on the inside of the little door, secured it as with a bolt. "There now," admiringly holding it off at arm's-length, "there now, let that soft-handed gentleman come now a' softly trying this little knob here, and let him keep a' trying till he finds his head as soft as his hand. Buy the traveler's patent lock, sir, only twenty-five cents."

"Dear me," cried the old man, "this beats printing. Yes, child, I will have one, and use it this very night."

With the phlegm of an old banker pouching the change, the boy now turned to the other: "Sell you one, sir?"

"Excuse me, my fine fellow, but I never use such blacksmiths' things."

"Those who give the blacksmith most work seldom do," said the boy, tipping him a wink expressive of a degree of indefinite knowingness, not uninteresting to consider in one of his years. But the wink was not marked by the old man, nor, to all appearances, by him for whom it was intended.

"Now then," said the boy, again addressing the old man. "With your traveler's lock on your door tonight, you will think yourself all safe, won't you?"

"I think I will, child."

"But how about the window?"

"Dear me, the window, child. I never thought of that. I must see to that."

"Never you mind about the window," said the boy, "nor, to be honor bright, about the traveler's lock either, (though I ain't sorry for selling one), do you just buy one of these little jokers," producing a number of suspender-like objects, which he dangled before the old man; "money-belts, sir; only fifty cents."

"Money-belt? never heard of such a thing."

"A sort of pocket-book," said the boy, "only a safer sort. Very good for travelers."

"Oh, a pocket-book. Queer looking pocket-books though, seems to me. Ain't they rather long and narrow for pocket-books?"

"They go round the waist, sir, inside," said the boy, "door open or locked, wide awake on your feet or fast asleep in your chair, impossible to be robbed with a money-belt."

"I see, I see. It *would* be hard to rob one's money-belt. And I was told to-day the Mississippi is a bad river for pick-pockets. How much are they?"

"Only fifty cents, sir."

"I'll take one. There!"

"Thank-ee. And now there's a present for ye," with which, drawing from his breast a batch of little papers, he threw one before the old man, who, looking at it, read *"Counterfeit Detector."*

"Very good thing," said the boy, "I give it to all my customers who trade seventy-five cents' worth; best present can be made them. Sell you a money-belt, sir?" turning to the cosmopolitan.

"Excuse me, my fine fellow, but I never use that sort of thing; my money I carry loose."

"Loose bait ain't bad," said the boy, "look a lie and find the truth; don't care about a Counterfeit Detector, do ye? or is the wind East, d'ye think?"

"Child," said the old man in some concern, "you mustn't sit up any longer, it affects your mind; there, go away, go to bed."

"If I had some people's brains to lie on, I would," said the boy, "but planks is hard, you know."

"Go, child—go, go!"

"Yes, child,—yes, yes," said the boy, with which roguish parody, by way of congé, he scraped back his hard foot on the woven flowers of the carpet, much as a mischievous steer in May scrapes back his horny hoof in the pasture; and then with a flourish of his hat—which, like the rest of his tatters, was, thanks to hard times, a belonging beyond his years, though not beyond his experience, being a grown man's cast-off beaver —turned, and with the air of a young Caffre, quitted the place.

"That's a strange boy," said the old man, looking after him. "I wonder who's his mother; and whether she knows what late hours he keeps?"

"The probability is," observed the other, "that his mother does not know. But if you remember, sir, you were saying something, when the boy interrupted you with his door."

"So I was.—Let me see," unmindful of his purchases for the moment, "what, now, was it? What was that I was saying? Do *you* remember?"

"Not perfectly, sir; but, if I am not mistaken, it was something like this: you hoped you did not distrust the creature; for that would imply distrust of the Creator."

"Yes, that was something like it," mechanically and unintelligently letting his eye fall now on his purchases.

"Pray, will you put your money in your belt tonight?"

"It's best, ain't it?" with a slight start. "Never too late to be cautious. 'Beware of pick-pockets' is all over the boat."

"Yes, and it must have been the Son of Sirach, or some other morbid cynic, who put them there. But that's not to the purpose. Since you are minded to it, pray, sir, let me help you about the belt. I think that, between us, we can make a secure thing of it."

"Oh no, no, no!" said the old man, not unperturbed, "no, no, I wouldn't trouble you for the world," then, nervously folding up the belt, "and I won't be so impolite as to do it for myself, before you, either. But, now that I think of it," after a pause, carefully taking a little wad from a remote corner of his vest pocket, "here are two bills they gave me at St. Louis, yesterday. No doubt they are all right; but just to pass time, I'll compare them with the Detector here. Blessed boy to make me such a present. Public benefactor, that little boy!"

Laying the Detector square before him on the table, he then, with something of the air of an officer bringing by the collar a brace of culprits to the bar, placed the two bills opposite the Detector, upon which, the examination began, lasting some time, prosecuted with no small research and vigilance, the forefinger of the right hand proving of lawyer-like efficacy in tracing out and pointing the evidence, whichever way it might go.

After watching him a while, the cosmopolitan said in a formal voice, "Well, what say you, Mr. Foreman; guilty, or not guilty?—Not guilty, ain't it?"

"I don't know, I don't know," returned the old man, perplexed, "there's so many marks of all sorts to go by, it makes it a kind of uncertain. Here, now, is this bill," touching one, "it looks to be a three dollar bill on the Vicksburgh Trust and Insurance Banking Company. Well, the Detector says—"

"But why, in this case, care what it says? Trust and Insurance! What more would you have?"

"No; but the Detector says, among fifty other things, that, if a good bill, it must have, thickened here and there into the substance of the paper, little wavy spots of red; and it says they must have a kind of silky feel, being made by the lint of a red silk handkerchief stirred up in the paper-maker's vat— the paper being made to order for the company."

"Well, and is—"

"Stay. But then it adds, that sign is not always to be relied on; for some good bills get so worn, the red marks get rubbed out. And that's the case with my bill here—see how old it is— or else it's a counterfeit, or else—I don't see right—or else—dear, dear me—I don't know what else to think."

"What a peck of trouble that Detector makes for you now; believe me, the bill is good; don't be so distrustful. Proves what I've always thought, that much of the want of confidence, in these days, is owing to these Counterfeit Detectors you see on every desk and counter. Puts people up to suspecting good bills. Throw it away, I beg, if only because of the trouble it breeds you."

"No; it's troublesome, but I think I'll keep it.—Stay, now, here's another sign. It says that, if the bill is good, it must have in one corner, mixed in with the vignette, the figure of a goose, very small, indeed, all but microscopic; and, for added precaution, like the figure of Napoleon outlined by the tree, not observable, even if magnified, unless the attention is directed to it. Now, pore over it as I will, I can't see this goose."

"Can't see the goose? why, I can; and a famous goose it is.

There" (reaching over and pointing to a spot in the vignette).

"I don't see it—dear me—I don't see the goose. Is it a real goose?"

"A perfect goose; beautiful goose."

"Dear, dear, I don't see it."

"Then throw that Detector away, I say again; it only makes you purblind; don't you see what a wild-goose chase it has led you? The bill is good. Throw the Detector away."

"No; it ain't so satisfactory as I thought for, but I must examine this other bill."

"As you please, but I can't in conscience assist you any more; pray, then, excuse me."

So, while the old man with much painstakings resumed his work, the cosmopolitan, to allow him every facility, resumed his reading. At length, seeing that he had given up his undertaking as hopeless, and was at leisure again, the cosmopolitan addressed some gravely interesting remarks to him about the book before him, and, presently, becoming more and more grave, said, as he turned the large volume slowly over on the table, and with much difficulty traced the faded remains of the gilt inscription giving the name of the society who had presented it to the boat, "Ah, sir, though every one must be pleased at the thought of the presence in public places of such a book, yet there is something that abates the satisfaction. Look at this volume; on the outside, battered as any old valise in the baggage-room; and inside, white and virgin as the hearts of lilies in bud."

"So it is, so it is," said the old man sadly, his attention for the first directed to the circumstance.

"Nor is this the only time," continued the other, "that I have observed these public Bibles in boats and hotels. All much like this—old without, and new within. True, this aptly typifies that internal freshness, the best mark of truth, however ancient; but then, it speaks not so well as could be wished for the good book's esteem in the minds of the traveling public. I may err, but it seems to me that if more confidence was put in it by the traveling public, it would hardly be so."

With an expression very unlike that with which he had bent over the Detector, the old man sat meditating upon his companion's remarks a while; and, at last, with a rapt look, said: "And yet, of all people, the traveling public most need to put trust in that guardianship which is made known in this book."

"True, true," thoughtfully assented the other.

"And one would think they would want to, and be glad to," continued the old man kindling; "for, in all our wanderings through this vale, how pleasant, not less than obligatory, to feel that we need start at no wild alarms, provide for no wild perils; trusting in that Power which is alike able and willing to protect us when we cannot ourselves."

His manner produced something answering to it in the cosmopolitan, who, leaning over towards him, said sadly: "Though this is a theme on which travelers seldom talk to each other, yet, to you, sir, I will say, that I share something of your sense of security. I have moved much about the world, and still keep at it; nevertheless, though in this land, and especially in these parts of it, some stories are told about steamboats and railroads fitted to make one a little apprehensive, yet, I may say that, neither by land nor by water, am I ever seriously disquieted, however, at times, transiently uneasy; since, with you, sir, I believe in a Committee of Safety, holding silent sessions over all, in an invisible patrol, most alert when we soundest sleep, and whose beat lies as much through forests as towns, along rivers as streets. In short, I never forgot that passage of Scripture which says, 'Jehovah shall be thy confidence.' The traveler who has not this trust, what miserable misgivings must be his; or, what vain, short-sighted care must he take of himself."

"Even so," said the old man, lowly.

"There is a chapter," continued the other, again taking the book, "which, as not amiss, I must read you. But this lamp, solar-lamp as it is, begins to burn dimly."

"So it does, so it does," said the old man with changed air, "dear me, it must be very late. I must to bed, to bed! Let me see," rising and looking wistfully all round, first on the stools and settees, and then on the carpet, "let me see, let me see;—is there anything I have forgot,—forgot? Something I a sort of dimly remember. Something, my son—careful man—told me at starting this morning, this very morning. Something about seeing to—something before I got into my berth. What could it be? Something for safety. Oh, my poor old memory!"

"Let me give a little guess, sir. Life-preserver?"

"So it was. He told me not to omit seeing I had a life-preserver in my state-room; said the boat supplied them, too. But where are they? I don't see any. What are they like?"

"They are something like this, sir, I believe," lifting a brown stool with a curved tin compartment underneath; "yes, this, I think, is a life-preserver, sir; and a very good one, I should say, though I don't pretend to know much about such things, never using them myself."

"Why, indeed, now! Who would have thought it? *that* a life-preserver? That's the very stool I was sitting on, ain't it?"

"It is. And that shows that one's life is looked out for, when he ain't looking out for it himself. In fact, any of these stools here will float you, sir, should the boat hit a snag, and go down in the dark. But, since you want one in your room, pray take this one," handing it to him. "I think I can recommend this one; the tin part," rapping it with his knuckles, "seems so perfect—sounds so very hollow."

"Sure it's *quite* perfect, though?" Then, anxiously putting on his spectacles, he scrutinized it pretty closely—"well soldered? quite tight?"

"I should say so, sir; though, indeed, as I said, I never use this sort of thing, myself. Still, I think that in case of a wreck, barring sharp-pointed timbers, you could have confidence in that stool for a special providence."

"Then, good-night, good-night; and Providence have both of us in its good keeping."

"Be sure it will," eying the old man with sympathy, as for the moment he stood, money-belt in hand, and life-preserver under arm, "be sure it will, sir, since in Providence, as in man, you and I equally put trust. But, bless me, we are being left in the dark here. Pah! what a smell, too."

"Ah, my way now," cried the old man, peering before him, "where lies my way to my state-room?"

"I have indifferent eyes, and will show you; but, first, for the good of all lungs, let me extinguish this lamp."

The next moment, the waning light expired, and with it the waning flames of the horned altar, and the waning halo round the robed man's brow; while in the darkness which ensued, the cosmopolitan kindly led the old man away. Something further may follow of this Masquerade.

EXPLANATORY NOTES

The passage in the text to which each note refers is indicated by two numbers: the first gives the page, the second gives the line on the page.

KEY

To collections and books most frequently cited in the Notes

Journal . . . 1849-1850: Journal of a Visit to London and the Continent, by Herman Melville, 1849-1850. Edited by Eleanor Melville Metcalf. Cambridge, Massachusetts, 1948.

Journal up the Straits: Journal up the Straits: October 11, 1856-May 5, 1857. Edited by Raymond Weaver. New York, 1935.

HCL-M: The Melville Collection in the Harvard College Library.

Log: Jay Leyda, *The Melville Log: A Documentary Life of Herman Melville, 1819-1891.* New York, 1951. 2 vols.

MHS: Massachusetts Historical Society.

Sealts: Merton M. Sealts, Jr., "Melville's Reading: A Check-List of Books Owned and Borrowed by Herman Melville," *Harvard Library Bulletin,* II (1948), 141-163, 378-392; III (1949), 119-130, 268-277, 407-421; IV (1950), 98-109.

Sealts, Supplement: Merton M. Sealts, Jr., "Melville's Reading: A Supplementary List of Books Owned and Borrowed," *Harvard Library Bulletin,* VI (1952), 239-247.

Thorp: *Herman Melville: Representative Selections, with Introduction, Bibliography, and Notes.* Edited by Willard Thorp. New York, 1938.

Wright: Nathalia Wright, *Melville's Use of the Bible,* Durham, N. C. 1949.

References to *Moby-Dick, Pierre, Piazza Tales,* and *Collected Poems of Herman Melville* are to the Collected Edition, as follows: *Moby-Dick: Or, The Whale.* Edited by Luther S. Mansfield and Howard P. Vincent. New York, 1952; *Pierre: Or, The Ambiguities.* Edited by Henry A. Murray. New York, 1949; *Piazza Tales.* Edited by Egbert S. Oliver. New York, 1948; *Collected Poems of Herman Melville.* Edited by Howard P. Vincent. Chicago, 1947.

1.3. *A BOAT ON THE MISSISSIPPI:* There are a number of possible reasons why Melville used the Mississippi and a river steamboat as the setting of his novel. As soon as he chose to pun on the term "confidence man," he was half committed to a big river boat; furthermore, his need to change the personality of his hero frequently was well served by the many stops at landings made by such a boat. Insofar as his book was to be a satire of national traits, the central artery of the United States was a natural choice for setting; "the Western spirit is, or will yet be (for no other is, or can be), the true American one," he had written in *Israel Potter* (Ch. 22). As setting for universal satire, the Father of Waters adds its microcosmic connotations to those supplied by the world-ship and its motley passengers; in the chapter on dreams in *Mardi* (Ch. 119) Melville had alluded to the way in which "the great Mississippi musters his watery nations: Ohio, with his leagued streams; Missouri, bringing down in torrents the clans from the highlands; Arkansas, his Tartar rivers from the plain," and this "linked analogy" remained in his mind. If, on the other hand, Melville merely wished to exploit the Mississippi, the wish is easy to account for. The publishers of *Putnam's Monthly,* who had brought out *The Piazza Tales* and to whom Melville had proposed a novel, probably *The Confidence-Man,* in the late spring of 1855 (see Introduction, p. xxiii), used a considerable amount of Western material; "We believe in the West," *Putnam's Monthly* had announced (January 1853).

Melville had seen the river when he visited his uncle Thomas Melville at Galena, Illinois, in 1840, and his numerous references to the Mississippi show an old interest in it and a varied knowledge of it; (see Harrison Hayford and Merrell Davis, "Herman Melville as Office-Seeker," *Modern Language Quarterly,* X [1949], 168-183, 377-388; see also *Log,* pp. 105-108; John W. Nichol, "Melville and the Midwest," *PMLA,* LXVI [1951], 613-625; William H. Gilman, *Melville's Early Life and Redburn,* New York,

1951, pp. 151-153; Leon Howard, *Herman Melville: A Biography,* Berkeley & Los Angeles, 1951, pp. 31-37; Mr. Nichol collects the allusions and descriptions from Melville's writings which, taken together, show that he probably saw at first hand from a steamboat that stretch of the Mississippi which is intermittently described in *The Confidence-Man,* that from St. Louis to Cairo, Illinois). In 1855, letters from Melville's Aunt Mary in Galena to the Hon. Lemuel Shaw speak of the fact that her son George was involved in "steamboat speculations" that "did not turn out very well" (letter of 19 April 1855, MHS), and remark in October that her son Robert is "as yet on a steamboat—he expects to go down South at the close of navigation here" (letter of 2 October 1855, MHS). Bookstores and magazines and reading-rooms were filled with sketches of travel up and down the Mississippi, stories of life on the river steamers, and yarns of crooks and gambling on those floating microcosms. (See the bibliographies in Ralph H. Rusk, *The Literature of the Middle Western Frontier,* New York, 1925, Vol. II.) *Harper's New Monthly Magazine,* to which Melville subscribed (Sealts, No. 240), carried a number of these sketches. See especially T. B. Thorpe, "Remembrances of the Mississippi," (XII [December 1855], 25-41); this long article is rich with miscellaneous information. Thorpe's description of the heterogeneous crowd on a Mississippi steamer, p. 34, is similar to Melville's and may have given Melville a suggestion or two.

Banvard had exhibited his famous Panorama of the Mississippi before thousands; and if by chance Melville failed to see these three miles of painted canvas, he could have read a full description of this "Largest Painting ever Executed by Man" in the pamphlet about it, *Banvard's Geographical Panorama . . .,* Boston, 1847. He certainly knew of the Panorama, for in his *Journal up the Straits,* pp. 35f., he says, speaking of the First Bridge in Constantinople: "Banvard should paint a few hundred miles of this pageant of moving processions." Whatever his sources, a comparison with descriptions and charts of the Mississippi shows that Melville's references to scenery and landings are correct, except, of course, that his Devil's Joke is an imaginary landing.

1.4 *suddenly as Manco Capac at the lake Titicaca:* This comparison of the advent of the man in cream colors to the advent of a deity—Manco Capac, child of the sun and legendary founder of the Inca dynasty of Peru—begins the constant double reference of the novel. There are several legends of Manco Capac; the one involving his sudden appearance at Lake Titicaca is told as follows by Garcilasso de la Vega, the Ynca (d. 1616): " 'Our Father the Sun,' said my uncle the Ynca, 'seeing the human race in the condition I have described, had compassion upon them, and sent down from heaven to the earth a son and daughter to instruct them in the knowledge of our Father the Sun, that they might adore Him, and adopt Him as their God; also to give them precepts and laws by which to live as reasonable and civilised men. . . . With these commands and intentions our Father the Sun placed his two children in the Lake Titicaca. . . . These children set out from Titicaca and travelled northwards.' " They founded Cuzco and established an Inca empire. The subjugated Indians " 'worshipped the strangers as children of the Sun, and obeyed them as kings.' " Garcilasso gives this first Inca's name as Manco Ccapak, and says that the "Indians of those and later times . . . believed most firmly that the first Ynca was a child of the Sun, . . . worshipping him as such. . . . They, therefore, believed that he was a divine man come down from heaven." (*First Part of the Royal Commentaries of the Yncas,* trans. and ed. by Sir Clements R. Markham, London, for the Hakluyt Society, 1869-1871, 2 vols.; I, 64f, 66, 83. Garcilasso's *Royal Commentaries* had appeared in English as early as 1688.) William H. Prescott summarizes this version of the myth of Manco Capac, and calls it "the tradition most familiar to the European scholar." (*History of the Conquest of Peru,* New York, 1847, 2 vols.; I, 8) See also note 199.19.

1.7. *His cheek was fair:* See the Introduction, pp. l-li, for the argument that this "lamb-like" man represents Christian religion or Christ in the allegory. Supported by other evidence of this meaning in Chapters I and II, the details of his "flaxen" hair and "fleecy" hat recall Melville's reference in *Moby-Dick* (Ch. 42) to the Vision of St. John and "the Holy One that sitteth there white like wool." The reference is to the description of "one like unto the Son of man" in Revelation 1:14: "His head and his hairs were white like wool, as white as snow. . . ."

1.14. *Fidèle:* The symbolism and irony of this name for Melville's microcosmic vessel soon become obvious. Hawthorne's allegorical use of the name *Faith* in "Young Goodman Brown" had caught Melville's attention; he wrote in his essay, "Hawthorne and His Mosses":

"And with Young Goodman, too, in allegorical pursuit of his Puritan wife, you cry out in your anguish:—

" 'Faith!' shouted Goodman Brown, in a voice of agony and desperation; and the echoes of the forest mocked him, crying, 'Faith! Faith!' as if bewildered wretches were seeking her all through the wilderness."

In the same passage Melville says that some of Hawthorne's titles are "directly calculated to deceive—egregiously deceive, the superficial skimmer of pages. . . . You would of course suppose that it ["Young Goodman Brown"] was a simple little tale, intended as a supplement to *Goody Two Shoes*. Whereas, it is deep as Dante." This method and manner, discovered in Hawthorne in 1850, became under his own hands the method and manner of *The Confidence-Man*. Perhaps the name Melville gave ironically to his climactic Confidence Man, Frank Goodman, also owed something to his recollections of "Young Goodman Brown." In naming his steamboat, he also probably had in mind the assumed name of Imogen in *Cymbeline;* he had used the lines: "With fairest flowers, Whilst summer lasts, and I live here, Fidele," from *Cymbeline*, IV, ii, 218-219, as an epigraph for "The Piazza."

John W. Shroeder ("Sources and Symbols for Melville's *Confidence-Man*," *PMLA*, LXVI [1951], 363-380) points out in *The Confidence-Man* many similarities and probable references to Hawthorne's sketch "The Celestial Railroad" and to the source of this sketch, Bunyan's *Pilgrim's Progress*. The *Fidèle*, he believes, combines Melville's "favorite symbol of the boat-as-world with Hawthorne's symbol of the vessel bound for Tophet." Also, the name *Fidèle* may owe something, he suggests, to Bunyan's character Faithful.

1.20. *impostor:* See the description of crooks and rackets on the Mississippi in Bernard DeVoto, *Mark Twain's America* (Boston, 1932).

2.7 *Measan . . . Murrel . . . the brothers Harpe:* Samuel Mason or Meason had been one of the more spectacular river pirates in the early days. (James Hall, *Sketches of History, Life, and Manners in the West*, Philadelphia, 1835, II, 88-89, and *Letters from the West*, London, 1828, pp. 278-279. Melville used Hall's *Sketches* for his account of Indian-hating and Moredock in Chs. 26 and 27, and probably used it here as well.) John A. Murrall or Murrel was a criminal on the grand scale, the story of whose clever swindles and bloody murders was written and rewritten in the 1830's and 1840's. When the steamboats began to threaten his business as a river pirate, he made a trip from New Orleans to Cincinnati, posing as an itinerant preacher, organizing the lawless into a great Mystic Clan for the purpose of stealing and reselling Negroes and horses, and murdering whenever convenient. He planned a great slave rebellion, but was caught in 1835 by Virgil Stewart, who published in the following year his history of Murrel's villainies and his capture. (*The History of Virgil A. Stewart*, New York, 1836) These hideous adventures were rewritten in narrative after narrative; the *National Police Gazette* carried a life of Murrel through most of 1846 and 1847, as one of its "series of biographies of criminals drawn from police records," and published it in paper covers in 1847. William Gilmore Simms's *Border Beagles*, of which there was a new edition in 1855, and *Richard Hurdis* are said by their editor, W. P. Trent, to be based upon the history of the Murrel gang. Melville must have known one or more of these versions; he could have derived from them not only a touch of Mississippi local color but, more important, some hints for his portrait of the Confidence Man, for Murrel like the Confidence Man hid his malice under saintliness: as he told Stewart, he dressed "rather in the Methodist order," was well versed in Scripture, preached "a hell of a good sermon," and after preaching found it easy to trade in counterfeit money with members of his audience. (Stewart, pp. 32-33)

The Harpes, less clever and more bloodthirsty, also had their saga. (T. Marshall Smith, *Legends of the War of Independence and of the Earlier Settlements in the West*, Louisville, Ky., 1855) Hall used their story a number of times in the 1820's and 1830's. He stresses their "deep rooted malignity against human nature"; one of the Harpes said, just before his death, that "he had been actuated by no inducement, but a settled hatred of his species, whom he had sworn to destroy without distinction." Perhaps the shadow of his misanthropy falls across the Confidence Man. (Hall, *Sketches* . . . , II, 87; *Letters* . . . , pp. 277-281; *The Harpe's Head; A Legend of Kentucky*, Philadelphia, 1833. The sentence about "a settled hatred of his species" occurs identically in *Letters* . . . , p. 277, and *The Harpe's Head*, p. 245.)

2.22 *Charity thinketh no evil:* This and the following legends held up by the lamblike man are from I Corinthians 13. In Melville's copy of the New Testament (in HCL-M), this chapter is marked with checks at the beginning and in a number of places; "Charity suffereth long and is kind" and "thinketh no evil" are checked.

4.28 *nigh the foot of a ladder there leading to a deck above:* Melville probably intended here to suggest Jacob's vision of the ladder to heaven with "the angels of God ascending and descending on it," God's promise of blessing to all the families of the earth through Jacob's seed, and perhaps also, through oblique reference to heaven, the resurrection. The first probability is fortified by the last comment which Melville in the next chapter puts in the mouths of spectators at this scene: " 'Jacob dreaming at Luz.' "

6.6. *Casper Hauser:* Kaspar Hauser (1812?-1833), a German youth of mysterious origin who appeared suddenly at Nuremberg in 1829. His identity and psychology were much discussed. He could, or would, tell nothing of his past. Melville had referred to his vacant mind in *Pierre*, p. 304.

6.21. *Jacob dreaming at Luz:* Genesis 28:12-15. Jacob's vision of the ladder to heaven is frequently mentioned by Melville, and is marked in his Bible (NYPL). (Wright, pp. 26, 10.)

6:30. *The great ship-canal of Ving-King-Ching:* Undoubtedly the Grand or Imperial Canal of Eastern China, called *Yun Ho* or *Cha Ho* by the Chinese. This great canal, connecting the Yangtze with the Pei River and the city of Hangchow with Tientsin, was partly opened in 486 B.C., was completed by Kublai Khan in 1289 A.D., and is still in some use. Melville's name for the Canal is apparently unknown to the Chinese. His memory of the Chinese name of a part of it was somewhat fresher five years earlier, when he wrote in *Moby-Dick* (p. 289): "For upon the great canal of Hang-Ho, or whatever they call it, in China, four or five laborers on the foot-path will draw a bulky freighted junk at the rate of a mile an hour." For a part of its course, the canal lies along a bed of the Hwang-ho, or Yellow River.

7.6 *the Fidèle, though, might at distance have been taken by strangers for some whitewashed fort:* One of the more obvious themes of the novel, the failure of Christians to live up to their professions of peace and charity, is symbolized here. Readers of *White-Jacket* will recall Melville's comparison of this world to a man-of-war and his ironic contrast between its Articles of War and the

Sermon on the Mount. These ideas also reappear in *Billy Budd* and elsewhere.

7.11. *Fine promenades:* Mr. Nichol says (p. 622) that this part of the description of the *Fidèle* owes more to Eastern ships of 1856 than to the river steamboats of 1840, when Melville had seen them; other details are, he says, authentic.

7.23. *Cocovarde mountains:* Corcovado (Hunchback), a 2,372-foot peak overlooking Rio de Janeiro. In *United States Exploring Expedition, 1838-1842* [Philadelphia, 184-?], 6 v., which Melville owned (Sealts, No. 532), he could have read that aqueducts bring water to the fountains of Rio de Janeiro from "the Corcovado and Tejuca Mountains, a distance of six or seven miles." (I, 49 in the Philadelphia edition of 1850.) The *United States*, the ship on which Melville was returning from the Pacific, lay in the harbor of Rio de Janeiro 16-24 August 1844; he did not go ashore, however (Charles Roberts Anderson, *Melville in the South Seas*, New York, 1939, p. 356). Many of the events of *White-Jacket* take place at Rio.

7.33. *high bluffs and shot-towers on the Missouri shore:* Melville's details are accurate; *The Western Pilot* mentions the high, rocky bluff that runs for eight or ten miles along the Missouri shore below St. Louis, and the shot factories at Herculaneum (Samuel Cummings, *The Western Pilot; Containing Charts . . . of the Mississippi from the Mouth of the Missouri to the Gulf of Mexico*, Cincinnati, 1848, pp. 79, 81).

8.8. *Chaucer's Canterbury pilgrims:* Melville quotes from Chaucer's portrait of the shipman, in *White-Jacket* (Ch. 86). He owned Robert Bell's edition of the *Poetical Works* "in eight vols.—good print." (Letter to Catherine G. Lansing, 12 Oct. 1876, in Victor Hugo Paltsits, ed., *The Family Correspondence of Herman Melville*, New York, 1929; see Sealts, Nos. 138, 141.)

8.14. *hunters after all these hunters:* Diddling, imposture, and humbug flourished in the 1850's, though perhaps no more luxuriantly than usual. The books of Jonathan Green, "reformed gambler," give a somewhat jumbled but adequate picture of some of the organized villainies of the West. His *The Secret Band of Brothers* (Philadelphia, 1846) is about a "wide-spread organization—pledged to gambling, theft, and villainy of all kinds. . . . It numbers among its members the professional man, the 'respectable citizen,' the prominent and wealthy of various towns throughout the Union; nay, it has sometimes invaded the house of God, and secured the services of those who are ostensibly its ministers." (Preface, p. 4; see also his *Twelve Days in the Tombs*, New York, 1850.) P. T. Barnum was at the height of his glittering career, and he made sure that the public was kept aware of the excitement of humbug. His *Life* . . ., written by himself, was published in 1855 (New York) and read far and wide. Melville may have seen it; he could have found in it not only amusing tales of imposture, quackery, and charlatanry, but also an account of travels in a Mississippi steamboat, the story of a trick played on the ship's barber by Barnum, whom the barber thought to be in league with the devil in a scene reminiscent of the next-to-last in *The Confidence-Man*, and a whole bagful of April Fool jokes. Melville had made fun of Barnum's advertisements and his hoaxes in 1847 (Luther S. Mansfield, "Melville's Comic Articles on Zachary Taylor," *American Literature*, IX [1938], 411-418).

8.23. *Dives and Lazarus:* See note on 81.32.

8.26. *an Anarchasis Cloots congress:* Baron Jean Baptiste de Clootz (1755-94), also known as World-Citizen Anacharsis Clootz, came to France after the Revolution began and led a delegation of "ambassadors of the human race" to the National Assembly. Carlyle describes his entrance on June 19, 1790: ". . . Anacharsis Clootz entering the august Salle de Manège, with the Human Species at his heels. Swedes, Spaniards, Polacks; Turks, Chaldeans, Greeks, dwellers in Mesopotamia; behold them all; they have come to claim place in the grand Federation. . . ." (*The French Revolution*, I, x.) Reference to Anacharsis Clootz was a favorite device of Melville's for establishing the representational, microcosmic character of his ships and their crews or passengers; the heterogeneous crew of the *Pequod* was "An Anacharsis Clootz deputation from all the isles of the sea, and all the ends of the earth, accompanying Old Ahab in the *Pequod* to lay the world's grievances before that bar from which not very many of them ever came back." (*Moby-Dick*, pp. 118 f.) In the opening paragraphs of *Billy Budd*, Melville speaks of a heterogeneous group of sailors as made up of "such an assortment of tribes and complexions as would have well fitted them to be marched up by Anacharsis Clootz before the bar of the first French Assembly as Representatives of the Human Race."

9.3. *In the forward part of the boat:* The reader will remember that the lamblike man was last seen on the forecastle.

9.4. *negro cripple . . . cut down to the stature of a Newfoundland dog:* See Introduction, p. lii, for a discussion of the symbolic significance of this Negro, who heads the list of Confidence Men. The Negro proves that he is an embodiment of the Confidence Man by claiming all the others as his sponsors and by the time-worn *double-entendre* with reference to them: " 'What knows me as well as dis poor old darkie knows hisself.' " His falseness comes out in his dishonest appropriation and use of Mr. Roberts' business card. Connotations of "cynic," "misanthrope," and "fawning insincerity" cluster about Melville's use of *dog* and *canine* throughout this novel, as will be seen particularly in Ch. 22. Descriptions of people are highly emblematic; the Negro's being "cut down to the stature of a Newfoundland dog" signifies the humility which he speciously represents. F. O. Matthiessen (*American Renaissance*, New York, 1941, p. 502) observes, in considering Melville's color symbolism, that whiteness connoted innocence and purity in the early novels *Typee* and *Redburn*, terror in *Moby-Dick*, ambiguity in *Pierre*, and innocence and purity again at the end in *Billy Budd*. In *The Confidence-Man* whiteness and blackness carry their conventional suggestions of good and evil respectively; the Negro's blackness is the first clue to the diabolic nature of the Confidence Man.

Some years before, probably in 1849 (see the argument for this date in the Explanatory Notes of *Moby-Dick*, p. 643), Melville had jotted down some ideas for a comic story about devils circulating in human society. Some of these ideas may have found their way into *Moby-Dick* and *Pierre*, as the Notes mentioned above suggest; but the tone of comedy, the method of parody, and the idea of the Devil disguised as a Quaker were an adumbration of *The Confidence-Man*, in which the powers of evil masquerade under the Christian virtues and one of their embodiments, in Ch. 10, appears briefly as a "somewhat elderly person, in the quaker dress." These jottings of Melville's were made in pencil on the last flyleaf of Volume VII of his set of Shakespeare (Sealts, No. 460): " 'Yes, Madam, Cain was a godless froward boy, & Reuben (Gen. 4:49 [49:4]) & Absolom' Many pious men have impious childer—(Devil as a Quaker) / A formal compact—Imprimis—First—Second. The aforesaid soul. said soul &c—Duplicates— 'How was it about the temptation on the hill?' &c Conversation upon Gabriel, Michael & Raphel—gentlemanly &c— D begs the hero to form one of a 'Society of D's,'—his name would be mighty &c—Leaves a letter to the D— 'My dear D'—'Terra Oblivionis' . . . —At the Astor find him making [illegible word]—Going to a ball takes a long time making toilette.—The Doctor's Coach stops the way.—'Do you beleive all that stuff? nonsense—The world was new [never?] made. —'[Illegible word] not this you mention *here*—in the scriptures?' Receives visits from the principal d's—'Gentlemen' &c *arguments* to persuade—'Would you not rather be below with kings than above with fools?' "

It is possible that Melville's interest in devils as dramatis personæ was renewed, or even originated, of course, by those skirmishes with the devil or devils that are so dramatically recorded in historical and homiletic literature of seventeenth-century New England. Many of the stories of his friend Nathaniel Hawthorne, it will be remembered, transmute this material. Cotton Mather had a very lively sense, especially during the witchcraft delusion, that "An Army of *Devils* is horribly broke in upon the place which is the *Center*, and after a sort, the *First-born* of our *English* Settlements," and that "at prodigious *Witch-Meetings*, the Wretches have proceeded so far, as to Concert and Consult the Methods of Rooting out the Christian Religion from this Country. . . ." (*The Wonders of the Invisible World. Observations As well Historical as Theological, upon the Nature, The Number, and the Operations of the Devils* . . ., Boston, 1693, § II) Increase Mather explained the devil's strategy of masquerade: "As the evil Spirit will speak good Words, so doth he sometimes appear in the likeness of good Men, to the end that he may the more effectually deceive and delude all such as shall be so unhappy as to entertain converses with him." (*An Essay for the Recording of Illustrious Providences,* 1684, p. 210) While it is not known that Melville read *The Wonders* . . . or the *Essay* . . ., it is probable that he did read Cotton Mather's *Magnalia Christi Americana,* which the Pittsfield Library Association acquired in 1853 ("Mather's Magnalia, 2 vols. 8vo.—One of the richest sources of New England history. A quaint, entertaining book." *Log,* p. 477) and which he refers to in "The Apple-Tree Table" (published in May 1856) in a way to suggest that he may have been reading it. Fraudulent ministers are the confidence men of the *Magnalia,* and they are the tools of the devil. "Wolves in sheep's cloathing" is the title of Chapter V of Book VII, *The Wars of the Lord; "Or, an history of several* impostors, *pretending to be* ministers *remarkably detected in the churches of* New England. . . ." Mather explains: "The *preaching of the gospel,* being that grand institution whereon depends the everlasting salvation of men, satan seeks it as a mighty triumph, to pervert it unto their everlasting destruction. . . . Or suppose the *new preachers* do broach no *new errors,* yet if they shall prove *cheats,* that have made the *preaching of the gospel* only a cloak for their *covetous* or *lacivious,* or other prophane designs. . . ." Mather has many pages about these satanic impostors, and a rogues' gallery of examples.

Most important in the satanic ancestry of the Confidence Man are the Bible and *Paradise Lost;* see notes 24.14, 35.24, 36.17, 148.4, 148.31, 151.17, 213.17, 254.28.

Melville had been rereading Burton's *Anatomy of Melancholy,* it seems, or at any rate thinking about this favorite old book of his (Sealts, Nos. 102, 103), when he went to New York in 1856 to arrange for the publication of *The Confidence-Man* (see Introduction, p. xxv). There are many lines in the *Anatomy* that anticipate ideas of Melville's novel; it is possible that a rereading of Burton helped precipitate the book and form the character of the Confidence Man. Burton speaks often of those who make a show of religion but in their hearts laugh at it, and of "our religious madness . . . so many professed Christians, yet so few imitators of Christ." And perhaps the protean Confidence Man owes something to this sentence from "old Burton": "To see a man turn himself into all shapes like a Chameleon, or as Proteus transform himself into all that is monstrous; to act twenty parts & persons at once for his advantage, to temporize & vary like Mercury the Planet, good with good, bad with bad; having a several face, garb, & character, for every one he meets; of all religions, humours, inclinations; to fawn like a spaniel, with lying and feigned obsequiousness, rage like a lion, bark like a cur, fight like a dragon, sting like a serpent, as meek as a lamb, & yet again grin like a tiger, weep like a crocodile, insult over some, & yet others domineer over him, here command, there crouch, tyrannize in one place, be baffled in another, a wise man at home, a fool abroad to make others merry." (Robert Burton, *The Anatomy of Melancholy,* ed. Floyd Dell and Paul Jordan-Smith, New York, 1927, p. 53)

Mr. Richard Chase says that elements from American folklore—the Yankee peddler, Brother Jonathan, Uncle Sam—combined with ideas of Orpheus and Christ, contribute to the composite character of the Confidence-Man. (*Herman Melville: A Critical Study,* New York, 1949, pp. 186-188)

Picaresque romances, a number of which Melville had read and from which he had borrowed in earlier books, certainly helped form the Confidence Man, who is "the first real anti-hero in Melville's novels to appear as the central character," as well as the novel as a whole, in which "Melville has used the structure and content of rogue fiction as the symbolic medium through which to express his profound ponderings of good and evil. . . ." (Richard Jackson Foster, "Melville and Roguery: A Study of the Relation of Melville's Writings to Picaresque Fiction," unpublished M.A. thesis, Oberlin College, 1950, pp. 120, 138)

Also to be reckoned among the possible ancestors of Melville's central character are the con men who impinged upon Melville's life. Picaresque vagabonds among his shipmates on whalers and among the beachcombers of the Pacific islands where he passed weeks and months of his adventurous youth may have lent a trait or a wile here or there to the Confidence Men. One of these, who had been his companion, under the name John B. Troy, aboard the *Lucy Ann* and on Tahiti and neighboring islands, and whom Melville later used as Doctor Long Ghost in *Omoo*, had a career which exploited such a variety of talents and aliases that it brings to the mind of at least one biographer, Mr. Jay Leyda, the various disguises of the Confidence Man. (*Log*, p. xxxiii) In a sense, Melville was the victim of another confidence man, someone who called himself "Herman Melville" and took orders for "his" books in Georgia and South Carolina in the summer of 1850. (*Log*, p. xxx) A few suggestions—for the name of the novel or an incident or so— may have come from the newspapers. The *Springfield Daily Republican* for 5 May 1855 reported the arrest of "The Original Confidence Man," a man named Thompson, who died in Sing Sing prison in October 1856. (I am indebted to Mr. Leyda for this news.) The *Berkshire County Eagle* for 21 December 1855 carried a news story of the discovery of fraud in the sale of bogus stock in the New Haven and New York road; one Schuyler had made false entries in the transfer book, and the company had provided no way to check on this sort of thing. Among the jokes in the *Berkshire County Eagle* for 1 February 1856 are these: "A 'Confidence' Man —the man who thinks he can help a good looking servant girl 'cord the bedstead,' without getting his head broke by his wife." "Confidence men' were never so plenty in the Police accounts of New York —apparently—as at present. Why don't they emigrate to Washington? Nobody there seems to have any confidence in anybody."

11.30. *The will of man is by his reason swayed: A Midsummer*

Night's Dream, II, ii, 115. Puck has just poured upon Lysander's eyelids the juice that makes anyone so anointed "madly dote Upon the next live creature that it sees." Lysander, awakening, attributes his sudden love for Helena to reason. The rest of Melville's passage is ironic, of course, and a good example of the involution of irony that is a cause of confusion in *The Confidence-Man.* Although Melville's point through a large part of the novel is the need for a sound, critical use of reason, he appears to disparage with his irony the justified skepticism of the crowd at this point. "Waywardness" is, to be sure, a more accurate term for the vacillating attitudes of the crowd than either skepticism or charity; but Melville's ironical undermining of "improved judgment" can be for the reader a small red herring.

12.35. *Oh yes, oh yes, ge'mmen, . . . dar is aboard here:* The Negro's list of his friends is, with two discrepancies, a list of the subsequent Confidence Men, or rather of the various manifestations of the Confidence Man, in the order of their appearance. There are, however, no "ge'mman in a yaller west" and "sodjer" in the novel, unless they be the Mississippi operator who is unmasked by the cosmopolitan in Chs. 25-35, and the cripple in the old regimental coat whom the herb-doctor dupes; but these men, though they are in the confidence game themselves, are actually more or less victimized by the real Confidence Man. It is likely that Melville changed or forgot his earlier intention regarding these two men; contrary to his usual practice, he did not see either the English or the American edition through the press.

14.9. *To where it belongs with your charity! to heaven with it!:* Plinlimmon in *Pierre* (Ch. 14) had also proposed that self-sacrificing charity be postponed to heaven. Melville makes the case for skepticism in the first part of *The Confidence-Man* and the case for charity and trust in the last. Several critics have believed that the gimlet-eyed, wooden-legged man expressed Melville's own views; readers who note the emblematic quality of all descriptions of persons in this novel will understand more correctly what Melville is saying here. In *Israel Potter* (Ch. 7), Melville had put the following words into the mouth of Benjamin Franklin: "Sad usage has made you sadly suspicious, my honest friend. An indiscriminate distrust of human nature is the worst consequence of a miserable condition, whether brought about by innocence or guilt. And though want of suspicion more than want of sense, sometimes leads a man into harm, yet too much suspicion is as bad as too little sense." In his copy of Chapman's translation of Homer's *Odyssey*, which was given him in November 1858 by George Duyckinck (Sealts, No. 278), Melville underlined this passage: "Blind Confidence, (The God of Fools)."

15.13. *under this captain of fools, in this ship of fools!:* "When we are born, we cry that we are come To this great stage of fools." (*King Lear,* IV, vi, 186f.)

16.18. *Might deter Timon:* See notes on 157.7 and 261.12, and other references on 260.2 and 265.20.

16.30. *Jeremy Diddler:* Jeremy Diddler, the hero of a farce by James Kenney, *Raising the Wind* (London, 1803), was a penniless gentleman who used his amiability, his status as a gentleman, and a little flattery to induce people to trust him with small loans, which he did not repay. This farce was long popular, and was played many times in New York in the years of Melville's residence there in the 1840's; it probably gave rise to the sense of *diddler* as "a mean cheat or swindler" (NED). Edgar Allan Poe's diddler, in his "Diddling Considered as One of the Exact Sciences," is "guided by self interest. He scorns to diddle for the mere *sake* of the diddle." But not so Melville's Confidence Man. Another diddler in Melville is Stubb in *Moby-Dick* (Ch. 91); Stubb, to use his own word, "diddled" the captain of the *Rosebud:* pretending to save him and his crew from a fever, he got the dead, ambergris-laden whale away from them. See another reference to Jeremy Diddler on 154.30.

20.22. *Werter's Charlotte, and the bread and butter:* Werther tells how he lost his heart to Charlotte when he saw her slicing a rye loaf for her six little brothers and sisters. (Johann Wolfgang von Goethe, *The Sorrows of Young Werther,* Book I, June 16.) Melville may have known not only Goethe's novel but also Thackeray's ballad, "Sorrows of Werther," which begins and ends:

> Werther had a love for Charlotte
>   Such as words could never utter;
> Would you know how first he met her?
>   She was cutting bread and butter.
>
>   · · · · ·
>
> Charlotte, having seen his body
>   Borne before her on a shutter,
> Like a well-conducted person,
>   Went on cutting bread and butter.

Thackeray's ballad appeared in *Putnam's Monthly* in the same issue with the last instalment of "Benito Cereno" (Dec. 1855), p. 626.

An allusion to *The Sorrows of Young Werther* comes quite appropriately from the man with the weed, who embodies eighteenth-century sentimental doctrines.

21.31. *potter's clay:* Isaiah 64:8: "But now, O Lord, thou art our father; we are the clay, and thou our potter. . . ."

24.14. *from the stock's descent its rise:* Henry F. Pommer, *Milton and Melville*, [Pittsburgh,] 1950, p. 31, points out Melville's echo here of a passage from *Paradise Lost* (II, 14-17; Mr. Pommer's italics):

> From this *descent*
> Celestial virtues *rising*, will appear
> More glorious and more dread *than from no fall*,
> And *trust themselves to fear no second fate.*

Thus the stock of the Black Rapids Coal Company is from the beginning associated with hell, and the Confidence Man, as he does later, uses the language of Satan. Mr. Pommer's careful study finds that Melville was more significantly influenced by Milton than was any other major American author, and by *Paradise Lost* more heavily than by any other of Milton's poems. Milton's Satan contributed greatly to the character of Ahab, as Mr. Pommer and others have shown; he contributed not so much to characterize as to identify the Confidence Man for the knowing reader.

27.25. *sophomore:* "sophomorean presumption and egotism" (*Pierre*, p. 324)

28.4. *In general a black and shameful period lies before me:* Melville's supposed quotation from Tacitus gives the gist of several passages in the *Histories* and the *Annals* of the Roman historian (55?–after 117?). The passage that Melville perhaps had in mind is in Tacitus' introduction to his history of the Roman Empire from 79 A.D. to the death of Domitian: "I enter upon a time rich in catastrophes, full of fierce battles and civic strife, a time when even peace had horrors of its own; a time during which four Emperors perished by the sword. . . . I shall have to tell of holy rites profaned, of adulteries in high places, of seas crowded with exiles, of islands stained with blood, and of horrors in the city greater still, where high birth, wealth, the acceptance of office, or the refusal of it, were accounted crimes, and where virtue proved the surest road to death. . . ." (*Histories* i. 2, trans. George Gilbert Ramsay.)

Other passages similar in thought to Melville's quotation are *Annals*
iii. 28; v. 3. In *Redburn* (Ch. 55) Melville speaks of "unmatchable
Tacitus," who "has embalmed his [Tiberius'] carrion."

28.28. *There is a subtle man, and the same is deceived:* This is
not an exact quotation but apparently a way of referring the reader
to a passage in Ecclesiasticus 19 that suits the colloquy between the
man in mourning and the sophomore: "23. There is a wickedness,
and the same is abomination; And there is a fool wanting in wisdom. . . . 25. There is an exquisite subtilty, and the same is unjust; And there is one that perverteth favour to gain a judgement.
26. There is one that doeth wickedly, that hangeth down his head
with mourning; But inwardly he is full of deceit."

28.34. *its wickedness—that is, its ugliness:* A fundamental doctrine in the ethical system of Anthony Ashley Cooper, Lord Shaftesbury, (1671-1713), appearing many times in the treatises that
make up his *Characteristics,* is that the moral sense is a faculty
which apprehends the beauty or deformity of actions in a world
which is essentially a harmony; morality, like art, is a matter of
Taste: ". . . the Taste of Beauty and the Relish of what is decent,
just, and amiable, perfects the character of the Gentleman and the
Philosopher. And the study of such a Taste or Relish will, as we
suppose, be ever the great employment and concern of him who
covets as well to be wise and good, as agreeable and polite." "And
thus, after all, the most natural beauty in the world is honesty and
moral truth. For all beauty is truth." ". . . virtue, which is itself
no other than the love of order and beauty in society." "So that
beauty, said I, and good with you, Theocles [Shaftesbury], I perceive, are still one and the same." (Shaftesbury, *Miscellany,* III,
Ch. 1; *An Essay on the Freedom of Wit and Humour,* Part IV, sec.
iii; *An Inquiry Concerning Virtue or Merit,* Book I, Part III, sec.
iii; *The Moralists,* Part III, sec. ii.) In a letter to Hawthorne, [June
[?] 1851], Melville referred to Shaftesbury: "Truth is ridiculous to
men. Thus easily in my room here do I, conceited and garrulous,
revere the test of my Lord Shaftesbury." (Thorp, pp. 390 and
434 n.1) In *Clarel* (Part III, vi), when Derwent calls Jesus "'Pon-
tiff of optimists supreme!'" Mortmain says, "'Twas Shaftesbury
first assumed your tone, Trying to cheerfulize Christ's moan.'"

29.9 *the cemeteries of Auburn and Greenwood:* This remark links
the man in mourning with the Graveyard School of poets, Robert
Blair, Edward Young, and their imitators, and with eighteenth-cen-

tury sentimental melancholy in general. Mt. Auburn Cemetery, Cambrige, Mass., "was for many years the only garden cemetery in the environs of Boston. It is still one of the most beautiful. Its grounds are thickly wooded with rare trees and shrubs, landscaped with occasional ponds and they rise to a commanding hill, from which is a dreamy view of the winding Charles River, Cambridge, Boston, and distant hills." It has the graves of many famous people. (*Massachusetts* . . ., American Guide Series, Boston, 1937, p. 202.) Greenwood Cemetery was the principal and best known cemetery in use in New York. Its naturally beautiful situation, in the extreme southeastern part of Brooklyn on Gowanus Heights, and its expensively ornamented grounds made it famous. It had been in use since 1840.

29.14. *Akenside—his 'Pleasures of Imagination':* Perhaps a sly way of tagging the shallow optimism of the man with the weed as Pleasures of Imagination; probably another way of indicating that the man with the weed represents eighteenth-century sentimental optimism (among other things). Akenside, a disciple of Shaftesbury and Hutcheson, in *The Pleasures of Imagination* (1744) presents a benevolent universe in which whatever is is right, where we trace,

> Through all its fabric, Wisdom's artful aim
> Disposing every part, and gaining still
> By means proportion'd her benignant end,

and where the "final cause" of pleasure from Beauty is the discovery and love of Truth and Goodness:

> Thus was Beauty sent from heaven,
> The lovely ministress of Truth and Good
> In this dark world; for Truth and Good are one,
> And Beauty dwells in them, and they in her,
> With like participation.

(*The Pleasures of Imagination,* II, 122-125; I, 372-376.) Mark Akenside's volume had been in Melville's childhood home, a gift from his father to his mother during their courtship. (R. M. Weaver, *Herman Melville: Mariner and Mystic,* New York, 1921, p. 57; Sealts, No. 8)

29.18. *Ovid, Horace, Anacreon, and the rest:* Melville bought in 1849 Harper's Classical Library, 37 vols., containing translations of Xenophon, Demosthenes, Sallust, Caesar, Cicero, Virgil, Aeschylus,

Sophocles, Euripides, Horace, *Phaedrus,* Ovid, Thucydides, Livy, Herodotus, Homer, Juvenal, Persius, Pindar, Anacreon. (See Sealts, No. 147)

30.33. *Astrea:* "a daughter of Zeus and Themis. According to the poets, she lived on earth during the golden age and was a source of blessing to men; but their impiety drove her to heaven during the brazen and iron ages, and she was placed among the constellations of the zodiac, under the name Virgo." (*Oxford Companion to English Literature.*)

35.24. *the devil is never so black as he is painted:* A hint at the diabolic nature of the Confidence Man, reinforced, a few lines further on, in " 'How much money did the devil make by gulling Eve?' "

36.17. *How much money did the devil make by gulling Eve?:* See Genesis 3:1-6. One of many references in this novel, through the Bible and through *Paradise Lost,* to the Garden of Eden myth of the temptation and fall, when the devil first played the role of confidence man.

39.2. *A GENTLEMAN WITH GOLD SLEEVE-BUTTONS:* One of Melville's earlier drafts of the title of this chapter conveys his intentions more explicitly: "A righteous man encounters a good man, and an enthusiast a gentleman] a man of common sense." In his final draft he added with a caret "in fine linen" after "gentleman," a revealing reference, probably, to "fine linen, clean and white: for the fine linen is the righteousness of saints." (Revelation 19:8) This gentleman is the only one in the novel who is neither dupe nor, on the other hand, knave, cynic, or hard-hearted egoist. He is the ideal, the all-good, the sound in both mind and heart; but he enjoys this state of preternatural goodness because, emblematically, he has always been separated from the sooty world, through his "very good luck"; he has never been submitted to the conditions of mortal life, the ineluctable damaging.

40.27. *like the Hebrew governor:* Probably Pontius Pilate, Roman governor of Judaea. Pilate washed his hands as a symbol of his innocence in the matter when the populace demanded the crucifixion of Jesus. (Matthew 27:24)

40.31 *Wilberforce:* William Wilberforce (1759-1833), the wealthy English philanthropist who, after his conversion to Evangelical Christianity, advocated in Parliament and elsewhere various humanitarian reforms, particularly the abolition of slavery in the

British colonies; wrote religious books; and labored for religious education and foreign missions. Evangelicalism was condemned as "enthusiastic" by the old High Church party. See Introduction, lv, for comment on the man in the gray coat as Wilberforce.

41.10. *Scarcely for a righteous man. . .* : Romans 5:7.

42.20. *that notion of Socrates that the soul is a harmony:* Merton M. Sealts, Jr. (in his doctoral dissertation, "Herman Melville's Reading in Ancient Philosophy," Yale University, 1942, pp. 111-113) discusses Melville's interest in Plato's tripartite division of the soul (in *Timaeus, Phaedrus,* and *The Republic*): "The good government of the soul, Socrates declares in the latter dialogue, consists in a harmony of these three principles: the rational or governing part, the irrational or concupiscent part, and the irascible part or will. In regulating bodily desires, the will becomes auxiliary to the reason in enforcing control over the third member and thus achieving harmony." "The psychological implications of Melville's use of this figure . . . indicate that he had the *Republic* [Bohn ed., II, 127, 129, 147, 244, 260f., 282] in mind when employing it," rather than the *Phaedo,* the only source assigned to it by K. H. Sundermann (*Herman Melvilles Gedankengut. . . ,* Berlin, 1937, p. 98 and note, p. 209). In *Redburn* (Ch. 49) Melville says: "Not in a spirit of foolish speculation altogether, in no merely transcendental mood, did the glorious Greek of old fancy the human soul to be essentially a harmony." There are many admiring references to Socrates in Melville's works.

43.1. *World's Fair in London:* At the Crystal Palace, in Hyde Park, 1851. In 1857, when Melville was in London, he jotted in his journal, under the dates 29 April-1 May, "Chrystal Palace—digest of universe. . . ." (*Journal up the Straits,* p. 172.)

43.10. *like a pin, one to make the head, and the other the point:* Adam Smith, *The Wealth of Nations:* "To take an example, therefore, from a very trifling manufacture; but one in which the division of labour has been very often taken notice of, the trade of the pin-maker. . . . One man draws out the wire, another straights it, a third cuts it, a fourth points it, a fifth grinds it at the top for receiving the head; to make the head requires two or three distinct operations; to put it on, is a peculiar business, to whiten the pins is another; it is even a trade by itself to put them into the paper. . . ." (11th ed., London, 1805, 3 vols., I, 3) Young Redburn read, or tried to read, *The Wealth of Nations* (*Redburn,* Ch. 18).

43.12. *"Protean easy chair"*: At the Great Exhibition of the Works of Industry of all Nations, held in London at the Crystal Palace in 1851, William Ragan, a manufacturer from Philadelphia, exhibited, and won honorable mention for, reclining chairs promising some of the comforts described by the man with the gray coat; these chairs "are intended for the use of invalids, and are so constructed that the degree of inclination is regulated with facility by the weight of the body," in the words of the *Official Descriptive and Illustrated Catalogue* (London, 1852), III, 1449. Mechanical reclining chairs or couches for invalids were also exhibited by two British manufacturers.

44.27. *Yes, I am no Fourier*: François Marie Charles Fourier (1772-1837), French socialist and inventor of a system of Utopian communism. His ideas were popularized in the United States after his death; Brook Farm was for a while organized according to Fourier's principles.

45.23. *the heathen not less than the Christian*: The *Berkshire County Eagle* for 7 Dec. 1855, in reporting the receipts of the American Bible Society, noted that some of them had been collected in the Sandwich Islands.

47.1. *Abraham reviling the angel*: Genesis 17:16, 17: "And I [God] will bless her [Sarah], and give thee a son also of her; yea, I will bless her, and she shall be a mother of nations; kings of people shall be of her.

"Then Abraham fell upon his face, and laughed, and said in his heart, Shall a child be born unto him that is an hundred years old? and shall Sarah, that is ninety years old, bear?"

47.11. *I have confidence to remove obstacles, though mountains*: I Corinthians 13:2: ". . . and though I have all faith, so that I could remove mountains, and have not charity, I am nothing."

47.18. *the millennial promise*: Revelation 20:1-6.

47.25. *gestures that were a Pentecost of added ones*: Acts 2:1-11. The Holy Spirit, descending upon the Apostles on the day of Pentecost, gave them the gift of tongues so that they spoke in other languages.

50.26. *I rejoice that I have confidence in you. . . .* : II Corinthians 7:16.

52.6. *the Black Rapids Coal Company*: The president and "transfer-agent" of this firm is, of course, the devil.

53.28. *spurious Jeremiahs; sham Heraclituses, . . . sham Laza-*

ruses: Jeremiah, the prophet of doom and judgment. Miss Wright finds that "among the four great prophets his name appears least often in Melville's pages—less than half a dozen times in all. Yet in itself this fact may signify little. . . . That he read Jeremiah is attested by the well-marked pages of this book in his Bible. . . . The details of Jeremiah's life, however, would seem to have had a peculiar appeal for him." (Wright, p. 84.) Miss Wright's admirable treatise also discusses the "apparent echoes" of Jeremiah's thought in Father Mapple's sermon in *Moby-Dick* and interesting similarities in style between some of Jeremiah's and some of Melville's passages. See another reference to Jeremiah on 154.32.

Heraclitus (c. 540-475 B.C.), Greek philosopher who taught the universality of change and was traditionally called "the weeping philosopher" because of his gloomy views. In his essay "Heraclitus" Fénelon says that he "entertained the greatest contempt for the actions of all men, and greatly deplored their blindness, so that it made him weep continually"; his "hatred of mankind made him at last resolve totally to abandon society"; he taught that "the gods exercise no providential care over" the universe. (François Salignac de la Motte Fénelon, *Lives of the Ancient Philosophers,* trans. Rev. John Cormack, New York, 1900, pp. 125ff.) In *Pierre* (p. 325) Melville says that the " 'Compensation,' or 'Optimist' school" cries: "Begone, Heraclitus! The lamentations of the rain are but to make us our rainbows!" Merton Sealts suggests as possible sources of Melville's knowledge of pre-Socratic philosophers, Fénelon's essay "Democritus and Heraclitus," in a school text used by Melville, *The English Reader* (NYPL-GL); some manual of philosophy; works of Bacon, Browne, R. Burton, P. Bayle; and the philosophers that Melville knew at first hand, such as Plato and Plutarch. ("Herman Melville's Reading in Ancient Philosophy," p. 168.)

"Lazarus" is used here, of course, in the generic sense of "diseased beggar."

54.6. *Good-Enough-Morgan:* William Morgan of Batavia, New York, disappeared mysteriously in 1826. A body found in the Niagara River was identified as Morgan's, but subsequently this identification was shown to be extremely doubtful. But, since Morgan's disappearance had been charged to the Masons, and much political capital had been made of the corpse, Thurlow Weed said that, whether it was Morgan's or not, it was "a good enough Morgan till after election." (*Dictionary of Americanisms,* ed. J. R. Bartlett.)

54.22. *musty old Seneca:* Melville owned, marked, and gave to his brother Thomas in 1854, *Seneca's Morals by Way of Abstract* (London, 1746); he also owned at some time Seneca's *Workes* . . . (London, 1614). (Sealts, Nos. 458, 457) Among the passages marked is one on the credulousness of the mob (p. 77) and this: "Our Fate is Decreed, and Things do not so much Happen, as in their due time proceed, and every Man's Portion of Joy, and Sorrow, is Predetermined" (p. 122). See William Braswell, "Melville's Use of Seneca," *American Literature,* XII (1940), 98-104. Melville refers to Seneca many times; "Seneca and the Stoics" was a phrase standing with him for calmness and brave endurance; also there are several references to events in Seneca's life, as, e.g., the one on p. 223 of *The Confidence-Man.* Seneca was the representative Stoic philosopher for Melville, according to Mr. Sealts ("Herman Melville's Reading in Ancient Philosophy," p. 159). Lucius Annaeus Seneca (c. 3 B.C.-65 A.D.), Roman Stoic Philosopher, dramatist, statesman.

55.30. *the maxim of Lord Bacon:* "My essays . . . come home, to men's business, and bosoms." From the dedication of the 1625 edition of *The Essays, Counsels, Civil and Morall* (first published 1597), of Francis Bacon, Baron Verulam and Viscount St. Albans (1561-1626), English philosopher and statesman. Mr. Sealts ("Herman Melville's Reading in Ancient Philosophy," p. 150, n. 87, and p. 151, n. 90) thinks that Melville's error, here and elsewhere, of calling him "Lord Bacon" may be a clue to the edition of Bacon used by Melville; that published in Philadelphia in 1844, in 3 vols., has as shelf-back title "The Works of Lord Bacon."

There are numerous references to Bacon in Melville's works; Bacon's philosophy is often disparaged as pragmatic and insufficiently open to the claims of imagination, intuition, and moral idealism; see, for example, *Pierre,* pp. 248, 232. The cited dissertation of Mr. Sealts contains an excellent brief analysis of Melville's attitude towards Bacon, his praise of Bacon on the ancients, and his possible debt to Bacon's *The Wisdom of the Ancients.* See also 154.6 and 223.36.

55.33. *New Jerusalem:* The following passage gives Melville opportunity for witty satirical reference to one of the flourishing swindles of the day in America, speculation in land-development projects and sale of non-existent sites. (See J. B. McMaster, "Paper

Towns," *History of the People of the United States.* . . , New York, 1883-1913, 8 vols., VII, 198-99.) Also Melville doubtless had in mind the New Jerusalem described in Revelation 21 and 22, the "holy city . . . coming down from heaven"; among the very few details describing the stock-salesman's city are its "perpetual fountain" and "lignum-vitae rostrums," which are strongly reminiscent of the New Jerusalem's "fountain of the water of life" (Revelation 21:6), the "pure river of water of life, clear as crystal, proceeding out of the throne of God and of the Lamb" (Revelation 22:1), and its "tree of life" on "either side of the river" (Revelation 22:2). Also, Melville may have had in mind, as Mr. Nichol conjectures ("Melville and the Midwest," p. 622), the founding of Nauvoo, Illinois, by Mormons driven out of Missouri in 1840.

56.9. *All standing*—bona fide: A *double-entendre* with a play on *bona fide*.

56.28. *Ariamius:* Probably a misspelling, or mistake of the copyist, for Arimanius, or Ahriman, the evil principle in Zoroastrianism. Pierre Bayle's *Dictionary,* an English translation of which Melville bought in 1849 (Sealts, No. 51), gives the spelling "Arimanius" among others. Between 1848 and 1851, Melville acquired considerable information about Persian religion, and remained interested in it to the end of his life. (Sealts, "Herman Melville's Reading in American Philosophy, pp. 139f.) For a brief discussion of Melville's interest in Zoroastrianism and Bayle's *Dictionary* as a likely source for some of his information on it, see F. O. Matthiessen, *American Renaissance,* New York, 1941, p. 439. Melville frequently refers to Zoroaster, Parsees, fire worship, and "Parthian magi." See also Millicent Bell's "Pierre Bayle and *Moby Dick,*" *PMLA,* LXVI (1951), 626-648, which demonstrates the influence of Zoroastrianism and Bayle's *Dictionary* upon Melville's persistent concern, particularly as it appears in *Moby-Dick,* with the questions whether the world is governed by evil as well as good, and, alternatively, whether it is governed at all.

57.12. *ODE ON THE INTIMATIONS OF DISTRUST IN MAN.* . . : Perhaps through the oblique allusion here to Wordsworth's "Ode: Intimations of Immortality from Recollections of Early Childhood," Melville is reminding the reader of the question of immortality and of the Confidence Man's message, "Trust God."

62.18. *the true book:* Mr. John Truman's authenticator is, I take it, the Bible. The investment that he offers, backed by its authority, is in heaven; but the investment that the faithful buy, with his connivance, is in hell. The satire is many-bladed.

64.5. *Nature . . . in Shakespeare's words, had meal and bran:* "Nature hath meal and bran, contempt and grace." *Cymbeline,* IV, ii, 27.

64.21. *African Zimmermann or Torquemada:* Johann Georg, Ritter von Zimmermann (1728-1795), Swiss philosophical writer, author of *Über die Einsamkeit,* was given to sentimentalism, enthusiasm, melancholy. See note for 154.4. Tomás de Torquemada (1420-1498), Spanish inquisitor general.

65.9. *the saying of Thrasea:* Publius Clodius (?) Paetus Thrasea (d. 66), Roman senator, Stoic, and leader of the republican opposition to Nero. Tacitus reports his speeches and death at some length; he says: "Nero after having butchered so many illustrious men, at last aspired to extirpate virtue itself by murdering Thrasea Paetus. . . ." (*Annals* xvi. 21, trans. Alfred J. Church and William J. Brodribb.) Though Thrasea had good reason for the remark Melville attributes to him, I do not find it among the ancient writers who mention him.

65.14. *Goneril:* Melville's copy of *King Lear* (Sealts, No. 460) is heavily marked, and annotated. (HCL-M) The name Goneril underlines the pessimism of Melville's story of "unmerited misery . . . brought about by unhindered arts of the wicked" and points to his symbolic intention by reminding the reader of that other tragedy. The following passage from Dr. Johnson's essay on *King Lear* (appended to the play in Melville's copy) is marked with a line in the margin: "A play in which the wicked prosper, and the virtuous miscarry, may doubtless be good, because it is a just representation of the common events of human life. . . ."

The idea that Melville's Goneril is a caricature of Fanny Kemble, as Egbert S. Oliver argues ("Melville's Goneril and Fanny Kemble," *New England Quarterly,* XVIII [1945], 489-500), seems to me untenable. Mr. Oliver rests his identification upon a slighting remark that Melville once made about Fanny Kemble and upon similarities between Fanny and her divorce from Pierce Butler and Goneril and her story. The identification must rest more on Melville's remark than on the similarities, because the differences are much greater than the similarities, and because it would be hard to describe any woman without turning out a few resemblances to the many-sided and variously understood Fanny Kemble, or any legal action involving the custody of a child without touching her story at some points. But Melville made this remark casually in a letter to Duyckinck six or seven years before he wrote *The Confidence-Man:* "Mrs. Butler too I have heard at her Readings. She makes a glorious Lady Macbeth but her Desdemona seems like a boarding school miss.—She's so unfemininely masculine that had she not, on unimpeachable authority, borne children, I should be curious to learn the result of a surgical examination of her person in private. The Lord help Butler . . . I marvel not he seeks being amputated off from his maternal half." (Letter of 24 February [1849]; see Thorp, p. 371.) In the years between this offhand, jocose remark, to a friend, and his composition of the Goneril chapter, Melville had been through the "hellfire" of *Moby-Dick*, the heart-searching of *Pierre*, the widening compassion of the short stories and *Israel Potter*, and distress and vicissitude in his own life, and there is no indication in all this time that his early impression of Fanny Kemble rankled in his mind, or that he thought of it at all. Evert Duyckinck, writing letters while visiting Melville in Pittsfield in 1850 and 1851, mentions Fanny Kemble, who lived not far from Pittsfield then, several times, always in either a neutral or an admiring tone. (See Luther S. Mansfield, "Glimpses of Herman Melville's Life in Pittsfield, 1850-51. . . ," *American Literature*, IX [1937], 25-48.) It is hard to believe that the light remark of the witty young literary lion, the Melville of 1849, had any kinship with the thoughts of the sober, chastened Melville of 1856.

But it is, to me at any rate, quite unthinkable that he should be guilty of savage, malicious personal satire (Mr. Oliver grants it is that), particularly in a book made out of his grief at the failure of Christian charity and his plea that all of us cripples at least "refrain from picking a fellow-limper to pieces." (The satire of Emerson, later on, is satire of a philosophy, and makes no cruel reference to personal shortcomings or personal tragedy.)

Even if he intended no one to guess the person caricatured, he could not himself have been thinking of Fanny Kemble, whose fault in his eyes six or seven years before had been only that she was so unfeminine in appearance (and perhaps so good in the role of Lady Macbeth) as to justify Butler's wish for divorce, when he wrote the terrible words in the first paragraph of the Goneril chapter about vice too evil for any good man to call it human, and so himself called the "unpledged tabernacle" which contained it "Goneril."

Melville knew the difference between unfeminine deportment and wickedness.

Goneril is, as Mr. Oliver finds, like Fanny Kemble (plus Melville's old impression of Fanny) in her straight figure, her lack of femininity, her health, her independence; the Unfortunate Man is like Pierce Butler in his jealousy, in withdrawing their child from her mother, in abandoning the mother, in doing nothing further about the matter for a while, in losing money and reputation. But the differences in appearance between Fanny and Goneril are at least as great as the one real similarity, her straight figure, and other differences are much greater. Goneril is a creature of cold, unlimited malignity, sensual but without love, a re-embodiment of that "gilded serpent" in *King Lear* (Melville underlined the phrase in his copy); Fanny Kemble was impulsive, loving, generous (she entered a profession she disliked in order to save her family's fortunes, she gave her large American earnings to her father when she married, she risked domestic unhappiness to speak out for Butler's slaves); the most biased view of Fanny could not mistake her fire for ice. Goneril's "touching" people embarrasses them; Fanny's charm delighted the thousands who came under it, and, unlike Goneril's curious attentions, it was shed no more upon the young men than upon old men, women, and children. Goneril hates frankness and innocence and torments her child; Fanny was unflinchingly honest, adored her two children and was loved by them, submitted to tyranny from Butler in order to be near them, suffered when banished by his ukase, and was at the peak of happiness in 1856, when *The Confidence-Man* was being written, because her elder daughter then reached her majority and could join her mother if she chose, as she did. Melville must have known all about this joyous conclusion of Fanny's long separation from her daughter, because Fanny's cottage was not far from Pittsfield, and her closest friends in Berkshire, the Sedgwicks, were acquaintances of Melville. The Unfortunate Man goes into "domestic exile," but it was Fanny, not her husband, who was forced into "domestic exile": Butler built separate quarters for her on Butler Farm and banished her from her children. The legal actions and subsequent events in the two stories are quite different; Goneril brings suit against her husband, he pleads her mental derangement, she tries to have him committed as a lunatic, he flees an outcast, she dies; but it was Butler who brought suit against Fanny; his complaint was her "wilful and malicious desertion, without reasonable cause, of her husband and his habitation, persisted in for two years"; Fanny's lawyer argued that she had been banished; Fanny, not the husband, left the country; both were alive in 1856.

It is the lying Confidence Man, not the good country merchant or Melville, who tries to explain away this story of "unmerited misery . . . brought about by unhindered arts of the wicked."

Melville's story of Goneril, I take it, was invented as a symbol to connote, even more than to dramatize, the kind of anomalous viciousness that one finds in *King Lear*, that Thrasea found in Nero's Rome, an evil simply unexplainable, an enigma to decent human beings. Therefore he makes it epicene and also half human, half extra-human, an eater of clay in preference to human food, for only a part of the day thawed "into but talking terms with humanity"; he gives it the hideous connotations of "Goneril"; he gives it an "Indian figure" because of the connotations of "Indian" in this book.

Possibly a relative's story gave Melville a hint of the human misery that can be caused when a woman turns against husband and children: Melville's aunt Mary A. A. Melville wrote from Galena, Illinois, 1 April 1856: "My son John's wife became deranged after her last confinement, more than two months ago, and was taken to the Asylum. I brought the three children home; last week she was pronounced cured and came to see her children with the expectation to remain here some time, but I fear that she was sent home too soon, perhaps meeting with her husband and family (for whom, she manifested all the dislike and suspicion common I believe to all deranged persons, may have caused a partial relapse, but I cannot but hope that it may wear off after a time.—She is at board now, and Robert the only one of the family that she is friendly with, can keep watch over her. John remains in Chicago." (Letter to Lemuel Shaw. MHS. Mr. Jay Leyda kindly brought this letter to my notice.)

65.19. *Her Indian figure:* Melville's allusions to Indians in touches which help establish the non-, sub-, or extra-human nature of Goneril are illuminating in view of the symbol which he makes of the Indian later in the book. In the Indian-hater chapters, the Indian embodies allegorically a primitive, or primal, malign, treacherous force in the universe that lures man into a false confidence and then betrays him, that by appealing to his highest human impulses, destroys his humanity.

70.5. *a grave American savan:* Melville perhaps heard this anecdote through a friend, or from the American savant himself; he came into direct or indirect contact with a number of great men of his time through his father-in-law, Chief Justice Lemuel Shaw of Massachusetts, and among his literary friends in New York and Boston, and also through his relatives in Albany. In the works of American "savants" who were in London during the years when the incident might have happened, I have found no anectdote about Sir Humphry that comes any closer to Melville's than this, told by John Quincy Adams, who met Sir Humphry at an evening party at Lord Carysfort's (on 8 June 1815), here described: "After dinner, there was a numerous party of both sexes who came, but there were no cards. Sir Humphry Davy, who has very lately returned from Italy, talked much upon his travel there, much upon agriculture and farming, much upon the art of sculpture, and the Laocoön, and the Venus, and much upon his own chemical discoveries. If modesty is an inseparable companion of genius, Sir Humphry is a prodigy." (*Memoirs of J. Q. Adams, 1795-1848*, Phila., 1874-1876, 12 vols., III, 217.) J. Q. Adams' sedate and scholarly manner, his unusual intellectual powers, his ardent interest in science, which was instrumental in the establishment of the Smithsonian Institution by Congressional Act,—these qualities, at any rate, would suit Melville's portrait of the grave American savant. Melville also mentions Sir Humphry Davy in *Mardi* (Ch. 19).

73.9. *Malakoff:* In the Crimean War, a fort important among the defenses of Sebastopol. Melville's remark that it is better to stick behind the secure Malakoff than to be tempted forth to hazardous skirmishes on the open ground, possibly indicates that this part of the novel was composed before September or October 1855. The Russians, trying to lift the siege of Sebastopol, had attacked the British and their allies at Inkerman, about four miles southeast of Sebastopol, on 5 November 1854, and had lost heavily without dislodging the enemy. Again on 16 August 1855, with the same purpose the Russians attacked French and Sardinian troops at the Chernaya River, and again drew off with heavy losses. The security of Malakoff was ended, however, on 8 September 1855, when the French took Malakoff by storm. The *Berkshire County Eagle* carried news of the siege of "impregnable Malakoff" throughout the summer of 1855, and did not announce its fall until 5 October 1855.

74.24. *In vino veritas:* There is truth in wine. "Proverbial from Pliny," according to the *Oxford Dictionary of Quotations*, which quotes from Pliny's *Historia Naturalis,* xiv. 141: "Vulgoque veritas iam attributa vino est."

76.1. *CHAPTER XIV:* Some very interesting early drafts of this chapter will be found in the Appendix, showing the labor that went to produce the even quietness, elegance, tautness, and ease that distinguish the style of *The Confidence-Man.*

This chapter has frequently been noticed by recent critics, who remark Melville as a forerunner of fruitful modern ideas about the novelist's art. Willard Thorp, in his admirable condensed discussion of Melville's life and works, points out that Melville's "conception of what constituted reality in fiction was utterly at variance with the dominant attitude of the mid-century, which had yet to be given the name realism, though it had manifested itself abundantly in art and literature and was already accepted as a fixed critical canon." In speaking of the strikingly modern quality of "Melville's heterodoxy on the subject of character portrayal," Mr. Thorp quotes remarks of D. H. Lawrence and Aldous Huxley which parallel Melville's objections to representing human nature in "transparency." (Thorp. pp. xliv-xlv and n. 59.)

Another example of the same doctrine in contemporary literature appears in André Gide's *Les Faux-Monnayeurs,* in Edouard's journal: "Inconséquence des caractères. Les personnages qui, d'un bout à l'autre du roman ou du drame, agissent exactement comme on aurait pu le prévoir. . . . On propose à notre admiration cette constance, à quoi je reconnais au contraire qu'ils sont artificiels et construits." (André Gide, *Les Faux-Monnayeurs,* Paris, 1937, p. 427.)

Melville had adumbrated the central idea of Chapter XIV in *Pierre,* particularly in the following passage from Book VII (pp. 165f.): "Like all youths, Pierre had conned his novel-lessons; had read more novels than most persons of his years; but their false, inverted attempts at systematizing eternally unsystemizable [*sic*] elements; their audacious, intermeddling impotency, in trying to unravel, and spread out, and classify, the more thin than gossamer threads which make up the complex web of life; these things over Pierre had no power now. Straight through their helpless miserableness he pierced. . . . By infallible presentiment he saw, that not always doth life's beginning gloom conclude in gladness; that wedding-bells peal not ever in the last scene of life's fifth act; that while the countless tribes of common novels laboriously spin veils of mystery, only to complacently clear them up at last; and while the countless tribe of common dramas do but repeat the same; yet the profounder emanations of the human mind, intended to illustrate all that can be humanly known of human life; these never unravel their own intricacies, and have no proper endings; but in imperfect, unanticipated, and disappointing sequels (as mutilated stumps), hurry to abrupt interminglings with the eternal tides of time and fate."

76.26. *expect to run and read:* "Write the vision, and make it plain upon tables, that he may run that readeth it." Habakkuk 2:2.

77.6. *the caterpillar into which it changes:* The biological error here is attributable to the difficulty that Melville's copyist had in trying to read a much revised passage; near the beginning of his labors on this sentence, Melville wrote: "as the catterpillar [*sic*] is to the butterfly it becomes." See Appendix, p. 386, for the revisions which caused the trouble.

77.14. *the duck-billed beaver of Australia:* the Platypus, *Ornithorhyncus Anatinus* (formerly *Paradoxus*). Robert Knox, a celebrated Edinburgh anatomist, wrote in 1823: "It is well known that specimens of this very extraordinary animal when first brought to Europe were considered by many to be impositions. They reached England by vessels which had navigated the Indian seas, a circumstance arousing the suspicions of scientists, aware of the monstrous impostures which the artful Chinese then practiced on European adventurers—these oriental taxidermists were quite notorious for their skill in constructing non-existent animals for sale to credulous seamen, such as the so-called 'eastern mermaid,' to be seen occasionally in curiosity shops to this day, consisting of the forepart of a monkey skilfully stitched to the tail of a fish." (Quoted in E. Troughton, *Furred Animals of Australia*, Sydney, 1943, p. 4.) Sir Richard Owen contributed a number of papers on the platypus to the *Transactions of the Zoological Society of London*.

78.9. *fearfully and wonderfully made:* "I will praise thee; for I am fearfully and wonderfully made. . . ." Psalms 139:14.

81.27. *Orpheus in his gay descent to Tartarus:* "But he, solacing love's anguish with his hollow shell, sang of thee, sweet wife—of thee, to himself on the lonely shore, of thee as day grew nigh, of thee as day declined. Even the jaws of Taenarus, the lofty portals of Dis, he entered, and the grove that is murky with black terror, and came to the dead, and the king of terrors, and the hearts that know not how to soften at human prayers. . . . Nay, the very halls of Hell were spell-bound, and inmost Tartarus, and the Furies with livid snakes entwined in their locks." (Virgil, *Georgics* iv. 464ff.; translation of H. R. Fairclough.) The story of Orpheus' descent to Hades to win back Euridice with his music is also told by Ovid in his *Metamorphoses*, Book X, and mentioned in his *Ars Amatoria*, Book III. See note on 29.18.

81.32. *Dives:* Luke 16:19-31 tells the story of the beggar Lazarus and a rich man who cried out in hell for Lazarus to come from heaven and cool his tongue with a drop of water. The rich man's epithet *"dives"* in the Vulgate Bible became almost universally current as his name. The story of Lazarus and Dives is one to which Melville frequently alludes, as Miss Wright points out (p. 23). See also a reference on 8.23.

82.24. *Cant, gammon!:* The miser is using cant, the secret language of thieves, professional beggars, etc. "Gammon" is "Thieves' slang. In phrases *To give gammon, To keep in gammon:* to engage (a person's) attention while a confederate is robbing him." Also: "Ridiculous nonsense suited to deceive simple persons only." (NED) "Bubble" means "To delude. . . ; to befoul, cheat, humbug." (NED) "Fetch" and "gouge" mean "to cheat." Richard Foster ("Melville and Roguery," p. 133) points out that misers and barbers are traditionally satirized and ridiculed in picaresque fiction, and also that the miser here is speaking rogues' cant.

84.28. *I confide:* Cf. Mark 9:24: "And straightway the father of the child cried out, and said with tears, Lord, I believe; help thou mine unbelief."

86.4 *The sky slides into blue:* The opening paragraph, poetic and glittering, is an appropriate prelude to the herb-doctor's eulogy of nature and hope. Melville's satire is social as well as philosophical in his sketch of that picturesque and ubiquitous national charlatan, the itinerant vendor of cure-alls. An amusing parallel to Melville's herb-doctor, calling upon eighteenth-century philosophy to justify "natural" medicine, turns up in the person of one Dr. Brandreth, who in 1834 began advertising his "purely vegetable" pills in these terms: "The laws of life are written upon the face of Nature. The Tempest, Whirlwind, and Thunderstorm bring health from the Solitudes of God. The Tides are the daily agitators and purifiers of the Mighty World of Waters.

"What the Providential means are as purifiers of the Atmosphere or Air, Brandreth's Pills are to man." (Quoted in P. T. Barnum, *The*

Humbugs of the World, New York, 1865, p. 68.) These "natural" pills were known to Melville, who suggests that a whale's dyspepsia might be cured by "three or four boatloads of Brandreth's pills." (*Moby-Dick,* Ch. 92.)

See Introduction, pp. lix-lxi, on the herb-doctor.

86.30. *good Samaritans:* Luke 10:30-37. A good Samaritan took care of a man who had been left for dead by thieves and whom others had avoided helping. There is another reference on 230.32.

87.26. *Calvin Edson:* This "living skeleton" appeared at various museums in New York through the 1830's and 1840's. On 1 February 1847 he joined the other curiosities at Barnum's American Museum; he was "forty-two years old, weighs but 49 lbs., 5 feet, 6 inches high," and had been so advertised, more or less, since 1830. (George C. D. Odell, *Annals of the New York Stage,* New York, 1927-1949, 15 vols.; V, 306; III, 476, 528, 592, 593.)

88.19. *Pharaoh's . . . sorcerers . . . Egyptians:* Exodus 7:11-12, 22.

88.33. *Solomon the Wise, who knew all vegetables:* Solomon's wisdom, which "excelled the wisdom of all the children of the east country, and all the wisdom of Egypt," included botanical knowledge: "And he spake of trees, from the cedar tree that is in Lebanon even unto the hyssop that springeth out of the wall." I Kings 4:30, 33. See also 229.26 and 248.12.

89.1 *Medea gathered the enchanted herbs: The Merchant of Venice,* V, i, 13f.

89.22 *Preisnitz:* Vincenz Preissnitz (1799-1851), a Silesian, author of a book on hydrotherapy and operator of a hydrotherapeutic establishment.

89.28. *get strength by confidence:* Cf. Isaiah 30:15: "For thus saith the Lord God, the Holy One of Israel; In returning and rest shall ye be saved: in quietness and in confidence shall be your strength."

91.1. *Hope is proportioned to confidence:* When blind men came to him to be cured, Jesus said to them: "Believe ye that I am able to do this? They said unto him, Yea, Lord. Then he touched their eyes, saying, According to your faith be it unto you." Matthew 9:28, 29.

93.34. *Prove all the vials:* I Thessalonians 5:21: "Prove all things; hold fast that which is good." This verse was a sort of motto of the New England Transcendentalists.

94.1. *From evil comes good:* Cf. the conclusion of Emerson's essay "Compensation": "And yet the compensations of calamity are made apparent to the understanding also, after long intervals of time. A fever, a mutilation, a cruel disappointment, a loss of wealth, a loss of friends seems at the moment unpaid loss, and unpayable. But the sure years reveal the deep remedial force that underlies all facts. The death of a dear friend, wife, brother, lover, which seemed nothing but privation, somewhat later assumes the aspect of a guide or genius. . . ."

94.6. *Japus in Virgil:* Melville's quotation is John Dryden's translation of Virgil's *Aeneid* iii.427-429. Dryden has "hands divine" instead of Melville's "power divine." Melville's "Japus" is "Iapis" in Dryden, "Iapyx" in Virgil. (See note 29.18.)

96.27. *haunted Cock Lane in London:* Mysterious noises heard at No. 33 Cock Lane, Smithfield, had been attributed to a ghost, had caused much excitement, and had been exposed as a hoax in 1762. Melville visited Cock Lane on Saturday, 10 November 1849, and recorded that he went "down Holborn Hill through Cock Lane (Dr. Johnson's Ghost) to Smithfield (West)." (*Journal . . . 1849-1850*, pp. 25f.) Melville bought in London in 1849 Boswell's *Johnson* ("10 vol. 18mo"; Sealts, No. 84) and evidently read it or parts of it. Yet he says, in *Moby-Dick* (p. 308): "Are you a believer in ghosts, my friends? There are other ghosts than the Cock-Lane one, and far deeper men than Doctor Johnson who believe in them." Boswell had taken pains to show that Doctor Johnson had been "ignorantly misrepresented as weakly credulous" upon the subject of ghosts in general and the Cock Lane ghost in particular; Churchill, Boswell said, in his poem "The Ghost" had "availed himself of the absurd credulity imputed to Johnson" and represented Johnson as a believer in the Cock Lane hoax; Boswell points out that Johnson "was one of those by whom the imposture was detected." (James Boswell, *The Life of Samuel Johnson,* under the year 1763.) In Cairo in 1857 some lonely, uninhabited houses made Melville think of "Haunted houses & Cock Lanes." (*Journal up the Straits,* p. 54.)

97.12. *Hey diddle, diddle:* Also in Edgar Allan Poe's essay "Diddling Considered as One of the Exact Sciences" this rhyme is attracted from the orbit of the nursery to that of the petty swindler.

98.7.*Adam to the thunder:* This particular image does not appear in either the Biblical or the Miltonic story, and may of course derive from Melville's dramatic imagination, if not from some pictorial representation or other literary source. A remote possibility is that Melville was thinking of Adam's words in *Paradise Lost* when, after his transgression, he longs for death, for then God's "dreadful voice no more Would thunder in my ears." (Bk. X, 11. 779f.)

101.8. *the Paris Bourse:* Melville recorded in his *Journal . . . 1849-1850* under 29 November: "Visited the Bourse—great hum round a mystic circle . . .," and mentioned visits on each of the two following days (pp. 53-55).

101.8. *Asmodeus:* a demon in *Le Diable Boiteux* by Alain René Le Sage (1668-1747), who lifts the roofs off houses to show his benefactor what is passing within. Various stage productions featuring Asmodeus and to a greater or less degree derived from Le Sage's novel played in New York in the 1840's and 1850's.

101.11. *as Hamlet says:* Horatio says: " 'Twere to consider too curiously, to consider so," in *Hamlet*, V, i, 227.

105.3. *Molino del Rey? Resaca de la Palma?:* Resaca de la Palma, an opening battle of the Mexican War, was fought on 9 May 1846, and won by Gen. Zachary Taylor before war was declared by Congress. Molino del Rey was taken 8 September 1847, in an assault led by Gen. William J. Worth. Melville published a series of good-natured, comic articles on "Old Zack" in *Yankee Doodle* in the summer of 1847. (See Luther S. Mansfield, "Melville's Comic Articles on Zachary Taylor," *American Literature*, IX [1938], 411-418.)

105.4. *Tombs!:* The Halls of Justice on Centre Street in New York City. In Melville's day the Tombs was "a large, heavy granite building constructed in the style of an Egyptian temple" which has since been replaced. It was described, in 1868, as sanitary but dark and overcrowded to a "fearful extent." (Edward W. Martin, *The Secrets of the Great City: A Work Descriptive of the Virtues and the Vices, the Mysteries, Miseries and Crimes of New York City*, Phila., 1868, pp. 98-101.)

105.29. *the other Lazarus:* who was raised from the dead; John 12. For the Lazarus who had sores, see note 81.32.

106.20. *the noble cripple, Epictetus:* Epictetus of Hieropolis (c. 60-140), eminent Stoic philosopher, born a slave and lame from early youth, gave as a formula for the good life, "Endure and renounce." His doctrines are known through the *Discourses* and *Manual* of his pupil, Arrian. Mr. Merton Sealts, Jr., thinks that Melville may have known Epictetus at first hand, and cites the mention of Arrian in *The Confidence-Man* (p. 218) and the last part of Babbalanja's soliloquy in *Mardi*, Ch. 78. Mr. Sealts finds Melville's thought closer to the *Discourses* of Epictetus than to the *Manual*. (Sealts, "Herman Melville's Reading in Ancient Philosophy," p. 162.)

107.6. *Mrs. Fry:* Elizabeth Gurney Fry (1780-1845), English philanthropist and Quaker, effected reforms in prisons in Great Britain and on the Continent. Her *Observations on . . . Female Prisoners* appeared in 1827, her *Memoirs* in 1847.

110.15 *Buena Vista . . . General Scott . . . Contreras:* At Buena Vista General Taylor fought a long and desperate battle in February 1847, and won a decisive victory over the Mexicans, against great odds. Contreras was the scene of a battle near Mexico City, on 19-20 August 1847, in the course of Gen. Winfield Scott's victorious march from Vera Cruz to Mexico City. Melville's cousin, Lieutenant Guert Gansevoort, commanding the *John Adams,* had been "one of the first to plant the American standard on the beach" at Vera Cruz; this is mentioned in Melville's poem "Bridegroom Dick." (*Log*, p. 238).

112.11 *those who are loved are chastened:* "For whom the Lord loveth he chasteneth. . . ." Hebrews 12:16. "As many as I love, I rebuke and chasten. . . ." Revelation 3:19.

117.28 *Mammoth Cave:* Consumptives lived in this great cave in Kentucky in the hope that its uniform temperature of 54° F. would be beneficial. Melville calls the sperm whale's stomach "the great Kentucky Mammoth Cave" in *Moby-Dick* (p. 330); the interior of the pyramids reminded him of the Cave (*Journal up the Straits,* p. 58). Mr. Nichol thinks he may have visited the Mammoth Cave in 1840 ("Melville and the Midwest," p. 624).

120.7. *ursine in aspect:* Melville used the bear several times for symbolic connotations. Priming, in *White-Jacket* (Ch. 44) was a "churlish, ill-tempered, unphilosophical, superstitious old bear of a quarter-gunner" who maintained a point of view opposite to the optimistic and sentimental. Ahab, because he shut himself off from companionship, was like the grizzly bear that, "burying himself in the hollow of a tree, lived out the winter there, sucking his own paws." (*Moby-Dick,* p. 150)

121.10. *Peter the Wild Boy:* A naked boy, about twelve years old, dumb and uncivilized, was found in a field near Hamelin in July 1724, brought to the town, and called Peter; a year later King

George I of England had him sent to Hanover and later still to London. "Just at this time the controversy about the existence of innate ideas was at its height; and PETER seemed the very subject for determining the question." The investigation of his "innate ideas" was entrusted to Dr. John Arbuthnot, who soon found that he was an idiot and that "no brilliant discoveries in psychology or anthropology could be expected" from his case. It was found that he had been lost in the woods for a time in 1723 and had been driven there again by his stepmother. He lived till 1785. The case of Peter the Wild Boy was famous. "SWIFT has immortalised him in his humorous production, *It cannot rain, but it pours; or London Strewed with Rarities.* LINNEUS gave him a niche in the *Systema Naturae* . . . : BUFFON, DE PAAUW, and J. J. ROUSSEAU, have extolled him as the true child of nature, the genuine unsophisticated man. MONBODDO is still more enthusiastic. . . ." (M. Lawrence, *Lectures on Physiology, Zoology, and the Natural History of Man, Delivered at the Royal College of Surgeons*, Salem, 1828, pp. 120-123.)

122.13. *I have confidence in nature?:* Melville commented frequently on the cruelty of nature, e.g.: "beholding the tranquil beauty and brilliancy of the ocean's skin, one forgets the tiger heart that pants beneath it." (*Moby-Dick*, pp. 485f.); "Flies on the eyes at noon. Nature feeding on man." (*Journal up the Straits*, p. 54); "A burning mountain—enumerate the monstrousness of the remorselessness of Nature—ravages of war &c—burned city." (*Ibid.*, p. 125).

122.20. *that soil will come back after many days:* Cf. Ecclesiastes 11:1: "Cast thy bread upon the waters: for thou shalt find it after many days." Cf. also Emerson in his essay "Compensation": "The nature and soul of things takes on itself the guaranty of the fulfillment of every contract, so that honest service cannot come to loss. If you serve an ungrateful master, serve him the more. Put God in your debt. Every stroke shall be repaid. The longer the payment is withholden, the better for you; for compound interest on compound interest is the rate and usage of this exchequer."

125.33. *the dungeoned Italian we read of:* Perhaps the Abbé Faria in *The Count of Monte Cristo*, by Alexandre Dumas, which had been translated into English in 1846. The Abbé Faria had been filled with thoughts of vengeance during his long imprisonment in a dungeon of the Chateau d'If, but the disinterested love of Edmond Dantès restored him to the feeling of charity towards his fellow men which had marked his early life. Melville read *The Queen's Neck-*

lace, by Dumas, while waiting for a steamer in Jaffa in 1857, and commented: "Excellent, Cagliostro's talk in opening chapter." (*Journal up the Straits,* p. 71.)

127.25. *If by abolitionist you mean a zealot:* The herb-doctor's stand is neither that of the abolitionists nor that of Melville. The herb-doctor's willingness to abolish the suffering of slavery by methods " 'opposed to nobody's interest, and therefore rousing nobody's enmity' " is either vapid sentimentalism or what Pitch calls it, " 'picked and prudent sentiments.' " In *Mardi* (Ch. 162) Melville had shown not only the distress he felt over slavery in the South but also a much greater understanding of the complexities of the situation than the abolitionists showed. " 'Humanity cries out against this vast enormity:—not one man knows a prudent remedy,' " says the philosopher of *Mardi.* " 'Time—all-healing Time . . . must befriend these thralls.' "

128.16. *Cape Giradeau:* Cape Girardeau, Mo., 142½ miles down river from St. Louis. (Samuel Cummings, *The Western Pilot,* Cincinnati, 1848)

129.2. *TUSCULAN DISPUTATIONS:* A philosophical treatise in the form partly of a dialogue, in which Marcus Tullius Cicero (106 B.C.-43 B.C.) discusses the conditions of happiness, from the point of view of a Stoic, and concludes that the wise and virtuous man can be happy even in the face of death and of physical and mental suffering. "In the Polite Spirit" is of course ironical. Cicero's language in the *Disputations* is that of friendly discussion, sometimes bantering, sometimes earnest, sometimes eloquent, but never petulant and badgering, or fawning and insistent, as in the "philosophical" disputation between the man from the Philosophical Intelligence Office and Pitch. Melville may intend some contrast between stoic and cynic in his dialogue.

129.3. *PHILOSOPHICAL INTELLIGENCE OFFICE:* "Intelligence Office" was a common term for an employment bureau for domestic help, and the magazines were full of jokes and cartoons about servants employed through intelligence offices. But Melville's title was probably suggested by Hawthorne's story, "The Intelligence Office," which Melville mentioned in his "Hawthorne and His Mosses"; it is one of many links of *The Confidence-Man* with Hawthorne's stories.

129.9. *baker-kneed man:* "Baker's knee, as it is called, or an inclining inwards of the right knee-joint until it closely resembles the right side of a letter K, is the almost certain penalty of habitually bearing any burden of bulk in the right hand." (Quoted in NED.)

131.25. *patient continuance in well-doing:* Romans 2:7: "To them who by patient continuance in well doing seek for glory and honour and immortality, eternal life. . . ."

131.33. *"You Praise-God-Barebones":* Praise-God Barebone or Barbon (c. 1596-1679), a London leather merchant and religious fanatic, was member of Cromwell's little group of "godly men" which formed the Little Parliament of July-December 1653. Enemies called it Barebone's Parliament.

132.13. *what Horace and others of the ancients say of servants:* Quintus Horatius Flaccus, Latin poet, 65-8 B.C. There are numerous passages in Horace's *Satires, Epodes,* and *Epistles* on "saucy slaves," "rascal slaves," and such small faults of slaves as stumbling and breaking a dish at a banquet (*Satires* II. viii. 72), stealing pasties and flesh-brushes (*Satires* II. vii. 102, 109-110), licking up the half-eaten fish and its sauce in a dish that is being removed from the table (*Satires* I. iii. 80ff.) Also Horace speaks several times of runaway slaves, and even of slaves who rob; e.g., discoursing on the disadvantages of wealth, Horace says: "What, to lie awake half-dead with fear, to be in terror night and day of wicked thieves, of fire, of slaves, who may rob you and run away—is this so pleasant?" (*Satires* I. i) Most interesting, in view of the sales talk of the P.I.O. man, is the speech that Horace puts in the mouth of someone who wants to sell you a slave: "Here's a handsome boy, comely from top to toe; . . . home-bred he is, apt for service at his owner's beck, knows a bit of Greek learning, and can master any art; the clay is soft—you will mould it to what you will. . . . Once he played truant, as boys will do, under the stairs, fearing the hanging strap. . . ." (*Epistles* II. ii. 3-16; this translation and that from *Satires* I. i is by H. Rushton Fairclough.) Marcus Porcius Cato (the Elder, 234-149 B.C.), writing about the duties of the overseer, says: "He must settle disputes among the slaves; and if anyone commits an offence he must punish him properly in proportion to the fault. . . . Let him keep them busy with their work—he will more easily keep them from wrong-doing and meddling. . . . He must keep the servants busy." (*On Agriculture* v, trans. Harrison Boyd Ash.) See note on 29.18.

133.24. *a perfect Chesterfield:* Philip Dormer Stanhope, fourth Earl of Chesterfield (1694-1773), famous as a gentleman of the world and a man of fashion; his *Letters . . . to His Son* give instruction in manners and worldly wisdom. Here Melville uses his name as a synonym for polished manners, later (193.3) for worldliness. In the library of Melville's father was Chesterfield's *Principles of Politeness, and of Knowing the World* . . . (Portsmouth, N. H., 1786; Sealts, No. 142). Melville refers to Chesterfield a number of times, chiefly as the polished gentleman. His first "Fragment from a Writing Desk," dated 4 May 1839, borrows more than a phrase from Lord Chesterfield; the young hero seems modeled on Lord Chesterfield's specifications for polite young men of the world. (William H. Gilman, *Melville's Early Life and Redburn*, New York, 1951, pp. 109-11, 113, 115)

135.2. *the child is father of the man:* From William Wordsworth's "My Heart Leaps Up."

136.1. *a wet sheet and a flowing sea!:* From Allan Cunningham's poem of that name in his *The Songs of Scotland, Ancient and Modern* (1825):

> A wet sheet and a flowing sea,
> A wind that follows fast
> And fills the white and rustling sails
> And bends the gallant mast.

141.36. *the founder of La Trappe:* Probably Melville means Abbot de Rancé (1626-1700), who reformed the Cistercian abbey of La Trappe, in the department of Orne, France, established its rules of extreme austerity, and has been called the founder of the Trappists. *La Grande Encyclopédie* says that "Sa vie fut, pendant longtemps, très dissipée," and that, according to legend, the cause of his conversion (about 1657) was calling upon his mistress and finding her dead. The man who actually founded the abbey, in 1140, was Rotrou, an obscure count of Perche.

141.37. *Ignatius Loyola:* Loyola (1491-1556), a Spaniard of noble birth, was brought up a courtier and for several years followed a military career. In 1521, when convalescent from a serious wound, he was converted to a desire for the religious life. He founded the Society of Jesus, led in the movement for Catholic reform, and is known as one of the principal Christian mystics. He was canonized in 1622.

142.15. *The best wisdom in this world:* John 13 through 17; also accounts of the Last Supper in Matthew 26:20-29, Mark 14:17-25, Luke 22:14-38.

142.34. *"St. Augustine on Original Sin":* Saint Augustine (354-

430) in his *The City of God* (Books XIII and XIV) treats of the fall of man, the corruption of human nature through Adam's sin, and the nature of that sin. His great argument for the doctrine of original sin, however, is in his Pelagian treatises. Mr. Sealts ("Herman Melville's Reading in Ancient Philosophy," p. 174) thinks it probable that Melville knew the works of Augustine at first hand.

143.11. *St. Augustine confesses that until his thirtieth year:* In his *Confessions,* written after his conversion to Christianity in 387, Saint Augustine tells of the passion and sensuality of his youth. In a dispute with Alypius he said he could not give up his habitual pleasures for celibacy. It was because he had found his own nature weak and sinful and incapable of throwing off the trammels of sensuality without divine help that Augustine was able to develop with such deep feeling the doctrine or original sin.

144.19. *your marines to whom you may say anthing:* The *Oxford Dictionary of English Proverbs* mentions appearances of this saying both earlier and later than Scott's version, in *Redgauntlet* (1824): "Tell that to the marines—the sailors won't believe it."

147.5. *AT Cairo:* Mr. Nichol says that this description of Cairo as unhealthful is correct, since at that time the city was not protected by dikes against inundation by the Ohio River, which here joins the Mississippi. ("Melville and the Midwest," p. 623)

147.7. *his hand . . . has not lost its cunning:* Psalms 137.5: "If I forget thee, O Jerusalem, let my right hand forget her cunning."

147.9. *Calvin Edson:* See note 87.26.

147.17. *Apemantus' dog:* Apemantus is a churlish cynic in Shakespeare's *Timon of Athens;* he is also mentioned in Plutarch's life of Antony as the only companion of the misanthropic Timon.

148.4. *Philosophy, knowledge, experience:* Mr. Pommer (*Milton and Melville,* p. 64) argues convincingly that the two sentences beginning thus are indebted to the following lines from *Paradise Lost* (III, 686-689):

> And oft, though Wisdom wake, Suspicion sleeps
> At Wisdom's gate, and to Simplicity
> Resigns her charge, while Goodness thinks no ill
> Where no ill seems.

These lines occur in the scene in which Satan, disguising himself as a "stripling cherub," deceives Uriel, the "sharpest-sighted Spirit of all in Heaven," and is told how to reach the earth and Eden. "For neither man nor angel can discern Hypocrisy," says Milton (11.

682f.) The parallel between the sharp-sighted Pitch and Uriel increases the probability that Melville was thinking of this scene.

148.31. *beast that windeth his way on his belly:* Another of the many allusions in this novel to the Biblical story of the fall of man, and one of the many associations of the Confidence Man with Satan and the serpent that tempted Eve. Part of the curse that the Lord lays upon the serpent after the temptation is: ". . . upon thy belly thou shalt go." (Genesis 3:14)

149.10. *Toucan fowl:* In *White-Jacket* (Ch. 56) Melville calls the toucan fowl "a magnificent, omnivorous, broad-billed bandit bird of prey, a native of Brazil. Its perch is on the loftiest trees, whence it looks down upon all humbler fowls, and, hawk-like, flies at their throats."

149.13. *stranger . . . a liberalist, in dress:* See Introduction for a discussion of the cosmopolitan, pp. lxxi f. Nathalia Wright, "The Confidence Men of Melville and Cooper: An American Indictment," *American Quarterly,* IV (1952), 266-268, holds that Melville's conception of the cosmopolitan, Frank Goodman, may have been influenced by James Fenimore Cooper's Steadfast Dodge in *Homeward Bound:* they are similar in appearance; each wears garments suggesting many nations, internationalism, the man of the world; these costumes are "emblematic of a character which is desperately gregarious." "The core of both Cooper's and Melville's novels is an attack on the twin American concepts that a democracy is a rule of the majority and that the majority is always right." (Pp. 266, 268)

150.12. *Signor Marzetti in the African pantomime:* A skit about Jocko, the Brazilian ape, was popular in New York for a number of years; there was an Ethiopian as well as a Brazilian version. During the period of Melville's residence in New York, *Jocko* was performed, in the summer of 1849, with Joseph Marzetti as the ape, at Niblo's Garden; it was also performed there the following winter by the same troupe. (Odell, V, 560, 563, and 240-263 *passim*)

151.17. *that good dish, man:* Mr. Shroeder (p. 371) notes that the cosmopolitan refers lovingly to man as a table delicacy repeatedly in this passage and later when he says that he has inspected Pitch's heart and "found it an inviting oyster in a forbidding shell"; and, says Mr. Shroeder, "We need not go to the Fathers of the Church for this reference. Modern writers from Poe to C. S. Lewis have noted the Devil's fondness for the human soul as a dish."

152.4. *hide his light under the bushel:* Matthew 5:15: "Neither do men light a candle, and put it under a bushel, but on a candlestick. . . ." See also Mark 4:21, Luke 11:33.

152.11. *Life is a pic-nic en costume:* Melville, who was "just recovering from a severe illness," attended a fancy-dress picnic, apparently in plain clothes himself, in Pittsfield on 7 September 1855. The costumes of some of the other guests, including those of his wife, his sister, and one of his sons, were described in the *Berkshire County Eagle* for 14 September 1855. (*Log,* 507) Leon Howard thinks that meditation on the conceit that "life is a pic-nic *en costume*" was the beginning of *The Confidence-Man.* (*Herman Melville: A Biography,* Berkeley and Los Angeles, 1951, p. 226)

152.35. *a jug of Santa Cruz:* Santa Cruz rum, from Santa Cruz island in the West Indies.

154.4. *Zimmermann:* Johann Georg, Ritter von (1728-1795), Swiss physician. He published his four volumes on solitude in 1784-1786, maintaining that such qualities of the soul as "fortitude, firmness, and stoic inflexibility, are much sooner acquired by silent meditation than amidst the noisy intercourse of mankind." (*Solitude,* New York, 1833, p. 125) See note 64.21.

154.5. *Hume's on Suicide:* The essay "Of Suicide" by David Hume (1711-1776) argues that it is superstitious, even blasphemous, to believe that a miserable man has no right to end his misery, and sets out to prove that suicide is not a "transgression of our duty either to God, our neighbor, or ourselves," that it is not prohibited by Scripture, and that it is but the use of that "prudence and skill" which were given men and animals "for their conduct in the world." (*Philosophical Works of David Hume,* Boston, 1854, 4 vols., IV, 535-546.) Melville's early work shows the influence of Hume, Mr. Thorp believes (p. xxvi, n. 18). Melville speaks of Hume's death—"Humble, composed, without bravado," his skepticism, and his "firm, creedless faith that embraces the spheres," in *Redburn.* (Ch. 58).

154.6. *Bacon's on Knowledge:* Any of Bacon's philosophical works might be called his book on knowledge, *The Advancement of Learning* (1650) or its larger form, the *De Augmentis Scientiarum,* or the *Novum Organum.* Bacon advocated experiment and carefully controlled observation as the path to knowledge; the cosmopolitan, like the other Confidence Men, advocates blind faith and decries the appeal to experience. Bacon says: "We will begin therefore with this precept, according to the ancient opinion, that the sinews of wisdom are slowness of belief and distrust" (*The Advancement of Learning*, II, xxiii, 16); the Confidence Man maintains that human nature is perfect, or at any rate that we ought not to mistrust it. Bacon, writing of the need for a truthful treatise on "the frauds, cautels, impostures, and vices of every profession," says that "we are much beholden to Machiavelli and others, that write what men do, and not what they ought to do. For it is not possible to join serpentine wisdom with the columbine innocency, except men know exactly all the conditions of the serpent; his baseness and going upon his belly, his volubility and lubricity, his envy and sting, and the rest; that is, all forms and natures of evil. For without this, virtue lieth open and unfenced. Nay, an honest man can do no good upon those that are wicked, to reclaim them, without the help of the knowledge of evil." (II, xxi, 9) See also references and notes 55.30 and 223.36.

154.19. *Rabelais's pro-wine Koran:* Melville borrowed "Rabelais Vol 2," "vol 3," and "vol 4" from Evert Duyckinck late in 1847– March 1848 (Sealts, No. 417), while he was writing *Mardi*. From the publication of *Mardi* to the present, many reviewers and critics have remarked the numerous similarities between the works of Rabelais and Melville and also the considerable influence of Rabelais. In his study of *Mardi*, Mr. Merrell Davis ranks the works of Rabelais high among the books which helped to cause Melville, while composing *Mardi*, to expand that novel from a South Sea romance into "a travelogue-satire with the wild songs, wild chronicles, and wilder speculations of characters whom he had created for that purpose," and thinks that Rabelais probably "suggested the possibility of combining such a romantic 'Quest for the Holy Bottle' with a sight-seeing tour through the islands of Mardi, which may already have been begun. To Rabelais, at least, he seems to have turned for the suggestion of the framework of his travelogue-satire. . . ." Besides this large debt of "artistic liberation" and artistic form, Melville owed to Rabelais suggestions for various incidents and situations, for "Rabelaisian burlesque of such legal documents" as John Jacob Astor's will, for comic parody of catalogues of "rarities" and of old books, including theological works. (Merrell Davis, *Melville's Mardi: A Chartless Voyage*, New Haven, 1952, pp. 194, 76-77, 65-66, 167n, 148, 153-155.) See also W. H. Wells, "Moby-Dick and Rabelais," *Modern Language Notes*, XXXVIII (1923), 123; and *Moby-Dick*, pp. xli, 581, 582, 706, 815. Soon after its publication,

The Confidence-Man was called "a Rabelaisian piece of patchwork without any of the Rabelaisian indecencies. . . ." (*New-York Evening Times*, 11 April 1857; the review is quoted in *Log*, p. 570.) The long tale of Gargantua, Pantagruel, and Panurge, by François Rabelais (1494?-1553), French humanist, satirist, and physician, might well be lightly called a "pro-wine Koran," for, besides the mighty eating and drinking which enliven it, the advice of the oracle of the Bottle, whom Pantagruel, Panurge, and others go on a long voyage to consult, is summed up in the word "Drink."

154.19. *Mahomet's anti-wine one:* The Koran prohibits intoxicants in Part III, Section 27, Verse 219, and in Ch. 5, Section 12, Verse 90. Melville borrowed Thomas Carlyle's *On Heroes, Hero-Worship, and the Heroic in History* (Sealts, No. 122) from Evert Duyckinck in 1850, but whether his knowledge of Islam was appreciably greater than Carlyle's second lecture, "The Hero as Prophet. Mahomet: Islam," could have made it, is not known. Carlyle mentions abstinence from wine as among the more rigorous requirements of Mahomet's religion. There are several rather general references to Islam, as, for example, to the fast of Ramadan in *Moby-Dick*, Chs. 16, 17, and to Mohammed in Melville's works; in *White-Jacket*, Ch. 65, he calls the prophet "that old exquisite, Mohammed, who so much loved to snuff perfumes and essences, and used to lounge out of the conservatories of Khadija, his wife, to give battle to the robust sons of Koriesh. . . ." The editors of *Moby-Dick* point out the probability that Goethe's analysis of the character of Mahomet suggested some of the traits of Ahab (p. 648), and they analyze and stress the similarities between Carlyle's characterization of the prophet and Melville's portrait of Ahab (pp. 650-651). Melville had bought *The Auto-Biography of Goethe. Truth and Poetry: From My Own Life* in two volumes in 1849 (Sealts, No. 228).

154.30. *Jeremy Diddler:* See note 16.30.

154.32. *Jeremy the prophet:* See note 53.28.

154.33. *Jeremy Taylor the divine:* English bishop and author, 1613-1667. Melville acquired his *The Rule and Exercise of Holy Dying* (Boston, [1864?]) in 1869; Sealts, Supplement, No. 495a.

157.1. *Primrose-hill:* Primrose Hill lies north of Regent's Park. Associated with it are a famous murder and a number of duels. In 1678 the body of the murdered Sir Edmond Berry Godfrey was found in a dry ditch at the foot of the hill. Primrose Hill was often chosen for duels as late as 1821. Its ugly history and its innocent name make it a suitable neighborhood for the Confidence Man. Across Albert Road from Primrose Hill are the Zoological Gardens of Regent's Park. Thither Melville had gone on 13 November 1849, after watching the public execution of the Mannings in London. Two days later Melville went by bus to Primrose Hill (*Journal* . . . *1849-1850*, pp. 30, 32).

157.2. *the Piazza, Covent Garden:* The scene of a pretty flower-market. The Piazza was an open corridor or arcade, originally built by Inigo Jones, along the north and east sides of Covent Garden market.

157.4. *Diogenes . . . a merry-andrew, in the flower-market:* Diogenes of Sinope (c. 412-323 B.C.), Greek Cynic philosopher. The cosmopolitan is, of course, the real cynic and misanthrope, the real Diogenes and Timon, of this and other scenes, as Pitch comprehends. Diogenes' biographer, Diogenes Laërtius, says in his *Lives* that Diogenes the Cynic was "great at pouring scorn on his contemporaries," that, "asked where he came from, he said, 'I am a citizen of the world'"; he relates many anecdotes of Diogenes' harsh and surly remarks in the market place. (Diogenes Laërtius, *Lives of Eminent Philosophers,* trans. R. D. Hicks, VI. ii; Melville owned, and annotated, the *Lives* in the Bohn ed. [1853]; see Sealts, No. 183a.) Lucian, in his "Philosophers for Sale," has Diogenes the Cynic say that he is "a citizen of the world," and that he will teach a pupil, among other things, this: " 'Frequent the most crowded place, and in those very places desire to be solitary and uncommunicative, greeting nor friend nor stranger.' " (Trans. A. M. Harmon).

157.7. *Lord Timon:* The noble Athenian Timon, hero of Shakespeare's *Timon of Athens,* after the fickleness of his friends drove him to bitter misanthropy, lived and railed alone in the woods outside Athens. Lucian and Plutarch are also possible sources of Melville's interest in Timon. In *Mardi* (Ch. 13) Melville says of the "ghastly White Shark" that "Timon-like, he always swims by himself. . . ." Pierre was "fairly Timonized" by some of his experiences (*Pierre,* pp. 297, 300). In his essay "Hawthorne and his Mosses," Melville speaks of Shakespeare's "dark characters," Hamlet, Timon, Lear, Iago. Melville's dark philosophic questioning in *The Confidence-Man* has led some critics to speak of his Timonism in this novel. But it is the Confidence Man, and not the creator of both this man and his victims, including the embattled Pitch, who is the real Misanthropos (as Timon names himself); and it is a question whether the Confidence Man is human at all. See note on 261.12 and other references to Timon on 16.18, 260.2, and 265.20.

157.23. *To you, an Ishmael:* The Biblical story of Ishmael, banished and sent out by Abraham into the wilderness (Gen. 21:9-21), supplied an allusion frequently used by Melville to underline the isolation and loneliness of a character. As everybody knows, the narrator of *Moby-Dick* called himself Ishmael; an Explanatory Note in *Moby-Dick* (pp. 586-591) discusses at length Melville's Ishmael concept and its possible sources in addition to the Biblical source. Miss Wright finds Ishmael to be the prototype of seven of Melville's characters: Redburn, White-Jacket, Ishmael, Pierre, Israel Potter, Pitch, and Ungar. "Pitch is perhaps of all Melville's Ishmaels the one who best reveals his deep sympathy with this character. Toward it he is never unsympathetic, but he never seems so serious as here." (Wright, 46, 55.)

158.9. *Colonel John Moredock:* "Among the members of the third territorial legislature [of Illinois], elected in 1816, was John Mordock [*sic*], representative from Monroe County." (Solon Justus Buck, *Illinois in 1818*, Springfield, Ill., 1917, p. 203 n.) The territorial papers of Indiana show John Moredock's signature to a recommendation (dated Vincennes, 28 December 1802) to President Jefferson, and his signature to a memorial to Congress. ("The Territory of Indiana, 1800-1810," *The Territorial Papers of the United States,* comp. and ed. by Clarence Edwin Carter, Washington, 1939, VII, 83, 143.) Melville's source was undoubtedly James Hall; see below, 163.2.

159.22. *eye like Lochiel's:* Sir Ewan (or Ewen or Evan) Cameron of Lochiel (1629-1719), famous Scottish highland chieftain who fought for Charles I and Charles II. Macaulay tells us: "In agility and skill at his weapons he had few equals among the inhabitants of the hills. He had repeatedly been victorious in single combat. He was a hunter of great fame. He made vigorous war on the wolves . . . ; and by his hand perished the last of the ferocious breed which is known to have wandered at large in our island." (Thomas Babington Macaulay, *The History of England from the Accession of James II,* Vol. III Philadelphia, 1856, p. 251. The London edition of Volume III appeared in 1855.)

159.36. *Pocahontas, . . . Massasoit, etc.:* Some of the Indians named by the cosmopolitan nullify his point about universal benevolence. Philip (d. 1676), a Wampanoag sachem and son of Massasoit, after trying to deal peacefully with the white settlers of New England, fought them bitterly in the savage and bloody King Philip's War, in the course of which he was killed, at Mount Hope, R. I. Tecumseh (1768-1813), Shawnee chief, tried to unite all Indian tribes east of the Mississippi in the Old Northwest and South, against the purchase of land by whites from individual tribes; he fought on the side of the British, as a brigadier general, in the War of 1812. Logan (1725-1780) lived in Pennsylvania for many years as a good friend of the whites; but after the massacre of his family by white settlers, Logan's heart changed, and in hatred and vengeance he instigated a war against them. In the Revolution he fought on the British side. The Five Nations were a powerful and warlike Iroquois league which fought on the side of the British in the French and Indian Wars; in the Revolution many of the chiefs fought against the colonists and raided and massacred white settlements in the West. The Araucanians, an important race of Indians in South America, independent, warlike, loosely organized, long resisted Spanish aggression. On the other hand, Pocahontas (d. 1617), daughter of Powhatan, by her marriage to John Rolfe in 1614, brought about peace and friendship between the white settlers of Virginia and their Indian neighbors. Massasoit (d. 1661), Wampanoag sachem, kept faithfully his treaty with the Plymouth settlers, in spite of unjust dealings on the part of white men. Red Jacket (c. 1756-1830), a chief of the Senecas, was known as an orator rather than a fighter, and was largely friendly towards the whites.

161.21. *James Hall, the judge:* James Hall (1793-1868), circuit judge in Illinois, founder of the *Illinois Monthly Magazine*, the first literary periodical west of Ohio, and author of sketches, stories, novels, and historical works about the West, is Melville's chief source for the two following chapters.

163.2. *INDIAN-HATING:* Melville's chief source for Chapters XXVI and XXVII was James Hall's "Indian hating.—Some of the sources of this animosity.—Brief account of Col. Moredock," in Hall's *Sketches of History, Life, and Manners, in the West* (Philadelphia, 1835), Vol. II, Ch. VI, pp. 74-82, which is given, slightly abridged, below.

The violent animosity which exists between the people of our frontier and the Indians, has long been a subject of remark. In the early periods of the history of our country, it was easily accounted for, on the ground of mutual aggression. The whites were continually encroaching upon the aborigines, and the latter avenging their wrongs by violent and sudden hostilities. The philanthropist is surprised, however, that such feelings should prevail now, when these atrocious wars have ceased, and when no immediate cause of enmity remains; at least upon our side. Yet the fact is, that the dweller upon the frontier continues to regard the Indian with a degree of terror and hatred, similar to that which he feels towards the rattlesnake or panther, and which can neither be removed by argument, nor appeased by anything but the destruction of its object.

In order to understand the cause and operation of these feelings, it is necessary to recollect that the backwoodsmen are a peculiar race. We allude to the pioneers, who, keeping continually in the advance of civilization, precede the denser population of our country in its progress westward, and live always upon the frontier. They are the descendants of a people whose habits were identically the same as their own. Their fathers were pioneers. . . . The great tide of emigration, as it rolls forward, beats upon them and rolls them onward, without either swallowing them up in its mass, or mingling its elements with theirs. . . . [Hostility and even hatred are created between the two races when the white man disputes with the Indian "the right to the soil, and the privilege of hunting game."]

Our pioneers have, as we have said, been born and reared on the frontier, and have, from generation to generation, by successive removal, remained in the same relative situation in respect to the Indians and to our own government. Every child thus reared, learns to hate an Indian, because he always hears him spoken of as an enemy. From the cradle, he listens continually to horrid tales of savage violence, and becomes familiar with narratives of aboriginal cunning and ferocity. Every family can remember some of its members or relatives among the victims of a midnight massacre, or can tell of some acquaintance who has suffered death at the stake. Traditions of horses stolen, and cattle driven off, and cabins burned, are numberless; are told with great minuteness, and listened to with intense interest. With persons thus reared, hatred towards an Indian becomes a part of their nature, and revenge an instinctive principle. Nor does the evil end here. . . . In the formation of each of the western territories and states, the backwoodsmen have, for a while, formed the majority of the population, and given the tone to public opinion.

If we attempt to reason on this subject, we must reason with a due regard to facts, and to the known principles of human nature. Is it to be wondered at, that a man should fear and detest an Indian, who has been always accustomed to hear him described only as a midnight prowler, watching to murder the mother as she bends over her helpless children, and tearing, with hellish malignity, the babe from the maternal breast? Is it strange, that he whose mother has fallen under the savage tomahawk, or whose father has died a lingering death at the stake, should indulge the passion of revenge towards the perpetrators of such atrocities? They know the story only as it was told to them. . . .

Besides that general antipathy which pervades the whole community under such circumstances, there have been many instances of individuals who, in consequence of some personal wrong, have vowed eternal hatred to the whole Indian race, and have devoted nearly all of their lives to the fulfilment of a vast scheme of vengeance. A familiar instance is before us in the life of a gentleman, who was known to the writer of this article, and whose history we have heard repeated by those who were intimately conversant with all the events. We allude to the late Colonel John Moredock, who was a member of the territorial legislature of Illinois, a distinguished militia officer, and a man universally known and respected by the early settlers of that region. . . .

John Moredock was the son of a woman who was married several times, and was as often widowed by the tomahawk of the savage. Her husbands had been pioneers, and with them she had wandered from one territory to another, living always on the frontier. She was at last left a widow, at Vincennes, with a large family of children, and was induced to join a party about to remove to Illinois, to which region a few American families had then recently removed. On the eastern side of Illinois there were no settlements of whites; on the shore of the Mississippi a few spots were occupied by the French; and it was now that our own backwoodsmen began to turn their eyes to this delightful country, and determined to settle in the vicinity of the French villages. Mrs. Moredock and her friends embarked at Vincennes in boats, with the intention of descending the Wabash and Ohio rivers, and ascending the Mississippi. They proceeded in safety until they reached the Grand Tower on the Mississippi, where, owing to the difficulty of the navigation for ascending boats, it became necessary for the boatmen to land, and drag their vessels round a rocky point, which was swept by a violent current. Here a party of Indians, lying in wait, rushed upon them, and murdered the whole party. Mrs. Moredock was among the victims, and *all* her children, except John, who was proceeding with another party.

John Moredock was just entering upon the years of manhood, when he was thus left in a strange land, the sole survivor of his race. He resolved upon executing vengeance, and immediately took measures to discover the actual perpetrators of the massacre. It was ascertained that the outrage was committed by a party of twenty or thirty Indians, belonging to different tribes, who had formed themselves into a lawless predatory band. Moredock watched the motions of this band for more than a year, before an opportunity suitable for his purpose occurred. At length he learned, that they were hunting on the Missouri side of the river, nearly opposite to the recent settlements of the Americans. He raised a party of young men and pursued them; but that time they escaped. Shortly after, he sought them at the head of another party, and had the good fortune to discover them one evening, on an island, whither they had retired to encamp the more securely for the night. Moredock and his friends, about equal in numbers to the Indians, waited until the dead of night, and then landed upon the island, turning adrift their own canoes and those of the enemy, and determined to sacrifice their own lives, or to exterminate the savage band. They were completely successful. Three only of the Indians escaped, by throwing themselves into the river; the rest were slain, while the whites lost not a man.

But Moredock was not satisfied while one of the murderers of his mother remained. He had learned to recognize the names and persons of the three that had escaped, and these he pursued with secret, but untiring diligence, until they all fell by his own hand. Nor was he yet satisfied. He had now become a hunter and warrior. He was a square-built, muscular man, of remarkable strength and activity. In athletic sports he had few equals; few men would willingly have encountered him in single combat. He was a man of determined courage, and great coolness and steadiness of purpose. He was expert in the use of the rifle and other weapons; and was complete master of those wonderful and numberless expedients by which the woodsman subsists in the forest, pursues the steps of an enemy with unerring sagacity, or conceals himself and his designs from the discovery of a watchful foe. He had resolved never to spare an Indian, and though he made no boast of this determination, and seldom avowed it, it became the ruling passion of his life. He thought it praiseworthy to kill an Indian; and would roam through the forest silently and alone, for days and weeks, with this single purpose. A solitary red man, who was so unfortunate as to meet him in the woods, was sure to become his victim; if he encountered a party of the enemy, he would either secretly pursue their footsteps until an opportunity for striking a blow occurred, or, if discovered, would elude them by his superior skill. He died about four years ago, an old man, and it is supposed never in his life failed to embrace an opportunity to kill a savage.

The reader must not infer from this description that Colonel Moredock was unsocial, ferocious, or by nature cruel. On the contrary, he was a man of warm feelings, and excellent disposition. At home he was like other men, conducting a large farm with industry and success, and gaining the good will of all his neighbours by his popular manners and benevolent deportment. He was cheerful, convivial, and hospitable; and no man in the territory was more generally known, or more universally respected. He was an officer in the ranging service during the war of 1813-14, and acquitted himself with credit; and was afterwards elected to the command of the militia of his country, at a time when such an office was honourable, because it imposed responsibility, and required the exertion of military skill. Colonel Moredock was a member of the legislative council of the territory of Illinois, and at the formation of the state government, was spoken of as a candidate for the office of governor, but refused to permit his name to be used.

The third paragraph of Melville's Chapter XXVI is not represented by anything in this sketch but probably owes its substratum to the following passages, which occur a little farther along in Hall's book (*Sketches. . .* , II, 86; 95-96) :

The genuine woodsman, the real pioneer, are [sic] independent, brave, and upright. . . .
The first stock [of Kentuckians] were hunters or military men—an athletic, vigorous race, with hardy frames, active minds, and bold spirits; and they lived for years surrounded by dangers which kept them continually alert, and drew them often into active military service. Obliged

to think and act for themselves, they acquired independence of thought and habitual promptitude of demeanor. . . . Courage would naturally be held in high estimation, by a people whose ancestors were brave and continually engaged in warfare. . . . They are daring, impetuous, and tenacious of their honour; chivalrous, fond of adventure, courteous to females, and hospitable to the stranger.

Probably also the following, from Hall's "The Backwoodsman" in his *Legends of the West* (Philadelphia, 1832), p. 3, contributed to Melville's description in paragraph three and to his description of Colonel Moredock in the next chapter; the rest of "The Backwoodsman" repeats some of Hall's material on Indian-hating.

If they [the backwoodsmen] travelled or walked abroad, it was with the wary step, and jealous vigilance, of the Indian: with an eye continually glancing into every thicket, with an ear prepared to catch the slightest alarm of danger. . . . Simple, honest, and inoffensive in their manners, kind and just to each other, they were intrepid, fierce, and vindictive in war. . . . impatient of fatigue, ardent in their temperament, warm hearted and hospitable.

Judge Hall was accustomed to use his literary material over and over, and told the story of an Indian-hater, with much the same explanation of his terrible addiction, at least three times. Two other treatments are "The Pioneer," in *Tales of the Border* (Philadelphia, 1833), and "The Indian Hater," in *Legends of the West,* in *The Western Souvenir, a Christmas and New Year's Gift for 1829* (Cincinnati, n.d.), and in *The Wilderness and the War Path* (New York, 1846).

The sworn Indian-hater, such as Melville describes, was, as Hall says, an actual phenomenon of the American frontier; he became a minor theme in history and story. The most renowned of many actual Indian-haters was one Lew Wetzel; probably the most famous in fiction was the Quaker, Nathan, the hero of Robert Montgomery Bird's *Nick of the Woods; or, The Jibbenainosay: A Tale of Kentucky* (1837). For good discussions of actual and fictional Indian-haters, the reader may consult Cecil B. Williams' introduction to his edition of *Nick of the Woods,* "American Fiction Series" (New York, 1939) and G. H. Orians, "The Indian-Hater in Early American Fiction," *Journal of American History,* XXVII (1933), 33-44. Mr. Williams thinks that Bird's picture of Indian-hating probably derived from Hall's account of the phenomenon. Bird's perennially popular *Nick of the Woods* perhaps had a part in Melville's conception of the Indian-hater; for one of Melville's additions to Hall's essay is the statement that to treat an Indian as though he were a Quaker is injudicious and dangerous. This is what Nathan does; and in return for his kindness he sees his wife, mother, and children murdered before his eyes. The Confidence Man himself may also owe something to Nathan, for the Quaker, after he has devoted himself to the systematic murder of Indians, still pretends to be the man of peace.

Francis Parkman's *The Conspiracy of Pontiac* (1851) contains material on Indians and Indian-hating that may also have helped Melville; for Melville knew Parkman's writings, and the historian's picture of Indian malignity and treachery is much closer to that in the bilious man's story than is Judge Hall's. Parkman records the fact of sworn Indian-hating: "The chronicles of the American border are filled with the deeds of men, who, having lost all by the merciless tomahawk, have lived for vengeance alone; and such men will never cease to exist so long as a hostile tribe remains within striking distance of an American settlement." (Francis Parkman, *The Conspiracy of Pontiac and the Indian War After the Conquest of Canada*, Champlain Edition, Boston, 1898, II, 255. See also Parkman's treatment of the Paxton men as a band of Indian-haters, *ibid.*, II, 257ff., and his mention of a Quaker betrayed by his trust, II, 239, n. 1.) Parkman also depicts the settled treachery of the Indian: Pontiac flourishing the peace pipe in one hand and preparing to give the signal for massacre with the other; Indians using their reputation as friends to gain admittance to a house and murder the people assembled there; Pontiac and other Indians enticing white men to trust them and accept their hospitality, and then betraying them to torture and death (*ibid.*, I, 234; II, 222-23; I, 246ff. and II, 59, 101ff.)

But Hall is Melville's main and certain source for the two chapters on Indian-hating. Comparison of Melville's redaction with Hall's original will show how closely Melville followed his source, how he changed the portrait of the Indian for his own purposes, as explained in the Introduction of the present volume, and how his superior literary craftsmanship vivified Hall's monotonous narrative.

Melville makes of the Indian a symbol, as he had done in a letter to Hawthorne (29 June 1851; in Raymond M. Weaver, *Herman Melville: Mariner and Mystic* New York, 1921, pp. 328-330): "This most persuasive season has now for weeks recalled me from certain crotchety and over-doleful chimeras, the like of which men like you and me, and some others, forming a chain of God's posts round the world, must be content to encounter now and then, and fight them the best way we can. But come they will,—for in the boundless, trackless, but still glorious wild wilderness through which these outposts run, the Indians do sorely abound, as well as the insignificant but still stinging mosquitoes." His humanitarian feelings towards real Indians appear a number of times, e.g., *Redburn*, Ch. 21; *Mardi*, Ch. 145.

A recent article by Roy Harvey Pearce, "Melville's Indian-Hater: A Note on a Meaning of *The Confidence-Man*," *PMLA*, LXVII (1952), 942-948, corrects the tendency of Mr. Shroeder's article, cited above, to make a sort of hero of the Indian-hater as the only person in the novel who is not "victimized into believing that 'the world has no dark side'" and in whose "vision of spiritual reality" there is no "distortion." "Now I submit," says Mr. Pearce (p. 942), "that there is nothing but distortion in the Indian-hater's vision of spiritual reality, that the price he pays for resisting the confidence-man is exactly as high as the price he would pay for surrendering to him. . . . The issue of blind confidence and blind hatred is in the end identical." What Mr. Pearce says cannot be too much emphasized; it is precisely the point, morally speaking, of the novel. "The attempt is, I think," he goes on (p. 946), "to make us know the terrors of hatred as directly and as fully as we have known and shall know those of false love and confidence." "Hatred is hatred; and Melville will not let us see it as anything but hatred. . . . Melville has no more praise for Indian-hating than he does for confidence. Both are false, blind, unreasoning." (P. 948)

Mr. Pearce's conclusion, however, does not follow necessarily—that man has no choice except one of these extremes: "What would seem to follow in the novel is that . . . only by becoming a hater *par excellence* can one resist the confidence-man. But then one destroys oneself and makes life into a continual celebration of black masses to hatred. There would seem to be no way out of the darkness, no hope except perhaps that of true Charity and the doctrine of the thirteenth chapter of First Corinthians. But even that hope, we must recall, virtually disappears after Chapter I." (P. 948)

But Melville, though a pessimistic moralist in this novel, is not, I take it, a despairing one. Like many another moralist, and writer of comedy, he is concerned to point the dangers of both extremes. It is true, of course, that to Melville the human condition is inescapably a dilemma; no one succeeds perfectly; heaven's way (which is perhaps hinted to us in the Sermon on the Mount and I Corinthians 13) is not earth's way (which Melville symbolizes by the Articles of War and the No-Trust sign), as he said over and over to the end of his life, and the best of mortals trying to walk in heaven's way finds his mortality a cause of stumbling. But there are degrees of success. Even Pitch, though his charity is buried deeper and deeper in him, does not become a hater. The reader's sympathy is made to lie with those victims of the Confidence Man who have failed because of their goodness. The following couplet, which Melville marked in both margins when he encountered it quoted from "the Persians" in Emerson's "Illusions," *The Conduct of Life* (which Melville acquired in 1870; Sealts, No. 203), probably sums up most of the moral: "Fooled thou must be, though wisest of the wise; Then be the fool of virtue, not of vice." The rest of the moral is that blind confidence may in the end destroy one's faith and one's charity.

164.25. *Hairy Orson:* In the French medieval romance about Valentine and Orson, Orson, born in a forest, is carried off by a bear and grows up a wild man; his twin brother is brought up a courtier. The romance, probably composed in the fifteenth century, belongs to the Charlemagne cycle. Arthur Dickson, *Valentine and Orson: A Study in Late Medieval Romance* (New York, 1929) lists sixty-three editions of versions of this story in English from its first appearance through 1850, and also cites innumerable literary references to the story.

164.34. *the Emperor Julian in Gaul:* Julian the Apostate, Roman emperor from 361 to 363, "shared the dangers and fatigues which he imposed on the meanest of the soldiers," according to Gibbon, who also says: "With the same firmness that he resisted the allurements of love, he sustained the hardships of war. When the Romans marched through the flat and flooded country, their sovereign, on foot, at the head of his legions, shared their fatigues, and animated their diligence." (Edward Gibbon, *The Decline and Fall of the Roman Empire*, London, 1807, 12 vols., III, 228; IV, 175.) *The Decline . . .* was "either owned or borrowed by Melville" (Sealts, No. 223b). He visited "Gibbon's Church" in Rome on 8 March 1857, and he based a poem, "The Age of the Antonines," on the first chapter of *The Decline* . . . (see his letter to John C. Hoadley, 31 March 1877, in *Log*, p. 760, and the note, p. 475, in *Collected Poems*).

165.7. *Peace Congress:* The first international Peace Convention, held in London in 1843, supported the principle that " 'war is inconsistent with the spirit of Christianity and the true interests of mankind.' Its object was to deliberate on the best means, 'under Divine blessing,' by which the world might be shown the evils and inexpediency of war and to promote permanent and universal peace." There were four mid-century international Peace Congresses, at Brussels (1848), at Paris (1849), at Frankfort (1850), and at London (1851), which announced similar principles and objectives. The chief new note at the last Peace Congress, held at the time of the Crystal Palace Exibition, was "the resolution which condemned the aggression of civilized nations on barbarian peoples." (Merle Eugene Curti, *The American Peace Crusade, 1815-1860*, Durham, N. C., 1929, pp. 138, 187, and *passim*.) Emerson read a lecture on "war" to the American Peace Society in 1838 (*The Complete Works of Ralph Waldo Emerson*, 12 vols., Boston, 1903-1907, XI, 149-176, and "Notes").

165.26. *the Newgate Calendar or the Annals of Europe:* "The New *Newgate Calendar*, or Malefactor's Bloody Register, containing Authentic and Circumstantial Acc'ts. of the Lives, Transactions, Exploits, Trials, Executions, Dying Speeches, Confessions, and Other Curious Particulars, Relating to all the most notorious Criminals . . . and Violators of the Laws of their Country, who have suffered Death and other Exemplary Punishments, in England, Scotland, and Ireland, from the Commencement of the Year 1700 to the Present Time." Newgate was a London prison from 1218 to 1902. *The Annals of Europe* was a yearbook published in London from 1739 to 1744. The *Annals* . . . for 1739 calls itself "A methodical and full Account of all the remarkable Occurrences which happened within that Year, either at Home or Abroad; with Copies or Extracts of the most important Treaties, and other public Papers, and an Abstract of the most remarkable Pamphlets published within that Period."

166.4. *Moyamensing:* Formerly a district in the southern part of Philadelphia County, Pennsylvania.

166.5. *a treaty-breaker like an Austrian:* Probably a reference to the promises made by the imperial Austrian government in March

1848, when revolution threatened to dissolve the empire, and broken in the autumn and in 1849, as counter-revolution gained strength: the constituent assembly promised in the spring of 1848 was dissolved within a year and its work disregarded; the constitutional freedoms granted to Bohemia in March were revoked by a Hapsburg army in June; the complete constitutional separatism within the empire granted to Hungary in April 1848 was ended in August 1849 by an imperial army with large aid from Russia.

166.7. *a judicial murderer and Jeffries:* George Jeffreys, first Baron Jeffreys of Wem (1648-1689), English lord chancellor, notorious for judicial murder. In the "Bloody Assizes" after Monmouth's Rebellion he was responsible for the hanging of 320, the transporting of 841, and the whipping and imprisonment of many. Melville speaks in *White-Jacket,* Ch. 71, of the Restoration as a period when "a hangman Judge Jeffreys sentenced a world's champion like Algernon Sidney to the block." Macaulay's *The History of England from the Accession of James II* devotes a large part of Vol. I (London, 1849), Ch. 5, to the trials presided over by Jeffreys.

167.32. *perfidious as Caesar Borgia:* Caesar Borgia (1476-1507), son of Pope Alexander VI, duke of Valentinois and Romagna, notorious for his unscrupulousness, fraud, and treachery. He promised, for example, to spare the life of Manfredi, ruler of Faenza, on his surrender, but broke his word. Machiavelli admired him, partly for the cleverness with which he made use of cruelty and perfidy, and praised him in *The Prince.*

168.34. *Daniel Boone:* Explorer and famous frontiersman in Kentucky and Missouri (1734-1820). "Two darling sons, and a brother, have I lost by savage hands," says Daniel Boone in his autobiography. Boone speaks much of the cruelty and barbarism of the savages, but does not particularly stress perfidy. His one instance of Indian perfidy perhaps takes it for granted. (*The Adventures of Colonel Daniel Boone* in George [Gilbert] Imlay's *A Topographical Description of the Western Territory of North America,* 2nd ed., London, 1793, p. 361 and *passim.*) Speaking of the lone whale, Melville says in *Moby-Dick* (p. 392): "Like venerable moss-bearded Daniel Boone, he will have no one near him but Nature herself. . . ."

170.4. *An intenser Hannibal, he makes a vow:* Hannibal (247?-183? B.C.), Carthaginian general. When nine years old, he coaxed his father to take him to Spain with him; his father "brought him up to the altars, and compelled him to lay his hand on the conse-crated victims, and swear, that as soon as it should be in his power, he would show himself an enemy to the Roman people." (Livy *The History of Rome* xxi. 1, trans. George Baker; Melville bought this translation of Livy in 1849; Sealts, No. 147.)

170.15. *a Leather-stocking Nemesis:* "Leatherstocking" is a nick-name of Natty Bumppo, the hero of James Fenimore Cooper's five Leatherstocking novels. Melville was an early reader of Cooper; see his letter of tribute in *Memorial of James Fenimore Cooper* (New York, 1852), p. 30, and also, edited by J. H. Birss, in *Notes and Queries*, CLXII (1932), 39. Melville reviewed Cooper's *The Sea Lions* and *The Red Rover* in the *Literary World*, IV, no. 117 (28 April 1849), 370, and VI, no. 163 (16 March 1850), 276-277, respectively. (See Sealts, Nos. 160, 159.)

170.20. *gone to his long home:* Ecclesiastes 12:5: "man goeth to his long home."

172.3. *THAT EMINENT ENGLISH MORALIST WHO SAID HE LIKED A GOOD HATER:* Samuel Johnson, of whom Mrs. Piozzi tells the anecdote: " 'Dear Bathurst (said he to me one day) was a man to my very heart's content: he hated a fool, and he hated a rogue, and he hated a *whig*; he was a very good *hater*.' " (*Anec-dotes of the Late Samuel Johnson, LL.D.*, by Hester Lynch Piozzi (1786), reprinted in *Johnsonian Miscellanies*, ed. George Birkbeck Hill, Oxford, 1897, 2 vols., I, 204.) Melville referred to the same anecdote in *Mardi*, Ch. 13.

173.3. *the rock of the Grand Tower:* Banvard, mentioning the imposing spectacles to be seen on the Mississippi River between the mouth of the Ohio River and St. Louis, says (p. 19): "We may mention among them that gigantic mass of rocks forming a singular island in the river, called the 'Grand Tower,' and the shot towers of Herculaneum."

174.4. *the voice calling through the garden:* Genesis 3:8-10: "And they heard the voice of the Lord God walking in the garden in the cool of the day. . . . And the Lord God called unto Adam, and said unto him, Where art thou? And he said, I heard thy voice in the garden, and I was afraid, because I was naked, and I hid myself."

175.21. *Hull's dubious surrender at Detroit:* Brig. Gen. William Hull (1753-1825) surrendered his army and fortifications at Detroit to the British under Gen. Isaac Brock, without a battle, on 16

August 1812. A court martial tried him on charges of treason, cowardice, and neglect of duty, and found him guilty upon the second and third counts. His sentence of execution was remanded by President Madison because of the services of Hull in the Revolutionary War. "These charges would hardly be sustained today." (*Dictionary of American Biography*)

178.5. *what Dr. Johnson said of the alleged Lisbon earthquake:* Mrs. Piozzi furnishes the anecdote: "I once asked him if he believed the story of the destruction of Lisbon by an earthquake when it first happened: 'Oh! not for six months (said he) at least: I *did* think that story too dreadful to be credited, and can hardly yet persuade myself that it was true to the full extent we all of us have heard.'" (*Johnsonian Miscellanies*, I, 244.) Macaulay also gives the anecdote in his "Boswell's *Life of Johnson*" in his *Essays . . .*, which Mr. Sealts concludes was among Melville's purchases in 1849. (Sealts, No. 359)

180.17. *Let us drink of the wine:* From Leigh Hunt's *Bacchus in Tuscany, A Dithyrambic Poem from the Italian of Francesco Redi . . .* (1825); Leigh Hunt's lines go:

> And drink of the wine of the vine benign
> That sparkles warm in Sansovine.

182.17. *Brinvilliarses:* Marie Madeleine Marguerite D'Aubray, Marquise de Brinvilliers (c. 1630-1676), famous French prisoner, a pretty woman with an innocent, childlike air. A short poem of Melville's, "The Marchioness of Brinvilliers," embodies a favorite theme of his, one that permeates *The Confidence-Man*—the ironic contrast between innocent appearance and murderous reality. The tendency of Melville's irony to go underground, which is seen in *The Confidence-Man,* reaches its end in the poem—complete disappearance into a region somewhere between the poem and the reader's independent knowledge; for the poem loses its point unless the reader knows that the candid, sweet, "fathomless mild eyes" that the poem describes were the windows of an unspeakably hideous soul. (*Collected Poems of Herman Melville,* Chicago, 1947, p. 234.) Voltaire tells in his *Siècle de Louis XIV* (Ch. 26) how the Marquise de Brinvilliers poisoned her father, two brothers, and sister; but he denies the story, which is credited by the *Encyclopaedia Britannica,* however, that she first tried out her poisons in hospitals where she charitably visited the sick.

184.6. *the Rochefoucaultites:* Melville quotes one of the famous and generally cynical maxims of the Duke de La Rochefoucauld (1613-1680) in his "Hawthorne and His Mosses" to the effect that "'we exalt the reputation of some, in order to depress that of others.'" Melville's annotated copy of La Rochefoucauld's *Reflections and Moral Maxims* (London, [187-]) survives (Sealts, No. 321). See also 276.9.

184.22. *nine good jokes:* The Lord promised Abraham that he would not destroy the wicked city Sodom if as many as ten righteous persons could be found there. Genesis 18:32.

185.7. *a man may smile . . . and be a villain:* Hamlet's words, more or less, about his treacherous uncle: "Meet it is I set it down, That one may smile, and smile, and be a villain." (*Hamlet*, I, v, 107f.)

185.23. *Aristotle—I think, in his "Politics":* (1) The cosmopolitan's belief that Aristotle's *Politics* "should not, without precaution, be placed in the hands of youth" is probably due to the opposition between the egalitarianism and brotherhood which he pretends and Aristotle's belief that some men are "natural slaves," Aristotle's sense of the superiority of Greeks and the political ineptness of barbarians, and Aristotle's view of human nature, which may be seen, for example, in his study of revolutions and their causes in Book V, and which is far too realistic for the cosmopolitan's optimism. As will be seen below, Melville seems not to have known Aristotle with any great familiarity and accuracy, in spite of the fact that his works contain numerous references to him. If he read the Bohn Classical Library edition of the *Politics and Economics* (London, 1853), his eye may have fallen on the following passages, which would have been sufficient to account for the cosmopolitan's carefully measured and qualified objection to Aristotle, the cosmopolitan himself being an advocate of Platonic, Shaftesburyan, and Schilleresque views: (a) "In explaining the origin of political society, Aristotle writes neither the satire nor the panegyric of human nature; which, by writers of less wisdom than fancy, have been alternately substituted for plain history. . . . Neither the cunning, cowardly principles asserted by Hobbes and Mandeville, nor the benevolent moral affections espoused by Shaftesbury and Hutcheson, according to our author's [Aristotle's] notions, ought to be involved in the solution of the present question." (John Gillies' "Introduction," p. xxxiii.) (b) In *Politics* ii. 3, Aristotle oppugns Plato's idea that perfect unity is desirable in a state, and that a community of wives and children is desirable. The translator's footnote here (p. 38) could have suggested to Melville that it would be appropriate to bring in Aristotle on the other side of the fence from the cosmopolitan: the translator calls the theory "cosmopolitan" which is opposed to Aristotle's and which "would merge all particular and social affections into a mere system of general benevolence." (My references are to the London edition of 1876, with the same introduction, translation, and notes as in the following edition, which was available to Melville: *The Politics and Economics of Aristotle*, Translated, with Notes . . . and Analyses. To which are Prefixed, An Introductory Essay and a Life of Aristotle, by Dr. Gillies. By Edward Walford . . ., London, H. G. Bohn, 1853.)

(2) The remark which the cosmopolitan thinks is in the *Politics*, that "the least lovable men in history" seem to have hated humor but like "practical punning," is not made in the *Politics*, nor, to my knowledge, anywhere else in Aristotle. Perhaps Melville thought the tyrant Periander's advice to Thrasybulus an example of "practical punning": "Periander said nothing to the messenger sent to him with reference to the matter of advice, but that he struck off those ears of corn which were higher than the rest, and so reduced the whole crop to a level; so that the messenger, without knowing the cause of what was done, related the fact to Thrasybulus, who understood from it that he must take off all the principal men in the city." (Trans. Edward Walford; *Politics* iii. 13; the story is also told in v. 10. In both instances Aristotle has been speaking of the evils of tyranny.)

Mr. Sealts' conclusion that "first-hand knowledge of Aristotle on Melville's part is not reflected to any extent in his works" ("Herman Melville's Reading in Ancient Philosophy," p. 172, n. 54) agrees with the evidence of this paragraph of *The Confidence-Man*. At some time Melville acquired translations of *The Organon* and *The Treatise on Rhetoric*, published in 1889-1890 and 1872 respectively (Sealts, Nos. 14a, 14b).

185.33. *Phalaris:* Tyrant of Acragas in Sicily in the sixth century B. C. The story of the horse-laugh is Melville's invention, probably a deliberate analogue of the often cited example of Phalaris' cruelty, the story of the brazen bull in which the tyrant burned enemies and others. "Phalaris I" and "Phalaris II," two declamations attributed to Lucian and written with an amusing irony not unlike that of

Melville in *The Confidence-Man,* pretend to whitewash Phalaris; they dramatize an imaginary scene in which Phalaris' bull is presented to the temple of Apollo at Delphi. Phalaris in his message denies charges of cruelty, and tells the story of the invention of the Bull by Perilaus and Perilaus' device for making the victim's groans and shrieks pass through flutes in the bull's nose and become musical lowings "When I heard this I was disgusted with the wicked ingenuity of the fellow and hated the idea of the contrivance, so I gave him a punishment that fitted his crime." He induced Perilaus to get inside the bull, closed it, and lighted a fire. (Trans. A. M. Harmon.) Aristotle does not tell the story of the brazen bull, but mentions Phalaris among the tyrants who rose to the tyranny from offices of honor in the state, in *Politics* v. 10. One of the *Extracts* at the beginning of *Moby-Dick* is from *"Tooke's Lucian. The True History,"* and Melville mentions Lucian elsewhere, e.g., *Pierre,* p. 420; *Israel Potter,* Ch. 13; see also Sgt. Ben D. Kimpel, "Two Notes on Herman Melville," *American Literature,* XVI (1944), 29-32.

187.17. *Jack Cade:* An English peasant who led "Jack Cade's Rebellion" in 1640; he appears in Shakespeare's *Henry VI, Part II* as an ignorant, vulgar, bloody rebel, destroying senselessly people and institutions.

187.26. *Kossuth and Mazzini:* Lajos Kossuth (1802-1894) and Giuseppe Mazzini (1805-1872), leaders of the abortive revolutions of 1848-1849 in Hungary and Italy respectively. These revolutions in Europe are the subject of *Mardi,* Ch. 153.

189.4. *Praise be unto the press:* Miss Wright (pp. 153-157) points out Melville's paraphrase, here and there in this paragraph, of Proverbs 23:29-31, and his creation of the Biblical tone "by the use of the Psalmist's 'extol,' 'magnify,' and 'praise be unto'; by the archaic 'giveth,' 'knitteth,' 'fuseth,' 'ye.' 'Breaketh the true morning' suggests Isaiah ('Then shall thy light break forth as the morning') and 'glad tidings' is from Luke and Paul. The allusion to Noah, of course, is to the account of his drunkenness." By breaking this speech up into lines and choruses, Miss Wright gives an interesting demonstration of the way in which Melville seems to have caught not only the tone but also the form of Hebrew poetry.

189.4. *the press, not Faust's:* Johann Fust or Faust was a German printer and partner of Gutenberg from c. 1450-1455, and continued to use the press constructed by Gutenberg after the business was dissolved.

190.31. *an apple . . . a wasp's nest:* These two receptacles are
perhaps emblematic of the two boon companions: the cosmopolitan
"flushed with red and gold to the life" but a Sodom apple in reality,
the operator somewhat more obviously the waspish, brimstone
thing that he is. The Apple of Sodom, or Dead Sea Fruit, traditionally fair in appearance but turning to dust and ashes in the mouth,
is a badge elsewhere in Melville for utter desolation and emptiness:
see, for example, "The Encantadas," *The Piazza Tales,* p. 152;
Clarel, Part II, Canto xxviii. On the other hand these two receptacles
may simply repeat the opposition between appearance and reality
which is constant in *The Confidence-Man;* if this is so, the wasp
nest, the rough outside hiding a warm and living heart, would be the
reverse of the apple, as Pitch is the reverse of the Cosmopolitan.

192.16. *the advice of Polonius to Laertes: Hamlet,* I, iii, 59-80.

192.25. *Puritans . . . whom Shakespeare laughs his fill at:*
"Though honesty be no puritan, yet it will do no hurt" (*All's Well
That Ends Well,* I, iii, 98); "But one puritan amongst them
[singers], and he sings psalms to hornpipes" (*The Winter's Tale,*
IV, iii, 45-46); "that she would make a puritan of the devil, if he
should cheapen a kiss of her" (*Pericles,* IV, vi, 9-10); in *Twelfth
Night* Maria says of Malvolio that "sometimes he is a kind of puritan" (II, iii, 152), and his Puritan foibles of self-righteousness and
censoriousness are ridiculed.

193.3. *Lord Chesterfield:* See note on 133.24.

193.7. *The friends thou hast:* "Those friends thou hast, and their
adoption tried, Grapple them unto thy soul with hoops of steel"
(*Hamlet,* I, iii, 62-63). Melville has "hooks" (Pope's reading).

193.21. *sell all thou hast and give to the poor:* Matthew 19:21;
"Jesus said unto him, If thou wilt be perfect, go and sell that thou
hast, and give to the poor. . . ." The antinomy between worldly,
self-regarding, prudential ethics, extracted here from Polonius and
a little later from Emerson, and the ethics of Christ is a common
one in Melville; Plinlimmon's pamphlet, in *Pierre,* gives it expression under the trope of horological and chronometrical time.

195.1. *Shakespeare has got to be a kind of deity:* Melville says
in "Hawthorne and His Mosses": "Shakespeare has grown to be a
part of our Anglo-Saxon superstitions. . . . You must believe in
Shakespeare's unapproachability, or quit the country. But what sort
of a belief is this for an American, a man who is bound to carry
republican progressiveness into Literature as well as into Life?"

His intention, of course, is not to diminish Shakespeare, or, as the Confidence Man does, to reserve any "latent thoughts concerning him."

195.7. *Autolycus:* The witty and light-fingered rogue in *The Winter's Tale.* "Ha, ha! what a fool Honesty is! and Trust, his sworn brother, a very simple gentleman!" he says (IV, iv, 605-607). Something of a confidence man himself, he pretends to be suffering from a beating, to win the sympathy of a clown, and, when the clown is helping him, steals his purse.

199.18. *free-and-easies:* "A saloon or place of low resort." (*Dictionary of American English*)

199.19. *gold in old Peru, which Pizarro found:* Garcilasso de la Vega, the Ynca, writes that in every royal palace of the Incas, "All the cups for the whole service of the house, as well for the table as for the kitchen, were, large and small, of gold and silver." (*Commentaries,* II, 100) His *Commentaries* contain many passages describing the gold plates lining the temples of the Sun and the palaces of the Incas, the Inca's throne of solid gold set on a gold board, and the figures of men, women, animals, birds, and plants, all of gold, that decorated palaces and gardens. Francisco Pizarro, Spanish conquistador (d. 1541), reached Cajamarca, Peru, and was received by the Inca in 1532. See also note 1.4.

200.5. *Jack Ketch:* A headsman known to history for his clumsy execution of Lord Russell (1683) and the Duke of Monmouth (1685).

201.23. *when the Spaniard first entered Atahalpa's treasure chamber:* Atahualpa, the Inca monarch, who had been most perfidiously captured by Pizarro, offered to fill a room seventeen feet broad by twenty-two feet long with gold to a height of nine feet, in return for his freedom. Pizarro accepted the offer, and golden articles were brought in from all parts of the Inca empire—"goblets, ewers, salvers, vases of every shape and size, ornaments and utensils for the temples and the royal palaces, tiles and plates for the decoration of the public edifices, curious imitations of different plants and animals." After accepting the ransom, Pizarro put Atahualpa to death. (Prescott, I, 433, 464.) The "want of confidence" which the cosmopolitan says Pizarro felt, and his rapping the vessels with his knuckles, seem to have been the invention of Melville's imagination, which gave dramatic reality to every scene that it envisioned.

203.2. *A METAMORPHOSIS MORE SURPRISING THAN*

ANY IN OVID: In 1849 Melville bought Harper's Classical Library containing two volumes of Ovid, translated by "Dryden, Pope, Congreve, Addison, and Others" (Sealts, No. 147).

204.5. *Cadmus glided into the snake:* Ovid *Metamorphoses* iv. 563-603 tells how Cadmus, who sowed the dragon's teeth and founded Thebes, was so beset by troubles in his old age that he prayed to be transformed into a serpent if his troubles had sprung from his having killed a sacred serpent, and how first Cadmus and then his wife were transformed into snakes.

208.4. *CHARLEMONT:* Melville had treated much the same story as Charlemont's in "Jimmy Rose," *Harper's New Monthly Magazine,* XI (Nov. 1855), 803-807.

212.2. *IN WHICH THE COSMOPOLITAN IS ACCOSTED BY A MYSTIC:* In an early draft called "Titles for Chapters," Melville composed a title, "The practical mystic," presumably intended to cover the material of this and the next two chapters; it indicates, I believe, that he originally conceived the mystic Winsome and his practical disciple Egbert as one person. Together they embody Emerson's philosophy, as Melville saw it and caricatured it. See Introduction, pp. lxxix ff., and Appendix, p. 380.

Emerson lectured in Pittsfield while *The Confidence-Man* was being written; the *Berkshire County Eagle* (7 and 14 March), speaking of his lecture on 13 March 1856, called him "the only one," "perhaps the most popular lecturer of the day."

A careful identification of Winsome with Emerson appears in Egbert S. Oliver, "Melville's Picture of Emerson and Thoreau in *The Confidence-Man,*" *College English,* VIII (1946), 61-72. Mr. Oliver's identification of Winsome's disciple Egbert with Thoreau, however, I do not find convincing. Mr. Oliver's most telling points in this identification are, in my opinion, (1) that Thoreau *was* a disciple of Emerson (though Emerson was certainly not Thoreau's "sublime master" in the 1850's) and (2) that Egbert's disquisition on friendship is very close in idea to some passages from Thoreau's *A Week on the Concord and Merrimack Rivers*; most admirably consonant is Thoreau's "When he . . . treats his Friend like a Christian, . . . then Friendship ceases to be Friendship, and becomes charity. . . ." Mr. Oliver's third set of identifying details, however, except perhaps the fact that Winsome and Egbert are about as far apart in years as Emerson and Thoreau, seems to me too far-fetched to be significant; they are (a) two details of appearance, which are completely overshadowed by the fact that on the whole Egbert looked the opposite of Thoreau, being a "well-dressed, commercial-looking gentleman, . . . strikingly deferential"; (b) a reference to Egbert as a "promenader" about the deck, which might suggest Thoreau, who was a great walker; and (c) Egbert's being a merchant "in the *West* India trade," which is taken by Mr. Oliver to refer to Thoreau's dealings with *East* Indian or Hindu mysticism (italics mine).

In arguing his first point, Thoreau's discipleship, Mr. Oliver quotes Lowell's *A Fable for Critics* to the effect that Thoreau trod in Emerson's tracks and indeed copied him. The difference between Winsome and Egbert, however, is not so much the difference between an originator and a disciple as between a mystic and a practical man, between the man of theory who confines himself to words and the man of action who puts that theory to work. Thoreau, of course, did put some of his and Emerson's theories to work; he went to jail for his principles, and demanded of Waldo why he was not there. This point, rather surprisingly, is omitted by Mr. Oliver. Perhaps Mr. Oliver omitted it because the principles of Mark Winsome, when put into practice, were supposed to lead a man "neither to the mad-house nor to the poor-house," nor, presumably, to jail, but rather, as practiced by Egbert, had proved economically "serviceable knowledge" and made him a thriving merchant. All this is at the antipodes from Thoreau. The difference between airy theory and lucrative practice is the essential difference between Winsome and Egbert, and this makes it very hard for me to see Egbert as Thoreau. To me he seems to objectify rather the practical half, the practical application of Emerson's philosophy.

One more point. Egbert says that he is following the precepts of his "sublime" master's Essay on Friendship, meaning, of course, Emerson's essay of that name. Insofar as Thoreau repeats Emerson's ideas in the *Week* . . ., Egbert's remarks are just as close to the ideas of the one sage as the other; that is, Egbert's contention that friendship would debase itself if it became charitable could come from either. Mr. Oliver, furthermore, does not cite any passages from Thoreau to account for two other points which Egbert makes and through which Melville is satirizing, as I think, Emerson: (1) that " 'there is something wrong about the man who wants help,' " and (2) that inconsistency is not to be shunned: " 'Inconsistency? Bah!' "

Melville heard Emerson lecture in Boston in 1849; "Say what they will, he's a great man," he wrote Evert Duyckinck (24 February; Thorp, pp. 370f.), whose magazine, *The Literary World*, was in the habit of treating with gentle ridicule both Transcendentalism and Emerson himself. Melville, defending himself in his next letter (3 [March]; Thorp, pp. 371-373) to his friend, declared that he did not "oscillate in Emerson's rainbow," but that he nevertheless thought the man "more than a brilliant fellow," "an uncommon man," if a humbug, then "no common humbug": "I was very agreeably disappointed in Mr. Emerson. I had heard of him as full of transcendentalisms, myths & oracular gibberish; I had only glanced at a book of his once in Putnam's store—that was all I knew of him, till I heard him lecture.—To my surprise, I found him quite intelligible, tho' to say truth, they told me that night he was unusually plain.—Now, there is something about every man elevated above mediocrity, which is, for the most part, instinctively perceptible. This I see in Mr. Emerson. And, frankly, for the sake of the argument, let us call him a fool;—Then had I rather be a fool than a wise man.—I love all men who dive. . . .

"I could readily see in Emerson, notwithstanding his merit, a gaping flaw. It was, the insinuation, that had he lived in those days when the world was made, he might have offered some valuable suggestions. These men are all cracked right across the brow. . . . But enough of this Plato who talks thro' his nose. . . .

"You complain that Emerson tho' a denizen of the land of gingerbread, is above munching a plain cake in company of jolly fellows, & swiging [*sic*] off his ale like you & me. Ah, my dear sir, that's his misfortune, not his fault. His belly, sir, is in his chest, & his brains descend down into his neck, & offer an obstacle to a draught of ale or a mouthful of cake."

Until recently, the only evidence that Melville read Emerson before he acquired the *Poems* in 1859, the *Essays*, first and second series, in 1862, and *The Conduct of Life* in 1870 (Sealts, Nos. 206, 204, 205, 203) has been internal evidence in his short stories and novels, particularly *Pierre* and *The Confidence-Man*; but this testimony can hardly be gainsaid. Now the publication of a letter from Mrs. Nathaniel Hawthorne to her mother provides the external evidence: speaking of Melville's visits to the Hawthorne home in the summer and early autumn of 1850, she says that "one morning he shut himself into the boudoir & read Mr. Emerson's Essays in presence of our beautiful picture" (an engraving of the Transfiguration presented by Emerson). (Eleanor Melville Metcalf, *Herman Melville: Cycle and Epicycle*, Cambridge, Mass., 1953, p. 91) Surely Melville also discussed his famous contemporary with Hawthorne, who had been a neighbor of Emerson in Concord from 1842 to 1846. Of the thirty essays in Melville's three volumes, fourteen are marked and annotated by Melville; since among the unmarked essays are "Compensation," "Self-Reliance," and "Friendship," to which passages in *Pierre* and *The Confidence-Man* almost certainly refer, one may reasonably surmise that Melville left these and probably others of the more famous compositions unmarked in the 1860's for the reason that he was already familiar with them.

Although Melville's marginal comments on Emerson's essays in these volumes were jotted down a number of years after the double portrait of Emerson in *The Confidence-Man* was drawn, it seems safe to use them to establish Melville's intention in this portrait, since their agreement with his criticism of Emerson in the letters of 1849 indicates that his general opinion of him did not change greatly.

212.8. *a blue-eyed man, . . . perhaps five-and-forty:* When Melville had heard Emerson lecture in Boston in 1849, Emerson was forty-six. (Letters to Evert Duyckinck, 24 February [1849] and 3 [March 1849]; Thorp, pp. 370-373.) According to Emerson's son, "Mr. Emerson was tall,—six feet in his shoes,—erect until his latter days, neither very thin nor stout in frame, with rather narrow and unusually sloping shoulders, and long neck, but very well poised head, and a dignity of carriage. His eyes were very blue, his hair dark brown, his complexion clear and always with good color." (E. W. Emerson, *Emerson in Concord: A Memoir*, Boston, 1889, p. 156.)

212.10. *a certain angularity:* Cf. Mrs. Hawthorne's description of Emerson skating: "Emerson, too weary to hold himself erect, pitching headforemost, half lying in the air." (Nathaniel Hawthorne, *The American Notebooks*, ed. Randall Stewart, New Haven, 1932, p. 311, n. 331.)

212.12. *Puritan sort . . . farmer dignity:* Such details as "Puritan," "farmer," and "clover" remind one of Emerson's identification, by his inheritance and through his thinking, with New England, and his life among the fields and orchards of Concord.

212.14. *youthfulness in maturity:* Cf. Charles Eliot Norton's poem, "To R. W. Emerson" (quoted in *Emerson in Concord,* p. 259), ending: "And thou, though full of days, shalt die in youth."

212.21. *shrewdness and mythiness, strangely jumbled:* Melville underlines the union of opposites in Winsome, Cf. his comments on Emerson in the letter to Evert Duyckinck given in note 212.2. "I had heard of him as full of transcendentalisms, myths & oracular gibberish. . . ." "But enough of this Plato who talks thro' his nose."

213.8. *a statue in the Pitti Palace:* Melville lost no time in visiting the Pitti Palace when he arrived in Florence in March 1857 (*Journal up the Straits,* pp. 145, 149.) In *A Fable for Critics* Lowell says of Emerson that "To the men he thinks worthy he frankly accords The design of a white marble statue in words."

213.10. *a beautiful soul:* In Emerson's Platonic trinity of goodness, truth, and beauty, love is implicit, being practically identified with virtue in the essay on "Friendship" and with beauty in the "Ode to Beauty": love, in the essay by that name, is an education of the soul through the beauty, virtue, and wisdom apprehended in the beloved; celestial love is the love of the oneness of all things, in the poem "Initial, Daemonic and Celestial Love."

213.14. *Yes, with you and Schiller:* See particularly the poem "The Artists" and the essay "On Grace and Dignity" of Johann Friedrich von Schiller (1759-1805). In the essay Schiller says: ". . . in that the mind (in virtue of a law that we cannot fathom) . . . itself prescribes to physical nature which accompanies it, its own state, and in that the state of moral perfection is precisely . . . the most favourable for the accomplishment of the physical conditions of beauty it follows that it is the mind which renders beauty possible. . . ." "It is then in a noble soul that is found the true harmony between reason and sense, between inclination and duty, and grace is the expression of this harmony in the sensuous world." (*Aesthetical and Philosophical Essays,* ed. Nathan H. Dole, *The Works of Friedrich Schiller,* Vol. I, Boston, 1902, pp. 197, 209.) Melville acquired Schiller's *Poems and Ballads* in 1849 (Sealts, No. 439). There are references to Schiller in a letter to Hawthorne (June [?] 1851; Thorp, p. 389) and in *Journal up the Straits* (p. 32), and to "The Veiled Statue at Sais" in *Moby-Dick* (p. 336).

213.17. *"The rattle-snake, whose lithe neck":* See Introduction, pp. lxxxiii f.

214.14. *So that whoever is destroyed by a rattlesnake, . . . it is his own fault:* There is "always a reason *in the man,* for his good or bad fortune. . . ." (*Works*, VI, 100). In perhaps the most striking passage in which Emerson admitted the existence of evil in the universe and tried to include it within his optimistic scheme of things, he said: "We like to see everything do its office after its kind, whether it be a milch-cow or a rattlesnake." ("Napoleon; or, The Man of the World," *Works*, IV, 235).

214.17. *Who will pity the charmer:* This introduces a series of references to the Apocrypha: "Who will pity a charmer bitten by a serpent?" Ecclesiasticus 12:13.

216.1. *a pleasing Arabian romance:* Emerson recounted an Arabian story of hospitality in "Heroism" (1841) (*Works*, II, 253-254), and copied another into his *Journals*, (Boston, 1909-1914, IX, 539).

216.5. *in the lasting condition of an untried abstraction:* Melville alluded several times to Emerson's unconvivial habits: for example, see Introduction, pp. lxxv f. Melville disagreed, in a marginal comment, with Emerson's statement in "The Poet" about the deterioration of men of genius who found exhilaration in pleasure; "He has his Dardanelles for his every Marmora," concluded Melville. Melville's copies of Emerson's writings, containing Melville's markings and marginal comments, are in HCL-M; for these marginalia, in print, see William Braswell, "Melville as a Critic of Emerson," *American Literature*, IX (1937), 317-334; F. O. Matthiessen, *American Renaissance* (New York, 1941), *passim*.

216.7. *Hafiz:* There are many oriental allusions in Emerson's writings. Besides scattered references and quotations throughout his works, Emerson wrote an essay, "Persian Poetry," the preface of the first American edition of Saadi's *Gulistan* (1865), translations of Hafiz (Persian lyric poet, d. 1389?) and other Persian writers, using a German translation, and original poems inspired by Persian and Hindu literature; see F. I. Carpenter, *Emerson and Asia* (Cambridge, 1930), especially his Chap. VI, "Persian Poetry," and Chap. VII, "Arabian Literature and the Koran." See also J. D. Yohannan, "Emerson's Translations of Persian Poetry from German Sources," *American Literature*, XIV (1942), 407-420, and his "The Influence of Persian Poetry on Emerson's Work," *American Literature*, XV (1943), 25-41; and Arthur Christy, *The Orient in American Transcendentalism* (New York, 1932).

216.33. *I seldom care to be consistent:* Cf. Emerson in "Self-Reliance" (1841): "Suppose you should contradict yourself; what then? . . . A foolish consistency is the hobgoblin of little minds. . . . With consistency a great soul has simply nothing to do. . . . speak what you think now in hard words and to-morrow speak what to-morrow thinks in hard words again, though it contradict everything you said to-day." (*Works*, II, 57)

217.18. *the ancient Egyptians . . . Proclus:* This "oracular gibberish" fits one of Melville's early impressions of Emerson; see note 212.2. For a discussion of Emerson's indebtedness to Plato in general, to Proclus, and to Iamblichus' *Mysteries of the Egyptians, Chaldeans, and Assyrians*, see J. S. Harrison, *The Teachers of Emerson* (New York, 1910). Melville had already mocked, in *Mardi* in a number of passages, the esoteric doctrine and the peculiar terminology of Proclus as "gibberish," as Merton M. Sealts, Jr. has demonstrated in "Melville's Neoplatonical Originals,'" *Modern Language Notes*, LXVII (1952), 80-86. "It is certain," he says, that Melville "was acquainted with *The Six Books of Proclus on the Theology of Plato*, . . . for unmistakable borrowings from it can be seen in several of the mock-philosophical passages of *Mardi*. His satirical treatment of this abstruse source-material and his later reference to Proclus in *The Confidence-Man* (1857), both so different in tone from Emerson's attitude, are an indication of Melville's hostility to certain characteristics of Transcendentalism, ancient and modern."

217.30. *A favor!:* See Melville's satire of Emerson's views on friendship in Chs. 39-41 of *The Confidence-Man*. See also Introduction, pp. lxxvi ff.

218.9. *Arrian:* Mr. Sealts ("Herman Melville's Reading in Ancient Philosophy," pp. 160, 162) takes this mention of Arrian as evidence of Melville's first-hand knowledge of Epictetus; Arrian (fl. second century), a disciple, preserved the thought of Epictetus in *The Discourses of Epictetus* and *Manual of Ethics of Epictetus*.

218.34. *talk not against mummies:* Cf. *A Fable for Critics*, 11. 565-576, on Emerson:

> So perfect a balance there is in his head,
> That he talks of things sometimes as if they were dead;
> Life, nature, love, God, and affairs of that sort,
> He looks at as merely ideas; in short,
> As if they were fossils stuck round in a cabinet,
> Of such vast extent that our earth's a mere dab in it; . . .
> With the quiet precision of science he'll sort 'em,
> But you can't help suspecting the whole a *post mortem*.

223.25. *meekly standing like a Raphael:* Mr. Pommer points out (p. 72) that Melville is echoing a line of *Paradise Lost* (VII, 217), which occurs in the dialogue between the archangel Raphael and Adam: "To whom thus Raphael answered heavenly meek." He notes other references to Raphael, also with Miltonic associations, in *Clarel*, III, xxxi, and in the brief prose sketch "Marquis de Grandvin."

223.25. *in golden accents old Memnon murmurs:* A colossus near ancient Egyptian Thebes (now Luxor and Karnak), actually a statue of King Amenōphis of the eighteenth dynasty, was given the name of Memnon by the Greeks; at morning, when the rays of the sun struck it, it gave forth a musical sound, which was said to be Memnon's greeting to his mother, Eos, goddess of the dawn. The cause of the sound was something of a "riddle"; Strabo and others thought it was a trick of the priests; it may have been naturally caused by the sun's action. The sound has not been heard since the partial destruction of the statue by earthquake. Memnon was an Ethiopian youth (later supposed to have lived in Egypt), son of Eos (Aurora) and Tithonus, who fought in the Trojan War and was killed by Achilles. Melville tells his story in *Pierre* (p. 159): "For Memnon was that dewy, royal boy, son of Aurora, born King of Egypt, who, with enthusiastic rashness flinging himself on another's account into a rightful quarrel, fought hand to hand with his overmatch, and met his boyish and most dolorous death beneath the walls of Troy. His wailing subjects built a monument in Egypt to commemorate his untimely fate. Touched by the breath of the bereaved Aurora, every sunrise that statue gave forth a mournful broken sound, as of a harp-string suddenly sundered, being too harshly wound."

223.30. *mystery . . . but still the plain truth remains:* Cf. *A Fable for Critics*, 11. 593-594, on Emerson: "E. sits in a mystery calm and intense, And looks coolly around him with sharp common sense."

223.35. *Was not Seneca a usurer?:* Lucius Annaeus Seneca (c. 3 B.C.–65 A.D.), Roman Stoic philosopher, dramatist, statesman, and tutor of Nero, through whose favor he amassed great wealth. Tacitus writes that Publius Suilius taunted Seneca, saying, among other things, " 'By what kind of wisdom or maxims of philosophy had Seneca within four years of royal favour amassed three hundred million sesterces? At Rome the wills [*testamenta*] of the childless were, so to say, caught in his snare, while Italy and the provinces were drained by a boundless usury [*inmenso faenore*].'" (*Annals* xiii. 42, trans. Alfred John Church.) *Dio's Roman History* (lxii. 2) gives as one reason for the uprising in Britain in 61 A.D. "the fact that Seneca, in the hope of receiving a good rate of interest, had lent to the islanders 40,000,000 sesterces that they did not want, and had afterwards called in this loan all at once and had resorted to severe measures in exacting it." (Trans. Earnest Cary.) See also note on 54.22.

223.36. *Bacon a courtier:* Bacon became adviser to the crown in 1604, keeper of the great seal in 1617, and lord chancellor in 1618. See also 55.30 and 154.6.

223.36 *and Swedenborg, though with one eye on the invisible:* Emanuel Swedenborg (1688-1772), Swedish scientist, philosopher, and theologian, whose family was ennobled in 1719 and who, in the first half of his life, became widely known for his skill as an engineer and his books on various sciences, and was assessor of the Royal College of Mines; but who in 1743-1744 began having mystic experiences in which he believed that revelations were made direct to him by God and which he made the basis for a number of theological works. Melville made friends with George J. Adler aboard the *Southampton* going to Europe in 1849; Adler talked with him about Swedenborg and other philosophers. (*Journal . . . 1849-1850*, p. 4.) There are brief references to Swedenborg in "I and My Chimney" and *Journal up the Straits* (p. 141).

229.26. *the sour mind of Solomon:* Proverbs 18:24: "A man that hath friends must shew himself friendly; and there is a friend that sticketh closer than a brother." Proverbs 27:10: "Thine own friend, and thy father's friend, forsake not; neither go into thy brother's house in the day of thy calamity, for better is a neighbor that is near than a brother far off." In the traditional fashion, Melville spoke of Solomon as the author of Proverbs, Ecclesiastes, and the Song of Songs. There are many references in Melville to Solomon; "I read Solomon more and more, and every time see deeper and deeper and unspeakable meanings in him," he wrote to Hawthorne ([June, 1851]; Thorp, p. 392). See also 88.33 and 248.12.

229.28. *Essay on Friendship:* See pp. lxxvi-lxxviii, 352, 354.

230.32. *the good Samaritan:* Also referred to on 86.30.

232.21. *the fate of the first-born of Egypt:* Exodus 12:29.

234.2. *CHINA ASTER:* In this name Melville calls to mind not only the common garden flower, in contrast with the exotic and epiphytic Orchis, but also, by etymology, the stars, like which China Aster sheds light "through the darkness of a planet benighted." See Melville's "Field Asters," in *Collected Poems*, p. 269. In 1870 Melville wrote "Sketch of Major Thomas Melvill by a Nephew," which recalls the language and to some extent the theme of his story of China Aster; speaking of his Uncle Thomas, he says:

> I remember his telling me that upon one occasion, after prosperously closing in London some considerable affair, he held in his hands, before a cheery coal fire, the proceeds—negotiable bills, and for so large a sum, that he said to himself—holding them at arm's length, "This much is sure—here it is—the future is uncertain. Break it off, then, and get thee back to Boston Common." But a false friend—Hope by name (not one of the noted Amsterdam House) advised the contrary.

Also of his Uncle Thomas: ". . . fortune and his own too sanguine temper were his undoing." A copy of Melville's "Sketch . . ." is in NYPL-GL; the quotations above are published in Gilman, *Melville's Early Life and Redburn*, pp. 65f.

Dan G. Hoffman, "Melville's 'Story of China Aster,'" *American Literature*, XXII (1950), 137-149, follows Richard Chase's general interpretation of *The Confidence-Man* and discusses this interpolated story as an "explication of the conflict between the two opposing forces which dominate the book: the Promethean-creative-civilizing impulse versus its opposite, the surrender of moral judgments and the perversion of the Promethean spirit to private ends at the expense of mankind," China Aster being the Prometheus of the story.

237.15. *as Eliphaz, Bildad, and Zophar did:* Their colloquy with Job occupies Job 3-31.

243.18. *Death himself on the pale horse:* Revelation 6:8.

243.26. *Come-Outers:* "The name originally applied to certain religious dissenters. . . . Such a group flourished in New England, about 1840, including that group of non-resistance Abolitionists." Cape Cod "Come-Outers" were opposed to a regular ministry, and "formed a holy alliance with the Transcendentalists." (Quoted in *Dictionary of American English.*)

248.12. *THE SOBER PHILOSOPHY OF SOLOMON THE WISE:* Melville had declared that: "The truest of all men was the Man of Sorrows, and the truest of all books is Solomon's, and Ecclesiastes is the fine hammered steel of woe. 'All is vanity.' ALL. This wilful world hath not got hold of unchristian Solomon's wisdom yet. But he who dodges hospitals and jails, and walks fast crossing graveyards, and would rather talk of operas than hell; calls Cowper, Young, Pascal, Rousseau, poor devils all of sick men; and throughout a care-free lifetime swears by Rabelais as passing wise, and therefore jolly;—not that man is fitted to sit down on tombstones, and break the green damp mould with unfathomably wondrous Solomon." (*Moby-Dick*, p. 422.) Many passages in Proverbs and Ecclesiastes, then commonly attributed to Solomon, would persuade against the "ardently bright view of life"; one of several that fit China Aster's case is Proverbs 25:19: "Confidence in an unfaithful man in time of trouble is like a broken tooth, and a foot out of joint." See other references to Solomon on 88.33 and 229.26. See also Wright, *passim*.

252.4. *Inconsistency? Bah!:* Emerson: "A foolish consistency is the hobgoblin of little minds. . . ." See 216.33 and note.

253.19. *All the world's a stage: As You Like It,* II, vii, 139-142. Melville has "Who" instead of "They" in 1.141. This quotation is, of course, a reminder of the Masquerade, which Egbert suddenly suspected.

254.8. *Souter John and Tam O'Shanter:* Tam's "ancient, trusty, drouthy crony" and himself, hero of Robert Burns' poem "Tam O'Shanter." The vision that drunken, bewildered Tam saw was of "warlocks and witches" and "auld Nick, in shape of beast." Somnus and Morpheus, gods of sleep and dreams respectively.

254.26. *just as the townsfold called the angels:* Genesis 19:5.

254.28. *the devils who, in man's form, haunted the tombs:* Matthew 8:28; Mark 5:2. In his journal of the trip to the Mediterranean and the Holy Land which he made immediately after finishing *The Confidence-Man,* Melville jotted down this, in a section called "Jerusalem": "*Wandering among the tombs*—till I began to think myself one of the possessed with devils." (*Journal up the Straits,* p. 79.)

255.35. *Thersites:* reviler of the Greek leaders in the *Iliad* (Book II), especially of Agamemnon, the chief leader and a valiant fighter. Melville had bought Pope's translation of Homer in 1849. He preferred Chapman's translation, as his annotations show; he took Chapman's *Iliad* and *Odyssey,* which George Duyckinck had given him in 1858, with him on his trip around Cape Horn in 1860. (See Sealts, Nos. 147, 277, 278, and p. 272, n. 108.) Possibly Melville also had in mind the Thersites and Agamemnon of Shakespeare's *Troilus and Cressida.*

260.2. *Timon:* See note on 157.7.

261.2. *VERY CHARMING:* An earlier draft of this title is more specific: "In which the Cosmopolitan . . . earns the title of the man-charmer but not in the same sense that certain East Indians are called snake-charmers . . . pretty much in the same rank with the snak[e]." See pp. lxxxiii, 384. The wide interest in Mesmerism and animal magnetism in the mid-nineteenth century might be sufficient to account for Melville's inclusion of hypnotic spells in his stories were it not for the singular and consistent use that he makes of enchantments; with rare exceptions (e.g., *Redburn,* Ch. 56), they are the means of the triumph of something malign. The magazines of the period were full of articles on Mesmerism and snake-charming; see, for example, *Harper's New Monthly Magazine,* to which Melville subscribed (Sealts, No. 240), for March 1855 and April 1856. Further evidence of Melville's interest comes from the Duyckinck diary quoted on p. xxv; Melville, talking with Duyckinck shortly after he finished writing *The Confidence-Man,* cited a story from the *Decameron* as "good," the story of the "*Enchantment* of the husband in the tree" (ninth story on the seventh day); Duyckinck's underlining suggests that the enchantment itself was the chief subject of Melville's interest.

261.12. *I am Philanthropos, and love mankind:* Cf. Timon's "I am misanthropos, and hate mankind." (*Timon of Athens,* IV, iii, 52.) See note on 157.7.

261.22. *the three kings of Cologne:* At Cologne are venerated relics supposed to be the bones of the three Magi who visited the infant Jesus. For the protection of Melville's joke, perhaps it ought to be said that the Magi are patrons of travelers and pilgrims, and Saints Cosmo and Damian are patrons of barbers and surgeons (S. Young, *The Annals of the Barber-Surgeons of London,* London, 1890, pp. 433, 435). The masts of the *Pequod* "stood stiffly up like the spines of the three old kings of Cologne" (*Moby-Dick,* p. 68). Melville saw "the tomb of the *Three Kings of Cologne*—their skulls" in the cathedral at Cologne on Sunday 9 December 1849 (*Journal . . . 1849-1850,* p. 62.)

267.34. *An enemy speaketh sweetly with his lips:* Ecclesiasticus 12:16.

267.25. *I believed not his many words:* "believe not his many words." Ecclesiasticus 13:11.

268.29. *but little change with me just now:* The reader will remember that he had fifty dollars in his pocket shortly before, when he acted the necromancer with Noble.

270.11. *original characters in fiction:* Cf. Melville's thoughts upon this subject in *Pierre* (pp. 304f.): "And in the inferior instances of an immediate literary success, in very young writers, it will be almost invariably observable, that for that instant success they were chiefly indebted to some rich and peculiar experience in life, embodied in a book, which because, for that cause, containing original matter, the author himself, forsooth, is to be considered original; in this way, many very original books, being the product of very unoriginal minds. Indeed, man has only to be but a little circumspect, and away flies the last rag of his vanity. The world is forever babbling of originality; but there never yet was an original man, in the sense intended by the world; the first man himself—who according to the Rabbins was also the first author—not being an original; the only original author being God. Had Milton's been the lot of Casper Hauser, Milton would have been vacant as he. For though the naked soul of man doth assuredly contain one latent element of intellectual productiveness; yet never was there a child born solely from one parent; the visible world of experience being that procreative thing which impregnates the muses; self-reciprocally efficient hermaphrodites being but a fable."

270.15. *Hamlet . . . Don Quixote . . . Milton's Satan:* Melville made most conspicuous use of *Hamlet* in *Pierre*, comparing and contrasting his youthful idealist with Shakespeare's; see particularly pp. 159, 197-201. "Don Quixote, that sagest sage that ever lived," he pronounced in "The Piazza," (*The Piazza Tales*, p. 7). See Introduction, p. xciv, n. 88, on Melville's reading and marking of *Don Quixote*. The influence of Milton's Satan upon Melville's works, especially upon *Moby-Dick*, has been most fully studied by Mr. Pommer in Ch. 6 of his *Milton and Melville*.

272.3. *a solar lamp:* the light of the Old and New Testaments, to judge from its two transparencies, the horned altar and the robed man with a halo. On Mount Sinai the Lord gave Moses directions for making the altar, with "the horns of it upon the four corners thereof" (Exodus 27:2); other references to the horned altar of the Old Testament are Exodus 29:12; Leviticus 8:15; 9:9; 16:18; I Kings 1:50, 51; 2:28; Psalms 118:27.

273.4. *Simeon:* Luke 3:25-35.

274.28. *With much communication he will tempt thee:* This passage is a patchwork of passages from Ecclesiasticus 13: verses 11: ". . . with much communication will he tempt thee . . ."; 6: ". . . he will . . . smile upon thee. . . ; he will speak thee fair, and say, What wantest thou?" 4: "If thou be for his profit, he will use thee. . . ." 5: ". . . he will make thee bare, and will not be sorry for it." 13: "Observe and take good heed . . .: when thou hearest these things, awake in thy sleep." Melville has "bear" for "bare."

276.6. *Take heed of thy friends:* Ecclesiasticus 6:13. Miss Nathalia Wright (p. 101) points out that the characters towards the end of the book "converse by quoting from Ecclesiasticus," and that these cynical quotations are antiphonal to the quotations from I Corinthians 13 at the beginning.

276.9. *Rochefoucault:* See note 184.6.

277.21. *Murillo's wild beggar-boy's:* In *Redburn* (Ch. 49) Melville had described an emigrant Italian boy as "such a boy as Murillo often painted, when he went among the poor and outcast, for subjects wherewith to captivate the eyes of rank and wealth; such a boy, as only Andalusian beggars are, full of poetry, gushing from every rent." While he was in London in 1849, he visited the Dulwich gallery: "The gallery is full of gems—Titians, Claudes, Salvators, Murillos.—The Peasant Boys—the Venus—the Peasant Girl. . . ." (*Journal . . . 1849-1850,* p. 34.)

280.11. *Counterfeit Detector: Van Court's Counterfeit Detector* was published semi-monthly at Philadelphia.

284.27. *Jehovah shall be thy confidence:* Proverbs 3:26: "For the Lord shall be thy confidence. . . ."

286.8. *Something further may follow:* This has been taken by many critics to indicate that Melville intended to write a sequel. Perhaps it does. In his *Journal up the Straits* he penciled "For the Story" opposite this jotting: "Pera, the headquarters of ambassadors, and where also an unreformed diplomacy is carried on by swindlers, gamblers, cheats, no place in the world fuller of knaves"; and in Venice he noted that his guide, Antonio, was "good character for Con. Man"; the notes that he took of Antonio's conversation show Antonio as a happy-go-lucky, somewhat cynical "philosopher," salty of speech. (*Journal up the Straits,* pp. 39, 157f.; "Con. Man" is mistranscribed as "com. man" in Weaver's edition.) Yet perhaps Melville meant that Antonio would have been, rather than will be, a good character for *The Confidence-Man;* and his note about Pera may have referred to an unrelated story that he had in mind, for Melville had already written a good many things more or less in the picaresque vein. Also, the fact that the ambiguous final sentence of *The Confidence-Man* is not in a separate paragraph is evidence of a sort that its reference is to the final event of the novel and its implications. Whether or not Melville intended to continue the Masquerade, the design of *The Confidence-Man* is whole and complete, and one wonders how he could have pushed his argument further in a sequel. For a summary of the evidence in favor of a sequel, see Howard C. Horsford, "Evidence of Melville's Plans for a Sequel to *The Confidence-Man*," *American Literature*, XXIV (1952), 85-89.

TEXTUAL NOTES

The present edition, except for the emendations noted below and omission of periods after title, chapter titles, and chapter numbers, follows that of the American first edition (New York: Dix, Edwards & Co., 1857). With this the first English edition (London: Longman, Brown, Green, Longmans, & Roberts, 1857) is here collated. These were the only editions of the novel published during the author's lifetime; he saw neither of them through the press.

The numbers below represent page and line numbers in the text of the novel, the first number standing for the page, the second for the line.

Emendations

To conform to his usage elsewhere in the basic text, and also, in most instances, in the English edition of 1857, Melville's spelling, punctuation, and use of italics have been changed as follows: 9.5: tamborine *to* tambourine; 15.27, 20.31, 60.4: aint *to* ain't; 19.2: ACQUANTANCE *to* ACQUAINTANCE; 37.34: Good-by *to* Good-bye; 39.24: prevailent *to* prevalent; 56.9 and 115.17: bona fide *to* *bona fide*; 155.28: coquets *to* coquettes; 167.3: red-man *to* red man; 193.11: principal *to* principle; 220.21: then *to* then,; 223.2: self-complaisant *to* self-complacent; 229.11: a-head *to* ahead.

The following errors, which were obviously or fairly obviously mistakes either of the printer or of the copyist, have been corrected as follows: viii.33: music *to* magic; 20.28: don't *to* "don't; 39.23: make *to* may make; 39.30: imperfectly qualified *to* was imperfectly qualified; 40.21: prejudices *to* prejudice; 41.2: there by *to* thereby; 54.24: standway *to* stand way; 75.3: brightening." *to* brightening.; 90.15: incurable?" *to* incurable."; 96.11: faces) ladies *to* faces), "ladies; 104.17: since *to* "since; 105.7: to wardsthe *to* towards the; 106.18: story *to* story?; 142.33: suppose. *to* suppose."; 144.27: boys' *to* boys,; 152.35: cured? *to* cured?'; 156.2: mean; it *to* mean it;; 156.5: worldlingg, lutton *to* worldling, glutton; 156.13: confinement? *to* confinement?"; 175.35: ands *to* and; 190.11: grave! *to* grave!"; 196.6: with in *to* within; 217.28: defition *to* definition; 217.29: favor. *to* favor."; 227.13: you, *to* you; 232.34: Charlie. *to* Charlie."; 233.3: him. *to* him."; 233.13: it. *to* it."; 243.22: At *to* "At; 248.30: ihat *to* that; 255.28: *Trust?*" "No *to Trust?* No; 262.33: hearts? *to* hearts?"; 274.3: so ciety *to* society; 276.24: wisdom. *to* wisdom."; 279.25: nor *to* "nor.

Variants

Variant American and British spellings are not indicated in these textual notes except in the following list. The words in this list, and their compounds and inflectional forms, are consistently given the first spelling in the American and the second spelling in the English edition:

> apologize, apologise; ardor, ardour; authorize, authorise; barreled, barrelled; biased, biassed; candor, candour; caviler, caviller; chiseled, chiselled; clamor, clamour; color, colour; corseted, corsetted; defense, defence; demeanor, demeanour; endeavor, endeavour; eying, eyeing; favor, favour; favorite, favourite; flavor, flavour; gormandizings, gourmandizings; harbor, harbour; harmonize, harmonise; honor, honour; humor, humour; labor, labour; neighbor, neighbour; organize, organise; parlor, parlour; practicing, practising; rattle-snake, rattlesnake; rumor, rumour; skeptic, sceptic; succor, succour; sympathize, sympathise; tasseled, tasselled; traveler, traveller; traveling, travelling; vapor, vapour; vitalize, vitalise; willful, wilful; worshiper, worshipper.

The American edition regularly uses the word "Chapter" throughout the Table of Contents and at the beginning of chapters; the British edition uses "Chap." in these places. The American edition supplies no page numbers for chapters in the Table of Contents.

ix.13 unbends,] unbends 1.19 nigh] near 1.21 East;] East— 1.25 theatre-bill] play-bill 2.14 such] so 3.4 illy] ill 3.29 was] were 4.10 "NO TRUST."] "NO TRUST;"— 4.11 An] an 4.25 alone] only 4.28 nigh] near 6.25 near] hard 9.5 tamborine] tambourine 10.2 rolls] roll 10.37 nigh to] near 12.15 proved] was found 12.15 whose condemnation was deemed . . . , so that they] his condemnation being deemed . . . , they 12.30 you?" here] you here?" 12.35 eagerly] eagarly 13.1 weed] weed° *footnote:* °Crape on his

hat. 13.12 ge'mmen's] ge'mman's 13.22 "Wild goose chase!"]
"Wild-goose-chace!" 13.23 nigh] near 14.18 inkept] inward 17.26
nigher] nearer 19.2 ACQUANTANCE] ACQUAINTANCE 19.7
office,] office 20.22 Werter's] Werther's 20.28 smiling, don't]
smiling, "don't 24.4 hear,] hear 24.10 name,] name 26.11 something] somewhat 27.25 sophomore] sophomore* *footnote:* *A student in his second year. 28.28 There] there 32.29 that,] that 33.24
squirm,] "squirm," 33.36 So,] So 34.20 who] whom 35.18 do,]
do 36.11 all] all that 36.16 deviltry] devilry 37.13 You] you 39.13
winsome] winning 39.15 as,] as 39.23 it make] it may make 39.24
prevailent] prevalent 40.5 inner-side] inner side 40.5 coat-skirts]
coat skirts 40.18 dyed] died 41.2 there by] thereby 42.23 tune,]
tune 44.28 financier] financier, 45.19 By-the-way] By the way
47.32 look] look of 48.26 xiii.] thirteenth 49.24 stranger,] stranger
— 49.33 me,] me 50.13 half-mourning,] half-mourning,— 50.17 As
] as

51.9 which] which, 51.26 you] You 51.27 relief,] relief— 52.2
ten-dollar] ten dollar 52.10 embarrassment] embarrasment 53.10
small,] small 53.23 How,] How 54.3 naturally-quiet] naturally
quiet 54.26 youth.] youth, 55.36 called,] called 56.9 bona fide]
bonâ fide 56.19 is, *bona*] is *bonâ* 56.25 Ha ha!—now] Ha, ha!—Now
56.26 forever] for ever 57.10 philosophes] *philosophes* 57.29 doubt,
] doubt 57.29 moonstruck] moon-struck 58.14 ode,] ode,— 59.21 the
] his 59.31 him] him, 60.4 aint] ain't 60.16 cabin-full] cabinfull 61.
30 pray,] pray? 63.6 A] It is a 63.6 superstition,] superstition 63.8
continually. True] continually;—true 63.24 away. To] away;—to 64.
30 gray] grey 66.11 large,] large 66.15 not considering] considering
66.18 nature,] nature 66.33 arm or hand] hand or arm 67.33 duty
] duty, 68.1 husband,] husband 68.9 Ere] *new paragraph:* Ere
70.5 savan] *savan* 70.9 savan's] *savan's* 10.13 friend] friend, 70.14
savan] *savan* 70.15 Humphrey] Humphry 70.25 savan] *savan*
71.30 something far] something 71.31 her,] her 72.28 that,] that
73.20 heart,] heart 73.20 points,] points 73.32 case;] case: 74.3
that,] that 74.16 Ah] ah 75.3 brightening."] brightening. 76.10
this,] this 76.27 page,] page 80.8 lost;] lost 81.20 slumber.—]
slumber. 83.4 aboard] abroad 83.23 an hundred] a hundred 86.5
gurgling,] gurgling 86.7 huzzar] hussar 86.12 over,] over 87.5
saying] saying, 88.32 names,] names 89.2 Æson?"] Æson"? 89.22
Preisnitz] Priessnitz 90.15 incurable?"] incurable." 92.22 reject.]
reject? 94.6 Japas] Iapus 96.1 possibly] Possibly 96.11 faces)]

faces,) 97.6 than] than, 97.37 war] war, 98.1 sighed,] sighed; 98.18 specific,] specific

102.11 stood,] stood 102.31 lady,] lady 103.24 huzzar] hussar 104.17 since] "since 105.7 to wardsthe] towards the 105.9 wizened] wizzened 105.10 paralyzed] paralysed 107.1 unfortunate,] unfortunate! 115.36 mighty,] mighty 116.2 sooner.—] sooner. 116.21 Jones street] Jones-street 116.22 Jones street] Jones-street 120.10 and] and, 120.19 greeting] "greeting" 123.18 deny,] deny 123.27 blind] blind, 124.14 Nature] nature 127.28 therefore,] therefore 128.13 thrust, "but] thrust. "But 130.19 represent,] represent 130.20 pass,] pass 130.31 skunks.] skunks 131.29 patent-office] patent office 134.21 rail-road] railroad 136.29 "well] well 139.13 sir,] sir 139.13 be)] be), 139.23 bearskin] bear-skin 139.25 bread,] bread 140.10 ones.] ones? 140.33 man',] man,' 142.18 You, you] You, you, 142.33 suppose.] suppose." 144.19 marines] marines, 144.27 boys'] boys, 146.7 alacrity,] alacrity 147.8 Typhus] Typhus, 147.16 it audibly] it 148.33 tobacco-smoke] tobacco smoke 149.14 than] but 150.2 Nuremburgh] Nuremberg

151.23 have . . . even] have even 151.35 eaves-dropper?] eaves-dropper. 152.1 Intelligence-office] intelligence-office 152.35 cured? 'Indeed] cured?' 'Indeed 153.11 "the] the 154.1 men.] men? 154.25 pieces,] pieces 155.28 coquets] coquettes 156.2 mean; it] mean it; 156.5 worldlingg, lutton] worldling, glutton 156.13 confinement?] confinement?" 157.1 Primrose-hill] Primrose Hill 157.4 humor,] humour 157.17 say—] say 157.19 With] *no paragraph:* With 157.20 tone,] tone 157.32 I] I, 160.4 mind."] mind 160.37 off,] off 161.5 vanished,] vanished 162.1 But,] But 166.10 burk] burke 167.3 red-man] red man 167.4 with] of 167.25 illy] ill 172.30 descending] to descend 174.34 qualities,] qualities 175.3 is,] is 175.10 retributive,] retributive 175.35 ands] and 178.20 is it] it is 181.18 me,] me 182.17 Brinvilliarses] Brinvillierses 185.2 accompanied] accompanies 186.1 otherwise:] otherwise; 187.21 involving,] involving 190.11 grave!] grave!" 192.8 things] things, 193.1 first.] first time. 193.11 principal] principle 195.14 oh] oh, 196.6 with in] within 197.8 testily,] testily 198.9 glass,] glass 198.18 forever] for ever 199.22 noonlight] moonlight

203.5 "and] and 206.5 that,] that 206.19 tolerantly] tolerably 215.33 reënter] re-enter 217.2 grand Erie canal] Grand Erie Canal 217.6 consistently-flat] consistently flat 217.28 defition] definition 217.29 favor.] favour." 217.31 ribands] ribbons 220.21 then is]

then, is 220.33 such] such, 222.3 subject] subject, 222.30 system. He] system, he 223.2 self-complaisant] self-complacent 227.11 than] but 227.13 Favor?] Favour?" 227.13 you,] you 227.16 loan] loan, 229.25 Frank.] Frank? 229.27 yet,] yet 229.32 business-friend] business friend 230.7 Surely,] Surely 232.34 Charlie.] Charlie." 233.3 him.] him" 233.13 it.] it." 235.9 illy] ill 237.33 lottery-prize] lottery prize 239.15 tell me] tell 239.16 Now,] Now 241.21 reëstablishing] re-establishing 247.21 day,] day 248.30 ihat] that

252.7 illy] ill 253.20 players,] players; 253.21 Who] They 259.20 up."] up?" 259.32 presuming] persuming 261.12 Philan-thropos] philanthropos 262.33 hearts?] hearts?" 262.34 forever] for ever 266.18 sight,] sight 270.23 up?] up. 270.31 forms] forms, 271.35 at unawares] unawares 272.25 also,] also 273.23 Still,] Still 274.3 so ciety] society 275.4 me] me, 275.6 me,] me 275.29 case,] case 275.31 here,] here 275.31 time,] time 275.36 moment,] moment 276.12 indeed!] indeed? 276.24 wisdom.] wisdom." 277.9 travelers'] traveller's 279.25 nor] "nor 283.7 wild-goose chase] wild-goose-chace 284.3 a while] awhile 286.10 O] THE END.

APPENDIX

SURVIVING MANUSCRIPTS

The manuscript of *The Confidence-Man* has presumably been destroyed, but fortunately four pieces remain of drafts of parts of the novel: "The River," two sets of chapter titles, and early drafts of Chapter 14. They are precious because they illuminate Melville's intention in a number of places, they reveal the artistic principles and the tireless revision which created the distinctive style of the novel, and they explain some of the reasons why *The Confidence-Man* has its obscurities.

These fragments are written on sixteen long sheets of blue paper and a number of shorter pieces and slips of the same paper. How did they alone survive? Miss Margaret Morewood, granddaughter of Melville's brother Allan (who had bought Arrowhead in 1863), explains that old paper stored in the attic at Arrowhead had been used to start fires, but that she preserved anything that she recognized as "Uncle Herman's," including these bits of manuscript. The fragments are now in HCL-M. They are here published for the first time, except that extracts from "The River" have been previously published; the Committee on Higher Degrees in American Civilization, Harvard University, has kindly given permission for the present publication.

The page-and-a-half sketch "The River" may never have been a part of *The Confidence-Man*, for no part of this sketch appears in the completed novel. Yet its subject relates it more closely to this novel than to any of Melville's other works, and its physical appearance and the circumstances of its survival suggest that it was written along with and possibly for this novel. Perhaps Melville discarded it because its imagery suggests other ideas than those which he wished to attach to the Mississippi in *The Confidence-Man*.

Of the two sets of chapter titles, the earlier is discussed above, pp. lxxix f. The second set, on five numbered pages and two pieces of pages, is without heading. In their final form, many of these titles are identical with those published.

The fourth piece of surviving manuscript requires more extended comment here. It consists of two fairly complete drafts of Chapter 14 plus additional versions of several passages of that chapter. These drafts show us that Chapter 14 passed through at least three and possibly six or more versions before Melville achieved the text that he allowed to be published. Each of these versions actually represents several versions, so painstakingly is every sentence rephrased and remolded through cancellations and additions.

The earliest surviving draft of the whole chapter is here called B; there are three earlier fragments, A1, A2, and A3. B covers two and a half of the long blue sheets, and is roughly represented in the text of Chapter 14 in the novel as follows: the first three paragraphs of B become the first three of the final text; paragraph 4 of B becomes, in the text, the first sentence of paragraph 4, the last two sentences of paragraph 5, paragraph 6 except the second and third sentences, and paragraph 7; paragraph 5 of B becomes paragraph 8 of the text. Melville probably wrote at least one complete draft of this chapter before B: the first page of B (through "flying-squirrel") is in the hand of a copyist; there remains a precedent version (A2 and A3) of the fourth paragraph of B; and there is a penciled half-sheet (A1), which is boiled down to a sentence in B. B is without title.

Having covered B with further revisions, even the neat page prepared by his copyist, Melville began making a new copy, in a large, careful hand, revising phrases and also adding whole passages as he went. Perhaps he had already carried these new passages through several versions; an earlier state of one of them survives, here called C. This new, expanded draft of his chapter is here called D; it furnishes most of the text printed below. It contains some very interesting and revealing passages which were deleted before the final text was sent off.

D has nine paragraphs, written on five of the long blue sheets and three half-sheets; Melville canceled some passages (by drawing a slant line through them) and rewrote some of these in other places in D, so that in content D is not so much longer than B as it looks. The second, third, and fourth pages are numbered "76 (3)," "77," "78"; they and the first pages are in Melville's best hand and follow B with no great changes in substance except that they add (and then cancel) two passages. But then Melville cut away the lower half of page 78, and the rest of D (a page, half a page, and a half-sheet) is written in a hasty scrawl, much of it lined out, some of it old material completely revised, some of it new. D stops short four sentences (three in the novel) before the end of the chapter.

E is a passage on a half-sheet, written to replace the canceled first half of paragraph 3 of D.

The text transcribed below is D (with E substituted for the passage it supersedes) and the last four sentences of B. It gives what was probably Melville's penultimate text, and is as close to the final one as surviving manuscripts will take us. But comparison with the text in the novel will show that much additional revision intervened before Melville let his chapter go to the printer.

How best to present this material has been an even harder problem than how to read it. It has finally seemed best to transcribe one complete version, to describe the others, and to transcribe from these others whenever a revision is significant. The alternative is to reproduce the other versions completely too, since every sentence has its variants; and this alternative seemed hardly justified.

Besides "The River," the chapter titles, and "Chap. 14," there are two or three phrases and sentences related to other parts of the novel. These tiny fragments are not transcribed.

Any reader who observes the changes that Melville made from verson to version will see some of the reasons why the novel is obscure. It is immediately apparent that Melville's fear of wounding religious sensibilities was a real one and strong enough to account for his having buried his religious allegory pretty effectively in his novel. For example, Melville liked the following sentence well enough to carry it over intact (except for a shift to the subjunctive) from B to D, but he deleted it before publication: "So that the worst that can be said of any author in this particular, is that he shares a fault, if fault it be, with the author of authors." He gradually softened the following sentence until the first part was gone altogether and the second reduced to the word "contrasts": "And it is with man as with his maker: what makes him hard to comprehend is his inconsistency."[1] Also, he finally struck out every phrase or sentence in D which makes a clear assertion of his agnosticism, e.g.: "And possibly it may be in the one case as the other [human nature and the divine nature], that the expression of ignorance is

[1] See n. 32 and the corresponding passage in D. See also nn. 34, 37, 45, 46, and the corresponding passages.

wisdom. . . ." He deleted a ringing sentence which says that sooner or later Nature "puts out every one who anyway pretends to be acquainted with the whole of her, which is indispensable to fitly comprehending any part of her." (Melville capitalizes "Nature" throughout D, but not "author of authors.")

Furthermore, the style that Melville invented or evolved for the expository parts of this novel desiderates understatement, underemphasis, litotes, and complexity that looks like simplicity. As we see him in his revisions moving always in these directions, and away from the loose structure, open clarity, and directness of his earliest versions of passages, we watch many ideas growing less and less obvious. Let us look in a general way at these revisions.

If any testimony were needed that artistry, taste, and genius presided at the composition of this novel, it could be found in the consistency with which Melville's tireless revision pushed towards one wished-for, clearly defined, and hitherto uncreated style, the style proper to the mood and matter of his unique novel.

In revision Melville tended to expand first, and later to contract. He expanded by pausing to emphasize or clarify a point (e.g., see notes 23 and 25 below and the corresponding passages in "Chap. 14"); by adding new material or allowing the old to ramify; and by adding qualifying words and phrases which almost invariably softened or weakened the meaning (e.g., "still be" becomes "still run the risk of being," and "fare . . . as" becomes "fare . . . something as"). He shortened in two ways: he cut out whole sentences and passages, almost every one of which would have been considered sacrilegious or infidel by many of his contemporaries; and with unsparing hand he pruned away superfluous words and predications.

Some of Melville's revisions of diction show him groping for the exact word. A very great many of them show him carefully converting statement to understatement: "proof sufficient" becomes "proof presumptive" and finally "some presumption"; "is" becomes "may prove"; "prove otherwise" becomes "prove not so much so"; "always" becomes "mainly"; "many characters" becomes "no few characters"; "is" becomes "would seem"; "it would" becomes "it ought to"; "a fatal objection" becomes "an adequate objection"; "always varies" becomes "subject to variation"; "are bound to" becomes "may." Only once or twice does Melville make his language stronger in revision: "different" becomes "conflicting"; "excluded" becomes "excluded with contempt."

In keeping with this hushing of the voice, this meticulous moderation of thought, this elegant avoidance of vulgar emphasis in language, is the toning down of color, of metaphor and simile: the sequestered youth is described first as "pine green," and then merely as "at fault" upon entering real life; a comparison of inconsistent characters with some of the beasts in Revelation is deleted. Only those comparisons are finally retained which are, not fanciful or decorative, but as functional as an axle.

The same consistency of purpose is seen in Melville's syntactical revisions. By combining sentences, shrinking predication, subordinating, he not only achieves a classical economy and purity but also diminishes the emphasis that some of his thoughts enjoyed while they stood alone; compare the last sentence of the fourth paragraph below, the next-to-last of the sixth, and their counterpart in the text of the novel (at the end of the fourth paragraph there). His favorite method of achieving understatement by subordination, an achievement which may be seen in the sentence just mentioned, is to set main thoughts on relative grounds by tucking them into the terms of a comparison and then to put the whole upon even more minor and tentative grounds by introducing it with "Upon the whole, it might rather be thought, that . . . ," or "Which may appear the less improbable if it be considered that . . . ," or "Yet, touching this point, it may prove suggestive that. . . ." Thus the very syntax abets the hinting and whispering which are the language of this novel.

The other object or end of Melville's syntactical revisions was tension, tautness, strength in sentence structure. He increased parallelism regularly and periodic structure frequently from revision to revision as he combined and reduced sentences. He reversed the terms of comparisons, sometimes to make them conform better to the logic of the context, but often to gain suspense and climax, as in the next-to-last paragraph. The sentences, particularly the balanced and periodic ones, uncoil like springs, with a lithe, inexorable, cool precision. But this relentless movement of the sentence is half hidden beneath the mild language, the hesitating modifications, and emerges at the period with the shock of wit. In his revisions we may see Melville with infinite pains achieving in his sentences that fine ironic contrast and tension between mild-mannered, leisurely surface and stern dialectic beneath, which is the mode of his novel.

The editor has allowed "Chap. 14" to determine the form to be used in transcribing all the manuscript. The variants in "The River" and the chapter titles are so few that the form in which they are indicated is of small concern to the reader, but "Chap. 14" demands special treatment. What is wanted in its transcription is not so much a final text separated from variants, as some sort of reproduction of Melville's manuscript which will allow the reader to follow Melville's constantly shifting revisions just as he might if he had the manuscript before him (and could read it!) Or so it seems to the editor, her reasons being that, since Melville's final text of "Chap. 14" appears in the novel, each of the earlier variants of any given passage is equally as valuable and interesting as any of the others, and that in the amorphous, still living and growing and shifting prose that one can see in the manuscript a reader can come closer to Melville's mind and art than in any momentarily achieved reading before the final one.

When Melville was writing for his own eyes or those of a copyist in the family, he wrote in a way that reduces a transcriber to guesswork and often to defeat. He left out letters, syllables, groups of syllables; he reversed the order of letters; he shadowed forth a word rather than wrote it. In the transcriptions below, words have been freely filled out with their full complement of letters, and letters in reverse order have been transposed, without indication of editorial assistance. The editor has called attention to some uncertain readings; it would be impossible to indicate all of them. The published text often helps one to read the chapter titles and "Chap. 14"; but "The River" is without counterpart in the novel and is also unusually illegible, so that, most unfortunately, the transcription of this fine piece of prose is full of conjectured readings.

Key

Square brackets—editorial matter
This (italic type)—a word canceled by a line drawn through it
Arrow brackets—matter added between the lines or in the margin
X—an illegible word
X̶—an illegible canceled word
Recalled matter is repeated; Melville drew a broken line under matter to be recalled.

Canceled words and phrases appear in the order in which they were apparently written and rejected by Melville; when there is a series of such phrases, the editor has not attempted to separate them from each other because it is often impossible to say with assurance which combinations Melville intended. The reader will be reading Melville's first version of a sentence if he skips matter in square brackets and matter in arrow brackets and reads only the first in any series of italicized (that is, canceled) phrases; he will be reading Melville's final version if he skips matter in square brackets and matter in italic type and reads matter in arrow brackets as though the brackets were not there. Melville's cancellation of punctuation is not indicated; such punctuation is retained when needed, omitted when not needed.

I

The Mississippi The River[2]

As the word Abraham means the father of a <great> multitude of men so the word Mississippi means the father of a great multitude of waters. His tribes stream in from east & west, exceeding fruitful the lands they enrich. In this granary of a continent this basin of the Mississippi must not the nations be greatly multiplied & blest?

Above the Falls of St: Anthony for the most part he winds evenly in between banks of flags or through[3] tracts of pine[4] over marbles[5] sands in waters so clear that the deepest fish have the visable [*sic*] flight of the bird. Undisturbed as the lonely[6] life in its bosom feeds the lonely[6] life on its shores, the coronetted elk & the deer, while in the watery form of some *couched* <*mossy*> couched rock in the channel, <furred over with moss,> the furred bear on the marge seems to eye his amphibious brother. Wood & wave wed, man is remote. The Unsung time,[7] the Golden Age of the billow.

By *the* <his> Fall, though he rise not again, the unhumbled

[2] Melville underlined both titles. For help in reading the manuscript of this sketch, I owe thanks to Professor Howard P. Vincent, Professor Harrison Hayford, and Mr. Sumner B. Foster.

[3] slight?
[4] trees?
[5] marshes?
[6] lowly?
[7] tune?

river ennobles himself now deepens[8] now purely expands, now first forms his character & begins that career whose majestic serenity if not overborne by fierce onsets of torrents shall end only with ocean.

Like a larger Susquehannah [*sic*] like a long-drawn bison herd he hurries on through the prairie, here & there expanding into archipelagoes cycladean in beauty, while fissured and verdant, a long China Wall, the bluffs sweep bluely away. Glad & & [*sic*] content the sacred river glides on.

But at St: Louis the course of this dream is run. Down on it like a Pawnee from ambush foams the yellow-jacket Missouri. The calm is gone, the grouped isles disappear, the shores are jagged & rent, the hue of the water is clayed, the before moderate current is rapid & vexed. The peace[9] of the Upper River seems broken in the Lower, nor it is ever[10] renewed.

The Missouri *X* sends rather *an* a hostile element than a filial flow. Longer stronger than the father of waters like Jupiter he dethrones his sire & reigns in his stead. Under the benign name Mississippi it is in short the Missouri that now rolls to the Gulf, the Missouri that with the *X* snows from his solitudes freezes[11] the warmth[12] of the genial zones, the Missouri that by open assault or artful sap sweeps away fruit & field grave-yard & barn, the Missouri that not a tributary but an outlaw[13] enters the sea, long disdaining to yield his white wave to the blue.

II

Titles for Chapters[14]

The hypothetical friends.
The practical mystic.

[8] deeper?
[9] green? prime? dream?
[10] e'er?
[11] frees?
[12] waters?
[13] union? overlord?
[14] These words are underlined. This set of chapter titles seems to represent an early stage in the invention of the story; see above, pp. lxxix f. The first seven titles are in ink, the next four in pencil, the twelfth in ink, the last in pencil. Melville drew a line down through them, canceling them all. Across the bottom of the page, upside down to the titles, is: "In the same moment apparently with his advent."

Distrust the bare basis for confidence.
What *is* confidence <is> in the most confiding.
The <Sad want of confidence in a> gentleman-madman.
The age of *charms conjuration* enchantment not yet over.
How confidence overcomes reason. (Miser)
The boon companions.
Showing that the age of charms & conjuration is not yet over.
A rupture.   Dedicated to victims of
                                                        Auto da Fe.

The soldier of fortune
A mute goes on board a *Mississippi* boat on the Mississippi.
The Philanthropist & Misanthrope. *The Rifle* & Pipe.[15]

III

[Chapter Titles]

A mute goes on board a boat at St. Louis.
Showing that many men *have* many minds [Entire title recalled.]
In which a variety of characters appear
Renewal of old acquaintance
In which The man with the weed *by his words and behavior &
words* X makes it *doubtful* <an even *doubt* question> whether he
be a great philosopher or a great simpleton
Repulses and advances.
<*In Which*> *A man in grey after meeting with*
Some
In which certain persons <*Some*> Certain persons prove deaf to
the call of charity.
A gentleman *in fine linen &* with X gold sleeve-buttons.
*A righteous man encounters a good man, and an enthusiast a
gentleman a man of common sense.*
A <truly> charitable lady.
Two business men transact a little business *and have a little talk.*
<Genial Life> In the cabin.
Only a page or two.
A page or two of <*Some*> *discourse too brief to be tedious.*
Story of the unfortunate man, *showing with what justice he is so*

[15] *The Pipe* & Rifle?

called <from which may be gathered whether *he* or not he *has* has been *he is* justly so *called* entiled.>

The man with the traveling cap evinces <by his discourse> much humanity and *sho pro* in a way which would seem to *prove* <show> him <to be one of the most amiable of> an optimist<s>.

Containing a hint. A dilemma

A hint or two about consistency which may go <pass> for what it is worth.

Worth <the> consideration *by* of those *who may think it worth while* <to whom it may be think it worth> considering

An valuable investment is made.

An <A certain> old man <upon suitable representations> is prevailed upon to *make* <venture> an investment

A herb doctor

XXX herb

A doctor & his patient.

A sick man after *much* <some> impatience *gives himself up to be* <becomes> <is induced to become> a patient.

The herb doctor

Showing among other things *with what perverse* <how> some men will *refu reject* turn away [Entire title canceled.]

The herb doctor not so successful as his X would seem to merit. Toward the end of which the herb doctor proves himself a forgiver of injuries.

Some wise <a jury of> *men hold* an inquest on *the character of* the character of the herb doctor.

The character of the herb doctor discussed, <and settled> *by and what he truly is, finally settled by one fully competent and finally settled*

A soldier of fortune.

Reappearance of one *who has* who *will perhaps* <may> be remembered

A hard case.

Containing some of the most important <encouraging> *hints*

Full of encouraging hints <encouragement> *to all those who keep house:* <housekeepers who> *employ servant laborers & servants.* <Among other things meriting *X* the attention of such housekeepers as> may have despaired in the matter of servants, particularly juvenile ones.

Return of the old fit

In which the effect of scenery *on the mind* is *strikingly* evinced *by* in the case of the bachelor who <in view of the aguish country about Cairo> has a return of his *old* <chilly> fit.

A philanthropist <X> *and a misanthrope. essays* <tries> <sets out> to convert a misanthrope, *and finally not in but fi and finally ends by* <but only succeeds in> <gets so far as to> *confuting him* but does not get beyond confuting him. *which he does* [The last clause is erased.]

The Cosmopolitan makes an acquaintance.

The metaphysics of Indian-hating, according to the views of one evidently not <so> prepossessed as Rosseau [*sic*] in favor of *Indians* <the savages.>

Some account of the greatest man

Some account of *a famous Indian hater* <a good hater> *one worthy the esteem* <a man of questionable X *morality* but who nevertheless would seem> *eminently* entitled to the esteem of that eminent *great* <English> moralist *Dr. Johnson who loved a* said he liked a good hater.

A discussion of the character of the <moot points touching the> late Colonel John Moredock

The boon companions.

Opening with a <grand> <poetical> eulogy of the press, and continuing with talk inspired by it.

Conta <Containing> A <genuine real> metamorphosis <&> *more surprising* more surprising than any <fictitious one> in Ovid.

Showing that the age of *charms* <enchanters &> enchantments is *not yet* <by no means> over.

Which may pass for *what it is* <whatever it may prove to be> worth.

Story <In which the Cosmopolitan tells the story> of the getleman-madman.

Charlie

Less than a page.

The Cosmopolitan is accosted by a *great* mystic, *and strange enough* <some mystical> *talk ensues—and* <whereupon ensues> <pretty much> such <obscure> talk as might be *looked* expected, *in the*

The master introduces *the* <his> disciple.

The disciple becomes sociable.

The hypothetical friends.

The story of China Aster

In which the story of China Aster is at second hand told by one who while *vouching for the facts* <not disapproving the moral> X disdains the spirit of the style, *a*[16]

Ending with a X quotation [Entire title recalled.]

Enter into the Barber's shop

More of the barber's shop [Title enclosed in brackets.]

In which the Cosmopolitan *shows himself earns the title of the man-charmer* <but not> *in the same sense that certain East Indians are called snake-charmers XXXX pretty much in the same rank with the snak*[sic] earns a title *XXXXXXXX* as certain East Indians are called snake charmers[17]

In which the last three words of the last chapter are made the text of discourse *such as it is* which will *be sure of a* <which will be sure> <receive more or less> *careful perusal of* <the the attention of from> *all such persons* <readers> *as* <those readers who> do not <*think best to*> <*altogether*> skip it.

Rather long. Very Long & serious.

is as serious as anything before; *and perhaps* <if anything> a little more so.[18]

(End)

IV

Chap. 14

Worth the consideration of those
to whom it may be worth considering.[19]

[1] As the last chapter was begun with a reminder looking forwards, the present must consist of one glancing backwards.

[2] To some, it may raise *a degree of* <more or less of> surprise, that one so full of <easy> confidence as the merchant has throughout shown himself up to the moment of his late sudden *outburst* <impulsiveness>, should in that instance have betrayed

---

16 This second title is on a separate slip of paper. On still another sheet is this sentence: "He was *un* <honest,> & <therefore> must have friends, *who would not refuse accept such a mortgage as receipt for a loan.*"

17 The title beginning "In which" is on a separate page, with the title given in n. 16 and the one referred to in n. 18.

18 The title beginning "is as serious" is on a separate page; see n. 17.

19 This title and "Chap. 14" are underlined.

such a *depth* <degree> of distrust. He may be thought inconsistent.[20]

[3] And even so he is.[21] Yet why find fault with the author for it? But, it may be *said* <urged>, there is nothing an *author* <writer of fiction> should more carefully see to, as there is nothing a sensible reader will more carefully look for, than that in the depiction of any character its consistency should be preserved.[22] *This indeed* <But this> though <at first blush> seeming *very* reasonable enough, *is* may yet *upon turn out* upon a closer view *seem very unreasonable prove the reverse* <X *otherwise*> <prove otherwise.> For how does it *agree* <square> with another requirement,[23] *deemed* equally *important* <insisted upon> perhaps, that while to <*portraying the qualities*> *a* fiction is allowed *a certain latitude of* <*liberal play of ornament* & some play of> invention, yet fiction should never *do violence to fact? In this* be <essentially> contradictory to fact? And <*Now*> is it not *a* <an essential> fact that in real life[24] a consistent character is a rara avis? Which being so, the

[20] The third paragraph of B begins with this rather than the next sentence. This sentence in B (before revision) reads: "It may be thought that the discordancy is such as to make him seem an inconsistent character."

[21] The first seven sentences of this paragraph, down through "perplexity as to understanding them," are transcribed from E. The corresponding sentences in D, after being almost hidden under revisions, were canceled. E follows the revised reading of D pretty faithfully except at one sentence (see n. 24). D follows B, changing a few words.

[22] In B Melville wrote: "But, it is urged, there is nothing a sensible reader more carefully looks for, or a sensible author will be more careful to see to, than consistency in the characters of fiction." Then he reversed the order of his terms to make the author precede the reader, as above in E, and made minor changes in diction and tense. In D he preserved these changes, generally, and tried out "discreet writer," "discreet reader," "that sort of keeping in character called consistency."

[23] In the preceding sentence and thus far in this one, E expands both B and D; the shortest reading (one of B's) is: "Reasonable enough. But is it, or is it not, in conflict with that other requirement . . .?" The expansion emphasizes and clarifies his point here, which was underwritten in the earlier versions, being conveyed there chiefly through "But."

[24] E omits a clause before this; B (first reading) has: "For this last being required of him, is it not taxing his powers rather too hard, also to require of him none but truly consistent characters, seeing that . . . in real life . . .?" Revision of B reduced wordiness. D follows B with minor substitutions. In B, after this sentence Melville added the following in the margin and then canceled it: "Surely *he who demands* <if> consistency be <is demanded> in an author <*it*> *should at least do so* <*be done*> *in consistent terms.* <the demand itself should *not at least* not X inconsistent X with other demands.>"

distaste of readers to meeting <in books> with the contrary sort *in books* can hardly arise from any sense of their untrueness; *more likely, it though perhaps it may* <it rather may be> from perplexity as to understanding them.[25] But if the acutest philosopher be perplexed to understand <the characters of> no few people he is in living contact with,[26] shall those who are no<t> philosophers expect to run and read *human nature* <character> in those *outlined* phantoms of it *of it* which flit along *the novelist's* <a> page like *the phantom* shadows along a wall?[27] That *fiction* <novel> where every character can by reason of its consistency be comprehended at a glance, either exhibits but *easy* sections of character, making them appear for wholes, or else is wholly untrue to reality. While, on the other hand, that author who draws a character, even though to common view incongruous[28] in its parts as the flying-squirrel[29] and at different periods as *contradictory to* <much at variance with> itself as the butterfly is *to* <with> the catterpillar *from* <into> which it *proceeded;* <*had come; issued* changes;>[30] may yet, in so doing, be not false, but faithful, to *Nature.* facts.

[4][31] *The principle that the popular* <many> *writers adopt of making* <To represent> human nature <as> *always* <more or

[25] B has (first reading): "One reason of that repugnance of readers to inconsistent characters in fiction, no doubt arises from the perplexity as to understanding them." D and E clarify and emphasize by adding the contrast. E shortens D, which goes: ". . . untrueness, however much some may think that the reason; though perhaps the repugnance may in part spring from. . . ."

[26] B has: ". . . understand <the> *many* characters of <many> people he is in *bodily* <living> contact with . . ."; this is reduced in the final text to ". . . understand living character. . . ."

[27] B has: ". . . read *characters* <human nature> in those *mere ghosts of them* <empty shapes of it> which flit *through a fiction* <along *a page* the novelist's page> like <the equally empty> shadows along a wall?"

[28] Variants in B: "inconsistent," "contradictory," "discordant," "incongruous."

[29] Page 1 of B, in a copyist's hand, ends here. The copyist mistook "view" for "men" and "flying-squirrel" for "flying-squall." Melville made the corrections.

[30] B: ". . . at different *times* <periods *of its development*> contrasting *with* <as contradictory to> itself as *entirely* <much> as the catterpillar *with* <is to the> butterfly <it X becomes>. . . ."

[31]This paragraph does not occur in B. Melville composed it on a halfsheet, C, and then neatly copied it into D in this place. Later he canceled it here and worked it in, with much revision, at the end of paragraph 6 below.

less> translucent, *<transparent>* <easy to be understood, as *X>*
reflects either great honor or great dishonor upon it; for waters that
can be so readily seen through, must needs be very pure or very
shallow. But *<in degree>* *it is with man as with his maker; for*
just as by the contrasts obvious in the workings of Providence, the
pious <religious> mind is forced *to* into a *<humble>* confession
of ignorance; so, by the *<equally inscrutable>* inconsistencies in
the workings of hum human conduct, the philosophic intellect is
driven to exclaim 'I know it not.'[32]

[5] In a word, if reason be judge,[33] no *author* <novelist writer>
has produced such inconsistent characters as Nature herself has. So
that the worst that can be said of any author in this particular, is
that he shares a fault, if fault it be, with the author of authors.[34] And
it must call for no little sagacity in a reader, unerringly to discriminate *<in a fiction* in a book> between the inconsistencies of conception & those of life.[35] Experience is the <only> *best* guide
<here>; but as no one man's experience, *with his learning to boot*
<added>, can be coextensive with what is,[36] it may be imprudent

[32] C: *"And* *<in degree* But> it is with man as with his maker: what
<to full X> makes him *<so impossible, often>* *hard to comprehend is*
his *<is whatever* is what *to us* seems a want of> <is, what for want of
a better word we call his> *inconsistency* *<want* XXXXX>; for just as by
the contrasts obvious in the workings of Providence *the* *<finite>* *mind is*
bewildered <the pious mind *XXXX* is forced> into a *<humble re-*
ligious> confession of ignorance, so by the *contrasts* <inconsistencies>
in the *actions thoughts & X feelings and actions of man,* workings of
human nature, the philosophic intellect, is *forced* driven to exclaim 'I
know it not.' "

[33] B: ". . . if *human* reason *is the measure standard of things* <be
judge>. . . ."

[34] This sentence was cut out before the final text. B has: ". . . can
<honestly> be said . . ." and ". . . fault, <if fault it is>. . . ."

[35] The predecessor of this sentence, and perhaps of the preceding one
as well, is a passage written on a half-sheet, Al: *"It is true that* <True,>
the *inconsistency of the fictitious character* inconsistency may arise from
the author's conception *of it involving incompatibles,* but *inasmuch as it*
is incompatibles which constitute the it does not follow but if so it can
X only be from its involving *incompatibles* <inconsistency>, *and since*
these <incompatibles> constitute what makes which is and since for this
real life gives X, he must *be* needs be a sagatious [sic] critic who can
discriminate between the inconsistencies of conception & those of Nature."
On the next line, perhaps to indicate the passage to follow this, is: "Duck
billed beaver." Below: "True, the inconsistency may be the author's
fault, but *if so he only he X."*

[36] Melville underlined "what is"; B has "truth," "facts."

sometimes <in any case absolutely> to rely *too much* upon *either experience or learning, beyond a certain point* <it>. When the duck-billed beaver of Australia was first brought stuffed to England; the *most eminent wise ones* <naturalists judging from *experience* their classifications> *long* believed that there was in reality no such creature, the bill in the specimen must be some way stuck on *for a hoax.* They thought that X the *conception* <mere idea> of such a monster was *incongruous* <inconsistent> with Nature, XX whereas the *only* inconsistency was between the *true monster* <creature> itself and their classifications. So we see that it is not the Fuselies <alone> whom Nature puts out. Sooner or later she puts out every one who anyway pretends to be acquainted with the whole of her, which is indispensable to *rightly* <fitly> comprehending any part of her.[37]

[6][38] But let Nature, *to the confusion* <bewilderment> *of the naturalists,* produce her duck-billed beavers as she may; *still an* <lesser> author<s>, some may hold, have no business to be *confusing readers* <puzzling people readers bewildering readers> with duck-billed characters.[39] Though indeed, if such can be depicted, and then dissected,—well and good; in fact, nothing better.[40] And accordingly it is found, that the more masterly novelists excell in nothing so much as in this very point. They will present a character *as full X of parts* apparently *as* <full of> incompatible<s> *as*

---

[37] The two preceding sentences, "They thought . . . part of her," are among those that D adds to B. The passage is canceled, however, in D and does not get into the final text.

[38] The first part of this paragraph, through "Boston of real life," where the text above shows a break, is all canceled except the first sentence and the one beginning "At least," and is rewritten below in paragraphs 7, 8, and 9. It follows B, paragraph 4, (which continues for three more sentences; see below, n. 52). Of B, paragraph 4, there is a precedent version, A2 and A3, which are the upper and lower parts of a single page, from the middle of which a strip almost two inches wide has been cut; the whole page had been canceled with a line from top to bottom.

[39] D omits the second half of this sentence in B: ". . . characters; *his business or if he do, he is bound to dissect them or the business of an* X *his business being not to puzzle, but solve.*" Variants in A2: ". . . *not to present problems but not to add to the natural obscurity of things, but to* X not to <present> *puzzle, but sol clear up to* X *make things plain* <solutions>."

[40] This sentence appears first in B, and is canceled finally here.

those which make up some of the beasts in Revelations;[41] *and this,*
with the sole view of afterwards reconciling them pursuant to the
rules of art; in this way, throwing open to the understandings even
of schoolboys the last windings of the most winding recess in Nature.[42] At least something like this is claimed for *some novelists*
<*certain writers them such authors* X psychological novelists>, nor
will the claim be here disputed.[43] But how comes it, that while Boston is *an intricate* <a crooked> town, *but yet* the rustic <visitor>
who carefully studies a true map of it, will hardly be put to his wits'
ends to find his way <about it>; yet the *secluded* <studious>
youth who may have pored over all the charts of *the* human nature
hitherto published by the psychologists of fiction will nevertheless
be too often at fault upon entering <the crooked Boston of> real
life?[44]

[41] This comparison with the beasts in Revelation makes its brief appearance in D only. B has, instead: *"carefully elaborating them."* A2 has:
". . . the more popular novelists delight in nothing so much as in the
XX intricate characters." This whole passage, "And accordingly . . .
recess in Nature," is canceled and rewritten below in paragraph 7.

[42] A3 and B: ". . . recess in Nature, the human heart." A3 continues:
*"True, but it Well, if there be such authors, all one can say is, that the
world owes them many thanks for."* This sentence about the masterly
novelists is rewritten below in paragraph 7.

[43] This sentence is repeated below as paragraph 8.

[44] Melville copied B (revising and enlarging) to here, and perhaps
further, in a large, clear hand; he cut away the lower half of a sheet
after the last sentence above, and wrote the rest of D, a page and two half
pages, in a rapid scribble. There are five versions of the last sentence
above; they show Melville expanding a little from version to version, re-
versing the terms of his comparison and then returning them in the end
to their first order as he fills out the details of his analogy, and changing
the general effect from something blunt, simple, and direct, to something
polished, relatively complex in syntax, delicate and firm in rhythm, modi-
fied, qualified, understated. A3: ". . . but *how comes it that after
reading to be a XX* how comes it *to be a fact* to be a fact that the <se-
questered> youth *study of them will* <who has studied all the> novels
hitherto published in the world, will *yet be* still *be green pine green*
<be *XX be* at fault> upon entering real life? Boston is an intricate town,
but *he* <the stranger> who carefully studies a true *plan* <map> of it,
and goes about X Boston with that map in his hand, will not be put at his
wits end to find his way." B revises this until it comes out like the first
reading of D, except that D omits "and goes about with it in hand," and
changes "not . . . always" to "hardly," "cloistered" to "secluded," "the
human heart" to "human nature." The other two versions may be seen
in paragraph 9 below and in the novel, paragraph 6.

Human nature is no such X <*obscure thing*> *they maintain, and if painted at all it should be painted* X *as transparent. They should make things clear* <*transparent*>. *Now, to represent human nature as transparent* X
<In every case> They should *draw* <represent> human nature *in its* <not in obscurity but> transparency; which indeed is the way with *many* <popular> writers, *But* and is XX <perhaps> felt to be a kind of *compliment to it from them* XX *to it by them. compliment* <honor> rendered by them to their kind. Yet whether it *truly be so or not* <involve *great* honor or *great dishonor* the *contrary* reverse> might seem uncertain, considering that if these X waters *which* <of human nature> can be *so* so readily seen through, *must be the reason may be either that they are very pure or* XX *it may be* XXXX it may either be that they are very pure or very shallow. *But* <But> It might rather be thought that *the* he who <considering its inconsistencies *of conduct*> says of human nature *that it* the same that <in view of *the considering its contrasts the* its contrasts *of its operations*> is said of the divine nature, that it is past finding out, <XXXXX> XXXXXXXXX <*evinces a deeper* appreciation of it than he who would X you that he knows all about it.>[45] *And possibly it may be in the one case as the other, that the expression of ignorance is wisdom besides by his confession of ignorance in such a point disclaiming of knowledge attesting his wisdom.*[46]

[7] But though there is a prejudice against <XXX> *the drawing of puzzling characters in fiction* X <*inconsistent* inconsistent> characters in *fiction* <books>, yet *there* the prejudice is the other way when <*by the skill of the writer*> *their obscurity can be enlightened* what *was* <was at first> their *obscurity* <inconsistency> *afterwards turns out to be their* afterwards <by the *skill of the wr masterly thought of the novelist* skill of the *novelist* author>

[45] See above, n. 32 and corresponding passage, for two earlier versions of this sentence. Besides making other changes, Melville omits "But in degree it is with man as with his maker."

[46] The material from the break above, beginning "Human nature is no such . . .," to the end of this paragraph is paragraph 4 above, canceled there, rewritten here, and very close to Melville's final text; the final text, however, omits the last sentence and amplifies the ending of the one before it.

turns out to be their *harmony* <X good keeping>.[47] The *masterly* <X great> *novelists* <*authors* masters> excell in nothing so much as in this *very* fact. They fill you with *wonder* <X astonishment> at the X <tangly skein> of a character & then fill you with still more *wonder* <*astonishment* admiration> at their *easy X of it,* unravelling of it. *With a* In this way, throwing open even to the understandings <even> of school boys *the last X in the most winding recess* <*mystery of the soul*> the last *mysteries* <complications> of a spirit X <affirmed by its Creator to be> fearfully & wonderfully made.

[8] At least something like this is claimed for certain psychological novelists, nor will the claim be here disputed.

[9] *But if there is a science of human nature, XXXXXXXXXXXX*
But <as touching this subject> it is *XXXX* <suggestive> that all those *bursts of speculation* <*XXXX bursts of thought* methodized sallies of ingenuity> having for their object the X <*exact* revelation> of human nature, *are* have <by the best judges> *always* <mainly> been excluded from the ranks of the sciences—Palmistry, physiognomy, phrenology, psychology, *and psychological. Nor is this to be While as for those analytic fictions* [The next seven lines are canceled and illegible except for a word here and there, e.g., "fortune-tellers," "the horoscopists."][48] *But scarcely with as much advantage as* while the mere fact that in all ages, the past included, *XXXXXXX* such widely different views of human nature have <by the most eminent minds> been taken, this in itself is *proof sufficient* <presumptive> of the *general* <universal> ignorance of it.[49] *Take even* <*By* After reading> X the *novels* <novels or the philosophies> even of the most sensible *novelists* <men>, the studious youth will still be <X too often> at fault upon entering real life; whereas, if *those novels had* he had been furnished with a true *map chart* <plan> of *it* <human nature>, it would fare with him as with a *man* <stranger> entering *a crooked town* Bos-

[47] This sentence replaces the second sentence in paragraph 6 above; the rest of this paragraph is a revised version of the third and fourth sentences of paragraph 6 above. In the chapter in the novel, see paragraph 5.

[48] The matter from the beginning of paragraph 9 to here, scribbled on a half-sheet, forms one of Melville's additions made in D. It becomes one sentence in the final text, the second in paragraph 6.

[49] This sentence is an addition made in D.